The Wendigo and Others

ALGERNON BLACKWOOD

The Wendigo and Others

Collected Short Fiction
Volume 3: 1910–1912

Edited by S. T. Joshi

Hippocampus Press

New York

Published by Hippocampus Press
P.O. Box 641, New York, NY 10156.
www.hippocampuspress.com

Cover illustration and design © 2026 by Jason Van Hollander.
Hippocampus Press logo designed by Anastasia Damianakos.

First edition
1 3 5 7 9 8 6 4 2

ISBN 978-1-61498-432-0 six-volume set
ISBN 978-1-61498-461-0 volume 3
ISBN 978-1-61498-474-0 ebook

Contents

Introduction

The stories in this volume were written at the height of Blackwood's period of leisure (1909–14), when the sales of *John Silence—Physician Extraordinary* (1908) allowed him to spend his time alternatively in England and Switzerland and devote his time to writing without the need to earn an income. Many of the tales were gathered in two landmark volumes, *The Lost Valley and Other Stories* (1910) and *Pan's Garden: A Volume of Nature Stories* (1912). Others appeared in *Ten Minute Stories* (1914) and later collections, but several remained uncollected in Blackwood's lifetime.

"The Wendigo" is perhaps Blackwood's most poignant and terrifying exhibition of the terrors of the natural world, set in a Canada that he had come to know well from numerous camping trips in the 1890s. Other "nature" stories fit readily into *Pan's Garden:* "The Sea Fit" (which broaches the idea of sea gods), "The Glamour of the Snow" (about a snow elemental), "The Temptation of the Clay" (a tale of nature's revenge on a man's abuse of its purity), "Sand" (an epic tale of the Egyptian desert), and "The Man Whom the Trees Loved," an exquisite novella of a man's literal merging of his personality with the forests neighboring his property.

But another key motif enters Blackwood's fiction at this time, although it had been anticipated in some earlier tales: reincarnation. He had met Mabel Stuart-King (1880?–1945), later the Baroness de Knoop, as early as 1906, but it was in the early 1910s that he developed a mystical belief that he, she, and perhaps her husband, the Russian nobleman Baron Johann de Knoop (1847–1918), were re-enacting a love triangle from centuries or even millennia ago. Such a scenario is the basis of the later novel *The Wave* (1916), but in the stories of 1910–12 Blackwood explores various aspects of the reincarnation theme: "Old Clothes," "Two in One," "The Destruction of Smith," and a few

7

others. Vampirism is at the basis of "The Singular Death of Morton" and "The Transfer," while ghosts, revenants, and apparitions are featured in numerous tales in this volume. Precognitive dreams are also a dominant theme. A few non-weird items are present in this volume as well.

Many stories appeared in the *Westminster Gazette,* one of the leading evening newspapers in London at this time. Several others appeared in the *Morning Post,* another major London newspaper, and the *Eye-Witness,* a weekly paper edited by Hilaire Belloc. The settings of the stories vary from England to France to Switzerland to Egypt, reflecting Blackwood's wide travels and intimate familiarity with the topography, culture, and history of these varied locales.

The diversity and richness of Algernon Blackwood's short fiction is well displayed in the stories in this volume.

—S. T. JOSHI

The Wendigo

I

A considerable number of hunting parties were out that year without finding so much as a fresh trail; for the moose were uncommonly shy, and the various Nimrods returned to the bosoms of their respective families with the best excuses the facts or their imaginations could suggest. Dr. Cathcart, among others, came back without a trophy; but he brought instead the memory of an experience which he declares was worth all the bull-moose that had ever been shot. But then Cathcart, of Aberdeen, was interested in other things besides moose—amongst them the vagaries of the human mind. This particular story, however, found no mention in his book on *Collective Hallucination* for the simple reason (so he confided once to a fellow colleague) that he himself played too intimate a part in it to form a competent judgment of the affair as a whole. . . .

Besides himself and his guide, Hank Davis, there was young Simpson, his nephew, a divinity student destined for the "Wee Kirk" (then on his first visit to Canadian backwoods), and the latter's guide, Défago. Joseph Défago was a French "Canuck," who had strayed from his native Province of Quebec years before, and had got caught in Rat Portage when the Canadian Pacific Railway was a-building; a man who, in addition to his unparalleled knowledge of woodcraft and bush-lore, could also sing the old *voyageur* songs and tell a capital hunting yarn into the bargain. He was deeply susceptible, moreover, to that singular spell which the wilderness lays upon certain lonely natures, and he loved the wild solitudes with a kind of romantic passion that amounted almost to an obsession. The life of the backwoods fascinated him—whence, doubtless, his surpassing efficiency in dealing with their mysteries.

On this particular expedition he was Hank's choice. Hank knew him and swore by him. He also swore at him, "jest as a pal might," and since he had a vocabulary of picturesque, if utterly meaningless, oaths, the conversation between the two stalwart and hardy woodsmen was often of a rather lively description. This river of expletives, however, Hank agreed to dam a little out of respect for his old "hunting boss," Dr. Cathcart, whom of course he addressed after the fashion of the country as "Doc"; and also because he understood that young Simpson was already a "bit of a parson." He had, however, one objection to Défago, and one only—which was, that the French Canadian sometimes exhibited what Hank described as "the output of a cursed and dismal mind," meaning apparently that he sometimes was true to type, Latin type, and suffered fits of a kind of silent moroseness when nothing could induce him to utter speech. Défago, that is to say, was imaginative and melancholy. And, as a rule, it was too long a spell of "civilisation" that induced the attacks, for a few days of the wilderness invariably cured them.

This, then, was the party of four that found themselves in camp the last week in October of that "shy moose year" 'way up in the wilderness north of Rat Portage—a forsaken and desolate country. There was also Punk, an Indian, who had accompanied Dr. Cathcart and Hank on their hunting trips in previous years, and who acted as cook. His duty was merely to stay in camp, catch fish, and prepare venison steaks and coffee at a few minutes' notice. He dressed in the worn-out clothes bequeathed to him by former patrons, and, except for his coarse black hair and dark skin, he looked in these city garments no more like a real redskin than a stage negro looks like a real African. For all that, however, Punk had in him still the instincts of his dying race; his taciturn silence and his endurance survived; also his superstition.

The party round the blazing fire that night were despondent, for a week had passed without a single sign of recent moose discovering itself. Défago had sung his song and plunged into a story, but Hank, in bad humour, reminded him so often that "he kep' mussing-up the fac's so, that it was 'most all nothin' but a petred-out lie," that the Frenchman had finally subsided into a sulky silence which nothing seemed likely to break. Dr. Cathcart and his nephew were fairly done after an exhausting day. Punk was washing up the dishes, grunting to himself under the lean-to of branches, where he later also slept. No one troubled to stir the slowly dying fire. Overhead the stars were brilliant in a

sky quite wintry, and there was so little wind that ice was already form-
ing stealthily along the shores of the still lake behind them. The silence
of the vast listening forest stole forward and enveloped them.

Hank broke in suddenly with his nasal voice.

"I'm in favour of breaking new ground to-morrow, Doc," he observed with energy, looking across at his employer. "We don't stand a
dead Dago's chance about here."

"Agreed," said Cathcart, always a man of few words. "Think the
idea's good."

"Sure Doc, it's good," Hank resumed with confidence. "S'pose,
now, you and I strike west, up Garden Lake way for a change! None of
us ain't touched that quiet bit o' land yet—"

"I'm with you."

"And you, Défago, take Mr. Simpson along in the small canoe,
skip across the lake, portage over into Fifty Island Water, and take a
good squint down that thar southern shore. The moose 'yarded' there
like hell last year, and for all we know they may be doin' it agin this
year jest to spite us."

Défago, keeping his eyes on the fire, said nothing by way of reply.
He was still offended, possibly, about his interrupted story.

"No one's been up that way this year, an' I'll lay my bottom dollar
on *that!*" Hank added with emphasis, as though he had a reason for
knowing. He looked over at his partner sharply. "Better take the little
silk tent and stay away a couple o' nights," he concluded, as though the
matter were definitely settled. For Hank was recognised as general or-
ganiser of the hunt, and in charge of the party.

It was obvious to any one that Défago did not jump at the plan,
but his silence seemed to convey something more than ordinary disapproval, and across his sensitive dark face there passed a curious expression like a flash of firelight—not so quickly, however, that the three
men had not time to catch it. "He funked for some reason, *I* thought,"
Simpson said afterwards in the tent he shared with his uncle. Dr.
Cathcart made no immediate reply, although the look had interested
him enough at the time for him to make a mental note of it. The expression had caused him a passing uneasiness he could not quite account for at the moment.

But Hank, of course, had been the first to notice it, and the odd thing was that instead of becoming explosive or angry over the other's reluctance, he at once began to humour him a bit.

"But there ain't no *speshul* reason why no one's been up there this year," he said, with a perceptible hush in his tone; "not the reason you mean, anyway! Las' year it was the fires that kep' folks out, and this year I guess—I guess it jest happened so, that's all!" His manner was clearly meant to be encouraging.

Joseph Défago raised his eyes a moment, then dropped them again. A breath of wind stole out of the forest and stirred the embers into a passing blaze. Dr. Cathcart again noticed the expression in the guide's face, and again he did not like it. But this time the nature of the look betrayed itself. In those eyes, for an instant, he caught the gleam of a man scared in his very soul. It disquieted him more than he cared to admit.

"Bad Indians up that way?" he asked, with a laugh to ease matters a little, while Simpson, too sleepy to notice this subtle by-play, moved off to bed with a prodigious yawn; "or—or anything wrong with the country?" he added, when his nephew was out of hearing.

Hank met his eye with something less than his usual frankness.

"He's jest skeered," he replied good-humouredly. "Skeered stiff about some ole feery tale! That's all, ain't it, ole pard?" And he gave Défago a friendly kick on the moccasined foot that lay nearest the fire.

Défago looked up quickly, as from an interrupted reverie, a reverie, however, that had not prevented his seeing all that went on about him.

"Skeered—*nuthin'!*" he answered, with a flush of defiance. "There's nuthin' in the Bush that can skeer Joseph Défago, and don't you forget it!" And the natural energy with which he spoke made it impossible to know whether he told the whole truth or only a part of it.

Hank turned towards the doctor. He was just going to add something when he stopped abruptly and looked round. A sound close behind them in the darkness made all three start. It was old Punk, who had moved up from his lean-to while they talked and now stood there just beyond the circle of firelight—listening.

"'Nother time, Doc!" Hank whispered, with a wink, "when the gallery ain't stepped down into the stalls!" And, springing to his feet, he slapped the Indian on the back and cried noisily, "Come up t' the fire an' warm yer dirty red skin a bit." He dragged him towards the blaze and threw more wood on. "That was a mighty good feed you give us an hour or two back," he continued heartily, as though to set the man's thoughts on another scent, "and it ain't Christian to let you stand out there freezin' yer ole soul to hell while we're gettin' all good an' toasted!" Punk moved in and warmed his feet, smiling darkly at the other's volubility which he only half understood, but saying nothing. And presently Dr. Cathcart, seeing that further conversation was impossible, followed his nephew's example and moved off to the tent, leaving the three men smoking over the now blazing fire.

It is not easy to undress in a small tent without waking one's companion, and Cathcart, hardened and warm-blooded as he was in spite of his fifty odd years, did what Hank would have described as "considerable of his twilight" in the open. He noticed, during the process, that Punk had meanwhile gone back to his lean-to, and that Hank and Défago were at it hammer and tongs, or, rather, hammer and anvil, the little French Canadian being the anvil. It was all very like the conventional stage picture of Western melodrama: the fire lighting up their faces with patches of alternate red and black; Défago, in slouch hat and moccasins in the part of the "badlands'" villain; Hank, open-faced and hatless, with that reckless fling of his shoulders, the honest and deceived hero; and old Punk, eavesdropping in the background, supplying the atmosphere of mystery. The doctor smiled as he noticed the details; but at the same time something deep within him—he hardly knew what—shrank a little, as though an almost imperceptible breath of warning had touched the surface of his soul and was gone again before he could seize it. Probably it was traceable to that "scared expression" he had seen in the eyes of Défago; "probably"—for this hint of fugitive emotion otherwise escaped his usually so keen analysis. Défago, he was vaguely aware, might cause trouble somehow. . . . He was not as steady a guide as Hank, for instance. . . . Further than that he could not get. . . .

He watched the men a moment longer before diving into the stuffy tent where Simpson already slept soundly. Hank, he saw, was swearing like a mad African in a New York nigger saloon; but it was the swearing of "affection." The ridiculous oaths flew freely now that the cause of their obstruction was asleep. Presently he put his arm almost tenderly upon his comrade's shoulder, and they moved off together into the shadows where their tent stood faintly glimmering.

Punk, too, a moment later followed their example and disappeared between his odorous blankets in the opposite direction.

Dr. Cathcart then likewise turned in, weariness and sleep still fighting in his mind with an obscure curiosity to know what it was had scared Défago about the country up Fifty Island Water way,—wondering, too, why Punk's presence had prevented the completion of what Hank had to say. Then sleep overtook him. He would know to-morrow. Hank would tell him the story while they trudged after the elusive moose.

Deep silence fell about the little camp, planted there so audaciously in the jaws of the wilderness. The lake gleamed like a sheet of black glass beneath the stars. The cold air pricked. In the draughts of night that poured their silent tide from the depths of the forest, with messages from distant ridges and from lakes just beginning to freeze, there lay already the faint, bleak odours of coming winter. White men, with their dull scent, might never have divined them; the fragrance of the wood-fire would have concealed from them these almost electrical hints of moss and bark and hardening swamp a hundred miles away. Even Hank and Défago, subtly in league with the soul of the woods as they were, would probably have spread their delicate nostrils in vain . . .

But an hour later, when all slept like the dead, old Punk crept from his blankets and went down to the shore of the lake like a shadow—silently, as only Indian blood can move. He raised his head and looked about him. The thick darkness rendered sight of small avail, but, like the animals, he possessed other senses that darkness could not mute. He listened—then sniffed the air. Motionless as a hemlock-stem he stood there. After five minutes again he lifted his head and sniffed, and yet once again. A tingling of the wonderful nerves that betrayed itself by no outer sign, ran through him as he tasted the keen air. Then, merging his figure into the surrounding blackness in a way that only wild men and animals understand, he turned, still moving like a shadow, and went stealthily back to his lean-to and his bed.

And soon after he slept, the change of wind he had divined stirred gently the reflection of the stars within the lake. Rising among the far ridges of the country beyond Fifty Island Water, it came from the direction in which he had stared, and it passed over the sleeping camp with a faint and sighing murmur through the tops of the big trees that was almost too delicate to be audible. With it, down the desert paths of night, though too faint, too high even for the Indian's hair-like nerves, there passed a curious, thin odour, strangely disquieting, an odour of something that seemed unfamiliar—utterly unknown.

The French Canadian and the man of Indian blood each stirred uneasily in his sleep just about this time, though neither of them woke. Then the ghost of that unforgettably strange odour passed away and was lost among the leagues of tenantless forest beyond.

II

In the morning the camp was astir before the sun. There had been a light fall of snow during the night and the air was sharp. Punk had done his duty betimes, for the odours of coffee and fried bacon reached every tent. All were in good spirits.

"Wind's shifted!" cried Hank vigorously, watching Simpson and his guide already loading the small canoe. "It's across the lake—dead right for you fellers. And the snow'll make bully trails! If there's any moose mussing around up thar, they'll not get so much as a tail-end scent of you with the wind as it is. Good luck, Monsieur Défago!" he added, facetiously giving the name its French pronunciation for once, *"bonne chance!"*

Défago returned the good wishes, apparently in the best of spirits, the silent mood gone. Before eight o'clock old Punk had the camp to himself, Cathcart and Hank were far along the trail that led westwards, while the canoe that carried Défago and Simpson, with silk tent and grub for two days, was already a dark speck bobbing on the bosom of the lake, going due east.

The wintry sharpness of the air was tempered now by a sun that topped the wooded ridges and blazed with a luxurious warmth upon the world of lake and forest below; loons flew skimming through the sparkling spray that the wind lifted; divers shook their dripping heads to the sun and popped smartly out of sight again; and as far as eye could reach rose the leagues of endless, crowding Bush, desolate in its lonely sweep and grandeur, untrodden by foot of man, and stretching its mighty and unbroken carpet right up to the frozen shores of Hudson Bay.

Simpson, who saw it all for the first time as he paddled hard in the bows of the dancing canoe, was enchanted by its austere beauty. His heart drank in the sense of freedom and great spaces just as his lungs drank in the cool and perfumed wind. Behind him in the stern seat, singing fragments of his native chanties, Défago steered the craft of birchbark like a thing of life, answering cheerfully all his companion's questions. Both were gay and light-hearted. On such occasions men lose the superficial, worldly distinctions; they become human beings working together for a common end. Simpson, the employer, and Défago the employed, among these primitive forces, were simply—two men, the "guider" and the "guided." Superior knowledge, of course, assumed control, and the younger man fell without a second thought into the quasi-subordinate position. He never dreamed of objecting when Défago dropped the "Mr.," and addressed him as "Say, Simpson," or "Simpson, boss," which was invariably the case before they reached the farther shore after a stiff paddle of twelve miles against a head wind. He only laughed, and liked it; then ceased to notice it at all.

For this "divinity student" was a young man of parts and character, though as yet, of course, untravelled; and on this trip—the first time he had seen any country but his own and little Switzerland—the huge scale of things somewhat bewildered him. It was one thing, he realised, to hear about primeval forests, but quite another to see them. While to dwell in them and seek acquaintance with their wild life was, again, an initiation that no intelligent man could undergo without a certain shifting of personal values hitherto held for permanent and sacred.

Simpson knew the first faint indication of this emotion when he held the new ·303 rifle in his hands and looked along its pair of faultless, gleaming barrels. The three days' journey to their headquarters, by lake and portage, had carried the process a stage farther. And now that he was about to plunge beyond even the fringe of wilderness where they were camped into the virgin heart of uninhabited regions as vast as Europe itself, the true nature of the situation stole upon him with an effect of delight and awe that his imagination was fully capable of appreciating. It was himself and Défago against a multitude—at least, against a Titan!

The bleak splendours of these remote and lonely forests rather overwhelmed him with the sense of his own littleness. That stern quality of the tangled backwoods which can only be described as merciless and terrible, rose out of these far blue woods swimming upon the horizon, and revealed itself. He understood the silent warning. He realised his own utter helplessness. Only Défago, as a symbol of a distant civilisation where man was master, stood between him and a pitiless death by exhaustion and starvation.

It was thrilling to him, therefore, to watch Défago turn over the canoe upon the shore, pack the paddles carefully underneath, and then proceed to "blaze" the spruce stems for some distance on either side of an almost invisible trail, with the careless remark thrown in, "Say, Simpson, if anything happens to me, you'll find the canoe all correc' by these marks;—then strike doo west into the sun to hit the home camp agin, see?"

It was the most natural thing in the world to say, and he said it without any noticeable inflection of the voice, only it happened to express the youth's emotions at the moment with an utterance that was symbolic of the situation and of his own helplessness as a factor in it. He was alone with Défago in a primitive world: that was all. The canoe, another symbol of man's ascendancy, was now to be left behind. Those small yellow patches, made on the trees by the axe, were the only indications of its hiding-place.

Meanwhile, shouldering the packs between them, each man carrying his own rifle, they followed the slender trail over rocks and fallen trunks and across half-frozen swamps; skirting numerous lakes that fairly gemmed the forest, their borders fringed with mist; and towards five o'clock found themselves suddenly on the edge of the woods, looking out across a large sheet of water in front of them, dotted with pine-clad islands of all describable shapes and sizes.

"Fifty Island Water," announced Défago wearily, "and the sun jest goin' to dip his bald old head into it!" he added, with unconscious poetry; and immediately they set about pitching camp for the night.

In a very few minutes, under those skilful hands that never made a movement too much or a movement too little, the silk tent stood taut and cosy, the beds of balsam boughs ready laid, and a brisk cooking-fire burned with the minimum of smoke. While the young Scotchman cleaned the fish they had caught trolling behind the canoe, Défago "guessed" he would "jest as soon" take a turn through the Bush for indications of moose. "May come across a trunk where they bin and rubbed horns," he said, as he moved off, "or feedin' on the last of the maple leaves"—and he was gone.

His small figure melted away like a shadow in the dusk, while Simpson noted with a kind of admiration how easily the forest absorbed him into herself. A few steps, it seemed, and he was no longer visible.

Yet there was little underbrush hereabouts; the trees stood somewhat apart, well spaced; and in the clearings grew silver-birch and maple, spear-like and slender, against the immense stems of spruce and hemlock. But for occasional prostrate monsters, and the boulders of grey rock that thrust uncouth shoulders here and there out of the ground, it might well have been a bit of park in the Old Country. Almost, one might have seen in it the hand of man. A little to the right, however, began the great burnt section, miles in extent, proclaiming its real character—*brulé*, as it is called, where the fires of the previous year had raged for weeks, and the blackened stumps now rose gaunt and ugly, bereft of branches, like gigantic match-heads stuck into the ground, savage and desolate beyond words. The perfume of charcoal and rain-soaked ashes still hung faintly about it.

The dusk rapidly deepened; the glades grew dark; the crackling of the fire and the wash of little waves along the rocky lake shore were the only sounds audible. The wind had dropped with the sun, and in all that vast world of branches nothing stirred. Any moment, it seemed, the woodland gods, who are to be worshipped in silence and loneliness, might stretch their mighty and terrific outlines among the trees. In front, through doorways pillared by huge straight stems, lay the stretch of Fifty Island Water, a crescent-shaped lake some fifteen miles from tip to tip, and perhaps five miles across where they were camped. A sky of rose and saffron, more clear than any atmosphere Simpson had ever known, still dropped its pale streaming fires across the waves, where the islands—a hundred, surely, rather than fifty—floated like the fairy barques of some enchanted fleet. Fringed with pines, whose crests fingered most delicately the sky, they almost seemed to move upwards as the light faded—about to weigh anchor and navigate the pathways of the heavens instead of the currents of their native and desolate lake.

And strips of coloured cloud, like flaunting pennons, signalled their departure to the stars. . . .

The beauty of the scene was strangely uplifting. Simpson smoked the fish and burnt his fingers into the bargain in his efforts to enjoy it and at the same time tend the frying-pan and the fire. Yet, ever at the back of his thoughts, lay that other aspect of the wilderness: the indifference to human life, the merciless spirit of desolation which took no note of man. The sense of his utter loneliness, now that even Défago had gone, came close as he looked about him and listened for the sound of his companion's returning footsteps.

There was pleasure in the sensation, yet with it a perfectly comprehensible alarm. And instinctively the thought stirred in him: "What should I—*could* I, do—if anything happened and he did not come back—?"

They enjoyed their well-earned supper, eating untold quantities of fish, and drinking unmilked tea strong enough to kill men who had not covered thirty miles of hard "going," eating little on the way. And when it was over, they smoked and told stories round the blazing fire, laughing, stretching weary limbs, and discussing plans for the morrow. Défago was in excellent spirits, though disappointed at having no signs of moose to report. But it was dark and he had not gone far. The *brulé*, too, was bad. His clothes and hands were smeared with charcoal. Simpson, watching him, realised with renewed vividness their position—alone together in the wilderness.

"Défago," he said presently, "these woods, you know, are a bit too big to feel quite at home in—to feel comfortable in, I mean! . . . Eh?" He merely gave expression to the mood of the moment; he was hardly prepared for the earnestness, the solemnity even, with which the guide took him up.

"You've hit it right, Simpson, boss," he replied, fixing his searching brown eyes on his face, "and that's the truth, sure. There's no end to 'em—no end at all." Then he added in a lowered tone as if to himself, "There's lots found out *that,* and gone plumb to pieces!"

But the man's gravity of manner was not quite to the other's liking; it was a little too suggestive for this scenery and setting; he was sorry he had broached the subject. He remembered suddenly how his uncle had told him that men were sometimes stricken with a strange fever of the wilderness, when the seduction of the uninhabited wastes caught them so fiercely that they went forth, half fascinated, half deluded, to their death. And he had a shrewd idea that his companion held something in sympathy with that queer type. He led the conversation on to other topics, on to Hank and the doctor, for instance, and the natural rivalry as to who should get the first sight of moose.

"If they went doo west," observed Défago carelessly, "there's sixty miles between us now—with ole Punk at half-way house eatin' himself full to bustin' with fish and corfee." They laughed together over the picture. But the casual mention of those sixty miles again made Simpson realise the prodigious scale of this land where they hunted; sixty miles was a mere step; two hundred little more than a step. Stories of lost hunters rose persistently before his memory. The passion and mystery of homeless and wandering men, seduced by the beauty of great forests, swept his soul in a way too vivid to be quite pleasant. He wondered vaguely whether it was the mood of his companion that invited the unwelcome suggestion with such persistence.

"Sing us a song, Défago, if you're not too tired," he asked; "one of those old *voyageur* songs you sang the other night." He handed his tobacco pouch to the guide and then filled his own pipe, while the Canadian, nothing loth, sent his light voice across the lake in one of those plaintive, almost melancholy chanties with which lumbermen and trappers lessen the burden of their labour. There was an appealing and romantic flavour about it, something that recalled the atmosphere of the old pioneer days when Indians and wilderness were leagued together, battles frequent, and the Old Country farther off than it is to-day. The sound travelled pleasantly over the water, but the forest at their backs seemed to swallow it down with a single gulp that permitted neither echo nor resonance.

It was in the middle of the third verse that Simpson noticed something unusual—something that brought his thoughts back with a rush from far-away scenes. A curious change had come into the man's voice. Even before he knew what it was, uneasiness caught him, and looking up quickly, he saw that Défago, though still singing, was peering about him into the Bush, as though he heard or saw something. His voice grew fainter—dropped to a hush—then ceased altogether. The same instant, with a movement amazingly alert, he started to his feet and stood upright—*sniffing the air*. Like a dog scenting game, he drew the air into his nostrils in short, sharp breaths, turning quickly as he did so in all directions, and finally "pointing" down the lake shore, eastwards. It was a performance unpleasantly suggestive and at the same time singularly dramatic. Simpson's heart fluttered disagreeably as he watched it.

"Lord, man! How you made me jump!" he exclaimed, on his feet beside him the same instant, and peering over his shoulder into the sea of darkness. "What's up? Are you frightened—?"

Even before the question was out of his mouth he knew it was foolish, for any man with a pair of eyes in his head could see that the Canadian had turned white down to his very gills. Not even sunburn and the glare of the fire could hide that.

The student felt himself trembling a little, weakish in the knees. "What's up?" he repeated quickly. "D'you smell moose? Or anything queer, anything—wrong?" He lowered his voice instinctively.

The forest pressed round them with its encircling wall; the nearer tree-stems gleamed like bronze in the firelight; beyond that—blackness, and, so far as he could tell, a silence of death. Just behind them a passing puff of wind lifted a single leaf, looked at it, then laid it softly down again without disturbing the rest of the covey. It seemed as if a million invisible causes had combined just to produce that single visible effect. *Other* life pulsed about them—and was gone.

Défago turned abruptly; the livid hue of his face had turned to a dirty grey.

"I never said I heered—or smelt—nuthin'," he said slowly and emphatically, in an oddly altered voice that conveyed somehow a touch of defiance. "I was only—takin' a look round—so to speak. It's always a mistake to be too previous with yer questions." Then he added suddenly with obvious effort, in his more natural voice, "Have you got the matches, Boss Simpson?" and proceeded to light the pipe he had half filled just before he began to sing.

Without speaking another word they sat down again by the fire, Défago changing his side so that he could face the direction the wind came from. For even a tenderfoot could tell that. Défago changed his position in order to hear and smell—all there was to be heard and smelt. And, since he now faced the lake with his back to the trees it was evidently nothing in the forest that had sent so strange and sudden a warning to his marvellously trained nerves.

"Guess now I don't feel like singing any," he explained presently of his own accord. "That song kinder brings back memories that's troublesome to me; I never oughter've begun it. It sets me on t' imagining things, see?"

Clearly the man was still fighting with some profoundly moving emotion. He wished to excuse himself in the eyes of the other. But the explanation, in that it was only a part of the truth, was a lie, and he knew perfectly well that Simpson was not deceived by it. For nothing could explain away the livid terror that had dropped over his face while he stood there sniffing the air. And nothing—no amount of blazing fire, or chatting on ordinary subjects—could make that camp exactly as it had been before. The shadow of an unknown horror, naked if unguessed, that had flashed for an instant in the face and gestures of the guide, had also communicated itself, vaguely and therefore more potently, to his companion. The guide's visible efforts to dissemble the truth only made things worse. Moreover, to add to the younger man's uneasiness, was the difficulty, nay, the impossibility he felt of asking questions, and also his complete ignorance as to the cause. . . . Indians, wild animals, forest fires—all these, he knew, were wholly out of the question. His imagination searched vigorously, but in vain. . . .

Yet, somehow or other, after another long spell of smoking, talking and roasting themselves before the great fire, the shadow that had so suddenly invaded their peaceful camp began to lift. Perhaps Défago's efforts, or the return of his quiet and normal attitude accomplished this; perhaps Simpson himself had exaggerated the affair out of all proportion to the truth; or possibly the vigorous air of the wilderness brought its own powers of healing. Whatever the cause, the feeling of immediate horror seemed to have passed away as mysteriously as it had come, for nothing occurred to feed it. Simpson began to feel that he had permitted himself the unreasoning terror of a child. He put it down partly to a certain subconscious excitement that this wild and immense scenery generated in his blood, partly to the spell of solitude, and partly to over fatigue. That pallor in the guide's face was, of course, uncommonly hard to explain, yet it *might* have been due in some way to an effect of firelight, or his own imagination. . . . He gave it the benefit of the doubt; he was Scotch.

When a somewhat unordinary emotion has disappeared, the mind always finds a dozen ways of explaining away its causes. . . . Simpson lit a last pipe and tried to laugh to himself. On getting home to Scotland it would make quite a good story. He did not realise that this laughter was a sign that terror still lurked in the recesses of his soul—that, in fact, it was merely one of the conventional signs by which a man, seriously alarmed, tries to persuade himself that he is *not* so.

Défago, however, heard that low laughter and looked up with surprise on his face. The two men stood, side by side, kicking the embers about before going to bed. It was ten o'clock—a late hour for hunters to be still awake.

"What's ticklin' yer?" he asked in his ordinary tone, yet gravely.

"I—I was thinking of our little toy woods at home, just at that moment," stammered Simpson, coming back to what really dominated his mind, and startled by the question, "and comparing them to—to all this," and he swept his arm round to indicate the Bush.

A pause followed in which neither of them said anything.

"All the same I wouldn't laugh about it, if I was you," Défago added, looking over Simpson's shoulder into the shadows. "There's places in there nobody won't never see into—nobody knows what lives in there either."

"Too big—too far off?" The suggestion in the guide's manner was immense and horrible.

Défago nodded. The expression on his face was dark. He, too, felt uneasy. The younger man understood that in a *hinterland* of this size there might well be depths of wood that would never in the life of the world be known or trodden. The thought was not exactly the sort he welcomed. In a loud voice, cheerfully, he suggested that it was time for bed. But the guide lingered, tinkering with the fire, arranging the stones needlessly, doing a dozen things that did not really need doing. Evidently there was something he wanted to say, yet found it difficult to "get at."

"Say, you, Boss Simpson," he began suddenly, as the last shower of sparks went up into the air, "you don't—smell nothing, do you—nothing pertickler, I mean?" The commonplace question, Simpson realised, veiled a dreadfully serious thought in his mind. A shiver ran down his back.

"Nothing but burning wood," he replied firmly, kicking again at the embers. The sound of his own foot made him start.

"And all the evenin' you ain't smelt—nothing?" persisted the guide, peering at him through the gloom; "nothing extrordiny, and different to anything else you ever smelt before?"

"No, no, man; nothing at all!" he replied aggressively, half angrily.

Défago's face cleared. "That's good!" he exclaimed, with evident relief. "That's good to hear."

"Have *you?*" asked Simpson sharply, and the same instant regretted the question.

The Canadian came closer in the darkness. He shook his head. "I guess not," he said, though without overwhelming conviction. "It must've been just that song of mine that did it. It's the song they sing in lumber-camps and god-forsaken places like that, when they're skeered the Wendigo's somewheres around, doin' a bit of swift travellin'—"

"And what's the Wendigo, pray?" Simpson asked quickly, irritated because again he could not prevent that sudden shiver of the nerves. He knew that he was close upon the man's terror and the cause of it. Yet a rushing passionate curiosity overcame his better judgment, *and* his fear.

Défago turned swiftly and looked at him as though he were suddenly about to shriek. His eyes shone, but his mouth was wide open. Yet all he said, or whispered rather, for his voice sank very low, was—

"It's nuthin'—nuthin' but what those lousy fellers believe when they've bin hittin' the bottle too long—a sort of great animal that lives up yonder," he jerked his head northwards, "quick as lightning in its tracks, an' bigger'n anything else in the Bush, an' ain't supposed to be very good to look at—*that's all!*"

"A backwoods superstition—" began Simpson, moving hastily towards the tent in order to shake off the hand of the guide that clutched his arm. "Come, come, hurry up for God's sake, and get the lantern going! It's time we were in bed and asleep if we're going to be up with the sun to-morrow. . . ."

The guide was close on his heels. "I'm coming," he answered out of the darkness, "I'm coming." And after a slight delay he appeared with the lantern and hung it from a nail in the front pole of the tent. The shadows of a hundred trees shifted their places quickly as he did so, and when he stumbled over the rope, diving swiftly inside, the whole tent trembled as though a gust of wind struck it.

The two men lay down, without undressing, upon their beds of soft balsam boughs, cunningly arranged. Inside, all was warm and cosy, but outside the world of crowding trees pressed close about them, marshalling their million shadows, and smothering the little tent that stood there like a wee white shell facing the ocean of tremendous forest.

Between the two lonely figures within, however, there pressed another shadow that was *not* a shadow from the night. It was the Shadow cast by the strange Fear, never wholly exorcised, that had leaped suddenly upon Défago in the middle of his singing. And Simpson, as he lay there, watching the darkness through the open flap of the tent, ready to plunge into the fragrant abyss of sleep, knew first that unique and profound stillness of a primeval forest when no wind stirs . . . and when the night has weight and substance that enters into the soul to bind a veil about it. . . . Then sleep took him. . . .

III

Thus it seemed to him, at least. Yet it was true that the lap of the water, just beyond the tent door, still beat time with his lessening pulses when he realised that he was lying with his eyes open and that another sound had recently introduced itself with cunning softness between the splash and murmur of the little waves.

And, long before he understood what this sound was, it had stirred in him the centres of pity and alarm. He listened intently, though at first in vain, for the running blood beat all its drums too noisily in his ears. Did it come, he wondered, from the lake, or from the woods? . . .

Then, suddenly, with a rush and a flutter of the heart, he knew that it was close beside him in the tent; and, when he turned over for a better hearing, it focussed itself unmistakably not two feet away. It was a sound of weeping: Défago upon his bed of branches was sobbing in the darkness as though his heart would break, the blankets evidently stuffed against his mouth to stifle it.

And his first feeling, before he could think or reflect, was the rush of a poignant and searching tenderness. This intimate, human sound, heard amid the desolation about them, woke pity. It was so incongruous, so pitifully incongruous—and so vain! Tears—in this vast and cruel wilderness: of what avail? He thought of a little child crying in mid-Atlantic. . . . Then, of course, with fuller realisation, and the memory of what had gone before, came the descent of the terror upon him, and his blood ran cold.

"Défago," he whispered quickly, "what's the matter?" He tried to make his voice very gentle. "Are you in pain—unhappy—?" There was no reply, but the sounds ceased abruptly. He stretched his hand out and touched him. The body did not stir.

"Are you awake?" for it occurred to him that the man was crying in his sleep. "Are you cold?" He noticed that his feet, which were un-covered, projected beyond the mouth of the tent. He spread an extra fold of his own blankets over them. The guide had slipped down in his bed, and the branches seemed to have been dragged with him. He was afraid to pull the body back again, for fear of waking him.

One or two tentative questions he ventured softly, but though he waited for several minutes there came no reply, nor any sign of move-ment. Presently he heard his regular and quiet breathing, and putting his hand again gently on the breast, felt the steady rise and fall beneath.

"Let me know if anything's wrong," he whispered, "or if I can do anything. Wake me at once if you feel—queer."

He hardly knew what to say. He lay down again, thinking and wondering what it all meant. Défago, of course, had been crying in his sleep. Some dream or other had afflicted him. Yet never in his life would he forget that pitiful sound of sobbing, and the feeling that the whole awful wilderness of woods listened. . . .

His own mind busied itself for a long time with the recent events, of which *this* took its mysterious place as one, and though his reason successfully argued away all unwelcome suggestions, a sensation of un-easiness remained, resisting ejection, very deep-seated—peculiar be-yond ordinary.

IV

But sleep, in the long run, proves greater than all emotions. His thoughts soon wandered again; he lay there, warm as a toast, exceed-ingly weary; the night soothed and comforted, blunting the edges of memory and alarm. Half-an-hour later he was oblivious of everything in the outer world about him.

Yet sleep, in this case, was his great enemy, concealing all approaches, smothering the warning of his nerves.

As, sometimes, in a nightmare events crowd upon each other's heels with a conviction of dreadfullest reality, yet some inconsistent detail accuses the whole display of incompleteness and disguise, so the events that now followed, though they actually happened, persuaded the mind somehow that the detail which could explain them had been overlooked in the confusion, and that therefore they were but partly true, the rest delusion. At the back of the sleeper's mind something remains awake, ready to let slip the judgment, "All this is not *quite* real; when you wake up you'll understand."

And thus, in a way, it was with Simpson. The events, not wholly inexplicable or incredible in themselves, yet remain for the man who saw and heard them a sequence of separate facts of cold horror, because the little piece that might have made the puzzle clear lay concealed or overlooked.

So far as he can recall, it was a violent movement, running downwards through the tent towards the door, that first woke him and made him aware that his companion was sitting bolt upright beside him—quivering. Hours must have passed, for it was the pale gleam of the dawn that revealed his outline against the canvas. This time the man was not crying; he was quaking like a leaf; the trembling he felt plainly through the blankets down the entire length of his own body. Défago had huddled down against him for protection, shrinking away from something that apparently concealed itself near the door-flaps of the little tent.

Simpson thereupon called out in a loud voice some question or other—in the first bewilderment of waking he does not remember exactly what—and the man made no reply. The atmosphere and feeling of true nightmare lay horribly about him, making movement and speech both difficult. At first, indeed, he was not sure where he was—whether in one of the earlier camps, or at home in his bed at Aberdeen. The sense of confusion was very troubling.

And next—almost simultaneous with his waking, it seemed—the profound stillness of the dawn outside was shattered by a most uncommon sound. It came without warning, or audible approach; and it was unspeakably dreadful. It was a voice, Simpson declares, possibly a human voice; hoarse yet plaintive—a soft, roaring voice close outside the tent, overhead rather than upon the ground, of immense volume, while in some strange way most penetratingly and seductively sweet. It rang out, too, in three separate and distinct notes, or cries, that bore in some odd fashion a resemblance, far-fetched yet recognisable, to the name of the guide: *"Dé—fa—go!"*

The student admits he is unable to describe it quite intelligently, for it was unlike any sound he had ever heard in his life, and combined a blending of such contrary qualities. "A sort of windy, crying voice," he calls it, "as of something lonely and untamed, wild and of abominable power. . . ."

And, even before it ceased, dropping back into the great gulfs of silence, the guide beside him had sprung to his feet with an answering though unintelligible cry. He blundered against the tent-pole with violence, shaking the whole structure, spreading his arms out frantically for more room, and kicking his legs impetuously free of the clinging blankets. For a second, perhaps two, he stood upright by the door, his outline dark against the pallor of the dawn; then, with a furious, rushing speed, before his companion could move a hand to stop him, he shot with a plunge through the flaps of canvas—and was gone. And as he went—so astonishingly fast that the voice could actually be heard dying in the distance—he called aloud in tones of anguished terror that at the same time held something strangely like the frenzied exultation of delight—

"Oh! oh! My feet of fire! My burning feet of fire! Oh! oh! This height and fiery speed!"

And then the distance quickly buried it, and the deep silence of very early morning descended upon the forest as before.

It had all come about with such rapidity that, but for the evidence of the empty bed beside him, Simpson could almost have believed it to have been the memory of a nightmare carried over from sleep. He still felt the warm pressure of that vanished body against his side; there lay the twisted blankets in a heap; the very tent yet trembled with the vehemence of the impetuous departure. The strange words rang in his ears, as though he still heard them in the distance—wild language of a suddenly stricken mind. Moreover, it was not only the senses of sight and hearing that reported uncommon things to his brain, for even while the man cried and ran, he had become aware that a strange perfume, faint yet pungent, pervaded the interior of the tent. And it was at this point, it seems, brought to himself by the consciousness that his nostrils were taking this distressing odour down into his throat, that he found his courage, sprang quickly to his feet—and went out.

The grey light of dawn that dropped, cold and glimmering, between the trees revealed the scene tolerably well. There stood the tent behind him, soaked with dew; the dark ashes of the fire, still warm; the lake, white beneath a coating of mist, the islands rising darkly out of it like objects packed in wool; and patches of snow beyond among the clearer spaces of the Bush—everything cold, still, waiting for the sun. But nowhere a sign of the vanished guide—still, doubtless, flying at frantic speed through the frozen woods. There was not even the sound of disappearing footsteps, nor the echoes of the dying voice. He had gone—utterly.

There was nothing; nothing but the sense of his recent presence, so strongly left behind about the camp; *and*—this penetrating, all-pervading odour.

And even this was now rapidly disappearing in its turn. In spite of his exceeding mental perturbation, Simpson struggled hard to detect its nature, and define it, but the ascertaining of an elusive scent, not recognised subconsciously and at once, is a very subtle operation of the mind. And he failed. It was gone before he could properly seize or name it. Approximate description, even, seems to have been difficult, for it was unlike any smell he knew. Acrid rather, not unlike the odour of a lion, he thinks, yet softer and not wholly unpleasing, with something almost sweet in it that reminded him of the scent of decaying garden leaves, earth, and the myriad, nameless perfumes that make up the odour of a big forest. Yet the "odour of lions" is the phrase with which he usually sums it all up.

Then—it was wholly gone, and he found himself standing by the ashes of the fire in a state of amazement and stupid terror that left him the helpless prey of anything that chose to happen. Had a musk-rat poked its pointed muzzle over a rock, or a squirrel scuttled in that instant down the bark of a tree, he would most likely have collapsed without more ado and fainted. For he felt about the whole affair the touch somewhere of a great Outer Horror . . . and his scattered powers had not as yet had time to collect themselves into a definite attitude of fighting self-control.

Nothing did happen, however. A great kiss of wind ran softly through the awakening forest, and a few maple leaves here and there rustled tremblingly to earth. The sky seemed to grow suddenly much lighter. Simpson felt the cool air upon his cheek and uncovered head; realised that he was shivering with the cold; and, making a great effort, realised next that he was alone in the Bush—*and* that he was called upon to take immediate steps to find and succour his vanished companion.

Make an effort, accordingly, he did, though an ill-calculated and futile one. With that wilderness of trees about him, the sheet of water cutting him off behind, and the horror of that wild cry in his blood, he did what any other inexperienced man would have done in similar bewilderment: he ran about, without any sense of direction, like a frantic child, and called loudly without ceasing the name of the guide—

"Défago! Défago! Défago!" he yelled, and the trees gave him back the name as often as he shouted, only a little softened—"Défago! Défago! Défago!"

He followed the trail that lay a short distance across the patches of snow, and then lost it again where the trees grew too thickly for snow to lie. He shouted till he was hoarse, and till the sound of his own voice in all that unanswering and listening world began to frighten him. His confusion increased in direct ratio to the violence of his efforts. His distress became formidably acute, till at length his exertions defeated their own object, and from sheer exhaustion he headed back to the camp again. It remains a wonder that he ever found his way. It was with great difficulty, and only after numberless false clues, that he at last saw the white tent between the trees, and so reached safety.

Exhaustion then applied its own remedy, and he grew calmer. He made the fire and breakfasted. Hot coffee and bacon put a little sense and judgment into him again, and he realised that he had been behaving like a boy. He now made another, and more successful attempt to face the situation collectedly, and, a nature naturally plucky coming to his assistance, he decided that he must first make as thorough a search as possible, failing success in which, he must find his way into the home camp as best he could and bring help.

And this was what he did. Taking food, matches and rifle with him, and a small axe to blaze the trees against his return journey, he set forth. It was eight o'clock when he started, the sun shining over the tops of the trees in a sky without clouds. Pinned to a stake by the fire he left a note in case Défago returned while he was away.

This time, according to a careful plan, he took a new direction, intending to make a wide sweep that must sooner or later cut into indications of the guide's trail; and, before he had gone a quarter of a mile he came across the tracks of a large animal in the snow, and beside it the light and smaller tracks of what were beyond question human feet— the feet of Défago. The relief he at once experienced was natural, though brief; for at first sight he saw in these tracks a simple explanation of the whole matter: these big marks had surely been left by a bull moose that, wind against it, had blundered upon the camp, and uttered its singular cry of warning and alarm the moment its mistake was apparent. Défago, in whom the hunting instinct was developed to the point of uncanny perfection, had scented the brute coming down the wind hours before. His excitement and disappearance were due, of course, to—to his—

Then the impossible explanation at which he grasped faded, as common sense showed him mercilessly that none of this was true. No guide, much less a guide like Défago, could have acted in so irrational a way, going off even without his rifle . . . ! The whole affair demanded a far more complicated elucidation, when he remembered the details of it all—the cry of terror, the amazing language, the grey face of horror when his nostrils first caught the new odour; that muffled sobbing in the darkness, and—for this, too, now came back to him dimly—the man's original aversion for this particular bit of country. . . .

Besides, now that he examined them closer, these were not the tracks of a bull moose at all! Hank had explained to him the outline of a bull's hoofs, of a cow's or calf's, too, for that matter; he had drawn them clearly on a strip of birchbark. And these were wholly different. They were big, round, ample, and with no pointed outline as of sharp hoofs. He wondered for a moment whether bear-tracks were like that. There was no other animal he could think of, for caribou did not come so far south at this season, and, even if they did, would leave hoof-marks.

They were ominous signs—these mysterious writings left in the snow by the unknown creature that had lured a human being away from safety—and when he coupled them in his imagination with that haunting sound that broke the stillness of the dawn, a momentary dizziness shook his mind, distressing him again beyond belief. He felt the *threatening* aspect of it all. And, stooping down to examine the marks more closely, he caught a faint whiff of that sweet yet pungent odour that made him instantly straighten up again, fighting a sensation almost of nausea.

Then his memory played him another evil trick. He suddenly recalled those uncovered feet projecting beyond the edge of the tent, and the body's appearance of having been dragged towards the opening; the man's shrinking from something by the door when he woke later. The details now beat against his trembling mind with concerted attack. They seemed to gather in those deep spaces of the silent forest about him, where the host of trees stood waiting, listening, watching to see what he would do. The woods were closing round him.

With the persistence of true pluck, however, Simpson went forward, following the tracks as best he could, smothering these ugly emotions that sought to weaken his will. He blazed innumerable trees as he went, ever fearful of being unable to find the way back, and calling aloud at intervals of a few seconds the name of the guide. The dull tapping of the axe upon the massive trunks, and the unnatural accents of his own voice became at length sounds that he even dreaded to make, dreaded to hear. For they drew attention without ceasing to his presence and exact whereabouts, and if it were really the case that something was hunting himself down in the same way that he was hunting down another—

With a strong effort, he crushed the thought out the instant it rose. It was the beginning, he realised, of a bewilderment utterly diabolical in kind that would speedily destroy him.

Although the snow was not continuous, lying merely in shallow flurries over the more open spaces, he found no difficulty in following the tracks for the first few miles. They went straight as a ruled line wherever the trees permitted. The stride soon began to increase in length, till it finally assumed proportions that seemed absolutely impossible for any ordinary animal to have made. Like huge flying leaps they became. One of these he measured, and though he knew that "stretch" of eighteen feet must be somehow wrong, he was at a complete loss to understand why he found no signs on the snow between the extreme points. But what perplexed him even more, making him feel his vision had gone utterly awry, was that Défago's stride increased in the same manner, and finally covered the same incredible distances. It looked as if the great beast had lifted him with it and carried him across these astonishing intervals. Simpson, who was much longer in the limb, found that he could not compass even half the stretch by taking a running jump.

And the sight of these huge tracks, running side by side, silent evidence of a dreadful journey in which terror or madness had urged to impossible results, was profoundly moving. It shocked him in the secret depths of his soul. It was the most horrible thing his eyes had ever looked upon. He began to follow them mechanically, absent-mindedly almost, ever peering over his shoulder to see if he, too, were being followed by something with a gigantic tread. . . . And soon it came about that he no longer quite realised what it was they signified—these impressions left upon the snow by something nameless and untamed, always accompanied by the footmarks of the little French Canadian, his guide, his comrade, the man who had shared his tent a few hours before, chatting, laughing, even singing by his side. . . .

V

For a man of his years and inexperience, only a canny Scot, perhaps, grounded in common sense and established in logic, could have preserved even that measure of balance that this youth somehow or other did manage to preserve through the whole adventure. Otherwise, two things he presently noticed, while forging pluckily ahead, must have sent him headlong back to the comparative safety of his tent, instead of only making his hands close more tightly upon the rifle-stock, while his heart, trained for the Wee Kirk, sent a wordless prayer winging its way to heaven. Both tracks, he saw, had undergone a change, and this change, so far as it concerned the footsteps of the man, was in some undecipherable manner—appalling.

It was in the bigger tracks he first noticed this, and for a long time he could not quite believe his eyes. Was it the blown leaves that produced odd effects of light and shade, or that the dry snow, drifting like finely-ground rice about the edges, cast shadows and high lights? Or was it actually the fact that the great marks had become faintly coloured? For round about the deep, plunging holes of the animal there now appeared a mysterious, reddish tinge that was more like an effect of light than of anything that dyed the substance of the snow itself. Every mark had it, and had it increasingly—this indistinct fiery tinge that painted a new touch of ghastliness into the picture.

But when, wholly unable to explain or credit it, he turned his attention to the other tracks to discover if they, too, bore similar witness, he noticed that these had meanwhile undergone a change that was infinitely worse, and charged with far more horrible suggestion. For, in the last hundred yards or so, he saw that they had grown gradually into the semblance of the parent tread. Imperceptibly the change had come about, yet unmistakably. It was hard to see where the change first began. The result, however, was beyond question. Smaller, neater, more cleanly modelled, they formed now an exact and careful duplicate of the larger tracks beside them. The feet that produced them had, therefore, also changed. And something in his mind reared up with loathing and with terror as he saw it.

Simpson, for the first time, hesitated; then, ashamed of his alarm and indecision, took a few hurried steps ahead; the next instant stopped dead in his tracks. Immediately in front of him all signs of the trail ceased; both tracks came to an abrupt end. On all sides, for a hundred yards and more, he searched in vain for the least indication of their continuance. There was—nothing.

The trees were very thick just there, big trees all of them, spruce, cedar, hemlock; there was no underbrush. He stood, looking about him, all distraught; bereft of any power of judgment. Then he set to work to search again, and again, and yet again, but always with the same result: *nothing*. The feet that printed the surface of the snow thus far had now, apparently, left the ground!

And it was in that moment of distress and confusion that the whip of terror laid its most nicely calculated lash about his heart. It dropped with deadly effect upon the sorest spot of all, completely unnerving him. He had been secretly dreading all the time that it would come— and come it did.

Far overhead, muted by great height and distance, strangely thinned and wailing, he heard the crying voice of Défago, the guide.

The sound dropped upon him out of that still, wintry sky with an effect of dismay and terror unsurpassed. The rifle fell to his feet. He stood motionless an instant, listening as it were with his whole body, then staggered back against the nearest tree for support, disorganised hopelessly in mind and spirit. To him, in that moment, it seemed the most shattering and dislocating experience he had ever known, so that his heart emptied itself of all feeling whatsoever as by a sudden draft.

"Oh! oh! This fiery height! Oh, my feet of fire! My burning feet of fire ... !" ran in far, beseeching accents of indescribable appeal this voice of anguish down the sky. Once it called—then silence through all the listening wilderness of trees.

And Simpson, scarcely knowing what he did, presently found himself running wildly to and fro, searching, calling, tripping over roots and boulders, and flinging himself in a frenzy of undirected pursuit after the Caller. Behind the screen of memory and emotion with which experience veils events, he plunged, distracted and half-deranged, picking up false lights like a ship at sea, terror in his eyes and heart and soul. For the Panic of the Wilderness had called to him in that far voice—the Power of untamed Distance—the Enticement of the Desolation that destroys. He knew in that moment all the pains of some one hopelessly and irretrievably lost, suffering the lust and travail of a soul in the final Loneliness. A vision of Défago, eternally hunted, driven and pursued across the skiey vastness of those ancient forests, fled like a flame across the dark ruin of his thoughts. . . .

It seemed ages before he could find anything in the chaos of his disorganised sensations to which he could anchor himself steady for a moment, and think. . . .

The cry was not repeated; his own hoarse calling brought no response; the inscrutable forces of the Wild had summoned their victim beyond recall—and held him fast.

Yet he searched and called, it seems, for hours afterwards, for it was late in the afternoon when at length he decided to abandon a useless pursuit and return to his camp on the shores of Fifty Island Water. Even then he went with reluctance, that crying voice still echoing in his ears. With difficulty he found his rifle and the homeward trail. The concentration necessary to follow the badly blazed trees, and a biting hunger that gnawed, helped to keep his mind steady. Otherwise, he admits, the temporary aberration he had suffered might have been prolonged to the point of positive disaster. Gradually the ballast shifted back again, and he regained something that approached his normal equilibrium.

But for all that the journey through the gathering dusk was miserably haunted. He heard innumerable following footsteps; voices that laughed and whispered; and saw figures crouching behind trees and boulders, making signs to one another for a concerted attack the moment he had passed. The creeping murmur of the wind made him start and listen. He went stealthily, trying to hide where possible, and making as little sound as he could. The shadows of the woods, hitherto protective or covering merely, had now become menacing, challenging; and the pageantry in his frightened mind masked a host of possibilities that were all the more ominous for being obscure. The presentiment of a nameless doom lurked ill-concealed behind every detail of what had happened.

It was really admirable how he emerged victor in the end; men of riper powers and experience might have come through the ordeal with less success. He had himself tolerably well in hand, all things considered, and his plan of action proves it. Sleep being absolutely out of the question, and travelling an unknown trail in the darkness equally impracticable, he sat up the whole of that night, rifle in hand, before a fire he never for a single moment allowed to die down. The severity of the haunted vigil marked his soul for life; but it was successfully accomplished; and with the very first signs of dawn he set forth upon the long return journey to the home-camp to get help. As before, he left a written note to explain his absence, and to indicate where he had left a plentiful *cache* of food and matches—though he had no expectation that any human hands would find them!

How Simpson found his way alone by the lake and forest might well make a story in itself, for to hear him tell it is to *know* the passionate loneliness of soul that a man can feel when the Wilderness holds him in the hollow of its illimitable hand—and laughs. It is also to admire his indomitable pluck.

He claims no skill, declaring that he followed the almost invisible trail mechanically, and without thinking. And this, doubtless, is the truth. He relied upon the guiding of the unconscious mind, which is instinct. Perhaps, too, some sense of orientation, known to animals and primitive men, may have helped as well, for through all that tangled region he succeeded in reaching the exact spot where Défago had hidden the canoe nearly three days before with the remark, "Strike doo west across the lake into the sun to find the camp."

There was not much sun left to guide him, but he used his compass to the best of his ability, embarking in the frail craft for the last twelve miles of his journey with a sensation of immense relief that the forest was at last behind him. And, fortunately, the water was calm; he took his line across the centre of the lake instead of coasting round the shores for another twenty miles. Fortunately, too, the other hunters were back. The light of their fires furnished a steering-point without which he might have searched all night long for the actual position of the camp.

It was close upon midnight all the same when his canoe grated on the sandy cove, and Hank, Punk and his uncle, disturbed in their sleep by his cries, ran quickly down and helped a very exhausted and broken specimen of Scotch humanity over the rocks towards a dying fire.

VI

The sudden entrance of his prosaic uncle into this world of wizardry and horror that had haunted him without interruption now for two days and two nights, had the immediate effect of giving to the affair an entirely new aspect. The sound of that crisp "Hulloa, my boy! And what's up *now?*" and the grasp of that dry and vigorous hand introduced another standard of judgment. A revulsion of feeling washed through him. He realised that he had let himself "go" rather badly. He even felt vaguely ashamed of himself. The native hard-headedness of his race reclaimed him.

And this doubtless explains why he found it so hard to tell that group round the fire—everything. He told enough, however, for the immediate decision to be arrived at that a relief party must start at the earliest possible moment, and that Simpson, in order to guide it capably, must first have food and, above all, sleep. Dr. Cathcart observing the lad's condition more shrewdly than his patient knew, gave him a very slight injection of morphine. For six hours he slept like the dead.

From the description carefully written out afterwards by this student of divinity, it appears that the account he gave to the astonished group omitted sundry vital and important details. He declares that, with his uncle's wholesome, matter-of-fact countenance staring him in the face, he simply had not the courage to mention them. Thus, all the search-party gathered, it would seem, was that Défago had suffered in the night an acute and inexplicable attack of mania, had imagined himself "called" by some one or something, and had plunged into the bush after it without food or rifle, where he must die a horrible and lingering death by cold and starvation unless he could be found and rescued in time. "In time," moreover, meant "at once."

In the course of the following day, however—they were off by seven, leaving Punk in charge with instructions to have food and fire always ready—Simpson found it possible to tell his uncle a good deal more of the story's true inwardness, without divining that it was drawn out of him as a matter of fact by a very subtle form of cross-examination. By the time they reached the beginning of the trail, where the canoe was laid up against the return journey, he had mentioned how Défago spoke vaguely of "something he called a 'Wendigo'"; how he cried in his sleep; how he imagined an unusual scent about the camp; and had betrayed other symptoms of mental excitement. He also admitted the bewildering effect of "that extraordinary odour" upon himself, "pungent and acrid like the odour of lions." And by the time they were within an easy hour of Fifty Island Water he had let slip the further fact—a foolish avowal of his own hysterical condition, as he felt afterwards—that he had heard the vanished guide call "for help." He omitted the singular phrases used, for he simply could not bring himself to repeat the preposterous language. Also, while describing how the man's footsteps in the snow had gradually assumed an exact miniature likeness of the animal's plunging tracks, he left out the fact that they measured a *wholly* incredible distance. It seemed a question, nicely balanced between individual pride and honesty, what he should reveal and what suppress. He mentioned the fiery tinge in the snow, for instance, yet shrank from telling that body and bed had been partly dragged out of the tent. . . .

With the net result that Dr. Cathcart, adroit psychologist that he fancied himself to be, had assured him clearly enough exactly where his mind, influenced by loneliness, bewilderment and terror, had yielded to the strain and invited delusion. While praising his conduct, he managed at the same time to point out where, when, and how his mind had gone astray. He made his nephew think himself finer than he was by judicious praise, yet more foolish than he was by minimising the value of his evidence. Like many another materialist, that is, he lied cleverly on the basis of insufficient knowledge, *because* the knowledge supplied seemed to his own particular intelligence inadmissible.

"The spell of these terrible solitudes," he said, "cannot leave any mind untouched, any mind, that is, possessed of the higher imaginative qualities. It has worked upon yours exactly as it worked upon my own when I was your age. The animal that haunted your little camp was undoubtedly a moose, for the 'belling' of a moose may have, sometimes, a very peculiar quality of sound. The coloured appearance of the big tracks was obviously a defect of vision in your own eyes produced by excitement. The size and stretch of the tracks we shall prove when we come to them. But the hallucination of an audible voice, of course, is one of the commonest forms of delusion due to mental excitement—an excitement, my dear boy, perfectly excusable, and, let me add, wonderfully controlled by you under the circumstances. For the rest, I am bound to say, you have acted with a splendid courage, for the terror of feeling oneself lost in this wilderness is nothing short of awful, and, had I been in your place, I don't for a moment believe I could have behaved with one quarter of your wisdom and decision. The only thing I find it uncommonly difficult to explain is—that—damned odour."

"It made me feel sick, I assure you," declared his nephew, "positively dizzy!" His uncle's attitude of calm omniscience, merely because he knew more psychological formulæ, made him slightly defiant. It was so easy to be wise in the explanation of an experience one has not personally witnessed. "A kind of desolate and terrible odour is the only way I can describe it," he concluded, glancing at the features of the quiet, unemotional man beside him.

"I can only marvel," was the reply, "that under the circumstances it did not seem to you even worse." The dry words, Simpson knew, hovered between the truth, and his uncle's interpretation of "the truth."

And so at last they came to the little camp and found the tent still standing, the remains of the fire, and the piece of paper pinned to a stake beside it—untouched. The *cache,* poorly contrived by inexperienced hands, however, had been discovered and opened—by muskrats, mink and squirrel. The matches lay scattered about the opening, but the food had been taken to the last crumb.

"Well, fellers, he ain't here," exclaimed Hank loudly after his fashion, "and that's as sartain as the coal supply down below! But whar he's got to by this time is 'bout as onsartain as the trade in crowns in t'other place." The presence of a divinity student was no barrier to his language at such a time, though for the reader's sake it may be severely edited. "I propose," he added, "that we start out at once an' hunt for'm like hell!"

The gloom of Défago's probable fate oppressed the whole party with a sense of dreadful gravity the moment they saw the familiar signs of recent occupancy. Especially the tent, with the bed of balsam branches still smoothed and flattened by the pressure of his body, seemed to bring his presence near to them. Simpson, feeling vaguely as if his word were somehow at stake, went about explaining particulars in a hushed tone. He was much calmer now, though overwearied with the strain of his many journeys. His uncle's method of explaining— "explaining away," rather—the details still fresh in his haunted memory helped, too, to put ice upon his emotions.

"And that's the direction he ran off in," he said to his two companions, pointing in the direction where the guide had vanished that morning in the grey dawn. "Straight down there he ran like a deer, in between the birch and the hemlock. . . ."

Hank and Dr. Cathcart exchanged glances.

"And it was about two miles down there, in a straight line," continued the other, speaking with something of the former terror in his voice, "that I followed his trail to the place where—it stopped—dead!"

"And where you heered him callin' an' caught the stench, an' all the rest of the wicked entertainment," cried Hank, with a volubility that betrayed his keen distress.

"And where your excitement overcame you to the point of producing illusions," added Dr. Cathcart under his breath, yet not so low that his nephew did not hear it.

* * *

It was early in the afternoon, for they had travelled quickly, and there were still a good two hours of daylight left. Dr. Cathcart and Hank lost no time in beginning the search, but Simpson was too exhausted to accompany them. They would follow the blazed marks on the trees, and where possible, his footsteps. Meanwhile the best thing he could do was to keep a good fire going, and rest.

But after something like three hours' search, the darkness already down, the two men returned to camp with nothing to report. Fresh snow had covered all signs, and though they had followed the blazed trees to the spot where Simpson had turned back, they had not discovered the smallest indications of a human being—or, for that matter, of an animal. There were no fresh tracks of any kind; the snow lay undisturbed.

It was difficult to know what was best to do, though in reality there was nothing more they *could* do. They might stay and search for weeks without much chance of success. The fresh snow destroyed their only hope, and they gathered round the fire for supper, a gloomy and despondent party. The facts, indeed, were sad enough, for Défago had a wife at Rat Portage, and his earnings were the family's sole means of support.

Now that the whole truth in all its ugliness was out, it seemed useless to deal in further disguise or pretence. They talked openly of the facts and probabilities. It was not the first time, even in the experience of Dr. Cathcart, that a man had yielded to the singular seduction of the Solitudes and gone out of his mind; Défago, moreover, was predisposed to something of the sort, for he already had a touch of melancholia in his blood, and his fibre was weakened by bouts of drinking that often lasted for weeks at a time. Something on this trip—one might never know precisely what—had sufficed to push him over the line, that was all. And he had gone, gone off into the great wilderness of trees and lakes to die by starvation and exhaustion. The chances against his finding camp again were overwhelming; the delirium that was upon him would also doubtless have increased, and it was quite likely he might do violence to himself and so hasten his cruel fate. Even while they talked, indeed, the end had probably come. On the suggestion of Hank, his old pal, however, they proposed to wait a little longer and devote the whole of the following day, from dawn to darkness, to the most systematic search they could devise. They would divide the territory between them. They discussed their plan in great detail. All that men could do they would do.

And, meanwhile, they talked about the particular form in which the singular Panic of the Wilderness had made its attack upon the mind of the unfortunate guide. Hank, though familiar with the legend in its general outline, obviously did not welcome the turn the conversation had taken. He contributed little, though that little was illuminating. For he admitted that a story ran over all this section of country to the effect that several Indians had "seen the Wendigo" along the shores of Fifty Island Water in the "fall" of last year, and that this was the true reason of Défago's disinclination to hunt there. Hank doubtless felt that he had in a sense helped his old pal to death by over-persuading him. "When an Indian goes crazy," he explained, talking to himself more than to the others, it seemed, "it's always put that he's 'seen the Wendigo.' An' pore old Défaygo was superstitious down to his very heels . . . !"

And then Simpson, feeling the atmosphere more sympathetic, told over again the full story of his astonishing tale; he left out no details this time; he mentioned his own sensations and gripping fears. He only omitted the strange language used.

"But Défago surely had already told you all these details of the Wendigo legend, my dear fellow," insisted the doctor. "I mean, he had talked about it, and thus put into your mind the ideas which your own excitement afterwards developed?"

Whereupon Simpson again repeated the facts. Défago, he declared, had barely mentioned the beast. He, Simpson, knew nothing of the story, and, so far as he remembered, had never even read about it. Even the word was unfamiliar.

Of course he was telling the truth, and Dr. Cathcart was reluctantly compelled to admit the singular character of the whole affair. He did not do this in words so much as in manner, however. He kept his back against a good, stout tree; he poked the fire into a blaze the moment it showed signs of dying down; he was quicker than any of them to notice the least sound in the night about them—a fish jumping in the lake, a twig snapping in the bush, the dropping of occasional fragments of frozen snow from the branches overhead where the heat loosened them. His voice, too, changed a little in quality, becoming a shade less confident, lower also in tone. Fear, to put it plainly, hovered close about that little camp, and though all three would have been glad to speak of other matters, the only thing they seemed able to discuss was this—the source of their fear. They tried other subjects in vain; there was nothing to say about them. Hank was the most honest of the group; he said next to nothing. He never once, however, turned his back to the darkness. His face was always to the forest, and when wood was needed he didn't go farther than was necessary to get it.

VII

A wall of silence wrapped them in, for the snow, though not thick, was sufficient to deaden any noise, and the frost held things pretty tight besides. No sound but their voices and the soft roar of the flames made itself heard. Only, from time to time, something soft as the flutter of a pine-moth's wings went past them through the air. No one seemed anxious to go to bed. The hours slipped towards midnight.

"The legend is picturesque enough," observed the doctor after one of the longer pauses, speaking to break it rather than because he had anything to say, "for the Wendigo is simply the Call of the Wild personified, which some natures hear to their own destruction."

"That's about it," Hank said presently. "An' there's no misunderstandin' when you hear it. It calls you by name right 'nough."

Another pause followed. Then Dr. Cathcart came back to the forbidden subject with a rush that made the others jump.

"The allegory *is* significant," he remarked, looking about him into the darkness, "for the Voice, they say, resembles all the minor sounds of the Bush—wind, falling water, cries of the animals, and so forth. And, once the victim hears *that*—he's off for good, of course! His most vulnerable points, moreover, are said to be the feet and the eyes; the feet, you see, for the lust of wandering, and the eyes for the lust of beauty. The poor beggar goes at such a dreadful speed that he bleeds beneath the eyes, and his feet burn."

Dr. Cathcart, as he spoke, continued to peer uneasily into the surrounding gloom. His voice sank to a hushed tone.

"The Wendigo," he added, "is said to burn his feet—owing to the friction, apparently caused by its tremendous velocity—till they drop off, and new ones form exactly like its own."

Simpson listened in horrified amazement; but it was the pallor on Hank's face that fascinated him most. He would willingly have stopped his ears and closed his eyes, had he dared.

"It don't always keep to the ground neither," came in Hank's slow, heavy drawl, "for it goes so high that he thinks the stars have set him all a-fire. An' it'll take great thumpin' jumps sometimes, an' run along the tops of the trees, carrying its partner with it, an' then droppin' him jest as a fish-hawk 'll drop a pickerel to kill it before eatin'. An' its food, of all the muck in the whole Bush is—moss!" And he laughed a short, unnatural laugh. "It's a moss-eater, is the Wendigo," he added, looking up excitedly into the faces of his companions, "moss-eater," he repeated, with a string of the most outlandish oaths he could invent.

But Simpson now understood the true purpose of all this talk. What these two men, each strong and "experienced" in his own way, dreaded more than anything else was—silence. They were talking against time. They were also talking against darkness, against the invasion of panic, against the admission reflection might bring that they were in an enemy's country—against anything, in fact, rather than allow their inmost thoughts to assume control. He himself, already initiated by the awful vigil with terror, was beyond both of them in this respect. He had reached the stage where he was immune. But these two, the scoffing, analytical doctor, and the honest, dogged backwoodsman, each sat trembling in the depths of his being.

Thus the hours passed; and thus, with lowered voices and a kind of taut inner resistance of spirit, this little group of humanity sat in the jaws of the wilderness and talked foolishly of the terrible and haunting legend. It was an unequal contest, all things considered, for the wilderness had already the advantage of first attack—and of a hostage. The fate of their comrade hung over them with a steadily increasing weight of oppression that finally became insupportable.

It was Hank, after a pause longer than the preceding ones that no one seemed able to break, who first let loose all this pent-up emotion in very unexpected fashion, by springing suddenly to his feet and letting out the most ear-shattering yell imaginable into the night. He could not contain himself any longer, it seemed. To make it carry even beyond an ordinary cry he interrupted its rhythm by shaking the palm of his hand before his mouth.

"That's for Défago," he said, looking down at the other two with a queer, defiant laugh, "for it's my belief'—the sandwiched oaths may be omitted—"that my ole partner's not far from us at this very minute."

There was a vehemence and recklessness about his performance that made Simpson, too, start to his feet in amazement, and betrayed even the doctor into letting the pipe slip from between his lips. Hank's face was ghastly, but Cathcart's showed a sudden weakness—a loosening of all his faculties, as it were. Then a momentary anger blazed into his eyes, and he too, though with deliberation born of habitual self-control, got upon his feet and faced the excited guide. For this was unpermissible, foolish, dangerous, and he meant to stop it in the bud.

What might have happened in the next minute or two one may speculate about, yet never definitely know, for in the instant of profound silence that followed Hank's roaring voice, and as though in answer to it, something went past through the darkness of the sky overhead at terrific speed—something of necessity very large, for it displaced much air, while down between the trees there fell a faint and windy cry of a human voice, calling in tones of indescribable anguish and appeal—

"Oh, oh! this fiery height! Oh, oh! My feet of fire! My burning feet of fire!"

White to the very edge of his shirt, Hank looked stupidly about him like a child. Dr. Cathcart uttered some kind of unintelligible cry, turning as he did so with an instinctive movement of blind terror towards the protection of the tent, then halting in the act as though frozen. Simpson, alone of the three, retained his presence of mind a little. His own horror was too deep to allow of any immediate reaction. He had heard that cry before.

Turning to his stricken companions, he said almost calmly—

"That's exactly the cry I heard—the very words he used!"

Then, lifting his face to the sky, he cried aloud, "Défago, Défago! Come down here to us! Come down—!"

And before there was time for anybody to take definite action one way or another, there came the sound of something dropping heavily between the trees, striking the branches on the way down, and landing with a dreadful thud upon the frozen earth below. The crash and thunder of it was really terrific.

"That's him, s'help me the good Gawd!" came from Hank in a whispering cry half choked, his hand going automatically towards the hunting-knife in his belt. "And he's coming! He's coming!" he added, with an irrational laugh of terror, as the sounds of heavy footsteps crunching over the snow became distinctly audible, approaching through the blackness towards the circle of light.

And while the steps, with their stumbling motion, moved nearer and nearer upon them, the three men stood round that fire, motionless and dumb. Dr. Cathcart had the appearance of a man suddenly withered; even his eyes did not move. Hank, suffering shockingly, seemed on the verge again of violent action; yet did nothing. He, too, was hewn of stone. Like stricken children they seemed. The picture was hideous. And, meanwhile, their owner still invisible, the footsteps came closer, crunching the frozen snow. It was endless—too prolonged to be quite real—this measured and pitiless approach. It was accursed.

VIII

Then at length the darkness, having thus laboriously conceived, brought forth—a figure. It drew forward into the zone of uncertain light where fire and shadows mingled, not ten feet away; then halted, staring at them fixedly. The same instant it started forward again with the spasmodic motion as of a thing moved by wires, and coming up closer to them, full into the glare of the fire, they perceived then that— it was a man; and apparently that this man was—Défago.

Something like a skin of horror almost perceptibly drew down in that moment over every face, and three pairs of eyes shone through it as though they saw across the frontiers of normal vision into the Unknown.

Défago advanced, his tread faltering and uncertain; he made his way straight up to them as a group first, then turned sharply and peered close into the face of Simpson. The sound of a voice issued from his lips—

"Here I am, Boss Simpson. I heered some one calling me." It was a faint, dried-up voice, made wheezy and breathless as by immense exertion. "I'm havin' a reg'lar hell-fire kind of a trip, I am." And he laughed, thrusting his head forward into the other's face.

But that laugh started the machinery of the group of wax-work figures with the wax-white skins. Hank immediately sprang forward with a stream of oaths so far-fetched that Simpson did not recognise them as English at all, but thought he had lapsed into Indian or some other lingo. He only realised that Hank's presence, thrust thus between them, was welcome—uncommonly welcome. Dr. Cathcart, though more calmly and leisurely, advanced behind him, heavily stumbling.

Simpson seems hazy as to what was actually said and done in those next few seconds, for the eyes of that detestable and blasted visage peering at such close quarters into his own utterly bewildered his senses at first. He merely stood still. He said nothing. He had not the trained will of the older men that forced them into action in defiance of all emotional stress. He watched them moving as behind a glass that half destroyed their reality: it was dream-like, perverted. Yet, through the torrent of Hank's meaningless phrases, he remembers hearing his uncle's tone of authority—hard and forced—saying several things about food and warmth, blankets, whisky and the rest; . . . and, further, that whiffs of that penetrating, unaccustomed odour, vile yet sweetly bewildering, assailed his nostrils during all that followed.

It was no less a person than himself, however—less experienced and adroit than the others though he was—who gave instinctive utterance to the sentence that brought a measure of relief into the ghastly situation by expressing the doubt and thought in each one's heart.

"It *is*—YOU, isn't it, Défago?" he asked under his breath, horror breaking his speech.

And at once Cathcart burst out with the loud answer before the other had time to move his lips. "Of course it is! Of course it is! Only—can't you see—he's nearly dead with exhaustion, cold and terror! Isn't *that* enough to change a man beyond all recognition?" It was said in order to convince himself as much as to convince the others. The over-emphasis alone proved that. And continually, while he spoke and acted, he held a handkerchief to his nose. That odour pervaded the whole camp.

For the "Défago" who sat huddled by the big fire, wrapped in blankets, drinking hot whisky and holding food in wasted hands, was no more like the guide they had last seen alive than the picture of a man of sixty is like a daguerreotype of his early youth in the costume

of another generation. Nothing really can describe that ghastly carica-
ture, that parody, masquerading there in the firelight as Défago. From
the ruins of the dark and awful memories he still retains, Simpson declares that the face was more animal than human, the features drawn
about into wrong proportions, the skin loose and hanging, as though
he had been subjected to extraordinary pressures and tensions. It made
him think vaguely of those bladder-faces blown up by the hawkers on
Ludgate Hill, that change their expression as they swell, and as they
collapse emit a faint and wailing imitation of a voice. Both face and
voice suggested some such abominable resemblance. But Cathcart long
afterwards, seeking to describe the indescribable, asserts that thus
might have looked a face and body that had been in air so rarified that,
the weight of atmosphere being removed, the entire structure threatened to fly asunder and become—*incoherent*. . . .

It was Hank, though all distraught and shaking with a tearing volume of emotion he could neither handle nor understand, who brought
things to a head without much ado. He went off to a little distance
from the fire, apparently so that the light should not dazzle him too
much, and shading his eyes for a moment with both hands, shouted in
a loud voice that held anger and affection dreadfully mingled—

"You ain't Défaygo! You ain't Défaygo at all! I don't give a ———
damn, but that ain't you, my ole pal of twenty years!" He glared upon
the huddled figure as though he would destroy him with his eyes. "An'
if it is I'll swab the floor of hell with a wad of cotton-wool on a tooth-
pick, s'help me the good Gawd!" he added, with a violent fling of horror and disgust.

It was impossible to silence him. He stood there shouting like one
possessed, horrible to see, horrible to hear—*because it was the truth*. He
repeated himself in fifty different ways, each more outlandish than the
last. The woods rang with echoes. At one time it looked as if he meant
to fling himself upon "the intruder," for his hand continually jerked
towards the long hunting-knife in his belt.

But in the end he did nothing, and the whole tempest completed
itself very shortly with tears. Hank's voice suddenly broke, he collapsed
on the ground, and Cathcart somehow or other persuaded him at last
to go into the tent and lie quiet. The remainder of the affair, indeed,

was witnessed by him from behind the canvas, his white and terrified face peeping through the crack of the tent door-flap.

Then Dr. Cathcart, closely followed by his nephew who so far had kept his courage better than all of them, went up with a determined air and stood opposite to the figure of Défago huddled over the fire. He looked him squarely in the face and spoke. At first his voice was firm.

"Défago, tell us what's happened—just a little, so that we can know how best to help you?" he asked in a tone of authority, almost of command. And at that point, it *was* command. At once afterwards, however, it changed in quality, for the figure turned up to him a face so piteous, so terrible and so little like humanity, that the doctor shrank back from him as from something spiritually unclean. Simpson, watching close behind him, says he got the impression of a mask that was on the verge of dropping off, and that underneath they would discover something black and diabolical, revealed in utter nakedness. "Out with it, man, out with it!" Cathcart cried, terror running neck and neck with entreaty. "None of us can stand this much longer . . . !" It was the cry of instinct over reason.

And then "Défago," smiling *whitely,* answered in that thin and fading voice that already seemed passing over into a sound of quite another character—

"I seen that great Wendigo thing," he whispered, sniffing the air about him exactly like an animal. "I been with it too—"

Whether the poor devil would have said more, or whether Dr. Cathcart would have continued the impossible cross-examination cannot be known, for at that moment the voice of Hank was heard yelling at the top of his voice from behind the canvas that concealed all but his terrified eyes. Such a howling was never heard.

"His feet! Oh, Gawd, his feet! Look at his great changed—feet!"

Défago, shuffling where he sat, had moved in such a way that for the first time his legs were in full light and his feet were visible. Yet Simpson had no time, himself, to see properly what Hank had seen. And Hank has never seen fit to tell. That same instant, with a leap like that of a frightened tiger, Cathcart was upon him, bundling the folds of blanket about his legs with such speed that the young student caught little more than a passing glimpse of something dark and oddly massed where moccasined feet ought to have been, and saw even that but with uncertain vision.

Then, before the doctor had time to do more, or Simpson time to even think a question, much less ask it, Défago was standing upright in front of them, balancing with pain and difficulty, and upon his shapeless and twisted visage an expression so dark and so malicious that it was, in the true sense, monstrous.

"Now *you* seen it too," he wheezed, "you seen my fiery, burning feet! And now—that is, unless you kin save me an' prevent—it's 'bout time for—"

His piteous and beseeching voice was interrupted by a sound that was like the roar of wind coming across the lake. The trees overhead shook their tangled branches. The blazing fire bent its flames as before a blast. And something swept with a terrific, rushing noise about the little camp and seemed to surround it entirely in a single moment of time. Défago shook the clinging blankets from his body, turned towards the woods behind, and with the same stumbling motion that had brought him—was gone: gone, before any one could move muscle to prevent him, gone with an amazing, blundering swiftness that left no time to act. The darkness positively swallowed him; and less than a dozen seconds later, above the roar of the swaying trees and the shout of the sudden wind, all three men, watching and listening with stricken hearts, heard a cry that seemed to drop down upon them from a great height of sky and distance—

"Oh, oh! This fiery height! Oh, oh! My feet of fire! My burning feet of fire . . . !" then died away, into untold space and silence.

Dr. Cathcart—suddenly master of himself, and therefore of the others—was just able to seize Hank violently by the arm as he tried to dash headlong into the Bush.

"But I want ter know, —— you!" shrieked the guide. "I want ter see! That ain't him at all, but some —— devil that's shunted into his place . . . !"

Somehow or other—he admits he never quite knew how he accomplished it—he managed to keep him in the tent and pacify him. The doctor, apparently, had reached the stage where reaction had set in and allowed his own innate force to conquer. Certainly he "managed" Hank admirably. It was his nephew, however, hitherto so wonderfully controlled, who gave him most cause for anxiety, for the cumulative strain had now produced a condition of lachrymose hysteria which made it necessary to isolate him upon a bed of boughs and blankets as far removed from Hank as was possible under the circumstances.

And there he lay, as the watches of that haunted night passed over the lonely camp, crying startled sentences, and fragments of sentences, into the folds of his blanket. A quantity of gibberish about speed and height and fire mingled oddly with biblical memories of the classroom. "People with broken faces all on fire are coming at a most awful, awful, pace towards the camp!" he would moan one minute; and the next would sit up and stare into the woods, intently listening, and whisper, "How terrible in the wilderness are—are the feet of them that—" until his uncle came across to change the direction of his thoughts and comfort him.

The hysteria, fortunately, proved but temporary. Sleep cured him, just as it cured Hank.

Till the first signs of daylight came, soon after five o'clock, Dr. Cathcart kept his vigil. His face was the colour of chalk, and there were strange flushes beneath the eyes. An appalling terror of the soul battled with his will all through those silent hours. These were some of the outer signs. . . .

At dawn he lit the fire himself, made breakfast, and woke the others, and by seven they were well on their way back to the home camp—three perplexed and afflicted men, but each in his own way having reduced his inner turmoil to a condition of more or less systematised order again.

IX

They talked little, and then only of the most wholesome and common things, for their minds were charged with painful thoughts that clamoured for explanation, though no one dared refer to them. Hank, being nearest to primitive conditions, was the first to find himself, for he was also less complex. In Dr. Cathcart "civilisation" championed his forces against an attack singular enough. To this day, perhaps, he is not *quite* sure of certain things. Anyhow, he took longer to "find himself."

Simpson, the student of divinity, it was who arranged his conclusions probably with the best, though not most scientific, appearance of order. Out there, in the heart of unreclaimed wilderness, they had surely witnessed something crudely and essentially primitive. Something that had survived somehow the advance of humanity had emerged terrifically, betraying a scale of life still monstrous and immature. He envisaged it rather as a glimpse into prehistoric ages, when superstitions, gigantic and uncouth, still oppressed the hearts of men; when the forces of nature were still untamed, the Powers that may have haunted a primeval universe not yet withdrawn. To this day he thinks of what he termed years later in a sermon "savage and formidable Potencies lurking behind the souls of men, not evil perhaps in themselves, yet instinctively hostile to humanity as it exists."

With his uncle he never discussed the matter in detail, for the barrier between the two types of mind made it difficult. Only once, years later, something led them to the frontier of the subject—of a single detail of the subject, rather—

"Can't you even tell me what—*they* were like?" he asked; and the reply, though conceived in wisdom, was not encouraging, "It is far better you should not try to know, or to find out."

"Well—that odour . . . ?" persisted the nephew. "What do you make of that?"

Dr. Cathcart looked at him and raised his eyebrows.

"Odours," he replied, "are not so easy as sounds and sights of telepathic communication. I make as much or as little, probably, as you do yourself."

He was not quite so glib as usual with his explanations. That was all.

At the fall of day, cold, exhausted, famished, the party came to the end of the long portage and dragged themselves into a camp that at first glimpse seemed empty. Fire there was none, and no Punk came forward to welcome them. The emotional capacity of all three was too overspent to recognise either surprise or annoyance; but the cry of spontaneous affection that burst from the lips of Hank, as he rushed ahead of them towards the fireplace, came probably as a warning that the end of the amazing affair was not quite yet. And both Cathcart and his nephew confessed afterwards that when they saw him kneel down in his excitement and embrace something that reclined, gently moving, beside the extinguished ashes, they felt in their very bones that this "something" would prove to be Défago—the true Défago, returned.

And, so, indeed, it was.

It is soon told. Exhausted to the point of emaciation, the French Canadian—what was left of him, that is—fumbled among the ashes, trying to make a fire. His body crouched there, the weak fingers obeying feebly the instinctive habit of a lifetime with twigs and matches. But there was no longer any mind to direct the simple operation. The mind had fled beyond recall. And with it, too, had fled memory. Not only recent events, but all previous life was a blank.

This time it was the real man, though incredibly and horribly shrunken. On his face was no expression of any kind whatever—fear, welcome, or recognition. He did not seem to know who it was that embraced him, or who it was that fed, warmed, and spoke to him the words of comfort and relief. Forlorn and broken beyond all reach of human aid, the little man did meekly as he was bidden. The "something" that had constituted him "individual" had vanished for ever.

In some ways it was more terribly moving than anything they had yet seen—that idiot smile as he drew wads of coarse moss from his swollen cheeks and told them that he was "a damned moss eater"; the continued vomiting of even the simplest food; and, worst of all, the piteous and childish voice of complaint in which he told them that his feet pained him—"burn like fire"—which was natural enough when Dr. Cathcart examined them and found that both were dreadfully frozen. Beneath the eyes there were faint indications of recent bleeding.

The details of how he survived the prolonged exposure, of where he had been, or of how he covered the great distance from one camp to the other, including an immense detour of the lake on foot since he had no canoe—all this remains unknown. His memory had vanished completely. And before the end of the winter whose beginning witnessed this strange occurrence, Défago, bereft of mind, memory, and soul, had gone with it. He lingered only a few weeks.

And what Punk was able to contribute to the story throws no further light upon it. He was cleaning fish by the lake shore about five o'clock in the evening—an hour, that is, before the search party returned—when he saw this shadow of the guide picking its way weakly into camp. In advance of him, he declares, came the faint whiff of a certain singular odour.

That same instant old Punk started for home. He covered the entire journey of three days as only Indian blood could have covered it. The terror of a whole race drove him. He knew what it all meant. Défago had "seen the Wendigo."

Old Clothes

I

Imaginative children with their odd questionings of life and their delicate nervous systems must be often a source of greater anxiety than delight to their parents, and Aileen, the child of my widowed cousin, impressed me from the beginning as being a strangely vivid specimen of her class. Moreover, the way she took to me from the first placed quasi-avuncular responsibilities upon my shoulders (in her mother's eyes), that I had no right, even as I had no inclination, to shirk. Indeed, I loved the queer, wayward, mysterious little being. Only it was not always easy to advise; and her somewhat marked peculiarities certainly called for advice of a skilled and special order.

It was not merely that her make-believe was unusually sincere and haunting, and that she would talk by the hour with invisible playmates (touching them, putting up her lips to be kissed, opening doors for them to pass in and out, and setting chairs, footstools, and even flowers for them), for many children in my experience have done as much and done it with a vast sincerity; but that she also accepted what *they told her* with so steady a degree of conviction that their words influenced her life and, accordingly, her health.

They told her stories, apparently, in which she herself played a central part, stories, moreover, that were neither comforting nor wise. She would sit in a corner of the room, as both her mother and myself can vouch, face to face with some make-believe Occupant of the chair so carefully arranged; the footstool had been placed with precision, and sometimes she would move it a little this way or that; the table whereon rested the invisible elbows was beside her with a jar of flowers that changed according to the particular visitor. And there she would wait motionless, perhaps an hour at a time, staring up into the viewless features of the person who was talking with her—who was telling her a story in which she played an exceedingly poignant part. Her face altered with the run of emotions, her eyes grew large and moist, and sometimes frightened; rarely she laughed, and rarely asked a whispered question, but more often sat there, tense and eager, uncannily absorbed in the inaudible tale falling from invisible lips—the tale of her own adventures.

But it was the terror inspired by these singular recitals that affected her delicate health as early as the age of eight, and when, owing to her mother's well-meant but ill-advised ridicule, she indulged them with more secrecy, the effect upon her nerves and character became so acute that I was summoned down upon a special advisory visit I scarcely appreciated.

"Now, George, what *do* you think I had better do? Dr. Hale insists upon more exercise and more companionship, sea air and all the rest of it, but none of these things seem to do any good."

"Have you taken her into your confidence, or rather has *she* taken you into hers?" I ventured mildly.

The question seemed to give offence a little.

"Of course," was the emphatic answer. "The child has no secrets from her mother. She is perfectly devoted to me."

"But you *have* tried to laugh her out of it, haven't you now?"

"Yes. But with such success that she holds these conversations far less than she used to—"

"Or more secretly?" was my comment, that was met with a superior shrug of the shoulders.

Then, after a further pause, in which my cousin's distress and my own affectionate interest in the whimsical imagination of my little niece combined to move me, I tried again—

"Make-believe," I observed, "is always a bit puzzling to us older folk, because, though we indulge in it all our lives, we no longer believe in it; whereas children like Aileen—"

She interrupted me quickly—

"You know what I feel anxious about," she said, lowering her voice. "I think there may be cause for serious alarm." Then she added frankly, looking up with grave eyes into my face, "George, I want your help—your best help, please. You've always been a true friend."

I gave it her in calculated words.

"Theresa," I said with grave emphasis, "there is no trace of insanity on either side of the family, and my own opinion is that Aileen is perfectly well-balanced in spite of this too highly developed imagination. But, above all things, you must not drive it inwards by making fun of it. Lead it out. E—ducate it. Guide it by intelligent sympathy. Get her to tell you all about it, and so on. I think Aileen wants careful observing, perhaps—but nothing more."

For some minutes she watched my face in silence, her eyes intent, her features slightly twitching. I knew at once from her manner what she was driving at. She approached the subject with awkwardness and circumlocution, for it was something she dreaded, not feeling sure whether it was of heaven or of hell.

"You are very wonderful, George," she said at length, "and you have theories about almost everything—"

"Speculations," I admitted.

"And your hypnotic power is helpful, you know. Now—if—if you thought it safe, and that Providence would not be offended—"

"Theresa," I stopped her firmly before she had committed herself to the point where she would feel hurt by a refusal, "let me say at once that I do *not* consider a child a fit subject for hypnotic experiment, and I feel quite sure that an intelligent person like yourself will agree with me that it's unpermissible."

"I was only thinking of a little 'suggestion,'" she murmured.

"Which would come far better from the mother."

"If the mother had not already lost her power by using ridicule," she confessed meekly.

"Yes, you never should have laughed. Why did you, I wonder?"

An expression came into her eyes that I knew to be invariably with hysterical temperaments the precursor of tears. She looked round to make sure no one was listening.

"George," she whispered, and into the dusk of that September evening passed some shadow between us that left behind an atmosphere of sudden and inexplicable chill, "George, I wish—I wish it was *quite* clear to me that it really is all make-believe, I mean—"

"What do you mean?" I said, with a severity that was assumed to hide my own uneasiness. But the tears came the same instant in a flood that made any intelligent explanation out of the question. The terror of the mother for her own blood burst forth.

"I'm frightened—horribly frightened," she said between the sobs.

"I'll go up and see the child myself," I said comfortingly at length when the storm had subsided. "I'll run up to the nursery. You mustn't be alarmed. Aileen's all right. I think I can help you in the matter a good deal."

II

In the nursery as usual Aileen was alone. I found her sitting by the open window, an empty chair opposite to her. She was staring at it— into it, but it is not easy to describe the certainty she managed to convey that there was some one sitting in that chair, talking with her. It was her manner that did it. She rose quickly, with a start as I came in, and made a half gesture in the direction of the empty chair as though to shake hands, then corrected herself quickly, and gave a friendly little nod of farewell or dismissal—then turned towards me. Incredible as it must sound, that chair looked at once slightly otherwise. It was empty.

"Aileen, what in the world are you up to?"

"*You* know, uncle," she replied, without hesitation.

"Oh, rather! *I* know!" I said, trying to get into her mood so as later to get her out of it, "because I do the same thing with the people in my own stories. I talk to them too—"

She came up to my side, as though it were a matter of life and death.

"But do they *answer?*"

I realised the overwhelming sincerity, even the seriousness, of the question to her mind. The shadow evoked down-stairs by my cousin had followed me up here. It touched me on the shoulder.

"Unless they answer," I told her, "they are not really alive, and the story hangs fire when people read it."

She watched me very closely a moment as we leaned out of the open window where the rich perfume of the Portuguese laurels came up from the lawns below. The proximity of the child brought a distinct atmosphere of its own, an atmosphere charged with suggestions, almost with faint pictures, as of things I had once known. I had often felt this before, and did not altogether welcome it, for the pictures seemed framed in some emotional setting that invariably escaped my analysis. I understood in a vague way what it was about the child that made her mother afraid. There flashed across me a fugitive sensation, utterly elusive yet painfully real, that she knew moments of suffering by rights she ought not to have known. Bizarre and unreasonable as the conception was, it was convincing. And it touched a profound sympathy in me.

Aileen undoubtedly was aware of this sympathy.

"It's Philip that talks to me *most* of the time," she volunteered, "and he's always, always explaining—but never quite finishes."

"Explaining what, dear little Child of the Moon?" I urged gently, giving her a name she used to love when she was smaller.

"Why he couldn't come in time to save me, of course," she said. "You see, they cut off both his hands."

I shall never forget the sensation these words of a child's mental adventure caused me, nor the kind of bitter reality they forced into me that they were true, and not merely a detail of some attempted rescue of a "Princess in a Tower." A vivid rush of thought seemed to focus my consciousness upon my own two wrists, as though I felt the pain of the operation she mentioned, and with a swift instinct that slipped into action before I could control it, I had hidden both hands from her sight in my coat pockets.

"And what else does 'Philip' tell you?" I asked gently.

Her face flushed. Tears came into her eyes, then fled away again lest they should fall from their softly-coloured nests.

"That he loved me *so awfully*," she replied; "and that he loved me to the very end, and that all his life after I was gone, and after they cut his hands off, he did nothing but pray for me—from the end of the world where he went to hide—"

I shook myself free with an effort from the enveloping atmosphere of tragedy, realising that her imagination must be driven along brighter channels and that my duty must precede my interest.

"But you must get Philip to tell you all his funny and jolly adventures, too," I said, "the ones he had, you know, when his hands grew again—"

The expression that came into her face literally froze my blood.

"That's only making-up stories," she said icily. "They never did grow again. There *were* no happy or funny adventures."

I cast about in my mind for an inspiration how to help her mind into more wholesome ways of invention. I realised more than ever before the profundity of my affection for this strange, fatherless child, and how I would give my whole soul if I could help her and teach her joy. It was a real love that swept me, rooted in things deeper than I realised.

But, before the right word was given me to speak, I felt her nestle up against my side, and heard her utter the very phrase that for some time I had been dreading in the secret places of my soul she *would* utter. The sentence seemed to shake me within. I knew a hurried, passing moment of unspeakable pain that is utterly beyond me to reason about.

"*You* know," was what she said, "because it's *you* who are Philip!"

And the way she said it—so quietly, the words touched somehow with a gentle though compassionate scorn, yet made golden by a burning love that filled her little person to the brim—robbed me momentarily of all power of speech. I could only bend down and put my arm about her and kiss her head that came up barely to the level of my chin. I swear I loved that child as I never loved any other human being.

"Then Philip is going to teach you all sorts of jolly adventures with his new hands," I remember saying, with blundering good intention, "because he's no longer sad, and is full of fun, and loves you twice as much as ever!"

And I caught her up and carried her down the long stairs of the house out into the garden, where we joined the dogs and romped together until the face of the motherly Kempster at an upper window shouted down something stupid about bed-time, supper, or the rest of it, and Aileen, flushed yet with brighter eyes, ran into the house and, turning at the door, showed me her odd little face wreathed in smiles and laughter.

For a long time I paced to and fro with a cigar between the box hedges of the old-time garden, thinking of the child and her queer imaginings, and of the profoundly moving and disquieting sensations she stirred in me at the same time. Her face flitted by my side through the shadows. She was not pretty, properly speaking, but her appearance possessed an original charm that appealed to me strongly. Her head was big and in some way old-fashioned; her eyes, dark but not large, were placed close together, and she had a wide mouth that was certainly not beautiful. But the look of distressed and yearning passion that sometimes swept over these features, not otherwise prepossessing, changed her look into sudden beauty, a beauty of the soul, a soul that knew suffering and was acquainted with grief. This, at least, is the way my own mind saw the child, and therefore the only way I can hope to make others see her. Were I a painter I might put her upon canvas in some imaginary portrait and call it, perhaps, "Reincarnation"—for I have never seen anything in child-life that impressed me so vividly with that odd idea of an old soul come back to the world in a new young body—a new Suit of Clothes.

But when I talked with my cousin after dinner, and consoled her with the assurance that Aileen was gifted with an unusually vivid imagination which time and ourselves must train to some more practical end—while I said all this, and more besides, two sentences the child had made use of kept ringing in my head. One—when she told me with merciless perception that I was only "making-up" stories; and the other, when she had informed me with that quiet rush of certainty and conviction that "Philip" was—myself.

III

A big-game expedition of some months put an end temporarily to my avuncular responsibilities; at least so far as action was concerned, for there were certain memories that held curiously vivid among all the absorbing turmoil of our camp life. Often, lying awake in my tent at night, or even following the tracks of our prey through the jungle, these pictures would jump out upon me and claim attention. Aileen's little face of suffering would come between me and the sight of my rifle; or her assurance that I was the "Philip" of her imagination would attack me with an accent of reality that seemed queer enough until I analysed it away. And more than once I found myself thinking of her dark and serious countenance when she told how "Philip" had loved her to the end, and would have saved her if they had not cut off his hands. My own imagination, it seemed, was weaving the details of her child's invention into a story, for I never could think of this latter detail without positively experiencing a sensation of smarting pain in my wrists . . . !

When I returned to England in the spring they had moved, I found, into a house by the sea, a tumbled-down old rookery of a building my cousin's father had rarely occupied during his lifetime, nor had she been able to let since it had passed into her possession. An urgent letter summoned me thither, and I travelled down the very day after my arrival to the bleak Norfolk coast with a sense of foreboding in my heart that increased almost to a presentiment when the cab entered the long drive and I recognised the grey and gloomy walls of the old mansion. The sea air swept the gardens with its salt wash, and the moan of the surf was audible even up to the windows.

"I wonder what possessed her to come here?" was the first thought in my mind. "Surely the last place in the world to bring a morbid or too-sensitive child to!" My further dread that something had happened to the little child I loved so tenderly was partly dispelled, however, when my cousin met me at the door with open arms and smiling face, though the welcome I soon found, was chiefly due to the relief she gained from my presence. Something *had* happened to little Aileen, though not the final disaster that I dreaded. She had suffered from nervous attacks of so serious a character during my absence that the doctor had insisted upon sea air, and my cousin, not with the best judgment, had seized upon the idea of making the old house serve the purpose. She had made a wing habitable for a few weeks; she hoped the entire change of scene would fill the little girl's mind with new and happier ideas. Instead—the result had been exactly the reverse. The child had wept copiously and hysterically the moment she set eyes on the old walls and smelt the odour of the sea.

But before we had been talking ten minutes there was a cry and a sound of rushing footsteps, and a scampering figure, with dark, flying hair, had dived headlong into my arms, and Aileen was sobbing—

"Oh, you've come, you've come at last! I *am* so awfully glad. I thought it would be the same as before, and you'd get caught." She ran from me next and kissed her mother, laughing with pleasure through her tears, and was gone from the room as quickly as she had come.

I caught my cousin's glance of frightened amazement.

"Now isn't *that* odd?" she exclaimed in a hushed voice. "Isn't *that* odd? Those are the tears of happiness,—the first time I've seen her smile since we came here last week."

But it rather nettled me, I think. "Why odd?" I asked. "Aileen loves me, it's delightful to—"

"Not that, not that!" she said quickly. "It's odd, I meant, she should have found you out so soon. She didn't even know you were back in England, and I'd sent her off to play on the sands with Kempster and the dogs so as to be sure of an opportunity of telling you everything before you saw her."

Our eyes met squarely, yet not with complete sympathy or comprehension.

"You see, she knew perfectly well you were here—the instant you came."

"But there's nothing in that," I asserted. "Children know things just as animals do. She scented her favourite uncle from the shore like a dog!" And I laughed in her face.

That laugh perhaps was a mistake on my part. Its well-meant cheerfulness was possibly overdone. Even to myself it did not ring quite true.

"I do believe you are in league with her—against me," was the remark that greeted it, accompanied by an increase of that expression of fear in the eyes I had divined the moment we met upon the doorstep. Finding nothing genuine to say in reply, I kissed the top of her head.

In due course, after the tea things had been removed, I learned the exact state of affairs, and even making due allowance for my cousin's excited exaggerations, there were things that seemed to me inexplicable enough on any ground of normal explanation. Slight as the details may seem when set down seriatim, their cumulative effect upon my own mind touched an impressive and disagreeable climax that I did my best to conceal from outward betrayal. As I sat in the great shadowy room, listening to my cousin's jerky description of "childish" things, it was borne in upon me that they might well have the profoundest possible significance. I watched her eager, frightened face, lit only by the flickering flames the sharp spring evening made necessary, and thought of the subject of our conversation flitting about the dreary halls and corridors of the huge old building, a little figure of tragedy, laughing, crying, and dreaming in a world entirely her own—and there stirred in me an unwelcome recognition of those mutinous and dishevelled forces that lie but thinly screened behind the common-place details of life and that now seemed ready to burst forth and play their mysterious rôle before our very eyes.

"Tell me *exactly* what has happened," I urged, with decision but sympathy.

"There's so little, when it's put into words, George; but—well, the thing that first upset me was that she—knew the whole place, though she's never been here before. She knew every passage and staircase, many of them that I did not know myself; she showed us an underground passage to the sea, that father himself didn't know; and she actually drew a scrawl of the house as it used to be three hundred years ago when the other wing was standing where the copper beeches grow now. It's accurate, too."

It seemed impossible to explain to a person of my cousin's temperament the theories of pre-natal memory and the like, or the possibility of her own knowledge being communicated telepathically to the brain of her own daughter. I said therefore very little, but listened with an uneasiness that grew horribly.

"She found her way about the gardens instantly, as if she had played in them all her life; and she keeps drawing figures of people—men and women—in old costumes, the sort of thing our ancestors wore, you know—"

"Well, well, well!" I interrupted impatiently; "what can be more natural? She is old enough to have seen pictures she can remember enough to copy—?"

"Of course," she resumed calmly, but with a calmness due to the terror that ate her very soul and swallowed up all minor emotions; "of course, but one of the faces she gets is—*a portrait.*"

She rose suddenly and came closer to me across the big stone hearth, lowering her voice to a whisper, "George," she whispered, "it's the very image of that awful—de Lorne!"

The announcement, I admit, gave me a thrill, for that particular ancestor on my father's side had largely influenced my boyish imagination by the accounts of his cruelty and wickedness in days gone by. But I think now the shiver that ran down my back was due to the thought of my little Aileen practising her memory and pencil upon so vile an object. That, and my cousin's pale visage of alarm, combined to shake me. I said, however, what seemed wise and reasonable at the moment.

"You'll be claiming next, Theresa, that the house is haunted," I suggested.

She shrugged her shoulders with an indifference that was very eloquent of the strength of this other more substantial terror.

"That would be so easy to deal with," she said, without even looking up. "A ghost stays in one place. Aileen could hardly take it about with her."

I think we both enjoyed the pause that followed. It gave *me* time to collect my forces for what I knew was coming. It gave *her* time to get her further facts into some pretence of coherence.

"I told you about the belt?" she asked at length, weakly, and as though unutterable things she longed to disown forced the question to her unwilling lips.

The sentence shot into me like the thrust of a naked sword. . . . I shook my head.

"Well, even a year or two ago she had that strange dislike of wearing a belt with her frocks. We thought it was a whim, and did not humour her. Belts are necessary, you know, George," she tried to smile feebly. "But now it has come to such a point that I've had to give in."

"She dislikes a belt round her waist, you mean?" I asked, fighting a sudden inexplicable spasm in my heart.

"It makes her scream. The moment anything encloses her waist she sets up such a hubbub, and struggles so, and hides away, and I've been obliged to yield."

"But really, Theresa—!"

"She declares it fastens her in, and she will never get free again, and all kinds of other things. Oh, her fear is dreadful, poor child. Her face gets that sort of awful grey, don't you know? Even Kempster, who if anything is too firm, had to give in."

"And what else, pray?" I disliked hearing these details intensely. It made me ache with a kind of anger that I could not at once relieve the child's pain.

"The way she spoke to me after Dr. Hale had left—you know how awfully kind and gentle he is, and how Aileen likes him and even plays with him and sits on his knee? Well, he was talking about her diet, regulating it and so forth, teasing her that she mustn't eat this and that, and the rest of it, when she turned that horrid grey again and jumped off his knee with her scream—that thin wailing scream she has that goes through me like a knife, George—and flew to the nursery and locked herself in with—what do you think?—with all the bread, apples, cold meat, and other eatables she could find!"

"Eatables!" I exclaimed, aware of another spasm of vivid pain.

"When I coaxed her out, hours later, she was trembling like a leaf and fell into my arms utterly exhausted, and all I could get her to tell me was this—which she repeated again and again with a sort of beseeching, appealing tone that made my heart bleed—"

She hesitated an instant.

"Tell me at once."

"'I shall starve again, I shall starve again,' were the words she used. She kept repeating it over and over between her sobs. 'I shall be without anything to eat. I shall starve!' And, would you believe it, while she hid in that nursery cupboard she had crammed so much cake and stuff into her little self that she was violently sick for a couple of days. Moreover, she now hates the sight of Dr. Hale so much, poor man, that it's useless for him to see her. It does more harm than good."

I had risen and begun to walk up and down the hall while she told me this. I said very little. In my mind strange thoughts tore and raced, standing erect before me out of unbelievably immense depths of shadow. There was nothing very pregnant I found to say, however, for theories and speculations are of small avail as practical help—unless two minds see eye to eye in them.

"And the rest?" I asked gently, coming behind the chair and resting both hands upon her shoulders. She got up at once and faced me. I was afraid to show too much sympathy lest the tears should come.

"Oh, George," she exclaimed, "I *am* relieved you have come. You are really strong and comforting. To feel your great hands on my shoulders gives me courage. But, you know, truly and honestly I am frightened out of my very wits by the child—"

"You won't stay here, of course?"

"We leave at the end of this week," she replied. "You will not desert me till then, I know. And Aileen will be all right as long as you are here, for you have the most extraordinary effect on her for good."

"Bless her little suffering imagination," I said. "You can count on me. I'll send to town to-night for my things."

And then she told me about the room. It was simple enough, but it conveyed a more horrible certainty of something true than all the other details put together. For there was a room on the ground floor, intended to be used on wet days when the nursery was too far for muddy boots—and into this room Aileen could not go. Why? No one could tell. The facts were that the first moment the child ran in, her mother close behind, she stopped, swayed, and nearly fell. Then, with shrieks that were even heard outside by the gardeners sweeping the gravel path, she flung herself headlong against the wall, against a particular corner of it that is to say, and beat it with her little fists until the skin broke and left stains upon the paper. It all happened in less than a minute. The words she cried so frantically her mother was too shocked and flabbergasted to remember, or even to hear properly. Aileen nearly upset her in her bewildered efforts next to find the door and escape. And the first thing she did when escape was accomplished, was to drop in a dead faint upon the stone floor of the passage outside.

"Now, is *that* all make-believe?" whispered Theresa, unable to keep the shudder from her lips. "Is that all merely part of a story she has made up and plays a part in?"

We looked one another straight in the eyes for a space of some seconds. The dread in the mother's heart leaped out to swell a terror in my own—a terror of another kind, but greater.

"It is too late to-night," I said at length, "for it would only excite her unnecessarily; but to-morrow I will talk with Aileen. And—if it seems wise—I might—I might be able to help in other ways too," I added.

So I did talk to her—next day.

IV

I always had her confidence, this little dark-eyed maid, and there was an intimacy between us that made play and talk very delightful. Yet as a rule, without giving myself a satisfactory reason, I preferred talking with her in the sunlight. She was not eerie, bless her little heart of queerness and mystery, but she had a way of suggesting other ways of life and existence shouldering about us that made me look round in the dark and wonder what the shadows concealed or what waited round the next corner.

We were on the lawn, where the bushy yews drop thick shade, the soft air making tea possible out of doors, my cousin out driving to distant calls; and Aileen had invited herself and was messing about with my manuscripts in a way that vexed me, for I had been reading my fairy tales to her and she kept asking me questions that shamed my limited powers. I remember, too, that I was glad the collie ran to and fro past us, scampering and barking after the swallows on the lawn.

"Only *some* of your stories are true, aren't they?" she asked abruptly.

"How do you know that, young critic?" I had been waiting for an opening supplied by herself. Anything forced on my part she would have suspected.

"Oh, I can tell."

Then she came up and whispered without any hint of invitation on my part, "Uncle, it is true, isn't it, that I've been in other places with you? And isn't it only the things we did *there* that make the true stories?"

The opening was delivered all perfect and complete into my hands. I cannot conceive how it was I availed myself of it so queerly—I mean, how it was that the words and the name slipped out of their own accord as though I was saying something in a dream.

"Of course, my little Lady Aileen, because in imagination, you see, we—"

But before I had time to finish the sentence with which I hoped to coax out the true inwardness of her own distress, she was upon me in a heap.

"Oh," she cried, with a sudden passionate outburst, "then you *do* know my name? You know all the story—*our* story!"

She was very excited, face flushed, eyes dancing, all the emotions of a life charged to the brim with experience playing through her little person.

"Of course, Miss Inventor, I know your name," I said quickly, puzzled, and with a sudden dismay that was hideous, clutching at my throat.

"And all that we did in this place?" she went on, pointing with increased excitement to the thick, ivy-grown walls of the old house.

My own emotion grew extraordinarily, a swift, rushing uneasiness upsetting all my calculations. For it suddenly came back to me that in calling her "Lady Aileen" I had not pronounced the name quite as usual. My tongue had played a trick with the consonants and vowels, though at the moment of utterance I had somehow failed to notice the change. "Aileen" and "Helen" are almost interchangeable sounds . . . ! And it was "Lady Helen" that I had actually said.

The discovery took my breath away for an instant—and the way she had leaped upon the name to claim it.

"No one else, you see, knows me as 'Lady Helen,'" she continued whispering, "because that's only in our story, isn't it? And now I'm just Aileen Langton. But as long as you know, it's all right. Oh, I am so awf'ly glad you knew, most awf'ly, *awf'ly* glad."

I was momentarily at a loss for words. Keenly desirous to guide the child's "pain-stories" into wiser channels, and thus help her to relief, I hesitated a moment for the right clue. I murmured something soothing about "our story," while in my mind I searched vigorously for the best way of leading her on to explain all her terror of the belt, the fear of starvation, the room that made her scream, and all the rest. All *that* I was most anxious to get out of her little tortured mind and then replace it by some brighter dream.

But the insidious experience had shaken my confidence a little, and these explicable emotions destroyed my elder wisdom. The little Inventor had caught me away into the reality of her own "story" with a sense of conviction that was even beyond witchery. And the next sentence she almost instantly let loose upon me completed my discomfiture—

"With you," she said, still half whispering, "with you I could even go into the room. I never could—alone—!"

The spring wind whispering in the yews behind us brought in that moment something upon me from vanished childhood days that made me tremble. Some wave of lost passion—lost because I guessed not its origin or nature—surged through the depths of me, sending faint messages to the surface of my consciousness. Aileen, little mischief-maker, changed before my very eyes as she stood there close—changed into a tall sad figure that beckoned to me across seas of time and distance, with the haze of ages in her eyes and gestures, . . . I was obliged to focus my gaze upon her with a deliberate effort to see her again as the tumble-haired girl I was accustomed to. . . .

Then, sitting in the creaky garden chair, I drew her down upon my knee, determined to win the whole story from her mind. My back was to the house; she was perched at an angle, however, that enabled her to command the doors and windows. I mention this because, scarcely had I begun my attack, when I saw that her attention wandered, and that she seemed curiously uneasy. Once or twice, as she shifted her position to get a view of something that was going on over my shoulder, I was aware that a slight shiver passed from her small person down to my knees. She seemed to be expecting something—with dread.

"We'll make a special expedition, armed to the teeth," I said, with a laugh, referring to her singular words about the room. "We'll send Pat in first to bark at the cobwebs, and we'll take lots of provisions and— and water in case of a siege—and a file—"

I cannot pretend to understand why I chose those precise words— or why it was as though other thoughts than those I had intended rose up, clamouring for expression. It seemed all I could manage not to say a lot of other things about the room that could only have frightened instead of relieving her.

"Will you talk *into the wall* too?" she asked, turning her eyes down suddenly upon me with a little rush and flame of passion. And though I had not the faintest conception what she meant, the question sent an agony of yearning pain through me. "Talking into the wall," I instantly grasped, referred to the core of her trouble, the very central idea that frightened her and provided the suffering and terror of all her imaginings.

But I had no time to follow up the clue thus mysteriously offered to me, for almost at the same moment her eyes fixed themselves upon something behind me with an expression of tense horror, as though she saw the approach of a danger that might—*kill*.

"Oh, oh!" she cried under her breath, "he's coming! He's coming to take me! Uncle George—Philip—!"

The same impulse operated upon us simultaneously, it seems, for I sprang up with my fists clenched at the very instant she shot off my knee and stood with all her muscles rigid as though to resist attack. She was shaking dreadfully. Her face went the colour of linen.

"*Who's* coming—?" I began sharply, then stopped as I saw the figure of a man moving towards us from the house. It was the butler— the new butler who had arrived only that very afternoon. It is impossible to say what there was in his swift and silent approach that was— abominable. The man was upon us, it seemed, almost as soon as I caught sight of him, and the same moment Aileen, with a bursting cry, looking wildly about her for a place to hide in, plunged headlong into my arms and buried her face in my coat.

Horribly perplexed, yet mortified that the servant should see my little friend in such a state, I did my best to pretend that it was all part of some mad game or other, and catching her up in my arms, I ran, calling the collie to follow with, "Come on, Pat! She's our prisoner!"— and only set her down when we were under the limes at the far end of the lawn. She was all white and ghostly from her terror, still looking frantically about her, trembling in such a way that I thought any minute she must collapse in a dead faint. She clung to me with very tight fingers. How I hated that man. Judging by the sudden violence of my loathing he might have been some monster who wanted to torture her. . . .

"Let's go away, oh, much farther, ever so far away!" she whispered, and I took her by the hand, comforting her as best I could with words, while realising that the thing she wanted was my big arm about her to protect. My heart ached, oh, so fiercely, for her, but the odd thing about it was that I could not find anything of real comfort to say that I felt would be *true*. If I "made up" soothing rubbish, it would not deceive either of us and would only shake her confidence in me, so that I should lose any power I had to help. Had a tiger come upon her out of the wood I might as well have assured her it would not bite!

I did stammer something, however—

"It's only the new butler. He startled me, too; he came so softly, didn't he?" Oh! how eagerly I searched for a word that might make the thing seem as ordinary as possible—yet how vainly.

"But you know who he is—*really!*" she said in a crying whisper, running down the path and dragging me after her; "and if he gets me again . . . oh! oh!" and she shrieked aloud in the anguish of her fear.

That fear chased both of us down the winding path between the bushes.

"Aileen, darling," I cried, surrounding her with both arms and holding her very tight, "you need not be afraid. I'll always save you. I'll always be with you, dear child."

"Keep me in your big arms, always, always, won't you, Uncle—Philip?" She mixed both names. The choking stress of her voice wrung me dreadfully. "Always, always, like in our story," she pleaded, hiding her little face again in my coat.

I really was at a complete loss to know what best to do; I hardly dared to bring her back to the house; the sight of the man, I felt, might be fatal to her already too delicately balanced reason, for I dreaded a fit or seizure if she chanced to run across him when I was not with her. My mind was easily made up on one point, however.

"I'll send him away at once, Aileen," I told her. "When you wake up to-morrow he'll be gone. Of course mother won't keep him."

This assurance seemed to bring her some measure of comfort, and at last, without having dared to win the whole story from her as I had first hoped, I got her back to the house by covert ways, and saw her myself up-stairs to her own quarters. Also I took it upon myself to give the necessary orders. She must set no eye upon the man. Only, why was it that in my heart of hearts I longed for him to do something outrageous that should make it possible for me to break his very life at its source and kill him . . . ?

But my cousin, alarmed to the point of taking even frantic measures, finally had a sound suggestion to offer, namely that I should take the afflicted little child away with me the very next day, run down to Harwich, and carry her off for a week of absolute change across the North Sea. And I, meanwhile, had reached the point where I had persuaded myself that the experiment I had hitherto felt unable to consent to had now become a permissible, even a necessary one. Hypnotism should win the story from that haunted mind without her being aware of it, and provided I could drive her deep enough into the trance state, I could then further wipe the memory from her outer consciousness so completely that she might know at last some happiness of childhood.

V

It was after ten o'clock, and I was still sitting in the big hall before the fire of logs, talking with lowered voice. My cousin sat opposite to me in a deep armchair. We had discussed the matter pretty fully, and the deep uneasiness we felt clothed not alone our minds but the very building with gloom. The fact that, instinctively, neither of us referred to the possible assistance of doctors is eloquent, I think, of the emotion that troubled us both so profoundly, the emotion, I mean, that sprang from the vivid sense of the reality of it all. No child's make-believe merely could have thus caught us away, or spread a net that entangled our minds to such a point of confusion and dismay. It was perfectly comprehensible to me now that my cousin should have cried in very helplessness before the convincing effects of the little girl's calamitous distress. Aileen was living through a Reality, not an Invention. This was the fact that haunted the shadowy halls and corridors behind us. Already I hated the very building. It seemed charged to the roof with the memories of melancholy and ancient pain that swept my heart with shivering, cold winds.

Purposely, however, I affected some degree of cheerfulness, and concealed from my cousin any mention of the attacks that certain emotions and alarms had made upon myself: I said nothing of my replacing "Lady Aileen" with "Lady Helen," nothing of my passing for "Philip," or of my sudden dashes of quasi-memory arising from the child's inclusion of myself in her "story," and my own singular acceptance of the rôle. I did not consider it wise to mention *all* that the sight of the new servant with his sinister dark face and his method of stealthy approach had awakened in my thoughts. None the less these things started constantly to the surface of my mind and doubtless betrayed themselves somewhere in my "atmosphere," sufficiently at least for a woman's intuition to divine them. I spoke passingly of the "room," and of Aileen's singular aversion for it, and of her remark about "talking to the wall." Yet strange thoughts pricked their way horribly into both our minds. In the hall the stuffed heads of deer and fox and badger stared upon us like masks of things still alive beneath their fur and dead skin.

"But what disturbs me more than all the rest of her delusions put together," said my cousin, peering at me with eyes that made no pretence of hiding dark things, "is her extraordinary knowledge of this place. I assure you, George, it was the most uncanny thing I've ever known when she showed me over and asked questions as if she had actually lived here." Her voice sank to a whisper, and she looked up startled. It seemed to me for a moment that some one was coming near to listen, moving stealthily upon us along the dark approaches to the hall.

"I can understand you found it strange," I began quickly. But she interrupted me at once. Clearly it gave her a certain relief to say the things and get them out of her mind where they hid, breeding new growths of abhorrence.

"George," she cried aloud, "there's a limit to imagination. Aileen *knows*. That's the awful thing—"

Something sprang into my throat. My eyes moistened.

"The horror of the belt—" she whispered, loathing her own words.

"Leave that thought alone," I said with decision. The detail pained me inexpressibly—beyond belief.

"I wish I could," she answered, "but if you had seen the look on her face when she struggled—and the—the frenzy she got into about the food and starving—I mean when Dr. Hale spoke—oh, if you had seen all that, you would understand that I—"

She broke off with a start. Some one had entered the hall behind us and was standing in the doorway at the far end. The listener had moved upon us from the dark. Theresa, though her back was turned, had felt the presence and was instantly upon her feet.

"You need not sit up, Porter," she said, in a tone that only thinly veiled the fever of apprehension behind, "we will put the lights out," and the man withdrew like a shadow. She exchanged a quick glance with me. A sensation of darkness that seemed to have come with the servant's presence was gone. It is wholly beyond me to explain why neither myself nor my cousin found anything to say for some minutes. But it was still more a mystery, I think, why the muscles of my two hands should have contracted involuntarily with a force that drove the nails into my palms, and why the violent impulse should have leaped into my blood to fling myself upon the man and strangle the life out of his neck before he could take another breath. I have never before or since experienced this apparently causeless desire to throttle anybody. I hope I never may again.

"He hangs about rather," was all my cousin said presently. "He's always watching us—" But my own thoughts were horribly busy, and I was marvelling how it was this ugly and sinister creature had ever come to be accepted in the story that Aileen lived, and that I was slowly coming to *believe* in.

It was a relief to me when, towards midnight, Theresa rose to go to bed. We had skirted through the horrors of the child's possessing misery without ever quite facing it, and as we stood there lighting the candles, our voices whispering, our minds charged with the strain of thoughts neither of us had felt it wise to utter, my cousin started back against the wall and stared up into the darkness above where the staircase climbed the well of the house. She uttered a cry. At first I thought she was going to collapse. I was only just in time to catch the candle.

All the emotions of fearfulness she had repressed during our long talk came out in that brief cry, and when I looked up to discover the cause I saw a small white figure come slowly down the wide staircase and just about to step into the hall. It was Aileen, with bare feet, her dark hair tumbling down over her nightgown, her eyes wide open, an expression in them of anguished expectancy that her tender years could never possibly have known. She was walking steadily, yet somehow not quite as a child walks.

"Stop!" I whispered peremptorily to my cousin, putting my hand quickly over her mouth, and holding her back from the first movement of rescue, "don't wake her. She's walking in her sleep."

Aileen passed us like a white shadow, scarcely audible, and went straight across the hall. She was utterly unaware of our presence. Avoiding all obstructions of chairs and tables, moving with decision and purpose, the little figure dipped into the shadows at the far end and disappeared from view in the mouth of the corridor that had once—three hundred years ago—led into the wing where now the copper beeches grew upon open lawns. It was clearly a way familiar to her. And the instant I recovered from my surprise and moved after her to act, Theresa found her voice and cried aloud—a voice that broke the midnight silence with shrill discordance—

"George, oh, George! She's going to that awful room . . . !"

"Bring the candle and come after me," I replied from half-way down the hall, "but do not interrupt unless I call for you," and was after the child at a pace to which the most singular medley of emotions I have ever known urged me imperiously. A sense of tragic disaster gripped my very vitals. All that I did seemed to rise out of some subconscious region of the mind where the haunting passions of a deeply buried past stirred in their sleep and woke.

"Helen!" I cried, "Lady Helen!" I was close upon the gliding figure. Aileen turned and for the first time saw me with eyes that seemed to waver between sleep and waking. They gazed straight at me over the flickering candle flame, then hesitated. In similar fashion the gesture of her little hands towards me was arrested before it had completed itself. She saw me, knew my presence, yet was uncertain who I was. It was astonishing the way I actually surprised this momentary indecision between the two personalities in her—caught the two phases of her consciousness at grips—discerned the Aileen of To-day in the act of waking to know me as her "Uncle George," and that other Aileen of her great dark story, the "Helen" of some far Yesterday, that drew her in this condition of somnambulism to the scene in the past where our two lives were linked in her imagination. For it was quite clear to me that the child was dreaming in her sleep the action of the story she lived through in the vivid moments of her waking terror.

But the choice was swift. I just had time to signal Theresa to set the candle upon a shelf and wait, when she came up, stretched her hands out in completion of the original gesture, and fell into my arms with a smothered cry of love and anguish that, coming from those childish lips, I think is the most thrilling human sound I have ever known. She knew and saw me, but not as "Uncle" George of this present life.

"Oh, Philip!" she cried, "then you have come after all—"

"Of course, dear heart," I whispered. "Of course I have come. Did I not give my promise that I would?"

Her eyes searched my face, and then settled upon my hands that held her little cold wrists so tightly.

"But—but," she stammered in comment, "they are not cut! They have made you whole again! You will save me and get me out, and we—we—"

The expressions of her face ran together into a queer confusion of perplexity, and she seemed to totter on her feet. In another instant she would probably have wakened; again she felt the touch of uncertainty and doubt as to my identity. Her hands resisted the pressure of my own; she drew back half a step; into her eyes rose the shallower consciousness of the present. Once awake it would drive out the profoundly strange passion and mystery that haunted the corridors of thought and memory and plunged so obscurely into the inmost recesses of her being. For, once awake, I realised that I should lose her, lose the opportunity of getting the complete story. The chance was unique. I heard my cousin's footsteps approaching behind us down the passage on tiptoe—and I came to an immediate decision.

In the state of deep sleep, of course, the trance condition is very close, and many experiments had taught me that the human spirit can be subjected to the influence of hypnotism far more speedily when asleep than when awake; for if hypnotism means chiefly—as I then held it to mean—the merging of the little ineffectual surface-consciousness with the deep sea of the greater subliminal consciousness below, then the process has already been partially begun in normal slumber and its completion need be no very long or difficult matter. It was Aileen's very active subconsciousness that "invented" or "remembered" the dark story which haunted her life, her subconscious region too readily within tap. . . . By deepening her sleep state I could learn the whole story. . . .

Stopping her mother's approach with a sign that I intended she should clearly understand, and which accordingly she did understand, I took immediate steps to plunge the spirit of this little sleep-walking child down again into the subconscious region that had driven her thus far, and wherein lay the potentialities of all her powers, of memory, knowledge, and belief. Only the simplest passes were necessary, for she yielded quickly and easily; that first look came back into her eyes; she no longer wavered or hesitated, but drew close against me, with the name of "Philip" upon her lips, and together we moved down the long passage till we reached the door of her horrid room of terror.

And there, whether it was that Theresa's following with the candle disturbed the child—for the subconscious tie with the mother is of such unalterable power—or whether anxiety weakened my authority over her fluctuating mental state, I noticed that she again wavered and hesitated, looking up with eyes that saw partly "Uncle George," partly the "Philip" she remembered.

"We'll go in," I said firmly, "and you shall see that there is nothing to be afraid of." I opened the door, and the candle from behind threw a triangle of light into the darkness. It fell upon a bare floor, pictureless walls, and just tipped the high white ceiling overhead. I pushed the door still wider open and we went in hand in hand, Aileen shaking like a leaf in the wind.

How the scene lives in my mind, even as I write it to-day so many years after it took place: the little child in her nightgown facing me in that empty room of the ancient building, all the passionate emotions of a tragic history in the small young eyes, her mother like a ghost in the passage, afraid to come in, the tossing shadows thrown by the candle and the soft moan of the night wind against the outside walls.

I made further passes over the small flushed face and pressed my thumbs gently along the temples. "Sleep!" I commanded; "sleep—and remember!" My will poured over her being to control and protect. She passed still deeper into the trance condition in which the somnambulistic lucidity manifests itself and the deeper self gives up its dead. Her eyes grew wider, rounder, charged with memories as they fastened themselves upon my own. The present, which a few minutes before had threatened to claim her consciousness by waking her, faded. She saw me no longer as her familiar Uncle George, but as the faithful friend and lover of her great story, Philip, the man who had come to save her. There she stood in the atmosphere of bygone days, in the very room where she had known great suffering—this room that three centuries ago had led by a corridor into the wing of the house where now the beeches grew upon the lawns.

She came up close and put her thin bare arms about my neck and stared with peering, searching eyes into mine.

"Remember what happened here," I said resolutely. "Remember, and tell me."

Her brows contracted slightly as with the effort, and she whispered, glancing over her shoulder towards the farther end where the corridor once began, "It hurts a little, but I—I'm in your arms, Philip dear, and you will get me out, I know—"

"I hold you safe and you are in no danger, little one," I answered. "You can remember and speak without it hurting you. Tell me."

The suggestion, of course, operated instantly, for her face cleared, and she dropped a great sigh of relief. From time to time I continued the passes that held the trance condition firm.

Then she spoke in a low, silvery little tone that cut into me like a sword and searched my inmost parts. I seemed to bleed internally. I could have sworn that she spoke of things I knew as though I had lived through them.

"This was when I last saw you," she said, "this was the room where you were to fetch me and carry me away into happiness and safety from—him," and it was the voice and words of no mere child that said it; "and this was where you did come on that night of snow and wind. Through that window you entered"; she pointed to the deep, embrasured window behind us. "Can't you hear the storm? How it howls and screams! And the boom of the surf on the beach below. . . . You left the horses outside, the swift horses that were to carry us to the sea and away from all his cruelties, and then—"

She hesitated and searched for words or memories; her face darkened with pain and loathing.

"Tell me the rest," I ordered, "but forget all your own pain." And she smiled up at me with an expression of unbelievable tenderness and confidence while I drew the frail form closer.

"*You* remember, Philip," she went on, "you know just what it was, and how he and his men seized you the moment you stepped inside, and how you struggled and called for me, and heard me answer—"

"Far away—outside—" I interrupted quickly, helping her out of some flashing memory in my own deep heart that seemed to burn and leave a scar. "You answered from the lawn!"

"*You* thought it was the lawn, but really, you see, it was there—in there," and she pointed to the side of the room on my right. She shook dreadfully, and her voice dwindled most oddly in volume, as though coming from a distance—almost muffled.

"In there?" I asked it with a shudder that put ice and fire mingled in my blood.

"In the wall," she whispered. "You see, some one had betrayed us, and he knew you were coming. He walled me up alive in there, and only left two little holes for my eyes so that I could see. You heard my voice calling through those holes, but you never knew where I was. And then—"

Her knees gave way, and I had to hold her. She looked suddenly with torture in her eyes down the length of the room—towards the old wing of the house.

"You won't let him come," she pleaded beseechingly, and in her voice was the agony of death. "I thought I heard him. Isn't that his footsteps in the corridor?" She listened fearfully, her eyes trying to pierce the wall and see out on to the lawn.

"No one is coming, dear heart," I said, with conviction and authority. "Tell it all. Tell me everything."

"I saw the whole of it because I could not close my eyes," she continued. "There was an iron band round my waist fastening me in—an iron belt I never could escape from. The dust got into my mouth—I bit the bricks. My tongue was scraped and bleeding, but before they put in the last stones to smother me I saw them—cut both your hands off so that you could never save me—never let me out."

She dashed without warning from my side and flew up to the wall, beating it with her hands and crying aloud—

"Oh, you poor, poor thing. I know how awful it was. I remember—when I was in you and you wore and carried me, poor, poor body! That thunder of the last brick as they drove it in against the mouth, and the iron clamp that cut into the waist, and the suffocation and hunger and thirst!"

"What are you talking to in there?" I asked sternly, crushing down the tears.

"The body I was in—the one he walled up—my body—my own body!"

She flew back to my side. But even before my cousin had uttered that "mother-cry" that broke in upon the child's deeper consciousness, disturbing the memories, I had given the command with all the force of my being to "forget" the pain. And only those few who are familiar with the instantaneous changes of emotion that can be produced by suggestion under hypnosis will understand that Aileen came back to me from that moment of "talking to the wall" with laughter on her lips and in her eyes.

The small white figure with the cascade of dark hair tumbling over the nightgown ran up and jumped into my arms.

"But I saved you," I cried, "you were never properly walled-up; I got you out and took you away from him over the sea, and we were happy ever afterwards, like the people in the fairy tales." I drove the words into her with my utmost force, and inevitably she accepted them as the truth, for she clung to me with love and laughter all over her child's face of mystery, the horror fading out, the pain swept clean away. With kaleidoscopic suddenness the change came.

"So they never really cut your poor dead hands off at all," she said hesitatingly.

"Look! How could they? There they are!" And I first showed them to her and then pressed them against her little cheeks, drawing her mouth up to be kissed. "They're big enough still and strong enough to carry you off to bed and stroke you into so deep a sleep that when you wake in the morning you will have forgotten everything about your dark story, about Philip, Lady Helen, the iron belt, the starvation, your cruel old husband, and all the rest of it. You'll wake up happy and jolly just like any other child—"

"If you say so, of course I shall," she answered, smiling into my eyes.

And it was just then there came in that touch of abomination that so nearly made my experiment a failure, for it came with a black force that threatened at first to discount all my "suggestion" and make it of no account. My new command that she should forget had apparently not yet fully registered itself in her being; the tract of deeper con- sciousness that constructed the "Story" had not sunk quite below the threshold. Thus she was still open to any detail of her former suffering that might obtrude itself with sufficient force. And such a detail *did* ob- trude itself. This touch of abomination was calculated with a really su- perhuman ingenuity.

"Hark!" she cried—and it was that *scream in a whisper* that only utter terror can produce—"Hark! I hear his steps! He's coming! Oh, I told you he was coming! He's in *that* passage!" pointing down the room.

And she first sprang from my arms as though something burned her, and then almost instantly again flew back to my protection. In that interval of a few seconds she tore into the middle of the room, put her hand to her ear to listen, and then shaded her eyes in the act of peering down through the wall at the far end. She stared at the very place where in olden days the corridor had led into the vanished wing. The window my great-uncle had built into the wall now occupied the exact spot where the opening had been.

Theresa then for the first time came forward with a rush into the room, dropping the candle-grease over the floor. She clutched me by the arm. The three of us stood there—listening—listening apparently to nought but the sighing of the sea-wind about the walls, Aileen with her eyes buried in my coat. I was standing erect trying in vain to catch the new sound. I remember my cousin's face of chalk with the fluttering eyes and the candle held aslant.

Then suddenly she raised her hand and pointed over my shoulder. I thought her jaw would drop from her face. And she and the child both spoke in the same breath the two sharp phrases that brought the climax of the vile adventure upon us in that silent room of night.

They were like two pistol-shots.

"My God! There's a face watching us . . . !" I heard her voice, all choked and dry.

And at the same second, Aileen—

"Oh, oh! He's seen us! . . . He's *here!* Look. . . . He'll get me . . . hide your hands, hide your poor hands . . . !"

And, turning to the place my cousin stared at, I saw sure enough that a face—apparently a living human face—was pressed against the window-pane, framed between two hands as it tried to peer upon us into the semi-obscurity of the room. I saw the swift momentary rolling of the two eyes as the candle glare fell upon them, and caught a glimpse even of the hunched-up shoulders behind, as their owner, standing outside upon the lawn, stooped down a little to see better. And though the apparition instantly withdrew, I recognised it beyond question as the dark and evil countenance of the butler. His breath still stained the window.

Yet the strange thing was that Aileen, struggling violently to bury herself amid the scanty folds of my coat, could not possibly have seen what we saw, for her face was turned from the window the entire time, and from the way I held her she could never for a single instant have been in a position to know. It all took place behind her back. . . . A moment later, with her eyes still hidden against me, I was carrying her swiftly in my arms across the hall and up the main staircase to the night nursery.

My difficulty with her was, of course, while she hovered between the two states of sleep and waking, for once I got her into bed and plunged her deeply again into the trance condition, I was easily able to control her slightest thought or emotion. Within ten minutes she was sleeping peacefully, her little face smoothed of all anxiety or terror, and my imperious command ringing from end to end of her consciousness that when she woke next morning all should be forgotten. She was finally to forget . . . utterly and completely.

And, meanwhile, of course, the man, when I went with loathing and anger in my heart to his room in the servants' quarters, had a perfectly plausible explanation. He was in the act of getting ready for bed, he declared, when the noise had aroused his suspicions, and, as in duty bound, he had made a tour of the house outside, thinking to discover burglars. . . .

With a month's wages in his pocket, and a considerable degree of wonder in his soul, probably—for the man was guilty of nothing worse than innocently terrifying a child's imagination!—he went back to London the following day; and a few hours later I myself was travelling with Aileen and old Kempster over the blue waves of the North Sea, carrying her off, curiously enough, to freedom and happiness in the very way her "imagination" had pictured her escape in the "story" of long ago, when she was Lady Helen, held in bondage by a cruel husband, and I was Philip, her devoted lover.

Only this time her happiness was lasting and complete. Hypnotic suggestion had wiped from her mind the last vestige of her dreadful memories; her face was wreathed in jolly smiles; her enjoyment of the journey and our week in Antwerp was absolutely unclouded; she played and laughed with all the radiance of an unhaunted childhood, and her imagination was purged and healed.

And when we got back her mother had again moved her household gods to the original family mansion where she had first lived. Thither it was I took the restored child, and there it was my cousin and I looked up the old family records and verified certain details of the history of De Lorne, that wicked and semi-fabulous ancestor whose portrait hung in the dark corner of the stairs. That his life was evil to the brim I had always understood, but neither myself nor Theresa had known—at least had not consciously remembered—that he had married twice, and that his first wife, Lady Helen, had mysteriously disappeared, and Sir Philip Lansing, a neighbouring knight, supposed to be her lover, had soon afterwards emigrated to France and left his lands and property to go to ruin.

But another discovery I made, and kept to myself, had to do with that "room of terror" in the old Norfolk house where, on the plea of necessary renovation, I had the stones removed, and in the very spot where Aileen used to beat her hands against the bricks and "talk to the wall," the workmen under my own eyes laid bare the skeleton of a woman, fastened to the granite by means of a narrow iron band that encircled the waist—the skeleton of some unfortunate who had been walled-up alive and had come to her dreadful death by the pangs of hunger, thirst, and suffocation centuries ago.

The Price of Wiggins's Orgy

I

It happened to be a Saturday when Samuel Wiggins drew the first cash sum on account of his small legacy—some twenty pounds, ten in gold and ten in notes. It felt in his pocket like a bottled-up prolongation of life. Never before had he seen so many dreams within practical reach. It produced in him a kind of high and elusive exaltation of the spirit. From time to time he put his hand down to make the notes crackle and let his fingers play through the running sovereigns as children play through sand.

For twenty years he had been secretary to a philanthropist interested in feeding—feeding the poor. Soup kitchens had been the keynote of those twenty years, the distribution of victuals his sole objective. And now he had his reward—a legacy of £100 a year for the balance of his days.

To him it was riches. He wore a shortish frock-coat, a low, spreading collar, a black made-up tie, and boots with elastic sides. On this particular day he wore also a new pair of rather bright yellow leather gloves. He was unmarried, over forty, bald, plump in the body, and possessed of a simple and emotional heart almost child-like. His brown eyes shone in a face that was wrinkled and dusty—all his dreams driven inwards by the long years of uninspired toil for another.

For the first time in his life, released from the dingy purlieus of soup kitchens and the like, he wandered towards evening among the gay and lighted streets of the "West End"—Piccadilly Circus where the flaming lamps positively hurt the eyes, and Leicester Square. It was bewildering and delightful, this freedom. It went to his head. Yet he ought to have known better.

"I'm going to dine at a restaurant to-night, by Jove," he said to himself, thinking of the gloomy boarding-house where he usually sat between a missionary and a typewriter. He fingered his money. "I'm going to celebrate my legacy. I've earned it." The thought of a motor-car flashed absurdly through his mind; it was followed by another: a holiday in Spain, Italy, Hungary—one of those sunny countries where music was cheap, in the open air, and of the romantic kind he loved. These thoughts show the kind of exaltation that possessed him.

"It's nearly, though not quite, £2 a week," he repeated to himself for the fiftieth time, reflecting upon his legacy. "I simply can't believe it!"

After indecision that threatened to be endless, he turned at length through the swinging glass doors of a big and rather gorgeous restaurant. Only once before in his life had he dined at a big London restaurant—a Railway Hotel! Passing with some hesitation through the gaudy *café* where a number of foreigners sat drinking at little marble tables, he entered the main dining-room, long, lofty, and already thronged. Here the light and noise and movement dazed him considerably, and for the life of him he could not decide upon a table. The people all looked so prosperous and important; the waiters so like gentlemen in evening dress—the kind that came to the philanthropist's table. The roar of voices, eating, knives and forks, rose about him and filled him with a certain dismay. It was all rather overwhelming.

"I should have liked a smaller place better," he murmured, "but still—" And again he fingered his money to gain confidence.

The choice of a table *was* intimidating, for he was absurdly retiring, was Wiggins; more at home with papers and the reports of philanthropic societies; his holidays spent in a boarding-house at Worthing with his sister and her invalid husband. Then relief came in the form of a sub-head waiter who, spying his helplessness, enquired with a bland grandeur of manner if he "looked perhaps for some one?"

"Oh, a table, thanks, only a table—"

The man, washing his hands in mid-air, swept down the crowded aisles and found one without the least difficulty. It emerged from nowhere so easily that Wiggins felt he had been a fool not to discover it alone. He wondered if he ought to tip the man half-a-crown now or later, but, before he could decide, another occupied his place, bland and smiling, with black eyes and plush-like hair, bending low before him and holding out a large pink programme.

He examined it, feeling that he ought to order dishes with outlandish names just to show that he knew his way about. Before he could steady his eye upon a single line, however, a third waiter, very youthful, suggested in broken English that Wiggins should leave his hat, coat, and umbrella elsewhere. This he did willingly, though without grace or dispatch, for the yellow gloves stuck ridiculously to his hands. Then he sat down and turned to the menu again.

It was a very ordinary restaurant really, in spite of the vast height of the gilded ceiling, the scale of its sham magnificence, and the excessive glitter of its hundred lights. The menu, disguised by various expensive and *recherché* dishes (which when ordered were invariably found to be "off"), was even more ordinary than the hall. But to the dazed Wiggins the words looked like a series of death-sentences printed in different languages, but all meaning the same thing: *order me—or die!* That waiter standing over him was the executioner. Unless he speedily ordered something really worth the proprietor's while to provide, the head waiter would be summoned and he, Wiggins, would be beheaded. Those stars against certain cheap dishes meant that they could only be ordered by privileged persons, and those crosses—

"This is *vairy* nice this sevening, sir," said the waiter, suddenly bending and pointing with a dirty finger to a dish that Wiggins found buried in a list uncommonly like "Voluntary Subscriptions" in his reports. It was entitled "Lancashire Hot-Pot . . . 2/0"—two shillings, not two pounds, as he first imagined! He leaped at it.

"Yes, thanks; that'll do, then—for to-night," he said, and the waiter ambled away indifferently, looking all round the room in search of sympathy.

By degrees, however, the other recovered his self-possession, and realised that to spend his legacy on mere Hot-Pot was to admit he knew not the values of life. He called the plush-beaded waiter back and with a rush of words ordered some oysters, soup, a fried sole, and half a partridge to follow.

"Then ze 'Ot-Pot, sir?" queried the man, with respect.

"I'll see about that later."

For he was already wondering what he should drink, knowing nothing of wines and vintages. At luncheon with the philanthropist he sometimes had a glass of sherry; at Worthing with his sister he drank beer. But now he wanted something really good, something generous that would help him to celebrate. He would have ordered champagne as a conciliation to the waiter, now positively obsequious, but some one had told him once that there was not enough champagne in the world to go round, and that hotels and restaurants were supplied with "something rather bad." Burgundy, he felt, would be more the thing—rich, sunny, full-bodied.

He studied the wine-card till his head swam. A waiter, while he was thus engaged, sidled up and watched him from an angle. Wiggins, looking up distractedly at the same moment, caught his eye. Whew! It was the Head Waiter himself, a man of quite infinite presence, who at once bowed himself forward, and with a gentle but commanding manner drew his attention to the wines he could "especially recommend." Something in the man's face struck him momentarily as familiar—vaguely familiar—then passed.

Now Wiggins, as has been said, did not know one wine from another; but the spirit of his foolish pose fairly had him by the throat at last, and each time this condescending individual indicated a new vintage he shook his head knowingly and shrugged his shoulders with the air of a connoisseur. This pantomime continued for several minutes.

"Something *really* good, you know," he mumbled after a while, determined to justify himself in the eyes of this high official who was taking such pains. "A rare wine—er—with body in it." Then he added, with a sudden impulse of confidence, "It's Saturday night, remember!" And he smiled knowingly, making a gesture that a man of the world was meant to understand.

Why he should have said this remains a mystery. Perhaps it was a semi-apologetic reference to the supposed habit of men to indulge themselves on a Saturday because they need not rise early to work next day. Perhaps it was meant in some way to excuse all the trouble he was giving. In any case, there can be no question that the manner of the Head Waiter instantly changed in a subtle way difficult to describe, and from mere official politeness passed into deferential attention. He bowed slightly. He increased his distance by an inch or two. Wiggins, noticing it and slightly bewildered, repeated his remark, for want of something to say more than anything else. "It's Saturday night, of course," he repeated, murmuring, yet putting more meaning into the words than they could reasonably hold.

"As Monsieur says," the man replied, with a marked respect in his tone not there before; "and we—close early."

"Of course," said the other, gaining confidence pleasantly, "you close early."

He had quite forgotten the fact, even if he ever knew it, but he spoke with decision. Glancing up from the wine-list, he caught the man's eye; then instantly lowered his gaze, for the Head Waiter was staring at him in a fixed and curious manner that seemed unnecessary. And once again that passing touch of familiarity appeared upon the features and was gone.

"Monsieur is here for the first time, if I may ask?" came next.

"Er—yes, I am," he replied, thinking all this attention a trifle excessive.

"Ah, *pardon,* of course, I understand," the Head Waiter added softly. "A new—a recent member, then—?"

A little non-plussed, a little puzzled, Wiggins agreed with a nod of the head. He did not know that head waiters referred to customers as "members." For an instant it occurred to him that possibly he was being mistaken for somebody else. It was really—but at that moment the oysters arrived. The Head Waiter said something in rapid Italian to his subordinate—something that obviously increased that plush-headed person's desire to please—bent over with his best manner to murmur, "And I will get monsieur the wine he will like, the right kind of wine!"—and was gone.

It was a new and delightful sensation. Wiggins, feeling proud, pleased, and important under the effect of this excellent service and attention, turned to his oysters. The wine would come presently. And, meanwhile, the music had begun. . . .

II

He began to enjoy himself thoroughly, and the wine—still, fragrant, soft—soon ran in his veins and drove out the last vestige of his absurd shyness. Behind the palm trees, somewhere out of sight, the orchestra played soothingly, and if the selections were somewhat bizarre it made no difference to him. He drank in the sound just as he drank in the wine—eagerly. Both fed the consciousness that he was enjoying himself, and the Danse Macabre gave him as much pleasure as did the Bohème, the Strauss Waltz, or Donizetti. Everything—wine, music, food, people—served to intensify his interest *in himself.* He examined his face in the big mirrors and realised what a dog he was and what a good time he was having. He watched the other customers, finding them splendid and distinguished. The whole place was really fine—he would come again and again, always ordering the same wine, for it was certainly an unusual wine, as the Head Waiter had called it, "the right kind." The price of it he never asked, for in his pocket lay the price of a whole case. His hand slipped down to finger the sovereigns—hot and slippery now—and the notes, somewhat moist and crumpled. . . . The needles of the big staring clock meanwhile swung onwards. . . .

Thus, aided by the tactful and occasional superintendence of the Head Waiter from a distance, the evening passed along in a happy rush of pleasurable emotion. The half-partridge had vanished, and Wiggins toyed now with a wonderful-looking "sweet"—the most expensive he could find. He did not eat much of it, but liked to see it on his plate. The wine helped things enormously. He had ordered another half-bottle some time ago, delighted to find that it exhilarated without confusing him. And every one else in the place was enjoying himself in the same way. He was thrilled to discover this.

Only one thing jarred a little. A very big man, with a round, clean-shaven face inclined to fatness, stared at him more than he cared about from a table in the corner diagonally across the room. He had only come in half-an-hour ago. His face was somehow or other dog-like—something between a boar-hound and a pup, Wiggins thought. Each time he looked up the fellow's large and rather fierce eyes were fixed upon him, then lingeringly withdrawn. It was unpleasant to be stared at in this way by an offensive physiognomy.

But most of the time he was too full of personal visions conjured up by the wine to trouble long about external matters. His head was simply brimming over with thoughts and ideas—about himself, about soup-kitchens, feeding the poor, the change of life effected by the legacy, and a thousand other details. Once or twice, however, in sharp, clear moments when the tide of alcohol ebbed a little, other questions assailed him: Why should the Head Waiter have become so obsequious and attentive? What was it in his face that seemed familiar? What was there about the remark "It's Saturday evening" to change his manner? And—what was it about the dinner, the restaurant, and the music that seemed just a little out of the ordinary?

Or was he merely thinking nonsense? And was it his imagination that this man stared so oddly? The alcohol rushed deliciously in his veins.

The vague uneasiness, however, was a passing matter, for the orchestra was tearing madly through a Csardas, and his thoughts and feelings were swept away in the wild rhythm. He drank his bottle out and ordered another. Was it the second or the third? He could not remember. Counting always made his head ache. He did not care anyhow. "Let 'er go! I'm enjoying myself! I've got a fat legacy—money lying in the bank—money I haven't earned!" The carefulness of years was destroyed in as many minutes. "That music's simply spiffing!"

Then he glanced up and caught the clean-shaven face bearing down upon him across the shimmering room like the muzzle of a moving gun. He tried to meet it, but found he could not focus it properly. The same moment he saw that he was mistaken; the man was merely staring at him. Two faces swam and wobbled into one. This movement, and the appearance of coming towards him, were both illusions produced by the alcohol. He drank another glass quickly to steady his vision—and then another. . . .

"I'll call for my bill. Itshtime to go . . . !" he murmured aloud later, with a very deep sigh. He looked about him for the waiter, who instantly appeared—with coffee and liqueurs, however.

"Dear me, yes. Qui' forgot I or'ered those," he observed offhand, smiling in the man's face, willing and anxious to say a lot of things, but not quite certain what.

"My bill," was what he said finally, "mush b'off!"

The waiter laughed pleasantly, but very politely, in reply. Wiggins repeated his remark about his bill.

"Oh, that will be all right, sir," returned the man, as though no such thing as payment was ever heard of in *this* restaurant. It was rather confusing. Wiggins laughed to himself, drank his liqueur, and forgot about everything except the ballet music of Délibes the strings were sprinkling in a silver shower about the hall. His mind ran after them through the glittering air.

"Just fancy if I could catch 'em and take 'em home in a bunch," he said to himself, immensely pleased. He was enjoying himself hugely by now.

And then, suddenly, he became aware that the place was rapidly thinning, lights being lowered, good-nights being said, and that everybody seemed—drunk.

"P'rapsh they've all got legacies!" he thought, flushing with excitement.

He rose unsteadily to his feet and was delighted to find that *he* was not in the least—drunk. He at once respected himself.

"Itsh really 'sgusting that fellows can't stop when they've had 'nough!" he murmured, making his way with steps that required great determination towards the door, and remembering before he got halfway that he had not paid his bill. Turning in a half-circle that brought an unnecessary quantity of the room round with him, he made his way back, lost his way, fumbled about in the increasing gloom, and found himself face to face with the—Head Waiter. The unexpected meeting braced him astonishingly. The dignity of the man had curiously increased.

"I'm looking for my bill," observed Wiggins thickly, wondering for the twentieth time of whom the man's face reminded him; "you haven't seen it about anywhere, I shuppose?" He sat down with more dignity than he could have supposed possible and produced a £5 note from his pocket, the lining of the pocket coming out with it like a dirty glove.

Most of the guests had gone out by this time, and the big hall was very dark. Two lights only remained, and these, reflected from mirror to mirror, made its proportions seem vast and unreal. They flew from place to place, too, distressingly—these lights.

"Half-a-crown will settle that, sir," replied the man, with a respectful bow.

"Nonshense!" replied the other. "Why, I ordered Lancashire hotch-potch, grilled shole, a—a bird or something of the kind, and the wine—"

"I beg your pardon, sir, but—if you will permit me to say so—the others will soon be here now, and—as there will be a specially large attendance, perhaps you would like to make sure of your place." He pocketed the half-crown with a bow, pointed to the far, dim corner of the room, and stepped aside a little to make space for Wiggins to pass.

And Wiggins did pass—though it is not quite clear how he managed to dodge the flying tables. With deep sighs, hot, confused, and puzzled, but too obfuscated to understand what it was all about, he obeyed the directions, at the same time wondering uneasily how it was he had forgotten what was afoot. He wandered towards the end of the hall with the uncertainty of a butterfly that makes many feints before it settles. . . . At a vast distance off the Head Waiter was moving to close the main doors, utterly oblivious now of his existence. He felt glad of that. Something about that fellow was disagreeable—downright nasty. This suddenly came over him with a flood of conviction. The man was more than peculiar: he was sinister. . . . The air smelt horribly of cooked food, tobacco smoke, breathing crowds, scented women, and the rest. Whiffs of it, hot and fœtid, brought him a little to his senses. . . . Then suddenly he noticed that the big man with the face that was dark and smooth like the muzzle of a cannon, was watching him keenly from a table on the other side where an electric light still burned.

"By George! There he is again, that feller! Wonder whatsh he's smiling at me for. Looking for'sh bill too, p'raps— Now, in a Soup Kishen nothing of the kind—"

He bowed in return, smiling insolently, holding himself steady by a chair to do so. He shoved and stumbled his way on into the shadows, half-mingling with the throng passing out into the street. Then, making a sharp turn back into the room unobserved, he took a few uncertain steps and collapsed silently and helplessly upon a chair that was hidden behind a big palm-tree in a dark corner.

And the last thing he remembered as he sank, boneless, like soft hay, into that corner was that the sham palm-tree bowed towards him, then ran off into the ceiling, and from that elevation, which in no way diminished its size, bowed to him yet again. . . .

It was just after his eyes closed that the door in the gilt panelling at the end of the room softly opened and a woman entered on tiptoe. She was followed by other women and several girls; these, again, from time to time, by men, all dressed in black, all silent, and all ushered by the majestic Head Waiter to their places. The big man with the face like a gun-muzzle superintended. And each individual, on entering, was held there at the secret doorway until a certain sentence had passed his lips. Evidently a password: "It is Saturday night," said the one being admitted, "and we close early," replied the Head Waiter and the big man. And then the door was closed until the next soft tapping came.

But Wiggins, plunged in the stupor of the first sleep, knew none of all this. His frock-coat was bunched about his neck, his black tie under his ear, his feet resting higher than his head. He looked like a collapsed air-ship in a hedge, and he snored heavily.

III

It was about an hour later when he opened his eyes, climbed painfully and heavily to his feet, staggered back against the wall utterly bewildered—and stared. At the far end of the great hall, its loftiness now dim, was a group of people. The big mirrors on all sides reflected them with the effect of increasing their numbers indefinitely. They stood and sat upon an improvised platform. The electric lights, shaded with black, dropped a pale glitter upon their faces. They were systematically grouped, the big man in the centre, the Head Waiter at a small table just behind him. The former was speaking in low, measured tones.

In his dark and distant corner Wiggins first of all seized the carafe and quenched his feverish thirst. Next he advanced slowly and with the utmost caution to a point nearer the group where he could hear what was being said. He was still a good deal confused in mind, and had no idea what the hour was or what he had been doing in the meantime. There were some twenty or thirty people, he saw, of both sexes, well dressed, many of them distinguished in appearance, and all wearing black; even their gloves were black; some of the women, too, wore black veils—very thick. But in all the faces without exception there was something—was it about the lips and mouths?—that was peculiar and—repellent.

Obviously this was a meeting of some kind. Some society had hired the hall for a private gathering. Wiggins, understanding this, began to feel awkward. He did not wish to intrude; he had no right to listen; yet to make himself known was to betray that he was still very considerably intoxicated. The problem presented itself in these simple terms to his dazed intelligence. He was also aware of another fact: about these black-robed people there was something which made him secretly and horribly—afraid.

The big man with the smooth face like a gun-muzzle sat down after a softly-uttered speech, and the group, instead of applauding with their hands, waved black handkerchiefs. The fluttering sound of them trickled along the wastes of hall towards the concealed eavesdropper. Then the Head Waiter rose to introduce the next speaker, and the instant Wiggins saw him he understood what it was in his face that was familiar. For the false beard no longer adorned his lips, the wig that altered the shape of his forehead and the appearance of his eyes had been removed, and the likeness he bore to the philanthropist, Wiggins's late employer, was too remarkable to be ignored. Wiggins just repressed a cry, but a low gasp apparently did escape him, for several members of the group turned their heads in his direction and stared.

The Head Waiter, meanwhile, saved him from immediate discovery by beginning to speak. The words were plainly audible, and the resemblance of the voice to that other voice he knew now to be stopped with dust, was one of the most dreadful experiences he had ever known. Each word, each trick of expression came as a new and separate shock.

". . . and the learned Doctor will say a few words upon the *rationale* of our subject," he concluded, turning with a graceful bow to make room for a distinguished-looking old gentleman who advanced shambling from the back of the improvised platform.

What Wiggins then heard—in somewhat disjointed sentences owing to the buzzing in his ears—was at first apparently meaningless. Yet it was freighted, he knew, with a creeping and sensational horror that would fully reveal itself the instant he discovered the clue. The old clever-faced scoundrel was saying vile things. He knew it. But the key to the puzzle being missing, he could not quite guess what it was all about. The Doctor, gravely and with balanced phrases, seemed to be speaking of the fads of the day with regard to food and feeding. He ridiculed vegetarianism, and all the other *isms*. He said that one and all were based upon ignorance and fallacy, declaring that the time had at last come in the history of the race when a rational system of feeding was a paramount necessity. The physical and psychical conditions of the times demanded it, and the soul of man could never be emancipated until it was adopted. He himself was proud to be one of the founders of their audacious and secret Society, revolutionary and pioneer in

the best sense, to which so many of the medical fraternity now belonged, and so many of the brave women too, who were in the van of
the feminist movements of the times. He said a great deal in this vein.
Wiggins, listening in growing amazement and uneasiness, waited for
the clue to it all.

In conclusion, the speaker referred solemnly to the fact that there
was a stream of force in their Society which laid them open to the melancholy charge of being called "hysterical." "But after all," he cried,
with rising enthusiasm and in accents that rang down the hall, "a Society without hysteria is a dull Society, just as a woman without hysteria
is a dull woman. Neither the Society nor the woman need yield to the
tendency; but that it is present potentially infers the faculty, so delicious in the eyes of all sane men—the faculty of running to extremes.
It is a sign of life, and of very vivid life. It is not for nothing, dear
friends, that we are named the—" But the buzzing in Wiggins's ears
was so loud at this moment that he missed the name. It sounded to
him something between "Can-I-believes" and "Camels," but for the
life of him he could not overtake the actual word. The Doctor had uttered it, moreover, in a lowered voice—a suddenly lowered voice. . . .
When the noise in his ears had passed he heard the speaker bring his
address to an end in these words: ". . . and I will now ask the secretaries to make their reports from their various sections, after which, I understand"—his tone grew suddenly thick and clouded—"we are to be
regaled with a collation—a sacramental collation—of the usual
kind. . . ." His voice hushed away to nothing. His mouth was working
most curiously. A wave of excitement unquestionably ran over the faces of the others. Their mouths also worked oddly. Dark and sombre
things were afoot in that hall.

Wiggins crouched a little lower behind the edge of the overhanging
table-cloth and listened. He was perspiring now, but there were touches of icy horror fingering about in the neighbourhood of his heart. His
mental and physical discomfort were very great, for the conviction that
he was about to witness some dreadful scene—black as the garments
of the participants in it—grew rapidly within him. He devised endless
plans for escape, only to reject them the instant they were formed.
There was no escape possible. He had to wait till the end.

A charming young woman was on her feet, addressing the audience in silvery tones; sweet and comely she was, her beauty only marred by that singular leer that visited the lips and mouths of all of them. The flesh of his back began to crawl as he listened. He would have given his whole year's legacy to be out of it, for behind that voice of silver and sweetness there crowded even to her lips the rush of something that was unutterable—loathsome. Wiggins felt it. The uncertainty as to its exact nature only added to his horror and distress.

". . . so this question of supply, my friends," she was saying, "is becoming more and more difficult. It resolves itself into a question of ways and means." She looked round upon her audience with a touch of nervous apprehension before she continued. "In my particular sphere of operations—West Kensington—I have regretfully to report that the suspicions and activity of the police, the foolish, old-fashioned police, have now rendered my monthly contributions no longer possible. There have been too many disappearances of late—" She paused, casting her eyes down. Wiggins felt his hair rise, drawn by a shivery wind. The words "contributions" and "disappearances" brought with them something quite freezing.

". . . As you know," the girl resumed, "it is to the doctors that we must look chiefly for our steadier supplies, and unfortunately in my sphere of operations we have but one doctor who is a member. . . . I do not like to—to resign my position, but I must ask for lenient consideration of my failure"—her voice sank lower still—". . . my failure to furnish to-night the materials—" She began to stammer and hesitate dreadfully; her voice shook; an ashen pallor spread to her very lips. ". . . the elements for our customary feast—"

A movement of disapproval ran over the audience like a wave; murmurs of dissent and resentment were heard. As the girl paled more perceptibly the singular beauty of her face stood out with an effect of almost shining against that dark background of shadows and black garments. In spite of himself, and forgetting caution for the moment, Wiggins peeped over the edge of the table to see her better. She was a lady, he saw, high-bred and spirited. That pallor, and the timidity it bespoke, was but evidence of a highly sensitive nature facing a situation of peculiar difficulty—and danger. He read in her attitude, in the poise of that slim figure standing there before disapproval and possible disaster, the bearing and proud courage of a type that would face execution with calmness and dignity. Wiggins was amazed that this thought should flash through him so vividly—from nowhere. Born of the feverish aftermath of alcohol, perhaps—yet born inevitably, too, of this situation before his eyes.

With a thrill he realised that the girl was speaking again, her voice steady, but faint with the gravity of her awful position.

". . . and I ask for that justice in consideration of my failure which— the difficulties of the position demand. I have had to choose between that bold and ill-considered action which might have betrayed us all to the authorities, and—the risk of providing nothing for to-night."

She sat down. Wiggins understood that it was a question of life and death. The air about him turned icy. He felt the perspiration trickling on several different parts of his body at once.

An old lady rose instantly to reply; her face was stern and dreadful, although the signature of breeding and culture was plainly there in the delicate lines about the nostrils and forehead. Her mien held something implacable. She was dressed in black silk that rustled, and she was certainly well over sixty; but what made Wiggins squirm there in his narrow hiding-place was the extraordinary resemblance she bore to Mrs. Sturgis, the superintendent of one of his late employer's soup kitchens. It was all diabolically grotesque. She glanced round upon the group of members, who clearly regarded her as a leader. The machinery of the whole dreadful scene then moved quicker.

"Then are we to understand from the West Kensington secretary," she began in firm, even tones, "that for to-night there is—nothing?" The young girl bowed her head without rising from her chair.

"I beg to move, then, Mr. Chairman," continued the terrible old lady in iron accents, "that the customary procedure be followed, and that a Committee of Three be appointed to carry it into immediate effect." The words fell like bomb-shells into the deserted spaces of the hall.

"I second the motion," was heard in a man's voice.

"Those in favour of the motion will show their hands," announced the big chairman with the clean-shaven face.

Several score of black-gloved hands waved in the air, with the effect of plumes upon a jolting hearse.

"And those who oppose it?"

No single hand was raised. An appalling hush fell upon the group.

"I appoint Signor Carnamorte as chairman of the sub-committee, with power to choose his associates," said the big man. And the "Head Waiter" bowed his acceptance of the duty imposed upon him. There was at once then a sign of hurried movement, and the figure of the young girl was lost momentarily to view as several members surged round her. The next instant they fell away and she stood clear, her hands bound. Her voice, soft as before but very faint, was audible through the hush.

"I claim the privilege belonging to the female members of the Society," she said calmly; "the right to find, if possible, a substitute."

"Granted," answered the chairman gravely. "The customary ten minutes will be allowed you in which to do so. Meanwhile, the preparations must proceed in the usual way."

With a dread that ate all other emotions, Wiggins watched keenly from his concealment, and the preparations that he saw in progress, though simple enough in themselves, filled him with a sense of ultimate horror that was freezing. The Committee of Three were very busy with something at the back of the improvised platform, something that was heavy and, on being touched, emitted a metallic and sonorous ring. As in the strangling terror and heat of nightmare the full meaning of events is often kept concealed until the climax, so Wiggins knew that this simple sound portended something that would only be revealed to him later—something appalling as Satan—sinister as the grave. That ring of metal was the Gong of Death. He heard it in his own heart, and the shock was so great that he could not prevent an actual physical movement. His jerking leg drove sharply against a chair. The chair—squeaked.

The sound pierced the deep silence of the big hall with so shrill a note that of course everybody heard it. Wiggins, expecting to have the whole crew of these black-robed people about his ears, held his breath in an agony of suspense. All those pairs of eyes, he felt, were searching the spot where he lay so thinly hidden by the table-cloth. But no steps came towards him. A voice, however, spoke: the voice of the girl: she had heard the sound and had divined its cause.

"Loosen my bonds," she cried, "for there is some one yonder among the shadows. I have found a substitute! And—I swear to heaven—*he is plump!*"

The sentence was so extraordinary, that Wiggins felt a spring of secret merriment touched somewhere deep within him, and a gush of uncontrollable laughter came up in his throat so suddenly that before he could get his hand to his mouth, it rang down the long dim hall and betrayed him beyond all question of escape. Behind it lay the strange need of violent expression. He had to do something. The life of this slender and exquisite girl was in danger. And the nightmare strain of the whole scene, the hints and innuendoes of a dark purpose, the implacable nature of the decree that threatened so fair a life—all resulted in a pressure that was too much for him. Had he not laughed, he would certainly have shrieked aloud. And the next minute he did shriek aloud. The screams followed his laughter with a dreadful clamour, and at the same instant he staggered noisily to his feet and rose into full view from behind the table. Everybody then saw him.

Across the length of that dimly-lighted hall he faced the group of people in all their hideous reality, and what he saw cleared from his fuddled brain the last fumes of the alcohol. The white visage of each member seemed already close upon him. He saw the glimmering pallor of their skins against the black clothes, the eyes ashine, the mouths working, fingers pointing at him. There was the Head Waiter, more than ever like the dead philanthropist whose life had been spent in feeding others; there the odious smooth face of the big chairman; there the stern-lipped old lady who demanded the sentence of death. The whole silent crew of them stared darkly at him, and in front of them, like some fair lily growing amid decay, stood the girl with the proud and pallid face, calm and self-controlled. Immediately beyond her, a little to one side, Wiggins next perceived the huge iron cauldron, already swinging from its mighty tripod, waiting to receive her into its capacious jaws. Beneath it gleamed and flickered the flames from a dozen spirit-lamps.

"My substitute!" rang out her clear voice. "My substitute! Unloose my hands! And seize him before he can escape!"

"He cannot escape!" cried a dozen angry voices.

"In darkness!" thundered the chairman, and at the same moment every light was extinguished from the switch-board—every light but one. The bulb immediately behind him in the wall was left burning.

And the crew were upon him, coming swiftly and stealthily down the empty aisles between the tables. He saw their forms advance and shift by the gleam of the lamps beneath the awful cauldron. With the advance came, too, the sound of rushing, eager breathing. He imagined, though he could not see, those evil mouths a-working. And at this moment the subconscious part of him that had kept the secret all this time, suddenly revealed in letters of flame the name of the Society which fifteen minutes before he had failed to catch. The subconscious self, that supreme stage manager, that arch conspirator, rose and struck him in the face as it were out of the darkness, so that he understood, with a shock of nauseous terror, the terrible nature of the net in which he was caught.

For this Secret Society, meeting for their awful rites in a great public restaurant of mid-London, were maniacs of a rare and singular description—vilely mad on one point but sane on all the rest. They were Cannibals!

Never before had he run with such speed, agility, and recklessness; never before had he guessed that he could leap tables, clear chairs with the flying manner of a hurdle race, and dodge palms and flower-pots as an athlete of twenty dodges collisions in the football field. But in each dark corner where he sought a temporary refuge, the electric light on the wall above immediately sprang into brilliance, one of the crew having remained by the switchboard to control this diabolically ingenious method of keeping him ever in sight.

For a long time, however, he evaded his crowding and clumsy pursuers. It was a vile and ghastly chase. His flying frock-coat streamed out behind him, and he felt the elastic side of his worn boots split under the unusual strain of the twisting, turning ankles as he leaped and ran. His pursuers, it seemed, sought to prolong the hunt on purpose. The passion of the chase was in their blood. Round and round that hall, up and down, over tables and under chairs, behind screens, shaking the handles of doors—all immovable, past gleaming dish-covers on the wheeled joint-tables, taking cover by swing doors, curtains, palms, everything and anything, Wiggins flew for his life from the pursuing forces of a horrible death.

And at last they caught him. Breathless and exhausted, he collapsed backwards against the wall in a dark corner. But the light instantly flashed out above him. He lay in full view, and in another second the advancing horde—he saw their eyes and mouths so close—would be upon him, when something utterly unexpected happened: his head in falling struck against a hard projecting substance and—a bell rang sharply out. It was a telephone!

How he ever managed to get the receiver to his lips, or why the answering exchange came so swiftly he does not pretend to know. He had just time to shout, "Help! Help! Send police X . . . Restaurant! Murder! Cannibals!" when he was seized violently by the collar, his arms and legs grasped by a dozen pairs of hands, and a struggle began that he knew from the start must prove hopeless.

The fact that help might be on the way, however, gave him courage. Wiggins smashed right and left, screamed, kicked, bit, and butted. His frock-coat was ripped from his back with a whistling tear of cloth and lining, and he found himself free at the edge of a group that clawed and beat everywhere about him. The dim light was now in his favour. He shot down the hall again like a hare, leaping tables on the way, and flinging dish-covers, carafes, menus at the pursuing crowd as fast as he could lay hands upon them.

Then came a veritable pandemonium of smashed glass and crockery, while a grip of iron caught his arms behind and pinioned them beyond all possibility of moving. Turning quickly, he found himself looking straight into the eyes of a big blue policeman, the door into the street open beside him. The crowd became at once inextricably mixed up and jumbled together. The chairman, and the girl who was to have been eaten, melted into a single person. The philanthropist and the old lady slid into each other. It was a horrible bit of confusion. He felt deadly sick and dizzy. Everything dropped away from his sight then, and darkness tore up round him from the carpet. He remembered nothing more for a long time.

Perhaps the most vivid recollection of what occurred afterwards—he remembers it to this day, and his memory may be trusted, for he never touched wine again—was the weary smile of the magistrate, and the still more weary voice as he said in the court two days later—

"Forty shillings, and be bound over to keep the peace in two sureties for six months. And £5 to the proprietor of the restaurant to pay damages for the broken windows and crockery. Next case . . . !"

The Eccentricity of Simon Parnacute

I

It was one of those mornings in early spring when even the London streets run beauty. The day, passing through the sky with clouds of flying hair, touched every one with the magic of its own irresponsible gaiety, as it alternated between laughter and the tears of sudden showers.

In the parks the trees, faintly clothed with gauze, were busying themselves shyly with the thoughts of coming leaves. The air held a certain sharpness, but the sun swam through the dazzling blue spaces with bursts of almost summer heat; and a wind, straight from the haunted south, laid its soft persuasion upon all, bringing visions too fair to last—long thoughts of youth, of cowslip-meadows, white sails, waves on yellow sand, and other pictures innumerable and enchanting.

So potent, indeed, was this spell of awakening spring that even Simon Parnacute, retired Professor of Political Economy—elderly, thin-faced, and ruminating in his big skull those large questions that concern the polity of nations—formed no exception to the general rule. For, as he slowly made his way down the street that led from his apartment to the Little Park, he was fully aware that this magic of the spring was in his own blood too, and that the dust which had accumulated with the years upon the surface of his soul was being stirred by one of the softest breezes he had ever felt in the whole course of his arduous and tutorial career.

And—it so happened—just as he reached the foot of the street where the houses fell away towards the open park, the sun rushed out into one of the sudden blue spaces of the sky, and drenched him in a wave of delicious heat that for all the world was like the heat of July.

Professor Parnacute, once lecturer, now merely ponderer, was an exact thinker, dealing carefully with the facts of life as he saw them. He was a good man and a true. He dealt in large emotions, becoming for one who studied nations rather than individuals, and of all diplomacies of the heart he was rudely ignorant. He lived always at the centre of the circle—his own circle—and eccentricity was a thing to him utterly abhorrent. Convention ruled him, body, soul, and mind. To know a disordered thought, or an unwonted emotion, troubled him as much as to see a picture crooked on a wall, or a man's collar projecting beyond his overcoat. Eccentricity was the symptom of a disease.

Thus, as he reached the foot of the street and felt the sun and wind upon his withered cheeks, this unexpected call of the spring came to him sharply as something altogether out of place and illegitimate—symptom of an irregular condition of mind that must be instantly repressed. And it was just here, while the crowd jostled and delayed him, that there smote upon his ear the song incarnate of the very spring whose spell he was in the act of relegating to its proper place in his personal economy: he heard the entrancing *singing of a bird!*

Transfixed with wonder and delight, he stood for a whole minute and listened. Then, slowly turning, he found himself staring straight into the small beseeching eyes of a—thrush; a thrush in a cage that hung upon the outside wall of a bird-fancier's shop behind him.

Perhaps he would not have lingered more than these few seconds, however, had not the crowd held him momentarily prisoner in a spot immediately opposite the shop, where his head, too, was exactly on a level with the hanging cage. Thus he was perforce obliged to stand, and watch, and listen; and, as he did so, the bird's rapturous and appealing song played upon the feelings already awakened by the spring, urging them upwards and outwards to a point that grew perilously moving.

Both sound and sight caught and held him spellbound.

The bird, once well-favoured perhaps, he perceived was now thin and bedraggled, its feathers disarrayed by continual flitting along its perch, and by endless fluttering of wings and body against the bars of its narrow cage. There was not room to open both wings properly; it frequently dashed itself against the sides of its wooden prison; and all the force of its vain and passionate desire for freedom shone in the two small and glittering eyes which gazed beseechingly through the bars at the passers-by. It looked broken and worn with the ceaseless renewal of the futile struggle. Hopping along the bar, cocking its dainty little head on one side, and looking straight into the Professor's eyes, it managed (by some inarticulate magic known only to the eyes of creatures in prison) to spell out the message of its pain—the poignant longing for the freedom of the open sky, the lift of the great winds, the glory of the sun upon its lustreless feathers.

Now it so chanced that this combined onslaught of sight and sound caught the elderly Professor along the line of least resistance— the line of an untried, and therefore unexhausted, sensation. Here, apparently, was an emotion hitherto unrealised, and so not yet regulated away into atrophy.

For, with an intuition as singular as it was searching, he suddenly understood something of the passion of the wild Caged Things of the world, and realised in a flash of passing vision something of their unutterable pain.

In one swift moment of genuine mystical sympathy he *felt with* their peculiar quality of unsatisfied longing exactly as though it were his own; the longing, not only of captive birds and animals, but of anguished men and women, trapped by circumstance, confined by weakness, cabined by character and temperament, all yearning for a freedom they knew not how to reach—caged by the smallness of their desires, by the impotence of their wills, by the pettiness of their souls—caged in bodies from which death alone could finally bring release.

Something of all this found its way into the elderly Professor's heart as he stood watching the pantomime of the captive thrush—the Caged Thing;—and, after a moment's hesitation that represented a vast amount of condensed feeling, he deliberately entered the low doorway of the shop and enquired the price of the bird.

"The thrush—er—singing in the small cage," he stammered.

"One *and* six only, sir," replied the coarse, red-faced man who owned the shop, looking up from a rabbit that he was pushing with clumsy fingers into a box; "only one shilling *and* sixpence,"—and then went on with copious remarks upon thrushes in general and the superior qualities of this one in particular. "Been 'ere four months and sings just lovely," he added, by way of climax.

"Thank you," said Parnacute quietly, trying to persuade himself that he did not feel mortified by his impulsive and eccentric action; "then I will purchase the bird—at once—er—if you please."

"Couldn't go far wrong, sir," said the man, shoving the rabbit to one side, and going outside to fetch the thrush.

"No, I shall not require the cage, but—er—you may put him in a cardboard box perhaps, so that I can carry him easily."

He referred to the bird as "him," though at any other time he would have said "it," and the change, noted surreptitiously as it were, added to his general sense of confusion. It was too late, however, to alter his mind, and after watching the man force the bird with gross hands into a cardboard box, he gathered up the noose of string with which it was tied and walked with as much dignity and self-respect as he could muster out of the shop.

But the moment he got into the street with this living parcel under his arm—he both heard and felt the scuttling of the bird's feet—the realisation that he had been guilty of what he considered an outrageous act of eccentricity almost overwhelmed him. For he had succumbed in most regrettable fashion to a momentary impulse, and had bought the bird in order to release it!

"Dear me!" he thought, "how ever could I have allowed myself to do so eccentric and impulsive a thing!"

And, but for the fact that it would merely have accentuated his eccentricity, he would then and there have returned to the shop and given back the bird. That, however, being now clearly impossible, he crossed the road and entered the Little Park by the first iron gateway he could find. He walked down the gravel path, fumbling with the string. In another minute the bird would have been out, when he chanced to glance round in order to make sure he was unobserved and saw against the shrubbery on his left—a policeman.

This, he felt, was most vexatious, for he had hoped to complete the transaction unseen. Straightening himself up, he nervously fastened the string again, and walked on slowly as though nothing had happened, searching for a more secluded spot where he should be entirely free from observation.

Professor Parnacute now became aware that his vexation— primarily caused by his act of impulse, and increased by the fact that he was observed—had become somewhat acute. It was extraordinary, he reflected, how policemen had this way of suddenly outlining themselves in the least appropriate—the least necessary—places. There was no reason why a policeman should have been standing against that innocent shrubbery, where there was nothing to do, no one to watch. At almost any other point in the Little Park he might have served some possibly useful purpose, and yet, forsooth, he must select the one spot where he was not wanted—where his presence, indeed, was positively objectionable.

The policeman, meanwhile, watched him steadily as he retreated with the obnoxious parcel. He carried it upside down now without knowing it. He felt as though he had been detected in a crime. He watched the policeman, too, out of the corner of his eye, longing to be done with the whole business.

"That policeman is a tremendous fellow," he thought to himself. "I have never seen a constable so large, so stalwart. He must be *the* policeman of the district"—whatever that might mean—"a veritable wall and tower of defence." The helmet made him think of a battering ram, and the buttons on his overcoat of the muzzles of guns.

He moved away round the corner with as much innocence as he could assume, as though he were carrying a package of books or some new article of apparel.

It is, no doubt, the duty of every alert constable to observe as acutely as possible the course of events passing before his eyes, yet this particular Bobby seemed far more interested than the circumstances warranted in Parnacute's cardboard box. He kept his gaze remorselessly upon it. Perhaps, thought the Professor, he heard the scutterings of the frightened bird within. Perhaps he thought it was a cat going to be drowned in the ornamental water. Perhaps—oh, dreadful idea!—he thought it was a baby!

The suspicions of an intelligent policeman, however, being past finding out, Simon Parnacute wisely ignored them, and just then passed round a corner where he was screened from this persistent observer by a dense growth of rhododendron bushes.

Seizing the opportune moment, and acting with a prompt decision born of the dread of the reappearing policeman, he cut the string, opened the lid of the box, and an instant later had the intense satisfaction of seeing the imprisoned thrush hop upon the cardboard edge and then fly with a beautiful curving dip and a whirr of wings off into the open sky. It turned once as it flew, and its bright brown eye looked at him. Then it was gone, lost in the sunshine that blazed over the shrubberies and beckoned it out over their waving tops across the river.

The prisoner was free. For the space of a whole minute, the Professor stood still, conscious of a sense of genuine relief. That sound of wings, that racing sweep of the little quivering body escaping into limitless freedom, that penetrating look of gratitude from the wee brown eyes—these stirred in him again the same prodigious emotion he had experienced for the first time that afternoon outside the bird-fancier's shop. The release of the "caged creature" provided him with a kind of vicarious experience of freedom and delight such as he had never before known in his whole life. It almost seemed as though he had escaped himself—out of his "circle."

Then, as he faced about, with the empty box dangling in his hand, the first thing he saw, coming slowly down the path towards him with measured tread, was—the big policeman.

Something very stern, something very forbidding, hung like an atmosphere of warning about this guardian of the law in a blue uniform. It brought him back sharply to the rigid facts of life, and the soft beauty of the spring day vanished and left him untouched. He accepted the reminder that life is earnest, and that eccentricities are invitations to disaster. Sooner or later the Policeman is bound to make his appearance.

However, this particular constable, of course, passed him without word or gesture, and as soon as he came to one of the little wire baskets provided for the purpose, the Professor dropped his box into it, and then made his way slowly and thoughtfully back to his apartment and his luncheon.

But the eccentricity of which he had been guilty circled and circled in his mind, reminding him with merciless insistence of a foolish act he should not have committed, and plaguing him with remorseless little stabs for having indulged in an impulsive and irregular proceeding.

For, to him, the inevitableness of life came as a fact to which he was resigned, rather than as a force to be appropriated for the ends of his own soul; and the sight of the happy bird escaping into sky and sunshine, with the figure of the inflexible and stern-lipped policeman in the background, made a deep impression upon him that would sooner or later be certain to bear fruit.

"Dear me," thought the Professor of Political Economy, giving mental expression to this sentiment, "I shall pay for this in the long run! Without question I shall pay for it!"

II

If it may be taken that there is no Chance, playing tricksy-wise behind the scenes of existence, but that all events falling into the lives of men are the calculated results of adequate causes, then Mr. Simon Parnacute, late Professor of Political Economy in C—— College, certainly did pay for his spring aberration, in the sense that he caught a violent chill which brought him to bed and speedily developed into pneumonia.

It was the evening of the sixth day, and he lay weary and feverish in his bedroom on the top floor of the building which held his little self-contained apartment. The nurse was down-stairs having her tea. A shaded lamp stood beside the bed, and through the window—the blinds being not yet drawn—he saw the sea of roofs and chimney-pots, and the stream of wires, sharply outlined against a sunset sky of gold and pink. High and thin above the dusk floated long strips of coloured cloud, and the first stars twinkled through the April vapours that gathered with the approach of night.

Presently the door opened and some one came in softly half-way across the room, and then stopped. The Professor turned wearily and saw that the maid stood there and was trying to speak. She seemed flustered, he noticed, and her face was rather white.

"What's the matter *now*, Emily?" he asked feebly, yet irritably.

"Please, Professor—there's a gentleman——" and there she stuck.

"Some one to see me? The doctor again already?" queried the patient, wondering in a vague, absent way why the girl should seem so startled.

As he spoke there was a sound of footsteps on the landing outside—heavy footsteps.

"But please, Professor, sir, it's *not* the doctor," the maid faltered, "only I couldn't get his name, and I couldn't stop him, an' he said you expected him—and I think he looks like—"

The approaching footsteps frightened the girl so much that she could not find words to complete her description. They were just outside the door now.

"—like a perliceman!" she finished with a rush, backing towards the door as though she feared the Professor would leap from his bed to demolish her.

"A *policeman!*" gasped Mr. Parnacute, unable to believe his ears. "A policeman, Emily! In my apartment?"

And before the sick man could find words to express his particular annoyance that any stranger (above all a constable) should intrude at such a time, the door was pushed wide open, the girl had vanished with a flutter of skirts, and the tall figure of a man stood in full view upon the threshold, and stared steadily across the room at the occupant of the bed on the other side.

It was indeed a policeman, and a very large policeman. Moreover, it was *the* policeman.

The instant the Professor recognised the familiar form of the man from the park his anger, for some quite unaccountable reason, vanished almost entirely; the sharp vexation he had felt a moment before died away; and, sinking back exhausted among the pillows, he only found breath to ask him to close the door and come in. The fact was, astonishment had used up the small store of energy at his disposal, and for the moment he could think of nothing else to do.

The policeman closed the door quietly and moved forward towards the centre of the room, so that the circle of light from the shaded lamp at the head of the bed reached his figure but fell just short of his face.

The invalid sat up in bed again and stared. As nothing seemed to happen he recovered his scattered wits a little.

"You are the policeman from the park, unless I mistake?" he asked feebly, with mingled pomposity and resentment.

The big man bowed in acknowledgment and removed his helmet, holding it before him in his hand. His face was peculiarly bright, almost as though it reflected the glow of a bull's-eye lantern concealed somewhere about his huge person.

"I thought I recognised you," went on the Professor, exasperated a little by the other's self-possession. "Are you perhaps aware that I am ill—too ill to see strangers, and that to force your way up in this fashion—!" He left the sentence unfinished for lack of suitable expletives.

"You are certainly ill," replied the constable, speaking for the first time; "but then—I am *not* a stranger." His voice was wonderfully pitched and modulated for a policeman.

"Then, by what right, pray, do you dare to intrude upon me at such a time?" snapped the other, ignoring the latter statement.

"My duty, sir," the man replied, with a rather wonderful dignity, "knows nothing of time or place."

Professor Parnacute looked at him a little more closely as he stood there helmet in hand. He was something more, he gathered, than an ordinary constable; an inspector perhaps. He examined him carefully; but he understood nothing about differences in uniform, of bands or stars upon sleeve and collar.

"If you are here in the prosecution of your duty, then," exclaimed the man of careful mind, searching feverishly for some possible delinquency on the part of his small staff of servants, "pray be seated and state your business; but as briefly as possible. My throat pains me, and my strength is low." He spoke with less acerbity. The dignity of the visitor began to impress him in some vague fashion he did not understand.

The big figure in blue bowed again, but made no sign of advance.

"You come from X—— Station, I presume?" Parnacute added, mentioning the police station round the corner. He sank deeper into his pillows, conscious that his strength was becoming exhausted.

"From Headquarters—I come," replied the colossus in a deep voice.

The Professor had only the vaguest idea what Headquarters meant, yet the phrase conveyed an importance that somehow was not lost upon him. Meanwhile his impatience grew with his exhaustion.

"I must request you, officer, to state your business with dispatch," he said tartly, "or to come again when I am better able to attend to you. Next week, no doubt—"

"There is no time *but* the present," returned the other, with an odd choice of words that escaped the notice of his perplexed hearer, as he

produced from a capacious pocket in the tail of his overcoat a note-
book bound with some shining metal like gold.

"Your name is Parnacute?" he asked, consulting the book.

"Yes," answered the other, with the resignation of exhaustion.

"*Simon* Parnacute?"

"Of course, yes."

"And on the third of April last," he went on, looking keenly over the top of the note-book at the sick man, "you, Simon Parnacute, entered the shop of Theodore Spinks in the Lower P—— Road, and purchased from him a certain living creature?"

"Yes," answered the Professor, beginning to feel hot at the discovery of his folly.

"A bird?"

"A bird."

"A thrush?"

"A thrush."

"A singing thrush?"

"Oh yes, it was a singing thrush, if you *must* know."

"In money you paid for this thrush the sum of one shilling *and* six pennies?" He emphasised the "and" just as the bird-fancier had done.

"One and six, yes."

"But in true value," said the policeman, speaking with grave emphasis, "it cost you a great deal more?"

"Perhaps." He winced internally at the memory. He was so astonished, too, that the visit had to do with himself and not with some of his servants.

"You paid for it with your heart?" insisted the other.

The Professor made no reply. He started. He almost writhed under the sheets.

"Am I right?" asked the policeman.

"That is the fact, I suppose," he said in a low voice, sorely puzzled by the catechism.

"You carried this bird away in a cardboard box to E—— Gardens by the river, and there you gave it freedom and watched it fly away?"

"Your statement is correct, I think, in every particular. But really— this absurd cross-examination, my good man—!"

"And your motive in so doing," continued the policeman, his

voice quite drowning the invalid's feeble tones, "was the unselfish one of releasing an imprisoned and tortured creature?"

Simon Parnacute looked up with the greatest possible surprise.

"I think—well, well!—perhaps it was," he murmured apologetically. "The extraordinary singing—it *was* extraordinary, you know, and the sight of the little thing beating its wings pained me."

The big policeman put away his note-book suddenly, and moved closer to the bed so that his face entered the circle of lamplight.

"In that case," he cried, *"you are my man!"*

"I am your man!" exclaimed the Professor, with an uncontrollable start.

"The man I want," repeated the other, smiling.

His voice had suddenly grown soft and wonderful, like the ringing of a silver gong, and into his face had come an expression of wistful tenderness that made it positively beautiful. It shone. Never before, out of a picture, had he seen such a look upon a human countenance, or heard such tones issue from the lips of a human being. He thought, swiftly and confusedly, of a woman, of *the* woman he had never found—of a dream, an enchantment as of music or vision upon the senses.

"Wants me!" he thought with alarm. "What have I done now? What new eccentricity have I been guilty of?"

Strange, bewildering ideas crowded into his mind, blurred in outline, preposterous in character. A sensation of cold caught at his fever and overmastered it, bathing him in perspiration, making him tremble, yet not with fear. A new and curious delight had begun to pluck at his heart-strings.

Then an extravagant suspicion crossed his brain, yet a suspicion not wholly unwarranted.

"Who are you?" he asked sharply, looking up. "Are you really only a policeman?"

The man drew himself up so that he appeared, if possible, even huger than before.

"I am a World-Policeman," he answered, "a guardian, perhaps, rather than a detective."

"Heavens above!" cried the Professor, thinking of madness and the crimes committed in madness.

"Yes," he went on in those calm, musical tones that before long began to have a reassuring effect upon his listener, "and it is my duty, among many others, to keep an eye upon eccentric people; to lock them up when necessary, and when their sentences have expired, to release them. Also," he added impressively, "as in your case, to let them out of their cages without pain—when they've earned it."

"Gracious goodness me!" exclaimed Parnacute, unaccustomed to the use of expletives, but unable to think of anything else to say.

"And sometimes to see that their cages do not destroy them—and that they do not beat themselves to death against the bars," he went on, smiling quite wonderfully. "Our duties are varied *and* numerous. I am one of a large force."

The man learned in political economy felt as though his head were spinning. He thought of calling for help. Indeed, he had already made a motion with his hand towards the bell when a gesture on the part of his strange visitor restrained him.

"Then why do you want *me,* if I may ask?" he faltered instead.

"To mark you down; and when the time comes to let you out of your cage easily, comfortably, without pain. That's one reward for your kindness to the bird."

The Professor's fears had now quite disappeared. The policeman seemed perfectly harmless after all.

"It's *very* kind of you," he said feebly, drawing his arm back beneath the bed-clothes. "Only—er—I was not aware, exactly, that I lived in a cage."

He looked up resignedly into the man's face.

"You only realise that when you get out," he replied. "They're all like that. The bird didn't quite understand what was wrong; it only knew that it felt miserable. Same with you. You feel unhappy in that body of yours, and in that little careful mind you regulate so nicely; but, for the life of you, you don't quite know what it is that's wrong. You want space, freedom, a taste of liberty. You want to fly, that's what you want!" he cried, raising his voice.

"I—want—to—fly?" gasped the invalid.

"Oh," smiling again, "we World-Policemen have thousands of cases just like yours. Our field is a large one, a very large one indeed."

He stepped into the light more fully and turned sideways.

"Here's my badge, if you care to see it," he said proudly.

He stooped a little so that the Professor's beady eyes could easily focus themselves upon the collar of his overcoat. There, just like the lettering upon the collar of an ordinary London policeman, only in bright gold instead of silver, shone the constellation of the Pleiades. Then he turned and showed the other side, and Parnacute saw the constellation of Orion slanting upwards, as he had often seen it tilting across the sky at night.

"Those are my badges," he repeated proudly, straightening himself up again and moving back into the shadow.

"And very fine they are, too," said the Professor, his increasing exhaustion suggesting no better observation. But with the sight of those starry figures had come to him a strange whiff of the open skies, space, and wind—the winds of the world.

"So that when the time comes," the World-Policeman resumed, "you may have confidence. I will let you out without pain or fear just as you let out the bird. And, meanwhile, you may as well realise that you live in a cage just as cramped and shut away from light and freedom as the thrush did."

"Thank you; I will certainly try," whispered Parnacute, almost fainting with fatigue.

There followed a pause, during which the policeman put on his helmet, tightened his belt, and then began to search vigorously for something in his coat-tail pockets.

"And now," ventured the sick man, feeling half fearful, half happy, though without knowing exactly why, "is there anything more I can do for you, Mr. World-Policeman?" He was conscious that his words were peculiar yet he could not help it. They seemed to slip out of their own accord.

"There's nothing more you can do for *me*, sir, thank you," answered the man in his most silvery tones. "But there's something more I can do for *you*! And that is to give you a preliminary taste of freedom, so that you may realise you do live in a cage, and be less confused and puzzled when you come to make the final Escape."

Parnacute caught his breath sharply—staring open-mouthed.

With a single stride the policeman covered the space between himself and the bed. Before the withered, fever-stricken little Professor could utter a word or a cry, he had caught up the wasted body out of the bed, shaken the bed-clothes off him like paper from a parcel, and slung him without ceremony across his gigantic shoulders. Then he crossed the room, and producing the key from his coat-tail pocket, he put it straight into the solid wall of the room. He turned it, and the entire side of the house opened like a door.

For one second Simon Parnacute looked back and saw the lamp, and the fire, and the bed. And in the bed he saw his own body lying motionless in profound slumber.

Then, as the policeman balanced, hovering upon the giddy edge, he looked outward and saw the network of street-lamps far below, and heard the deep roar of the city smite upon his ears like the thunder of a sea.

The next moment the man stepped out into space, and he saw that they were rising up swiftly towards the dark vault of sky, where stars twinkled down upon them between streaks of thin flying clouds.

III

Once outside, floating in the night, the policeman gave his shoulder a mighty jerk and tossed his small burden into free space.

"Jump away!" he cried. "You're quite safe!"

The Professor dropped like a bullet towards the pavement; then suddenly began to rise again, like a balloon. All traces of fever or bodily discomfort had left him utterly. He felt light as air, and strong as lightning.

"Now, where shall we go to?" The voice sounded above him.

Simon Parnacute was no flyer. He had never indulged in those strange flying-dreams that form a weird pleasure in the sleep-lives of many people. He was terrified beyond belief until he found that he did not crash against the earth, and that he had within him the power to regulate his movements, to rise or sink at will. Then, of course, the wildest fury of delight and freedom he had ever known flashed all over him and burned in his brain like an intoxication.

"The big cities, or the stars?" asked the World-Policeman.

"No, no," he cried, "the country—the open country! And other lands!"

For Simon Parnacute had never travelled. Incredible as it may seem, the Professor had never in his life been farther out of England than in a sailing-boat at Southend. His body had travelled even less than his imagination. With this suddenly increased capacity for motion, the desire to race about and see became a passion.

"Woods! Mountains! Seas! Deserts! Anything but houses and people!" he shouted, rising upwards to his companion without the smallest effort.

An intense longing to see the desolate, unfrequented regions of the earth seized him and tore its way out into words strangely unlike his normal and measured mode of speech. All his life he had paced to and fro in a formal little garden with the most precise paths imaginable. Now he wanted a trackless world. The reaction was terrific. The desire of the Arab for the desert, of the gipsy for the open heaths, the "desire of the snipe for the wilderness"—the longing of the eternal wander-er—possessed his soul and found vent in words.

It was just as though the passion of the released thrush were re-producing itself in him and becoming articulate.

"I am haunted by the faces of the world's forgotten places," he cried aloud impetuously. "Beaches lying in the moonlight, all forsaken in the moonlight—"

His utterance, like the bird's, had become lyrical.

"Can this be what the thrush felt?" he wondered.

"Let's be off then," the policeman called back. "There's no time *but the present,* remember." He rushed through space like a huge projec-tile. He made a faint whistling noise as he went. Parnacute followed suit. The lightest desire, he found, gave him instantly the ease and speed of thought.

The policeman had taken off his helmet, overcoat, and belt, and dropped them down somewhere into a London street. He now ap-peared as a mere blue outline of a man, scarcely discernible against the dark sky—an outline filled with air. The Professor glanced down at himself and saw that he, too, was a mere outline of a man—a pallid outline filled with the purple air of night.

"Now then," sang out this "Bobby-of-the-World."

Side by side they shot up with a wild rush, and the lights of Lon-don, town and suburbs, flashed away beneath them in streaming lines and patches. In a second darkness filled the huge gap, pouring behind them like a mighty wave. Other streams and patches of light succeeded quickly, blurred and faint, like lamps of railway stations from a night express, as other towns dropped past them in a series and were swallowed up in the gulf behind.

A cool salt air smote their faces, and Parnacute heard the soft crashing of waves as they crossed the Channel, and swept on over the fields and forests of France, glimmering below like the squares of a mighty chess-board. Like toys, village after village shot by, smelling of peat-smoke, cattle, and the faint windiness of coming spring.

Sometimes they passed below the clouds and lost the stars, sometimes above them and lost the world; sometimes over forests roaring like the sea, sometimes above vast plains still and silent as the grave; but always Parnacute saw the constellations of Orion and Pleiades shining on the coat-collar of the soaring policeman, their little patterns picked out as with tiny electric lamps.

Below them lay the huge map of the earth, raised, scarred, darkly coloured, and breathing—a map *alive*.

Then came the Jura, soft and purple, carpeted with forests, rolling below them like a dream, and they looked down into slumbering valleys and heard far below the tumbling of water and the singing of countless streams.

"Glory, glory!" cried the Professor. "And do the birds know *this?*"

"Not the imprisoned ones," was the reply. And presently they whipped across large gleaming bodies of water as the lakes of Switzerland approached. Then, entering the zones of icy atmosphere, they looked down and saw white towers and pinnacles of silver, and the forms of scarred and mighty glaciers that rose and fell among the fields of eternal snow, folding upon the mountains in vast procession.

"I think—I'm frightened!" gasped Parnacute, clutching at his companion, but seizing only the frigid air.

The policeman shouted with laughter.

"This is nothing—compared to Mars or the moon," he cried, soaring till the Alps looked like a patch of snowdrops shining in a Surrey garden. "You'll soon get accustomed to it."

The Professor of Political Economy rose after him. But presently they sank again in an immense curving sweep and touched the tops of the highest mountains with their toes. This sent them instantly aloft again, bounding with the impetus of rockets, and so they careered on through the perfumed, pathless night till they came to Italy and left the Alps behind them like the shadowy wall of another world that had silently moved up close to them through space.

"Mother of Mountains!" shouted the delighted man of colleges. "And did the thrush know this too?"

"It has you to thank, if so," the policeman answered.

"And I have you to thank."

"No—yourself," replied his flying guide.

And then the desert! They had crossed the scented Mediterranean and reached the zones of sand. It rose in clouds and sheets as a mighty wind stirred across the leagues of loneliness that stretched below them into blue distance. It whirled about them and stung their faces.

"Thin ropes of sand which crumble ere they bind!" cried the Professor with a peal of laughter, not knowing what he said in the delirium of his pleasure.

The hot smell of the sand excited him; the knowledge that for hundreds of miles he could not see a house or a human being thrilled him dizzily with the incalculable delight of freedom. The splendour of the night, mystical and incommunicable, overcame him. He rose, laughing wildly, shaking the sand from his hair, and taking gigantic curves into the starry space about him. He remembered vividly the sight of those bedraggled wings in the little cramped cage—and then looked down and realised that here the winds sank exhausted from the very weariness of too much space. Oh, that he could tear away the bars of every cage the world had ever known—set free all captive creatures—restore to all wild, winged life the liberty of open spaces that is theirs by right!

He cried again to the stars and winds and deserts, but his words found no intelligible expression, for their passion was too great to be confined in any known medium. The World-Policeman alone understood, perhaps, for he flew down in circles round the little Professor and laughed and laughed and laughed.

And it seemed as if tremendous figures formed themselves out of the sky to listen, and bent down to lift him with a single sweep of their immense arms from the earth to the heavens. Such was the torrential power and delight of escape in him, that he almost felt as if he could skim the icy abysses of Death itself—without being ever caught. . . .

The colossal shapes of Egypt, terrible and monstrous, passed far below in huge and shadowy procession, and the desolate Lybian Mountains drew him hovering over their wastes of stone. . . . And this was only a beginning! Asia, India, and the Southern Seas all lay within reach! All could be visited in turn. The interstellar spaces, the far planets, and the white moon were yet to know!

"We must be thinking of turning soon," he heard the voice of his companion, and then remembered how his own body, hot and feverish, lay in that stuffy little room at the other end of Europe. It was indeed caged—the withered body in the room, and himself in the withered body—doubly caged. He laughed and shuddered. The wind swept through him, licking him clean. He rose again in the ecstasy of free flight, following the lead of the policeman on the homeward journey, and the mountains below became a purple line on the map. In a series of great sweeps they rested on the top of the Pyramid, and then upon the forehead of the Sphinx, and so onwards, touching the earth at intervals, till they heard once more the waves upon the coast-line, and soared aloft again across the sea, racing through Spain and over the Pyrenees. The thin blue outline of the policeman kept ever at his side.

"From all the far blue hills of heaven these winds of freedom blow!" he shouted into space, following it with a peal of laughter that made his guide circle round and round him, chuckling as he flew. A curious, silvery chuckle it was—yet it sounded as though it came to him through a much greater distance than before. It came, as it were, through barriers. . . .

The picture of the bird-fancier's shop came again vividly before him. He saw the beseeching and frightened little eyes; heard the ceaseless pattering of the imprisoned feet, wings beating against the bars, and soft furry bodies pushing vainly to get out. He saw the red face of Theodore Spinks, the proprietor, gloating over the scene of captive life that gave him the means to live—the means to enjoy his own little measure of freedom. He saw the sea-gull drooping in its corner, and the owl, its eyes filled with the dust of the street, its feathered ears twitching;—and then he thought again of the caged human beings of the world—men, women, and children, and a pain, like the pain of a whole universe, burned in his soul and set his heart aflame with yearning . . . to set them all instantly free.

And, unable to find words to give expression to what he felt, he found relief again in his strange, impetuous singing.

Simon Parnacute, Professor of Political Economy, sang in mid-heaven!

But this was the last vivid memory he knew. It all began to fade a little after that. It changed swiftly like a dream when the body nears the point of waking. He tried to seize and hold it, to delay the moment when it must end; but the power was beyond him. He felt heavy and tired, and flew closer to the ground; the intervals between the curves of flight grew smaller and smaller, the impetus weaker and weaker as he became every moment more dense and stupid. His progress across the fields of the south of England, as he made his way almost laboriously homewards, became rather a series of long, low leaps than actual flight. More and more often he found himself obliged to touch the earth to acquire the necessary momentum. The big policeman seemed suddenly to have quite melted away into the blue of night.

Then he heard a door open in the sky over his head. A star came down rather too close and half blinded his eyes. Instinctively he called for help to his friend, the world-policeman.

"It's time for your soup now," was the only answer he got. And it did not seem the right answer, or the right voice either. A terror of being permanently lost came over him, and he cried out again louder than before.

"And the medicine first," dropped the thin, shrill voice out of endless space.

It was not the policeman's voice at all. He knew now, and understood. A sensation of weariness, of sickening disgust and boredom came over him. He looked up. The sky had turned white; he saw curtains and walls and a bright lamp with a red shade. This was the star that had nearly blinded him—a lamp merely, in a sick-room!

And, standing at the farther end of the room, he saw the figure of the nurse in cap and apron. Below him lay his body in the bed. His sensation of disgust and boredom became a positive horror. But he sank down exhausted into it—into his cage.

"Take this soup, sir, after the medicine, and then perhaps you'll get another bit of sleep," the nurse was saying with gentle authority, bending over him.

IV

The progress of Professor Parnacute towards recovery was slow and tedious, for the illness had been severe and it left him with a dangerously weak heart. And at night he still had the delights of the flying dreams. Only, by this time, he had learned to fly alone. His phantom friend, the big World-Policeman, no longer accompanied him.

And his chief occupation during these weary hours of convalescence was curious and, the nurse considered, not very suitable for an invalid: for he spent the time with endless calculations, poring over the list of his few investments, and adding up times without number the total of his savings of nearly forty years. The bed was strewn with papers and documents; pencils were always getting lost among the clothes; and each time the nurse collected the paraphernalia and put them aside, he would wait till she was out of the room, and then crawl over to the table and carry them all back into bed with him.

Then, finally, she gave up fighting with him, and acquiesced, for his restlessness increased and he could not sleep unless his beloved half-sheets and pencils lay strewn upon the counterpane within instant reach.

Even to the least observant it was clear that the Professor was hatching the preliminary details of a profound plot.

And his very first visitor, as soon as he was permitted to see anybody, was a gentleman with parchment skin and hard, dry, peeping eyes who came by special request—a solicitor, from the firm of Messrs. Costa & Delay.

"I will ascertain the price of the shop and stock-in-trade and inform you of the result at the earliest opportunity, Professor Parnacute," said the man of law in his gritty, professional voice, as he at length took his departure and left the sick-room with the expressionless face of one to whom the eccentricities of human nature could never be new or surprising.

"Thank you; I shall be *most* anxious to hear," replied the other, turning in his long easy-chair to save his papers, and at the same time to defend himself against the chiding of the good-natured nurse.

"I knew I should have to pay for it," he murmured, thinking of his original sin; "but I hope,"—here he again consulted his pencilled figures—"I think I can manage it—just. Though with Consols so low—"

He fell to musing again. "Still, I can always sublet the shop, of course, as they suggest," he concluded with a sigh, turning to appeal to the bewildered nurse and finding for the first time that she had gone out of the room.

He fell to pondering deeply. Presently the "list enclosed" by the solicitors caught his eye among the pillows, and he began listlessly to examine it. It was type-written and covered several sheets of foolscap. It was split up into divisions headed as "Lot 1, Lot 2, Lot 3," and so on. He began to read slowly half aloud to himself; then with increasing excitement—

> "50 Linnets, guaranteed not straight from the fields; *all caged.*"
> "10 fierce singing Linnets."
> "10 grand cock Throstles, *just on song.*"
> "5 Pear-Tree Goldfinches, with deep, square blazes, well buttoned and mooned."
> "4 Devonshire Woodlarks, guaranteed full song; *caged three months.*"

The Professor sat up and gripped the paper tightly. His face wore a pained, intent expression. A convulsive movement of his fingers, automatic perhaps, crumpled the sheet and nearly tore it across. He went on reading, shedding rugs and pillows as though they oppressed him. His breath came a little faster.

> "5 cock Blackbirds, full plumage, *lovely songsters.*"
> "1 Song-Thrush, show-cage and hamper; *splendid whistler,* picked bird."
> "1 beautiful, large upstanding singing Skylark; *sings all day; been caged positively five months.*"

Simon Parnacute uttered a curious little cry. It was deep down in his throat. He was conscious of a burning desire to be rich—a millionaire; powerful—an autocratic monarch. After a pause he brought back his attention with an effort to the type-written page and the consideration of further "Lots"—

> "3 cock Skylarks; can hear them 200 yards off when singing."

"Two hundred yards off when singing," muttered the Professor into his one remaining pillow. He read on, kicking his feet, somewhat viciously for a sick man, against the wicker rest at the end of the lounge chair.

"1 special, select, singing cock Skylark; guaranteed caged three months; *sings his wild note.*"

He suddenly dashed the list aside. The whole chair creaked and groaned with the violence of his movement. He kicked three times running at the wicker foot-rest, and evidently rejoiced that it was still stiff enough to make it worth while to kick again—harder.

"Oh, that I had all the money in the world!" he cried to himself, letting his eyes wander to the window and the clear blue spaces between the clouds; "all the money in the world!" he repeated with growing excitement. He saw one of London's sea-gulls circling high, high up. He watched it for some minutes, till it sailed against a dazzling bit of white cloud and was lost to view.

"*'Sings his wild note'*—*'guaranteed caged three months'*—*'can be heard two hundred yards off.'*" The phrases burned in, his brain like consuming flames.

And so the list went on. He was glancing over the last page when his eye fell suddenly upon an item that described a lot of—

"8 Linnets caged four months; *raving with song.*"

He dropped the list, rose with difficulty from his chair, and paced the room, muttering to himself "raving with song, raving with song, raving with song." His hollow cheeks were flushed, his eyes aglow.

"*Caged, caged, caged,*" he repeated under his breath, while his thoughts travelled to that racing flight across Europe, over seas and mountains.

"*Sings his wild note!*" He heard again the whistling wind about his ears as he flew through the zones of heated air above the desert sands.

"*Raving with song!*" He remembered the passion of his own cry—that strange lyrical outburst of his heart when the magic of freedom caught him, and he had soared at will through the uncharted regions of the night.

And then he saw once more the blinking owl, its eyes blinded by the dust of the London street, its feathery ears twitching as it heard the wind sighing past the open doorway of the dingy shop. And again the thrush looked into his face and poured out the rapture of its spring song.

And half-an-hour later he was so exhausted by the unwonted emotion and exercise that the nurse herself was obliged to write at his dictation the letter he sent in reply to the solicitors, Messrs. Costa & De-lay in Southampton Row.

But the letter was posted that night and the Professor, still mumbling to himself about "having to pay for it," went to bed with the first hour of the darkness, and plunged straight into another of his delightful flying dreams almost the very moment his eyes had closed.

V

". . . Thus, all the animals have been disposed of according to your instructions," ran the final letter from the solicitors, "and we beg to append list of items so allotted, together with country addresses to which they have been sent. We think you may feel assured that they are now in homes where they will be well cared for.

"We still retain the following animals against your further instructions—

> 2 Zonure Lizards,
> 1 Angulated Tortoise,
> 2 Mealy Rosellas,
> 2 Scaly-breasted Lorikeets.

"With regard to these we should advise . . .

"The caged birds, meanwhile, which you intend the children shall release, are being cared for satisfactorily; and the premises will be ready for taking over as from June 1. . . ."

And, with the assistance of the nurse, he then began to issue a steady stream of letters to the parents of children he knew in the country, carefully noting and tabulating the replies, and making out little white labels inscribed in plain lettering with the words "Lot 1," "Lot 2," and so on, precisely as though he were in the animal business himself, and were getting ready for a sale.

But the sale which took place a fortnight later on June 1 was no ordinary sale.

It was a brilliant hot day when Simon Parnacute, still worn and shaky from his recent illness, made his way towards the shop of the "retired" bird-fancier. The sale of the premises and stock-in-trade, and the high price obtained, had made quite a stir in the "Fancy," but of that the Professor was sublimely ignorant as he crossed the street in front of a truculent motor-omnibus and stood before the dingy three-storey red-brick house.

He produced the key sent to him by Messrs. Costa & Delay, and opened the door. It was cool after the glare of the burning street, and delightfully silent. He remembered the chorus of crying birds that had greeted his last appearance. The silence now was eloquent.

"Good, good," he said to himself, with a quiet smile, as he noticed the temporary counter built across the front room for cloaks and parcels, "very good indeed."

Then he went up-stairs, climbing painfully, for he was still easily exhausted. There was hardly a stick of furniture in the house, nor an inch of carpet on the floor and stairs, but the rooms had been swept and scrubbed; everything was fresh and scrupulously clean, and the tenant to whom he was to sub-let could have no fault to find on that score.

In the first-floor rooms he saw with pleasure the flowers arranged about the boards as he had directed. The air was sweet and perfumed. The windows at the back—the sills deep with jars of roses—opened upon a small bit of green garden, and Parnacute looked out and saw the blue sky and the clouds floating lazily across it.

"Good, very good," he exclaimed again, sitting down on the stairs a moment to recover his breath. The excitement and the heat of the day tired him. And, as he sat, he put his hand to his ear and listened attentively. A sound of birds singing reached him faintly from the upper part of the house.

"Ah!" he said, drawing a deep breath, and colour coming into his cheeks. "Ah! Now I hear them."

The sound of singing came nearer, as on a passing wind. He climbed laboriously to the top floor, and then, after resting again, scrambled up a ladder through an open skylight on to the roof. The moment he put his perspiring face above the tiles a wild chorus of singing birds greeted him with a sound like a whole country-side in spring.

"If only my friend, the park policeman, could see this!" he said aloud, with a delighted chuckle, "and hear it!" He sought a precarious resting-place upon the butt of a chimney-stack, mopping his forehead.

All around him the sea of London roofs and chimneys rolled away in a black sea, but here, like an oasis in a desert, was a roof of limited extent, and not very high compared to others, converted into a perfect garden. Flowers—but why describe them, when he himself did not even know the names? It was enough that his orders had been carried out to his entire satisfaction, and that this little roof was a world of living colour, moving in the wind, scenting the air, welcoming the sunshine.

Everywhere among the pots and boxes of flowers stood the cages. And in the cages the thrushes and blackbirds, the larks and linnets, poured their hearts out with a chorus of song that was more exquisite, he thought, than anything he had ever heard. And there in the corner by the big chimney, carefully shaded from the glare, stood the large cage containing the owls.

"I can almost believe they have guessed my purpose after all," exclaimed the Professor.

For a long time he sat there, leaning against the chimney, oblivious of a blackened collar, listening to the singing, and feasting his eyes upon the garden of flowers all about him. Then the sound of a bell ringing down-stairs roused him suddenly into action, and he climbed with difficulty down again to the hall door.

"Here they come," he thought, greatly excited. "Dear me, I do trust I shall not make any mistakes."

He felt in his pocket for his note-book, and then opened the door into the street.

"Oh, it's only you!" he exclaimed, as his nurse came in with her arms full of parcels.

"Only me," she laughed, "but I've brought the lemonade and the biscuits. The others will be here now any minute. It's after three. There's just time to arrange the glasses and plates. We must expect about fifty according to the letters you got. And mind you don't get over-tired."

"Oh, I'm all right!" he answered.

She ran up-stairs. Before her steps had sounded once on the floor above, a carriage-and-pair stopped at the door, and a footman came up smartly and asked if Professor Parnacute was at home.

"Indeed I am," answered the old man, blushing and laughing at the same time, and then going down himself to the carriage to welcome the little girl and boy who got out. He bowed stiffly and awkwardly to the pretty lady in the victoria, who thanked him for his kindness with a speech he did not hear properly, and then led his callers into the house. They were very shy at first, and hardly knew what to make of it all, but once inside, the boy's sense of adventure was stirred by the sight of the empty shop, and the counter, and the strange array of flowers upon the floor.

He remembered the letter his father had read out from Professor Parnacute a week ago.

"My Lot is No. 7, isn't it, Mr. Professor?" he cried. "I let out a cage of linnets, and get a guinea-pig and a mealy-something-or-other as a present, don't I?"

Mr. Parnacute, shaky and beaming, consulted his note-book hurriedly, and replied that this was "perfectly correct."

"Master Edwin Burton," he read out; "to release—Lot 7. To take away—one guinea-pig, and one mealy rosella."

"I'm Lot 8, please," piped the voice of the little girl, standing with wide-open eyes beside him.

"Oh, are you, my dear?" said he; "yes, yes, I believe you are." He fumbled anew with the note-book. "Here it is," he added, reading aloud again—

"Miss Angelina Burton"; he peered closely in the gloom to decipher the writing; "To release—Lot 8—that's woodlarks, my dear, you know. To take away—one angulated tortoise. Quite correct, yes; quite correct."

He called to the nurse up-stairs to show the children their presents hidden away in boxes among the flowers—their rosella and tortoise— and then went again to the door to receive his other guests, who now began to arrive in a steady stream. To the number of twenty or thirty they came, and not one of them appeared to be much over twelve. And the majority of them left their elders at the door and came in unattended.

The marshalling of this array of youngsters among the birds and flowers was a matter of some difficulty, but here the nurse came to the Professor's assistance with energy and experience, so that his strength was economised and the children were arranged without danger to any one.

And upon that little roof the sight was certainly a unique one. There they all stood, an extraordinary patchwork of colour for the tiles of South-west London—the bright frocks of the girls, the plumage of the birds, the blues and yellows and scarlets of the flowers; while the singing and voices sent up a chorus that brought numerous surprised faces to the windows of the higher buildings about them, and made people stop in the street below and ask themselves with startled faces where in the world these sounds came from this still June afternoon!

"Now!" cried Simon Parnacute, when all lots and owners had been placed carefully side by side. "The moment I give the word of command, open your cages and let the prisoners escape! And point in the direction of the park."

The children stooped and picked up their cages. The voices and the singing in a hundred busy little throats ceased. A hush fell upon the roof and upon the strange gathering. The sun poured blazingly down over everything, and the Professor's face streamed.

"One," he cried, his voice tremulous with excitement, "two, three—and away!"

There was a rattling sound of opening doors and wire bars and then a sudden burst of half-suppressed, long-drawn "Ahhhhs." At once there followed a rush of fluttering feathers, a rapid vibration of the air, and the small host of prisoners shot out like a cloud into the air, and a moment later with a great whirring of wings had disappeared over the walls beyond the forest of chimneys and were lost to view. Blackbirds, thrushes, linnets, and finches were gone in a twinkling, so that the eye could hardly follow them. Only the sea-gulls, puzzled by their sudden freedom, with wings still stiff after their cramped quarters, lingered on the edge of the roof for a few minutes, and looked about them in a dazed fashion, until they, too, realised their liberty and sailed off into the open sky to search for splendours of the sea.

A second hush, deeper even than the first, fell over all for a moment, and then the children with one accord burst into screams of delight and explanation, shouting, for all who cared to listen, the details of how their birds, respectively, had flown; where they had gone; what they thought and looked like; and a hundred other details as to where they would build their nests and the number of eggs they would lay.

And then came the descent for the presents and refreshment. One by one they approached the Professor, holding out the tickets with the number of their "lot" and the description of animal they were to receive and find a home for. The few accompanied by elders came first.

"The owls, I think?" said the pink-faced clergyman who had chaperoned other children besides his own, picking his way across the roof as the crowd tapered off down the skylight. "Two owls," he repeated, with a smile. "In the windy towers of my belfry under the Mendips, I hope—"

"Oh, the very thing, the very place," replied Parnacute, with pleasure, remembering his correspondent. For, of course, the owls had not been released with the other birds.

"And for my little girl you thought, perhaps, a lorikeet—"

"A scaly-breasted lorikeet, papa," she interrupted, with a degree of excitement too intense for smiles, and pronouncing the name as she had learned it—in a single word; "*and* a lizard."

They moved off towards the trap-door, the owl cage under the clergyman's arm. They would receive the lorikeet and lizard downstairs from the nurse on presenting their ticket.

"And remember," added Parnacute slyly, addressing the child, "to comb their feathered trousers with a *very* fine comb!"

The clergyman turned a moment at the skylight as he helped the owls and children to squeeze through.

"I shall have something to say about this in my sermon next Sunday," he said. He smiled as his head disappeared.

"Oh, but, my dear sir—" cried the Professor, tripping over a flower-pot in his pleasure and embarrassment, and just reaching the skylight in time to add, "And, remember, there are cakes and lemonade on the floor below!"

The animals had all been provided with happy homes; the last cab had driven away, and the nurse had gone to find the flower-man. Parnacute had strewn the roof with food, and with moss and hair-material for nesting, in case any of the birds returned. He stood alone and watched the sunset pour its gold over the myriad houses—the cages of the men and women of London town. He felt exhausted; the sky was soothing and pleasant to behold. . . .

He sat down to rest, conscious of a great weakness now that the excitement was over and the reaction had begun to set in. Probably he had exerted himself unduly.

His mind reverted to his first impulsive eccentricity of two months before.

"I knew I should pay for it," he murmured, with a smile, "and I have. But it was worth it."

He stopped abruptly and caught his breath a moment. He was thoroughly over-tired; the excitement of it all had been too much for him. He must get home as quickly as possible to rest. The nurse would be back any minute now.

A sound of wings rapidly beating the air passed overhead, and he looked up and saw a flight of pigeons wheeling by. He fancied, too, that he just caught the notes of a thrush singing far away in the park at the end of the street. He recalled the phrases of that dreadfully haunting list. "Wild singing note," "Can be heard two hundred yards off," "Raving with song." A momentary spasm passed through his frame. Far up in the air the sea-gulls still circled, making their way with all the splendour of real freedom to the sea.

"To-night," he thought, "they will roost on the marshes, or perched upon the lonely cliffs. Good, good, *very* good!"

He got up, stiffly and with difficulty, to watch the pigeons better, and to hear the thrush, and, as he did so, the bell rang down-stairs to admit the nurse and the flower-man.

"Odd," he thought; "I gave her the key!"

He made his way towards the skylight, picking his way with uncertain tread between the flower-boxes; but before he could reach it a head and shoulders suddenly appeared above the opening.

"Odd," he thought again, "that she should have come up so quickly—"

But he did not complete the thought. It was not the nurse at all. A very different figure followed the emerging head and shoulders, and there in front of him on the roof stood—a policeman.

It was *the* policeman.

"Oh," said Parnacute quietly, "it's *you!*" A wild tumult of yearning and happiness caught at his heart and made it impossible to think of anything else to say.

The big blue figure smiled his shining smile.

"One more flight, sir," said the silvery, ringing voice respectfully, "and the last."

The pigeons wheeled past overhead with a sharp whirring of wings. Both men looked up significantly at their vanishing outline over the roofs. A deep silence fell between them. Parnacute was aware that he was smiling and contented.

"I am quite ready, I think," he said in a low tone. "You promised—"

"Yes," returned the other in the voice that was like the ringing of a silver gong, "I promised—without pain."

The Policeman moved softly over to him; he made no sound; the constellations of Orion and the Pleiades shone on his coat-collar. There was another whirring rush as the pigeons swept again overhead and wheeled abruptly, but this time there was no one on the roof to watch them go, and it seemed that their flying wedge, as they flashed away, was larger and darker than before. . . .

And when the nurse returned with the man for the boxes, they came up to the roof and found the body of Simon Parnacute, late Professor of Political Economy, lying face upwards among the flowers. The human cage was empty. Some one had opened the door.

The Message of the Clock

S uddenly, in most singular fashion, Smith, the patent agent, became aware of the clock upon his mantelpiece.

His mind was an exact one, dealing soberly with life as he saw it, and the way he saw it was as a series of hard, pellet-like facts, behind which he never divined a possible flaming glory. The artistic temperament touched him not. Religion, beauty, wonder—all that tended to make clients unreasonable or things in life seem other than they are—he loathed. Yet here he was, on the eve of Easter, still postponing his country visit, simply because the poor woman in the flat below—who painted pictures and starved in the process—lay dying. Here he was, lingering on in town almost against his will, scarcely knowing why he did so, held there by something that was not a fact, and despising himself (with a kind of curious amazement) for so doing.

For it was not the blunt fact of the woman's dying that kept him; it was something intangible connected with her dying. This much he realised: it was something queer.

And thus, as he sat pondering the matter between the hour of tea and dinner, he became suddenly aware, in this curious fashion, of the presence of the clock. It was startling.

Now, a clock was merely a piece of mechanism—clumsy mechanism—for had he not filed hundreds of specifications to improve them? His own specimen was square and ugly, with a dirty white face, and holes for two keys. Never before had he noticed how it ticked even, and it had no "strike." Yet now, with abrupt insistence, he became aware in the stillness that its steady little hammering note claimed attention—that it ticked, indeed, almost like a voice. For the first time he realised that it was there—busy and important—fussy! It was a Presence. He was no longer *quite* alone. So strong, indeed, was the feeling that he turned to look at it, as he might have turned to some one who stood waiting beside him with a message. And this was an extraordinary idea to enter the mind of Smith, the patent agent: a clock, ticking out a communication!

"Quarter to seven," he observed. "And probably wants winding."

This last he added by way of explanation to himself. He moved forward to insert the key—then stopped short. "Can't be that," he murmured. "I wound it only this morning—"

Puffing hard at his pipe, he stood and stared; he listened. By some process of the mind he did not understand—and instinctively opposed—it was borne in upon him that this ticking of the clock led up to something—to a certain moment. It was like a telegraph instrument clicking out a message, a little voice consciously drawing his attention to something—to something that was *about to happen*. Without understanding it quite, Smith experienced the imaginative truth that, if the mind dwells long enough upon an object, that object becomes invested with a personality. The voice of that clock became alive, and held intercourse with him. But why it should have led him to think something was going to happen—and happen at seven o'clock—perplexed him to the point of positive annoyance.

This was a state of mind the patent agent regarded with suspicion and dislike. He deliberately tried to think of something else; yet without success. His thoughts always turned back to the personality of the woman down-stairs who lay dying, the artist whom he had seen, though never spoken with, and about whom he had gathered all kinds of intimate details owing to that curious leakage that turns a House of Flats into a huge Whispering Gallery.

Her mode of life, he always felt, in some inexplicable way challenged his own, as though character created an atmosphere that could spread mysteriously through bricks and mortar like an emanation, to affect other minds. Insensibly, often, he had found himself contrasting her life with his: his self-centred, utilitarian, highly moral existence, believing only in "facts"; and hers, the vain fluttering of a soul after Beauty—achieving nothing, yet shedding about her an atmosphere of light, considering all she possessed as belonging to every one in need of it. He knew, for instance, how she often kept her models when she had no work for them, and even fed them to her own want. The servants carried some rather wonderful stories about—stories that made him feel uncomfortable till he banished them. . . . So that when he had heard a few days before that she lay dangerously ill—lonely, perhaps dying—he contrasted his jolly Easter in the country with her own dismal prospects, and the instinct stirred in him to stay on a little in town . . . perhaps to help . . . perhaps only to *know* . . . he scarcely understood himself . . . yet he had stayed. . . .

Again the ticking of the clock interrupted his reverie.

"Ten minutes to seven," he read.

It was very curious; he could not keep his mind from her. On the floor below all was silent. A wind sang mournfully past the walls, carrying a million raindrops that beat their tiny hammers upon the windows. Queer new thoughts attacked his mind, showing him in swift, fugitive vision possibilities of life that a temperament like hers might hold. Perhaps the truth was that this little wave of unwonted sympathy touched into being a new corner of his own consciousness. The figure of the woman, as he had once passed her on the stairs, rose with haunting persistence before him. She had no beauty, strictly speaking, this elderly Irish woman, but her face had that touch of soul that painted it sometimes with a burning glory, and was gone, so that all who saw it experienced a sudden and inexpressible yearning for high things.

And he, Smith, had caught her once or twice with that look. It was very wonderful, very radiant. It had made him pause and ask himself whether, after all, it was she that was wasting time, or himself. Her motto, he had heard, was "Help others, and pass on"; and she practised it, passing on without reward; she gave herself freely, not counting the cost—time, money, sympathy. Yet, here she was at this moment dying, almost in want, nothing saved, nothing put by, nothing achieved—a failure. Was it worthwhile—this life of unpractical dreaming? He had wondered about it before. He wondered about it now. . . .

Again the voice of the clock drew his attention.

"Five minutes to seven."

It was very haunting, this persistent calling of the clock; he began to feel unaccountably ill at ease and restless. A sensation of eeriness came over him. He wished the hour of seven were past. He drew the curtains closer to shut out the sighing of the wind. More than once he looked over his shoulder, expecting something, he knew not what. . . . Once he even thought of going downstairs to enquire of the nurse. . . . Perhaps he might be able to help.

He was still sitting, however, in his armchair opposite the mirror
when the sound of the door opening softly behind him drew his attention. The curtain on the rod made it swish audibly. He instantly looked
up and saw the figure of the very woman he had been thinking about
reflected in the glass before him. In her eyes was that flame seen sometimes in the eyes of the mad, sometimes in those of religious enthusi-
asts—that lightning of the disturbed soul which seeks to reconcile an
inner glory with the common light of the sun. Only, with her now, the
soul was not disturbed; the flame was steady and permanent; and an
expression of peace and happiness, extraordinarily beautiful, rested
upon her features as the mirror gave them back to him.

She was sleep-walking—he realised that, of course—under the
stress of fever or delirium. He must act promptly and get her down-
stairs again, or call for the nurse. Yet he found himself able to do none
of these things. He could only stare, with a sense of wonder so exquisite that it was pain—stare at the radiant and beatific expression in the
mirror before him.

Amazed, and yet not amazed—conscious, too, of a kind of elevat-
ing terror—he then stood bolt upright and tried to turn and face her.
Finding this was somehow impossible, he tried to speak. This also
failed him. He could not move his lips. The beauty of that look held
him spellbound and speechless. He stood motionless, staring at her
image in the glass—the image of this dying woman, silent and wonderful behind him—unbelievably glorious!

Then, with extraordinary softness, the whisper of a voice floated
to his ear:

"It is more wonderful even than I dreamed. It is—and it was—worthwhile!"

Smith suddenly realised something new, and his heart gave a horrid jump. He turned sharply round, a terror of the unknown clutching
him. The room was absolutely empty.

The ticking of the clock, sounding up till now like a tiny hammer
in his brain, had ceased; and he saw that the hands pointed to seven.
The mechanism had accountably run down. . . . It was only on the following day, however, he learned that the human mechanism had also
run down at the same moment.

The vision he dismissed easily as a dream, but that running down
of the clock puzzled him dreadfully for years.

The Sea Fit

The sea that night sang rather than chanted; all along the far-running shore a rising tide dropped thick foam, and the waves, white-crested, came steadily in with the swing of a deliberate purpose. Overhead, in a cloudless sky, that ancient Enchantress, the full moon, watched their dance across the sheeted sands, guiding them carefully while she drew them up. For through that moonlight, through that roar of surf, there penetrated a singular note of earnestness and meaning—almost as though these common processes of Nature were instinct with the flush of an unusual activity that sought audaciously to cross the borderland into some subtle degree of conscious life. A gauze of light vapour clung upon the surface of the sea, far out—a transparent carpet through which the rollers drove shorewards in a moving pattern.

In the low-roofed bungalow among the sand-dunes the three men sat. Foregathered for Easter, they spent the day fishing and sailing, and at night told yarns of the days when life was younger. It was fortunate that there were three—and later four—because in the mouths of several witnesses an extraordinary thing shall be established—when they agree. And although whisky stood upon the rough table made of planks nailed to barrels, it is childish to pretend that a few drinks invalidate evidence, for alcohol, up to a certain point, intensifies the consciousness, focusses the intellectual powers, sharpens observation; and two healthy men, certainly three, must have imbibed an absurd amount before they all see, or omit to see, the same things.

The other bungalows still awaited their summer occupants. Only the lonely tufted sand-dunes watched the sea, shaking their hair of coarse white grass to the winds. The men had the whole spit to themselves—with the wind, the spray, the flying gusts of sand, and that great Easter full moon. There was Major Reese of the Gunners and his half-brother, Dr. Malcolm Reese, and Captain Erricson, their host, all men whom the kaleidoscope of life had jostled together a decade ago in many adventures, then flung for years apart about the globe. There was also Erricson's body-servant, "Sinbad," sailor of big seas, and a man who had shared on many a ship all the lust of strange adventure that distinguished his great blonde-haired owner—an ideal servant and dog-faithful, divining his master's moods almost before they were born. On the present occasion, besides crew of the fishing-smack, he was cook, valet, and steward of the bungalow smoking-room as well.

"Big Erricson," Norwegian by extraction, student by adoption, wanderer by blood, a Viking reincarnated if ever there was one, belonged to that type of primitive man in whom burns an inborn love and passion for the sea that amounts to positive worship—devouring tide, a lust and fever in the soul. "All genuine votaries of the old sea-gods have it," he used to say, by way of explaining his carelessness of worldly ambitions. "We're never at our best away from salt water—never quite right. I've got it bang in the heart myself. I'd do a bit before the mast sooner than make a million on shore. Simply can't help it, you see, and never could! It's our gods calling us to worship." And he had never tried to "help it," which explains why he owned nothing in the world on land except this tumble-down, one-storey bungalow—more like a ship's cabin than anything else, to which he sometimes asked his bravest and most faithful friends—and a store of curious reading gathered in long, becalmed days at the ends of the world. Heart and mind, that is, carried a queer cargo. "I'm sorry if you poor devils are uncomfortable in here. You must ask Sinbad for anything you want and don't see, remember." As though Sinbad could have supplied comforts that were miles away, or converted a draughty wreck into a snug, taut, brand-new vessel.

Neither of the Reeses had cause for grumbling on the score of comfort, however, for they knew the keen joys of roughing it, and both weather and sport besides had been glorious. It was on another score this particular evening that they found cause for uneasiness, if not for actual grumbling. Erricson had one of his queer sea fits on—the Doctor was responsible for the term—and was in the thick of it, plunging like a straining boat at anchor, talking in a way that made them both feel vaguely uncomfortable and distressed. Neither of them knew exactly perhaps why he should have felt this growing *malaise,* and each was secretly vexed with the other for confirming his own unholy instinct that something uncommon was astir. The loneliness of the sand-spit and that melancholy singing of the sea before their very door may have had something to do with it, seeing that both were lands-men; for Imagination is ever Lord of the Lonely Places, and adventurous men remain children to the last. But, whatever it was that affected both men in different fashion, Malcolm Reese, the doctor, had not thought it necessary to mention to his brother that Sinbad had tugged his sleeve on entering and whispered in his ear significantly: "Full moon, sir, please, and he's better without too much! These high spring tides get him all caught off his feet sometimes—clean sea-crazy"; and the man had contrived to let the doctor see the hilt of a small pistol he carried in his hip-pocket.

For Erricson had got upon his old subject: that the gods were not dead, but merely withdrawn, and that even a single true worshipper was enough to draw them down again into touch with the world, into the sphere of humanity, even into active and visible manifestation. He spoke of queer things he had seen in queerer places. He was serious, vehement, voluble; and the others had let it pour out unchecked, hoping thereby for its speedier exhaustion. They puffed their pipes in comparative silence, nodding from time to time, shrugging their shoulders, the soldier mystified and bewildered, the doctor alert and keenly watchful.

"And I like the old idea," he had been saying, speaking of these departed pagan deities, "that sacrifice and ritual feed their great beings, and that death is only the final sacrifice by which the worshipper becomes absorbed into them. The devout worshipper"—and there was a singular drive and power behind the words—"should go to his death singing, as to a wedding—the wedding of his soul with the particular deity he has loved and served all his life." He swept his tow-coloured beard with one hand, turning his shaggy head towards the window, where the moonlight lay upon the procession of shaking waves. "It's playing the whole game, I always think, man-fashion. . . . I remember once, some years ago, down there off the coast by Yucatan—"

And then, before they could interfere, he told an extraordinary tale of something he had seen years ago, but told it with such a horrid earnestness of conviction—for it was dreadful, though fine, this adventure—that his listeners shifted in their wicker chairs, struck matches unnecessarily, pulled at their long glasses, and exchanged glances that attempted a smile yet did not quite achieve it. For the tale had to do with sacrifice of human life and a rather haunting pagan ceremonial of the sea, and at its close the room had changed in some indefinable manner—was not exactly as it had been before perhaps—as though the savage earnestness of the language had introduced some new element that made it less cosy, less cheerful, even less warm. A secret lust in the man's heart, born of the sea, and of his intense admiration of the pagan gods called a light into his eye not altogether pleasant.

"They were great Powers, at any rate, those ancient fellows," Erricson went on, refilling his huge pipe bowl; "too great to disappear altogether, though to-day they may walk the earth in another manner. I swear they're still going it—especially the—" (he hesitated for a mere second) "the old water Powers—the Sea Gods. Terrific beggars, every one of 'em."

"Still move the tides and raise the winds, eh?" from the Doctor.

Erricson spoke again after a moment's silence, with impressive dignity. "And I like, too, the way they manage to keep their names before us," he went on, with a curious eagerness that did not escape the Doctor's observation, while it clearly puzzled the soldier. "There's old Hu, the Druid god of justice, still alive in 'Hue and Cry'; there's Typhon hammering his way against us in the typhoon; there's the mighty Hurakar, serpent god of the winds, you know, shouting to us in hurricane and *ouragan;* and there's—"

"Venus still at it as hard as ever," interrupted the Major, facetiously, though his brother did not laugh because of their host's almost sacred earnestness of manner and uncanny grimness of face. Exactly how he managed to introduce that element of gravity—of conviction—into such talk neither of his listeners quite understood, for in discussing the affair later they were unable to pitch upon any definite detail that betrayed it. Yet there it was, alive and haunting, even distressingly so. All day he had been silent and morose, but since dusk, with the turn of the tide, in fact, these queer sentences, half mystical, half unintelligible, had begun to pour from him, till now that cabin-like room among the sand-dunes fairly vibrated with the man's emotion.

And at last Major Reese, with blundering good intention, tried to shift the key from this portentous subject of sacrifice to something that might eventually lead towards comedy and laughter, and so relieve this growing pressure of melancholy and incredible things. The Viking fellow had just spoken of the possibility of the old gods manifesting themselves visibly, audibly, physically, and so the Major caught him up and made light mention of spiritualism and the so-called "materialisation séances," where physical bodies were alleged to be built up out of the emanations of the medium and the sitters. This crude aspect of the Supernatural was the only possible link the soldier's mind could manage. He caught his brother's eye too late, it seems, for Malcolm Reese realised by this time that something untoward was afoot, and no longer needed the memory of Sinbad's warning to keep him sharply on the look-out. It was not the first time he had seen Erricson "caught" by the sea; but he had never known him quite so bad, nor seen his face so flushed and white alternately, nor his eyes so oddly shining. So that Major Reese's well-intentioned allusion only brought wind to fire.

The man of the sea, once Viking, roared with a rush of boisterous laughter at the comic suggestion, then dropped his voice to a sudden hard whisper, awfully earnest, awfully intense. Any one must have started at the abrupt change and the life-and-death manner of the big man. His listeners undeniably both did.

"Bunkum!" he shouted, "bunkum, and be damned to it all! There's only one real materialisation of these immense Outer Beings possible, and that's when the great embodied emotions, which are their sphere of action"—his words became wildly incoherent, painfully struggling to get out—"derived, you see, from their honest worshippers the world over—constituting their Bodies, in fact—come down into matter and get condensed, crystallised into form—to claim that final sacrifice I spoke about just now, and to which any man might feel himself proud and honoured to be summoned. . . . No dying in bed or fading out from old age, but to plunge full-blooded and alive into the great Body of the god who has deigned to descend and fetch you—"

The actual speech may have been even more rambling and incoherent than that. It came out in a torrent at white heat. Dr. Reese kicked his brother beneath the table, just in time. The soldier looked thoroughly uncomfortable and amazed, utterly at a loss to know how he had produced the storm. It rather frightened him.

"I know it because I've seen it," went on the sea man, his mind and speech slightly more under control. "Seen the ceremonies that brought these whopping old Nature gods down into form—seen 'em carry off a worshipper into themselves—seen that worshipper, too, go off singing and happy to his death, proud and honoured to be chosen."

"Have you really—by George!" the Major exclaimed. "You tell us a queer thing, Erricson"; and it was then for the fifth time that Sinbad cautiously opened the door, peeped in and silently withdrew after giving a swiftly comprehensive glance round the room.

The night outside was windless and serene, only the growing thunder of the tide near the full woke muffled echoes among the sanddunes.

"Rites and ceremonies," continued the other, his voice booming with a singular enthusiasm, but ignoring the interruption, "are simply means of losing one's self by temporary ecstasy in the God of one's choice—the God one has worshipped all one's life—of being partially absorbed into his being. And sacrifice completes the process—"

"At death, you said?" asked Malcolm Reese, watching him keenly.

"Or voluntary," was the reply that came flash-like. "The devotee becomes wedded to his Deity—goes bang into him, you see, by fire or water or air—as by a drop from a height—according to the nature of the particular God; at-one-ment, of course. A man's death that! Fine, you know!"

The man's inner soul was on fire now. He was talking at a fearful pace, his eyes alight, his voice turned somehow into a kind of singsong that chimed well, singularly well, with the booming of waves outside, and from time to time he turned to the window to stare at the sea and the moon-blanched sands. And then a look of triumph would come into his face—that giant face framed by slow-moving wreaths of pipe smoke.

Sinbad entered for the sixth time without any obvious purpose, busied himself unnecessarily with the glasses and went out again, lingeringly. In the room he kept his eye hard upon his master. This time he contrived to push a chair and a heap of netting between him and the window. No one but Dr. Reese observed the manœuvre. And he took the hint.

"The port-holes fit badly, Erricson," he laughed, but with a touch of authority. "There's a five-knot breeze coming through the cracks worse than an old wreck!" And he moved up to secure the fastening better.

"The room *is* confoundedly cold," Major Reese put in; "has been for the last half-hour, too." The soldier looked what he felt—cold—distressed—creepy. "But there's no wind really, you know," he added.

Captain Erricson turned his great bearded visage from one to the other before he answered; there was a gleam of sudden suspicion in his blue eyes. "The beggar's got that back door open again. If he's sent for any one, as he did once before, I swear I'll drown him in fresh water for his impudence—or perhaps—can it be already that he expects—?" He left the sentence incomplete and rang the bell, laughing with a boisterousness that was clearly feigned. "Sinbad, what's this cold in the place? You've got the back door open. Not expecting any one, are you?"

"Everything's shut tight, Captain. There's a bit of a breeze coming up from the east. And the tide's drawing in at a raging pace—"

"We can all hear *that*. But are you expecting any one? I asked," repeated his master, suspiciously, yet still laughing. One might have said he was trying to give the idea that the man had some land flirtation on hand. They looked one another square in the eye for a moment, these two. It was the straight stare of equals who understood each other well.

"Some one—might be—on the way, as it were, Captain. Couldn't say for certain."

The voice almost trembled. By a sharp twist of the eye, Sinbad managed to shoot a lightning and significant look at the Doctor.

"But this cold—this freezing, damp cold in the place? Are you sure no one's come—by the back ways?" insisted the master. He whispered it. "Across the dunes, for instance?" His voice conveyed awe and delight, both kept hard under.

"It's all over the house, Captain, already," replied the man, and moved across to put more sea-logs on the blazing fire. Even the soldier noticed then that their language was tight with allusion of another kind. To relieve the growing tension and uneasiness in his own mind he took up the word "house" and made fun of it.

"As though it were a mansion," he observed, with a forced chuckle, "instead of a mere sea-shell!" Then, looking about him, he added: "But, all the same, you know, there *is* a kind of fog getting into the room—from the sea, I suppose; coming up with the tide, or something, eh?" The air had certainly in the last twenty minutes turned thickish; it was not all tobacco smoke, and there was a moisture that began to precipitate on the objects in tiny, fine globules. The cold, too, fairly bit.

"I'll take a look round," said Sinbad, significantly, and went out. Only the Doctor perhaps noticed that the man shook, and was white down to the gills. He said nothing, but moved his chair nearer to the window and to his host. It was really a little bit beyond comprehension how the wild words of this old sea-dog in the full sway of his "sea fit" had altered the very air of the room as well as the personal equations of its occupants, for an extraordinary atmosphere of enthusiasm that was almost splendour pulsed about him, yet vilely close to something that suggested terror! Through the armour of every-day common sense that normally clothed the minds of these other two, had crept the faint wedges of a mood that made them vaguely wonder whether the incredible could perhaps sometimes—by way of bewildering exceptions—actually come to pass. The moods of their deepest life, that is to say, were already affected. An inner, and thoroughly unwelcome, change was in progress. And such psychic disturbances once started are hard to arrest. In this case it was well on the way before either the Army or Medicine had been willing to recognise the fact. There was something coming—coming from the sand-dunes or the sea. And it was invited, welcomed at any rate, by Erricson. His deep, volcanic enthusiasm and belief provided the channel. In lesser degree they, too, were caught in it. Moreover, it was terrific, irresistible.

And it was at this point—as the comparing of notes afterwards established—that Father Norden came in, Norden, the big man's nephew, having bicycled over from some point beyond Corfe Castle and raced along the hard Studland sand in the moonlight, and then hullood till a boat had ferried him across the narrow channel of Poole Harbour. Sinbad simply brought him in without any preliminary question or announcement. He could not resist the splendid night and the spring air, explained Norden. He felt sure his uncle could "find a hammock" for him somewhere aft, as he put it. He did not add that

Sinbad had telegraphed for him just before sundown from the coast-guard hut. Dr. Reese already knew him, but he was introduced to the Major. Norden was a member of the Society of Jesus, an ardent, not clever, and unselfish soul.

Erricson greeted him with obviously mixed feelings, and with an extraordinary sentence: "It doesn't really matter," he exclaimed, after a few commonplaces of talk, "for all religions are the same if you go deep enough. All teach sacrifice, and, without exception, all seek final union by absorption into their Deity." And then, under his breath, turning sideways to peer out of the window, he added a swift rush of half-smothered words that only Dr. Reese caught: "The Army, the Church, the Medical Profession, and Labour—if they would only all come! What a fine result, what a grand offering! Alone—I seem so unworthy—insignificant . . . !"

But meanwhile young Norden was speaking before any one could stop him, although the Major did make one or two blundering attempts. For once the Jesuit's tact was at fault. He evidently hoped to introduce a new mood—to shift the current already established by the single force of his own personality. And he was not quite man enough to carry it off.

It was an error of judgment on his part. For the forces he found established in the room were too heavy to lift and alter, their impetus being already acquired. He did his best, anyhow. He began moving with the current—it was not the first sea fit he had combated in this extraordinary personality—then found, too late, that he was carried along with it himself like the rest of them.

"Odd—but couldn't find the bungalow at first," he laughed, somewhat hardly. "It's got a bit of sea-fog all to itself that hides it. I thought perhaps my pagan uncle—"

The Doctor interrupted him hastily, with great energy. "The fog *does* lie caught in these sand hollows—like steam in a cup, you know," he put in. But the other, intent on his own procedure, missed the cue.

"—thought it was smoke at first, and that you were up to some heathen ceremony or other," laughing in Erricson's face; "sacrificing to the full moon or the sea, or the spirits of the desolate places that haunt sand-dunes, eh?"

No one spoke for a second, but Erricson's face turned quite radiant.

"My uncle's such a pagan, you know," continued the priest, "that as I flew along those deserted sands from Studland I almost expected to hear old Triton blow his wreathèd horn . . . or see fair Thetis's tinsel-slippered feet. . ."

Erricson, suppressing violent gestures, highly excited, face happy as a boy's, was combing his great yellow beard with both hands, and the other two men had begun to speak at once, intent on stopping the flow of unwise allusion. Norden, swallowing a mouthful of cold soda-water, had put the glass down, spluttering over its bubbles, when the sound was first heard at the window. And in the back room the man-servant ran, calling something aloud that sounded like "It's coming, God save us, it's coming in . . . !" Though the Major swears some name was mentioned that he afterwards forgot—Glaucus—Proteus—Pontus—or some such word. The sound itself, however, was plain enough—a kind of imperious tapping on the window-panes as of a multitude of objects. Blown sand it might have been or heavy spray or, as Norden suggested later, a great water-soaked branch of giant sea-weed. Every one started up, but Erricson was first upon his feet, and had the window wide open in a twinkling. His voice roared forth over those moonlit sand-dunes and out towards the line of heavy surf ten yards below.

"All along the shore of the Ægean," he bellowed, with a kind of hoarse triumph that shook the heart, "that ancient cry once rang. But it was a lie, a thumping and audacious lie. And He is not the only one. Another still lives—and, by Poseidon, He comes! He knows His own and His own know Him—and His own shall go to meet Him . . . !"

That reference to the Ægean "cry"! It was so wonderful. Every one, of course, except the soldier, seized the allusion. It was a comprehensive, yet subtle, way of suggesting the idea. And meanwhile all spoke at once, shouted rather, for the Invasion was somehow—monstrous.

"Damn it—that's a bit too much. Something's caught my throat!" The Major, like a man drowning, fought with the furniture in his amazement and dismay. Fighting was his first instinct, of course. "Hurts so infernally—takes the breath," he cried, by way of explaining the extraordinarily violent impetus that moved him, yet half ashamed of himself for seeing nothing he could strike. But Malcolm Reese struggled to get between his host and the open window, saying in tense voice something like "Don't let him get out! Don't let him get out!" While the shouts of warning from Sinbad in the little cramped back offices added to the general confusion. Only Father Norden stood quiet—watching with a kind of admiring wonder the expression of magnificence that had flamed into the visage of Erricson.

"Hark, you fools! Hark!" boomed the Viking figure, standing erect and splendid.

And through that open window, along the far-drawn line of shore from Canford Cliffs to the chalk bluffs of Studland Bay, there certainly ran a sound that was no common roar of surf. It was articulate—a message from the sea—an announcement—a thunderous warning of approach. No mere surf breaking on sand could have compassed so deep and multitudinous a voice of dreadful roaring—far out over the entering tide, yet at the same time close in along the entire sweep of shore, shaking all the ocean, both depth and surface, with its deep vibrations. Into the bungalow chamber came—the SEA!

Out of the night, from the moonlit spaces where it had been steadily accumulating, into that little cabined room so full of humanity and tobacco smoke, came invisibly—the Power of the Sea. Invisible, yes, but mighty, pressed forward by the huge draw of the moon, soft-coated with brine and moisture—the great Sea. And with it, into the minds of those three other men, leaped instantaneously, not to be denied, overwhelming suggestions of water-power, the tear and strain of thousand-mile currents, the irresistible pull and rush of tides, the suction of giant whirlpools—more, the massed and awful impetus of whole driven oceans. The air turned salt and briny, and a welter of seaweed clamped their very skins.

"Glaucus! I come to Thee, great God of the deep Waterways. . . . Father and Master!" Erricson cried aloud in a voice that most marvellously conveyed supreme joy.

The little bungalow trembled as from a blow at the foundations, and the same second the big man was through the window and running down the moonlit sands towards the foam.

"God in heaven! Did you all see *that?*" shouted Major Reese, for the manner in which the great body slipped through the tiny window-frame was incredible. And then, first tottering with a sudden weakness, he recovered himself and rushed round by the door, followed by his brother. Sinbad, invisible, but not inaudible, was calling aloud from the passage at the back. Father Norden, slimmer than the others—well controlled, too—was through the little window before either of them reached the fringe of beach beyond the sand-dunes. They joined forces half-way down to the water's edge. The figure of Erricson, towering in the moonlight, flew before them, coasting rapidly along the wave-line.

No one of them said a word; they tore along side by side, Norden a trifle in advance. In front of them, head turned seawards, bounded Erricson in great flying leaps, singing as he ran, impossible to overtake.

Then, what they witnessed all three witnessed; the weird grandeur of it in the moonshine was too splendid to allow the smaller emotions of personal alarm, it seems. At any rate, the divergence of opinion afterwards was unaccountably insignificant. For, on a sudden, that heavy roaring sound far out at sea came close in with a swift plunge of speed, followed simultaneously—accompanied, rather—by a dark line that was no mere wave moving: enormously, up and across, between the sea and sky it swept close in to shore. The moonlight caught it for a second as it passed, in a cliff of her bright silver.

And Erricson slowed down, bowed his great head and shoulders, spread his arms out and . . .

And what? For no one of those amazed witnesses could swear exactly what then came to pass. Upon this impossibility of telling it in language they all three agreed. Only those eyeless dunes of sand that watched, only the white and silent moon overhead, only that long, curved beach of empty and deserted shore retain the complete record, to be revealed some day perhaps when a later Science shall have learned to develop the photographs that Nature takes incessantly upon her secret plates. For Erricson's rough suit of tweed went out in ribbons across the air; his figure somehow turned dark like strips of tide-sucked seaweed; something enveloped and overcame him, half shrouding him from view. He stood for one instant upright, his hair wild in the moonshine, towering, with arms again outstretched; then bent forward, turned, drew out most curiously sideways, uttering the singing sound of tumbling waters. The next instant, curving over like a falling wave, he swept along the glistening surface of the sands—and was gone. In fluid form, wave-like, his being slipped away into the Being of the Sea. A violent tumult convulsed the surface of the tide near in, but at once, and with amazing speed, passed careering away into the deeper water—far out. To his singular death, as to a wedding, Erricson had gone, singing, and well content.

"May God, who holds the sea and all its powers in the hollow of His mighty hand, take them *both* into Himself!" Norden was on his knees, praying fervently.

The body was never recovered . . . and the most curious thing of all was that the interior of the cabin, where they found Sinbad shaking with terror when they at length returned, was splashed and sprayed, almost soaked, with salt water. Up into the bigger dunes beside the bungalow, and far beyond the reach of normal tides, lay, too, a great streak and furrow as of a large invading wave, caking the dry sand. A hundred tufts of the coarse grass tussocks had been torn away.

The high tide that night, drawn by the Easter full moon, of course, was known to have been exceptional, for it fairly flooded Poole Harbour, flushing all the coves and bays towards the mouth of the Frome. And the natives up at Arne Bay and Wych always declare that the noise of the sea was heard far inland even up to the nine Barrows of the Purbeck Hills—triumphantly singing.

The Singular Death of Morton

Dusk was melting into darkness as the two men slowly made their way through the dense forest of spruce and fir that clothed the flanks of the mountain. They were weary with the long climb, for neither was in his first youth, and the July day had been a hot one. Their little inn lay further in the valley among the orchards that separated the forest from the vineyards.

Neither of them talked much. The big man led the way, carrying the knapsack, and his companion, older, shorter, evidently the more fatigued of the two, followed with small footsteps. From time to time he stumbled among the loose rocks. An exceptionally observant mind would possibly have divined that his stumbling was not entirely due to fatigue, but to an absorption of spirit that made him careless how he walked.

"All right behind?" the big man would call from time to time, half glancing back.

"Eh? What?" the other would reply, startled out of a reverie.

"Pace too fast?"

"Not a bit. I'm coming." And once he added: "You might hurry on and see to supper, if you feel like it. I shan't be long behind you."

But his big friend did not adopt the suggestion. He kept the same distance between them. He called out the same question at intervals. Once or twice *he* stopped and looked back too.

In this way they came at length to the skirts of the wood. A deep hush covered all the valley; the limestone ridges they had climbed gleamed down white and ghostly upon them from the fading sky. Midway in its journeys, the evening wind dropped suddenly to watch the beauty of the moonlight—to hold the branches still so that the light might slip between and weave its silver pattern on the moss below.

And, as they stood a moment to take it in, a step sounded behind them on the soft pine-needles, and the older man, still a little in the rear, turned with a start as though he had been suddenly called by name.

"There's that girl—again!" he said, and his voice expressed a curious mingling of pleasure, surprise and—apprehension.

Into a patch of moonlight passed the figure of a young girl, looked at them as though about to stop yet thinking better of it, smiled softly, and moved on out of sight into the surrounding darkness. The moon just caught her eyes and teeth, so that they shone; the rest of her body stood in shadow; the effect was striking—almost as though head and shoulders hung alone in mid air, watching them with this shining smile, then fading away.

"Come on, for heaven's sake," the big man cried. There was impatience in his manner, not unkindness. The other lingered a moment, peering closely into the gloom where the girl had vanished. His friend repeated his injunction, and a moment later the two had emerged upon the high road with the village lights in sight beyond, and the forest left behind them like a vast mantle that held the night within its folds.

For some minutes neither of them spoke; then the big man waited for his friend to draw up alongside.

"About all this valley of the Jura," he said presently, "there seems to me something—rather weird." He shifted the knapsack vigorously on his back. It was a gesture of unconscious protest.

"Something uncanny," he added, as he set a good pace.

"But extraordinarily beautiful—"

"It attracts you more than it does me, I think," was the short reply.

"The picturesque superstitions still survive here," observed the older man. "They touch the imagination in spite of oneself."

A pause followed during which the other tried to increase the pace. The subject evidently made him impatient for some reason.

"Perhaps," he said presently. "Though I think myself it's due to the curious loneliness of the place. I mean, we're in the middle of tourist-Europe here, yet so utterly remote. It's such a neglected little corner of the world. The contradiction bewilders. Then, being so near the frontier, too, with the clock changing an hour a mile from the village, makes one think of time as unreal and imaginary." He laughed. He produced several other reasons as well. His friend admitted their value, and agreed half-heartedly. He still turned occasionally to look back. The mountain ridge where they had climbed was clearly visible in the moonlight.

"Odd," he said, "but I don't see that farmhouse where we got the milk anywhere. It ought to be easily visible from here."

"Hardly—in this light. It was a queer place rather, I thought," he added. He did not deny the curiously suggestive atmosphere of the region, he merely wanted to find satisfactory explanations. "A case in point, I mean. I didn't like it quite—that farmhouse—yet I'm hanged if I know why. It made me feel uncomfortable. That girl appeared so suddenly, although the place seemed deserted. And her silence was so odd. Why in the world couldn't she answer a single question? I'm glad I didn't take the milk. I spat it out. I'd like to know where she got it from, for there was no sign of a cow or a goat to be seen anywhere!"

"I swallowed mine—in spite of the taste," said the other, half smiling at his companion's sudden volubility.

Very abruptly, then, the big man turned and faced his friend. Was it merely an effect of the moonlight, or had his skin really turned pale beneath the sunburn?

"I say, old man," he said, his face grave and serious, "what do you think she was? What made her seem like that, and why the devil do you think she followed us?"

"I think," was the slow reply, "it was *me* she was following."

The words, and particularly the tone of conviction in which they were spoken, clearly were displeasing to the big man, who already regretted having spoken so frankly what was in his mind. With a companion so imaginative, so impressionable, so nervous, it had been foolish and unwise. He led the way home at a pace that made the other arrive five minutes in his rear, panting, limping, and perspiring as if he had been running.

"I'm rather for going on into Switzerland tomorrow, or the next day," he ventured that night in the darkness of their two-bedded room. "I think we've had enough of this place. Eh? What do you think?"

But there was no answer from the bed across the room, for its occupant was sound asleep and snoring.

"Dead tired, I suppose!" he muttered to himself, and then turned over to follow his friend's example. But for a long time sleep refused him. Queer, unwelcome thoughts and feelings kept him awake—of a kind he rarely knew, and thoroughly disliked. It was rubbish, yet it made him uncomfortable so that his nerves tingled. He tossed about in the bed. "I'm overtired," he persuaded himself, "that's all."

The strange feelings that kept him thus awake were not easy to analyse, perhaps, but their origin was beyond all question: they grouped themselves about the picture of that deserted, tumble-down châlet on the mountain ridge where they had stopped for refreshment a few hours before. It was a farmhouse, dilapidated and dirty, and the name stood in big black letters against a blue background on the wall above the door: "La Chenille." Yet not a living soul was to be seen anywhere about it; the doors were fastened, windows shuttered; chimneys smokeless; dirt, neglect, and decay everywhere in evidence.

Then, suddenly, as they had turned to go, after much vain shouting and knocking at the door, a face appeared for an instant at a window, the shutter of which was half open. His friend saw it first, and called aloud. The face nodded in reply, and presently a young girl came round the corner of the house, apparently by a back door, and stood staring at them both from a little distance.

And from that very instant, so far as he could remember, these queer feelings had entered his heart—fear, distrust, misgiving. The thought of it now, as he lay in bed in the darkness, made his hair rise. There was something about that girl that struck cold into the soul. Yet she was a mere slip of a thing, very pretty, seductive even, with a certain serpent-like fascination about her eyes and movements; and although she only replied to their questions as to refreshment with a smile, uttering no single word, she managed to convey the impression that she was a managing little person who might make herself very disagreeable if she chose. In spite of her undeniable charm there was about her an atmosphere of something sinister. He himself did most of the questioning, but it was his older friend who had the benefit of her smile. Her eyes hardly ever left his face, and once she had slipped quite close to him and touched his arm.

The strange part of it now seemed to him that he could not remember in the least how she was dressed, or what was the colouring of her eyes and hair. It was almost as though he had *felt*, rather than seen, her presence.

The milk—she produced a jug and two wooden bowls after a brief disappearance round the corner of the house—was—well, it tasted so odd that he had been unable to swallow it, and had spat it out. His friend, on the other hand, savage with thirst, had drunk his bowl to the last drop too quickly to taste it even, and, while he drank, had kept his eyes fixed on those of the girl, who stood close in front of him.

And from that moment his friend had somehow changed. On the way down he said things that were unusual, talking chiefly about the "Chenille," and the girl, and the delicious, delicate flavour of the milk, yet all phrased in such a way that it sounded singular, unfamiliar, unpleasant even. Now that he tried to recall the sentences the actual words evaded him; but the memory of the uneasiness and apprehension they caused him to feel remained. And night ever italicises such memories!

Then, to cap it all, the girl had followed them. It was wholly foolish and absurd to feel the things he did feel; yet there the feelings were, and what was the good of arguing? That girl frightened him; the change in his friend was in some way or other a danger signal. More than this he could not tell. An explanation might come later, but for the present his chief desire was to get away from the place and to get his friend away, too.

And on this thought sleep overtook him—heavily.

The windows were wide open; outside was a garden with a rather high enclosing wall, and at the far end a gate that was kept locked because it led into private fields and so, by a back way, to the cemetery and the little church. When it was open the guests of the inn made use of it and got lost in the network of fields and vines, for there was no proper route that way to the road or the mountains. They usually ended up prematurely in the cemetery, and got back to the village by passing through the church, which was always open; or by knocking at the kitchen doors of the other houses and explaining their position. Hence the gate was locked now to save trouble.

After several hours of hot, unrefreshing sleep the big man turned in his bed and woke. He tried to stretch, but couldn't; then sat up panting with a sense of suffocation. And by the faint starlight of the summer night, he saw next that his friend was up and moving about the room. Remembering that sometimes he walked in his sleep, he called to him gently:

"Morton, old chap," he said in a low voice, with a touch of authority in it, "go back to bed! You've walked enough for one day!"

And the figure, obeying as sleep-walkers often will, passed across the room and disappeared among the shadows over his bed. The other plunged and burrowed himself into a comfortable position again for sleep, but the heat of the room, the shortness of the bed, and this tiresome interruption of his slumbers made it difficult to lose consciousness. He forced his eyes to keep shut, and his body to cease from fidgeting, but there was something nibbling at his mind like a spirit mouse that never permitted him to cross the frontier into actual oblivion. He slept with one eye open, as the saying is. Odours of hay and flowers and baked ground stole in through the open window; with them, too, came from time to time sounds—little sounds that disturbed him without being ever loud enough to claim definite attention.

Perhaps, after all, he did lose consciousness for a moment—when, suddenly, a thought came with a sharp rush into his mind and galvanised him once more into utter wakefulness. It amazed him that he had not grasped it before. It was this: the figure he had seen was *not the figure of his friend.*

Alarm gripped him at once before he could think or argue, and a cold perspiration broke out all over his body. He fumbled for matches, couldn't find them; then, remembering there was electric light, he scraped the wall with his fingers—and turned on the little white switch. In the sudden glare that filled the room he saw instantly that his friend's bed was no longer occupied. And his mind, then acting instinctively, without process of conscious reasoning, flew like a flash to their walk of the day—to the tumble-down "Chenille," the glass of milk, the odd behaviour of his friend, and—to the girl.

At the same second he noticed that the odour in the room which hitherto he had taken to be the composite odour of fields, flowers, and night, was really something else: it was the odour of freshly turned earth. Immediately on the top of this discovery came another. Those slight sounds he had heard outside the window were not ordinary night-sounds, the murmur of wind and insects: they were footsteps moving softly, stealthily down the little paths of crushed granite.

He was dressed in wonderful short order, noticing as he did so that his friend's night-garments lay upon the bed, and that he, too, had therefore dressed; further—that the door had been unlocked and stood half an inch ajar. There was now no question that he *had* slept again: between the present and the moment when he had seen the figure there had been a considerable interval. A couple of minutes later he had made his way cautiously down-stairs and was standing on the garden path in the moonlight. And as he stood there, his mind filled with the stories the proprietor had told a few days before of the superstitions that still lived in the popular imagination and haunted this little, remote pine-clad valley. The thought of that girl sickened him. The odour of newly-turned earth remained in his nostrils and made his gorge rise. Utterly and vigorously he rejected the monstrous fictions he had heard, yet for all that, could not prevent their touching his imagination as he stood there in the early hours of the morning, alone with night and silence. The spell was undeniable; only a mind without sensibility could have ignored it.

He searched the little garden from end to end. Empty! Opposite the high gate he stopped, peering through the iron bars, wet with dew to his hands. Far across the intervening fields he fancied something moved. A second later he was sure of it. Something down there to the right beyond the trees was astir. It was in the cemetery.

And this definite discovery sent a shudder of terror and disgust through him from head to foot. He framed the name of his friend with his lips, yet the sound did not come forth. Some deeper instinct warned him to hold it back. Instead, after incredible efforts, he climbed that iron gate and dropped down into the soaking grass upon the other side. Then, taking advantage of all the cover he could find, he ran, swiftly and stealthily, towards the cemetery. On the way, without quite knowing why he did so, he picked up a heavy stick; and a moment later he stood beside the low wall that separated the fields from the churchyard—stood and stared.

There, beside the tombstones, with their hideous metal wreaths and crowns of faded flowers, he made out the figure of his friend; he was stooping, crouched down upon the ground; behind him rose a couple of bushy yew trees, against the dark of which his form was easily visible. He was not alone; in front of him, bending close over him it seemed, was another figure—a slight, shadowy, slim figure.

This time the big man found his voice and called aloud:

"Morton, Morton!" he cried. "What, in the name of heaven, are you doing? What's the matter—?"

And the instant his deep voice broke the stillness of the night with its clamour, the little figure, half hiding his friend, turned about and faced him. He saw a white face with shining eyes and teeth as the form rose; the moonlight painted it with its own strange pallor; it was weird, unreal, horrible; and across the mouth, downwards from the lips to the chin, ran a deep stain of crimson.

The next moment the figure slid with a queer, gliding motion towards the trees, and disappeared among the yews and tombstones in the direction of the church. The heavy stick, hurled whirling after it, fell harmlessly half-way, knocking a metal cross from its perch upon an upright grave; and the man who had thrown it raced full speed towards the huddled up figure of his friend, hardly noticing the thin, wailing cry that rose trembling through the night air from the vanished form. Nor did he notice more particularly that several of the graves, newly made, showed signs of recent disturbance, and that the odour of turned earth he had noticed in the room grew stronger. All his attention was concentrated upon the figure at his feet.

"Morton, man, get up! Wake for God's sake! You've been walking in—"

Then the words died upon his lips. The unnatural attitude of his friend's shoulders, and the way the head dropped back to show the neck, struck him like a blow in the face. There was no sign of movement. He lifted the body up and carried it, all limp and unresisting, by ways he never remembered afterwards, back to the inn.

It was all a dreadful nightmare—a nightmare that carried over its ghastly horror into waking life. He knew that the proprietor and his wife moved busily to and fro about the bed, and that in due course the village doctor was upon the scene, and that he was giving a muddled and feverish description of all he knew, telling how his friend was a confirmed sleep-walker and all the rest. But he did not realise the truth until he saw the face of the doctor as he straightened up from the long examination.

"Will you wake him?" he heard himself asking, "or let him sleep it out till morning?" And the doctor's expression, even before the reply came to confirm it, told him the truth. "Ah, monsieur, your friend will not ever wake again, I fear! It is the heart, you see; *hélas,* it is sudden failure of the heart!"

The final scenes in the little tragedy which thus brought his holiday to so abrupt and terrible a close need no description, being in no way essential to this strange story. There were one or two curious details, however, that came to light afterwards. One was, that for some weeks before there had been signs of disturbance among newly-made graves in the cemetery, which the authorities had been trying to trace to the nightly wanderings of the village madman—in vain; and another, that the morning after the death a trail of blood had been found across the church floor, as though some one had passed through from the back entrance to the front. A special service was held that very week to cleanse the holy building from the evil of that stain; for the villagers, deep in their superstitions, declared that nothing human had left that trail; nothing could have made those marks but a vampire disturbed at midnight in its awful occupation among the dead.

Apart from such idle rumours, however, the bereaved carried with him to this day certain other remarkable details which cannot be so easily dismissed. For he had a brief conversation with the doctor, it appears, that impressed him profoundly. And the doctor, an intelligent man, prosaic as granite into the bargain, had questioned him rather closely as to the recent life and habits of his dead friend. The account of their climb to the "Chenille" he heard with an amazement he could not conceal.

"But no such châlet exists," he said. "There is no 'Chenille.' A long time ago, fifty years or more, there was such a place, but it was destroyed by the authorities on account of the evil reputation of the people who lived there. They burnt it. Nothing remains today but a few bits of broken wall and foundation."

"Evil reputation—?"

The doctor shrugged his shoulders. "Travellers, even peasants, disappeared," he said. "An old woman lived there with her daughter, and poisoned milk was supposed to be used. But the neighbourhood accused them of worse than ordinary murder—"

"In what way?"

"Said the girl was a vampire," answered the doctor shortly.

And, after a moment's hesitation, he added, turning his face away as he spoke:

"It was a curious thing, though, that tiny hole in your friend's throat, small as a pin-prick, yet so deep. And the heart—did I tell you?—was almost completely drained of blood."

Imagination

Having dined upon a beefsteak and a pint of bitter, Jones went home to work. The trouble with Jones—his first name William—was that he possessed creative imagination: that luggage upon which excess charges have to be paid all through life—to the critic, the stupid, the orthodox, the slower minds without the "flash." He was alone in his brother's flat. It was after nine o'clock. He was half-way into a story, and had—stuck! Sad to relate, the machinery that carries on the details of an original inspiration had blocked. And to invent he knew not how. Unless the imagination "produced" he would not allow his brain to devise mere episodes—-dull and lifeless substitutes. Jones, poor fool, was also artist.

And the reason he had "stuck" was not surprising, for his story was of a kind that might well tax the imagination of any sane man. He was writing at the moment about a being who had survived his age—a study of one of those rare and primitive souls who walk the earth to-day in a man's twentieth-century body, while yet the spirit belongs to the Golden Age of the world's history. You may come across them sometimes, rare, ingenuous, delightful beings, the primal dews still upon their eyelids, the rush and glow of earth's pristine fires pulsing in their veins, careless of gain, indifferent to success, lost, homeless, exiled—*dépaysés*. . . . The idea had seized him. He had met such folk. He burned to describe their exile, the pathos of their loneliness, their yearnings and their wanderings—rejected by a world they had outlived. And for his type, thus representing some power of unexpended mythological values strayed back into modern life to find itself denied and ridiculed—he had chosen a Centaur! For he wished it to symbolise what he believed was to be the next stage in human evolution: Intuition no longer neglected, but developed equally with Reason. His Centaur was to stand for instinct (the animal body close to Nature)

159

combined with, yet not dominated by, the upright stature moving towards deity. The conception was true and pregnant.

And—he had stuck. The detail that blocked him was the man's *appearance*. How would such a being look? In what details would he betray that, though outwardly a man, he was inwardly this survival of the Golden Age, escaped from some fair Eden, splendid, immense, simple, and beneficent, yet—a Centaur?

Perhaps it was just as well he had "stuck," for his brother would shortly be in, and his brother was a successful business man with the money-sense and commercial instincts strongly developed. He dealt in rice and sugar. With his brother in the flat no Centaur could possibly survive for a single moment. "It'll come to me when I'm not thinking about it," he sighed, knowing well the waywardness of his particular genius. He threw the reins upon the subconscious self and moved into an armchair to read in the evening paper the things the public loved— that public who refused to buy his books, pleading they were "queer." He waded down the list of immoralities, murders, and assaults with a dreamy eye, and had just reached the witness's description of finding the bloody head in the faithless wife's bedroom, when there came a hurried, pelting knock at, the door, and William Jones, glad of the relief, went to open it. There, facing him, stood the bore from the flat below. Horrors!

It was not, however, a visit after all. "Jones," he faltered, "there's an odd sort of chap here asking for you or your brother. Rang my bell by mistake."

Jones murmured some reply or other, and as the bore vanished with a hurry unusual to him, there passed into the flat a queer shape, born surely of the night and stars and desolate places. He seemed in some undefinable way bent, humpbacked, very large. With him came a touch of open spaces, winds, forests, long clean hills, and dew-drenched fields.

"Come in, please . . ." said Jones, instantly aware that the man was not for his brother. "You have something to—er—" he was going to use the word "ask," then changed it instinctively—"*say* to me, haven't you?"

The man was ragged, poor, outcast. Clearly it was a begging episode; and yet he trembled violently, while in his veins ran fire. The caller refused a seat, but moved over to the curtains by the window, drawing them slightly aside so that he could see out. And the window was high above old smoky London—open. It felt cold. Jones bent down, always keeping his caller in view, and lit the gas-stove. "You wish to see me," he said, rising again to an upright position. Then he added more hurriedly, stepping back a little towards the rack where the walking-sticks were, "Please let me know what I can do for you!"

Bearded, unkempt, with massive shoulders and huge neck, the caller stood a moment and stared. "Your name and address," he said at length, "were given to me"—he hesitated a moment, then added— "you know by whom." His voice was deep and windy and echoing. It made the stretched cords of the upright piano ring against the wall. "He told me to call," the man concluded.

"Ah yes; of course," Jones stammered, forgetting for the moment who or where he was. "Let me see—where are you"—the word did not want to come out—"staying?" The caller made an awful and curious movement; it seemed so much bigger than his body. "In what way—er—can I be of assistance?" Jones hardly knew what he said. The other volunteered so little. He was frightened. Then, before the man could answer, he caught a dreadful glimpse, as of something behind the outline. It moved. Was it shadow that thus extended his form? Was it the glare of that ugly gas-stove that played tricks with the folds of the curtain, driving bodily outline forth into mere vacancy? For the figure of his strange caller seemed to carry with it the idea of projections, extensions, growths, in themselves not monstrous, fine and comely, rather—yet awful.

The man left the window and moved towards him. It was a movement both swift and enormous. It was instantaneous.

"Who are you—*really?*" asked Jones, his breath catching, while he went pluckily out to meet him, irresistibly drawn. "And what is it you *really* want of me?" He went very close to the shrouded form, caught the keen air from the open window behind, sniffed a wind that was not London's stale and weary wind, then stopped abruptly, frozen with terror and delight. The man facing him was splendid and terrific, exhaling something that overwhelmed.

"What can I . . . do . . . for . . . you?" whispered Jones, shaking like a leaf. A delight of racing clouds was in him.

The answer came in a singular roaring voice that yet sounded far away, as though among mountains. Wind might have brought it down.

"There is nothing you can do for me! But, by Chiron, there is something I can do for you!"

"And that is?" asked Jones faintly, feeling something sweep against his feet and legs like the current of a river in flood.

The man eyed him appallingly a moment.

"Let you see me!" he roared, while his voice set the piano singing again, and his outline seemed to swim over the chairs and tables like a fluid mass. "Show myself to you!"

The figure stretched out what looked like arms, reared gigantically aloft towards the ceiling, and swept towards him. Jones saw the great visage close to his own. He smelt the odour of caves, river-beds, hillsides—space. In another second he would have been lost—

His brother made a great rattling as he opened the door. The atmosphere of rice and sugar and office desks came in with him.

"Why, Billy, old man, you look as if you'd seen a ghost. You're white!"

William Jones mopped his forehead. "I've been working rather hard," he answered. "Feel tired. Fact is—I got stuck in a story for a bit."

"Too bad. Got it straightened out at last, I hope?"

"Yes, thanks. *It came to me*—in the end."

The other looked at him. "Good," he said shortly. "Rum thing, imagination, isn't it?" And then he began talking about his day's business—in tons and tons of food.

The Empty Sleeve

I

The Gilmer brothers were a couple of fussy and pernickety old bachelors of a rather retiring, not to say timid, disposition. There was grey in the pointed beard of John, the elder, and if any hair had remained to William it would also certainly have been of the same shade. They had private means. Their main interest in life was the collection of violins, for which they had the instinctive *flair* of true connoisseurs. Neither John nor William, however, could play a single note. They could only pluck the open strings. The production of tone, so necessary before purchase, was done vicariously for them by another.

The only objection they had to the big building in which they occupied the roomy top floor was that Morgan, liftman and caretaker, insisted on wearing a billycock with his uniform after six o'clock in the evening, with a result disastrous to the beauty of the universe. For "Mr. Morgan," as they called him between themselves, had a round and pasty face on the top of a round and conical body. In view, however, of the man's other rare qualities—including his devotion to themselves—this objection was not serious.

He had another peculiarity that amused them. On being found fault with, he explained nothing, but merely repeated the words of the complaint.

"Water in the bath wasn't really hot this morning, Morgan!"

"Water in the bath not reely 'ot, wasn't it, sir?"

Or, from William, who was something of a faddist:

"My jar of sour milk came up late yesterday, Morgan."

"Your jar sour milk come up late, sir, yesterday?"

Since, however, the statement of a complaint invariably resulted in

163

its remedy, the brothers had learned to look for no further explanation. Next morning the bath *was* hot, the sour milk *was* "brort up" punctually. The uniform and billycock hat, though, remained an eyesore and source of oppression.

On this particular night John Gilmer, the elder, returning from a Masonic rehearsal, stepped into the lift and found Mr. Morgan with his hand ready on the iron rope.

"Fog's very thick outside," said Mr. John pleasantly; and the lift was a third of the way up before Morgan had completed his customary repetition: "Fog very thick outside, yes, sir." And Gilmer then asked casually if his brother were alone, and received the reply that Mr. Hyman had called and had not yet gone away.

Now this Mr. Hyman was a Hebrew, and, like themselves, a connoisseur in violins, but, unlike themselves, who only kept their specimens to look at, he was a skilful and exquisite player. He was the only person they ever permitted to handle their pedigree instruments, to take them from the glass cases where they reposed in silent splendour, and to draw the sound out of their wondrous painted hearts of golden varnish. The brothers loathed to see his fingers touch them, yet loved to hear their singing voices in the room, for the latter confirmed their sound judgment as collectors, and made them certain their money had been well spent. Hyman, however, made no attempt to conceal his contempt and hatred for the mere collector. The atmosphere of the room fairly pulsed with these opposing forces of silent emotion when Hyman played and the Gilmers, alternately writhing and admiring, listened. The occasions, however, were not frequent. The Hebrew only came by invitation, and both brothers made a point of being in. It was a very formal proceeding—something of a sacred rite almost.

John Gilmer, therefore, was considerably surprised by the information Morgan had supplied. For one thing, Hyman, he had understood, was away on the Continent.

"Still in there, you say?" he repeated, after a moment's reflection.

"Still in there, Mr. John, sir." Then, concealing his surprise from the liftman, he fell back upon his usual mild habit of complaining about the billycock hat and the uniform.

"You really should try and remember, Morgan," he said, though kindly. "That hat does *not* go well with that uniform!"

Morgan's pasty countenance betrayed no vestige of expression. "'At don't go well with the yewniform, sir," he repeated, hanging up the disreputable bowler and replacing it with a gold-braided cap from the peg. "No, sir, it don't, do it?" he added cryptically, smiling at the transformation thus effected.

And the lift then halted with an abrupt jerk at the top floor. By somebody's carelessness the landing was in darkness, and, to make things worse, Morgan, clumsily pulling the iron rope, happened to knock the billycock from its peg so that his sleeve, as he stooped to catch it, struck the switch and plunged the scene in a moment's complete obscurity.

And it was then, in the act of stepping out before the light was turned on again, that John Gilmer stumbled against something that shot along the landing past the open door. First he thought it must be a child, then a man, then—an animal. Its movement was rapid yet stealthy. Starting backwards instinctively to allow it room to pass, Gilmer collided in the darkness with Morgan, and Morgan incontinently screamed. There was a moment of stupid confusion. The heavy framework of the lift shook a little, as though something had stepped into it and then as quickly jumped out again. A rushing sound followed that resembled footsteps, yet at the same time was more like gliding— some one in soft slippers or stockinged feet, greatly hurrying. Then came silence again. Morgan sprang to the landing and turned up the electric light. Mr. Gilmer, at the same moment, did likewise to the switch in the lift. Light flooded the scene. Nothing was visible.

"Dog or cat, or something, I suppose, wasn't it?" exclaimed Gilmer, following the man out and looking round with bewildered amazement upon a deserted landing. He knew quite well, even while he spoke, that the words were foolish.

"Dog or cat, yes, sir, or—something," echoed Morgan, his eyes narrowed to pin-points, then growing large, but his face stolid.

"The light should have been on." Mr. Gilmer spoke with a touch of severity. The little occurrence had curiously disturbed his equanimity. He felt annoyed, upset, uneasy.

For a perceptible pause the liftman made no reply, and his employer, looking up, saw that, besides being flustered, he was white about the jaws. His voice, when he spoke, was without its normal assurance. This time he did not merely repeat. He explained.

"The light *was* on, sir, when last *I* come up!" he said, with emphasis, obviously speaking the truth. "Only a moment ago," he added.

Mr. Gilmer, for some reason, felt disinclined to press for explanations. He decided to ignore the matter.

Then the lift plunged down again into the depths like a diving-bell into water; and John Gilmer, pausing a moment first to reflect, let himself in softly with his latch-key, and, after hanging up hat and coat in the hall, entered the big sitting-room he and his brother shared in common.

The December fog that covered London like a dirty blanket had penetrated, he saw, into the room. The objects in it were half shrouded in the familiar yellowish haze.

II

In dressing-gown and slippers, William Gilmer, almost invisible in his armchair by the gas-stove across the room, spoke at once. Through the thick atmosphere his face gleamed, showing an extinguished pipe hanging from his lips. His tone of voice conveyed emotion, an emotion he sought to suppress, of a quality, however, not easy to define.

"Hyman's been here," he announced abruptly. "You must have met him. He's this very instant gone out."

It was quite easy to see that something had happened, for "scenes" leave disturbance behind them in the atmosphere. But John made no immediate reference to this. He replied that he had seen no one— which was strictly true—and his brother thereupon, sitting bolt upright in the chair, turned quickly and faced him. His skin, in the foggy air, seemed paler than before.

"That's odd," he said nervously.

"What's odd?" asked John.

"That you didn't see—anything. You ought to have run into one another on the doorstep." His eyes went peering about the room. He was distinctly ill at ease. "You're positive you saw no one? Did Morgan take him down before you came? Did Morgan see him?" He asked several questions at once.

"On the contrary, Morgan told me he was still here with you. Hyman probably walked down, and didn't take the lift at all," he replied. "That accounts for neither of us seeing him." He decided to say nothing about the occurrence in the lift, for his brother's nerves, he saw plainly, were on edge.

William then stood up out of his chair, and the skin of his face changed its hue, for whereas a moment ago it was merely pale, it had now altered to a tint that lay somewhere between white and a livid grey. The man was fighting internal terror. For a moment these two brothers of middle age looked each other straight in the eye. Then John spoke:

"What's wrong, Billy?" he asked quietly. "Something's upset you. What brought Hyman in this way—unexpectedly? I thought he was still in Germany."

The brothers, affectionate and sympathetic, understood one another perfectly. They had no secrets. Yet for several minutes the younger one made no reply. It seemed difficult to choose his words apparently.

"Hyman played, I suppose—on the fiddles?" John helped him, wondering uneasily what was coming. He did not care much for the individual in question, though his talent was of such great use to them.

The other nodded in the affirmative, then plunged into rapid speech, talking under his breath as though he feared some one might overhear. Glancing over his shoulder down the foggy room, he drew his brother close.

"Hyman came," he began, "unexpectedly. He hadn't written, and I hadn't asked him. You hadn't either, I suppose?"

John shook his head.

"When I came in from the dining-room I found him in the passage. The servant was taking away the dishes, and he had let himself in while the front door was ajar. Pretty cool, wasn't it?"

"He's an original," said John, shrugging his shoulders. "And you welcomed him?" he asked.

"I asked him in, of course. He explained he had something glorious for me to hear. Silenski had played it in the afternoon, and he had bought the music since. But Silenski's 'Strad' hadn't the power—it's thin on the upper strings, you remember, unequal, patchy—and he said no instrument in the world could do it justice but our 'Joseph'—

the small Guarnerius, you know, which he swears is the most perfect in the world."

"And what was it? Did he play it?" asked John, growing more uneasy as he grew more interested. With relief he glanced round and saw the matchless little instrument lying there safe and sound in its glass case near the door.

"He played it—divinely: a Zigeuner Lullaby, a fine, passionate, rushing bit of inspiration, oddly misnamed 'lullaby.' And, fancy, the fellow had memorised it already! He walked about the room on tiptoe while he played it, complaining of the light—"

"Complaining of the light?"

"Said the thing was crepuscular, and needed dusk for its full effect. I turned the lights out one by one, till finally there was only the glow of the gas logs. He insisted. You know that way he has with him? And then he got over me in another matter: insisted on using some special strings he had brought with him, and put them on, too, himself— thicker than the A and E *we* use."

For though neither Gilmer could produce a note, it was their pride that they kept their precious instruments in perfect condition for playing, choosing the exact thickness and quality of strings that suited the temperament of each violin; and the little Guarnerius in question always "sang" best, they held, with thin strings.

"Infernal insolence," exclaimed the listening brother, wondering what was coming next. "Played it well, though, didn't he, this Lullaby thing?" he added, seeing that William hesitated. As he spoke he went nearer, sitting down close beside him in a leather chair.

"Magnificent! Pure fire of genius!" was the reply with enthusiasm, the voice at the same time dropping lower. "Staccato like a silver hammer; harmonics like flutes, clear, soft, ringing; and the tone—well, the G string was a baritone, and the upper registers creamy and mellow as a boy's voice. John," he added, "that Guarnerius is the very pick of the period and"—again he hesitated—"Hyman loves it. He'd give his soul to have it."

The more John heard, the more uncomfortable it made him. He had always disliked this gifted Hebrew, for in his secret heart he knew that he had always feared and distrusted him. Sometimes he had felt half afraid of him; the man's very forcible personality was too insistent to be pleasant. His type was of the dark and sinister kind, and he possessed a violent will that rarely failed of accomplishing its desire.

"Wish I'd heard the fellow play," he said at length, ignoring his brother's last remark, and going on to speak of the most matter-of-fact details he could think of. "Did he use the Dodd bow, or the Tourte? That Dodd I picked up last month, you know, is the most perfectly balanced I have ever—"

He stopped abruptly, for William had suddenly got upon his feet and was standing there, searching the room with his eyes. A chill ran down John's spine as he watched him.

"What is it, Billy?" he asked sharply. "Hear anything?"

William continued to peer about him through the thick air.

"Oh, nothing, probably," he said, an odd catch in his voice; "only— I keep feeling as if there was somebody listening. Do you think, perhaps"—he glanced over his shoulder—"there is some one at the door? I wish—I wish you'd have a look, John."

John obeyed, though without great eagerness. Crossing the room slowly, he opened the door, then switched on the light. The passage leading past the bathroom towards the bedrooms beyond was empty. The coats hung motionless from their pegs.

"No one, of course," he said, as he closed the door and came back to the stove. He left the light burning in the passage. It was curious the way both brothers had this impression that they were not alone, though only one of them spoke of it.

"Used the Dodd or the Tourte, Billy—which?" continued John in the most natural voice he could assume.

But at that very same instant the water started to his eyes. His brother, he saw, was close upon the thing he really had to tell. But he had stuck fast.

III

By a great effort John Gilmer composed himself and remained in his chair. With detailed elaboration he lit a cigarette, staring hard at his brother over the flaring match while he did so. There he sat in his dressing-gown and slippers by the fireplace, eyes downcast, fingers playing idly with the red tassel. The electric light cast heavy shadows across the face. In a flash then, since emotion may sometimes express itself in attitude even better than in speech, the elder brother understood that Billy was about to tell him an unutterable thing.

By instinct he moved over to his side so that the same view of the room confronted him.

"Out with it, old man," he said, with an effort to be natural. "Tell me what you saw."

Billy shuffled slowly round and the two sat side by side, facing the fog-draped chamber.

"It was like this," he began softly, "only I was standing instead of sitting, looking over to that door as you and I do now. Hyman moved to and fro in the faint glow of the gas logs against the far wall, playing that 'crepuscular' thing in his most inspired sort of way, so that the music seemed to issue from himself rather than from the shining bit of wood under his chin, when—I noticed something coming over me that was"—he hesitated, searching for words—"that wasn't *all* due to the music," he finished abruptly.

"His personality put a bit of hypnotism on you, eh?"

William shrugged his shoulders.

"The air was thickish with fog and the light was dim, cast upwards upon him from the stove," he continued. "I admit all that. But there wasn't light enough to throw shadows, you see, and—"

"Hyman looked queer?" the other helped him quickly.

Billy nodded his head without turning.

"Changed there before my very eyes"—he whispered it—"turned animal—"

"Animal?" John felt his hair rising.

"That's the only way I can put it. His face and hands and body turned otherwise than usual. I lost the sound of his feet. When the bow-hand or the fingers on the strings passed into the light, they were"—he uttered a soft, shuddering little laugh—"furry, oddly divided, the fingers massed together. And he paced stealthily. I thought every instant the fiddle would drop with a crash and he would spring at me across the room."

"My dear chap—"

"He moved with those big, lithe, striding steps one sees"—John held his breath in the little pause, listening keenly—"one sees those big brutes make in the cages when their desire is aflame for food or escape, or—or fierce, passionate desire for anything they want with their whole nature—"

"The big felines!" John whistled softly.

"And every minute getting nearer and nearer to the door, as though he meant to make a sudden rush for it and get out."

"With the violin! Of course you stopped him?"

"In the end. But for a long time, I swear to you, I found it difficult to know what to do, even to move. I couldn't get my voice for words of any kind; it was like a spell."

"It *was* a spell," suggested John firmly.

"Then, as he moved, still playing," continued the other, "he seemed to grow smaller; to shrink down below the line of the gas. I thought I should lose sight of him altogether. I turned the light up suddenly. There he was over by the door—crouching."

"Playing on his knees, you mean? "

William closed his eyes in an effort to visualise it again.

"Crouching," he repeated, at length, "close to the floor. At least, I think so. It all happened so quickly, and I felt so bewildered, it was hard to see straight. But at first I could have sworn he was half his natural size. I called to him, I think I swore at him—I forget exactly, but I know he straightened up at once and stood before me down there in the light"—he pointed across the room to the door—"eyes gleaming, face white as chalk, perspiring like midsummer, and gradually filling out, straightening up, whatever you like to call it, to his natural size and appearance again. It was the most horrid thing I've ever seen."

"As an—animal, you saw him still?"

"No; human again. Only much smaller."

"What did he say?"

Billy reflected a moment.

"Nothing that I can remember," he replied. "You see, it was all over in a few seconds. In the full light, I felt so foolish, and nonplussed at first. To see him normal again baffled me. And, before I could collect myself, he had let himself out into the passage, and I heard the front door slam. A minute later—the same second almost, it seemed—you came in. I only remember grabbing the violin and getting it back safely under the glass case. The strings were still vibrating."

The account was over. John asked no further questions. Nor did he say a single word about the lift, Morgan, or the extinguished light on the landing. There fell a longish silence between the two men; and then, while they helped themselves to a generous supply of whisky-and-soda before going to bed, John looked up and spoke:

"If you agree, Billy," he said quietly, "I think I might write and suggest to Hyman that we shall no longer have need for his services."

And Billy, acquiescing, added a sentence that expressed something of the singular dread lying but half concealed in the atmosphere of the room, if not in their minds as well:

"Putting it, however, in a way that need not offend him."

"Of course. There's no need to be rude, is there?"

Accordingly, next morning the letter was written; and John, saying nothing to his brother, took it round himself by hand to the Hebrew's rooms near Euston. The answer he dreaded was forthcoming:

"Mr. Hyman's still away abroad," he was told. "But we're forwarding letters; yes. Or I can give you 'is address if you'll prefer it." The letter went, therefore, to the number in Konigstrasse, Munich, thus obtained.

Then, on his way back from the insurance company where he went to increase the sum that protected the small Guarnerius from loss by fire, accident, or theft, John Gilmer called at the offices of certain musical agents and ascertained that Silenski, the violinist, was performing at the time in Munich. It was only some days later, though, by diligent enquiry, he made certain that at a concert on a certain date the famous virtuoso had played a Zigeuner Lullaby of his own composition—the very date, it turned out, on which he himself had been to the Masonic rehearsal at Mark Masons' Hall.

John, however, said nothing of these discoveries to his brother William.

IV

It was about a week later when a reply to the letter came from Munich—a letter couched in somewhat offensive terms, though it contained neither words nor phrases that could actually be found fault with. Isidore Hyman was hurt and angry. On his return to London a month or so later, he proposed to call and talk the matter over. The offensive part of the letter lay, perhaps, in his definite assumption that he could persuade the brothers to resume the old relations. John, however, wrote a brief reply to the effect that they had decided to buy no new fiddles; their collection being complete, there would be no occasion for them to invite his services as a performer. This was final. No answer came, and the matter seemed to drop. Never for one moment, though, did it leave the consciousness of John Gilmer. Hyman had said that he would come, and come assuredly he would. He secretly gave Morgan instructions that he and his brother for the future were always "out" when the Hebrew presented himself.

"He must have gone back to Germany, you see, almost at once after his visit here that night," observed William—John, however, making no reply.

One night towards the middle of January the two brothers came home together from a concert in Queen's Hall, and sat up later than usual in their sitting-room discussing over their whisky and tobacco the merits of the pieces and performers. It must have been past one o'clock when they turned out the lights in the passage and retired to bed. The air was still and frosty; moonlight over the roofs—one of those sharp and dry winter nights that now seem to visit London rarely.

"Like the old-fashioned days when we were boys," remarked William, pausing a moment by the passage window and looking out across the miles of silvery, sparkling roofs.

"Yes," added John; "the ponds freezing hard in the fields, rime on the nursery windows, and the sound of a horse's hoofs coming down the road in the distance, eh?" They smiled at the memory, then said good night, and separated. Their rooms were at opposite ends of the corridor; in between were the bathroom, dining-room, and sitting-room. It was a long, straggling flat. Half an hour later both brothers were sound asleep, the flat silent, only a dull murmur rising from the great city outside, and the moon sinking slowly to the level of the chimneys.

Perhaps two hours passed, perhaps three, when John Gilmer, sitting up in bed with a start, wide-awake and frightened, knew that some one was moving about in one of the three rooms that lay between him and his brother. He had absolutely no idea why he should have been frightened, for there was no dream or nightmare-memory that he brought over from unconsciousness, and yet he realised plainly that the fear he felt was by no means a foolish and unreasoning fear. It had a cause and a reason. Also—which made it worse—it was fully warranted. Something in his sleep, forgotten in the instant of waking, had happened that set every nerve in his body on the watch. He was positive only of two things—first, that it was the entrance of this person, moving so quietly there in the flat, that sent the chills down his spine; and, secondly; that this person was *not* his brother William.

John Gilmer was a timid man. The sight of a burglar, his eyes black-masked, suddenly confronting him in the passage, would most likely have deprived him of all power of decision—until the burglar had either shot him or escaped. But on this occasion some instinct told him that it was no burglar, and that the acute distress he experienced was not due to any message of ordinary physical fear. The thing that had gained access to his flat while he slept had first come—he felt sure of it—into his room, and had passed very close to his own bed, before going on. It had then doubtless gone to his brother's room, visiting them both stealthily to make sure they slept. And its mere passage through his room had been enough to wake him and set these drops of cold perspiration upon his skin. For it was—he felt it in every fibre of his body—something hostile.

The thought that it might at that very moment be in the room of his brother, however, brought him to his feet on the cold floor, and set him moving with all the determination he could summon towards the door. He looked cautiously down an utterly dark passage; then crept on tiptoe along it. On the wall were old-fashioned weapons that had belonged to his father; and feeling a curved, sheathless sword that had come from some Turkish campaign of years gone by, his fingers closed tightly round it, and lifted it silently from the three hooks whereon it lay. He passed the doors of the bathroom and dining-room, making instinctively for the big sitting-room where the violins were kept in their glass cases. The cold nipped him. His eyes smarted with the effort to see in the darkness. Outside the closed door he hesitated.

Putting his ear to the crack, he listened. From within came a faint sound of some one moving. The same instant there rose the sharp, delicate "ping" of a violin-string being plucked; and John Gilmer, with nerves that shook like the vibrations of that very string, opened the door wide with a fling and turned on the light at the same moment. The plucked string still echoed faintly in the air.

The sensation that met him on the threshold was the well-known one that things had been going on in the room which his unexpected arrival had that instant put a stop to. A second earlier and he would have discovered it all in the act. The atmosphere still held the feeling of rushing, silent movement with which the things had raced back to their normal, motionless positions. The immobility of the furniture was a mere attitude hurriedly assumed, and the moment his back was turned the whole business, whatever it might be, would begin again. With this presentment of the room, however—a purely imaginative one—came another, swiftly on its heels.

For one of the objects, less swift than the rest, had not quite regained its "attitude" of repose. It still moved. Below the window curtains on the right, not far from the shelf that bore the violins in their glass cases, he made it out, slowly gliding along the floor. Then, even as his eye caught it, it came to rest.

And, while the cold perspiration broke out all over him afresh, he knew that this still moving item was the cause both of his waking and of his terror. This was the disturbance whose presence he had divined in the flat without actual hearing, and whose passage through his room, while he yet slept, had touched every nerve in his body as with ice. Clutching his Turkish sword tightly, he drew back with the utmost caution against the wall and watched, for the singular impression came to him that the movement was not that of a human being crouching, but rather of something that pertained to the animal world. He remembered, flash-like, the movements of reptiles, the stealth of the larger felines, the undulating glide of great snakes. For the moment, however, it did not move, and they faced one another.

The other side of the room was but dimly lighted, and the noise he made clicking up another electric lamp brought the thing flying forward again—towards himself. At such a moment it seemed absurd to think of so small a detail, but he remembered his bare feet, and, genuinely frightened, he leaped upon a chair and swished with his sword through the air about him. From this better point of view, with the increased light to aid him, he then saw two things—first, that the glass case usually covering the Guarnerius violin had been shifted; and, secondly, that the moving object was slowly elongating itself into an up-right position. Semi-erect, yet most oddly, too, like a creature on its hind legs, it was coming swiftly towards him. It was making for the door—and escape.

The confusion of ghostly fear was somehow upon him so that he was too bewildered to see clearly, but he had sufficient self-control, it seemed, to recover a certain power of action; for the moment the advancing figure was near enough for him to strike, that curved scimitar flashed and whirred about him, with such misdirected violence, however, that he not only failed to strike it even once, but at the same time lost his balance and fell forward from the chair whereon he perched—straight into it.

And then came the most curious thing of all, for as he dropped, the figure also dropped, stooped low down, crouched, dwindled amazingly in size, and rushed past him close to the ground like an animal on all fours. John Gilmer screamed, for he could no longer contain himself. Stumbling over the chair as he turned to follow, cutting and slashing wildly with his sword, he saw half-way down the darkened corridor beyond the scuttling outline of, apparently, an enormous—cat!

The door into the outer landing was somehow ajar, and the next second the beast was out, but not before the steel had fallen with a crashing blow upon the front disappearing leg, almost severing it from the body.

It was dreadful. Turning up the lights as he went, he ran after it to the outer landing. But the thing he followed was already well away, and he heard, on the floor below him, the same oddly gliding, slithering, stealthy sound, yet hurrying, that he had heard weeks before when something had passed him in the lift, and Morgan, in his terror, had likewise cried aloud.

For a time he stood there on that dark landing, listening, thinking, trembling; then turned into the flat and shut the door. In the sitting-room he carefully replaced the glass case over the treasured violin, puzzled to the point of foolishness, and strangely routed in his mind. For the violin itself, he saw, had been dragged several inches from its cushioned bed of plush.

Next morning, however, he made no allusion to the occurrence of the night. His brother apparently had not been disturbed.

V

The only thing that called for explanation—an explanation not fully forthcoming—was the curious aspect of Mr. Morgan's countenance. The fact that this individual gave notice to the owners of the building, and at the end of the month left for a new post, was, of course, known to both brothers; whereas the story he told in explanation of his face was known only to the one who questioned him about it—John. And John, for reasons best known to himself, did not pass it on to the other. Also, for reasons best known to himself, he did not cross-question the liftman about those singular marks, or report the matter to the police.

Mr. Morgan's pasty visage was badly scratched, and there were red lines running from the cheek into the neck that had the appearance of having been produced by sharp points viciously applied—claws. He had been disturbed by a noise in the hall, he said, about three in the morning. A scuffle had ensued in the darkness, but the intruder had got clear away. . . .

"A cat, or something of the kind, no doubt," suggested John Gilmer at the end of the brief recital. And Morgan replied in his usual way: "A cat, or something of the kind, Mr. John, no doubt."

All the same, he had not cared to risk a second encounter, but had departed to wear his billycock and uniform in a building less haunted.

Hyman, meanwhile, made no attempt to call and talk over his dismissal. The reason for this was only apparent, however, several months later when, quite by chance, coming along Piccadilly in an omnibus, the brothers found themselves seated opposite to a man with a thick black beard and blue glasses. William Gilmer hastily rang the bell and got out, saying something half intelligible about feeling faint. John followed him.

"Did you see who it was?" he whispered to his brother the moment they were safely on the pavement.

John nodded.

"Hyman, in spectacles. He's grown a beard, too."

"Yes, but didn't you also notice—"

"What?"

"He had an empty sleeve."

"An empty sleeve?"

"Yes," said William; "he's lost an arm."

There was a long pause before John spoke. At the door of their club the elder brother added:

"Poor devil! He'll never again play on"—then, suddenly changing the preposition—"*with* a pedigree violin!"

And that night in the flat, after William had gone to bed, he looked up a curious old volume he had once picked up on a second-hand bookstall, and read therein quaint descriptions of how the "desire-body of a violent man" may assume animal shape, operate on concrete matter even at a distance; and, further, how a wound inflicted thereon can reproduce itself upon its physical counterpart by means of the mysterious so-called phenomenon of "re-percussion."

The Deferred Appointment

The little "Photographic Studio" in the side-street beyond Shepherd's Bush had done no business all day, for the light had been uninviting to even the vainest sitter, and the murky sky that foreboded snow had hung over London without a break since dawn. Pedestrians went hurrying and shivering along the pavements, disappearing into the gloom of countless ugly little houses the moment they passed beyond the glare of the big electric standards that lit the thundering motor-buses in the main street. The first flakes of snow, indeed, were already falling slowly, as though they shrank from settling in the grime. The wind moaned and sang dismally, catching the ears and lifting the shabby coat-tails of Mr. Mortimer Jenkyn, "Photographic Artist," as he stood outside and put the shutters up with his own cold hands in despair of further trade. It was five minutes to six.

With a lingering glance at the enlarged portrait of a fat man in masonic regalia who was the pride and glory of his window-front, he fixed the last hook of the shutter, and turned to go indoors. There was developing and framing to be done upstairs, not very remunerative work, but better, at any rate, than waiting in an empty studio for customers who did not come—wasting the heat of two oil-stoves into the bargain. And it was then, in the act of closing the street-door behind him, that he saw a man standing in the shadows of the narrow passage, staring fixedly into his face.

Mr. Jenkyn admits that he jumped. The man was so very close, yet he had not seen him come in; and in the eyes was such a curiously sad and appealing expression. He had already sent his assistant home, and there was no other occupant of the little two-storey house. The man must have slipped past him from the dark street while his back was turned. Who in the world could he be, and what could he want? Was he beggar, customer, or rogue?

"Good evening," Mr. Jenkyn said, washing his hands, but using only half the oily politeness of tone with which he favoured sitters. He was just going to add "sir," feeling it wiser to be on the safe side, when the stranger shifted his position so that the light fell directly upon his face, and Mr. Jenkyn was aware that he—recognised him. Unless he was greatly mistaken, it was the second-hand bookseller in the main street.

"Ah, it's you, Mr. Wilson!" he stammered, making half a question of it, as though not quite convinced. "Pardon me; I did not quite catch your face—er—I was just shutting up." The other bowed his head in reply. "Won't you come in? Do, please."

Mr. Jenkyn led the way. He wondered what was the matter. The visitor was not among his customers; indeed, he could hardly claim to know him, having only seen him occasionally when calling at the shop for slight purchases of paper and what not. The man, he now realised, looked fearfully ill and wasted, his face pale and haggard. It upset him rather, this sudden, abrupt call. He felt sorry, pained. He felt uneasy.

Into the studio they passed, the visitor going first as though he knew the way, Mr. Jenkyn noticing through his flurry that he was in his "Sunday best." Evidently he had come with a definite purpose. It was odd. Still without speaking, he moved straight across the room and posed himself in front of the dingy background of painted trees, facing the camera. The studio was brightly lit. He seated himself in the faded armchair, crossed his legs, drew up the little round table with the artificial roses upon it in a tall, thin vase, and struck an attitude. He meant to be photographed. His eyes, staring straight into the lens, draped as it was with the black velvet curtain, seemed, however, to take no account of the Photographic Artist. But Mr. Jenkyn, standing still beside the door, felt a cold air playing over his face that was not merely the winter cold from the street. He felt his hair rise. A slight shiver ran down his back. In that pale, drawn face, and in those staring eyes across the room that gazed so fixedly into the draped camera, he read the signature of illness that no longer knows hope. It was Death that he saw.

In a flash the impression came and went—less than a second. The whole business, indeed, had not occupied two minutes. Mr. Jenkyn pulled himself together with a strong effort, dismissed his foolish obsession, and came sharply to practical considerations. "Forgive me," he said, a trifle thickly, confusedly, "but I—er—did not quite realise. You desire to sit for your portrait, of course. I've had such a busy day, and—

'ardly looked for a customer so late." The clock, as he spoke, struck six. But he did not notice the sound. Through his mind ran another reflection: "A man shouldn't 'ave his picture taken when he's ill and next door to dying. Lord! He'll want a lot of touching-up and finishin', too!"

He began discussing the size, price, and length—the usual rigmarole of his "profession," and the other, sitting there, still vouchsafed no comment or reply. He simply made the impression of a man in a great hurry, who wished to finish a disagreeable business without unnecessary talk. Many men, reflected the photographer, were the same; being photographed was worse to them than going to the dentist. Mr. Jenkyn filled the pauses with his professional running talk and patter, while the sitter, fixed and motionless, kept his first position and stared at the camera. The photographer rather prided himself upon his ability to make sitters look bright and pleasant; but this man was hopeless. It was only afterwards Mr. Jenkyn recalled the singular fact that he never once touched him—that, in fact, something connected possibly with his frail appearance of deadly illness had prevented his going close to arrange the details of the hastily assumed pose.

"It must be a flashlight, of course, Mr. Wilson," he said, fidgeting at length with the camera-stand, shifting it slightly nearer; while the other moved his head gently yet impatiently in agreement. Mr. Jenkyn longed to suggest his coming another time when he looked better, to speak with sympathy of his illness; to say something, in fact, that might establish a personal relation. But his tongue in this respect seemed utterly tied. It was just this personal relation which seemed impossible of approach—absolutely and peremptorily impossible. There seemed a barrier between the two. He could only chatter the usual professional commonplaces. To tell the truth, Mr. Jenkyn thinks he felt a little dazed the whole time—not quite his usual self. And, meanwhile, his uneasiness oddly increased. He hurried. He, too, wanted the matter done with and his visitor gone.

At length everything was ready, only the flashlight waiting to be turned on, when, stooping, he covered his head with the velvet cloth and peered through the lens—at no one! When he says "at no one," however, he qualifies it thus: "There was a quick flash of brilliant white light and a face in the middle of it—my gracious heaven! But such a face—'im, yet not 'im—like a sudden rushing glory of a face! It shot off like lightning out of the camera's field of vision. It left me blinded, I assure you, 'alf blinded, and that's a fac'. It was sheer dazzling!"

It seems Mr. Jenkyn remained entangled a moment in the cloth, eyes closed, breath coming in gasps, for when he got clear and straightened up again, staring once more at his customer over the top of the camera, he stared for the second time at—no one. And the cap that he held in his left hand he clapped feverishly over the uncovered lens. Mr. Jenkyn staggered . . . looked hurriedly round the empty studio, then ran, knocking a chair over as he went, into the passage. The hall was deserted, the front door closed. His visitor had disappeared "almost as though he hadn't never been there at all"—thus he described it to himself in a terrified whisper. And again he felt the hair rise on his scalp; his skin crawled a little, and something put back the ice against his spine.

After a moment he returned to the studio and somewhat feverishly examined it. There stood the chair against the dingy background of trees; and there, close beside it, was the round table with the flower vase. Less than a minute ago Mr. Thomas Wilson, looking like death, had been sitting in that very chair. "It wasn't *all* a sort of dreamin', then," ran through his disordered and frightened mind. "I did see something . . . !" He remembered vaguely stories he had read in the newspapers, stories of queer warnings that saved people from disasters, apparitions, faces seen in dream, and so forth. "Maybe," he thought with confusion, "something's going to 'appen to *me!*" Further than that he could not get for some little time, as he stood there staring about him, almost expecting that Mr. Wilson might reappear as strangely as he had disappeared. He went over the whole scene again and again, reconstructing it in minutest detail. And only then, for the first time, did he plainly realise two things which somehow or other he had not thought strange before, but now thought very strange. For his visitor, he remembered, had not uttered a single word, nor had he, Mr. Jenkyn, once touched his person. . . . And, thereupon, without more ado, he put on his hat and coat and went round to the little shop in the main street to buy some ink and stationery which he did not in the least require.

The shop seemed all as usual, though Mr. Wilson himself was not visible behind the littered desk. A tall gentleman was talking in low tones to the partner. Mr. Jenkyn bowed as he went in, then stood examining a case of cheap stylographic pens, waiting for the others to finish. It was impossible to avoid overhearing. Besides, the little shop had distinguished customers sometimes, he had heard, and this evidently was one of them. He only understood part of the conversation, but he remembers all of it. "Singular, yes, these last words of dying men," the tall man was saying, "very singular. You remember Newman's: 'More light,' wasn't it?" The bookseller nodded. "Fine," he said, "fine, that!" There was a pause. Mr. Jenkyn stooped lower over the pens. "This, too, was fine in its way," the gentleman added, straightening up to go; "the old promise, you see, unfulfilled but not forgotten. Cropped up suddenly out of the delirium. Curious, very curious! A good, conscientious man to the last. In all the twenty years I've known him he never broke his word . . ."

A motor-bus drowned a sentence, and then was heard in the bookseller's voice, as he moved towards the door. ". . . You see, he was half-way down the stairs before they found him, always repeating the same thing, 'I promised the wife, I promised the wife.' And it was a job, I'm told, getting him back again . . . he struggled so. That's what finished him so quick, I suppose. Fifteen minutes later he was gone, and his last words were always the same, 'I promised the wife' . . ."

The tall man was gone, and Mr. Jenkyn forgot about his purchases. "When did it 'appen?" he heard himself asking in a voice he hardly recognised as his own. And the reply roared and thundered in his ears as he went down the street a minute later to his house: "Close on six o'clock—a few minutes before the hour. Been ill for weeks, yes. Caught him out of bed with high fever on his way to your place, Mr. Jenkyn, calling at the top of his voice that he'd forgotten to see you about his picture being taken. Yes, very sad, very sad indeed."

But Mr. Jenkyn did not return to his studio. He left the light burning there all night. He went to the little room where he slept out, and next day gave the plate to be developed by his assistant. "Defective plate, sir," was the report in due course; "shows nothing but a flash of light—uncommonly brilliant." "Make a print of it all the same," was the reply. Six months later, when he examined the plate and print, Mr. Jenkyn found that the singular streaks of light had disappeared from both. The uncommon brilliance had faded out completely as though it had never been there.

The Impulse

My dear chap," cried Jones, throwing his hands out in a gesture of distress he thought was quite real, "nothing would give me greater pleasure—if only I could manage it. But the fact is I'm as hard up as yourself!"

The little pale-faced man of uncertain age opposite shrugged his shoulders ever so slightly.

"In a month or so, perhaps—" Jones added, hedging instinctively, "If it's not too late then—I should be delighted—"

The other interrupted quickly, a swift flush emphasising momentarily the pallor of his strained and tired face. Overworked, overweary he looked.

"Oh, thanks, but it's really of no consequence. I felt sure you wouldn't mind my asking, though." And Jones replied heartily that he only wished he were "flush" enough to lend it. They talked weather and politics then—after a pause, finished their drinks, Jones refusing the offer of another, and, presently, the elder man said good-night and left the Club. Jones, with a slight sigh of boredom, as though life went hard with him, passed upstairs to the card-room to find partners for a game.

Jones was not a bad fellow really; he was untaught. Experience had neglected him a little, so that his sympathies knew not those sweet though difficult routes by which interest travels away from self— towards others. He entirely lacked that acuter sense of life which only comes to those who have known genuine want and hardship. A fat income had always tumbled into his bank without effort on his part, the harvest of another's sweat; yet, as with many such, he imagined that he earned his thousand a year, and figured somehow to himself that he deserved it. He was neither evil-liver nor extravagant; he knew not values, that was all—least of all money values; and at the moment when his cousin asked for twenty pounds to help his family to a holiday, he

184

found that debts pressed a bit hard, that he owed still on his motor-car, and that some recent speculations seemed suddenly very doubtful. He was hard up, yes. . . . Perhaps, if the cards were lucky, he might do it after all. But the cards were not lucky. Soon after midnight he took a taxi home to his rooms in St. James's Street. And then it was he found a letter marked "Urgent" placed by his man upon the table by the door so that he could not miss it.

The letter kept him awake most of the night in keen distress—for himself. It was anonymous, signed "Your Well-wisher." It warned him, in words that proved the writer to be well informed, that the speculation in which he, Jones, had plunged so recklessly a week before would mean a total loss unless he instantly took certain steps to retrieve himself. Such steps, moreover, were just possible, provided he acted immediately.

Jones, as he read it, turned pale, if such a thing were possible, all over his body; then he turned hot and cold. He sweated, groaned, sighed, raged; sat down and wrote urgent instructions to solicitors and others; tore the letters up and wrote others. The loss of that money would reduce his income by at least half, alter his whole plan and scale of living, make him poor. He tried to reflect, but the calmness necessary to sound reflection lay far from him. Action was what he needed, but action was just then out of the question, for all the machinery of the world slept—solicitors, company secretaries, influential friends, law-courts. The telephone on the wall merely grinned at him uselessly. Sleep was as vain a remedy as the closed and silent banks. There was absolutely nothing he could do till the morning; and he realised that the letters he wrote were futile even while he wrote them—and tore them up the next minute. Personal interviews the first thing in the morning, energetic talk and action based upon the best possible advice, were the only form relief could take, and these personal interviews he could obtain even before the letters would be delivered, or as soon. For him that money seemed as good as already lost . . . and tossing upon his sleepless bed he faced the change of life the loss involved—bitterly, savagely, with keen pain: the lowered scale of self-indulgence, the clipped selfishness, restricted pleasures, fewer clothes, cheaper rooms, difficult and closely calculated travelling, and all the rest. It bit him hard—this first grinding of the little wheels of possible development in an ordinary selfish, though not evil, heart. . . .

And then it was, as the grey dawn-light crept past the blinds, that the sharpness of his pain and the keen flight of his stirred imagination, projecting itself as by these forced marches into new, untried conditions, produced a slight reaction. The swing of the weary pendulum went a little beyond himself. He fell to wondering vaguely, and with poor insight, yet genuinely, what other men might feel, and how they managed on smaller incomes than his own—smaller than his would be even with the loss. Gingerly, tentatively, he snatched fearful glimpses (fearful, they seemed, to him, at least) into the enclosures of these more restricted lives of others. He knew a mild and weak extension of himself, as it were, that fringed the little maps of lives less happy and indulgent than his own. And the novel sensation brought a faint relief. The small, clogged wheels of sympathy acquired faster movement, almost impetus. It seemed as though the heat and fire of his pain, though selfish pain, generated some new energy that made them turn.

Jones, in all his useless life, had never *thought;* his mind had reflected images perhaps, but had never taken hold of a real idea and followed it by logical process to an end. His mind was heavy and confused, for his nature, as with so many, only moved to calculated action when a strong enough desire instinctively showed the quickest, easiest way by which two and two could be made into four. His reflections upon comparative poverty—the poverty he was convinced now faced him cruelly—were therefore obscure and trivial enough, while wholly honest. Wealth, he divined dimly, was relative, and money represented the value of what is wanted, perhaps of what is needed rather, and usually of what cannot be obtained. Some folk are poor because they cannot afford a second motor-car, or spend more than £100 upon a trip abroad; others because the moors and sea are out of reach; others, again, because they are glad of cast-off clothing and only dare "the gods" one night a week or take the free standing-room at Sunday concerts. . . . He suddenly recalled the story of some little penniless, elderly governess in Switzerland who made her underskirts from the silk of old umbrellas because she liked the frou-frou sound. Again and again this thought for others slipped past the network of his own distress, making his own selfish pain spread wider and therefore less acutely. For even with a mere £500 his life, perhaps, need not be too hard and unhappy. . . . The little wheels moved faster. His pain struck sparks. He saw strange glimpses of a new, far country, a fairer land than he had ever dreamed of, with endless horizons, and flowers, small and very simple, yet so lovely that he would have liked to pick them for their perfume. A sense of joy came for a moment on some soft wind of beauty, fugitive, but sweet. It vanished instantly again, but the vision caught for a moment, too tiny to be measured even by a fraction of a second, had flamed like summer lightning through his heart. It almost seemed as though his grinding selfish pain had burned the dense barriers that hid another world, bringing a light that just flamed above those huge horizons before they died. For they did die—and quickly, yet left behind a touch of singular joy and peace that somehow glowed on through all his subsequent self-pity. . . .

And then, abruptly, with a vividness of detail that shocked him, he saw the Club smoking-room, and the worn face of his cousin close before him—the overworked hack-writer, who had asked a temporary £20, a little sum he would assuredly have paid back before the end of the year, a sum he asked, not for himself, but that he might send his wife and children to the sea.

Impulse, usually deplored as weakness, may prove first seed of habit. Whether Jones afterwards regretted his unconsidered action may be left unrecorded—whether he *would* have regretted it, rather, if the saving of his dreaded loss had not subsequently been effected. As matters stand, he only knew a sense of flattering self-congratulation that he had slipped that letter—the only one he left untorn—into the pillar-box at the corner before the sun rose, and that it contained a pink bit of paper that should bring to another the relief he himself had, for the first time in his life, known imaginatively upon that sleepless bed. Before the day was over the letter reached its destination, and his own affairs had been put right. And two days later, when they met in the Club, and Jones noticed the obvious happiness in the other's eyes and manner, he only answered to his words of thanks:

"I wish I could have given it at once. The fact is I found letters on getting home that night which—er—made it possible, you see . . . !"

But in his heart, as he said it, flamed again quite suddenly the memory of that fair land with endless horizons he had sighted for a second, and the sentence that ran unspoken through his mind was: "By Jove, that's something I must do again. It's worth it . . . !"

The Prayer

There was a glitter in the eye of O'Malley when they met. "I've got it!" he said under his breath, holding out a tiny phial with the ominous red label.

"Got what?" asked Jones, as though he didn't know. Both were medical students; both of a speculative and adventurous turn of mind as well; the Irishman, however, ever the leader in mischief.

"The stuff!" was the reply. "The recipe the Hindu gave me. Your night's free, isn't it? Mine, too. We'll try it. Eh?"

They eyed the little bottle with its shouting label—Poison. Jones took it up, fingered it, drew the cork, sniffed it. "Ugh!" he exclaimed, "it's got an awful smell. Don't think I could swallow that!"

"You don't swallow it," answered O'Malley impatiently. "You sniff it up through the nose—just a drop. It goes down the throat that way."

"Irish swallowing, eh?" laughed Jones uneasily. "It looks wicked to me." He played with the bottle, till the other snatched it away.

"Look out, man! Begad, there's enough there to kill a Cabinet Minister, or a horse. It's the real stuff, I tell you. I told him it was for a psychical experiment. You remember the talk we had that night—"

"Oh, I remember well enough. But it's not worth while in my opinion. It will only make us sick." He said it almost angrily. "Besides, we've got enough hallucinations in life already without inducing others—"

O'Malley glanced up quickly. "Nothing of the sort," he snapped. "You're backing out. You swore you'd try it with me if I got it. The effect—"

"Well, what is the effect?"

The Irishman looked keenly at him. He answered very low. Evidently he said something he really believed. There was gravity, almost solemnity, in his voice and manner.

"Opens the inner sight," he whispered darkly. "Makes you sensitive to thoughts and thought-forces." He paused a moment, staring hard into the other's eyes. "For instance," he added slowly, earnestly, "if somebody's thinking hard about *you,* I should twig it. See? I should *see* the thought-stream getting at you—influencing you—making you do this and that. The air is full of loose and wandering thoughts from other minds. I should see these thoughts hovering about your mind like flies trying to settle. Understand? The cause of a sudden change of mood in a man, an inspiration, a helping thought—a temptation—!"

"Bosh!"

"Are you afraid?"

"No. But it's a poisonous doctrine—that such experiments are worth while even if—if—"

But O'Malley knew his pal. . . . They took the prescribed dose together, laughing, scoffing, hoping. Then they went out to dine. "We must eat very little," explained the Irishman. "The stomach must be comparatively empty. And drink nothing at all."

"What a bore!" said Jones, who was always hungry, and usually thirsty. The prescribed hour passed between the taking of the dose and dinner. They felt nothing more than what Jones described as a "beastly uncomfortable sort of inner heat."

Opposite them, at a table alone, sat a small man, over-dressed according to their standards, and wearing diamond rings. His face had a curious mixture of refinement and wickedness—like a man naturally sensitive whom circumstances, indulgence, or some special temptation had led astray. He did not notice their somewhat close attention because, in his turn, he was closely watching—somebody else. He ate and drank soberly, but drew his dinner out. The "somebody else" he watched, obviously enough, was a country couple, up probably for the festivities due to the presence of a foreign Potentate in town. They were bewildered by big London. They carried hand-bags. From time to time the old man fingered his breast-pocket. He looked about him nervously. The be-ringed man was kind to them, lent them his newspaper, passed the salt, gave them scraps of favoured, kind, and sympathetic conversation. He was very gentle with them.

"Feel anything yet?" asked O'Malley for the tenth time, noticing a curious, passing look on his companion's face. "I don't feel a blessed thing meself! I believe that chemist fooled me, gave me diluted stuff or something—" He stopped short, caught by the other's eye. They had been dining very sparingly, much to the disgust of the waiter, who wanted their table for more remunerative customers.

"I do feel something, yes," was the quiet reply. "Or, rather, I *see* something. It's odd; but I really do—"

"What? Out with it! Tell me!"

"A sort of wavy line of gold," said Jones calmly, "gold and shining. And sometimes it's white. It flits about that fellow's head—that fellow over there." He indicated the man with the rings. "Almost as if—it were trying to get into him—"

"Bosh!" said O'Malley, who was ever the last to believe in the success of his own experiments. "You swear it?"

The other's face convinced him, and a thrill went down his Irish spine.

"Hush," said Jones in a lower tone, "don't shout. I see it right enough. It's like a little wavy stream of light. It's going all about his head and eyes. By gad, it's lovely, though—it's like a flower now, a floating blossom—and now a strip of thin soft gold. It's got him! By George, I tell you, it's got him—!"

"Got him?" echoed the Irishman, genuinely impressed.

"Got *into* him, I meant. It's disappeared—gone clean into his head. Look!"

O'Malley looked hard, but saw nothing. "Me boy!" he cried, "the stuff *was* real. It's working. Watch it. I do believe you've seen a thought—a thought from somebody else—a wandering thought. It's got into his mind. It may affect his actions, movements, decisions. Good Lord! The stuff was not diluted, after all. You've seen a thought-force!" He was tremendously excited. Jones, however, was too absorbed in what he saw to feel excitement. Whether it was due to the drug or not, he knew he saw a real thing.

"Wonder if it's a good one or a bad one!" whispered the Irishman. "Wonder what sort of mind it comes from! Where? How far away?" He wondered a number of things. He chattered below his breath like a dying gramophone. But his companion just sat, staring in rapt silence.

"What are *you* doing here?" said a voice from the table behind them quietly. And O'Malley, turning—Jones was too preoccupied—recognised a plain-clothes detective whom he chanced to know from having been associated with him in a recent poisoning case.

"Nothing particular; just having dinner," he answered. "And you?"

The detective made no secret of his object. "Watching the crowds for their own safety," he said, "that's all. London's full of prey just now—all up from the country, with their bags in their hands, their money in their breast-pockets, and good-natured folks ready every-where to help 'em, and help themselves at the same time." He laughed, nodding towards the man with the rings. "All the crooks are on the job," he added significantly. "There's an old friend of ours. He doesn't know *me*, but I know him right enough. He's usually made up as a cler-gyman; and to-night he's after that old couple at the nex' table, or my name ain't Joe Leary! Don't stare, or he'll notice." He turned his head the other way.

O'Malley, however, was far too interested in hoping for a psychical experience of his own, and in watching the "alleged phenomena" of his companion, to feel much interest in a mere detective's hunt for pickpockets. He turned towards his friend again. "What's up now?" he asked, with his back to the detective; "see anything more?"

"It's perfectly wonderful," whispered Jones softly. "It's out again. I can see the gold thread, all shining and alive, clean down in the man's mind and heart, then out, then in again. It's making him different—I swear it is. By George, it's like a blessed chemical experiment. I can't explain it as I see it, but he's getting sort of bright within—golden like the thread." Jones was wrought up, excited, moved. It was impossible to doubt his earnestness. He described a thing he really saw. O'Malley listened with envy and resentment.

"Blast it all!" he exclaimed. "I see nothing. I didn't take enough!" And he drew the little phial out of his pocket.

"Look! He's *changed!*" exclaimed Jones, interrupting the movement so suddenly that O'Malley dropped the phial and it smashed to atoms against the iron edge of the umbrella-stand. "His thought's altered. He's going out. The gold has spread all through him—!"

"By gosh!" put in O'Malley, so loud that people stared, "it's helped him—made him a better man—turned him from evil. It's that blessed wandering thought! Follow it, follow it! Quick!" And in the general confusion that came with the paying of bills, cleaning up the broken glass, and the rest, the "crook" slipped out into the crowd and was lost, the detective murmured something about "wonder what made him leave so good a trail!" and the Irishman filled in the pauses with hurried, nervous sentences—"Keep your eye on the line of gold! We'll follow it! We'll trace it to its source. Never mind the tip! Hurry, hurry! Don't lose it!"

But Jones was already out, drawn by the power of his obvious conviction. They went into the street. Regardless of the blaze of lights and blur of shadows, the noise of traffic and the rush of the crowds, they followed what Jones described as the "line of wavy gold."

"Don't lose it! For heaven's sake, don't lose it!" O'Malley cried, dodging with difficulty after the disappearing figure. "It's a genuine thought-force from another mind. Follow it! Trace it! We'll track it to its source—some noble thinker somewhere—some gracious woman— some exalted, golden source, at any rate!" He was wholly caught away now by the splendour of the experiment's success. A thought that could make a criminal change his mind must issue from a radiant well of rare and purest thinking. He remembered the Hindu's words: "You will *see* thoughts in colour—bad ones, lurid and streaked—good ones, sweet and shining, like a line of golden light—and if you follow, you may trace them to the mind that sent them out."

"It goes so fast!" Jones called back, "I can hardly keep up. It's in the air, just over the heads of the crowd. It leaves a trail like a meteor. Come on, come on!"

"Take a taxi," shouted the Irishman. "It'll escape us!" They laughed, and panted, dodged past the stream of people, crossed the street.

"Shut up!" answered Jones. "Don't talk so much. I lose it when you talk. It's in my mind. I really see it, but your chatter blurs it. Come on, come on!"

And so they came at last to the region of mean streets, where the traffic was less, the shadows deeper, the lights dim, streets that visiting Emperors do not change. No match-sellers, bootlace venders, or "dreadful shadows proffering toys," blocked their way on the pavement edge, because here were none to buy.

"It's changed from gold to white," Jones whispered breathlessly.

"It shines now—by gad, it shines—like a bit of escaped sunrise. And others have joined it. Can't you see 'em? Why, they're like a network. They're rays—rays of glory. And—hullo! I see where they come from now! It's that house over there. Look, man, look! They're streaming like a river of light out of that high window, that little attic window up there"—he pointed to a dingy house standing black against the murk of the sky. "They come out in a big stream, and then separate in all directions. It's simply wonderful!"

O'Malley gasped and panted. He said nothing. Jones, the phlegmatic, heavy Jones, had got a real vision, whereas he who always imagined "visions" got nothing. He followed the lead. Jones, he understood, was taking his instinct where it led him. He would not interfere.

And the instinct led him to the door. They stopped dead, hesitating for the first time. "Better not go in, you know," said O'Malley, breaking the decision he had just made. Jones looked up at him, slightly bewildered. "I've lost it," he whispered, "lost the line—" A taxi-cab drew up with a rattling thunder just in front and a man got out, came up to the door, and stood beside them. It was the crook.

For a second or two the three men eyed each other. Clearly the new arrival did not recognise them. "Pardon, gentlemen," he said, pushing past to pull the bell. They saw his rings. The taxi boomed away down the little dark street that knew more of coal-carts than of motors. "You're coming in?" the man asked, as the door opened and he stepped inside. O'Malley, usually so quick-witted, found no word to say, but Jones had a question ready. The Irishman never understood how he asked it, and got the answer, too, without giving offence. The instinct guided him in choice of words and tone and gesture—somehow or other. He asked who lived upstairs in the front attic room, and the man, as he quietly closed the door upon them, gave the information—"My father."

And, for the rest, all they ever learnt—by a little diligent enquiry up and down the street, engineered by Jones—was that the old man, bedridden for a dozen years, was never seen, and that an occasional district-visitor, or such like, were his only callers. But they all agreed that he was good. "They do say he lies there praying day and night—jest praying for the world." It was the grocer at the corner who told them that.

The Return

It was curious—that sense of dull uneasiness that came over him so suddenly, so stealthily at first he scarcely noticed it, but with such marked increase after a time that he presently got up and left the theatre. His seat was on the gangway of the dress circle, and he slipped out awkwardly in the middle of what seemed to be the best and jolliest song of the piece. The full house was shaking with laughter; so infectious was the gaiety that even strangers turned to one another as much as to say: "Now, isn't *that* funny—?"

It was curious, too, the way the feeling first got into him at all, here in the full swing of laughter, music, light-heartedness, for it came as a vague suggestion: "I've forgotten something—something I meant to do—something of importance. What in the world was it, now?" And he thought hard, searching vainly through his mind; then dismissed it as the dancing caught his attention. It came back a little later again, during a passage of long-winded talk that bored him and set his attention free once more, but came more strongly this time, insisting on an answer. What could it have been that he had overlooked, left undone, omitted to see to? It went on nibbling at the subconscious part of him. Several times this happened, this dismissal and return, till at last the thing declared itself more plainly—and he felt bothered, troubled, distinctly uneasy.

He was wanted somewhere. There was somewhere else he ought to be. That describes it best, perhaps. Some engagement of moment had entirely slipped his memory—an engagement that involved another person, too. But where, what, with whom? And, at length, this vague uneasiness amounted to positive discomfort, so that he felt unable to enjoy the piece—and left abruptly. Like a man to whom comes suddenly the horrible idea that the match he lit his cigarette with and flung into the waste-paper basket on leaving was not really out—a sort of panic distress—he jumped into a taxi-cab and hurried to his flat: to find everything in order, of course; no smoke, no fire, no smell of burning.

But his evening was spoilt. He sat smoking in his armchair at home—this business man of forty, practical in mind, of character some called stolid—cursing himself for an imaginative fool. It was now too late to go back to the theatre; the club bored him; he spent an hour with the evening papers, dipping into books, sipping a long cool drink; doing odds and ends about the flat; "I'll go to bed early for a change," he laughed, but really all the time fighting—yes, deliberately fighting—this strange attack of uneasiness that so insidiously grew upwards, outwards from the buried depths of him that sought so strenuously to deny it. It never occurred to him that he was ill. He was *not* ill. His health was thunderingly good. He was robust as a coal-heaver.

The flat was roomy, high up on the top floor, yet in a busy part of town, so that the roar of traffic mounted round it like a sea. Through the open windows came the fresh night air of June. He had never noticed before how sweet the London night air could be, and that not all the smoke and dust could smother a certain touch of wild fragrance that tinctured it with perfume—yes, almost perfume—as of the country. He swallowed a draught of it as he stood there, staring out across the tangled world of roofs and chimney-pots. He saw the procession of the clouds; he saw the stars; he saw the moonlight falling in a shower of silver spears upon the slates and wires and steeples. And something in him quickened—something that had never stirred before.

He turned with a horrid start, for the uneasiness had of a sudden leaped within him like an animal. There was some one in the flat.

Instantly, with action, even this slight action, the fancy vanished; but, all the same, he switched on the electric lights and made a search. For it seemed to him that some one had crept up close behind him while he stood there watching the Night—some one, moreover, whose silent presence fingered with unerring touch both this new thing that had quickened in his heart *and* that sense of original deep uneasiness. He was amazed at himself, angry; indignant that he could be thus foolishly upset over nothing, yet at the same time profoundly distressed at this vehement growth of a new thing in his well-ordered personality.

Growth? He dismissed the word the moment it occurred to him. But it had occurred to him. It stayed. While he searched the empty flat, the long passages, the gloomy bedroom at the end, the little hall where he kept his overcoats and golf sticks—it stayed. Growth! It was oddly disquieting. Growth, to him, involved—though he neither acknowledged nor recognised the truth perhaps—some kind of undesirable changeableness, instability, unbalance.

Yet, singular as it all was, he realised that the uneasiness and the sudden appreciation of Beauty that was so new to him had both entered by the same door into his being. When he came back to the front room he noticed that he was perspiring. There were little drops of moisture on his forehead. And down his spine ran positively chills— little, faint quivers of cold. He was shivering.

He lit his big meerschaum pipe, and left the lights all burning. The feeling that there was something he had overlooked, forgotten, left undone, had vanished. Whatever the original cause of this absurd uneasiness might be—he called it absurd on purpose, because he now realised in the depths of him that it was really more vital than he cared about—it was much nearer to discovery than before. It dodged about just below the threshold of discovery. It was as close as that. Any moment he would know what it was: he would remember. Yes, he would *remember*. Meanwhile, he was in the right place. No desire to go elsewhere afflicted him, as in the theatre. Here was the place, here in the flat.

And then it was, with a kind of sudden burst and rush—it seemed to him the only way to phrase it—memory gave up her dead.

At first he only caught her peeping round the corner at him, drawing aside a corner of an enormous curtain, as it were; striving for more complete entrance as though the mass of it were difficult to move. But he understood; he knew; he recognised. It was enough for that. An entrance into his being—heart, mind, soul—was being attempted, and the entrance, because of his stolid temperament, was difficult of accomplishment. There was effort, strain. Something in him had first to be opened up, widened, made soft and ready as by an operation, before full entrance could be effected. This much he grasped, though for the life of him he could not have put it into words. Also, he knew *who* it was that sought an entrance. Deliberately from himself he withheld the name. But he knew, as surely as though Straughan stood in the room and faced him with a knife, saying, "Let me in, let me in. I wish you to know I'm here. I'm clearing a way . . . ! You recall our promise . . . ?"

He rose from his chair and went to the open window again, the strange fear slowly passing. The cool air fanned his cheeks. Beauty, till now, had scarcely ever brushed the surface of his soul. He had never troubled his head about it. It passed him by, indifferent; and he had ever loathed the mouthy prating of it on others' lips. He was practical; beauty was for dreamers, for women, for men who had means and leisure. He had not exactly scorned it; rather it had never touched his life, to sweeten, cheer, uplift. Artists for him were like monks—another sex almost, useless beings who never helped the world go round. He was for action always, work, activity, achievement—as he saw them. He remembered Straughan vaguely—Straughan, the ever impecunious, friend of his youth, always talking of colour, sound—mysterious, ineffective things. He even forgot what they had quarrelled about, if they *had* quarrelled at all even; or why they had gone apart all these years ago. And, certainly, he had forgotten any promise. Memory, as yet, only peeped round the corner of that huge curtain at him, tentatively, suggestively, yet—he was obliged to admit it—somewhat winningly. He was conscious of this gentle, sweet seductiveness that now replaced his fear.

And, as he stood now at the open window, peering over huge London, Beauty came close and smote him between the eyes. She came blindingly, with her train of stars and clouds and perfumes. Night, mysterious, myriad-eyed, and flaming across her sea of haunted shadows, invaded his heart and shook him with her immemorial wonder and delight. He found no words, of course, to clothe the new, unwonted sensations. He only knew that all his former dread, uneasiness, distress, and with them this idea of "growth" that had seemed so repugnant to him, were merged, swept up, and gathered magnificently home into a wave of Beauty that enveloped him. "See it . . . and understand," ran a secret inner whisper across his mind. He saw. He understood. . . .

He went back and turned the lights out. Then he took his place again at that open window, drinking in the night. He saw a new world; a species of intoxication held him. He sighed . . . as his thoughts blundered for expression among words and sentences that knew him not.

But the delight was there, the wonder, the mystery. He watched, with heart alternately tightening and expanding, the transfiguring play of moon and shadow over the sea of buildings. He saw the dance of the hurrying clouds, the open patches into outer space, the veiling and unveiling of that ancient silvery face; and he caught strange whispers of the hierophantic, sacerdotal Power that has echoed down the world since Time began and dropped strange magic phrases into every poet's heart since first "God dawned on Chaos"—the Beauty of the Night. . . .

A long time passed—it may have been one hour, it may have been three—when at length he turned away and went slowly to his bedroom. A deep peace lay over him. Something quite new and blessed had crept into his life and thought. He could not quite understand it all. He only knew that it uplifted. There was no longer the least sign of affliction or distress. Even the inevitable reaction that, of course, set in could not destroy that.

And then, as he lay in bed, nearing the borderland of sleep, suddenly and without any obvious suggestion to bring it, he remembered another thing. He remembered the promise. Memory got past the big curtain for an instant, and showed her face. She looked into his eyes. It must have been a dozen years ago when Straughan and he had made that foolish, solemn promise that whoever died first should show himself, if possible, to the other.

He had utterly forgotten it—till now. But Straughan had not forgotten it. The letter came three weeks later, from India. That very evening Straughan had died—at nine o'clock. And he had come back—in the Beauty that he loved.

Two in One

Some idle talker, playing with half-truths, had once told him that he was too self-centred to fall into love—out of himself; he was unwilling to lose himself in another; and that was the reason he had never married. But Le Maitre was not really more of an egoist than is necessary to make a useful man. A too selfless person is ever ineffective. The suggestion, nevertheless, had remained to distress, for he was no great philosopher—merely a writer of successful tales—tales of wild Nature chiefly; the "human interest" (a publisher's term) was weak; the great divine enigma of an undeveloped soul—certainly of a lover's or a woman's soul—had never claimed his attention enough, perhaps. He was somewhat too much detached from human life. Nature had laid so powerful a spell upon his heart. . . .

"I hope she won't be late," ran the practical thought across his mind as he waited that early Sunday morning in the Great Central Station and reflected that it was the cleanest, brightest, and most airy terminus of all London. He had promised her the whole day out—a promise somewhat long neglected. He was not conscious of doing an unselfish act, yet on the whole, probably, he would rather—or just as soon—have been alone.

The air was fragrant, and the sunshine blazed in soft white patches on the line. The maddening loveliness of an exceptional spring danced everywhere into his heart. Yes, he rather wished he were going off into the fields and woods alone, instead of with her. Only—she was really a dear person, more, far more now, than secretary and typist; more, even, than the devoted girl who had nursed him through that illness. A friend she was; the years of their working together had made her that; and she was wise and gentle. Oh, yes; it would be delightful to have her with him. How she would enjoy the long sunny day!

Then he saw her coming towards him through the station. In a patch of sunshine she came, as though the light produced her—came suddenly from the middle of a group of men in flannels carrying golf-sticks. And he smiled his welcome a little paternally, trying to kill the selfish thought that he would rather have been alone. Soft things fluttered about her. The big hat was becoming. She was dressed in brown, he believed.

He bought a Sunday paper. "I must buy one too," she laughed. She chose one with pictures, chose it at random rather. He had never heard its name even. And in a first-class carriage alone—he meant to do it really well—they raced through a world of sunshine and brilliant fields to Amersham. She was very happy. She tried every seat in turn; the blazing sheets of yellow—such a spring for buttercups there had never been—drew her from side to side. She put her head out, and nearly lost her big hat, and that soft fluttering thing she wore streamed behind her like the colour of escaping flowers. She opened both windows. The very carriage held the perfume of May that floated over the whole country-side.

He was very nice to her, but read his paper—though always ready with a smile and answer when she asked for them. She teased and laughed and chattered. The luncheon packages engaged her serious attention. Never for a moment was she still, trying every corner in turn, putting her feet up, and bouncing to enjoy the softness of the first-class cushions. "You'll be sitting in the rack next," he suggested. But her head was out of the window again and she did not hear him. She was radiant as a child. His paper interested him—book reviews or something. "I've asked you that three times, you know, already," he heard her laughing opposite. And with a touch of shame he tossed the paper through the window. "There! I'd quite forgotten her again!" he thought, with a touch of shame. "I must pull myself together." For it was true. He had for the moment—more than once—forgotten her existence, just as though he really *were* alone.

Together they strolled down through the beech wood towards Amersham, he for ever dropping the luncheon packages, which she picked up again and tried to stuff into his pockets. For she refused to carry anything at all. "It's *my* day out, not yours, remember! *I* do no work to-day!" And he caught her happiness, pausing to watch her while she picked flowers and leaves and all the rest, and disentangling without the least impatience that soft fluttering thing she wore when it caught in thorns, and even talking with her about this wild spring glory as though she were just the companion that he needed out of all the world. He no longer felt quite so conscious of her objective presence as at first. In the train, for instance, he had felt so vividly aware that she was there. Alternately he had forgotten and remembered her presence. Now it was better. They were more together, as it were. "I wish I were alone," he thought once more as the beauty of the spring called to him tumultuously and he longed to lie and dream it all, unhampered by another's presence. Then, even while thinking it, he realised that he was——alone. It was curious.

This happened even in their first wood when they went downhill into Amersham. As they left it and passed again into the open it came. And on its heels, as he watched her moving here and there, light-footed as a child or nymph, there came this other instinctive thought—"I wish I were ten years younger than I am!"—the first time in all his life, probably, that such a thought had ever bothered him. Apparently he said it aloud, laughingly, as he watched her dancing movements. For she turned and ran up to his side quickly, her little face quite grave beneath the big hat's rim. "You *are!*" That answer struck him as rather wonderful. Who was she after all . . . ?

And in Amersham they hired from the Griffin a rickety old cart, drawn by a still more rickety horse, to drive them to Penn's Woods. She, with her own money, bought stone-bottle ginger-beer—two bottles. It made her day complete to have those bottles, though unless they had driven she would have done without them. The street was deserted, drenched in blazing sunshine. Rooks were cawing in the elms behind the church. Not a soul was about as they crawled away from the houses and passed upwards between hedges smothered in cow-parsley over the hill. She had kept her picture-paper. It lay on her lap all the way. She never opened it or turned a single page; but she held it in her lap. They drove in silence. The old man on the box was like a faded, weather-beaten farmer dressed in somebody else's cast-off Sunday coat. He flicked the horse with a tattered whip. Sometimes he grunted. Plover rose from the fields, cuckoos called, butterflies danced sideways past the carriage, eyeing them . . . and, as they passed through Penn Street, Le Maitre started suddenly and said something. For, again, he had quite forgotten she was there. "What a selfish beast I am! Why can't I forget myself and my own feelings, and look after her and make her feel amused and happy? It's *her* day out, not mine!" This, some-how, was the way he put it to himself, just as any ordinary man would have put it. But, when he turned to look at her, he received a shock. Here was something new and unexpected. With a thud it dropped down into his mind—crash!

For at the sound of his voice she looked up confused and startled into his face. She had forgotten *him!* For the first time in all the years together, years of work, of semi-official attention to his least desire, yet of personal devotion as well, because she respected him and thought him wonderful—she had forgotten *he* was there. She had forgotten his existence beside her as a separate person. She, too, had been—alone.

It was here, perhaps, he first realised this singular thing that set this day apart from every other day that he had ever known. In reality, of course, it had come far sooner—begun with the exquisite spring dawn before either of them was awake, had tentatively fluttered about his soul even while he stood waiting for her in the station, come softly nearer all the way in the train, dropped threads of its golden web about him, especially in that first beech wood, then moved with its swifter yet unhurried rush—until, here, now, in this startling moment, he realised it fully. Thus steal those changes o'er the sky, perhaps, that the day it-self knows at sunrise, but that unobservant folk do not notice till the sun bursts out with fuller explanation, and they say, "The weather's changed; how delightful! how unexpected!" Le Maitre had never been observant very—of people.

And then in this deep, lonely valley, too full of sunshine to hold anything else, it seemed, they stopped where the beech woods trooped to the edge of the white road. No wind was here; it was still and silent; the leaves glittered, motionless. They entered the thick trees together, she carrying the ginger-beer bottles *and* that picture-paper. He noticed that: the way she held it, almost clutched it, still unopened. Her face, he saw, was pale. Or was it merely the contrast of the shade? The trees were very big and wonderful. No birds sang, the network of dazzling sunshine-patches in the gloom bewildered a little.

At first they did not talk at all, and then in hushed voices. But it was only when they were some way into the wood, and she had put down the bottles—though not the paper—to pick a flower or spray of leaves, that he traced the singular secret thrill to its source and understood why he had felt—no, not uneasy, but so strangely moved. For he had asked the sleepy driver of the way, and how they might best reach Beaconsfield across these Penn Woods, and the old man's mumbled answer took no note of—her:

"It's a bit rough, maybe, on t'other side, stony like and steep, but that ain't nothing for a gentleman—when he's alone . . . !"

The words disturbed him with a sense of darkness, yet of wonder. As though the old man had not noticed her; almost as though he had seen only one person—himself.

They lunched among heather and bracken just beside a pool of sunshine. In front lay a copse of pines, with little beeches in between. The roof was thick just there, the stillness haunting. All the countryside, it seemed, this Sunday noon, had gone to sleep, he and she alone left out of the deep, soft dream. He watched those pines, mothering the slim young beeches, the brilliant fresh green of whose lower branches, he thought, were like little platforms of level sunlight amid the general gloom—patches that had left the ground to escape by the upper air and had then been caught.

"Look," he heard, "they make one think of laughter crept in unawares among a lot of solemn monks—or of children lost among grave elder beings whose ways are dull and sombre!" It was his own thought continued . . . yet it was she, lying there beside him, who said it. . . .

And all that wonderful afternoon she had this curious way of picking the thoughts out of his mind and putting them into words for him. "Look," she said again later, "you can always tell whether the wind loves a tree or not by the way it blows the branches. If it loves them, it tries to draw them out to go away with it. The others it merely shakes carelessly as it passes!" It was the very thought in his own mind, too. Indeed, he had been on the point of saying it, but had desisted, feeling she would not understand—with the half wish—though far less strong than before—that he were alone to enjoy it all in his own indulgent way. Then, even more swiftly, came that other strange sensation that he *was* alone all the time; more—that he was for the first time in his life most wonderfully complete and happy, all sense of isolation gone.

He turned quickly the instant she had said it. But not quickly enough. By the look in her great grey eyes, by the expression on the face where the discarded hat no longer hid it, he read the same amazing enigma he had half divined before. She, too, was—alone. She had forgotten him again—forgotten his presence—radiant and happy without him, enjoying herself in her own way. She had merely uttered her delightful thought aloud, as if speaking to herself!

How the afternoon, with its long sunny hours, passed so quickly away, he never understood, nor how they made their way eventually to Beaconsfield through other woods and over other meadows. He remembers only that the whole time he kept forgetting that she was with him, and then suddenly remembering it again. And once on the grass, when they rested to drink the cold tea from his rather musty flask, he lit his pipe, and after a bit he—dozed. He actually slept; for ten minutes at her side, yes, he slept. He heard her laughing at him, but the laughter was faint and very far away; it might just as well have been the wind in the cow-parsley that said, "If you sleep, I shall change you— change you while you sleep!" And for some minutes after he woke again, it hardly seemed queer to him that he did not see her, for when he noticed her coming towards him from the hedgerow, her arms full of flowers and things, he only thought, "Oh, there she is"—as though her absence, or his own absence in sleep, were not quite the common absences of the world.

And he remembered that on the walk to the village her shoe hurt her, and he offered to carry her, and that then she took her shoe off and ran along the grass beside the lane the whole way. But it was at the inn where they had their supper that the oddest thing of all occurred, for the deaf and rather stupid servant girl would insist on laying the table on the lawn for—one.

"Oh, expectin' some one, are yer?" she said at last. "Is that it?" and so brought plates and knives for two. The girl never once looked at his companion—almost as though she did not see her and seemed unaware of her presence. Le Maitre began to feel that he was dreaming. This was a dream-country, where the people had curious sight. He remembered the driver. . . .

In the dusk they made their way to the station. They spoke no word. He kept losing sight of her. Once or twice he forgot who he was. But the whole amazing thing blazed into him most strongly, showing how it had seized upon his mind, when he stood before the ticket-window and hesitated—for a second—how many tickets he should buy. He stammered at length for two first-class, but he was absurdly flustered for a second. It had actually occurred to him that they needed only one ticket. . . .

And suddenly in the train he understood—and his heart came up in his throat. They were alone. He turned to her where she lay in the corner, feet up, weary, crumpled among the leaves and flowers she had gathered. Like a hedgerow flower she looked, tired by the sunshine and the wind. In one hand was the picture-paper, still unopened and unread, symbol of everyday reality. She was dozing certainly, if not actually asleep. So he woke her with a touch, calling her name aloud.

There were no words at first. He looked at her, coming up very close to do so, and she looked back at him—straight into his eyes— just as she did at home when they were working and he was explaining something important. And then her own eyes dropped, and a deep blush spread over all her face.

"I wasn't asleep—really," she said, as he took her at last into his arms; "I was wondering—when—you'd find out—"

"Come to myself, you mean?" he asked tremblingly.

"Well," she hesitated, as soon as she got breath, "that I *am* yourself—and that you are me. Of course, we're really only one. I knew it years—oh, years and years ago . . ."

Accessory Before the Fact

At the moorland cross-roads Martin stood examining the sign-post for several minutes in some bewilderment. The names on the four arms were not what he expected, distances were not given, and his map, he concluded with impatience, must be hopelessly out of date. Spreading it against the post, he stooped to study it more closely. The wind blew the corners flapping against his face. The small print was almost indecipherable in the fading light. It appeared, how-ever—as well as he could make out—that two miles back he must have taken the wrong turning.

He remembered that turning. The path had looked inviting; he had hesitated a moment, then followed it, caught by the usual lure of walk-ers that it "might prove a short cut." The short-cut snare is old as hu-man nature. For some minutes he studied the sign-post and the map alternately. Dusk was falling, and his knapsack had grown heavy. He could not make the two guides tally, however, and a feeling of uncer-tainty crept over his mind. He felt oddly baffled, frustrated. His thought grew thick. Decision was most difficult. "I'm muddled," he thought; "I must be tired," as at length he chose the most likely arm. "Sooner or lat-er it will bring me to an inn, though not the one I intended." He accept-ed his walker's luck, and started briskly. The arm read, "Over Litacy Hill" in small, fine letters that danced and shifted every time he looked at them; but the name was not discoverable on the map. It was, how-ever, inviting like the short cut. A similar impulse again directed his choice. Only this time it seemed more insistent, almost urgent.

And he became aware, then, of the exceeding loneliness of the country about him. The road for a hundred yards went straight, then curved like a white river running into space; the deep blue-green of heather lined the banks, spreading upwards through the twilight; and occasional small pines stood solitary here and there, all unexplained.

The curious adjective, having made its appearance, haunted him. So many things that afternoon were similarly—unexplained: the short cut, the darkened map, the names on the sign-post, his own erratic impulses, and the growing strange confusion that crept upon his spirit. The entire country-side needed explanation, though perhaps "interpretation" was the truer word. Those little lonely trees had made him see it. Why had he lost his way so easily? Why did he suffer vague impressions to influence his direction? Why was he here—exactly *here?* And why did he go now "over Litacy Hill"?

Then, by a green field that shone like a thought of daylight amid the darkness of the moor, he saw a figure lying in the grass. It was a blot upon the landscape, a mere huddled patch of dirty rags, yet with a certain horrid picturesqueness too; and his mind—though his German was of the schoolroom order—at once picked out the German equivalents as against the English. *Lump* and *Lumpen* flashed across his brain most oddly. They seemed in that moment right, and so expressive, almost like onomatopœic words, if that were possible of sight. Neither "rags" nor "rascal" would have fitted what he saw. The adequate description was in German.

Here was a clue tossed up by the part of him that did not reason. But it seems he missed it. And the next minute the tramp rose to a sitting posture and asked the time of evening. In German he asked it. And Martin, answering without a second's hesitation, gave it, also in German, *"halb sieben"*—half-past six. The instinctive guess was accurate. A glance at his watch when he looked a moment later proved it. He heard the man say, with the covert insolence of tramps, "T'ank you; much opliged." For Martin had not shown his watch—another intuition subconsciously obeyed.

He quickened his pace along that lonely road, a curious jumble of thoughts and feelings surging through him. He had somehow known the question would come, and come in German. Yet it flustered and dismayed him. Another thing had also flustered and dismayed him. He had expected it in the same queer fashion: it was right. For when the ragged brown thing rose to ask the question, a part of it remained lying on the grass—another brown, dirty thing. There were two tramps. And he saw both faces clearly. Behind the untidy beards, and below the old slouch hats, he caught the look of unpleasant, clever faces that watched him closely while he passed. The eyes followed him. For a second he looked straight into those eyes, so that he could not fail to know them. And he understood, quite horridly, that both faces were too sleek, refined, and cunning for those of ordinary tramps. The men were not really tramps at all. They were disguised.

"How covertly they watched me!" was his thought, as he hurried along the darkening road, aware in dead earnestness now of the loneliness and desolation of the moorland all about him.

Uneasy and distressed, he increased his pace. Midway in thinking what an unnecessarily clanking noise his nailed boots made upon the hard white road, there came upon him with a rush together the company of these things that haunted him as "unexplained." They brought a single definite message: That all this business was not really meant for him at all, and hence his confusion and bewilderment; that he had intruded into some one else's scenery, and was trespassing upon another's map of life. By some wrong *inner* turning he had interpolated his person into a group of foreign forces which operated in the little world of some one else. Unwittingly, somewhere, he had crossed the threshold, and now was fairly in—a trespasser, an eavesdropper, a Peeping Tom. He was listening, peeping; overhearing things he had no right to know, because they were intended for another. Like a ship at sea he was intercepting wireless messages he could not properly interpret, because his Receiver was not accurately tuned to their reception. And more—these messages were warnings!

Then fear dropped upon him like the night. He was caught in a net of delicate, deep forces he could not manage, knowing neither their origin nor purpose. He had walked into some huge psychic trap elaborately planned and baited, yet calculated for another than himself. Something had lured him in, something in the landscape, the time of day, his mood. Owing to some undiscovered weakness in himself he had been easily caught. His fear slipped easily into terror.

What happened next happened with such speed and concentration that it all seemed crammed into a moment. At once and in a heap it happened. It was quite inevitable. Down the white road to meet him a man came swaying from side to side in drunkenness quite obviously feigned—a tramp; and while Martin made room for him to pass, the lurch changed in a second to attack, and the fellow was upon him. The blow was sudden and terrific, yet even while it fell Martin was aware that behind him rushed a second man, who caught his legs from under him and bore him with a thud and crash to the ground. Blows rained then; he saw a gleam of something shining; a sudden deadly nausea plunged him into utter weakness where resistance was impossible. Something of fire entered his throat, and from his mouth poured a thick sweet thing that choked him. The world sank far away into darkness. . . . Yet through all the horror and confusion ran the trail of two clear thoughts: he realised that the first tramp had sneaked at a fast double through the heather and so come down to meet him; and that something heavy was torn from fastenings that clipped it tight and close beneath his clothes against his body. . . .

Abruptly then the darkness lifted, passed utterly away. He found himself peering into the map against the sign-post. The wind was flapping the corners against his cheek, and he was poring over names that now he saw quite clear. Upon the arms of the sign-post above were those he had expected to find, and the map recorded them quite faithfully. All was accurate again and as it should be. He read the name of the village he had meant to make—it was plainly visible in the dusk, two miles the distance given. Bewildered, shaken, unable to think of anything, he stuffed the map into his pocket unfolded, and hurried forward like a man who has just wakened from an awful dream that had compressed into a single second all the detailed misery of some prolonged, oppressive nightmare.

He broke into a steady trot that soon became a run; the perspiration poured from him; his legs felt weak, and his breath was difficult to manage. He was only conscious of the overpowering desire to get away as fast as possible from the sign-post at the cross-roads where the dreadful vision had flashed upon him. For Martin, accountant on a holiday, had never dreamed of any world of psychic possibilities. The entire thing was torture. It was worse than a "cooked" balance of the books that some conspiracy of clerks and directors proved at his innocent door. He raced as though the country-side ran crying at his heels. And always still ran with him the incredible conviction that none of this was really meant for himself at all. He had overheard the secrets of another. He had taken the warning for another into himself, and so altered its direction. He had thereby prevented its right delivery. It all shocked him beyond words. It dislocated the machinery of his just and accurate soul. The warning was intended for another, who could not—would not—now receive it.

The physical exertion, however, brought at length a more comfortable reaction and some measure of composure. With the lights in sight, he slowed down and entered the village at a reasonable pace. The inn was reached, a bedroom inspected and engaged, and supper ordered with the solid comfort of a large Bass to satisfy an unholy thirst and complete the restoration of balance. The unusual sensations largely passed away, and the odd feeling that anything in his simple, wholesome world required explanation was no longer present. Still with a vague uneasiness about him, though actual fear quite gone, he went into the bar to smoke an after-supper pipe and chat with the natives, as his pleasure was upon a holiday, and so saw two men leaning upon the counter at the far end with their backs towards him. He saw their faces instantly in the glass, and the pipe nearly slipped from between his teeth. Clean-shaven, sleek, clever faces—and he caught a word or two as they talked over their drinks— German words. Well dressed they were, both men, with nothing about them calling for particular attention; they might have been two tourists holiday-making like himself in tweeds and walking-boots. And they presently paid for their drinks and went out. He never saw them face to face at all; but the sweat broke out afresh all over him, a feverish rush of heat and ice together ran about his body; beyond question he recognised the two tramps, this time not disguised—*not yet* disguised.

He remained in his corner without moving, puffing violently at an extinguished pipe, gripped helplessly by the return of that first vile terror. It came again to him with an absolute clarity of certainty that it was not with himself they had to do, these men, and, further, that he had no right in the world to interfere. He had no *locus standi* at all; it would be immoral . . . even if the opportunity came. And the opportunity, he felt, would come. He had been an eavesdropper, and had come upon private information of a secret kind that he had no right to make use of, even that good might come—even to save life. He sat on in his corner, terrified and silent, waiting for the thing that should happen next.

But night came without explanation. Nothing happened. He slept soundly. There was no other guest at the inn but an elderly man, apparently a tourist like himself. He wore gold-rimmed glasses, and in the morning Martin overheard him asking the landlord what direction he should take for Litacy Hill. His teeth began then to chatter and a weakness came into his knees. "You turn to the left at the cross-roads," Martin broke in before the landlord could reply; "you'll see the sign-post about two miles from here, and after that it's a matter of four miles more." How in the world did he know, flashed horribly through him. "I'm going that way myself," he was saying next; "I'll go with you for a bit—if you don't mind!" The words came out impulsively and ill-considered; of their own accord they came. For his own direction was exactly opposite. *He did not want the man to go alone.* The stranger, however, easily evaded his offer of companionship. He thanked him with the remark that he was starting later in the day. . . . They were standing, all three, beside the horse-trough in front of the inn, when at that very moment a tramp, slouching along the road, looked up and asked the time of day. And it was the man with the gold-rimmed glasses who told him.

"T'ank you; much opliged," the tramp replied, passing on with his slow, slouching gait, while the landlord, a talkative fellow, proceeded to remark upon the number of Germans that lived in England and were ready to swell the Teutonic invasion which *he*, for his part, deemed imminent.

But Martin heard it not. Before he had gone a mile upon his way he went into the woods to fight his conscience all alone. His feebleness, his cowardice, were surely criminal. Real anguish tortured him. A dozen times he decided to go back upon his steps, and a dozen times the singular authority that whispered he had no right to interfere prevented him. How could he act upon knowledge gained by eavesdropping? How interfere in the private business of another's hidden life merely because he had overheard, as at the telephone, its secret dangers? Some inner confusion prevented straight thinking altogether. The stranger would merely think him mad. He had no "fact" to go upon. . . . He smothered a hundred impulses . . . and finally went on his way with a shaking, troubled heart.

The last two days of his holiday were ruined by doubts and questions and alarms—all justified later when he read of the murder of a tourist upon Litacy Hill. The man wore gold-rimmed glasses, and carried in a belt about his person a large sum of money. His throat was cut. And the police were hard upon the trail of a mysterious pair of tramps, said to be—Germans.

Clairvoyance

In the darkest corner, where the firelight could not reach him, he sat listening to the stories. His young hostess occupied the corner on the other side; she was also screened by shadows; and between them stretched the horseshoe of eager, frightened faces that seemed all eyes. Behind yawned the blackness of the big room, running as it were without a break into the night.

Some one crossed on tiptoe and drew a blind up with a rattle, and at the sound all started: through the window, opened at the top, came a rustle of the poplar leaves that stirred like footsteps in the wind. "There's a strange man walking past the shrubberies," whispered a nervous girl; "I saw him crouch and hide. I saw his eyes!" "Nonsense!" came sharply from a male member of the group; "it's far too dark to see. You heard the wind." For mist had risen from the river just below the lawn, pressing close against the windows of the old house like a soft grey hand, and through it the stir of leaves was faintly audible. . . . Then, while several called for lights, others remembered that the hop-pickers were still about in the lanes, and the tramps this autumn over-bold and insolent. All, perhaps, wished secretly for the sun. Only the elderly man in the corner sat quiet and unmoved, contributing nothing. He had told no fearsome story. He had evaded, indeed, many openings expressly made for him, though fully aware that to his well-known interest in psychical things was partly due his presence in the week-end party. "I never have experiences—that way," he said shortly when some one asked him point blank for a tale; "I have no unusual powers." There was perhaps the merest hint of contempt in his tone, but the hostess from her darkened corner quickly and tactfully covered his retreat. And he wondered. For he knew why she invited him. The haunted room, he was well aware, had been specially allotted to him.

And then, most opportunely, the door opened noisily and the host came in. He sniffed at the darkness, rang at once for lamps, puffed at his big curved pipe, and generally, by his mere presence, made the group feel rather foolish. Light streamed past him from the corridor. His white hair shone like silver. And with him came the atmosphere of common sense, of shooting, agriculture, motors, and the rest. Age entered at that door. And his young wife sprang up instantly to greet him, as though his disapproval of this kind of entertainment might need humouring.

It may have been the light—that witchery of half-lights from the fire and the corridor, or it may have been the abrupt entrance of the Practical upon the soft Imaginative that traced the outline with such pitiless, sharp conviction. At any rate, the contrast—for those who had this inner clairvoyant sight all had been prating of so glibly!—was unmistakably revealed. It was poignantly dramatic, pain somewhere in it—naked pain. For, as she paused a moment there beside him in the light, this childless wife of three years' standing, picture of youth and beauty, there stood upon the threshold of that room the presence of a true ghost story.

And most marvellously she changed—her lineaments, her very figure, her whole presentment. Etched against the gloom, the delicate, unmarked face shone suddenly keen and anguished, and a rich maturity, deeper than any mere age, flushed all her little person with its secret grandeur. Lines started into being upon the pale skin of the girlish face, lines of pleading, pity, and love the daylight did not show, and with them an air of magic tenderness that betrayed, though for a second only, the full soft glory of a motherhood denied, yet somehow mysteriously enjoyed. About her slenderness rose all the deep-bosomed sweetness of maternity, a potential mother of the world, and a mother, though she might know no dear fulfilment, who yet yearned to sweep into her immense embrace all the little helpless things that ever lived.

Light, like emotion, can play strangest tricks. The change pressed almost upon the edge of revelation. . . . Yet, when a moment later lamps were brought, it is doubtful if any but the silent guest who had told no marvellous tale, knew no psychical experience, and disclaimed the smallest clairvoyant faculty, had received and registered the vivid, poignant picture. For an instant it had flashed there, mercilessly clear for all to see who were not blind to subtle spiritual wonder thick with pain. And it was not so much mere picture of youth and age ill-matched, as of youth that yearned with the oldest craving in the world, and of age that had slipped beyond the power of sympathetically divining it. . . . It passed, and all was as before.

The husband laughed with genial good-nature, not one whit annoyed. "They've been frightening you with stories, child," he said in his jolly way, and put a protective arm about her. "Haven't they now? Tell me the truth. Much better," he added, "have joined me instead at billiards, or for a game of Patience, eh?" She looked up shyly into his face, and he kissed her on the forehead. "Perhaps they have—a little, dear," she said, "but now that you've come, I feel all right again." "Another night of this," he added in a graver tone, "and you'd be at your old trick of putting guests to sleep in the haunted room. I was right after all, you see, to make it out of bounds." He glanced fondly, paternally down upon her. Then he went over and poked the fire into a blaze. Some one struck up a waltz on the piano, and couples danced. All trace of nervousness vanished, and the butler presently brought in the tray with drinks and biscuits. And slowly the group dispersed. Candles were lit. They passed down the passage into the big hall, talking in lowered voices of to-morrow's plans. The laughter died away as they went up the stairs to bed, the silent guest and the young wife lingering a moment over the embers.

"You have not, after all then, put me in your haunted room?" he asked quietly. "You mentioned, you remember, in your letter—"

"I admit," she replied at once, her manner gracious beyond her years, her voice quite different, "that I wanted you to sleep there—some one, I mean, who really knows, and is not merely curious. But—forgive my saying so—when I *saw* you"—she laughed very slowly—"and when you told no marvellous story like the others, I somehow felt—"

"But I never *see* anything—" he put in hurriedly.

"You *feel*, though," she interrupted swiftly, the passionate tenderness in her voice but half suppressed. "I can tell it from your—"

"Others, then," he interrupted abruptly, almost bluntly, "have slept there—sat up, rather?"

"Not recently. My husband stopped it." She paused a second, then added, "I had that room—for a year—when first we married."

The other's anguished look flew back upon her little face like a shadow and was gone, while at the sight of it there rose in himself a sudden deep rush of wonderful amazement beckoning almost towards worship. He did not speak, for his voice would tremble.

"I had to give it up," she finished, very low.

"Was it so terrible?" after a pause he ventured.

She bowed her head. "I had to change," she repeated softly.

"And since then—*now*—you see nothing?" he asked.

Her reply was singular. "Because I will not, not because it's gone." . . . He followed her in silence to the door, and as they passed along the passage, again that curious great pain of emptiness, of loneliness, of yearning rose upon him, as of a sea that never, never can swim beyond the shore to reach the flowers that it loves . . .

"Hurry up, child, or a ghost will catch you," cried her husband, leaning over the banisters, as the pair moved slowly up the stairs towards him. There was a moment's silence when they met. The guest took his lighted candle and went down the corridor. Good-nights were said again. They moved away, she to her loneliness, he to his unhaunted room. And at his door he turned. At the far end of the passage, silhouetted against the candle-light, he watched them—the fine old man with his silvered hair and heavy shoulders, and the slim young wife with that amazing air as of some great bountiful mother of the world for whom the years yet passed hungry and unharvested. They turned the corner, and he went in and closed his door.

Sleep took him very quickly, and while the mist rose up and veiled the country-side, something else, veiled equally for all other sleepers in that house but two, drew on towards its climax. . . . Some hours later he awoke; the world was still, and it seemed the whole house listened; for with that clear vision which some bring out of sleep, he remembered that there had been no direct denial, and of a sudden realised that this big, gaunt chamber where he lay was after all the haunted room. For him, however, the entire world, not merely separate rooms in it, was ever haunted; and he knew no terror to find the space about him charged with thronging life quite other than his own. . . . He rose and lit the candle, crossed over to the window where the mist shone grey, knowing that no barriers of walls or door or ceiling could keep out this host of Presences that poured so thickly everywhere about him. It was like a wall of being, with peering eyes, small hands stretched out, a thousand pattering wee feet, and tiny voices crying in a chorus very faintly and beseeching. . . . The haunted room! Was it not, rather, a temple vestibule, prepared and sanctified by yearning rites few men might ever guess, for all the childless women of the world? How could she know that *he* would understand—this woman he had seen but twice in all his life? And how entrust to him so great a mystery that was her secret? Had she so easily divined in him a similar yearning to which, long years ago, death had denied fulfilment? Was she clairvoyant in the true sense, and did all faces bear on them so legibly this great map that sorrow traced? . . .

And then, with awful suddenness, mere feelings dipped away, and something concrete happened. The handle of the door had faintly rattled. He turned. The round brass knob was slowly moving. And first, at the sight, something of common fear did grip him, as though his heart had missed a beat, but on the instant he heard the voice of his own mother, now long beyond the stars, calling to him to go softly yet with speed. He watched a moment the feeble efforts to undo the door, yet never afterwards could swear that he saw actual movement, for something in him, tragic as blindness, rose through a mist of tears and darkened vision utterly. . . .

He went towards the door. He took the handle very gently, and very softly then he opened it. Beyond was darkness. He saw the empty passage, the edge of the banisters where the great hall yawned below, and, dimly, the outline of the Alpine photograph and the stuffed deer's head upon the wall. And then he dropped upon his knees and opened wide his arms to something that came in upon uncertain, viewless feet. All the young winds and flowers and dews of dawn passed with it . . . filling him to the brim . . . covering closely his breast and eyes and lips. There clung to him all the small beginnings of life that cannot stand alone . . . the little helpless hands and arms that have no confidence . . . and when the wealth of tears and love that flooded his heart seemed to break upon the frontiers of some mysterious yet impossible fulfilment, he rose and went with curious small steps towards the window to taste the cooling, misty air of that other dark Emptiness that waited so patiently there above the entire world. He drew the sash up. The air felt soft and tender as though there were somewhere children in it too—children of stars and flowers, of mists and wings and music, all that the Universe contains unborn and tiny. . . . And when at length he turned again the door was closed. The room was empty of any life but that which lay so wonderfully blessed within himself. And this, he felt, had marvellously increased and multiplied. . . .

Sleep then came back to him, and in the morning he left the house before the others were astir, pleading some overlooked engagement. For he had seen Ghosts indeed, but yet not ghosts that he could talk about with others round an open fire.

Dream Trespass

The little feathers of the dusk were drifting through the autumn leaves when we came so unexpectedly upon the inn that was not marked upon our big-scaled map. And most opportunely, for Ducommun, my friend, was clearly overtired. An irritability foreign to his placid temperament had made the last few hours' trudge a little difficult, and I felt we had reached that narrow frontier which lies between non-success and failure.

"Another five miles to the inn we chose this morning," I told him; "but we'll soon manage it at a steady pace."

And he groaned, "I'm done! I simply couldn't do it."

He sank down upon the bit of broken wall to rest, while the darkness visibly increased, and the wind blew damp and chill across the marshes on our left. But behind the petulance of his tone, due to exhaustion solely, lay something else as well, something that had been accumulating for days. For our walking tour had not turned out quite to measure, distances always under-calculated; the inns, moreover, bad; the people surly and inhospitable; even the weather cross.

And Ducommun's disappointment had in a sense been double, so that I felt keen sympathy with him. For this was the country where his ancestors once reigned as proprietors, grand seigneurs, and the rest; he had always longed to visit it; and secretly in his imagination had cherished a reconstructed picture in which he himself would somehow play some high, distinguished rôle his proud blood entitled him to. Clerk to-day in a mere insurance office, but descendant of romantic, ancient stock, he knew the history of the period intimately; the holiday had been carefully, lovingly planned; and—the unpleasantness of the inhabitants had shattered his dream thus fostered and so keenly anticipated. The breaking-point had been reached. Was not this inn we hoped to reach by dark a portion of the very château—he had established it from musty records enough—where once his family dwelt in

218

old-time splendour? And had he not indulged all manner of delightful secret dreaming in advance? . . .

It was here, then, returning from a little private reconnoitring on my own account, that I reported my brave discovery of an unexpected half-way house, and found him almost asleep upon the stones, unwilling to believe the short half-mile I promised. "Only another nest of robbery and insolence," he laughed sourly, "and, anyhow, not the inn we counted on." He dragged after me in silence, eyeing askance the tumbled, ivy-covered shanty that stood beside the roadway, yet gladly going in ahead of me to rest his weary limbs, and troubling himself no whit with bargaining that he divined might be once more unpleasant.

Yet the inn proved a surprise in another way—it was entirely delightful. There was a glowing fire of peat in a biggish hall, the *patron* and his wife were all smiles and pleasure, welcoming us with an old-fashioned dignity that made bargaining impossible, and in ten minutes we felt as much at home as if we had arrived at a country house where we had been long expected.

"So few care to stop here now," the old woman told us, with a gracious gesture that was courtly rather than deferential, "we stand no longer upon the old high road," and showed in a hundred nameless ways that all they had was entirely at our disposal. Till even Ducommun melted and turned soft: "Only in France could this happen," he whispered with a touch of pride, as though claiming that this fragrance of gentle life, now fast disappearing from the world, still lingered in the land of his descent and in his own blood too. He patted the huge, rough deer-hound that seemed to fill the little room where we awaited supper, and the friendly creature, bounding with a kind of subdued affection, added another touch of welcome. His face and manners were evidence of kind treatment; he was proud of his owners and of his owners' guests. I thought of well-loved pets in our English country houses. "This beast," I laughed, "has surely lived with gentlemen." And Ducommun took the compliment to himself with personal satisfaction.

It is difficult to tell afterwards with accuracy the countless little touches that made the picture all so gentle—they were so delicately suggested, painted in silently with such deft spiritual discretion. It stands out in my memory, set in some strange, high light, as the most enchanting experience of many a walking tour; and yet, about it all, like a veil of wonder that evades description, an atmosphere of something at the same time—I use the best available word—truly singular. This touch of something remote, indefinite, unique, began to steal over me from the very first, bringing with it an incalculable, queer charm. It lulled like a drug all possible suspicions. And in my friend—detail of the picture nearest to my heart, that is—it first betrayed itself, with a degree of surprise, moreover, not entirely removed from shock.

For as he passed before me underneath that low-browed porch, quite undeniably he—altered. This indefinable change clothed his entire presentment to my eyes; to tired eyes, I freely grant, as also that it was dusk, and that the transforming magic of the peat fire was behind him. Yet, eschewing paragraphs of vain description, I may put a portion of it crudely thus, perhaps: that his lankiness turned suddenly all grace; the atmosphere of the London office stool, as of the clerk a-holidaying, vanished; and that the way he bowed his head to enter the dark-beamed lintel of the door was courtly and high bred, instinct with native elegance, and in the real sense aristocratic. It came with an instant and complete conviction. It was wonderful to see; and it gave me a moment's curious enchantment. All that I divined and loved in the man, usually somewhat buried, came forth upon the surface. A note of explanation followed readily enough, half explanation at any rate—that houses alter people because, like dressing-up with women and children, they furnish a new setting to the general appearance, and the points one is accustomed to undergo a readjustment. Yet with him this subtle alteration did not pass; it not only clung to him during the entire evening, but most curiously increased. He maintained, indeed, his silence the whole time, but it was a happy, dreaming silence holding the charm of real companionship, his disappointment gone as completely as the memory of our former cheerless inns and ill-conditioned people.

I cannot pretend, though, that I really watched him carefully, since an attack from another quarter divided my attention equally, and the charm of the daughter of the house, in whose eyes, it seemed to me, lay all the quiet sadness of the country we had walked through—*triste, morne*, forsaken land—claimed a great part of my observant sympathy. The old people left us entirely to her care, and the way she looked after us, divining our wants before we ventured to express them, was more suggestive of the perfect hostess than merely of some one who would take payment for all that she supplied. The question of money, indeed, did not once intrude, though I cannot say whence came my impression that this hospitality was, in fact, offered without the least idea of remuneration in silver and gold. That it did come, I can swear; also, that behind it lay no suggestion of stiff prices to be demanded at the last moment on the plea that terms had not been settled in advance. We were made welcome like expected guests, and my heart leaped to encounter this spirit of old-fashioned courtesy that the greed of modern life has everywhere destroyed.

"To-morrow or the next day, when you are rested," said the maiden softly, sitting beside us after supper and tending the fire, "I will take you through the *Allée des tilleuls* towards the river, and show you where the fishing is so good."

For it seemed natural that she should sit and chat with us, and only afterwards I remembered sharply that the river was a good five miles from where we housed, across marshes that could boast no trees at all, *tilleuls* least of all, and of avenues not a vestige anywhere.

"We'll start," Ducommun answered promptly, taking my breath a little, "in the dawn"; and presently then made signs to go to bed.

She brought the candles, lit them for us with a spill of paper from the peat, and handed one to each, a little smile of yearning in her deep, soft eyes that I remember to this day.

"You will sleep long and well," she said half shyly, accompanying us to the foot of the stairs. "I made and aired the beds with my own hands."

And the last I saw of her, as we turned the landing corner overhead, was her graceful figure against the darkness, with the candle-light falling upon the coiled masses of her dark-brown hair. She gazed up after us with those large grey eyes that seemed to me so full of yearning, and yet so sad, so patient, so curiously resigned. . . .

Ducommun pulled me almost roughly by the arm. "Come," he said with sudden energy, and as though everything was settled. "We have an early start, remember!"

I moved unwillingly; it was all so strange and dream-like, the beauty of the girl so enchanting, the change in himself so utterly perplexing.

"It's like staying with friends in a country house," I murmured, lingering in a moment of bewilderment by his door. "Old family retainers almost, proud and delighted to put one up, eh?"

And his answer was so wholly unexpected that I waited, staring blankly into his altered eyes:

"I only hope we shall get away all right," he muttered. "I mean, that is—get off."

Evidently his former mood had flashed a moment back. "You feel tired?" I suggested sympathetically, "so do I."

"Dog-tired, yes," he answered shortly, then added in a slow, suggestive whisper—"And I feel cold, too—extraordinarily cold."

The significant, cautious way he said it made me start. But before I could prate of chills and remedies, he quickly shut the door upon me, leaving those last words ringing in my brain—"cold, extraordinarily cold." And an inkling stole over me of what he meant; uninvited and unwelcome it came, then passed at once, leaving a vague uneasiness behind. For the cold he spoke of surely was not bodily cold. About my own heart, too, moved some strange touch of chill. Cold sought an entrance. But it was not common cold. Rather it was in the mind and thoughts, and settled down upon the spirit. In describing his own sensations he had also described my own; for something at the very heart of me seemed turning numb. . . .

I got quickly into bed. The night was still and windless, but, though I was tired, sleep held long away. Uneasiness continued to affect me. I lay, listening to the blood hurrying along the thin walls of my veins, singing and murmuring, and, when at length I dropped off, two vivid pictures haunted me into unconsciousness—his face in the doorway as he made that last remark, and the face of the girl as she had peered up so yearningly at him over the shaded candle.

Then—at once, it seemed—I was wide awake again, aware, however, that an interval had passed, but aware also of another thing that was incredible, and somehow dreadful, namely, that while I slept, the house had undergone a change. It caught me, shivering in my bed, utterly unprepared, as though unfair advantage had been taken of me while I lay unconscious. This startling idea of external alteration made me shudder. How I so instantly divined it lies beyond all explanation. I somehow realised that, while the room I woke in was the same as before, the building of which it formed a little member had known in the darkness some transmuting, substituting change that had turned it otherwise. My terror I also cannot explain, nor why, almost immediately, instead of increasing, it subtly shifted into that numbness I have already mentioned—a curious, deep bemusement of the spirit that robbed it of really acute distress. It seemed as if only a part of me—the wakened part—knew what was going on, and that some other part remained in sleep and ignorance.

For the house was now enormous. It *had* experienced this weird transformation. The roof, I somehow knew, rose soaring through the darkness; the walls ran over acres; it had towers, wings, and battlements, broad balconies, and magnificent windows. It had grown both dignified and ancient . . . and had swallowed up our little inn as comfortably as a palace includes a single bedroom. The blackness about me of course concealed it, but I *felt* the yawning corridors, the gape of lofty halls, high ceilings, spacious chambers, till I seemed lost in the being of some stately building that extended itself with imposing majesty upon the night.

Then came the instinct—more, perhaps, a driving impulse than a mere suggestion—to go out and see. See what? I asked myself, as I made my way towards the window gropingly, unwilling or afraid to strike a light. And the answer, utterly without explanation, came hard and sharp like this—

"To catch them on the lawn."

And the curious phrase I knew was right, for the surroundings had changed equally with the house. I drew aside the curtain and peered out upon a lawn that a few hours ago had been surely a rather desolate, plain roadway, and beyond it into spacious gardens, bounded by park-like timber, where before had been but dreary, half-cultivated fields.

Through a risen mist the light of the moon shone faintly, and everywhere my sight confirmed the singular impression of extension I have mentioned, for away to the left another mass of masonry that was like the wing of some great mansion rose dimly through the air, and beneath my very eyes a projecting balcony obscured pathways and beds of flowers. Next, where a gleam of moonlight caught it, I saw the broad, slow bend of river edging the lawn through clumps of willows. Even the river had come close. And while I stared, striving to force from so much illusion a single fact that might explain, a little tree upon the lawn just underneath moved slightly nearer, and I saw it was a human figure—a figure that I recognised. Wrapped in some long, loose garment, the daughter of the house stood there in an attitude of waiting. And the waiting was at once explained, for another figure—this time the figure of a man that seemed to me both strange and familiar at the same time—emerged from the shadows of the house to join her. She slipped into his arms. Then came a sound of horses neighing in their stalls, and the couple moved away with sudden swiftness, silently as ghosts, disappearing in the mist, while three minutes later I heard the crunch of hoofs on gravel, dying rapidly away into the distance of the night.

And here a sudden, wild reaction, not easy of analysis, rushed over me, as if that other part of me that had not waked now came sharply to the rescue, set free from the inhibition of some drug. I felt anger, disgust, resentment, and a wave of indignation that somehow I was being tricked. Impulsively—there seemed no time for judgment or reflection—I crossed the landing, now so oddly deep and lofty, and, without knocking, ran headlong into my friend's room. The bed, I saw at once, was empty, the sheets not even lain in. The furniture was in disorder, garments strewn about the floor, signs of precipitate flight in all directions. And Ducommun, of course, was gone.

What happened next confuses me when I try to think of it, for my only recollection is of hurrying distractedly to and fro between his bedroom and my own. There was a rush and scuttling in the darkness, and then I blundered heavily against walls or furniture or both, and the darkness rose up over my mind with a smothering thick curtain that blinded everything . . . and I came to my senses in the open road, my friend standing over me, enormous in the dusk, and the bit of broken wall where he had rested while I reconnoitred, just behind us. The moon was rising, the air was damp and chill, and he was shouting in my ear, "I thought you were never coming back again. I'm rested now. We'd better hurry on and do those beastly five miles to the inn."

We started, walking so briskly that we reached it in something over seventy minutes, and passing on the way no single vestige of a house nor of any kind of building. I was the silent one, but when Ducommun talked it was only to curse the desolate, sad country, and wonder why his forbears had ever chosen such a wilderness to live in. And when at length we put up at this inn which he made out was a part of his original family estate, he spent the evening poring over maps and papers, by means of which he admitted finally his calculations were all wrong. "The house itself," he said, "must have stood farther back along the road we came by. The river, you see," pointing to the dirty old chart, "has changed its course a bit since then. Its older bed lay much nearer to the château, flanking the garden lawn below the park." And he pointed again to the place with a finger that obviously now held office pens.

News *v.* Nourishment

The first thing I saw of him was the dome of his bald head and the strip of wandering black hair that strayed across it like a bit of seaweed left by an ebbing tide. The rest was hidden behind the opened newspaper which he devoured while waiting for his luncheon. He was a little man. I saw the tips of square boots with knobs on them projecting beneath the table, and later I noted that his nose was aquiline, and that he had large comfortable ears. He may have been something in a Forwarding Office; he was not spruce enough for banking or insurance circles. He read that evening edition as if the future of the race depended on it.

Then the girl, a lackadaisical, bird-like creature, brought his plate of "braised beef an' carruts" swimming in thick brown gravy, and set it down with noisy clatter upon the marble table. He was so absorbed that the dishes came as a surprise; and as he looked up, startled, the paper descended softly upon the thick brown gravy. This was the first disaster; for when he lifted it to find his place the columns of print resembled a successful fly-paper. He looked round at everybody, bewildered. For the moment, however, I was so interested in the wandering strip of seaweed on his skull that I hardly noticed his efforts to free the newspaper, himself, his neighbours, and the cruet-stand from the adhesive entanglement of this portion of his luncheon. There was a sound of scattering—then the girl had somehow managed it for him with her grimy napkin. But that remnant of a tide forgotten, as I came to regard it, fascinated me. It strayed, lonely as a cloud; it was so admirably fastened down; the angle, curve, and general adjustment had been evidently chosen with so much care. Its "lie" upon that dome of silence had been calculated to a nicety, so that it should relieve with the best possible effect the open waste around it. It was like a mathematical problem. Only when his grave, dark eyes met mine did I realise that I was staring rudely.

But long before my own hurried luncheon came, the difficulties in which this stranger opposite was involved had fascinated me afresh. The contents of the now mutilated evening paper absorbed him to the point of positive conflict. It may have been the racing news, police reports, or a breach of promise case; it may have been some special article and leader, or it may have been merely advertisements, perhaps; I cannot say. But his efforts to read and eat at the same time made me wonder with a growing excitement for the final issue of the battle. Had I not been alone, I would have laid a bet—with odds, I think, against "braised beef an' carruts."

He did it all so gravely and so earnestly, aware of the claims of both contestants, yet determined to be conscientious. Determined he most certainly was. A man doing anything with all his heart is always interesting to watch, but a man solemnly doing two things at once wins admiration and respect as well. My sympathies went out to him. I longed to give him hints. And the only time my attention wandered from this contest between news and nourishment was when I watched that strip of lonely seaweed rise and fall, vanish and reappear, with the movement of his head in eating. The way it dived to meet the fork, then rose again to greet the paper, was like the motion of a swimmer among waves.

He arranged his sight so cleverly, dividing it in some swift, extraordinary manner, yet without squinting, between the occupants of the arena. An eye and a half on each alternately seemed to be the plan, the extra half left over being free to bring immediate first-aid when needed; but his mind, I felt, was really with the paper all along. The nourishment was pleasure, the news was duty. There was heroism in this little man.

He would heap his fork with a marvellously balanced pyramid of beef and carrots and bread, smear it over with thick gravy, top it with a dash of salt—all with one hand, this!—then leave it hovering above the plate while he looked back keenly at the paper, searching to find his place. For between mouthfuls he always lost his place. It distressed me till he found it again, my interest centred on the piled-up fork. But what distressed me even more was that every time he found it and shot an eye back again to the loaded implement—that pyramid tumbled! Three times out of four, at least, it dropped its burden in this way; and the look of weariness, surprise, and disappointment on his face at each collapse was almost more than I could bear—in silence. He looked at that fork as some men look at a dog—with mortified astonishment. "I'm surprised at you," his expression said, "after all those years, too!" I longed to ask, "Why *did* you add that carrot to the top? You might have known by this time—!" But his own expression said quite plainly, "I built you up so very carefully—all with one hand, too. You really *might* have stayed!"

My own tension became too keen then for mere amusement. I found myself taking sides alternately with the beef and paper. I was conscious of a desire to steady the fork for him while he read, and then to guide it straight into his mouth. For it next became most painfully obvious that he rarely found the opening—at the first attempt. With that over-loaded, over-balanced fork, a dripping carrot perched on the apex of the pile, he jabbed successively his lower lip, his cheek, his chin, and once at least the tip of his nose, before the proper terminus was reached and delivery accomplished. Small beauty-spots of brown remained dotted here and there to mark the inaccuracy of his aim and the firmness of his persistence.

For he was *so* patient. Both jobs he did so thoroughly. I began to wonder if he did two things at once at other times as well: whether, for instance, he buttoned his collar with one hand while with the other he led that strip of seaweed into safety for the day's adventure. Surely, it seemed, he must excel at those parlour tricks which involve patting the breast with one hand and rubbing it up and down with the other simultaneously. Something of the sort he surely practised. Although the way, with a piece of bread speared on his fork, he groped all round the table for the gravy that was cooling on his plate, made me question his absolute skill sometimes.

He was too absorbed to notice things around him. The stout, bespectacled woman, for instance, who sat beside him on the leather couch, might not have existed at all. The way she looked him up and down, hinting for more room, was utterly lost upon him. So was the way she moved her glass of steaming milk and her under-sized bananas to and fro to dodge the paper he constantly flapped beneath her very nose. He took far more than his proper share of space, and she clearly resented it most bitterly, yet was afraid to speak. The movements of her glass and fruit were like a game of chess: he played the stronger gambit and forced her moves. She sulked—and lost.

The girl came up and whisked his unfinished plate away, asking him with a sideways bend of the head, bird-like rather, if he wished to order anything else, and his face shot up above the edge of the paper as though she had interrupted him in the midst of a serious business transaction.

"Didn't I order something, miss?" he was heard to enquire resentfully, one eye glued still to the sheet.

"Nothing not yet," came the disinterested reply.

"Bring me sultana pudding hot—no, cold, I mean—with sauce, please," he said, as if remembering some quotation learnt by heart—and down he plunged once more beneath that sea of print.

But with the arrival of the cold sultana pudding came the crisis of the battle. For the pudding was slippery. It stood on end amid its paste-like sauce, impatient of amateur attack, inviting more skill than evidently he possessed. He caught my warning eye once or twice upon him, but disregarded it. These whole-hearted people never take advice. Smothering the toppling form with sugar, he seized a fork and aimed; but, before striking, buried his eyes again in the paper. The shot flew wild. The pyramid of dough went slithering round the plate as though alive, scattering sauce upon the marble table. A second shot, delivered with impatience, took off the top and side. He speared the broken piece—still without looking up to direct it properly—gathered a little sauce and sugar on the way; then, flushed with success, the face turned sideways towards the paper, rushed recklessly for his mouth—and bit an empty fork. The load had slipped aside *en route;* or, rather, the paper, holding the best position in the field, had taken it prisoner. For it fell with a soft and sticky thud into the column nearest to his waistcoat. This time he *spooned* it up, and for a little time after that he had success. The paper and the pudding ran neck and neck along the home-stretch. He read with absorbing interest; he ate without waste of attention. I watched him with amazement. This performance of a divided personality must be given somewhere every day at the luncheon hour. The mood of the afternoon hung probably upon its accomplishment without disaster. The pudding had dwindled to its last titbit without attempting further *ausflüge,* and his eyes had just begun to feast upon a freshly turned page of the newspaper, when, crash, bang—there came complete discomfiture.

Drunk with success, he made a violent misdirected shot. He had waited long for that titbit, had nursed it carefully, keeping a little pool of sauce and sugar especially for it, when this careless aim sent it flying off the plate several inches into the middle of the table. The woman with the milk and the banana gave a little scream—of indignation. He turned abruptly, noticing her presence for the first time. He realised that he had edged her almost off the couch. He also realised, with the other eye, that the bit of pudding lay beyond redemption or recapture. Several people were watching him. He could not possibly, without total loss of dignity, restore it to an edible condition. He shunted down the seat with the sideways movement of a penguin, quietly replaced the errant morsel on his plate, called for his bill, then waited resignedly with a sigh, a defeated man.

Our eyes met in that moment full and square across the room. "I told you so," mine said; "you were too reckless with it." But in his own there shone a look of misery and regret I shall not easily forget. For a single instant his face vanished behind the crumpled but victorious paper, to emerge, scarlet, a moment later with the strip of seaweed drawn out of its normal bed into an unaccustomed route towards one tilted eyebrow. In his distress the man had passed a hand absent-mindedly across his forehead. The woman, putting on her spectacles, eyed with relief his preparations for departure. He went. But he took the paper with him.

And through the window I caught my final glimpse of him as he climbed outside a passing omnibus. He was small and rotund. His eyes shone in a flushed and disappointed face. His coat-tails spread sideways in the wind. Like an irate and very swollen sparrow he looked, defeated in some wretched gutter combat, yet eager for more, and certain to return to the arena as long as life should last—about the luncheon hour.

The Glamour of the Snow

I

Hibbert, always conscious of two worlds, was in this mountain village conscious of three. It lay on the slopes of the Valais Alps, and he had taken a room in the little post office, where he could be at peace to write his book, yet at the same time enjoy the winter sports and find companionship in the hotels when he wanted it.

The three worlds that met and mingled here seemed to his imaginative temperament very obvious, though it is doubtful if another mind less intuitively equipped would have seen them so well-defined. There was the world of tourist English, civilised, quasi-educated, to which he belonged by birth, at any rate; there was the world of peasants to which he felt himself drawn by sympathy—for he loved and admired their toiling, simple life; and there was this other—which he could only call the world of Nature. To this last, however, in virtue of a vehement poetic imagination, and a tumultuous pagan instinct fed by his very blood, he felt that most of him belonged. The others borrowed from it, as it were, for visits. Here, with the soul of Nature, hid his central life.

Between all three was conflict—potential conflict. On the skating-rink each Sunday the tourists regarded the natives as intruders; in the church the peasants plainly questioned: "Why do you come? We are here to worship; you to stare and whisper!" For neither of these two worlds accepted the other. And neither did Nature accept the tourists, for it took advantage of their least mistakes, and indeed, even of the peasant-world "accepted" only those who were strong and bold enough to invade her savage domain with sufficient skill to protect themselves from several forms of—death.

Now Hibbert was keenly aware of this potential conflict and want of harmony; he felt outside, yet caught by it—torn in the three directions because he was partly of each world, but wholly in only one. There grew in him a constant, subtle effort—or, at least, desire—to unify them and decide positively to which he should belong and live in. The attempt, of course, was largely subconscious. It was the natural instinct of a richly imaginative nature seeking the point of equilibrium, so that the mind could feel at peace and his brain be free to do good work.

Among the guests no one especially claimed his interest. The men were nice but undistinguished—athletic schoolmasters, doctors snatching a holiday, good fellows all; the women, equally various—the clever, the would-be-fast, the dare-to-be-dull, the women "who understood," and the usual pack of jolly dancing girls and "flappers." And Hibbert, with his forty odd years of thick experience behind him, got on well with the lot; he understood them all; they belonged to definite, predigested types that are the same the world over, and that he had met the world over long ago.

But to none of them did he belong. His nature was too "multiple" to subscribe to the set of shibboleths of any one class. And, since all liked him, and felt that somehow he seemed outside of them—spectator, looker-on—all sought to claim him.

In a sense, therefore, the three worlds fought for him: natives, tourists, Nature. . . .

It was thus began the singular conflict for the soul of Hibbert. *In his own soul*, however, it took place. Neither the peasants nor the tourists were conscious that they fought for anything. And Nature, they say, is merely blind and automatic.

The assault upon him of the peasants may be left out of account, for it is obvious that they stood no chance of success. The tourist world, however, made a gallant effort to subdue him to themselves. But the evenings in the hotel, when dancing was not in order, were—English. The provincial imagination was set upon a throne and worshipped heavily through incense of the stupidest conventions possible. Hibbert used to go back early to his room in the post office to work.

"It is a mistake on my part to have *realised* that there is any conflict at all," he thought, as he crunched home over the snow at midnight after one of the dances. "It would have been better to have kept outside it all and done my work. Better," he added, looking back down the silent village street to the church tower, "and—safer."

The adjective slipped from his mind before he was aware of it. He turned with an involuntary start and looked about him. He knew perfectly well what it meant—this thought that had thrust its head up from the instinctive region. He understood, without being able to express it fully, the meaning that betrayed itself in the choice of the adjective. For if he had ignored the existence of this conflict he would at the same time have remained outside the arena. Whereas now he had entered the lists. Now this battle for his soul must have issue. And he knew that the spell of Nature was greater for him than all other spells in the world combined—greater than love, revelry, pleasure, greater even than study. He had always been afraid to let himself go. His pagan soul dreaded her terrific powers of witchery even while he worshipped.

The little village already slept. The world lay smothered in snow. The châlet roofs shone white beneath the moon, and pitch-black shadows gathered against the walls of the church. His eye rested a moment on the square stone tower with its frosted cross that pointed to the sky: then travelled with a leap of many thousand feet to the enormous mountains that brushed the brilliant stars. Like a forest rose the huge peaks above the slumbering village, measuring the night and heavens. They beckoned him. And something born of the snowy desolation, born of the midnight and the silent grandeur, born of the great listening hollows of the night, something that lay 'twixt terror and wonder, dropped from the vast wintry spaces down into his heart—and called him. Very softly, unrecorded in any word or thought his brain could compass, it laid its spell upon him. Fingers of snow brushed the surface of his heart. The power and quiet majesty of the winter's night appalled him. . . .

Fumbling a moment with the big unwieldy key, he let himself in and went upstairs to bed. Two thoughts went with him—apparently quite ordinary and sensible ones:

"What fools these peasants are to sleep through such a night!" And the other:

"Those dances tire me. I'll never go again. My work only suffers in the morning." The claims of peasants and tourists upon him seemed thus in a single instant weakened.

The clash of battle troubled half his dreams. Nature had sent her

Beauty of the Night and won the first assault. The others, routed and dismayed, fled far away.

II

"Don't go back to your dreary old post office. We're going to have supper in my room—something hot. Come and join us. Hurry up!"

There had been an ice carnival, and the last party, tailing up the snow slope to the hotel, called him. The Chinese lanterns smoked and sputtered on the wires; the band had long since gone. The cold was bitter and the moon came only momentarily between high, driving clouds. From the shed where the people changed from skates to snow-boots he shouted something to the effect that he was "following"; but no answer came; the moving shadows of those who had called were already merged high up against the village darkness. The voices died away. Doors slammed. Hibbert found himself alone on the deserted rink.

And it was then, quite suddenly, the impulse came to—stay and skate alone. The thought of the stuffy hotel room, and of those noisy people with their obvious jokes and laughter, oppressed him. He felt a longing to be alone with the night, to taste her wonder all by himself there beneath the stars, gliding over the ice. It was not yet midnight, and he could skate for half an hour. That supper party, if they noticed his absence at all, would merely think he had changed his mind and gone to bed.

It was an impulse, yes, and not an unnatural one; yet even at the time it struck him that something more than impulse lay concealed behind it. More than invitation, yet certainly less than command, there was a vague queer feeling that he stayed because he had to, almost as though there was something he had forgotten, overlooked, left undone. Imaginative temperaments are often thus; and impulse is ever weakness. For with such ill-considered opening of the doors to hasty action may come an invasion of other forces at the same time—forces merely waiting their opportunity perhaps!

He caught the fugitive warning even while he dismissed it as absurd, and the next minute he was whirling over the smooth ice in delightful curves and loops beneath the moon. There was no fear of collision. He could take his own speed and space as he willed. The shadows of the towering mountains fell across the rink, and a wind of ice came from the forests, where the snow lay ten feet deep. The hotel lights winked and went out. The village slept. The high wire netting could not keep out the wonder of the winter night that grew about him like a presence. He skated on and on, keen exhilarating pleasure in his tingling blood, and weariness all forgotten.

And then, midway in the delight of rushing movement, he saw a figure gliding behind the wire netting, watching him. With a start that almost made him lose his balance—for the abruptness of the new arrival was so unlooked for—he paused and stared. Although the light was dim he made out that it was the figure of a woman and that she was feeling her way along the netting, trying to get in. Against the white background of the snow-field he watched her rather stealthy efforts as she passed with a silent step over the banked-up snow. She was tall and slim and graceful; he could see that even in the dark. And then, of course, he understood. It was another adventurous skater like himself, stolen down unawares from hotel or châlet, and searching for the opening. At once, making a sign and pointing with one hand, he turned swiftly and skated over to the little entrance on the other side.

But, even before he got there, there was a sound on the ice behind him and, with an exclamation of amazement he could not suppress, he turned to see her swerving up to his side across the width of the rink. She had somehow found another way in.

Hibbert, as a rule, was punctilious, and in these free-and-easy places, perhaps, especially so. If only for his own protection he did not seek to make advances unless some kind of introduction paved the way. But for these two to skate together in the semi-darkness without speech, often of necessity brushing shoulders almost, was too absurd to think of. Accordingly he raised his cap and spoke. His actual words he seemed unable to recall, nor what the girl said in reply, except that she answered him in accented English with some commonplace about doing figures at midnight on an empty rink. Quite natural it was, and right. She wore grey clothes of some kind, though not the customary long gloves or sweater, for indeed her hands were bare, and presently when he skated with her, he wondered with something like astonishment at their dry and icy coldness.

And she was delicious to skate with—supple, sure, and light, fast as a man yet with the freedom of a child, sinuous and steady at the same time. Her flexibility made him wonder, and when he asked where she had learned she murmured—he caught the breath against his ear and recalled later that it was singularly cold—that she could hardly tell, for she had been accustomed to the ice ever since she could remember.

But her face he never properly saw. A muffler of white fur buried her neck to the ears, and her cap came over the eyes. He only saw that she was young. Nor could he gather her hotel or châlet, for she pointed vaguely, when he asked her, up the slopes. "Just over there—" she said, quickly taking his hand again. He did not press her; no doubt she wished to hide her escapade. And the touch of her hand thrilled him more than anything he could remember; even through his thick glove he felt the softness of that cold and delicate softness.

The clouds thickened over the mountains. It grew darker. They talked very little, and did not always skate together. Often they separated, curving about in corners by themselves, but always coming together again in the centre of the rink; and when she left him thus Hibbert was conscious of—yes, of missing her. He found a peculiar satisfaction, almost a fascination, in skating by her side. It was quite an adventure—these two strangers with the ice and snow and night!

Midnight had long since sounded from the old church tower before they parted. She gave the sign, and he skated quickly to the shed, meaning to find a seat and help her take her skates off. Yet when he turned—she had already gone. He saw her slim figure gliding away across the snow . . . and hurrying for the last time round the rink alone he searched in vain for the opening she had twice used in this curious way.

"How very queer!" he thought, referring to the wire netting. "She must have lifted it and wriggled under . . . !"

Wondering how in the world she managed it, what in the world had possessed him to be so free with her, and who in the world she was, he went up the steep slope to the post office and so to bed, her promise to come again another night still ringing delightfully in his ears. And curious were the thoughts and sensations that accompanied him. Most of all, perhaps, was the half suggestion of some dim memory that he had known this girl before, had met her somewhere, more—that she knew him. For in her voice—a low, soft, windy little voice it was, tender and soothing for all its quiet coldness—there lay some faint reminder of two others he had known, both long since gone: the voice of the woman he had loved, and—the voice of his mother.

But this time through his dreams there ran no clash of battle. He was conscious, rather, of something cold and clinging that made him think of sifting snowflakes climbing slowly with entangling touch and thickness round his feet. The snow, coming without noise, each flake so light and tiny none can mark the spot whereon it settles, yet the mass of it able to smother whole villages, wove through the very texture of his mind—cold, bewildering, deadening effort with its clinging network of ten million feathery touches.

III

In the morning Hibbert realised he had done, perhaps, a foolish thing. The brilliant sunshine that drenched the valley made him see this, and the sight of his work-table with its typewriter, books, papers, and the rest, brought additional conviction. To have skated with a girl alone at midnight, no matter how innocently the thing had come about, was unwise—unfair, especially to her. Gossip in these little winter resorts was worse than in a provincial town. He hoped no one had seen them. Luckily the night had been dark. Most likely none had heard the ring of skates.

Deciding that in future he would be more careful, he plunged into work, and sought to dismiss the matter from his mind.

But in his times of leisure the memory returned persistently to haunt him. When he "ski-d," "luged," or danced in the evenings, and especially when he skated on the little rink, he was aware that the eyes of his mind for ever sought this strange companion of the night. A hundred times he fancied that he saw her, but always sight deceived him. Her face he might not know, but he could hardly fail to recognise her figure. Yet nowhere among the others did he catch a glimpse of that slim young creature he had skated with alone beneath the clouded stars. He searched in vain. Even his enquiries as to the occupants of the private châlets brought no results. He had lost her. But the queer thing was that he felt as though she were somewhere close; he *knew* she had not really gone. While people came and left with every day, it never once occurred to him that she had left. On the contrary, he felt assured that they would meet again.

This thought he never quite acknowledged. Perhaps it was the wish that fathered it only. And, even when he did meet her, it was a question how he would speak and claim acquaintance, or whether *she* would recognise himself. It might be awkward. He almost came to dread a meeting, though "dread," of course, was far too strong a word to describe an emotion that was half delight, half wondering anticipation.

Meanwhile the season was in full swing. Hibbert felt in perfect health, worked hard, ski-d, skated, luged, and at night danced fairly often—in spite of his decision. This dancing was, however, an act of subconscious surrender; it really meant he hoped to find her among the whirling couples. He was searching for her without quite acknowledging it to himself; and the hotel-world, meanwhile, thinking it had won him over, teased and chaffed him. He made excuses in a similar vein; but all the time he watched and searched and—waited.

For several days the sky held clear and bright and frosty, bitterly cold, everything crisp and sparkling in the sun; but there was no sign of fresh snow, and the ski-ers began to grumble. On the mountains was an icy crust that made "running" dangerous; they wanted the frozen, dry, and powdery snow that makes for speed, renders steering easier and falling less severe. But the keen east wind showed no signs of changing for a whole ten days. Then, suddenly, there came a touch of softer air and the weather-wise began to prophesy.

Hibbert, who was delicately sensitive to the least change in earth or sky, was perhaps the first to feel it. Only he did not prophesy. He knew through every nerve in his body that moisture had crept into the air, was accumulating, and that presently a fall would come. For he responded to the moods of Nature like a fine barometer.

And the knowledge, this time, brought into his heart a strange little wayward emotion that was hard to account for—a feeling of unexplained uneasiness and disquieting joy. For behind it, woven through it rather, ran a faint exhilaration that connected remotely somewhere with that touch of delicious alarm, that tiny anticipating "dread," that so puzzled him when he thought of his next meeting with his skating companion of the night. It lay beyond all words, all telling, this queer relationship between the two; but somehow the girl and snow ran in a pair across his mind.

Perhaps for imaginative writing-men, more than for other workers, the smallest change of mood betrays itself at once. His work at any rate revealed this slight shifting of emotional values in his soul. Not that his writing suffered, but that it altered, subtly as those changes of sky or sea or landscape that come with the passing of afternoon into evening—imperceptibly. A subconscious excitement sought to push outwards and express itself ... and, knowing the uneven effect such moods produced in his work, he laid his pen aside and took instead to reading that he had to do.

Meanwhile the brilliance passed from the sunshine, the sky grew slowly overcast; by dusk the mountain tops came singularly close and sharp; the distant valley rose into absurdly near perspective. The moisture increased, rapidly approaching saturation point, when it must fall in snow. Hibbert watched and waited.

And in the morning the world lay smothered beneath its fresh white carpet. It snowed heavily till noon, thickly, incessantly, chokingly, a foot or more; then the sky cleared, the sun came out in splendour, the wind shifted back to the east, and frost came down upon the mountains with its keenest and most biting tooth. The drop in the temperature was tremendous, but the ski-ers were jubilant. Next day the "running" would be fast and perfect. Already the mass was settling, and the surface freezing into those moss-like, powdery crystals that make the ski run almost of their own accord with the faint "sishing" as of a bird's wings through the air.

IV

That night there was excitement in the little hotel-world, first because there was a *bal costumé,* but chiefly because the new snow had come. And Hibbert went—felt drawn to go; he did not go in costume, but he wanted to talk about the slopes and ski-ing with the other men, and at the same time. . . .

Ah, there was the truth, the deeper necessity that called. For the singular connection between the stranger and the snow again betrayed itself, utterly beyond explanation as before, but vital and insistent. Some hidden instinct in his pagan soul—heaven knows how he phrased it even to himself, if he phrased it at all—whispered that with the snow the girl would be somewhere about, would emerge from her hiding place, would even look for him.

Absolutely unwarranted it was. He laughed while he stood before the little glass and trimmed his moustache, tried to make his black tie sit straight, and shook down his dinner jacket so that it should lie upon the shoulders without a crease. His brown eyes were very bright. "I look younger than I usually do," he thought. It was unusual, even significant, in a man who had no vanity about his appearance and certainly never questioned his age or tried to look younger than he was. Affairs of the heart, with one tumultuous exception that left no fuel for lesser subsequent fires, had never troubled him. The forces of his soul and mind, not called upon for "work" and obvious duties, all went to Nature. The desolate, wild places of the earth were what he loved; night, and the beauty of the stars and snow. And this evening he felt their claims upon him mightily stirring. A rising wildness caught his blood, quickened his pulse, woke longing and passion too. But chiefly snow. The snow whirred softly through his thoughts like white, seductive dreams. . . . For the snow had come; and She, it seemed, had somehow come with it—into his mind.

And yet he stood before that twisted mirror and pulled his tie and coat askew a dozen times, as though it mattered. "What in the world is up with me?" he thought. Then, laughing a little, he turned before leaving the room to put his private papers in order. The green morocco desk that held them he took down from the shelf and laid upon the table. Tied to the lid was the visiting card with his brother's London address "in case of accident." On the way down to the hotel he wondered why he had done this, for though imaginative, he was not the kind of man who dealt in presentiments. Moods with him were strong, but ever held in leash.

"It's almost like a warning," he thought, smiling. He drew his thick coat tightly round the throat as the freezing air bit at him. "Those warnings one reads of in stories sometimes . . . !"

A delicious happiness was in his blood. Over the edge of the hills across the valley rose the moon. He saw her silver sheet the world of snow. Snow covered all. It smothered sound and distance. It smothered houses, streets, and human beings. It smothered—life.

V

In the hall there was light and bustle; people were already arriving from the other hotels and châlets, their costumes hidden beneath many wraps. Groups of men in evening dress stood about smoking, talking "snow" and "ski-ing." The band was tuning up. The claims of the hotel world clashed about him faintly as of old. At the big glass windows of the verandah, peasants stopped a moment on their way home from the *café* to peer. Hibbert thought laughingly of that conflict he used to imagine. He laughed because it suddenly seemed so unreal. He belonged so utterly to Nature and the mountains, and especially to those desolate slopes where now the snow lay thick and fresh and sweet, that there was no question of a conflict at all. The power of the newly fallen snow had caught him, proving it without effort. Out there, upon those lonely reaches of the moonlit ridges, the snow lay ready—masses and masses of it—cool, soft, inviting. He longed for it. It awaited him. He thought of the intoxicating delight of ski-ing in the moonlight. . . .

Thus, somehow, in vivid flashing vision, he thought of it while he stood there smoking with the other men and talking all the "shop" of ski-ing.

And, ever mysteriously blended with this power of the snow, poured also through his inner being the power of the girl. He could not disabuse his mind of the insinuating presence of the two together. He remembered that queer skating-impulse of ten days ago, the impulse that had let her in. That any mind, even an imaginative one, could pass beneath the sway of such a fancy was strange enough; and Hibbert, while fully aware of the disorder, yet found a curious joy in yielding to it. This insubordinate centre that drew him towards old pagan beliefs had assumed command. With a kind of sensuous pleasure he let himself be conquered.

And snow that night seemed in everybody's thoughts. The dancing couples talked of it; the hotel proprietors congratulated one another; it meant good sport and satisfied their guests; every one was planning trips and expeditions, talking of slopes and telemarks, of flying speed and distance, of drifts and crust and frost. Vitality and enthusiasm pulsed in the very air; all were alert and active, positive, radiating currents of creative life even into the stuffy atmosphere of that crowded ball-room.

And the snow had caused it, the snow had brought it; all this discharge of eager sparkling energy was due primarily to the—Snow.

But in the mind of Hibbert, by some swift alchemy of his pagan yearnings, this energy became transmuted. It rarefied itself, gleaming in white and crystal currents of passionate anticipation, which he transferred, as by a species of electrical imagination, into the personality of the girl—the Girl of the Snow. She somewhere was waiting for him, expecting him, calling to him softly from those leagues of moonlit mountain. He remembered the touch of that cool, dry hand; the soft and icy breath against his cheek; the hush and softness of her presence in the way she came and the way she had gone again—like a flurry of snow the wind sent gliding up the slopes. She, like himself, belonged out there. He fancied that he heard her little windy voice come sifting to him through the snowy branches of the trees, calling his name . . . that haunting little voice that dived straight to the centre of his life as once, long years ago, two other voices used to do. . . .

But nowhere among the costumed dancers did he see her slender figure. He danced with one and all, distrait and absent, a stupid partner as each girl discovered, his eyes ever turning towards the door and windows, hoping to catch the luring face, the vision that did not come . . . and at length, hoping even against hope. For the ball-room thinned; groups left one by one, going home to their hotels and châlets; the band tired obviously; people sat drinking lemon-squashes at the little tables, the men mopping their foreheads, everybody ready for bed.

It was close on midnight. As Hibbert passed through the hall to get his overcoat and snow-boots, he saw men in the passage by the "sport-room," greasing their ski against an early start. Knapsack luncheons were being ordered by the kitchen swing doors. He sighed. Lighting a cigarette a friend offered him, he returned a confused reply to some question as to whether he could join their party in the morning. It seemed he did not hear it properly. He passed through the outer vestibule between the double glass doors, and went into the night.

The man who asked the question watched him go, an expression of anxiety momentarily in his eyes.

"Don't think he heard you," said another, laughing. "You've got to shout to Hibbert, his mind's so full of his work."

"He works too hard," suggested the first, "full of queer ideas and dreams."

But Hibbert's silence was not rudeness. He had not caught the invitation, that was all. The call of the hotel-world had faded. He no longer heard it. Another wilder call was sounding in his ears.

For up the street he had seen a little figure moving. Close against the shadows of the baker's shop it glided—white, slim, enticing.

VI

And at once into his mind passed the hush and softness of the snow—yet with it a searching, crying wildness for the heights. He knew by some incalculable, swift instinct she would not meet him in the village street. It was not there, amid crowding houses, she would speak to him. Indeed, already she had disappeared, melted from view up the white vista of the moonlit road. Yonder, he divined, she waited where the highway narrowed abruptly into the mountain path beyond the châlets.

It did not even occur to him to hesitate; mad though it seemed, and was—this sudden craving for the heights with her, at least for open spaces where the snow lay thick and fresh—it was too imperious to be denied. He did not remember going up to his room, putting the sweater over his evening clothes, and getting into the fur gauntlet gloves and the helmet cap of wool. Most certainly he had no recollection of fastening on his ski; he must have done it automatically. Some faculty of normal observation was in abeyance, as it were. His mind was out beyond the village—out with the snowy mountains and the moon.

Henri Défago, putting up the shutters over his *café* windows, saw him pass, and wondered mildly: "Un monsieur qui fait du ski à cette heure! Il est Anglais, donc . . . !" He shrugged his shoulders, as though a man had the right to choose his own way of death. And Marthe Perotti, the hunchback wife of the shoemaker, looking by chance from her window, caught his figure moving swiftly up the road. She had other thoughts, for she knew and believed the old traditions of the witches and snow-beings that steal the souls of men. She had even heard, 'twas said, the dreaded "synagogue" pass roaring down the street at night, and now, as then, she hid her eyes. "They've called to him . . . and he must go," she murmured, making the sign of the cross.

But no one sought to stop him. Hibbert recalled only a single incident until he found himself beyond the houses, searching for her along the fringe of forest where the moonlight met the snow in a bewildering frieze of fantastic shadows. And the incident was simply this—that he remembered passing the church. Catching the outline of its tower against the stars, he was aware of a faint sense of hesitation. A vague uneasiness came and went—jarred unpleasantly across the flow of his excited feelings, chilling exhilaration. He caught the instant's discord, dismissed it, and—passed on. The seduction of the snow smothered the hint before he realised that it had brushed the skirts of warning.

And then he saw her. She stood there waiting in a little clear space of shining snow, dressed all in white, part of the moonlight and the glistening background, her slender figure just discernible.

"I waited, for I knew you would come," the silvery little voice of windy beauty floated down to him. "You *had* to come."

"I'm ready," he answered, "I knew it too."

The world of Nature caught him to its heart in those few words— the wonder and the glory of the night and snow. Life leaped within him. The passion of his pagan soul exulted, rose in joy, flowed out to her. He neither reflected nor considered, but let himself go like the veriest schoolboy in the wildness of first love.

"Give me your hand," he cried, "I'm coming . . . !"

"A little farther on, a little higher," came her delicious answer. "Here it is too near the village—and the church."

And the words seemed wholly right and natural; he did not dream of questioning them; he understood that, with this little touch of civilisation in sight, the familiarity he suggested was impossible. Once out upon the open mountains, 'mid the freedom of huge slopes and towering peaks, the stars and moon to witness and the wilderness of snow to watch, they could taste an innocence of happy intercourse free from the dead conventions that imprison literal minds.

He urged his pace, yet did not quite overtake her. The girl kept always just a little bit ahead of his best efforts. . . . And soon they left the trees behind and passed on to the enormous slopes of the sea of snow that rolled in mountainous terror and beauty to the stars. The wonder of the white world caught him away. Under the steady moonlight it was more than haunting. It was a living, white, bewildering power that deliciously confused the senses and laid a spell of wild perplexity upon the heart. It was a personality that cloaked, and yet revealed, itself through all this sheeted whiteness of snow. It rose, went with him, fled before, and followed after. Slowly it dropped lithe, gleaming arms about his neck, gathering him in. . . .

Certainly some soft persuasion coaxed his very soul, urging him ever forwards, upwards, on towards the higher icy slopes. Judgment and reason left their throne, it seemed, completely, as in the madness of intoxication. The girl, slim and seductive, kept always just ahead, so that he never quite came up with her. He saw the white enchantment of her face and figure, something that streamed about her neck flying like a wreath of snow in the wind, and heard the alluring accents of her whispering voice that called from time to time: "A little farther on, a little higher. . . . Then we'll run home together!"

Sometimes he saw her hand stretched out to find his own, but each time, just as he came up with her, he saw her still in front, the hand and arm withdrawn. They took a gentle angle of ascent. The toil seemed nothing. In this crystal, wine-like air fatigue vanished. The sishing of the ski through the powdery surface of the snow was the only sound that broke the stillness; this, with his breathing and the rustle of her skirts, was all he heard. Cold moonshine, snow, and silence held the world. The sky was black, and the peaks beyond cut into it like frosted wedges of iron and steel. Far below the valley slept, the village long since hidden out of sight. He felt that he could never tire. . . . The sound of the church clock rose from time to time faintly through the air—more and more distant.

"Give me your hand. It's time now to turn back."

"Just one more slope," she laughed. "That ridge above us. Then we'll make for home." And her low voice mingled pleasantly with the purring of their ski. His own seemed harsh and ugly by comparison.

"But I have never come so high before. It's glorious! This world of silent snow and moonlight—and *you*. You're a child of the snow, I swear. Let me come up—closer—to see your face—and touch your little hand."

Her laughter answered him.

"Come on! A little higher. Here we're quite alone together."

"It's magnificent," he cried. "But why did you hide away so long?

I've looked and searched for you in vain ever since we skated—" he was going to say "ten days ago," but the accurate memory of time had gone from him; he was not sure whether it was days or years or minutes. His thoughts of earth were scattered and confused.

"You looked for me in the wrong places," he heard her murmur just above him. "You looked in places where I never go. Hotels and houses kill me. I avoid them." She laughed—a fine, shrill, windy little laugh.

"I loathe them too—"

He stopped. The girl had suddenly come quite close. A breath of ice passed through his very soul. She had touched him.

"But this awful cold!" he cried out, sharply, "this freezing cold that takes me. The wind is rising; it's a wind of ice. Come, let us turn . . . !"

But when he plunged forward to hold her, or at least to look, the girl was gone again. And something in the way she stood there a few feet beyond, and stared down into his eyes so steadfastly in silence, made him shiver. The moonlight was behind her, but in some odd way he could not focus sight upon her face, although so close. The gleam of eyes he caught, but all the rest seemed white and snowy as though he looked beyond her—out into space. . . .

The sound of the church bell came up faintly from the valley far below, and he counted the strokes—five. A sudden, curious weakness seized him as he listened. Deep within it was, deadly yet somehow sweet, and hard to resist. He felt like sinking down upon the snow and lying there. . . . They had been climbing for five hours. . . . It was, of course, the warning of complete exhaustion.

With a great effort he fought and overcame it. It passed away as suddenly as it came.

"We'll turn," he said with a decision he hardly felt. "It will be dawn before we reach the village again. Come at once. It's time for home."

The sense of exhilaration had utterly left him. An emotion that was akin to fear swept coldly through him. But her whispering answer turned it instantly to terror—a terror that gripped him horribly and turned him weak and unresisting.

"Our home is—*here!*" A burst of wild, high laughter, loud and shrill, accompanied the words. It was like a whistling wind. The wind *had* risen, and clouds obscured the moon. "A little higher—where we cannot hear the wicked bells," she cried, and for the first time seized him deliberately by the hand. She moved, was suddenly close against his face. Again she touched him.

And Hibbert tried to turn away in escape, and so trying, found for the first time that the power of the snow—that other power which does not exhilarate but deadens effort—was upon him. The suffocating weakness that it brings to exhausted men, luring them to the sleep of death in her clinging soft embrace, lulling the will and conquering all desire for life—this was awfully upon him. His feet were heavy and entangled. He could not turn or move.

The girl stood in front of him, very near; he felt her chilly breath upon his cheeks; her hair passed blindingly across his eyes; and that icy wind came with her. He saw her whiteness close; again, it seemed, his sight passed through her into space as though she had no face. Her arms were round his neck. She drew him softly downwards to his knees. He sank; he yielded utterly; he obeyed. Her weight was upon him, smothering, delicious. The snow was to his waist. . . . She kissed him softly on the lips, the eyes, all over his face. And then she spoke his name in that voice of love and wonder, the voice that held the accent of two others—both taken over long ago by Death—the voice of his mother, and of the woman he had loved.

He made one more feeble effort to resist. Then, realising even while he struggled that this soft weight about his heart was sweeter than anything life could ever bring, he let his muscles relax, and sank back into the soft oblivion of the covering snow. Her wintry kisses bore him into sleep.

VII

They say that men who know the sleep of exhaustion in the snow find no awakening on the hither side of death. . . . The hours passed and the moon sank down below the white world's rim. Then, suddenly, there came a little crash upon his breast and neck, and Hibbert—woke.

He slowly turned bewildered, heavy eyes upon the desolate mountains, stared dizzily about him, tried to rise. At first his muscles would not act; a numbing, aching pain possessed him. He uttered a long, thin cry for help, and heard its faintness swallowed by the wind. And then he understood vaguely why he was only warm—not dead. For this

very wind that took his cry had built up a sheltering mound of driven
snow against his body while he slept. Like a curving wave it ran beside
him. It was the breaking of its over-toppling edge that caused the
crash, and the coldness of the mass against his neck that woke him.

Dawn kissed the eastern sky; pale gleams of gold shot every peak
with splendour; but ice was in the air, and the dry and frozen snow
blew like powder from the surface of the slopes. He saw the points of
his ski projecting just below him. Then he—remembered. It seems he
had just strength enough to realise that, could he but rise and stand, he
might fly with terrific impetus towards the woods and village far beneath. The ski would carry him. But if he failed and fell . . . !

How he contrived it Hibbert never knew; this fear of death somehow called out his whole available reserve force. He rose slowly, balanced a moment, then, taking the angle of an immense zigzag, started
down the awful slopes like an arrow from a bow. And automatically
the splendid muscles of the practised ski-er and athlete saved and
guided him, for he was hardly conscious of controlling either speed or
direction. The snow stung face and eyes like fine steel shot; ridge after
ridge flew past; the summits raced across the sky; the valley leaped up
with bounds to meet him. He scarcely felt the ground beneath his feet
as the huge slopes and distance melted before the lightning speed of
that descent from death to life.

He took it in four mile-long zigzags, and it was the turning at each
corner that nearly finished him, for then the strain of balancing taxed
to the verge of collapse the remnants of his strength.

Slopes that have taken hours to climb can be descended in a short
half-hour on ski, but Hibbert had lost all count of time. Quite other
thoughts and feelings mastered him in that wild, swift dropping through
the air that was like the flight of a bird. For ever close upon his heels
came following forms and voices with the whirling snow-dust. He heard
that little silvery voice of death and laughter at his back. Shrill and wild,
with the whistling of the wind past his ears, he caught its pursuing tones;
but in anger now, no longer soft and coaxing. And it was accompanied;
she did not follow alone. It seemed a host of these flying figures of the
snow chased madly just behind him. He felt them furiously smite his
neck and cheeks, snatch at his hands and try to entangle his feet and
ski in drifts. His eyes they blinded, and they caught his breath away.

The terror of the heights and snow and winter desolation urged him forward in the maddest race with death a human being ever knew; and so terrific was the speed that before the gold and crimson had left the summits to touch the ice-lips of the lower glaciers, he saw the friendly forest far beneath swing up and welcome him.

And it was then, moving slowly along the edge of the woods, he saw a light. A man was carrying it. A procession of human figures was passing in a dark line laboriously through the snow. And—he heard the sound of chanting.

Instinctively, without a second's hesitation, he changed his course. No longer flying at an angle as before, he pointed his ski straight down the mountain-side. The dreadful steepness did not frighten him. He knew full well it meant a crashing tumble at the bottom, but he also knew it meant a doubling of his speed—with safety at the end. For, though no definite thought passed through his mind, he understood that it was the village *curé* who carried that little gleaming lantern in the dawn, and that he was taking the Host to a châlet on the lower slopes—to some peasant *in extremis*. He remembered her terror of the church and bells. She feared the holy symbols.

There was one last wild cry in his ears as he started, a shriek of the wind before his face, and a rush of stinging snow against closed eye-lids—and then he dropped through empty space. Speed took sight from him. It seemed he flew off the surface of the world.

Indistinctly he recalls the murmur of men's voices, the touch of strong arms that lifted him, and the shooting pains as the ski were unfastened from the twisted ankle . . . for when he opened his eyes again to normal life he found himself lying in his bed at the post office with the doctor at his side. But for years to come the story of "mad Hibbert's" ski-ing at night was recounted in that mountain village. He went, it seems, up slopes, and to a height that no man in his senses ever tried before. The tourists were agog about it for the rest of the season, and the very same day two of the bolder men went over the actual ground and photographed the slopes. Later Hibbert saw these photographs. He noticed one curious thing about them—though he did not mention it to any one:

There was only a single track.

The Transfer

The child first began to cry in the early afternoon—about three o'clock, to be exact. I remember the hour, because I had been listening with secret relief to the sound of the departing carriage. Those wheels fading into distance down the gravel drive with Mrs. Frene, and her daughter Gladys to whom I was governess, meant for me some hours' welcome rest, and the June day was oppressively hot. Moreover, there was this excitement in the little country household that had told upon us all, but especially upon myself. This excitement, running delicately behind all the events of the morning, was due to some mystery, and the mystery was of course kept concealed from the governess. I had exhausted myself with guessing and keeping on the watch. For some deep and unexplained anxiety possessed me, so that I kept thinking of my sister's dictum that I was really much too sensitive to make a good governess, and that I should have done far better as a professional clairvoyante.

Mr. Frene, senior, "Uncle Frank," was expected for an unusual visit from town about tea-time. That I knew. I also knew that his visit was concerned somehow with the future welfare of little Jamie, Gladys' seven-year-old brother. More than this, indeed, I never knew, and this missing link makes my story in a fashion incoherent—an important bit of the strange puzzle left out. I only gathered that the visit of Uncle Frank was of a condescending nature, that Jamie was told he must be upon his very best behaviour to make a good impression, and that Jamie, who had never seen his uncle, dreaded him horribly already in advance. Then, trailing thinly through the dying crunch of the carriage wheels this sultry afternoon, I heard the curious little wail of the child's crying, with the effect, wholly unaccountable, that every nerve in my body shot its bolt electrically, bringing me to my feet with a tingling of unequivocal alarm. Positively, the water ran into my eyes. I recalled his white distress that morning when told that Uncle Frank was motoring

250

down for tea and that he was to be "very nice indeed" to him. It had gone into me like a knife. All through the day, indeed, had run this nightmare quality of terror and vision.

"The man with the 'normous face?" he had asked in a little voice of awe, and then gone speechless from the room in tears that no amount of soothing management could calm. That was all I saw; and what he meant by "the 'normous face" gave me only a sense of vague presentiment. But it came as anti-climax somehow—a sudden revelation of the mystery and excitement that pulsed beneath the quiet of the stifling summer day. I feared for him. For of all that commonplace household I loved Jamie best, though professionally I had nothing to do with him. He was a high-strung, ultra-sensitive child, and it seemed to me that no one understood him, least of all his honest, tender-hearted parents; so that his little wailing voice brought me from my bed to the window in a moment like a call for help.

The haze of June lay over that big garden like a blanket; the wonderful flowers, which were Mr. Frene's delight, hung motionless; the lawns, so soft and thick, cushioned all other sounds; only the limes and huge clumps of guelder roses hummed with bees. Through this muted atmosphere of heat and haze the sound of the child's crying floated faintly to my ears—from a distance. Indeed, I wonder now that I heard it at all, for the next moment I saw him down beyond the garden, standing in his white sailor suit alone, two hundred yards away. He was down by the ugly patch where nothing grew—the Forbidden Corner. A faintness then came over me at once, a faintness as of death, when I saw him *there* of all places—where he never was allowed to go, and where, moreover, he was usually too terrified to go. To see him standing solitary in that singular spot, above all to hear him crying there, bereft me momentarily of the power to act. Then, before I could recover my composure sufficiently to call him in, Mr. Frene came round the corner from the Lower Farm with the dogs, and, seeing his son, performed that office for me. In his loud, good-natured, hearty voice he called him, and Jamie turned and ran as though some spell had broken just in time—ran into the open arms of his fond but uncomprehending father, who carried him indoors on his shoulder, while asking "what all this hubbub was about?" And, at their heels, the tail-less sheep-dogs followed, barking loudly, and performing what Jamie called their "Gravel Dance," because they ploughed up the moist, rolled gravel with their feet.

I stepped back swiftly from the window lest I should be seen. Had I witnessed the saving of the child from fire or drowning the relief could hardly have been greater. Only Mr. Frene, I felt sure, would not say and do the right thing quite. He would protect the boy from his own vain imaginings, yet not with the explanation that could really heal. They disappeared behind the rose trees, making for the house. I saw no more till later, when Mr. Frene, senior, arrived.

To describe the ugly patch as "singular" is hard to justify, perhaps, yet some such word is what the entire family sought, though never—oh, never!—used. To Jamie and myself, though equally we never mentioned it, that treeless, flowerless spot was more than singular. It stood at the far end of the magnificent rose garden, a bald, sore place, where the black earth showed uglily in winter, almost like a piece of dangerous bog, and in summer baked and cracked with fissures where green lizards shot their fire in passing. In contrast to the rich luxuriance of the whole amazing garden it was like a glimpse of death amid life, a centre of disease that cried for healing lest it spread. But it never did spread. Behind it stood the thick wood of silver birches and, glimmering beyond, the orchard meadow, where the lambs played.

The gardeners had a very simple explanation of its barrenness—that the water all drained off it owing to the lie of the slopes immediately about it, holding no remnant to keep the soil alive. I cannot say. It was Jamie—Jamie who felt its spell and haunted it, who spent whole hours there, even while afraid, and for whom it was finally labelled "strictly out of bounds" because it stimulated his already big imagination, not wisely but too darkly—it was Jamie who buried ogres there and heard it crying in an earthy voice, swore that it shook its surface sometimes while he watched it, and secretly gave it food in the form of birds or mice or rabbits he found dead upon his wanderings. And it was Jamie who put so extraordinarily into words the *feeling* that the horrid spot had given me from the moment I first saw it.

"It's bad, Miss Gould," he told me.

"But, Jamie, nothing in Nature is bad—exactly; only different from the rest sometimes."

"Miss Gould, if you please, then it's empty. It's not fed. It's dying because it can't get the food it wants."

And when I stared into the little pale face where the eyes shone so dark and wonderful, seeking within myself for the right thing to say to him, he added, with an emphasis and conviction that made me suddenly turn cold: "Miss Gould"—he always used my name like this in all his sentences—"it's hungry, don't you see? But *I* know what would make it feel all right."

Only the conviction of an earnest child, perhaps, could have made so outrageous a suggestion worth listening to for an instant; but for me, who felt that things an imaginative child believed were important, it came with a vast disquieting shock of reality. Jamie, in this exaggerated way, had caught at the edge of a shocking fact—a hint of dark, undiscovered truth had leaped into that sensitive imagination. Why there lay horror in the words I cannot say, but I think some power of darkness trooped across the suggestion of that sentence at the end, "I know what would make it feel all right." I remember that I shrank from asking explanation. Small groups of other words, veiled fortunately by his silence, gave life to an unspeakable possibility that hitherto had lain at the back of my own consciousness. The way it sprang to life proves, I think, that my mind already contained it. The blood rushed from my heart as I listened. I remember that my knees shook. Jamie's idea was—had been all along—my own as well.

And now, as I lay down on my bed and thought about it all, I understood why the coming of his uncle involved somehow an experience that wrapped terror at its heart. With a sense of nightmare certainty that left me too weak to resist the preposterous idea, too shocked, indeed, to argue or reason it away, this certainty came with its full, black blast of conviction; and the only way I can put it into words, since nightmare horror really is not properly tellable at all, seems this: that there *was* something missing in that dying patch of garden; something lacking that it ever searched for; something, once found and taken, that would turn it rich and living as the rest; more—that there *was* some living person who could do this for it. Mr. Frene, senior, in a word, "Uncle Frank," was this person who out of his abundant life could supply the lack—unwittingly.

For this connection between the dying, empty patch and the person of this vigorous, wealthy, and successful man had already lodged itself in my subconsciousness before I was aware of it. Clearly it must have lain there all along, though hidden. Jamie's words, his sudden pallor, his vibrating emotion of fearful anticipation had developed the plate, but it was his weeping alone there in the Forbidden Corner that had printed it. The photograph shone framed before me in the air. I hid my eyes. But for the redness—the charm of my face goes to pieces unless my eyes are clear—I could have cried. Jamie's words that morning about the "'normous face" came back upon me like a battering-ram.

Mr. Frene, senior, had been so frequently the subject of conversation in the family since I came, I had so often heard him discussed, and had then read so much about him in the papers—his energy, his philanthropy, his success with everything he laid his hand to—that a picture of the man had grown complete within me. I knew him as he was—within; or, as my sister would have said—clairvoyantly. And the only time I saw him (when I took Gladys to a meeting where he was chairman, and later *felt* his atmosphere and presence while for a moment he patronisingly spoke with her) had justified the portrait I had drawn. The rest, you may say, was a woman's wild imagining; but I think rather it was that kind of divining intuition which women share with children. If souls could be made visible, I would stake my life upon the truth and accuracy of my portrait.

For this Mr. Frene was a man who drooped alone, but grew vital in a crowd—because he used their vitality. He was a supreme, unconscious artist in the science of taking the fruits of others' work and living—for his own advantage. He vampired, unknowingly no doubt, every one with whom he came in contact; left them exhausted, tired, listless. Others fed him, so that while in a full room he shone, alone by himself and with no life to draw upon he languished and declined. In the man's immediate neighbourhood you felt his presence draining you; he took your ideas, your strength, your very words, and later used them for his own benefit and aggrandisement. Not evilly, of course; the man was good enough; but you felt that he was dangerous owing to the facile way he absorbed into himself all loose vitality that was to be had. His eyes and voice and presence devitalised you. Life, it seemed, not highly organised enough to resist, must shrink from his too near approach and hide away for fear of being appropriated, for fear, that is, of—death.

Jamie, unknowingly, put in the finishing touch to my unconscious portrait. The man carried about with him some silent, compelling trick of drawing out all your reserves—then swiftly pocketing them. At first you would be conscious of taut resistance; this would slowly shade off into weariness; the will would become flaccid; then you either moved away or yielded—agreed to all he said with a sense of weakness pressing ever closer upon the edges of collapse. With a male antagonist it might be different, but even then the effort of resistance would generate force that *he* absorbed and not the other. He never gave out. Some instinct taught him how to protect himself from that. To human beings, I mean, he never gave out. This time it was a very different matter. He had no more chance than a fly before the wheels of a huge—what Jamie used to call—"attraction" engine.

So this was how I saw him—a great human sponge, crammed and soaked with the life, or proceeds of life, absorbed from others—stolen. My idea of a human vampire was satisfied. He went about carrying these accumulations of the life of others. In this sense his "life" was not really his own. For the same reason, I think, it was not so fully under his control as he imagined.

And in another hour this man would be here. I went to the window. My eye wandered to the empty patch, dull black there amid the rich luxuriance of the garden flowers. It struck me as a hideous bit of emptiness yawning to be filled and nourished. The idea of Jamie playing round its bare edge was loathsome. I watched the big summer clouds above, the stillness of the afternoon, the haze. The silence of the overheated garden was oppressive. I had never felt a day so stifling, motionless. It lay there waiting. The household, too, was waiting—waiting for the coming of Mr. Frene from London in his big motor-car.

And I shall never forget the sensation of icy shrinking and distress with which I heard the rumble of the car. He had arrived. Tea was all ready on the lawn beneath the lime trees, and Mrs. Frene and Gladys, back from their drive, were sitting in wicker chairs. Mr. Frene, junior, was in the hall to meet his brother, but Jamie, as I learned afterwards, had shown such hysterical alarm, offered such bold resistance, that it had been deemed wiser to keep him in his room. Perhaps, after all, his presence might not be necessary. The visit clearly had to do with something on the uglier side of life—money, settlements, or what not; I never knew exactly; only that his parents were anxious, and that Uncle Frank had to be propitiated. It does not matter. That has nothing to do with the affair. What has to do with it—or I should not be telling the story—is that Mrs. Frene sent for me to come down "in my nice white dress, if I didn't mind," and that I was terrified, yet pleased, because it meant that a pretty face would be considered a welcome addition to the visitor's landscape. Also, most odd it was, I felt my presence was somehow inevitable, that in some way it was intended that I should witness what I did witness. And the instant I came upon the lawn—I hesitate to set it down, it sounds so foolish, disconnected—I could have sworn, as my eyes met his, that a kind of sudden darkness came, taking the summer brilliance out of everything, and that it was caused by troops of small black horses that raced about us from his person—to attack.

After a first momentary approving glance he took no further notice of me. The tea and talk went smoothly; I helped to pass the plates and cups, filling in pauses with little under-talk to Gladys. Jamie was never mentioned. Outwardly all seemed well, but inwardly everything was awful—skirting the edge of things unspeakable, and so charged with danger that I could not keep my voice from trembling when I spoke.

I watched his hard, bleak face; I noticed how thin he was, and the curious, oily brightness of his steady eyes. They did not glitter, but they drew you with a sort of soft, creamy shine like Eastern eyes. And everything he said or did announced what I may dare to call the *suction* of his presence. His nature achieved this result automatically. He dominated us all, yet so gently that until it was accomplished no one noticed it.

Before five minutes had passed, however, I was aware of one thing only. My mind focussed exclusively upon it, and so vividly that I marvelled the others did not scream, or run, or do something violent to prevent it. And it was this: that, separated merely by some dozen yards or so, this man, vibrating with the acquired vitality of others, stood within easy reach of that spot of yawning emptiness, waiting and eager to be filled. Earth scented her prey.

These two active "centres" were within fighting distance; he so thin, so hard, so keen, yet really spreading large with the loose "surround" of others' life he had appropriated, so practised and triumphant;

that other so patient, deep, with so mighty a draw of the whole earth behind it, and—ugh!—so obviously aware that its opportunity at last had come.

I saw it all as plainly as though I watched two great animals prepare for battle, both unconsciously; yet in some inexplicable way I saw it, of course, within me, and not externally. The conflict would be hideously unequal. Each side had already sent out emissaries, how long before I could not tell, for the first evidence *he* gave that something was going wrong with him was when his voice grew suddenly confused, he missed his words, and his lips trembled a moment and turned flabby. The next second his face betrayed that singular and horrid change, growing somehow loose about the bones of the cheek, and larger, so that I remembered Jamie's miserable phrase. The emissaries of the two kingdoms, the human and the vegetable, had met, I make it out, in that very second. For the first time in his long career of battening on others, Mr. Frene found himself pitted against a vaster kingdom than he knew and, so finding, shook inwardly in that little part that was his definite actual self. He felt the huge disaster coming.

"Yes, John," he was saying, in his drawling, self-congratulating voice, "Sir George gave me that car—gave it to me as a present. Wasn't it char—?" and then broke off abruptly, stammered, drew breath, stood up, and looked uneasily about him. For a second there was a gaping pause. It was like the click which starts some huge machinery moving—that instant's pause before it actually starts. The whole thing, indeed, then went with the rapidity of machinery running down and beyond control. I thought of a giant dynamo working silently and invisible.

"What's that?" he cried, in a soft voice charged with alarm. "What's that horrid place? And some one's crying there—who is it?"

He pointed to the empty patch. Then, before any one could answer, he started across the lawn towards it, going every minute faster. Before any one could move he stood upon the edge. He leaned over—peering down into it.

It seemed a few hours passed, but really they were seconds, for time is measured by the quality and not the quantity of sensations it contains. I saw it all with merciless, photographic detail, sharply etched amid the general confusion. Each side was intensely active, but only one side, the human, exerted all its force—in resistance. The other merely stretched out a feeler, as it were, from its vast, potential strength; no more was necessary. It was such a soft and easy victory. Oh, it was rather pitiful! There was no bluster or great effort on one side at least. Close by his side I witnessed it, for I, it seemed, alone had moved and followed him. No one else stirred, though Mrs. Frene clattered noisily with the cups, making some sudden impulsive gesture with her hands, and Gladys, I remember, gave a cry—it was like a little scream—"Oh, mother, it's the heat, isn't it?" Mr. Frene, her father, was speechless, pale as ashes.

But the instant I reached his side, it became clear what had drawn me there thus instinctively. Upon the other side, among the silver birches, stood little Jamie. He was watching. I experienced—for him— one of those moments that shake the heart; a liquid fear ran all over me, the more effective because unintelligible really. Yet I felt that if I could know all, and what lay actually behind, my fear would be more than justified; that the thing *was* awful, full of awe.

And then it happened—a truly wicked sight—like watching a universe in action, yet all contained within a small square foot of space. I think he understood vaguely that if some one could only take his place he might be saved, and that was why, discerning instinctively the easiest substitute within reach, he saw the child and called aloud to him across the empty patch, "James, my boy, come here!"

His voice was like a thin report, but somehow flat and lifeless, as when a rifle misses fire, sharp, yet weak; it had no "crack" in it. It was really supplication. And, with amazement, I heard my own ring out imperious and strong, though I was not conscious of saying it, "Jamie, don't move. Stay where you are!" But Jamie, the little child, obeyed neither of us. Moving up nearer to the edge, he stood there—laughing! I heard that laughter, but could have sworn it did not come from him. The empty, yawning patch gave out that sound.

Mr. Frene turned sideways, throwing up his arms. I saw his hard, bleak face grow somehow wider, spread through the air, and downwards. A similar thing, I saw, was happening at the same time to his entire person, for it drew out into the atmosphere in a stream of movement. The face for a second made me think of those toys of green india-rubber that children pull. It grew enormous. But this was an external impression only. What actually happened, I clearly understood, was that all this vitality and life he had transferred from others to himself for years was now in turn being taken from him and transferred—elsewhere.

One moment on the edge he wobbled horribly, then with that queer sideways motion, rapid yet ungainly, he stepped forward into the middle of the patch and fell heavily upon his face. His eyes, as he dropped, faded shockingly, and across the countenance was written plainly what I can only call an expression of destruction. He looked utterly destroyed. I caught a sound—from Jamie?—but this time not of laughter. It was like a gulp; it was deep and muffled and it dipped away into the earth. Again I thought of a troop of small black horses galloping away down a subterranean passage beneath my feet—plunging into the depths—their tramping growing fainter and fainter into buried distance. In my nostrils was a pungent smell of earth.

And then—all passed. I came back into myself. Mr. Frene, junior, was lifting his brother's head from the lawn where he had fallen from the heat, close beside the tea-table. He had never really moved from there. And Jamie, I learned afterwards, had been the whole time asleep upon his bed upstairs, worn out with his crying and unreasoning alarm. Gladys came running out with cold water, sponge, and towel, brandy too—all kinds of things. "Mother, it was the heat, wasn't it?" I heard her whisper, but I did not catch Mrs. Frene's reply. From her face it struck me that she was bordering on collapse herself. Then the butler followed, and they just picked him up and carried him into the house. He recovered even before the doctor came.

But the queer thing to me is that I was convinced the others all had seen what I saw, only that no one said a word about it; and to this day no one *has* said a word. And that was, perhaps, the most horrid part of all.

From that day to this I have scarcely heard a mention of Mr. Frene, senior. It seemed as if he dropped suddenly out of life. The papers never mentioned him. His activities ceased, as it were. His after-life, at any rate, became singularly ineffective. Certainly he achieved nothing worth public mention. But it may be only that, having left the employ of Mrs. Frene, there was no particular occasion for me to hear anything.

The after-life of that empty patch of garden, however, was quite otherwise. Nothing, so far as I know, was done to it by gardeners, or in the way of draining it or bringing in new earth, but even before I left in the following summer it had changed. It lay untouched, full of great, luscious, driving weeds and creepers, very strong, full-fed, and bursting thick with life.

The Messenger

I have never been afraid of ghostly things, attracted rather with a curious live interest, though it is always out of doors that strange Presences get nearest to me, and in Nature I have encountered warnings, messages, presentiments, and the like, that, by way of help or guidance, have later justified themselves. I have, therefore, welcomed them. But in the little rooms of houses things of much value rarely come, for the thick air chokes the wires, as it were, and distorts or mutilates the clear delivery.

But the other night, here in the carpenter's house, where my attic windows beckon to the mountains and the woods, I woke with the uncomfortably strong suggestion that something was on the way, and that I was not ready. It came along the by-ways of deep sleep. I woke abruptly, alarmed before I was even properly awake. Something was approaching with great swiftness—and I was unprepared.

Across the lake there were faint signs of colour behind the distant Alps, but terraces of mist still lay grey above the vineyards, and the slim poplar, whose tip was level with my face, no more than rustled in the wind of dawn. A shiver, not brought to me by any wind, ran through my nerves, for I knew with a certainty no arguing could lessen nor dispel that something from immensely far away was deliberately now approaching me. The touch of wonder in advance of it was truly awful; its splendour, size, and grandeur belonged to conditions I had surely never known. It came through empty spaces—from another world. While I lay asleep it had been already on the way.

I stood there a moment, seeking for some outward sign that might betray its nature. The last stars were fading in the northern sky, and blue and dim lay the whole long line of the Jura, cloaked beneath still slumbering forests. There was a rumbling of a distant train. Now and then a dog barked in some outlying farm. The Night was up and walking, though as yet she moved but slowly from the sky. Shadows still draped the world. And the warning that had reached me first in sleep rushed through my tingling nerves once more with a certainty not far removed from shock. Something from another world was drawing every minute nearer, with a speed that made me tremble and half-breathless. It would presently arrive. It would stand close beside me and look straight into my face. Into these very eyes that searched the mist and shadow for an outward sign it would gaze intimately with a Message brought for me alone. But into these narrow walls it could only come with difficulty. The message would be maimed. There still was time for preparation. And I hurried into clothes and made my way downstairs and out into the open air.

Thus, at first, by climbing fast, I kept ahead of it, and soon the village lay beneath me in its nest of shadow, and the limestone ridges far above dropped nearer. But the awe and terrible deep wonder did not go. Along these mountain paths, whose every inch was so intimate that I could follow them even in the dark, this sense of breaking grandeur clung to my footsteps, keeping close. Nothing upon the earth—familiar, friendly, well-known, little earth—could have brought this sense that pressed upon the edges of true reverence. It was the awareness that some speeding messenger from spaces far, far beyond the world would presently stand close and touch me, would gaze into my little human eyes, would leave its message as of life or death, and then depart upon its fearful way again—it was this that conveyed the feeling of apprehension that went with me.

And instinctively, while rising higher and higher, I chose the darkest and most sheltered way. I sought the protection of the trees, and ran into the deepest vaults of the forest. The moss was soaking wet beneath my feet, and the thousand tapering spires of the pines dipped upwards into a sky already brightening with palest gold and crimson. There was a whispering and a rustling overhead as the trees, who know everything before it comes, announced to one another that the thing I sought to hide from was already very, very near. Plunging deeper into the woods to hide, this detail of sure knowledge followed me and laughed: that the speed of this august arrival was one which made the greatest speed I ever dreamed of a mere standing still. . . .

I hid myself where possible in the darkness that was growing every minute more rare. The air was sharp and exquisitely fresh. I heard birds calling. The low, wet branches kissed my face and hair. A sense of glad relief came over me that I had left the closeness of the little attic chamber, and that I should eventually meet this huge New-comer in the wide, free spaces of the mountains. There must be room where I could hold myself unmanacled to meet it. . . . The village lay far beneath me, a patch of smoke and mist and soft red-brown roofs among the vineyards. And then my gaze turned upwards, and through a rift in the close-wrought ceiling of the trees I saw the clearness of the open sky. A strip of cloud ran through it, carrying off the Night's last little dream . . . and down into my heart dropped instantly that cold breath of awe I have known but once in life, when staring through the stupendous mouth within the Milky Way—that opening into the outer spaces of eternal darkness, unlit by any single star, men call the Coal Hole.

The futility of escape then took me bodily, and I renounced all further flight. From this speeding Messenger there was no hiding possible. His splendid shoulders already brushed the sky. I heard the rushing of his awful wings . . . yet in that deep, significant silence with which light steps upon the clouds of morning.

And simultaneously I left the woods behind me and stood upon a naked ridge of rock that all night long had watched the stars.

Then terror passed away like magic. Cool winds from the valleys bore me up. I heard the tinkling of a thousand cowbells from pastures far below in a score of hidden valleys. The cold departed, and with it every trace of little fears. My eyes seemed for an instant blinded, and I knew that deep sense of joy which seems so "unearthly" that it almost stains the sight with the veil of tears. The soul sank to her knees in prayer and worship.

For the messenger from another world had come. He stood beside me on that dizzy ledge. Warmth clothed me, and I knew myself akin to deity. He stood there, gazing straight into my little human eyes. He touched me everywhere. Above the distant Alps the sun came up. His eye looked close into my own.

The Golden Fly

It fell upon him out of a clear sky just when existence seemed on its very best behaviour, and he savagely resented the undeserved affliction of it. Involving him in an atrocious scandal that reflected directly upon his honour, it destroyed in a moment the erection his entire life had so laboriously built up—his reputation. In the eyes of the world he was a broken, discredited man, at the very moment, moreover, when his most cherished ambitions touched fulfilment. And the cruelty of it appalled his sense of justice, for it was impossible to vindicate himself without inculpating others who were dearer to him than life. It seemed more than he could bear; and the grim course he contemplated—decision itself as yet hung darkly waiting in the background—appeared the only way of escape that offered.

He had discussed the matter with friends until his brain whirled. Their sympathy maddened him, with hints of *qui s'excuse s'accuse,* and he turned at last in desperation to something that could not answer back. For the first time in his life he turned to Nature—to that dead, inanimate Nature he had left to poets and rhapsodising women: "I must face it alone," he put it. For the Finger of God was a phrase without meaning to him, and his entire being contained no trace of the religious instinct. He was a business man, honest, selfish, and ambitious; and the collapse of his worldly position was paramount to the collapse of the universe itself—his universe, at any rate. This "crumbling of the universe" was the thought he took out with him. He left the house by the path that led into solitude, and reached the heathery expanse that formed one of the breathing-places of the New Forest. There he flung himself down wearily in the shadow of a little pine-copse. And his crumbled universe lay down with him, for he could not escape it.

Taking the pistol from the hip-pocket where it hurt him, he lay upon his back and watched the clouds. Half stunned, half dazed, he stared into the sky. The perfumed wind played softly on his eyes; he smelt the heather-honey; golden flies hung motionless in the air, like coloured pins fastening the sunshine against the blue curtain of the summer, while dragon-flies, like darting shuttles, wove across its pattern their threads of gleaming bronze. He heard the petulant crying of the peewits, and watched their tumbling flight. Below him tinkled a rivulet, its brown water rippling between banks of peaty earth. Everywhere was singing, peace, and careless unconcern.

And this lordly indifference of Nature calmed and soothed him. Neither human pain nor the injustice of man could shift the key of the water, alter the peewits' cry a single tone, nor influence one fraction of an inch those cloudy frigates of vapour that sailed the sky. The earth bulged sunwards as she had bulged for centuries. The power of her steady gait, superbly calm, breathed everywhere with grandeur— undismayed, unhasting, and supremely confident.... And, like the flash of those golden flies, there leaped suddenly upon him this vivid thought: that his world of agony lay neatly buttoned up within the tiny space of his own brain. Outside himself it had no existence at all. His mind contained it—the minute interior he called his heart. From this vaster world about him it lay utterly apart, like deeds in the black boxes of japanned tin he kept at the office, shut off from the universe, huddled in an overcrowded space within his skull.

How this commonplace thought reached him, garbed in such startling novelty, was odd enough; for it seemed as though the fierceness of his pain had burned away something. His thoughts it merely enflamed; but this other thing it consumed. Something that had obscured clear vision shrivelled before it as a piece of paper, eaten up by fire, dwindles down into a thimbleful of unimportant ashes. The thicket of his mind grew half transparent. At the farther end he saw, for the first time—light. The perspective of his inner life, hitherto so enormous, telescoped into the proportions of a miniature. Just as momentous and significant as before, it was somehow abruptly different—seen from another point of view. The suffering had burned up rubbish he himself had piled over the head of a little Fact. Like a point of metal that glows yet will not burn, he discerned in the depths of him the essential shining fact that not all this ruinous conflagration could destroy. And this brilliant, indestructible kernel was—his Innocence. The rest was self-reared rubbish: opinion of the world. He had magnified an atom into a universe. . . .

Pain, as it seemed, had cleared a way for the sublimity of Nature to approach him. The calm old Universe rolled past. The deep, majestic Day gave him a push, as though the shoulder of some star had brushed his own. He had thought his feelings were the world: instead, they were merely his way of looking at it. The actual "world" was some glorious, unchanging thing he never saw direct. His attitude of mind was but a peephole into it. The choice of his particular peephole, moreover, lay surely within the power of his individual will. The anguish, centred upon so small a point, had seemed to affect the entire spread universe around him, whereas in reality it affected nothing but his attitude of mind towards it. The truism struck him like a blow between the eyes, that a man is what he thinks or feels himself to be. It leaped the barrier between words and meaning. The intellectual concept became a hard-edged fact, because he realised it—for the first time in his very circumscribed life. And this dreadful pain that had made even suicide seem desirable was entirely a fabrication of his own mind. The universe about him rolled on just the same in the majesty of its eternal purpose. His tiny inner world was clouded, but the glory of this stupendous world about him was undimmed, untroubled, unaffected. Even death itself . . .

With a swift smash of the hand he crushed the golden fly that settled on his knee. The murder was done impulsively, utterly without intention. He watched the little point of gold quiver for a moment among the hairs of the rough tweed; lie still for ever . . . but the scent of heather-honey filled the air as before; the wind passed sighing through the pines; the clouds still sailed their uncharted sea of blue. There lay the whole spread surface of the Forest in the sun. Only the attitude of the golden fly towards it all was gone. A single, tiny point of view had disappeared. Nature passed on calmly and unhasting; she took no note.

Then, with a rush of awe, another thought flashed through him: Nature *had* taken note. There was a difference everywhere. Not a sparrow falleth, he remembered, without God knowing. God was certainly in Nature somewhere. His clumsy senses could not register this difference, yet it was there. His own small world, fed by these senses, was after all the merest little corner of Existence. To the whole of Existence, that included himself, the golden fly, the sun, and all the stars, he must somehow answer for his crime. It was a wanton interference with a sublime and sovereign Purpose that he now divined for the first time. He looked at the wee point of gold lying still and silent in the forest of hairs. He realised the enormity of his act. It could not have been graver had he put out the sun, or the little, insignificant flame of his own existence. He had done a criminal, evil thing, for he had put an end to a certain point of view; had wiped it out; made it impossible. Had the fly been quicker, less easily overwhelmed, or more tenacious of the scrap of universal life it used, Nature would at this instant be richer for its little contribution to the whole of things—to which he himself also belonged. And wherein, he asked himself, did he differ from that fly in the importance, the significance of his contribution to the universe? The soul . . . ? He had never given the question a single thought; but if the scrap of life he owned was called a soul, why should that point of golden glory not comprise one too? Its minute size, its trivial purpose, its few hours of apparently futile existence . . . these formed no true criterion . . . !

Similarly, the thought rushed over him, a Hand was being stretched out to crush himself. His pain was the shadow of its approach; anger in his heart, the warning. Unless he were quick enough, adroit and skilled enough, he also would be wiped out, while Nature continued her slow, unhasting way without him. His attitude towards the personal pain was really the test of his ability, of his merit—of his right to survive. Pain teaches, pain develops, pain brings growth: he had heard it since his copybook days. But now he realised it, as again thought leaped the barrier between familiar words and meaning. In his attitude of mind to his catastrophe lay his salvation or his . . . death.

In some such confused and blundering fashion, because along unaccustomed channels, the truth charged into him to overwhelm, yet bringing with it an unwonted sense of joy that seemed to break a crust which long had held back—life. Thus tapped, these sources gushed forth and bubbled over, spread about his being, flooded him with hope and courage, above all with—calmness. Nature held forces just as real and living as human sympathy, and equally able to modify the soul. And Nature was always accessible. A sense of huge companionship, denied him by the littleness of his fellow-men, stole sweetly over him. It was amazingly uplifting, yet fear came close behind it, as he realised the presumption of his former attitude of cynical indifference. These Powers were aware of his petty insolence, yet had not crushed him. . . . It was, of course, the awakening of the religious instinct in a man who hitherto had worshipped merely a rather low-grade form of intellect.

And, while the enormous confusion of it shook him, this sense of incommunicable sweetness remained. Bright haunting eyes, with love in them, gazed at him from the blue; and this thing that came so close, stood also far away upon the line of the horizon. It was everywhere. It filled the hollows, but towered over him as well towards the pinnaces of cloud. It was in the sharpness of the peewits' cry, and in the water's murmur. It whispered in the pine-boughs, and blazed in every patch of sunlight. And it was glory, pure and simple. It filled him with a sense of strength for which he could find but one description—Triumph.

And so, first, the anger faded from his mind and crept away. Resentment then slunk after it. Revolt and disappointment also melted, and bitterness gave place to the most marvellous peace the man had ever known. Then came resignation to fill the empty places. Pain, as a means and not an end, had cleared the way, though the accomplishment was like a miracle. But Conversion *is* a miracle. No ordinary pain can bring it. This anguish he understood now in a new relation to life—as something to be taken willingly into himself and dealt with, all regardless of public opinion. What people said and thought was in their world, not in his. It was less than nothing. The pain cultivated dormant tracts. The terror also purged. It disclosed. . . .

He watched the wind, and even the wind brought revelation; for without obstacles in its path it would be silent. He watched the sunshine, and the sunshine taught him too; for without obstacles to fling it back against his eye, he could never see it. He would neither hear the tinkling water nor feel the summer heat unless both one and other overcame some reluctant medium in their pathways. And, similarly with his moral being—his pain resulted from the friction of his personal ambitions against the stress of some noble Power that sought to lift him higher. That Power he could not know direct, but he recognised its strain against him by the resistance it generated in the inertia of his selfishness. His attitude of mind had switched completely round. It was what the preachers termed development through suffering.

Moreover, he had acquired this energy of resistance somehow from the wind and sun and the beauty of a common summer's day. Their peace and strength had passed into himself. Unconsciously on his way home he drew upon it steadily. He tossed the pistol into a pool of water. Nature had healed him; and Nature, should he turn weak again, was always there. It was very wonderful. He wanted to sing. . . .

The Heath Fire

The men at luncheon in Rennie's Surrey cottage that September day were discussing, of course, the heat. All agreed it had been exceptional. But nothing unusual was said until O'Hara spoke of the heath fires. They had been rather terrific, several in a single day, devouring trees and bushes, endangering human life, and spreading with remarkable rapidity. The flames, too, had been extraordinarily high and vehement for heath fires. And O'Hara's tone had introduced into the commonplace talk something new—the element of mystery; it was nothing definite he said, but manner, eyes, hushed voice and the rest conveyed it. And it was genuine. What he *felt* reached the others rather than what he said. The atmosphere in the little room, with the honeysuckle trailing sweetly across the open windows, changed; the talk became of a sudden less casual, frank, familiar; and the men glanced at one another across the table, laughing still, yet with an odd touch of constraint marking little awkward, unfilled pauses. Being a group of normal Englishmen, they disliked mystery; it made them feel uncomfortable; for the things O'Hara hinted at had touched that kind of elemental terror that lurks secretly in all human beings. Guarded by "culture," but never wholly concealed, the unwelcome thing made its presence known—the hint of primitive dread that, for instance, great thunder-storms, tidal waves, or violent conflagrations rouse.

And instinctively they fell at once to discussing the obvious causes of the fires. The stockbroker, scenting imagination, edged mentally away, sniffing. But the journalist was full of brisk information, "simply given."

"The sun starts them in Canada, using a dewdrop as a lens," he said, "and an engine's spark, remember, carries an immense distance without losing its heat."

"But hardly miles," said another, who had not been really listening.

"It's my belief," put in the critic keenly, "that a lot were done on purpose. Bits of live coal wrapped in cloth were found, you know." He was a little, weasel-faced iconoclast, dropping the acid of doubt and disbelief wherever he went, but offering nothing in the place of what he destroyed. His head was turret-shaped, lips tight and thin, nose and chin running to points like gimlets, with which he bored into the un-remunerative clays of life.

"The general unrest, yes," the journalist supported him, and tried to draw the conversation on to labour questions. But their host pre-ferred the fire talk. "I must say," he put in gravely, "that some of the blazes hereabouts were uncommonly—er—queer. They started, I mean, so oddly. You remember, O'Hara, only last week that suspicious one over Kettlebury way—?"

It seemed he wished to draw the artist out, and that the artist, feel-ing the general opposition, declined.

"Why seek an unusual explanation at all?" the critic said at length, impatiently. "It's all natural enough, if you ask me."

"Natural! Oh yes!" broke in O'Hara, with a sudden vehemence that betrayed feeling none had as yet suspected; "provided you don't limit the word to mean only what we understand. There's nothing any-where—unnatural."

A laugh cut short the threatened tirade, and the journalist ex-pressed the general feeling with "Oh *you*, Jim! You'd see a devil in a dust-storm, or a fairy in the tea-leaves of your cup!"

"And why not, pray? Devils and fairies arc every bit as true as formulæ."

Some one tactfully guided them away from a profitless discussion, and they talked glibly of the damage done, the hideousness of the de-stroyed moors, the gaunt, black, ugly slopes, fifty-foot flames, roaring noises, and the splendour of the enormous smoke-clouds that had filled the skies. And Rennie, still hoping to coax O'Hara, repeated tales the beaters had brought in that crying, as though living things were caught, had been heard in places, and that some had seen tall shapes of fire passing headlong through the choking smoke. For the note O'Hara had struck refused to be ignored. It went on sounding under-neath the commonest remark; and the atmosphere to the end retained that curious tinge that he had given to it—of the strange, the ominous, the mysterious and unexplained. Until, at last, the artist, having added nothing further to the talk, got up with some abruptness and left the room. He complained briefly that the fever he had suffered from still bothered him and he would go and lie down a bit. The heat, he said, oppressed him.

A silence followed his departure. The broker drew a sigh as though the market had gone up. But Rennie, old, comprehending friend, looked anxious. "Excitement," he said, "not oppression, is the word he meant. He's always a bit strung up when that Black Sea fever gets him. He brought it with him from Batoum." And another brief silence followed.

"Been with you most of the summer, hasn't he?" enquired the journalist, on the trail of a "par," "painting those wild things of his that no one understands." And their host, weighing a moment how much he might in fairness tell, replied—among friends it was—"Yes; and this summer they have been more—er—wild and wonderful than usual—an extraordinary rush of colour—splendid schemes, 'conceptions,' I believe you critics call 'em, of fire, as though, in a way, the unusual heat had possessed him for interpretation."

The group expressed its desultory interest by uninspired interjections.

"That was what he meant just now when he said the fires had been mysterious, required explanation, or something—the way they started, rather," concluded Rennie.

Then he hesitated. He laughed a moment, and it was an uneasy, apologetic little laugh. How to continue he hardly knew. Also, he wished to protect his friend from the cheap jeering of miscomprehension. "He is very imaginative, you know," he went on, quietly, as no one spoke. "You remember that glorious mad thing he did of the Fallen Lucifer—driving a star across the heavens till the heat of the descent set a light to half the planets, scorched the old moon to the white cinder that she now is, and passed close enough to earth to send our oceans up in a single jet of steam? Well, this time—he's been at something every bit as wild, only truer—finer. And what is it? Briefly, then, he's got the idea, it seems, that the unusual heat from the sun this year has penetrated deep enough—in places—especially on these unprotected heaths that retain their heat so cleverly—to reach another kindred expression—to waken a response—in sympathy, you see—from the central fires of the earth."

He paused again a moment awkwardly, conscious how clumsily he expressed it. "The parent getting into touch again with its lost child, eh? See the idea? Return of the Fire Prodigal, as it were?"

His listeners stared in silence, the broker looking his obvious relief that O'Hara was not on 'Change, the critic's eyes glancing sharply down that pointed, boring nose of his.

"And the central fires have felt it and risen in response," continued Rennie in a lower voice. "You see the idea? It's big, to say the least. The volcanoes have answered too—there's old Etna, the giant of 'em all, breaking out in fifty new mouths of flame. Heat is latent in everything, only waiting to be called out. That match you're striking, this coffee-pot, the warmth in our bodies, and so on—their heat comes first from the sun, and is therefore an actual part of the sun, the origin of all heat and life. And so O'Hara, you know, who sees the universe as a single homogeneous *One* and—and—well, I give it up. Can't explain it, you see. You must get him to do that. But somehow this year—cloudless—the protecting armour of water all gone too—the sun's rays managed to sink in and reach their kind buried deep below. Perhaps, later, we may get him to show us the studies that he's made— whew!—the most—er—amazing things you ever saw!"

The "superiority" of unimaginative minds was inevitable, making Rennie regret that he had told so much. It was almost as if he had been untrue to his friend. But at length the group broke up for the afternoon. They left messages for O'Hara. Two motored, and the journalist took the train. The critic followed his sharp nose to London, where he might ferret out the failures that his mind delighted in. And when they were gone the host slipped quickly upstairs to find his friend. The heat was unbearable to suffocation, the little bedroom like an oven. But Jim O'Hara was not in it.

For, instead of lying down as he had said, a fierce revolt, stirred by the talk of those unvisioned minds below, had wakened, and the deep, sensitive, poet's soul in him had leaped suddenly to the acceptance of an impossible thing. He had escaped, driven forth by the secret call of wonder. He made full speed for the destroyed moors. Fever or no fever, he must see for himself. Did no one understand? Was he the only one? . . . Walking quickly, he passed the Frensham Ponds, came through that spot of loneliness and beauty, the Lion's Mouth, noting that even there the pool of water had dried up and the rushes waved in the hot air over a bed of hard, caked mud, and so reached within the hour the wide expanse of Thursley Common. On every side the world stretched dark and burnt, a cemetery of cinders. Great thrills rushed through his heart; and with the power of a tide that yet came at flashing speed the truth rose up in him. . . . Half running now, he plunged forward another mile or two, and found himself, the only living thing, amid the great waste of heather-land. The blazing sunlight drenched it. It lay, a sheet of weird dark beauty, spreading like a black, enormous garden as far as the eye could reach.

Then, breathless, he paused and looked about him. Within his heart something, long smouldering, ran into sudden flame. Light blazed upon his inner world. For as the scorch of vehement passion may quicken tracts of human consciousness that lie ordinarily inert and unproductive, so here the surface of the earth had turned alive. He knew; he saw; he understood.

Here, in these open sun-traps that gathered and retained the heat, the fire of the Universe had dropped and lain, increasing week by week. These parched, dry months, the soil, free from rejecting and protective moisture, had let it all accumulate till at length it had sunk downwards, inwards, and the sister fires below, responding to the touch of their ancient parent source, too long unfelt, had answered with a swift uprising roar. They had come up with answering joy, and here and there had actually reached the surface, and had leaped out with dancing cry, wild to escape from an age-long prison back to their huge, eternal origin.

This sunshine, ah! what was it? These farthing dips of heat men complained about in their tiny, cage-like houses! It scorched the grass and fields, yes; but the surface never held it long enough to let it sink to union with its kindred of the darker fires beneath! These cried for it, but union was ever denied and stifled by the weight of cooled and cooling rock. And the ages of separation had almost cooled remembrance too—fire—the kiss and strength of fire—the flaming embrace and burning lips of the father sun himself. . . . He could have cried with the fierce delight of it all, and the picture he would paint rose there before him, burnt gloriously into the canvas of the entire heavens. Was not his own heat and life also from the sun? . . .

He stared about him in the deep silence of the afternoon. The world was still. It basked in the windless heat. No living thing stirred, for the common forms of life had fled away. Earth waited. He, too, waited. And then some touch of intuition, blown to white heat, supplied the link the pedestrian intellect missed, and he knew that what he waited for was on the way. For he would *see*. The message he should paint would come before his outer eye as well, though not, as he had first stupidly expected, on some grand, enormous scale. Rather would it be the equivalent of that still, small voice that once had inspired an entire nation. . . .

The wind passed very softly across the un-burnt patch of heather where he lay; he heard it rustling in the skeletons of scorched birch trees, and in the gorse and furze bushes that the flame had left so ghostly pale. Farther off it sang in the isolated pines, dying away like surf upon some far-off reef. He smelt the bitter perfume of burnt soil, the pungent, acrid odour of beaten ashes. The purple-black of the moors yawned like openings in the side of the earth. In all directions for miles stretched the deep emptiness of the heather-lands, an immense, dark, magic garden, still black with the feet of wonder that had flown across it and left it so beautifully scarred. The shadow of the terrible embrace still trailed and lingered as though Midnight had screened a time of passion with this curtain of her softest plumes.

And *they* had called it ugly, had spoken of its marred beauty, its hideousness! He laughed exultantly as he drank it in, for the weird and savage splendour everywhere broke loose and spread, passing from the earth into the receptive substance of his own mind. Even the roots of gorse and heather, like petrified, shadow-eating snakes, charged with the mystery of that eternal underworld whence they had risen, lay waiting for the return of the night of sleep whence Fire had wakened them. Lost ghosts of a salamander army that the flame had swept above the ground, they lay anguished and frightened in the glare of the unaccustomed sun. . . .

And waiting, he stared about him in the deep silence of the afternoon. Hazy with distance he saw the peak of Crooksbury, dim in its sheet of pines, waving a blue-plumed crest into the sky for signal; and close about him rose the more sombre glory of the lesser knolls and boulders, still cloaked in the swarthy magic of the smoke. Amid pools of ashes in the nearer hollows he saw the blue beauty of the fire-weed that rushes instantly into life behind all conflagrations. It was blowing softly in the wind. And here and there, set like emeralds upon some dusky bosom, lay the brilliant spires of young bracken that rose to clap a thousand tiny hands in the heart of exquisite desolation. In a cloud of green they rustled in the wind above the sea of black. . . . And so within himself O'Hara realised the huge excitement of the flame this fragment of the earth had felt. For Fire, mysterious symbol of universal life, spirit that prodigally gives itself without itself diminishing, had passed in power across this ancient heather-land, leaving the soul of it all naked and unashamed. The sun had loved it. The fires below had risen up and answered. They had known that union with their source which some call death. . . .

And the fires were rising still. The poet's heart in him became suddenly and awfully aware. Ye stars of fire! This patch of unburnt heather where he lay had been untouched as yet, but now the flame in his soul had brought the little needed link and he would *see*. The thing of wonder that the Universe should teach him how to paint was already on the way. Called by the sun, tremendous, splendid parent, the central fires were still rising.

And he turned, weakness and exultation racing for possession of him. The wind passed softly over his face, and with it came a faint, dry sound. It was distant and yet close beside him. At the stir of it there rose also in himself a strange vast thing that was bigger than the bulk of the moon and wide as the extension of swept forests, yet small and gentle as a blade of grass that pricks the lawn in spring. And he realised then that "within" and "without" had turned one, and that over the entire moorland arrived this thing that was happening too in a white-hot point of his own heart. He was linked with the sun and the farthest star, and in his little finger glowed the heat and fire of the universe itself. In sympathy *his own fires were rising too.*

The sound was born—a faint, light noise of crackling in the heather at his feet. He bent his head and searched, and among the obscure and tiny underways of the roots he saw a tip of curling smoke rise slowly upwards. It moved in a thin, blue spiral past his face. Then terror took him that was like a terror of the mountains, yet with it at the same time a realisation of beauty that made the heart leap within him into dazzling radiance. For the incense of this fairy column of thin smoke drew his soul out with it—upwards towards its source. He rose to his feet, trembling. . . .

He watched the line rise slowly to the sky and vanish into blue. The whole expanse of blackened heather-land watched too. Wind sank away; the sunshine dropped to meet it. A sense of deep expectancy, profound and reverent, lay over all that sun-baked moor; and the entire sweep of burnt world about him knew with joy that what was taking place in that wee, isolated patch of Surrey heather was the thing the Hebrew mystic knew when the Soul of the Universe became manifest in the bush that burned, yet never was consumed. In that faint sound of crackling, as he stood aside to listen and to watch, O'Hara knew a form of the eternal Voice of Ages. There was no flame, but it seemed to him that all his inner being passed in fiery heat outwards towards its source. . . . He saw the little patch of dried-up heather sink to the level of the black surface all about it—a sifted pile of delicate, pale-blue ashes. The tiny spiral vanished; he watched it disappear, winding upwards out of sight in a little ghostly trail of beauty. So small and soft and simple was this wonder of the world. It was gone. And something in himself had broken, dropped in ashes, and passed also outwards like a tiny mounting flame.

But the picture O'Hara had thought himself designed to paint was never done. It was not even begun. The great canvas of "The Fire Worshipper" stood empty on the easel, for the artist had not strength to lift a brush. Within two days the final breath passed slowly from his lips. The strange fever that so perplexed the doctor by its rapid development and its fury took him so easily. His temperature was extraordinary. The heat, as of an internal fire, fairly devoured him, and the smile upon his face at the last—so Rennie declared—was the most perplexingly wonderful thing he had ever seen. "It was like a great, white flame," he said.

The Biter Bit

It was in the smoking room of the little mountain hotel—after dinner; and round an open fire of pine-logs. Ski-talk had been exhausted. I drew back into my corner to watch and listen—the interplay of personal forces among a group of men conversationally inclined is always fascinating—and wondered what subject they would finally decide on. The man with the scarred nose (a bad telemark did that!) turned to light his pipe, and his eye fell on the newspaper beside him. He offered a remark on the cotton strike. But no one bit. "I wonder if a rubber of bridge would be possible?" asked a grey-haired father whose children had forced him to ski against his will all day. "Why not?" said another, and "I should think so." But no one moved. They tried a number of subjects, all barren, until at length some one chanced to mention dogs, and dogs at once became the favourite. Everybody talked dogs. It was easy, prevented argument, opened the way for stories with a sufficient flavour of personal advertisement to be attractive. The man who started it was a genius, for he struck the keynote of the group, or rather the L.C.M. Dogs went into each of them without remainder. All talked dogs at once with gusto. It was like a kennel. The quiet man attached to a huge calabash pipe was responsible for the masterly lead: "The proprietor's dog," he observed, apropos of nothing, "is like a wolf. I'm told his mother was a wolf." And everybody braced themselves for the fray. But it was the big man in the corner who rushed in first. He had a pontifical utterance that dominated the group. His speech was final, hard to contradict. He had a deep and terrible voice, and his face was full of determination. He knew.

"I wouldn't trust the brute a moment," he announced decisively. "Never trust a half-breed, whether dog or human." He looked darkly round him. No one said him nay. There was a pause. The big man's position was established. "They're always treacherous," he added, clinching it.

"That may be so," observed a timid voice, "but I have a spaniel—"

278

He was drowned by a chorus as every one, taking courage from his lead, rushed in with comments and suggestions. His sentence remained unfinished. He was a gentle, bald-headed, little fellow, hardly visible above the table where he occupied an uncomfortable chair outside the main group. He subsided, and was instantly forgotten.

"Don't you believe it," said Pontiff, in his booming voice, when the others had finished. That voice and manner demolished the lot of them. "They're treacherous beasts always, these half-bred things. I'm not afraid of any dog I ever saw, but—you never can be sure of them. Even hounds are dangerous." And he told a story of a huntsman who entered the kennels at night and was torn to pieces. A friend of his, also a huntsman, never went among the pack without his red coat on.

"His what?" asked Calabash.

"Red coat, I said," replied Pontiff, glaring, as though he scented a denial.

"Ah, yes; of course," said Calabash, with an air of thanks. "They respected the red coat—associated it with the whip, I presume." He told a pointless story about a bloodhound that once had followed him down a Devonshire lane. "It was a nasty business," he concluded. "Most uncomfortable, indeed, I'm sure," added Paterfamilias. "Hmm," objected Pontiff, "but that's quite different. A bloodhound won't attack a man for nothing." "Oh, no; not *that*," assented the narrator, feeling he had struck a false or foolish note.

"A spaniel I once had," began the voice from little Baldhead outside the circle—and again was instantly overwhelmed. There was no conviction in his tone, for one thing. Such voices are always lost in general conversation, when all wish to speak at once. This time it was the man with the scarred nose who won the victory. He told a capital story in few words, and with a grave face, fixing his eyes on his pipe and puffing hard between the sentences, although the pipe was really well alight. He never once raised his eyes till the end, and then he looked each of his listeners straight in the eye, as who should say, "There! What d'you think of that, eh?"

"I am a poor swimmer," he began. "One day in the Isle of Wight a friend made me swim out a quarter of a mile. As we turned to come in I saw a big Newfoundland dog, who had followed us from shore. The brute came up and took my neck in his teeth. He thought I was in danger. He was trying to save me. We both went under, and I swallowed a lot of water. 'Look out!' my friend cried, as I came to the surface again. 'He'll do for you.' He swam up close to help me. He said we must drown the brute or be drowned ourselves. My neck was torn and bleeding. 'You take his front paws and I'll take his tail,' yelled my spluttering friend. I did so, but my friend had the best place. The dog's front paws fairly tore my chest to pieces." He passed a hand up and down his shirt-front to indicate the attack, still with both eyes fixed upon the pipe. "We all three went under. I swallowed more water. 'Leave the beast and swim for your life,' my friend shouted. We did so. But the dog followed—me." A guffaw from Pontiff suggested the story was already long enough. He had one to tell himself now. The group got restless. All had a story to tell. They listened with boredom. "And how *did* you escape in the end?" asked Paterfamilias.

"Boat came out and took us. Men had seen us from the shore. A sailor bashed the brute on the head with an oar," concluded Scarred Nose gruffly. For he was offended; he considered this impatience very bad manners. "And the owner?" queried another, who shared his opinion and wished to help him out a little. "Said it was only the magnificent instinct of his pet asserting itself! That dog had drowned others before with his magnificent instinct. Later the town authorities sent him away." "I should think so, indeed," said Pontiff.

"I've got a little water-spaniel here," came from little Baldhead. But Pontiff squelched him for the tenth time—utterly. He had a story about a chow that bit him once. He himself had behaved grandly in the matter. Again Baldhead ventured into the fray with his little water-spaniel, and again was overwhelmed by Pontiff. "I merely wished to tell you that my spaniel—"

"That reminds me," broke in the other impudently, "of the best way to stop fighting dogs." And he told it. He had some humour in his noisy constitution, but always humour that glorified himself. He described the foolish way a man feels when his dog starts a prolonged fight in a public street, and how, for his part, he always vanished into the nearest shop and bought something till it was over. But on one occasion there was no shop handy. A crowd collected. He shouted "come off yer brutes!" till he was hoarse. Then a countryman came up and offered to separate them for a shilling. He took the tail of one dog in his mouth and bit it. The dog turned to see what on earth was the matter—letting go his adversary. The countryman then bit the other dog in the same way. He earned his shilling. "I gave half a crown," Pontiff concluded proudly.

The talk then became very general, though still—dogs, dogs, dogs. Calabash mentioned hydrophobia. A man he knew was bitten in the hand. Nothing happened. But, a year later he "got an awful thirst, had convulsions, and died." Pontiff easily demolished him. "A bit remote, *I* call it," he decided. "Rabies is very rare. There's as little chance of a dog with rabies biting you as there is of getting tetanus from a scratch with a knife."

"My water-spaniel," came Baldhead once more feebly to the attack. But the group resented him by this time. Everybody jumped in at once with anecdotes and theories. They talked of the Pyrenees dogs, of treacherous collies, of big hairy brutes that follow a man from lonely mountain farms, and Calabash described how a tiny toy dog gave him a nasty bite once at an afternoon call, and described his suppressed anger when the hostess assured him "it was only his play," and he had to smile sweetly when really he wanted to kick the little beast across the room. "I had to go to a doctor for it," he added amid the general laughter.

"This spaniel of mine, I ought to say—" began little Baldhead finally, as a last attempt.

But it was no good. The group had by this time had enough of dogs. They shifted in their chairs. Pontiff got up with energy. His manner indicated that the session was at an end. I think I was, perhaps, the only one who saw the shadow enter by the door that stood ajar into the corridor. Pontiff pushed his chair back with a bold gesture, as though he were bravely attacking a bloodhound—then yelled with pain. His foot had stepped upon the little shadow. The commotion was terrific. Pontiff was white and frightened, but I laughed so that I was obliged to leave the room in a hurry. For Pontiff had stepped on the front paw of a real dog this time, and had been sharply bitten in the calf.

"Why the—!" he began, quite furious.

"It's only my little spaniel," I heard Baldhead saying as I made my exit. "You must have hurt him. He is rather treacherous in his temper."

"Then, why the —— didn't you tell me?" roared the injured victim.

"I tried to," was the meek reply. "But you wouldn't let me."

The Destruction of Smith

Ten years ago, in the western States of America, I once met Smith. But he was no ordinary member of the clan: he was Ezekiel B. Smith of Smithville. He *was* Smithville, for he founded it and made it live.

It was in the oil region, where towns spring up on the map in a few days like mushrooms, and may be destroyed again in a single night by fire and earthquake. On a hunting expedition Smith stumbled upon a natural oil well, and instantly staked his claim; a few months later he was rich, grown into affluence as rapidly as that patch of wilderness grew into streets and houses where you could buy anything from an evening's gambling to a tin of Boston baked pork-and-beans. Smith was really a tremendous fellow, a sort of human dynamo of energy and pluck, with rare judgment in his great square head—the kind of judgment that in higher walks of life makes statesmen. His personality cut through the difficulties of life with the clean easy force of putting his whole life into anything he touched. "God's own luck," his comrades called it; but really it was sheer ability and character and personality. The man had power.

From the moment of that "oil find" his rise was very rapid, but while his brains went into a dozen other big enterprises, his heart remained in little Smithville, the flimsy mushroom town he had created. His own life was in it. It was his baby. He spoke tenderly of its hideousness. Smithville was an intimate expression of his very self.

Ezekiel B. Smith I saw once only, for a few minutes; but I have never forgotten him. It was the moment of his death. And we came across him on a shooting trip where the forests melt away towards the vast plains of the Arizona desert. The personality of the man was singularly impressive. I caught myself thinking of a mountain, or of some elemental force of Nature so sure of itself that hurry is never necessary. And his gentleness was like the gentleness of women. Great strength often—the greatest always—has tenderness in it, a depth of tenderness unknown to pettier life.

Our meeting was coincidence, for we were hunting in a region where distances are measured by hours and the chance of running across white men very rare. For many days our nightly camps were pitched in spots of beauty where the loneliness is akin to the loneliness of the Egyptian Desert. On one side the mountain slopes were smothered with dense forest, hiding wee meadows of sweet grass like English lawns; and on the other side, stretching for more miles than a man can count, ran the desolate alkali plains of Arizona where tufts of sagebrush are the only vegetation till you reach the lips of the Colorado Canyons. Our horses were tethered for the night beneath the stars. Two backwoodsmen were cooking dinner. The smell of bacon over a wood fire mingled with the keen and fragrant air—when, suddenly, the horses neighed, signalling the approach of one of their own kind. Indians, white men—probably another hunting party—were within scenting distance, though it was long before my city ears caught any sound, and still longer before the cause itself entered the circle of our firelight.

I saw a square-faced man, tanned like a redskin, in a hunting shirt and a big sombrero, climb down slowly from his horse and move towards us, keenly searching with his eyes; and at the same moment Hank, looking up from the frying-pan where the bacon and venison spluttered in a pool of pork-fat, exclaimed, "Why, it's Ezekiel B.!" The next words, addressed to Jake, who held the kettle, were below his breath: "And if he ain't all broke up! Jest look at the eyes on him!" I saw what he meant—the face of a human being distraught by some extraordinary emotion, a soul in violent distress, yet betrayal well kept under. Once, as a newspaper man, I had seen a murderer walk to the electric chair. The expression was similar. Death was *behind* the eyes, not in them. Smith brought in with him—terror.

In a dozen words we learned he had been hunting for some weeks, but was now heading for Tranter, a "stop-off" station where you could flag the daily train 140 miles south-west. He was making for Smithville, the little town that was the apple of his eye. Something "was wrong" with Smithville. No one asked him what—it is the custom to wait till information is volunteered. But Hank, helping him presently to venison (which he hardly touched), said casually, "Good hunting, Boss, your way?"; and the brief reply told much, and proved how eager he was to relieve his mind by speech. "I'm glad to locate your camp, boys," he said. "That's luck. There's something going wrong"—and a catch came into his voice—"with Smithville." Behind the laconic statement emerged somehow the terror the man experienced. For Smith to confess cowardice and in the same breath admit mere "luck," was equivalent to the hysteria that makes city people laugh or cry. It was genuinely dramatic. I have seen nothing more impressive by way of human tragedy—though hard to explain why—than this square-jawed, dauntless man, sitting there with the firelight on his rugged features, and saying this simple thing. For how in the world could he know it—?

In the pause that followed, his Indians came gliding in, tethered the horses, and sat down without a word to eat what Hank distributed. But nothing was to be read on their impassive faces. Redskins, whatever they may feel, show little. Then Smith gave us another pregnant sentence. "*They* heard it too," he said, in a lower voice, indicating his three men; "they saw it jest as I did." He looked up into the starry sky a second. "It's hard upon our trail right now," he added, as though he expected something to drop upon us from the heavens. And from that moment I swear we all felt creepy. The darkness round our lonely camp hid terror in its folds; the wind that whispered through the dry sage-brush brought whispers and the shuffle of watching figures; and when the Indians went softly out to pitch the tents and get more wood for the fire, I remember feeling glad the duty was not mine. Yet this feeling of uneasiness is something one rarely experiences in the open. It belongs to houses, overwrought imaginations, and the presence of evil men. Nature gives peace and security. That we all felt it proves how real it was. And Smith, who felt it most, of course, had brought it.

"There's something gone wrong with Smithville" was an ominous statement of disaster. He said it just as a man in civilised lands might say, "My wife is dying; a telegram's just come. I must take the train." But how he felt so sure of it, a thousand miles away in this uninhabited corner of the wilderness, made us feel curiously uneasy. For it was an incredible thing—yet true. We all felt *that*. Smith did not imagine things. A sense of gloomy apprehension settled over our lonely camp, as though things were about to happen. Already they stalked across the great black night, watching us with many eyes. The wind had risen, and there were sounds among the trees. I, for one, felt no desire to go to bed. The way Smith sat there, watching the sky and peering into the sheet of darkness that veiled the Desert, set my nerves all jangling. He expected something—but what? It was following him. Across this tractless wilderness, apparently above him against the brilliant stars, Something was "hard upon his trail."

Then, in the middle of painful silences, Smith suddenly turned loquacious—further sign with him of deep mental disturbance. He asked questions like a schoolboy—asked them of me too, as being "an edicated man." But there were such queer things to talk about round an Arizona camp-fire that Hank clearly wondered for his sanity. He knew about the "wilderness madness" that attacks some folks. He let his green cigar go out and flashed me signals to be cautious. He listened intently, with the eyes of a puzzled child, half cynical, half touched with superstitious dread. For, briefly, Smith asked me what I knew about stories of dying men appearing at a distance to those who loved them much. He had read such tales, "heard tell of 'em," but "are they dead true, or are they jest little feery tales?" I satisfied him as best I could with one or two authentic stories. Whether he believed or not I cannot say; but his swift mind jumped in a flash to the point. "Then, if that kind o' stuff is true," he asked, simply, "it looks as though a feller had a dooplicate of himself—sperrit maybe—that gits loose and active at the time of death, and heads straight for the party it loves best. Ain't that so, Boss?" I admitted the theory was correct. And then he startled us with a final question that made Hank drop an oath below his breath—sure evidence of uneasy excitement in the old backwoodsman. Smith whispered it, looking over his shoulder into the night: "Ain't it jest possible then," he asked, "seeing that men an' Nature is all made of a piece like, that places too have this dooplicate appearance of theirselves that gits loose when they go under?"

It was difficult, under the circumstances, to explain that such a theory *had* been held to account for visions of scenery people sometimes have, and that a city may have a definite personality made up of all its inhabitants—moods, thoughts, feelings, and passions of the multitude who go to compose its life and atmosphere, and that hence is due the odd changes in a man's individuality when he goes from one city to another. Nor was there any time to do so, for hardly had he asked his singular question when the horses whinnied, the Indians leaped to their feet as if ready for an attack, and Smith himself turned the colour of the ashes that lay in a circle of whitish-grey about the burning wood. There was an expression in his face of death, or, as the Irish peasants say, "destroyed."

"That's Smithville," he cried, springing to his feet, then tottering so that I thought he must fall into the flame; "that's my baby town— got loose and huntin' for me, who made it, and love it better'n anything on Gawd's green earth!" And then he added with a kind of gulp in his throat as of a man who wanted to cry but couldn't: "And it's going to bits—it's dying—and I'm not thar to save it—!"

He staggered and I caught his arm. The sound of his frightened, anguished voice, and the shuffling of our many feet among the stones, died away into the night. We all stood, staring. The darkness came up closer. The horses ceased their whinnying. For a moment nothing happened. Then Smith turned slowly round and raised his head towards the stars as though he saw something. "Hear that?" he whispered. "It's coming up close. That's what I've bin hearing now, on and off, two days and nights. Listen!" His whispering voice broke horribly; the man was suffering atrociously. For a moment he became vastly, horribly animated—then stood still as death.

But in the hollow silence, broken only by the sighing of the wind among the spruces, we at first heard nothing. Then, most curiously, something like rapid driven mist came trooping down the sky, and veiled a group of stars. With it, as from an enormous distance, but growing swiftly nearer, came noises that were beyond all question the noises of a city rushing through the heavens. From all sides they came; and with them there shot a reddish, streaked appearance across the misty veil that swung so rapidly and softly between the stars and our eyes. Lurid it was, and in some way terrible. A sense of helpless bewilderment came over me, scattering my faculties as in scenes of fire, when the mind struggles violently to possess itself and act for the best. Hank, holding his rifle ready to shoot, moved stupidly round the group, equally at a loss, and swearing incessantly below his breath. For this overwhelming certainty that Something living had come upon us from the sky possessed us all, and I, personally, felt as if a gigantic Being swept against me through the night, destructive and enveloping, and yet that it was not one, but many. Power of action left me. I could not even observe with accuracy what was going on. I stared, dizzy and bewildered, in all directions; but my power of movement was gone, and my feet refused to stir. Only I remember that the Redskins stood like figures of stone, unmoved.

And the sounds about us grew into a roar. The distant murmur came past us like a sea. There was a babel of shouting. Here, in the deep old wilderness that knew no living human beings for hundreds of leagues, there was a tempest of voices calling, crying, shrieking; men's hoarse clamouring, and the high screaming of women and children. Behind it ran a booming sound like thunder. Yet all of it, while apparently so close above our heads, seemed in some inexplicable way far off in the distance—muted, faint, thinning out among the quiet stars. More like a *memory* of turmoil and tumult it seemed than the actual uproar heard at first hand. And through it ran the crash of big things tumbling, breaking, falling in destruction with an awful detonating thunder of collapse. I thought the hills were toppling down upon us. A shrieking city, it seemed, fled past us through the sky.

How long it lasted it is impossible to say, for my power of measuring time had utterly vanished. A dreadful wild anguish summed up all the feelings I can remember. It seemed I watched, or read, or dreamed some desolating scene of disaster in which human life went overboard wholesale, as though one threw a hatful of insects into a blazing fire. This idea of burning, of thick suffocating smoke and savage flame, coloured the entire experience. And the next thing I knew was that it had passed away as completely as though it had never been at all; the stars shone down from an air of limpid clearness, and—there was a smell of burning leather in my nostrils. I just stepped back in time to save my feet. I had moved in my excitement against the circle of hot ashes. Hank pushed me back roughly with the barrel of his rifle.

But, strangest of all, I understood, as by some flash of divine intuition, the reason of this abrupt cessation of the horrible tumult. The Personality of the town, set free and loosened in the moment of death, had returned to him who gave it birth, who loved it, and of whose life it was actually an expression. The Being of Smithville was literally a projection, an emanation of the dynamic, vital personality of its puissant creator. And, in death, it had returned on him with the shock of an accumulated power impossible for a human being to resist. For years he had provided it with life—but *gradually*. It now rushed back to its source, thus concentrated, in a single terrific moment.

"That's him," I heard a voice saying from a great distance as it seemed. "He's fired his last shot—!" and saw Hank turning the body over with his rifle-butt. And, though the face itself was calm beneath the stars, there was an attitude of limbs and body that suggested the bursting of an enormous shell that had twisted every fibre by its awful force yet somehow left the body as a whole intact.

We carried "it" to Tranter, and at the first real station along the line we got the news by telegraph: "Smithville wiped out by fire. Burned two days and nights. Loss of life, 3000." And all the way in my dreams I seemed still to hear that curious, dreadful cry of Smithville, the shrieking city rushing headlong through the sky.

The Man Whom the Trees Loved

I

He painted trees as by some special divining instinct of their essential qualities. He understood them. He knew why in an oak forest, for instance, each individual was utterly distinct from its fellows, and why no two beeches in the whole world were alike. People asked him down to paint a favourite lime or silver birch, for he caught the individuality of a tree as some catch the individuality of a horse. How he managed it was something of a puzzle, for he never had painting lessons, his drawing was often wildly inaccurate, and, while his perception of a Tree Personality was true and vivid, his rendering of it might almost approach the ludicrous. Yet the character and personality of that particular tree stood there alive beneath his brush—shining, frowning, dreaming, as the case might be, friendly or hostile, good or evil. It emerged.

There was nothing else in the wide world that he could paint; flowers and landscapes he only muddled away into a smudge; with people he was helpless and hopeless; also with animals. Skies he could sometimes manage, or effects of wind in foliage, but as a rule he left these all severely alone. He kept to trees, wisely following an instinct that was guided by love. It was quite arresting, this way he had of making a tree look almost like a being—alive. It approached the uncanny.

"Yes, Sanderson knows what he's doing when he paints a tree!" thought old David Bittacy, C.B., late of the Woods and Forests. "Why, you can almost hear it rustle. You can smell the thing. You can hear the rain drip through its leaves. You can almost see the branches move. It grows." For in this way somewhat he expressed his satisfaction, half to persuade himself that the twenty guineas were well spent (since his wife thought otherwise), and half to explain this uncanny reality of life that lay in the fine old cedar framed above his study table.

Yet in the general view the mind of Mr. Bittacy was held to be austere, not to say morose. Few divined in him the secretly tenacious love of nature that had been fostered by years spent in the forests and jungles of the eastern world. It was odd for an Englishman, due possibly to that Eurasian ancestor. Surreptitiously, as though half ashamed of it, he had kept alive a sense of beauty that hardly belonged to his type, and was unusual for its vitality. Trees, in particular, nourished it. He, also, understood trees, felt a subtle sense of communion with them, born perhaps of those years he had lived in caring for them, guarding, protecting, nursing, years of solitude among their great shadowy presences. He kept it largely to himself, of course, because he knew the world he lived in. He also kept it from his wife—to some extent. He knew it came between them, knew that she feared it, was opposed. But what he did not know, or realise at any rate, was the extent to which she grasped the power which they wielded over his life. Her fear, he judged, was simply due to those years in India, when for weeks at a time his calling took him away from her into the jungle forests, while she remained at home dreading all manner of evils that might befall him. This, of course, explained her instinctive opposition to the passion for woods that still influenced and clung to him. It was a natural survival of those anxious days of waiting in solitude for his safe return.

For Mrs. Bittacy, daughter of an evangelical clergyman, was a self-sacrificing woman, who in most things found a happy duty in sharing her husband's joys and sorrows to the point of self-obliteration. Only in this matter of the trees she was less successful than in others. It remained a problem difficult of compromise.

He knew, for instance, that what she objected to in this portrait of the cedar on their lawn was really not the price he had given for it, but the unpleasant way in which the transaction emphasised this breach between their common interests—the only one they had, but deep.

Sanderson, the artist, earned little enough money by his strange talent; such cheques were few and far between. The owners of fine or interesting trees who cared to have them painted singly were rare indeed, and the "studies" that he made for his own delight he also kept for his own delight. Even were there buyers, he would not sell them. Only a few, and these peculiarly intimate friends, might even see them, for he disliked to hear the undiscerning criticisms of those who did not understand. Not that he minded laughter at his craftsmanship—he admitted it with scorn—but that remarks about the personality of the tree itself could easily wound or anger him. He resented slighting observations concerning them, as though insults offered to personal friends who could not answer for themselves. He was instantly up in arms.

"It really *is* extraordinary," said a Woman who Understood, "that you can make that cypress seem an individual, when in reality all cypresses are so *exactly* alike."

And though the bit of calculated flattery had come so near to saying the right, true thing, Sanderson flushed as though she had slighted a friend beneath his very nose. Abruptly he passed in front of her and turned the picture to the wall.

"Almost as queer," he answered rudely, copying her silly emphasis, "as that *you* should have imagined individuality in your husband, Madame, when in reality all men are so *exactly* alike!"

Since the only thing that differentiated her husband from the mob was the money for which she had married him, Sanderson's relations with that particular family terminated on the spot, chance of prospective "orders" with it. His sensitiveness, perhaps, was morbid. At any rate the way to reach his heart lay through his trees. He might be said to love trees. He certainly drew a splendid inspiration from them, and the source of a man's inspiration, be it music, religion, or a woman, is never a safe thing to criticise.

"I do think, perhaps, it was just a little extravagant, dear," said Mrs. Bittacy, referring to the cedar cheque, "when we want a lawn-mower so badly too. But, as it gives you such pleasure—"

"It reminds me of a certain day, Sophia," replied the old gentleman, looking first proudly at herself, then fondly at the picture, "now long gone by. It reminds me of another tree—that Kentish lawn in the spring, birds singing in the lilacs, and some one in a muslin frock waiting patiently beneath a certain cedar—not the one in the picture, I know, but—"

"I was not waiting," she said indignantly, "I was picking fir cones for the schoolroom fire—"

"Fir-cones, my dear, do not grow on cedars, and schoolroom fires were not made in June in my young days."

"And anyhow it isn't the same cedar."

"It has made me fond of all cedars for its sake," he answered, "and it reminds me that you are the same young girl still—"

She crossed the room to his side, and together they looked out of the window where, upon the lawn of their Hampshire cottage, a ragged Lebanon stood in a solitary state.

"You're as full of dreams as ever," she said gently, "and I don't regret the cheque a bit—really. Only it would have been more real if it had been the original tree, wouldn't it?"

"That was blown down years ago. I passed the place last year, and there's not a sign of it left," he replied tenderly. And presently, when he released her from his side, she went up to the wall and carefully dusted the picture Sanderson had made of the cedar on their present lawn. She went all round the frame with her tiny handkerchief, standing on tiptoe to reach the top rim.

"What I like about it," said the old fellow to himself when his wife had left the room, "is the way he has made it live. All trees have it, of course, but a cedar taught it to me first—the 'something' trees possess that make them know I'm there when I stand close and watch. I suppose I felt it then because I was in love, and love reveals life everywhere." He glanced a moment at the Lebanon looming gaunt and sombre through the gathering dusk. A curious wistful expression danced a moment through his eyes. "Yes, Sanderson has seen it as it is," he murmured, "solemnly dreaming there its dim hidden life against the Forest edge, and as different from that other tree in Kent as I am from—from the vicar, say. It's quite a stranger, too. I don't know anything about it really. That other cedar I loved; this old fellow I respect. Friendly though—yes, on the whole quite friendly. He's painted the friendliness right enough. He saw that. I'd like to know that man better," he added. "I'd like to ask him how he saw so clearly that it stands there between this cottage and the Forest—yet somehow more in sympathy with us than with the mass of woods behind—a sort of go-between. *That* I never noticed before. I see it now—through his eyes. It stands there like a sentinel—protective rather."

He turned away abruptly to look through the window. He saw the great encircling mass of gloom that was the Forest, fringing their little lawn. It pressed up closer in the darkness. The prim garden with its formal beds of flowers seemed an impertinence almost—some little coloured insect that sought to settle on a sleeping monster—some gaudy fly that danced impudently down the edge of a great river that could engulf it with a toss of its smallest wave. That Forest with its thousand years of growth and its deep spreading being was some such slumbering monster, yes. Their cottage and garden stood too near its running lip. When the winds were strong and lifted its shadowy skirts of black and purple . . . He loved this feeling of the Forest Personality; he had always loved it.

"Queer," he reflected, "awfully queer, that trees should bring me such a sense of dim, vast living! I used to feel it particularly, I remember, in India; in Canadian woods as well; but never in little English woods till here. And Sanderson's the only man I ever knew who felt it too. He's never said so, but there's the proof," and he turned again to the picture that he loved. A thrill of unaccustomed life ran through him as he looked. "I wonder; by Jove, I wonder," his thoughts ran on, "whether a tree—er—in any lawful meaning of the term can be—alive. I remember some writing fellow telling me long ago that trees had once been moving things, animal organisms of some sort, that had stood so long feeding, sleeping, dreaming, or something, in the same place, that they had lost the power to get away . . . !"

Fancies flew pell-mell about his mind, and, lighting a cheroot, he dropped into an armchair beside the open window and let them play. Outside the blackbirds whistled in the shrubberies across the lawn. He smelt the earth and trees and flowers, the perfume of mown grass, and the bits of open heath-land far away in the heart of the woods. The summer wind stirred very faintly through the leaves. But the great New Forest hardly raised her sweeping skirts of black and purple shadow.

Mr. Bittacy, however, knew intimately every detail of that wilderness of trees within. He knew all the purple coombs splashed with yellow waves of gorse; sweet with juniper and myrtle, and gleaming with clear and dark-eyed pools that watched the sky. There hawks hovered, circling hour by hour, and the flicker of the peewit's flight with its melancholy, petulant cry, deepened the sense of stillness. He knew the solitary pines, dwarfed, tufted, vigorous, that sang to every lost wind, travellers like the gipsies who pitched their bush-like tents beneath them; he knew the shaggy ponies, with foals like baby centaurs; the chattering jays, the milky call of the cuckoos in the spring, and the boom of the bittern from the lonely marshes. The undergrowth of watching hollies, he knew too, strange and mysterious, with their dark, suggestive beauty, and the yellow shimmer of their pale dropped leaves.

Here all the Forest lived and breathed in safety, secure from mutilation. No terror of the axe could haunt the peace of its vast subconscious life, no terror of devastating Man afflict it with the dread of premature death. It knew itself supreme; it spread and preened itself without concealment. It set no spires to carry warnings, for no wind brought messages of alarm as it bulged outwards to the sun and stars.

But, once its leafy portals left behind, the trees of the country-side were otherwise. The houses threatened them; they knew themselves in danger. The roads were no longer glades of silent turf, but noisy, cruel ways by which men came to attack them. They were civilised, cared for—but cared for in order that some day they might be put to death. Even in the villages, where the solemn and immemorial repose of giant chestnuts aped security, the tossing of a silver birch against their mass, impatient in the littlest wind, brought warning. Dust clogged their leaves. The inner humming of their quiet life became inaudible beneath the scream and shriek of clattering traffic. They longed and prayed to enter the great Peace of the Forest yonder, but they could not move. They knew, moreover, that the Forest with its august, deep splendour despised and pitied them. They were a thing of artificial gardens, and belonged to beds of flowers all forced to grow one way. . . .

"I'd like to know that artist fellow better," was the thought upon which he returned at length to the things of practical life. "I wonder if Sophia would mind him here for a bit—?" He rose with the sound of the gong, brushing the ashes from his speckled waistcoat. He pulled the waistcoat down. He was slim and spare in figure, active in his movements. In the dim light, but for that silvery moustache, he might easily have passed for a man of forty. "I'll suggest it to her anyhow," he decided on his way upstairs to dress. His thought really was that Sanderson could probably explain this world of things he had always felt about—trees. A man who could paint the soul of a cedar in that way must know it all.

"Why not?" she gave her verdict later over the bread-and-butter pudding; "unless you think he'd find it dull without companions."

"He would paint all day in the Forest, dear. I'd like to pick his brains a bit, too, if I could manage it."

"You can manage anything, David," was what she answered, for this elderly childless couple used an affectionate politeness long since deemed old-fashioned. The remark, however, displeased her, making her feel uneasy, and she did not notice his rejoinder, smiling his pleasure and content—"Except yourself and our bank account, my dear." This passion of his for trees was of old a bone of contention, though very mild contention. It frightened her. That was the truth. The Bible, her Baedeker for earth and heaven, did not mention it. Her husband, while humouring her, could never alter that instinctive dread she had. He soothed, but never changed her. She liked the woods, perhaps as spots for shade and picnics, but she could not, as he did, love them.

And after dinner, with a lamp beside the open window, he read aloud from *The Times* the evening post had brought, such fragments as he thought might interest her. The custom was invariable, except on Sundays, when, to please his wife, he dozed over Tennyson or Farrar as their mood might be. She knitted while he read, asked gentle questions, told him his voice was a "lovely reading voice," and enjoyed the little discussions that occasions prompted because he always let her win them with "Ah, Sophia, I had never thought of it quite in *that* way before; but now you mention it I must say I think there's something in it. . . ."

For David Bittacy was wise. It was long after marriage, during his months of loneliness spent with trees and forests in India, his wife waiting at home in the Bungalow, that his other, deeper side had developed the strange passion that she could not understand. And after one or two serious attempts to let her share it with him, he had given up and learned to hide it from her. He learned, that is, to speak of it only casually; for since she knew it was there, to keep silence altogether would only increase her pain. So from time to time he skimmed the surface just to let her show him where he was wrong and think she won the day. It remained a debatable land of compromise. He listened with patience to her criticisms, her excursions and alarms, knowing that while it gave her satisfaction, it could not change himself. The thing lay in him too deep and true for change. But, for peace' sake, some meeting place was desirable, and he found it thus.

It was her one fault in his eyes, this religious mania carried over from her up-bringing, and it did no serious harm. Great emotion could shake it sometimes out of her. She clung to it because her father taught it her and not because she had thought it out for herself. Indeed, like many women, she never really *thought* at all, but merely reflected the images of others' thinking which she had learned to see. So, wise in his knowledge of human nature, old David Bittacy accepted the pain of being obliged to keep a portion of his inner life shut off from the woman he deeply loved. He regarded her little biblical phrases as oddities that still clung to a rather fine, big soul—like horns and little useless things some animals have not yet lost in the course of evolution while they have outgrown their use.

"My dear, what is it? You frightened me!" She asked it suddenly, sitting up so abruptly that her cap dropped sideways almost to her ear. For David Bittacy behind his crackling paper had uttered a sharp exclamation of surprise. He had lowered the sheet and was staring at her over the tops of his gold glasses.

"Listen to this, if you please," he said, a note of eagerness in his voice, "listen to this, my dear Sophia. It's from an address by Francis Darwin before the Royal Society. He is president, you know, and son of the great Darwin. Listen carefully, I beg you. It is *most* significant."

"I *am* listening, David," she said with some astonishment, looking up. She stopped her knitting. For a second she glanced behind her. Something had suddenly changed in the room, and it made her feel wide awake, though before she had been almost dozing. Her husband's voice and manner had introduced this new thing. Her instincts rose in warning. "*Do* read it, dear." He took a deep breath, looking first again over the rims of his glasses to make quite sure of her attention. He had evidently come across something of genuine interest, although she herself she often found the passages from these "Addresses" somewhat heavy.

In a deep, emphatic voice he read aloud:

"'It is impossible to know whether or not plants are conscious; but it is consistent with the doctrine of continuity that in all living things there is something psychic, and if we accept this point of view—'"

"*If,*" she interrupted, scenting danger.

He ignored the interruption as a thing of slight value he was accustomed to.

"'If we accept this point of view,'" he continued, "'we must believe that in plants there exists a faint copy of *what we know as consciousness in ourselves*.'"

He laid the paper down and steadily stared at her. Their eyes met. He had italicised the last phrase.

For a minute or two his wife made no reply or comment. They stared at one another in silence. He waited for the meaning of the words to reach her understanding with full import. Then he turned and read them again in part, while she, released from that curious driving look in his eyes, instinctively again glanced over her shoulder round the room. It was almost as if she felt some one had come into them unnoticed.

"We must believe that in plants there exists a faint copy of what we know as consciousness in ourselves."

"*If,*" she repeated lamely, feeling before the stare of those questioning eyes she must say something, but not yet having gathered her wits together quite.

"*Consciousness,*" he rejoined. And then he added gravely: "That, my dear, is the statement of a scientific man of the twentieth century."

Mrs. Bittacy sat forward in her chair so that her silk flounces crackled louder than the newspaper. She made a characteristic little sound between sniffling and snorting. She put her shoes closely together, with her hands upon her knees.

"David," she said quietly, "I think these scientific men are simply losing their heads. There is nothing in the Bible that I can remember about any such thing whatsoever."

"Nothing, Sophia, that I can remember either," he answered patiently. Then, after a pause, he added, half to himself perhaps more than to her: "And, now that I come to think about it, it seems that Sanderson once said something to me that was similar."

"Then Mr. Sanderson is a wise and thoughtful man, and a safe man," she quickly took up, "if he said that."

For she thought her husband referred to her remark about the Bible, and not to her judgment of the scientific men. And he did not correct her mistake.

"And plants, you see, dear, are not the same thing as trees," she drove her advantage home, "not quite, that is."

"I agree," said David quietly; "but both belong to the great vegetable kingdom."

There was a moment's pause before she answered.

"Pah! the vegetable kingdom, indeed!" She tossed her pretty old head. And into the words she put a degree of contempt that, could the vegetable kingdom have heard it, might have made it feel ashamed for covering a third of the world with its wonderful tangled network of roots and branches, delicate shaking leaves, and its millions of spires that caught the sun and wind and rain. Its very right to existence seemed in question.

II

Sanderson accordingly came down, and on the whole his short visit was a success. Why he came at all was a mystery to those who heard of it, for he never paid visits and was certainly not the kind of man to court a customer. There must have been something in Bittacy he liked.

Mrs. Bittacy was glad when he left. He brought no dress-suit for one thing, not even a dinner-jacket, and he wore very low collars with big balloon ties like a Frenchman, and let his hair grow longer than was nice, she felt. Not that these things were important, but that she considered them symptoms of something a little disordered. The ties were unnecessarily flowing.

For all that he was an interesting man, and, in spite of his eccentricities of dress and so forth, a gentleman. "Perhaps," she reflected in her genuinely charitable heart, "he had other uses for the twenty guineas, an invalid sister or an old mother to support!" She had no notion of the cost of brushes, frames, paints, and canvases. Also she forgave him much for the sake of his beautiful eyes and his eager enthusiasm of manner. So many men of thirty were already blasé.

Still, when the visit was over, she felt relieved. She said nothing about his coming a second time, and her husband, she was glad to notice, had likewise made no such suggestion. For, truth to tell, the way the younger man engrossed the older, keeping him out for hours in the Forest, talking on the lawn in the blazing sun, and in the evenings when the damp of dusk came creeping out from the surrounding woods, all regardless of his age and usual habits, was not quite to her taste. Of course, Mr. Sanderson did not know how easily those attacks of Indian fever came back, but David surely might have told him.

They talked trees from morning to night. It stirred in her the old subconscious trail of dread, a trail that led ever into the darkness of big woods; and such feelings, as her early evangelical training taught her, were temptings. To regard them in any other way was to play with danger.

Her mind, as she watched these two, was charged with curious thoughts of dread she could not understand, yet feared the more on that account. The way they studied that old mangy cedar was a trifle unnecessary, unwise, she felt. It was disregarding the sense of proportion which deity had set upon the world for men's safe guidance.

Even after dinner they smoked their cigars upon the low branches that swept down and touched the lawn, until at length she insisted on their coming in. Cedars, she had somewhere heard, were not safe after sundown; it was not wholesome to be too near them; to sleep beneath them was even dangerous, though what the precise danger was she had forgotten. The upas was the tree she really meant.

At any rate she summoned David in, and Sanderson came presently after him.

For a long time, before deciding on this peremptory step, she had watched them surreptitiously from the drawing-room window—her husband and her guest. The dusk enveloped them with its damp veil of gauze. She saw the glowing tips of their cigars, and heard the drone of voices. Bats flitted overhead, and big, silent moths whirred softly over the rhododendron blossoms. And it came suddenly to her, while she watched, that her husband had somehow altered these last few days—since Mr. Sanderson's arrival in fact. A change had come over him, though what it was she could not say. She hesitated, indeed, to search. That was the instinctive dread operating in her. Provided it passed she would rather not know. Small things, of course, she noticed; small outward signs. He had neglected *The Times* for one thing, left off his speckled waistcoats for another. He was absent-minded sometimes; showed vagueness in practical details where hitherto he showed decision. And—he had begun to talk in his sleep again.

These and a dozen other small peculiarities came suddenly upon her with the rush of a combined attack. They brought with them a faint distress that made her shiver. Momentarily her mind was startled, then confused, as her eyes picked out the shadowy figures in the dusk, the cedar covering them, the Forest close at their backs. And then, before she could think, or seek internal guidance as her habit was, this whisper, muffled and very hurried, ran across her brain: "It's Mr. Sanderson. Call David in at once!"

And she had done so. Her shrill voice crossed the lawn and died away into the Forest, quickly smothered. No echo followed it. The sound fell dead against the rampart of a thousand listening trees.

"The damp is so very penetrating, even in summer," she murmured when they came obediently. She was half surprised at her open audacity, half repentant. They came so meekly at her call. "And my husband is sensitive to fever from the East. No, *please* do not throw away your cigars. We can sit by the open window and enjoy the evening while you smoke."

She was very talkative for a moment; subconscious excitement was the cause.

"It is so still—so wonderfully still," she went on, as no one spoke, "so peaceful, and the air so very sweet . . . and God is always near to those who need His aid." The words slipped out before she realised quite what she was saying, yet fortunately, in time to lower her voice, for no one heard them. They were, perhaps, an instinctive expression of relief. It flustered her that she could have said the thing at all.

Sanderson brought her shawl and helped to arrange the chairs; she thanked him in her old-fashioned, gentle way, declining the lamps which he had offered to light. "They attract the moths and insects so, I think!"

The three of them sat there in the gloaming, Mr. Bittacy's white moustache and his wife's yellow shawl gleaming at either end of the little horseshoe, Sanderson with his wild black hair and shining eyes midway between them. The painter went on talking softly, continuing evidently the conversation begun with his host beneath the cedar. Mrs. Bittacy, on her guard, listened—uneasily.

"For trees, you see, rather conceal themselves in daylight. They reveal themselves fully only after sunset. I never *know* a tree," he bowed here slightly towards the lady as though to apologise for something he felt she would not quite understand or like, "until I've seen it in the night. Your cedar, for instance," looking towards her husband again so that Mrs. Bittacy caught the gleaming of his turned eyes, "I failed with badly at first, because I did it in the morning. You shall see to-morrow what I mean—that first sketch is upstairs in my portfolio; it's quite another tree to the one you bought. That view"—he leaned forward, lowering his voice—"I caught one morning about two o'clock in very faint moonlight and the stars. I saw the naked being of the thing—"

"You mean that you went out, Mr. Sanderson, at that hour?" the old lady asked with astonishment and mild rebuke. She did not care particularly for his choice of adjectives either.

"I fear it was rather a liberty to take in another's house, perhaps," he answered courteously. "But, having chanced to wake, I saw the tree from my window, and made my way downstairs."

"It's a wonder Boxer didn't bite you; he sleeps loose in the hall," she said.

"On the contrary. The dog came out with me. I hope," he added, "the noise didn't disturb you, though it's rather late to say so. I feel quite guilty." His white teeth showed in the dusk as he smiled. A smell of earth and flowers stole in through the window on a breath of wandering air.

Mrs. Bittacy said nothing at the moment. "We both sleep like tops," put in her husband, laughing. "You're a courageous man, though, Sanderson; and, by Jove, the picture justifies you. Few artists would have taken so much trouble, though I read once that Holman Hunt, Rossetti, or some one of that lot, painted all night in his orchard to get an effect of moonlight that he wanted."

He chattered on. His wife was glad to hear his voice; it made her feel more easy in her mind. But presently the other held the floor again, and her thoughts grew darkened and afraid. Instinctively she feared the influence on her husband. The mystery and wonder that lie in woods, in forests, in great gatherings of trees everywhere, seemed so real and present while he talked.

"The Night transfigures all things in a way," he was saying; "but nothing so searchingly as trees. From behind a veil that sunlight hangs before them in the day they emerge and show themselves. Even buildings do that—in a measure—but trees particularly. In the daytime they sleep; at night they wake, they manifest, turn active—live. You remember," turning politely again in the direction of his hostess, "how clearly Henley understood that?"

"That socialist person, you mean?" asked the lady. Her tone and accent made the substantive sound criminal. It almost hissed, the way she uttered it.

"The poet, yes," replied the artist tactfully, "the friend of Stevenson, you remember, Stevenson who wrote those charming children's verses."

He quoted in a low voice the lines he meant. It was, for once, the time, the place, and the setting all together. The words floated out across the lawn towards the wall of blue darkness where the big Forest swept the little garden with its league-long curve that was like the shore-line of a sea. A wave of distant sound that was like surf accompanied his voice, as though the wind was fain to listen too:

> Not to the staring Day,
> For all the importunate questionings he pursues
> In his big, violent voice,
> Shall those mild things of bulk and multitude,
> The trees—God's sentinels . . .
> Yield of their huge, unutterable selves.
>
> .   .   .   .   .
>
> But at the word
> Of the ancient, sacerdotal Night,
> Night of many secrets, whose effect—
> Transfiguring, hierophantic, dread—
> Themselves alone may fully apprehend,
> They tremble and are changed:
> In each the uncouth, individual soul
> Looms forth and glooms
> Essential, and, their bodily presences
> Touched with inordinate significance,
> Wearing the darkness like a livery
> Of some mysterious and tremendous guild,
> They brood—they menace—they appal.

The voice of Mrs. Bittacy presently broke the silence that followed. "I like that part about God's sentinels," she murmured. There was no sharpness in her tone; it was hushed and quiet. The truth, so musically uttered, muted her shrill objections though it had not lessened her alarm. Her husband made no comment; his cigar, she noticed, had gone out.

"And old trees in particular," continued the artist, as though to himself, "have very definite personalities. You can offend, wound, please them; the moment you stand within their shade you feel whether they come out to you, or whether they withdraw." He turned abruptly towards his host. "You know that singular essay of Prentice Mulford's, no doubt, 'God in the Trees'—extravagant perhaps, but yet with a fine true beauty in it? You've never read it, no?" he asked.

But it was Mrs. Bittacy who answered; her husband keeping his curious deep silence.

"I never did!" It fell like a drip of cold water from the face muffled in the yellow shawl; even a child could have supplied the remainder of the unspoken thought.

"Ah," said Sanderson gently, "but there *is* 'God' in the trees, God in a very subtle aspect and sometimes—I have known the trees express it too—that which is *not* God—dark and terrible. Have you ever noticed, too, how clearly trees show what they want—choose their companions, at least? How beeches, for instance, allow no life too near them—birds or squirrels in their boughs, nor any growth beneath? The silence in the beech wood is quite terrifying often! And how pines like bilberry bushes at their feet and sometimes little oaks—all trees making a clear, deliberate choice, and holding firmly to it? Some trees obviously—it's very strange and marked—seem to prefer the human."

The old lady sat up crackling, for this was more than she could permit. Her stiff silk dress emitted little sharp reports.

"We know," she answered, "that He was said to have walked in the garden in the cool of the evening"—the gulp betrayed the effort that it cost her—"but we are nowhere told that He hid in the trees, or anything like that. Trees, after all, we must remember, are only large vegetables."

"True," was the soft answer, "but in everything that grows, has life, that is, there's mystery past all finding out. The wonder that lies hidden in our own souls lies also hidden, I venture to assert, in the stupidity and silence of a mere potato."

The observation was not meant to be amusing. It was *not* amusing. No one laughed. On the contrary, the words conveyed in too literal a sense the feeling that haunted all that conversation. Each one in his own way realised—with beauty, with wonder, with alarm—that the talk had somehow brought the whole vegetable kingdom nearer to that of man. Some link had been established between the two. It was not wise, with that great Forest listening at their very doors, to speak so plainly. The Forest edged up closer while they did so.

And Mrs. Bittacy, anxious to interrupt the horrid spell, broke suddenly in upon it with a matter-of-fact suggestion. She did not like her husband's prolonged silence, stillness. He seemed so negative—so changed.

"David," she said, raising her voice, "I think you're feeling the dampness. It's grown chilly. The fever comes so suddenly, you know, and it might be wise to take the tincture. I'll go and get it, dear, at once. It's better." And before he could object she had left the room to bring the homœopathic dose that she believed in, and that, to please her, he swallowed by the tumbler-full from week to week.

And the moment the door closed behind her, Sanderson began again, though now in quite a different tone. Mr. Bittacy sat up in his chair. The two men obviously resumed the conversation—the real conversation interrupted beneath the cedar—and left aside the sham one which was so much dust merely thrown in the old lady's eyes.

"Trees love you, that's the fact," he said earnestly. "Your service to them all these years abroad has made them know you."

"Know me?"

"Made them, yes,"—he paused a moment, then added—"made them *aware of your presence;* aware of a force outside themselves that deliberately seeks their welfare, don't you see?"

"By Jove, Sanderson—!" This put into plain language actual sensations he had felt, yet had never dared to phrase in words before. "They get into touch with me, as it were?" he ventured, laughing at his own sentence, yet laughing only with his lips.

"Exactly," was the quick, emphatic reply. "They seek to blend with something they feel instinctively to be good for them, helpful to their essential beings, encouraging to their best expression—their life."

"Good Lord, Sir!" Bittacy heard himself saying, "but you're putting my own thoughts into words. D'you know, I've felt something like that for years. As though—" he looked round to make sure his wife was not there, then finished the sentence—"as though the trees were after me!"

"'Amalgamate' seems the best word, perhaps," said Sanderson slowly. "They would draw you to themselves. Good forces, you see, always seek to merge; evil to separate; that's why Good in the end must always win the day—everywhere. The accumulation in the long run becomes overwhelming. Evil tends to separation, dissolution, death. The comradeship of trees, their instinct to run together, is a vital symbol. Trees in a mass are good; alone, you may take it generally, are—well, dangerous. Look at a monkey-puzzler, or better still, a holly. Look at it, watch it, understand it. Did you ever see more plainly an evil thought made visible? They're wicked. Beautiful too, oh yes! There's a strange, miscalculated beauty often in evil—"

"That cedar, then—?"

"Not evil, no; but alien, rather. Cedars grow in forests all together. The poor thing has drifted, that is all."

They were getting rather deep. Sanderson, talking against time, spoke so fast. It was too condensed. Bittacy hardly followed that last bit. His mind floundered among his own less definite, less sorted thoughts, till presently another sentence from the artist startled him into attention again.

"That cedar will protect you here, though, because you both have humanised it by your thinking so lovingly of its presence. The others can't get past it, as it were."

"Protect me!" he exclaimed. "Protect me from their love?"

Sanderson laughed. "We're getting rather mixed," he said; "we're talking of one thing in the terms of another really. But what I mean is—you see—that their love for you, their 'awareness' of your personality and presence involves the idea of winning you—across the border—into themselves—into their world of living. It means, in a way, taking you over."

The ideas the artist started in his mind ran furious wild races to and fro. It was like a maze sprung suddenly into movement. The whirling of the intricate lines bewildered him. They went so fast, leaving but half an explanation of their goal. He followed first one, then another, but a new one always dashed across to intercept before he could get anywhere.

"But India," he said, presently in a lower voice, "India is so far away—from this little English forest. The trees, too, are utterly different for one thing?"

The rustle of skirts warned of Mrs. Bittacy's approach. This was a sentence he could turn round another way in case she came up and pressed for explanation.

"There is communion among trees all the world over," was the strange quick reply. "They always know."

"They always know! You think then—?"

"The winds, you see—the great, swift carriers! They have their ancient rights of way about the world. An easterly wind, for instance, carrying on stage by stage as it were—linking dropped messages and meanings from land to land like the birds—an easterly wind—"

Mrs. Bittacy swept in upon them with the tumbler—

"There, David," she said, "that will ward off any beginnings of attack. Just a spoonful, dear. Oh, oh! not *all!*" for he had swallowed half the contents at a single gulp as usual; "another dose before you go to bed, and the balance in the morning, first thing when you wake."

She turned to her guest, who put the tumbler down for her upon a table at his elbow. She had heard them speak of the east wind. She emphasised the warning she had misinterpreted. The private part of the conversation came to an abrupt end.

"It is the one thing that upsets him more than any other—an east wind," she said, "and I am glad, Mr. Sanderson, to hear you think so too."

III

A deep hush followed, in the middle of which an owl was heard calling its muffled note in the forest. A big moth whirred with a soft collision against one of the windows. Mrs. Bittacy started slightly, but no one spoke. Above the trees the stars were faintly visible. From the distance came the barking of a dog.

Bittacy, relighting his cigar, broke the little spell of silence that had caught all three.

"It's rather a comforting thought," he said, throwing the match out of the window, "that life is about us everywhere, and that there is really no dividing line between what we call organic and inorganic."

"The universe, yes," said Sanderson, "is all one, really. We're puzzled by the gaps we cannot see across, but as a fact, I suppose, there are no gaps at all."

Mrs. Bittacy rustled ominously, holding her peace meanwhile. She feared long words she did not understand. Beelzebub lay hid among too many syllables.

"In trees and plants especially, there dreams an exquisite life that no one yet has proved unconscious."

"Or conscious either, Mr. Sanderson," she neatly interjected. "It's only man that was made after His image, not shrubberies and things. . . ."

Her husband interposed without delay.

"It is not necessary," he explained suavely, "to say that they're alive in the sense that we are alive. At the same time," with an eye to his wife, "I see no harm in holding, dear, that all created things contain some measure of His life Who made them. It's only beautiful to hold that He created nothing dead. We are not pantheists for all that!" he added soothingly.

"Oh, no! Not that, I hope!" The word alarmed her. It was worse than pope. Through her puzzled mind stole a stealthy, dangerous thing . . . like a panther.

"I like to think that even in decay there's life," the painter murmured. "The falling apart of rotten wood breeds sentiency; there's force and motion in the falling of a dying leaf, in the breaking up and crumbling of everything indeed. And take an inert stone: it's crammed with heat and weight and potencies of all sorts. What holds its particles together indeed? We understand it as little as gravity or why a needle always turns to the 'North.' Both things may be a mode of life. . . ."

"You think a compass has a soul, Mr. Sanderson?" exclaimed the lady with a crackling of her silk flounces that conveyed a sense of outrage even more plainly than her tone. The artist smiled to himself in the darkness, but it was Bittacy who hastened to reply.

"Our friend merely suggests that these mysterious agencies," he said quietly, "may be due to some kind of life we cannot understand.

Why should water only run downhill? Why should trees grow at right angles to the surface of the ground and towards the sun? Why should the worlds spin for ever on their axes? Why should fire change the form of everything it touches without really destroying them? To say these things follow the law of their being explains nothing. Mr. Sanderson merely suggests—poetically, my dear, of course—that these may be manifestations of life, though life at a different stage to ours."

"The '*breath* of life,' we read, 'He breathed into them.' These things do not breathe." She said it with triumph.

Then Sanderson put in a word. But he spoke rather to himself or to his host than by way of serious rejoinder to the ruffled lady.

"But plants do breathe too, you know," he said. "They breathe, they eat, they digest, they move about, and they adapt themselves to their environment as men and animals do. They have a nervous system too . . . at least a complex system of nuclei which have some of the qualities of nerve cells. They may have memory too. Certainly, they know definite action in response to stimulus. And though this may be physiological, no one has proved that it is only that, and not— psychological."

He did not notice, apparently, the little gasp that was audible behind the yellow shawl. Bittacy cleared his throat, threw his extinguished cigar upon the lawn, crossed and recrossed his legs.

"And in trees," continued the other, "behind a great forest, for instance," pointing towards the woods, "may stand a rather splendid Entity that manifests through all the thousand individual trees—some huge collective life, quite as minutely and delicately organised as our own. It might merge and blend with ours under certain conditions, so that we could understand it by *being* it, for a time at least. It might even engulf human vitality into the immense whirlpool of its own vast dreaming life. The pull of a big forest on a man can be tremendous and utterly overwhelming."

The mouth of Mrs. Bittacy was heard to close with a snap. Her shawl, and particularly her crackling dress, exhaled the protest that burned within her like a pain. She was too distressed to be overawed, but at the same time too confused 'mid the litter of words and meanings half understood, to find immediate phrases she could use. Whatever the actual meaning of his language might be, however, and whatever subtle dangers lay concealed behind them meanwhile, they certainly wove a kind of gentle spell with the glimmering darkness that held all three delicately enmeshed there by that open window. The odors of dewy lawn, flowers, trees, and earth formed part of it.

"The moods," he continued, "that people waken in us are due to their hidden life affecting our own. Deep calls to deep. A person, for instance, joins you in an empty room: you both instantly change. The new arrival, though in silence, has caused a change of mood. May not the moods of Nature touch and stir us in virtue of a similar prerogative? The sea, the hills, the desert, wake passion, joy, terror, as the case may be; for a few, perhaps," he glanced significantly at his host so that Mrs. Bittacy again caught the turning of his eyes, "emotions of a curious, flaming splendour that are quite nameless. Well . . . whence come these powers? Surely from nothing that is . . . dead! Does not the influence of a forest, its sway and strange ascendancy over certain minds, betray a direct manifestation of life? It lies otherwise beyond all explanation, this mysterious emanation of big woods. Some natures, of course, deliberately invite it. The authority of a host of trees,"—his voice grew almost solemn as he said the words—"is something not to be denied. One feels it here, I think, particularly."

There was considerable tension in the air as he ceased speaking. Mr. Bittacy had not intended that the talk should go so far. They had drifted. He did not wish to see his wife unhappy or afraid, and he was aware—acutely so—that her feelings were stirred to a point he did not care about. Something in her, as he put it, was "working up" towards explosion.

He sought to generalise the conversation, diluting this accumulated emotion by spreading it.

"The sea is His and He made it," he suggested vaguely, hoping Sanderson would take the hint, "and with the trees it is the same. . . ."

"The whole gigantic vegetable kingdom, yes," the artist took him up, "all at the service of man, for food, for shelter and for a thousand purposes of his daily life. Is it not striking what a lot of the globe they cover . . . exquisitely organised life, yet stationary, always ready to our hand when we want them, never running away? But the taking them, for all that, not so easy. One man shrinks from picking flowers, another from cutting down trees. And, it's curious that most of the forest tales and legends are dark, mysterious, and somewhat ill-omened. The forest-beings are rarely gay and harmless. The forest life was felt as terrible. Tree-worship still survives to-day. Woodcutters . . . those who take the life of trees . . . you see a race of haunted men. . . ."

He stopped abruptly, a singular catch in his voice. Bittacy felt something even before the sentences were over. His wife, he knew, felt it still more strongly. For it was in the middle of the heavy silence following upon these last remarks, that Mrs. Bittacy, rising with a violent abruptness from her chair, drew the attention of the others to something moving towards them across the lawn. It came silently. In outline it was large and curiously spread. It rose high, too, for the sky above the shrubberies, still pale gold from the sunset, was dimmed by its passage. She declared afterwards that it moved in "looping circles," but what she perhaps meant to convey was "spirals."

She screamed faintly. "It's come at last! And it's you that brought it!"

She turned excitedly, half afraid, half angry, to Sanderson. With a breathless sort of gasp she said it, politeness all forgotten. "I knew it . . . if you went on. I knew it. Oh! Oh!" And she cried again, "Your talking has brought it out!" The terror that shook her voice was rather dreadful.

But the confusion of her vehement words passed unnoticed in the first surprise they caused. For a moment nothing happened.

"What is it you think you see, my dear?" asked her husband, startled. Sanderson said nothing. All three leaned forward, the men still sitting, but Mrs. Bittacy had rushed hurriedly to the window, placing herself of a purpose, as it seemed, between her husband and the lawn. She pointed. Her little hand made a silhouette against the sky, the yellow shawl hanging from the arm like a cloud.

"Beyond the cedar—between it and the lilacs." The voice had lost its shrillness; it was thin and hushed. "There . . . now you see it going round upon itself again—going back, thank God! . . . going back to the Forest." It sank to a whisper, shaking. She repeated, with a great dropping sigh of relief—"Thank God! I thought . . . at first . . . it was coming here . . . to us! . . . David . . . to *you!*"

She stepped back from the window, her movements confused, feeling in the darkness for the support of a chair, and finding her husband's outstretched hand instead. "Hold me, dear, hold me, please . . .

tight. Do not let me go." She was in what he called afterwards "a regular state." He drew her firmly down upon her chair again.

"Smoke, Sophie, my dear," he said quickly, trying to make his voice calm and natural. "I see it, yes. It's smoke blowing over from the gardener's cottage. . . ."

"But, David,"—and there was a new horror in her whisper now—"it made a noise. It makes it still. I hear it swishing." Some such word she used—swishing, sishing, rushing, or something of the kind. "David, I'm very frightened. It's something awful! That man has called it out . . . !"

"Hush, hush," whispered her husband. He stroked her trembling hand beside him.

"It is in the wind," said Sanderson, speaking for the first time, very quietly. The expression on his face was not visible in the gloom, but his voice was soft and unafraid. At the sound of it, Mrs. Bittacy started violently again. Bittacy drew his chair a little forward to obstruct her view of him. He felt bewildered himself, a little, hardly knowing quite what to say or do. It was all so very curious and sudden.

But Mrs. Bittacy was badly frightened. It seemed to her that what she saw came from the enveloping forest just beyond their little garden. It emerged in a sort of secret way, moving towards them as with a purpose, stealthily, difficultly. Then something stopped it. It could not advance beyond the cedar. The cedar—this impression remained with her afterwards too—prevented, kept it back. Like a rising sea the Forest had surged a moment in their direction through the covering darkness, and this visible movement was its first wave. Thus to her mind it seemed . . . like that mysterious turn of the tide that used to frighten and mystify her in childhood on the sands. The outward surge of some enormous Power was what she felt . . . something to which every instinct in her being rose in opposition because it threatened her and hers. In that moment she realised the Personality of the Forest . . . menacing.

In the stumbling movement that she made away from the window and towards the bell she barely caught the sentence Sanderson—or was it her husband?—murmured to himself: "It came because we talked of it; our thinking made it aware of us and brought it out. But the cedar stops it. It cannot cross the lawn, you see . . ."

All three were standing now, and her husband's voice broke in with authority while his wife's fingers touched the bell.

"My dear, I should *not* say anything to Thompson." The anxiety he felt was manifest in his voice, but his outward composure had returned. "The gardener can go. . . ."

Then Sanderson cut him short. "Allow me," he said quickly. "I'll see if anything's wrong." And before either of them could answer or object, he was gone, leaping out by the open window. They saw his figure vanish with a run across the lawn into the darkness.

A moment later the maid entered, in answer to the bell, and with her came the loud barking of the terrier from the hall.

"The lamps," said her master shortly, and as she softly closed the door behind her, they heard the wind pass with a mournful sound of singing round the outer walls. A rustle of foliage from the distance passed within it.

"You see, the wind *is* rising. It *was* the wind!" He put a comforting arm about her, distressed to feel that she was trembling. But he knew that he was trembling too, though with a kind of odd elation rather than alarm. "And it *was* smoke that you saw coming from Stride's cottage, or from the rubbish heaps he's been burning in the kitchen garden. The noise we heard was the branches rustling in the wind. Why should you be so nervous?"

A thin whispering voice answered him:

"I was afraid for *you,* dear. Something frightened me for *you.* That man makes me feel so uneasy and uncomfortable for his influence upon you. It's very foolish, I know. I think . . . I'm tired; I feel so overwrought and restless." The words poured out in a hurried jumble and she kept turning to the window while she spoke.

"The strain of having a visitor," he said soothingly, "has taxed you. We're so unused to having people in the house. He goes to-morrow." He warmed her cold hands between his own, stroking them tenderly. More, for the life of him, he could not say or do. The joy of a strange, internal excitement made his heart beat faster. He knew not what it was. He knew only, perhaps, whence it came.

She peered close into his face through the gloom, and said a curious thing. "I thought, David, for a moment . . . you seemed . . . different. My nerves are all on edge to-night." She made no further reference to her husband's visitor.

A sound of footsteps from the lawn warned of Sanderson's return, as he answered quickly in a lowered tone—"There's no need to be afraid on my account, dear girl. There's nothing wrong with me, I assure you; I never felt so well and happy in my life."

Thompson came in with the lamps and brightness, and scarcely had she gone again when Sanderson in turn was seen climbing through the window.

"There's nothing," he said lightly, as he closed it behind him. "Somebody's been burning leaves, and the smoke is drifting a little through the trees. The wind," he added, glancing at his host a moment significantly, but in so discreet a way that Mrs. Bittacy did not observe it, "the wind, too, has begun to roar . . . in the Forest . . . further out."

But Mrs. Bittacy noticed about him two things which increased her uneasiness. She noticed the shining of his eyes, because a similar light had suddenly come into her husband's; and she noticed, too, the apparent depth of meaning he put into those simple words that "the wind had begun to roar in the Forest . . . further out." Her mind retained the disagreeable impression that he meant more than he said. In his tone lay quite another implication. It was not actually "wind" he spoke of, and it would not remain "further out" . . . rather, it was coming in. Another impression she got too—still more unwelcome—was that her husband understood his hidden meaning.

IV

"David, dear," she observed gently as soon as they were alone upstairs, "I have a horrible uneasy feeling about that man. I cannot get rid of it." The tremor in her voice caught all his tenderness.

He turned to look at her. "Of what kind, my dear? You're so imaginative sometimes, aren't you?"

"I think," she hesitated, stammering a little, confused, still frightened, "I mean—isn't he a hypnotist, or full of those theofosical ideas, or something of the sort? You know what I mean—"

He was too accustomed to her little confused alarms to explain them away seriously as a rule, or to correct her verbal inaccuracies, but to-night he felt she needed careful, tender treatment. He soothed her as best he could.

"But there's no harm in that, even if he is," he answered quietly. "Those are only new names for very old ideas, you know, dear." There was no trace of impatience in his voice.

"That's what I mean," she replied, the texts he dreaded rising in an unuttered crowd behind the words. "He's one of those things that we are warned would come—one of those Latter-Day things." For her mind still bristled with the bogeys of the Antichrist and Prophecy, and she had only escaped the Number of the Beast, as it were, by the skin of her teeth. The Pope drew most of her fire usually, because she could understand him; the target was plain and she could shoot. But this tree-and-forest business was so vague and horrible. It terrified her. "He makes me think," she went on, "of Principalities and Powers in high places, and of things that walk in darkness. I did *not* like the way he spoke of trees getting alive in the night, and all that; it made me think of wolves in sheep's clothing. And when I saw that awful thing in the sky above the lawn—"

But he interrupted her at once, for that was something he had decided it was best to leave unmentioned. Certainly it was better not discussed.

"He only meant, I think, Sophie," he put in gravely, yet with a little smile, "that trees may have a measure of conscious life—rather a nice idea on the whole, surely,—something like that bit we read in the *Times* the other night, you remember—and that a big forest may possess a sort of Collective Personality. Remember, he's an artist, and poetical."

"It's dangerous," she said emphatically. "I feel it's playing with fire, unwise, unsafe—"

"Yet all to the glory of God," he urged gently. "We must not shut our ears and eyes to knowledge—of any kind, must we?"

"With you, David, the wish is always farther than the thought," she rejoined. For, like the child who thought that "suffered under Pontius Pilate" was "suffered under a bunch of violets," she heard her proverbs phonetically and reproduced them thus. She hoped to convey her warning in the quotation. "And we must always try the spirits whether they be of God," she added tentatively.

"Certainly, dear, we can always do that," he assented, getting into bed.

But, after a little pause, during which she blew the light out, David

Bittacy settling down to sleep with an excitement in his blood that was new and bewilderingly delightful, realised that perhaps he had not said quite enough to comfort her. She was lying awake by his side, still frightened. He put his head up in the darkness.

"Sophie," he said softly, "you must remember, too, that in any case between us and—and all that sort of thing—there is a great gulf fixed, a gulf that cannot be crossed—er—while we are still in the body."

And hearing no reply, he satisfied himself that she was already asleep and happy. But Mrs. Bittacy was not asleep. She heard the sentence, only she said nothing because she felt her thought was better unexpressed. She was afraid to hear the words in the darkness. The Forest outside was listening and might hear them too—the Forest that was "roaring further out."

And the thought was this: That gulf, of course, existed, but Sanderson had somehow bridged it.

It was much later that night when she awoke out of troubled, uneasy dreams and heard a sound that twisted her very nerves with fear. It passed immediately with full waking, for, listen as she might, there was nothing audible but the inarticulate murmur of the night. It was in her dreams she heard it, and the dreams had vanished with it. But the sound was recognisable, for it was that rushing noise that had come across the lawn; only this time closer. Just above her face while she slept had passed this murmur as of rustling branches in the very room, a sound of foliage whispering. "A going in the tops of the mulberry trees," ran through her mind. She had dreamed that she lay beneath a spreading tree somewhere, a tree that whispered with ten thousand soft lips of green; and the dream continued for a moment even after waking.

She sat up in bed and stared about her. The window was open at the top; she saw the stars; the door, she remembered, was locked as usual; the room, of course, was empty. The deep hush of the summer night lay over all, broken only by another sound that now issued from the shadows close beside the bed, a human sound, yet unnatural, a sound that seized the fear with which she had waked and instantly increased it. And, although it was one she recognised as familiar, at first she could not name it. Some seconds certainly passed—and, they were very long ones— before she understood that it was her husband talking in his sleep.

The direction of the voice confused and puzzled her, moreover, for it was not, as she first supposed, beside her. There was distance in it. The next minute, by the light of the sinking candle flame, she saw his white figure standing out in the middle of the room, half-way towards the window. The candle-light slowly grew. She saw him move then nearer to the window, with arms outstretched. His speech was low and mumbled, the words running together too much to be distinguishable.

And she shivered. To her, sleep-talking was uncanny to the point of horror; it was like the talking of the dead, mere parody of a living voice, unnatural.

"David!" she whispered, dreading the sound of her own voice, and half afraid to interrupt him and see his face. She could not bear the sight of the wide-opened eyes. "David, you're walking in your sleep. Do—come back to bed, dear, *please!*"

Her whisper seemed so dreadfully loud in the still darkness. At the sound of her voice he paused, then turned slowly round to face her. His widely-opened eyes stared into her own without recognition; they looked through her into something beyond; it was as though he knew the direction of the sound, yet could not see her. They were shining, she noticed, as the eyes of Sanderson had shone several hours ago; and his face was flushed, distraught. Anxiety was written upon every feature. And, instantly, recognising that the fever was upon him, she forgot her terror temporarily in practical considerations. He came back to bed without waking. She closed his eyelids. Presently he composed himself quietly to sleep, or rather to deeper sleep. She contrived to make him swallow something from the tumbler beside the bed.

Then she rose very quietly to close the window, feeling the night air blow in too fresh and keen. She put the candle where it could not reach him. The sight of the big Baxter Bible beside it comforted her a little, but all through her under-being ran the warnings of a curious alarm. And it was while in the act of fastening the catch with one hand and pulling the string of the blind with the other, that her husband sat up again in bed and spoke in words this time that were distinctly audible. The eyes had opened wide again. He pointed. She stood stock still and listened, her shadow distorted on the blind. He did not come out towards her as at first she feared.

The whispering voice was very clear, horrible, too, beyond all she had ever known.

"They are roaring in the Forest further out . . . and I . . . must go and see." He stared beyond her as he said it, to the woods. "They are needing me. They sent for me. . . ." Then his eyes wandering back again to things within the room, he lay down, his purpose suddenly changed. And that change was horrible as well, more horrible, perhaps, because of its revelation of another detailed world he moved in far away from her.

The singular phrase chilled her blood; for a moment she was utterly terrified. That tone of the somnambulist, differing so slightly yet so distressingly from normal, waking speech, seemed to her somehow wicked. Evil and danger lay waiting thick behind it. She leaned against the window-sill, shaking in every limb. She had an awful feeling for a moment that something was coming in to fetch him.

"Not yet, then," she heard in a much lower voice from the bed, "but later. It will be better so. . . . I shall go later. . . ."

The words expressed some fringe of these alarms that had haunted her so long, and that the arrival and presence of Sanderson seemed to have brought to the very edge of a climax she could not even dare to think about. They gave it form; they brought it closer; they sent her thoughts to her Deity in a wild, deep prayer for help and guidance. For here was a direct, unconscious betrayal of a world of inner purposes and claims her husband recognised while he kept them almost wholly to himself.

By the time she reached his side and knew the comfort of his touch, the eyes had closed again, this time of their own accord, and the head lay calmly back upon the pillows. She gently straightened the bed clothes. She watched him for some minutes, shading the candle carefully with one hand. There was a smile of strangest peace upon the face.

Then, blowing out the candle, she knelt down and prayed before getting back into bed. But no sleep came to her. She lay awake all night thinking, wondering, praying, until at length with the chorus of the birds and the glimmer of the dawn upon the green blind, she fell into a slumber of complete exhaustion.

But while she slept the wind continued roaring in the Forest further out. The sound came closer—sometimes very close indeed.

V

With the departure of Sanderson the significance of the curious incidents waned, because the moods that had produced them passed away.
Mrs. Bittacy soon afterwards came to regard them as some growth of
disproportion that had been very largely, perhaps, in her own mind. It
did not strike her that this change was sudden, for it came about quite
naturally. For one thing her husband never spoke of the matter, and
for another she remembered how many things in life that had seemed
inexplicable and singular at the time turned out later to have been quite
commonplace.

Most of it, certainly, she put down to the presence of the artist and
to his wild, suggestive talk. With his welcome removal, the world
turned ordinary again and safe. The fever, though it lasted as usual a
short time only, had not allowed of her husband's getting up to say
good-bye, and she had conveyed his regrets and adieux. In the morning Mr. Sanderson had seemed ordinary enough. In his town hat and
gloves, as she saw him go, he seemed tame and unalarming.

"After all," she thought as she watched the pony-cart bear him off,
"he's only an artist!" What she had thought he might be otherwise her
slim imagination did not venture to disclose. Her change of feeling was
wholesome and refreshing. She felt a little ashamed of her behaviour.
She gave him a smile—genuine because the relief she felt was genuine—as he bent over her hand and kissed it, but she did not suggest a
second visit, and her husband, she noted with satisfaction and relief,
had said nothing either.

The little household fell again into the normal and sleepy routine
to which it was accustomed. The name of Arthur Sanderson was rarely
if ever mentioned. Nor, for her part, did she mention to her husband
the incident of his walking in his sleep and the wild words he used. But
to forget it was equally impossible. Thus it lay buried deep within her
like a centre of some unknown disease of which it was a mysterious
symptom, waiting to spread at the first favourable opportunity. She
prayed against it every night and morning: prayed that she might forget
it—that God would keep her husband safe from harm.

For in spite of much surface foolishness that many might have
read as weakness, Mrs. Bittacy had balance, sanity, and a fine deep

faith. She was greater than she knew. Her love for her husband and her God were somehow one, an achievement only possible to a single-hearted nobility of soul.

There followed a summer of great violence and beauty; of beauty, because the refreshing rains at night prolonged the glory of the spring and spread it all across July, keeping the foliage young and sweet; of violence, because the winds that tore about the south of England brushed the whole country into dancing movement. They swept the woods magnificently, and kept them roaring with a perpetual grand voice. Their deepest notes seemed never to leave the sky. They sang and shouted, and torn leaves raced and fluttered through the air long before their usually appointed time. Many a tree, after days of roaring and dancing, fell exhausted to the ground. The cedar on the lawn gave up two limbs that fell upon successive days, at the same hour too— just before dusk. The wind often makes its most boisterous effort at that time, before it drops with the sun, and these two huge branches lay in dark ruin covering half the lawn. They spread across it and towards the house. They left an ugly gaping space upon the tree, so that the Lebanon looked unfinished, half destroyed, a monster shorn of its old-time comeliness and splendour. Far more of the Forest was now visible than before; it peered through the breach of the broken defences. They could see from the windows of the house now—especially from the drawing-room and bedroom windows—straight out into the glades and depths beyond.

Mrs. Bittacy's niece and nephew, who were staying on a visit at the time, enjoyed themselves immensely helping the gardeners carry off the fragments. It took two days to do this, for Mr. Bittacy insisted on the branches being moved entire. He would not allow them to be chopped; also, he would not consent to their use as firewood. Under his superintendence the unwieldy masses were dragged to the edge of the garden and arranged upon the frontier line between the Forest and the lawn. The children were delighted with the scheme. They entered into it with enthusiasm. At all costs this defence against the inroads of the Forest must be made secure. They caught their uncle's earnestness, felt even something of a hidden motive that he had, and the visit, usually rather dreaded, became the visit of their lives instead. It was Aunt

Sophia this time who seemed discouraging and dull.

"She's got so old and funny," opined Stephen.

But Alice, who felt in the silent displeasure of her aunt some secret thing that half alarmed her, said:

"I think she's afraid of the woods. She never comes into them with us, you see."

"All the more reason then for making this wall impreg—all fat and thick and solid," he concluded, unable to manage the longer word. "Then nothing—simply *nothing*—can get through. Can't it, Uncle David?"

And Mr. Bittacy, jacket discarded and working in his speckled waistcoat, went puffing to their aid, arranging the massive limb of the cedar like a hedge.

"Come on," he said, "whatever happens, you know, we must finish before it's dark. Already the wind is roaring in the Forest further out." And Alice caught the phrase and instantly echoed it. "Stevie," she cried below her breath, "look sharp, you lazy lump. Didn't you hear what Uncle David said? It'll come in and catch us before we've done!"

They worked like Trojans, and, sitting beneath the wistaria tree that climbed the southern wall of the cottage, Mrs. Bittacy with her knitting watched them, calling from time to time insignificant messages of counsel and advice. The messages passed, of course, unheeded. Mostly, indeed, they were unheard, for the workers were too absorbed. She warned her husband not to get too hot, Alice not to tear her dress, Stephen not to strain his back with pulling. Her mind hovered between the homœopathic medicine-chest upstairs and her anxiety to see the business finished.

For this breaking up of the cedar had stirred again her slumbering alarms. It revived memories of the visit of Mr. Sanderson that had been sinking into oblivion; she recalled his queer and odious way of talking, and many things she hoped forgotten drew their heads up from that subconscious region to which all forgetting is impossible. They looked at her and nodded. They were full of life; they had no intention of being pushed aside and buried permanently. "Now look!" they whispered, "didn't we tell you so?" They had been merely waiting the right moment to assert their presence. And all her former vague distress crept over her. Anxiety, uneasiness returned. That dreadful sinking of the heart came too.

This incident of the cedar's breaking up was actually so unimportant, and yet her husband's attitude towards it made it so significant. There was nothing that he said in particular, or did, or left undone that frightened her, but his general air of earnestness seemed so unwarranted. She felt that he deemed the thing important. He was so exercised about it. This evidence of sudden concern and interest, buried all the summer from her sight and knowledge, she realised now had been buried purposely; he had kept it intentionally concealed. Deeply submerged in him there ran this tide of other thoughts, desires, hopes. What were they? Whither did they lead? The accident to the tree betrayed it most unpleasantly; and, doubtless, more than he was aware.

She watched his grave and serious face as he worked there with the children, and as she watched she felt afraid. It vexed her that the children worked so eagerly. They unconsciously supported him. The thing she feared she would not even name. But it was waiting.

Moreover, as far as her puzzled mind could deal with a dread so vague and incoherent, the collapse of the cedar somehow brought it nearer. The fact that, all so ill-explained and formless, the thing yet lay in her consciousness, out of reach but moving and alive, filled her with a kind of puzzled, dreadful wonder. Its presence was so very real, its power so gripping, its partial concealment so abominable. Then, out of the dim confusion, she grasped one thought and saw it stand quite clear before her eyes. She found difficulty in clothing it in words, but its meaning perhaps was this: That cedar stood in their life for something friendly; its downfall meant disaster; a sense of some protective influence about the cottage, and about her husband in particular, was thereby weakened.

"Why do you fear the big winds so?" he had asked her several days before, after a particularly boisterous day; and the answer she gave surprised her while she gave it. One of those heads poked up unconsciously, and let slip the truth:

"Because, David, I feel they—bring the Forest with them," she faltered. "They blow something from the trees—into the mind—into the house."

He looked at her keenly for a moment.

"That must be why I love them then," he answered. "They blow the souls of the trees about the sky like clouds."

The conversation dropped. She had never heard him talk in quite that way before.

And another time, when he had coaxed her to go with him down one of the nearer glades, she asked why he took the small hand-axe with him, and what he wanted it for.

"To cut the ivy that clings to the trunks and takes their life away," he said.

"But can't the verdurers do that?" she asked. "That's what they're paid for, isn't it?"

Whereupon he explained that ivy was a parasite the trees knew not how to fight alone, and that the verdurers were careless and did not do it thoroughly. They gave a chop here and there, leaving the tree to do the rest for itself if it could.

"Besides, I like to do it for them. I love to help them and protect," he added, the foliage rustling all about his quiet words as they went.

And these stray remarks, as his attitude towards the broken cedar, betrayed this curious, subtle change that was going forward in his personality. Slowly and surely all the summer it had increased.

It was growing—the thought startled her horribly—just as a tree grows, the outer evidence from day to day so slight as to be unnoticeable, yet the rising tide so deep and irresistible. The alteration spread all through and over him, was in both mind and actions, sometimes almost in his face as well. Occasionally, thus, it stood up straight outside himself and frightened her. His life was somehow becoming linked so intimately with trees, and with all that trees signified. His interests became more and more their interests, his activity combined with theirs, his thoughts and feelings theirs, his purpose, hope, desire, his fate—

His fate! The darkness of some vague, enormous terror dropped its shadow on her when she thought of it. Some instinct in her heart she dreaded infinitely more than death—for death meant sweet translation for his soul—came gradually to associate the thought of him with the thought of trees, in particular with these Forest trees. Sometimes, before she could face the thing, argue it away, or pray it into silence, she found the thought of him running swiftly through her mind like a thought of the Forest itself, the two most intimately linked and joined together, each a part and complement of the other, one being.

The idea was too dim for her to see it face to face. Its mere possibility dissolved the instant she focussed it to get the truth behind it. It was too utterly elusive, mad, protæan. Under the attack of even a minute's concentration the very meaning of it vanished, melted away. The idea lay really behind any words that she could ever find, beyond the touch of definite thought. Her mind was unable to grapple with it. But, while it vanished, the trail of its approach and disappearance flickered a moment before her shaking vision. The horror certainly remained.

Reduced to the simple human statement that her temperament sought instinctively it stood perhaps at this: Her husband loved her, and he loved the trees as well; but the trees came first, claimed parts of him she did not know. *She* loved her God and him. *He* loved the trees and her.

Thus, in guise of some faint, distressing compromise, the matter shaped itself for her perplexed mind in the terms of conflict. A silent, hidden battle raged, but as yet raged far away. The breaking of the cedar was a visible outward fragment of a distant and mysterious encounter that was coming daily closer to them both. The wind, instead of roaring in the Forest further out, now came nearer, booming in fitful gusts about its edge and frontiers.

Meanwhile the summer dimmed. The autumn winds went sighing through the woods; leaves turned to golden red, and the evenings were drawing in with cosy shadows before the first sign of anything seriously untoward made its appearance. It came then with a flat, decided kind of violence that indicated mature preparation beforehand. It was not impulsive nor ill-considered. In a fashion it seemed expected, and indeed inevitable. For within a fortnight of their annual change to the little village of Seillans above St. Raphael—a change so regular for the past ten years that it was not even discussed between them—David Bittacy abruptly refused to go.

Thompson had laid the tea-table, prepared the spirit lamp beneath the urn, pulled down the blinds in that swift and silent way she had, and left the room. The lamps were still unlit. The firelight shone on the chintz armchairs, and Boxer lay asleep on the black horse-hair rug. Upon the walls the gilt picture frames gleamed faintly, the pictures themselves indistinguishable. Mrs. Bittacy had warmed the teapot and was in the act of pouring the water in to heat the cups when her husband, looking up from his chair across the hearth, made the abrupt announcement:

"My dear," he said, as though following a train of thought of which she only heard this final phrase, "it's really quite impossible for me to go."

And so abrupt, inconsequent, it sounded that she at first misunderstood. She thought he meant to go out into the garden or the woods. But her heart leaped all the same. The tone of his voice was ominous.

"Of course not," she answered, "it would be *most* unwise. Why should you—?" She referred to the mist that always spread on autumn nights upon the lawn; but before she finished the sentence she knew that *he* referred to something else. And her heart then gave its second horrible leap.

"David! You mean abroad?" she gasped.

"I mean abroad, dear, yes."

It reminded her of the tone he used when saying good-bye years ago, before one of those jungle expeditions she dreaded. His voice then was so serious, so final. It was serious and final now. For several moments she could think of nothing to say. She busied herself with the teapot. She had filled one cup with hot water till it overflowed, and she emptied it slowly into the slop-basin, trying with all her might not to let him see the trembling of her hand. The firelight and the dimness of the room both helped her. But in any case he would hardly have noticed it. His thoughts were far away. . . .

VI

Mrs. Bittacy had never liked their present home. She preferred a flat, more open country that left approaches clear. She liked to see things coming. This cottage on the very edge of the old hunting grounds of William the Conqueror had never satisfied her ideal of a safe and pleasant place to settle down in. The sea-coast, with treeless downs behind and a clear horizon in front, as at Eastbourne, say, was her ideal of a proper home.

It was curious, this instinctive aversion she felt to being shut in— by trees especially; a kind of claustrophobia almost; probably due, as has been said, to the days in India when the trees took her husband off and surrounded him with dangers. In those weeks of solitude the feeling had matured. She had fought it in her fashion, but never conquered it. Apparently routed, it had a way of creeping back in other forms. In this particular case, yielding to his strong desire, she thought the battle won, but the terror of the trees came back before the first month had passed. They laughed in her face.

She never lost knowledge of the fact that the leagues of forest lay about their cottage like a mighty wall, a crowding, watching, listening presence that shut them in from freedom and escape. Far from morbid naturally, she did her best to deny the thought, and so simple and un-artificial was her type of mind that for weeks together she would wholly lose it. Then, suddenly it would return upon her with a rush of bleak reality. It was not only in her mind; it existed apart from any mere mood; a separate fear that walked alone; it came and went, yet when it went—went only to watch her from another point of view. It was in abeyance—hidden round the corner.

The Forest never let her go completely. It was ever ready to encroach. All the branches, she sometimes fancied, stretched one way—towards their tiny cottage and garden, as though it sought to draw them in and merge them in itself. Its great, deep-breathing soul resented the mockery, the insolence, the irritation of the prim garden at its very gates. It would absorb and smother them if it could. And every wind that blew its thundering message over the huge sounding-board of the million, shaking trees conveyed the purpose that it had. They had angered its great soul. At its heart was this deep, incessant roaring.

All this she never framed in words, the subtleties of language lay far beyond her reach. But instinctively she felt it; and more besides. It troubled her profoundly. Chiefly, moreover, for her husband. Merely for herself, the nightmare might have left her cold. It was David's peculiar interest in the trees that gave the special invitation.

Jealousy, then, in its most subtle aspect came to strengthen this aversion and dislike, for it came in a form that no reasonable wife could possibly object to. Her husband's passion, she reflected, was natural and inborn. It had decided his vocation, fed his ambition, nourished his dreams, desires, hopes. All his best years of active life had been spent in the care and guardianship of trees. He knew them, understood their secret life and nature, "managed" them intuitively as other men "managed" dogs and horses. He could not live for long away from them without a strange, acute nostalgia that stole his peace of mind and consequently his strength of body. A forest made him happy and at peace; it nursed and fed and soothed his deepest moods. Trees influenced the sources of his life, lowered or raised the very heart-beat in him. Cut off from them he languished as a lover of the sea can droop inland, or a mountaineer may pine in the flat monotony of the plains.

This she could understand, in a fashion at least, and make allowances for. She had yielded gently, even sweetly, to his choice of their English home; for in the little island there is nothing that suggests the woods of wilder countries so nearly as the New Forest. It has the genuine air and mystery, the depth and splendour, the loneliness, and here and there the strong, untamable quality of old-time forests as Bittacy of the Department knew them.

In a single detail only had he yielded to her wishes. He consented to a cottage on the edge, instead of in the heart of it. And for a dozen years now they had dwelt in peace and happiness at the lips of this great spreading thing that covered so many leagues with its tangle of swamps and moors and splendid ancient trees.

Only with the last two years or so—with his own increasing age, and physical decline perhaps—had come this marked growth of passionate interest in the welfare of the Forest. She had watched it grow, at first had laughed at it, then talked sympathetically so far as sincerity permitted, then had argued mildly, and finally come to realise that its treatment lay altogether beyond her powers, and so had come to fear it with all her heart.

The six weeks they annually spent away from their English home, each regarded very differently, of course. For her husband it meant a painful exile that did his health no good; he yearned for his trees—the sight and sound and smell of them; but for herself it meant release from a haunting dread—escape. To renounce those six weeks by the sea on the sunny, shining coast of France, was almost more than this little woman, even with her unselfishness, could face.

After the first shock of the announcement, she reflected as deeply as her nature permitted, prayed, wept in secret—and made up her mind. Duty, she felt clearly, pointed to renouncement. The discipline would certainly be severe—she did not dream at the moment how severe!—but this fine, consistent little Christian saw it plain; she accepted it, too, without any sighing of the martyr, though the courage she showed was of the martyr order. Her husband should never know the cost. In all but this one passion his unselfishness was ever as great as her own. The love she had borne him all these years, like the love she bore her anthropomorphic deity, was deep and real. She loved to suffer for them both. Besides, the way her husband had put it to her was singular. It did not take the form of a mere selfish predilection. Something higher than two wills in conflict seeking compromise was in it from the beginning.

"I feel, Sophia, it would be really more than I could manage," he said slowly, gazing into the fire over the tops of his stretched-out muddy boots. "My duty and my happiness lie here with the Forest and with you. My life is deeply rooted in this place. Something I can't define connects my inner being with these trees, and separation would make me ill—might even kill me. My hold on life would weaken; here is my source of supply. I cannot explain it better than that." He looked up steadily into her face across the table so that she saw the gravity of his expression and the shining of his steady eyes.

"David, you feel it as strongly as that!" she said, forgetting the tea things altogether.

"Yes," he replied, "I do. And it's not of the body only, I feel it in my soul."

The reality of what he hinted at crept into that shadow-covered room like an actual Presence and stood beside them. It came not by the windows or the door, but it filled the entire space between the walls and ceiling. It took the heat from the fire before her face. She felt suddenly cold, confused a little, frightened. She almost felt the rush of foliage in the wind. It stood between them.

"There are things—some things," she faltered, "we are not intended to know, I think." The words expressed her general attitude to life, not alone to this particular incident.

And after a pause of several minutes, disregarding the criticism as though he had not heard it—"I cannot explain it better than that, you see," his grave voice answered. "There *is* this deep, tremendous link,—some secret power they emanate that keeps me well and happy and—alive. If you cannot understand, I feel at least you may be able to—forgive." His tone grew tender, gentle, soft. "My selfishness, I know, must seem quite unforgivable. I cannot help it somehow; these trees, this ancient Forest, both seem knitted into all that makes me live, and if I go—"

There was a little sound of collapse in his voice. He stopped abruptly, and sank back in his chair. And, at that, a distinct lump came up into her throat which she had great difficulty in managing while she went over and put her arms about him.

"My dear," she murmured, "God will direct. We will accept His guidance. He has always shown the way before."

"My selfishness afflicts me—" he began, but she would not let him finish.

"David, He will direct. Nothing shall harm you. You've never once been selfish, and I cannot bear to hear you say such things. The way will open that is best for you—for both of us." She kissed him, she would not let him speak; her heart was in her throat, and she felt for him far more than for herself.

And then he had suggested that she should go alone perhaps for a shorter time, and stay in her brother's villa with the children, Alice and Stephen. It was always open to her as she well knew.

"You need the change," he said, when the lamps had been lit and the servant had gone out again; "you need it as much as I dread it. I could manage somehow until you returned, and should feel happier that way if you went. I cannot leave this Forest that I love so well. I even feel, Sophie dear"—he sat up straight and faced her as he half whispered it—"that I can *never* leave it again. My life and happiness lie here together."

And even while scorning the idea that she could leave him alone with the Influence of the Forest all about him to have its unimpeded way, she felt the pangs of that subtle jealousy bite keen and close. He loved the Forest better than herself, for he placed it first. Behind the words, moreover, hid the unuttered thought that made her so uneasy. The terror Sanderson had brought revived and shook its wings before her very eyes. For the whole conversation, of which this was a fragment, conveyed the unutterable implication that while he could not spare the trees, they equally could not spare him. The vividness with which he managed to conceal and yet betray the fact brought a profound distress that crossed the border between presentiment and warning into positive alarm.

He clearly felt that the trees would miss him—the trees he tended, guarded, watched over, loved.

"David, I shall stay here with you. I think you need me really,— don't you?" Eagerly, with a touch of heart-felt passion, the words poured out.

"Now more than ever, dear. God bless you for your sweet unselfishness. And your sacrifice," he added, "is all the greater because you cannot understand the thing that makes it necessary for me to stay."

"Perhaps in the spring instead—" she said, with a tremor in the voice.

"In the spring—perhaps," he answered gently, almost beneath his breath. "For they will not need me then. All the world can love them in the spring. It's in the winter that they're lonely and neglected. I wish to stay with them particularly then. I even feel I ought to—and I must."

And in this way, without further speech, the decision was made. Mrs. Bittacy, at least, asked no more questions. Yet she could not bring herself to show more sympathy than was necessary. She felt, for one thing, that if she did, it might lead him to speak freely, and to tell her things she could not possibly bear to know. And she dared not take the risk of that.

VII

This was at the end of summer, but the autumn followed close. The conversation really marked the threshold between the two seasons, and marked at the same time the line between her husband's negative and aggressive state. She almost felt she had done wrong to yield; he grew so bold, concealment all discarded. He went, that is, quite openly to the woods, forgetting all his duties, all his former occupations. He even sought to coax her to go with him. The hidden thing blazed out without disguise. And, while she trembled at his energy, she admired the virile passion he displayed. Her jealousy had long ago retired before her fear, accepting the second place. Her one desire now was to protect. The wife turned wholly mother.

He said so little, but—he hated to come in. From morning to night he wandered in the Forest; often he went out after dinner; his mind was charged with trees—their foliage, growth, development; their wonder, beauty, strength; their loneliness in isolation, their power in a herded mass. He knew the effect of every wind upon them; the danger from the boisterous north, the glory from the west, the eastern dryness, and the soft, moist tenderness that a south wind left upon their thinning boughs. He spoke all day of their sensations: how they drank the fading sunshine, dreamed in the moonlight, thrilled to the kiss of stars. The dew could bring them half the passion of the night, but frost sent them plunging beneath the ground to dwell with hopes of a later coming softness in their roots. They nursed the life they carried—insects, larvae, chrysalis—and when the skies above them melted, he spoke of them standing "motionless in an ecstasy of rain," or in the noon of sunshine "self-poised upon their prodigy of shade."

And once in the middle of the night she woke at the sound of his voice, and heard him—wide awake, not talking in his sleep—but talking towards the window where the shadow of the cedar fell at noon:

> O art thou sighing for Lebanon
> In the long breeze that streams to thy delicious East?
> Sighing for Lebanon,
> Dark cedar;

and, when, half charmed, half terrified, she turned and called to him by name, he merely said—

"My dear, I felt the loneliness—suddenly realised it—the alien desolation of that tree, set here upon our little lawn in England when all her Eastern brothers call her in sleep." And the answer seemed so queer, so "un-evangelical," that she waited in silence till he slept again. The poetry passed her by. It seemed unnecessary and out of place. It made her ache with suspicion, fear, jealousy.

The fear, however, seemed somehow all lapped up and banished soon afterwards by her unwilling admiration of the rushing splendour of her husband's state. Her anxiety, at any rate, shifted from the religious to the medical. She thought he might be losing his steadiness of mind a little. How often in her prayers she offered thanks for the guidance that had made her stay with him to help and watch is impossible to say. It certainly was twice a day.

She even went so far once—when Mr. Mortimer, the vicar, called, and brought with him a more or less distinguished doctor—as to tell the professional man privately some symptoms of her husband's queerness. And his answer that there was "nothing he could prescribe for" added not a little to her sense of unholy bewilderment. No doubt Sir James had never been "consulted" under such unorthodox conditions before. His sense of what was becoming naturally overrode his acquired instincts as a skilled instrument that might help the race.

"No fever, you think?" she asked insistently with hurry, determined to get something from him.

"Nothing that *I* can deal with, as I told you, Madam," replied the offended allopathic Knight.

Evidently he did not care about being invited to examine patients in this surreptitious way before a teapot on the lawn, chance of a fee most problematical. He liked to see a tongue and feel a thumping pulse; to know the pedigree and bank account of his questioner as well. It was most unusual, in abominable taste besides. Of course it was. But the drowning woman seized the only straw she could.

For now the aggressive attitude of her husband overcame her to the point where she found it difficult even to question him. Yet in the house he was so kind and gentle, doing all he could to make her sacrifice as easy as possible.

"David, you really *are* unwise to go out now. The night is damp and very chilly. The ground is soaked in dew. You'll catch your death of cold."

His face lightened. "Won't you come with me, dear,—just for once? I'm only going to the corner of the hollies to see the beech that stands so lonely by itself."

She had been out with him in the short dark afternoon, and they had passed that evil group of hollies where the gipsies camped. Nothing else would grow there, but the hollies thrive upon the stony soil.

"David, the beech is all right and safe." She had learned his phraseology a little, made clever out of due season by her love. "There's no wind to-night."

"But it's rising," he answered, "rising in the east. I heard it in the bare and hungry larches. They need the sun and dew, and always cry out when the wind's upon them from the east."

She sent a short unspoken prayer most swiftly to her deity as she heard him say it. For every time now, when he spoke in this familiar, intimate way of the life of the trees, she felt a sheet of cold fasten tight against her very skin and flesh. She shivered. How *could* he possibly know such things?

Yet, in all else, and in the relations of his daily life, he was sane and reasonable, loving, kind, and tender. It was only on the subject of the trees he seemed unhinged and queer. Most curiously it seemed that, since the collapse of the cedar they both loved, though in different fashion, his departure from the normal had increased. Why else did he watch them as a man might watch a sickly child? Why did he linger especially in the dusk to catch their "mood of night" as he called it? Why think so carefully upon them when the frost was threatening or the wind appeared to rise?

As she put it so frequently now herself—How could he possibly *know* such things?

He went. As she closed the front door after him she heard the distant roaring in the Forest. . . .

And then it suddenly struck her: How could she know them too?

It dropped upon her like a blow that she felt at once all over, upon body, heart, and mind. The discovery rushed out from its ambush to overwhelm. The truth of it, making all arguing futile, numbed her faculties. But though at first it deadened her, she soon revived, and her being rose into aggressive opposition. A wild yet calculated courage like that which animates the leaders of splendid forlorn hopes flamed in her little person—flamed grandly, and invincible. While knowing herself insignificant and weak, she knew at the same time that power at her back which moves the worlds. The faith that filled her was the weapon in her hands, and the right by which she claimed it; but the spirit of utter, selfless sacrifice that characterised her life was the means by which she mastered its immediate use. For a kind of white and faultless intuition guided her to the attack. Behind her stood her Bible and her God.

How so magnificent a divination came to her at all may well be a matter for astonishment, though some clue of explanation lies, perhaps, in the very simpleness of her nature. At any rate, she saw quite clearly certain things; saw them in moments only—after prayer, in the still silence of the night, or when left alone those long hours in the house with her knitting and her thoughts—and the guidance which then flashed into her remained, even after the manner of its coming was forgotten.

They came to her, these things she saw, formless, wordless; she could not put them into any kind of language; but by the very fact of being uncaught in sentences they retained their original clear vigour.

Hours of patient waiting brought the first, and the others followed easily afterwards, by degrees, on subsequent days, a little and a little. Her husband had been gone since early morning, and had taken his luncheon with him. She was sitting by the tea things, the cups and teapot warmed, the muffins in the fender keeping hot, all ready for his return, when she realised quite abruptly that this thing which took him off, which kept him out so many hours day after day, this thing that was against her own little will and instincts—was enormous as the sea. It was no mere prettiness of single Trees, but something massed and mountainous. About her rose the wall of its huge opposition to the sky, its scale gigantic, its power utterly prodigious. What she knew of it hitherto as green and delicate forms waving and rustling in the winds was but, as it were, the spray of foam that broke into sight upon the nearer edge of viewless depths far, far away. The trees, indeed, were sentinels set visibly about the limits of a camp that itself remained invisible. The awful hum and murmur of the main body in the distance passed into that still room about her with the firelight and hissing kettle. Out yonder—in the Forest further out—the thing that was ever roaring at the centre was dreadfully increasing.

The sense of definite battle, too—battle between herself and the Forest for his soul—came with it. Its presentiment was as clear as though Thompson had come into the room and quietly told her that the cottage was surrounded. "Please, ma'am, there are trees come up about the house," she might have suddenly announced. And equally might have heard her own answer: "It's all right, Thompson. The main body is still far away."

Immediately upon its heels, then, came another truth, with a close

reality that shocked her. She saw that jealousy was not confined to the
human and animal world alone, but ran though all creation. The Vegetable Kingdom knew it too. So-called inanimate nature shared it with
the rest. Trees felt it. This Forest just beyond the window—standing
there in the silence of the autumn evening across the little lawn—this
Forest understood it equally. The remorseless, branching power that
sought to keep exclusively for itself the thing it loved and needed,
spread like a running desire through all its million leaves and stems and
roots. In humans, of course, it was consciously directed; in animals it
acted with frank instinctiveness; but in trees this jealousy rose in some
blind tide of impersonal and unconscious wrath that would sweep opposition from its path as the wind sweeps powdered snow from the
surface of the ice. Their number was a host with endless reinforcements, and once it realised its passion was returned the power increased. . . . Her husband loved the trees. . . . They had become aware
of it. . . . They would take him from her in the end. . . .

Then, while she heard his footsteps in the hall and the closing of
the front door, she saw a third thing clearly;—realised the widening of
the gap between herself and him. This other love had made it. All
these weeks of the summer when she felt so close to him, now especially when she had made the biggest sacrifice of her life to stay by his
side and help him, he had been slowly, surely—drawing away. The es-
trangement was here and now—a fact accomplished. It had been all
this time maturing; there yawned this broad deep space between them.
Across the empty distance she saw the change in merciless perspective.
It revealed his face and figure, dearly-loved, once fondly worshipped,
far on the other side in shadowy distance, small, the back turned from
her, and moving while she watched—moving away from her.

They had their tea in silence then. She asked no questions, he volunteered no information of his day. The heart was big within her, and
the terrible loneliness of age spread through her like a rising icy mist.
She watched him, filling all his wants. His hair was untidy and his
boots were caked with blackish mud. He moved with a restless, swaying
motion that somehow blanched her cheek and sent a miserable shivering down her back. It reminded her of trees. His eyes were very bright.

He brought in with him an odour of the earth and forest that
seemed to choke her and make it difficult to breathe; and—what she

noticed with a climax of almost uncontrollable alarm—upon his face beneath the lamplight shone traces of a mild, faint glory that made her think of moonlight falling upon a wood through speckled shadows. It was his new-found happiness that shone there, a happiness uncaused by her and in which she had no part.

In his coat was a spray of faded yellow beech leaves. "I brought this from the Forest for you," he said, with all the air that belonged to his little acts of devotion long ago. And she took the spray of leaves mechanically with a smile and a murmured "thank you, dear," as though he had unknowingly put into her hands the weapon for her own destruction and she had accepted it.

And when the tea was over and he left the room, he did not go to his study, or to change his clothes. She heard the front door softly shut behind him as he again went out towards the Forest.

A moment later she was in her room upstairs, kneeling beside the bed—the side he slept on—and praying wildly through a flood of tears that God would save and keep him to her. Wind brushed the window panes behind her while she knelt.

VIII

One sunny November morning, when the strain had reached a pitch that made repression almost unmanageable, she came to an impulsive decision, and obeyed it. Her husband had again gone out with luncheon for the day. She took adventure in her hands and followed him. The power of seeing-clear was strong upon her, forcing her up to some unnatural level of understanding. To stay indoors and wait inactive for his return seemed suddenly impossible. She meant to know what he knew, feel what he felt, put herself in his place. She would dare the fascination of the Forest—share it with him. It was greatly daring; but it would give her greater understanding how to help and save him and therefore greater Power. She went upstairs a moment first to pray.

In a thick, warm skirt, and wearing heavy boots—those walking boots she used with him upon the mountains about Seillans—she left the cottage by the back way and turned towards the Forest. She could not actually follow him, for he had started off an hour before and she knew not exactly his direction. What was so urgent in her was the wish to be with him in the woods, to walk beneath leafless branches just as he did: to be there when he was there, even though not together. For it had come to her that she might thus share with him for once this horrible mighty life and breathing of the trees he loved. In winter, he had said, they needed him particularly; and winter now was coming. Her love *must* bring her something of what he felt himself—the huge attraction, the suction and the pull of all the trees. Thus, in some vicarious fashion, she might share, though unknown to himself, this very thing that was taking him away from her. She might thus even lessen its attack upon himself.

The impulse came to her clairvoyantly, and she obeyed without a sign of hesitation. Deeper comprehension would come to her of the whole awful puzzle. And come it did, yet not in the way she imagined and expected.

The air was very still, the sky a cold pale blue, but cloudless. The entire Forest stood silent, at attention. It knew perfectly well that she had come. It knew the moment when she entered; watched and followed her; and behind her something dropped without a sound and shut her in. Her feet upon the glades of mossy grass fell silently, as the oaks and beeches shifted past in rows and took up their positions at her back. It was not pleasant, this way they grew so dense behind her the instant she had passed. She realised that they gathered in an ever-growing army, massed, herded, trooped, between her and the cottage, shutting off escape. They let her pass so easily, but to get out again she would know them differently—thick, crowded, branches all drawn and hostile. Already their increasing numbers bewildered her. In front, they looked so sparse and scattered, with open spaces where the sunshine fell; but when she turned it seemed they stood so close together, a serried army, darkening the sunlight. They blocked the day, collected all the shadows, stood with their leafless and forbidding rampart like the night. They swallowed down into themselves the very glade by which she came. For when she glanced behind her—rarely—the way she had come was shadowy and lost.

Yet the morning sparkled overhead, and a glance of excitement ran quivering through the entire day. It was what she always knew as "children's weather," so clear and harmless, without a sign of danger, nothing ominous to threaten or alarm. Steadfast in her purpose, looking back as little as she dared, Sophia Bittacy marched slowly and deliberately into the heart of the silent woods, deeper, ever deeper. . . .

And then, abruptly, in an open space where the sunshine fell unhindered, she stopped. It was one of the breathing-places of the forest. Dead, withered bracken lay in patches of unsightly grey. There were bits of heather too. All round the trees stood looking on—oak, beech, holly, ash, pine, larch, with here and there small groups of juniper. On the lips of this breathing-space of the woods she stopped to rest, disobeying her instinct for the first time. For the other instinct in her was to go on. She did not really want to rest.

This was the little act that brought it to her—the wireless message from a vast Emitter.

"I've been stopped," she thought to herself with a horrid qualm.

She looked about her in this quiet, ancient place. Nothing stirred. There was no life nor sign of life; no birds sang; no rabbits scuttled off at her approach. The stillness was bewildering, and gravity hung down upon it like a heavy curtain. It hushed the heart in her. Could this be part of what her husband felt—this sense of thick entanglement with stems, boughs, roots, and foliage?

"This has always been as it is now," she thought, yet not knowing why she thought it. "Ever since the Forest grew it has been still and secret here. It has never changed." The curtain of silence drew closer while she said it, thickening round her. "For a thousand years—I'm here with a thousand years. And behind this place stand all the forests of the world!"

So foreign to her temperament were such thoughts, and so alien to all she had been taught to look for in Nature, that she strove against them. She made an effort to oppose. But they clung and haunted just the same; they refused to be dispersed. The curtain hung dense and heavy as though its texture thickened. The air with difficulty came through.

And then she thought that curtain stirred. There was movement somewhere. That obscure dim thing which ever broods behind the visible appearances of trees came nearer to her. She caught her breath and stared about her, listening intently. The trees, perhaps because she saw them more in detail now, it seemed to her had changed. A vague, faint alteration spread over them, at first so slight she scarcely would admit it, then growing steadily, though still obscurely, outwards. "They tremble and are changed," flashed through her mind the horrid line that Sanderson had quoted. Yet the change was graceful for all the uncouthness attendant upon the size of so vast a movement. They had turned in her direction. That was it. *They saw her.*

In this way the change expressed itself in her groping, terrified thought. Till now it had been otherwise: she had looked at them from her own point of view; now they looked at her from theirs. They stared her in the face and eyes; they stared at her all over. In some unkind, resentful, hostile way, they watched her. Hitherto in life she had watched them variously, in superficial ways, reading into them what her own mind suggested. Now they read into her the things they actually *were,* and not merely another's interpretation of them.

They seemed in their motionless silence there instinct with life, a life, moreover, that breathed about her a species of terrible soft enchantment that bewitched. It branched all through her, climbing to the brain. The Forest held her with its huge and giant fascination. In this secluded breathing-spot that the centuries had left untouched, she had stepped close against the hidden pulse of the whole collective mass of them. They were aware of her and had turned to gaze with their myriad, vast sight upon the intruder. They shouted at her in the silence. For she wanted to look back at them, but it was like staring at a crowd, and her glance merely shifted from one tree to another, hurriedly, finding in none the one she sought. They saw her so easily, each and all. The rows that stood behind her also stared. But she could not return the gaze. Her husband, she realised, could. And their steady stare shocked her as though in some sense she knew that she was naked. They saw so much of her: she saw of them—so little.

Her efforts to return their gaze were pitiful. The constant shifting increased her bewilderment. Conscious of this awful and enormous sight all over her, she let her eyes first rest upon the ground; and then she closed them altogether. She kept the lids as tight together as ever they would go.

But the sight of the trees came even into that inner darkness behind the fastened lids, for there was no escaping it. Outside, in the light, she still knew that the leaves of the hollies glittered smoothly, that the dead foliage of the oaks hung crisp in the air about her, that the needles of the little junipers were pointing all one way. The spread perception of the Forest was focussed on herself, and no mere shutting of the eyes could hide its scattered yet concentrated stare—the all-inclusive vision of great woods.

There was no wind, yet here and there a single leaf hanging by its dried-up stalk shook all alone with great rapidity—rattling. It was the sentry drawing attention to her presence. And then, again, as once long weeks before, she felt their Being as a tide about her. The tide had turned. That memory of her childhood sands came back, when the nurse said, "The tide has turned now; we must go in," and she saw the mass of piled-up waters, green and heaped to the horizon, and realised that it was slowly coming in. The gigantic mass of it, too vast for hurry, loaded with massive purpose, she used to feel, was moving towards herself. The fluid body of the sea was creeping along beneath the sky to the very spot upon the yellow sands where she stood and played. The sight and thought of it had always overwhelmed her with a sense of awe—as though her puny self were the object of the whole sea's advance. "The tide has turned; we had better go in now."

This was happening now about her—the same thing was happening in the woods—slow, sure, and steady, and its motion as little discernible as the sea's. The tide had turned. The small human presence that had ventured among its green and mountainous depths, moreover, was its objective.

That all was clear within her while she sat and waited with tight-shut lids. But the next moment she opened her eyes with a sudden realisation of something more. The presence that it sought was after all not hers. It was the presence of some one other than herself. And then she understood. Her eyes had opened with a click, it seemed; but the sound, in reality, was outside herself. Across the clearing where the sunshine lay so calm and still, she saw the figure of her husband moving among the trees—a man, like a tree, walking.

With hands behind his back, and head uplifted, he moved quite slowly, as though absorbed in his own thoughts. Hardly fifty paces separated them, but he had no inkling of her presence there so near. With mind intent and senses all turned inwards, he marched past her like a figure in a dream, and like a figure in a dream she saw him go. Love, yearning, pity rose in a storm within her, but as in nightmare she found no words or movement possible. She sat and watched him go— go from her—go into the deeper reaches of the green enveloping woods. Desire to save, to bid him stop and turn, ran in a passion through her being, but there was nothing she could do. She saw him go away from her, go of his own accord and willingly beyond her; she saw the branches drop about his steps and hide him. His figure faded out among the speckled shade and sunlight. The trees covered him. The tide just took him, all unresisting and content to go. Upon the bosom of the green soft sea he floated away beyond her reach of vision. Her eyes could follow him no longer. He was gone.

And then for the first time she realised, even at that distance, that the look upon his face was one of peace and happiness—rapt, and caught away in joy, a look of youth. That expression now he never showed to her. But she *had* known it. Years ago, in the early days of their married life, she had seen it on his face. Now it no longer obeyed the summons of her presence and her love. The woods alone could call it forth; it answered to the trees; the Forest had taken every part of him—from her—his very heart and soul. . . .

Her sight that had plunged inwards to the fields of faded memory now came back to outer things again. She looked about her, and her love, returning empty-handed and unsatisfied, left her open to the invading of the bleakest terror she had ever known. That such things could be real and happen found her helpless utterly. Terror invaded the quietest corners of her heart, that had never yet known quailing. She could not—for moments at any rate—reach either her Bible or her God. Desolate in an empty world of fear she sat with eyes too dry and hot for tears, yet with a coldness as of ice upon her very flesh. She stared, unseeing, about her. That horror which stalks in the stillness of the noonday, when the glare of an artificial sunshine lights up the motionless trees, moved all about her. In front and behind she was aware of it. Beyond this stealthy silence, just within the edge of it, the things of another world were passing. But she could not know them. Her husband knew them, knew their beauty and their awe, yes, but for her they were out of reach. She might not share with him the very least of them. It seemed that behind and through the glare of this wintry noonday in the heart of the woods there brooded another universe of life and passion, for her all unexpressed. The silence veiled it, the stillness hid it; but he moved with it all and understood. His love interpreted it.

She rose to her feet, tottered feebly, and collapsed again upon the moss. Yet for herself she felt no terror; no little personal fear could touch her whose anguish and deep longing streamed all out to him whom she so bravely loved. In this time of utter self-forgetfulness, when she realised that the battle was hopeless, thinking she had lost even her God, she found Him again quite close beside her like a little Presence in this terrible heart of the hostile Forest. But at first she did not recognise that He was there; she did not know Him in that strangely unacceptable guise. For He stood so very close, so very intimate, so very sweet and comforting, and yet so hard to understand—as Resignation.

Once more she struggled to her feet, and this time turned successfully and slowly made her way along the mossy glade by which she came. And at first she marvelled, though only for a moment, at the ease with which she found the path. For a moment only, because almost at once she saw the truth. The trees were glad that she should go. They helped her on her way. The Forest did not want her.

The tide was coming in, indeed, yet not for her.

And so, in another of those flashes of clear-vision that of late had lifted life above the normal level, she saw and understood the whole terrible thing complete.

Till now, though unexpressed in thought or language, her fear had been that the woods her husband loved would somehow take him from her—to merge his life in theirs—even to kill him in some mysterious way. This time she saw her deep mistake, and so seeing, let in upon herself the fuller agony of horror. For their jealousy was not the petty jealousy of animals or humans. They wanted him because they loved him, but they did not want him dead. Full charged with his splendid life and enthusiasm they wanted him. They wanted him—alive.

It was she who stood in their way, and it was she whom they intended to remove.

This was what brought the sense of abject helplessness. She stood upon the sands against an entire ocean slowly rolling in against her.

For, as all the forces of a human being combine unconsciously to eject a grain of sand that has crept beneath the skin to cause discomfort, so the entire mass of what Sanderson had called the Collective Consciousness of the Forest strove to eject this human atom that stood across the path of its desire. Loving her husband, she had crept beneath its skin. It was her they would eject and take away; it was her they would destroy, not him. Him, whom they loved and needed, they would keep alive. They meant to take him living.

She reached the house in safety, though she never remembered how she found her way. It was made all simple for her. The branches almost urged her out.

But behind her, as she left the shadowed precincts, she felt as though some towering Angel of the Woods let fall across the threshold the flaming sword of a countless multitude of leaves that formed behind her a barrier, green, shimmering, and impassable. Into the Forest she never walked again.

And she went about her daily duties with a calm and quietness that was a perpetual astonishment even to herself, for it hardly seemed of this world at all. She talked to her husband when he came in for tea—after dark. Resignation brings a curious large courage—when there is nothing more to lose. The soul takes risks, and dares. Is it a curious short-cut sometimes to the heights?

"David, I went into the Forest, too, this morning; soon after you I went. I saw you there."

"Wasn't it wonderful?" he answered simply, inclining his head a little. There was no surprise or annoyance in his look; a mild and gentle *ennui* rather. He asked no real question. She thought of some garden tree the wind attacks too suddenly, bending it over when it does not want to bend—the mild unwillingness with which it yields. She often saw him this way now, in the terms of trees.

"It was very wonderful indeed, dear, yes," she replied low, her voice not faltering though indistinct. "But for me it was too—too strange and big."

The passion of tears lay just below the quiet voice all unbetrayed. Somehow she kept them back.

There was a pause, and then he added:

"I find it more and more so every day." His voice passed through the lamp-lit room like a murmur of the wind in branches. The look of youth and happiness she had caught upon his face out there had wholly gone, and an expression of weariness was in its place, as of a man distressed vaguely at finding himself in uncongenial surroundings where he is slightly ill at ease. It was the house he hated—coming back to rooms and walls and furniture. The ceilings and closed windows confined him. Yet, in it, no suggestion that he found *her* irksome. Her presence seemed of no account at all; indeed, he hardly noticed her. For whole long periods he lost her, did not know that she was there. He had no need of her. He lived alone. Each lived alone.

The outward signs by which she recognised that the awful battle was against her and the terms of surrender accepted were pathetic. She put the medicine-chest away upon the shelf; she gave the orders for his pocket-luncheon before he asked; she went to bed alone and early, leaving the front door unlocked, with milk and bread and butter in the hall beside the lamp—all concessions that she felt impelled to make. For more and more, unless the weather was too violent, he went out after dinner even, staying for hours in the woods. But she never slept until she heard the front door close below, and knew soon afterwards his careful step come creeping up the stairs and into the room so softly. Until she heard his regular deep breathing close beside her, she lay awake. All strength or desire to resist had gone for good. The thing against her was too huge and powerful. Capitulation was complete, a fact accomplished. She dated it from the day she followed him to the Forest.

Moreover, the time for evacuation—her own evacuation—seemed approaching. It came stealthily ever nearer, surely and slowly as the rising tide she used to dread. At the high-water mark she stood waiting calmly—waiting to be swept away. Across the lawn all those terrible days of early winter the encircling Forest watched it come, guiding its silent swell and currents towards her feet. Only she never once gave up her Bible or her praying. This complete resignation, moreover, had somehow brought to her a strange great understanding, and if she could not share her husband's horrible abandonment to powers outside himself, she could, and did, in some half-groping way grasp at shadowy meanings that might make such abandonment—possible, yes, but more than merely possible—in some extraordinary sense not evil.

Hitherto she had divided the beyond-world into two sharp halves—spirits good or spirits evil. But thoughts came to her now, on soft and very tentative feet, like the footsteps of the gods which are on wool, that besides these definite classes, there might be other Powers as well, belonging definitely to neither one nor the other. Her thought stopped dead at that. But the big idea found lodgment in her little mind, and, owing to the largeness of her heart, remained there unejected. It even brought a certain solace with it.

The failure—or unwillingness, as she preferred to state it—of her God to interfere and help, that also she came in a measure to understand. For here, she found it more and more possible to imagine, was perhaps no positive evil at work, but only something that usually stands away from humankind, something alien and not commonly recognised. There *was* a gulf fixed between the two, and Mr. Sanderson *had* bridged it, by his talk, his explanations, his attitude of mind. Through these her husband had found the way into it. His temperament and natural passion for the woods had prepared the soul in him, and the moment he saw the way to go he took it—the line of least resistance. Life was, of course, open to all, and her husband had the right to choose it where he would. He had chosen it—away from her, away from other men, but not necessarily away from God. This was an enormous concession that she skirted, never really faced; it was too revolutionary to face. But its possibility peeped into her bewildered mind. It might delay his progress, or it might advance it. Who could know? And why should God, who ordered all things with such magnificent detail, from the pathway of a sun to the falling of a sparrow, object to his free choice, or interfere to hinder him and stop?

She came to realise resignation, that is, in another aspect. It gave her comfort, if not peace. She fought against all belittling of her God. It was, perhaps, enough that He—knew.

"You are not alone, dear, in the trees out there?" she ventured one night, as he crept on tiptoe into the room not far from midnight. "God is with you?"

"Magnificently," was the immediate answer, given with enthusiasm, "for He is everywhere. And I only wish that you—"

But she stuffed the clothes against her ears. That invitation on his lips was more than she could bear to hear. It seemed like asking her to hurry to her own execution. She buried her face among the sheets and blankets, shaking all over like a leaf.

IX

And so the thought that she was the one to go remained and grew. It was, perhaps, first sign of that weakening of the mind which indicated the singular manner of her going. For it was her mental opposition, the trees felt, that stood in their way. Once that was overcome, obliterated, her physical presence did not matter. She would be harmless.

Having accepted defeat, because she had come to feel that his obsession was not actually evil, she accepted at the same time the conditions of an atrocious loneliness. She stood now from her husband farther than from the moon. They had no visitors. Callers were few and far between, and less encouraged than before. The empty dark of winter was before them. Among the neighbours was none in whom, without disloyalty to her husband, she could confide. Mr. Mortimer, had he been single, might have helped her in this desert of solitude that preyed upon her mind, but his wife was the obstacle; for Mrs. Mortimer wore sandals, believed that nuts were the complete food of man, and indulged in other idiosyncrasies that classed her inevitably among the "latter signs" which Mrs. Bittacy had been taught to dread as dangerous. She stood most desolately alone.

Solitude, therefore, in which the mind unhindered feeds upon its own delusions, was the assignable cause of her gradual mental disruption and collapse.

With the definite arrival of the colder weather her husband gave up his rambles after dark; evenings were spent together over the fire; he read *The Times;* they even talked about their postponed visit abroad in the coming spring. No restlessness was on him at the change; he seemed content and easy in his mind; spoke little of the trees and woods; enjoyed far better health than if there had been change of scene, and to herself was tender, kind, solicitous over trifles, as in the distant days of their first honeymoon.

But this deep calm could not deceive her; it meant, she fully understood, that he felt sure of himself, sure of her, and sure of the trees as well. It all lay buried in the depths of him, too secure and deep, too intimately established in his central being to permit of those surface fluctuations which betray disharmony within. His life was hid with trees. Even the fever, so dreaded in the damp of winter, left him free. She now knew why. The fever was due to their efforts to obtain him, his efforts to respond and go—physical results of a fierce unrest he had never understood till Sanderson came with his wicked explanations. Now it was otherwise. The bridge was made. And—he had gone.

And she, brave, loyal, and consistent soul, found herself utterly alone, even trying to make his passage easy. It seemed that she stood at the bottom of some huge ravine that opened in her mind, the walls whereof instead of rock were trees that reached enormous to the sky, engulfing her. God alone knew that she was there. He watched, permitted, even perhaps approved. At any rate—He knew.

During those quiet evenings in the house, moreover, while they sat over the fire listening to the roaming winds about the house, her husband knew continual access to the world his alien love had furnished for him. Never for a single instant was he cut off from it. She gazed at the newspaper spread before his face and knees, saw the smoke of his cheroot curl up above the edge, noticed the little hole in his evening socks, and listened to the paragraphs he read aloud as of old. But this was all a veil he spread about himself of purpose. Behind it—he escaped. It was the conjurer's trick to divert the sight to unimportant details while the essential thing went forward unobserved. He managed wonderfully; she loved him for the pains he took to spare her distress; but all the while she knew that the body lolling in that armchair before her eyes contained the merest fragment of his actual self. It was little better than a corpse. It was an empty shell. The essential soul of him was out yonder with the Forest—farther out near that ever-roaring heart of it.

And, with the dark, the Forest came up boldly and pressed against the very walls and windows, peering in upon them, joining hands above the slates and chimneys. The winds were always walking on the lawn and gravel paths; steps came and went and came again; some one seemed always talking in the woods, some one was in the building too. She passed them on the stairs, or running soft and muffled, very large and gentle, down the passages and landings after dusk, as though loose fragments of the Day had broken off and stayed there caught among the shadows, trying to get out. They blundered silently all about the house. They waited till she passed, then made a run for it. And her husband always knew. She saw him more than once deliberately avoid them—because *she* was there. More than once, too, she saw him stand and listen when he thought she was not near, then heard herself the long bounding stride of their approach across the silent garden. Already *he* had heard them in the windy distance of the night, far, far away. They sped, she well knew, along that glade of mossy turf by which she last came out; it cushioned their tread exactly as it had cushioned her own.

It seemed to her the trees were always in the house with him, and in their very bedroom. He welcomed them, unaware that she also knew, and trembled.

One night in their bedroom it caught her unawares. She woke out of deep sleep and it came upon her before she could gather her forces for control.

The day had been wildly boisterous, but now the wind had dropped; only its rags went fluttering through the night. The rays of the full moon fell in a shower between the branches. Overhead still raced the scud and wrack, shaped like hurrying monsters; but below the earth was quiet. Still and dripping stood the hosts of trees. Their trunks gleamed wet and sparkling where the moon caught them. There was a strong smell of mould and fallen leaves. The air was sharp—heavy with odour.

And she knew all this the instant that she woke; for it seemed to her that she had been elsewhere—following her husband—as though she had been *out!* There was no dream at all, merely the definite, haunting certainty. It dived away, lost, buried in the night. She sat upright in bed. She had come back.

The room shone pale in the moonlight reflected through the windows, for the blinds were up, and she saw her husband's form beside her, motionless in deep sleep. But what caught her unawares was the horrid thing that by this fact of sudden, unexpected waking she had surprised these other things in the room, beside the very bed, gathered close about him while he slept. It was their dreadful boldness—herself of no account as it were—that terrified her into screaming before she could collect her powers to prevent. She screamed before she realised what she did—a long, high shriek of terror that filled the room, yet made so little actual sound. For wet and shimmering presences stood grouped all round that bed. She saw their outline underneath the ceiling, the green, spread bulk of them, their vague extension over walls and furniture. They shifted to and fro, massed yet translucent, mild yet thick, moving and turning within themselves to a hushed noise of multitudinous soft rustling. In their sound was something very sweet and winning that fell into her with a spell of horrible enchantment. They were so mild, each one alone, yet so terrific in their combination. Cold seized her. The sheets against her body had turned to ice.

She screamed a second time, though the sound hardly issued from her throat. The spell sank deeper, reaching to the heart; for it softened all the currents of her blood and took life from her in a stream—towards themselves. Resistance in that moment seemed impossible.

Her husband then stirred in his sleep, and woke. And, instantly, the forms drew up, erect, and gathered themselves in some amazing way together. They lessened in extent—then scattered through the air like an effect of light when shadows seek to smother it. It was tremendous, yet most exquisite. A sheet of pale-green shadow that yet had form and substance filled the room. There was a rush of silent movement, as the Presences drew past her through the air,—and they were gone.

But, clearest of all, she saw the manner of their going; for she recognised in their tumult of escape by the window open at the top, the same wide "looping circles"—spirals as it seemed—that she had seen upon the lawn those weeks ago when Sanderson had talked. The room once more was empty.

In the collapse that followed, she heard her husband's voice, as though coming from some great distance. Her own replies she heard as well. Both were so strange and unlike their normal speech, the very words unnatural:

"What is it, dear? Why do you wake me *now?*" And his voice whispered it with a sighing sound, like wind in pine boughs.

"A moment since something went past me through the air of the room. Back to the night outside it went." Her voice, too, held the same note as of wind entangled among too many leaves.

"My dear, it *was* the wind."

"But it called, David. It was calling *you*—by name!"

"The stir of the branches, dear, was what you heard. Now, sleep again, I beg you, sleep."

"It had a crowd of eyes all through and over it—before and behind—" Her voice grew louder. But his own in reply sank lower, far away, and oddly hushed.

"The moonlight, dear, upon the sea of twigs and boughs in the rain, was what you saw."

"But it frightened me. I've lost my God—and you—I'm cold as death!"

"My dear, it is the cold of the early morning hours. The whole world sleeps. Now sleep again yourself."

He whispered close to her ear. She felt his hand stroking her. His voice was soft and very soothing. But only a part of him was there; only a part of him was speaking; it was a half-emptied body that lay beside her and uttered these strange sentences, even forcing her own singular choice of words. The horrible, dim enchantment of the trees was close about them in the room—gnarled, ancient, lonely trees of winter, whispering round the human life they loved.

"And let me sleep again," she heard him murmur as he settled down among the clothes, "sleep back into that deep, delicious peace from which you called me. . . ."

His dreamy, happy tone, and that look of youth and joy she discerned upon his features even in the filtered moonlight, touched her again as with the spell of those shining, mild green presences. It sank down into her. She felt sleep grope for her. On the threshold of slumber one of those strange vagrant voices that loss of consciousness lets loose cried faintly in her heart—

"There is joy in the Forest over one sinner that—"

Then sleep took her before she had time to realise even that she was vilely parodying one of her most precious texts, and that the irreverence was ghastly. . . .

And though she quickly slept again, her sleep was not as usual, dreamless. It was not woods and trees she dreamed of, but a small and curious dream that kept coming again and again upon her: that she stood upon a wee, bare rock in the sea, and that the tide was rising. The water first came to her feet, then to her knees, then to her waist. Each time the dream returned, the tide seemed higher. Once it rose to her neck, once even to her mouth, covering her lips for a moment so that she could not breathe. She did not wake between the dreams; a period of drab and dreamless slumber intervened. But, finally, the water rose above her eyes and face, completely covering her head.

And then came explanation—the sort of explanation dreams bring. She understood. For, beneath the water, she had seen the world of seaweed rising from the bottom of the sea like a forest of dense green—long, sinuous stems, immense thick branches, millions of feelers spreading through the darkened watery depths the power of their ocean foliage. The Vegetable Kingdom was even in the sea. It was everywhere. Earth, air, and water helped it, way of escape there was none.

And even underneath the sea she heard that terrible sound of roaring—was it surf or wind or voices?—further out, yet coming steadily towards her.

And so, in the loneliness of that drab English winter, the mind of Mrs. Bittacy, preying upon itself, and fed by constant dread, went lost in disproportion. Dreariness filled the weeks with dismal, sunless skies and a clinging moisture that knew no wholesome tonic of keen frosts. Alone with her thoughts, both her husband and her God withdrawn into distance, she counted the days to Spring. She groped her way, stumbling down the long dark tunnel. Through the arch at the far end lay a brilliant picture of the violet sea sparkling on the coast of France. There lay safety and escape for both of them, could she but hold on. Behind her the trees blocked up the other entrance. She never once looked back.

She drooped. Vitality passed from her, drawn out and away as by some steady suction. Immense and incessant was this sensation of her powers draining off. The taps were all turned on. Her personality, as it were, streamed steadily away, coaxed outwards by this Power that never wearied and seemed inexhaustible. It won her as the full moon wins the tide. She waned; she faded; she obeyed.

At first she watched the process, and recognised exactly what was going on. Her physical life, and that balance of the mind which depends on physical well-being, were being slowly undermined. She saw that clearly. Only the soul, dwelling like a star apart from these and independent of them, lay safe somewhere—with her distant God. That she knew—tranquilly. The spiritual love that linked her to her husband was safe from all attack. Later, in His good time, they would merge together again because of it. But meanwhile, all of her that had kinship with the earth was slowly going. This separation was being remorselessly accomplished. Every part of her the trees could touch was being steadily drained from her. She was being—removed.

After a time, however, even this power of realisation went, so that she no longer "watched the process" or knew exactly what was going on. The one satisfaction she had known—the feeling that it was sweet to suffer for his sake—went with it. She stood utterly alone with this terror of the trees . . . mid the ruins of her broken and disordered mind.

She slept badly; woke in the morning with hot and tired eyes; her head ached dully; she grew confused in thought and lost the clues of daily life in the most feeble fashion. At the same time she lost sight, too, of that brilliant picture at the exit of the tunnel; it faded away into a tiny semicircle of pale light, the violet sea and the sunshine the merest point of white, remote as a star and equally inaccessible. She knew now that she could never reach it. And through the darkness that stretched behind, the power of the trees came close and caught her, twining about her feet and arms, climbing to her very lips. She woke at night, finding it difficult to breathe. There seemed wet leaves pressing against her mouth, and soft green tendrils clinging to her neck. Her feet were heavy, half rooted, as it were, in deep, thick earth. Huge creepers stretched along the whole of that black tunnel, feeling about her person for points where they might fasten well, as ivy or the giant parasites of the Vegetable Kingdom settle down on the trees themselves to sap their life and kill them.

Slowly and surely the morbid growth possessed her life and held her. She feared those very winds that ran about the wintry forest. They were in league with it. They helped it everywhere.

"Why don't you sleep, dear?" It was her husband now who played the rôle of nurse, tending her little wants with an honest care that at least aped the services of love. He was so utterly unconscious of the raging battle he had caused. "What is it keeps you so wide awake and restless?"

"The winds," she whispered in the dark. For hours she had been watching the tossing of the trees through the blindless windows. "They go walking and talking everywhere to-night, keeping me awake. And all the time they call so loudly to you."

And his strange whispered answer appalled her for a moment until the meaning of it faded and left her in a dark confusion of the mind that was now becoming almost permanent.

"The trees excite them in the night. The winds are the great swift carriers. Go with them, dear—and not against. You'll find sleep that way if you do."

"The storm is rising," she began, hardly knowing what she said.

"All the more then—go with them. Don't resist. They'll take you to the trees, that's all."

Resist! The word touched on the button of some text that once had helped her.

"Resist the devil and he will flee from you," she heard her whispered answer, and the same second had buried her face beneath the clothes in a flood of hysterical weeping.

But her husband did not seem disturbed. Perhaps he did not hear it, for the wind ran just then against the windows with a booming shout, and the roaring of the Forest farther out came behind the blow, surging into the room. Perhaps, too, he was already asleep again. She slowly regained a sort of dull composure. Her face emerged from the tangle of sheets and blankets. With a growing terror over her—she listened. The storm was rising. It came with a sudden and impetuous rush that made all further sleep for her impossible.

Alone in a shaking world, it seemed, she lay and listened. That storm interpreted for her mind the climax. The Forest bellowed out its victory to the winds; the winds in turn proclaimed it to the Night. The whole world knew of her complete defeat, her loss, her little human pain. This was the roar and shout of victory that she listened to.

For, unmistakably, the trees were shouting in the dark. There were sounds, too, like the flapping of great sails, a thousand at a time, and sometimes reports that resembled more than anything else the distant booming of enormous drums. The trees stood up—the whole beleaguering host of them stood up—and with the uproar of their million branches drummed the thundering message out across the night. It seemed as if they all had broken loose. Their roots swept trailing over field and hedge and roof. They tossed their bushy heads beneath the clouds with a wild, delighted shuffling of great boughs. With trunks upright they raced leaping through the sky. There was upheaval and adventure in the awful sound they made, and their cry was like the cry of a sea that has broken through its gates and poured loose upon the world. . . .

Through it all her husband slept peacefully as though he heard it not. It was, as she well knew, the sleep of the semi-dead. For he was out with all that clamouring turmoil. The part of him that she had lost was there. The form that slept so calmly at her side was but the shell, half emptied. . . .

And when the winter's morning stole upon the scene at length, with a pale, washed sunshine that followed the departing tempest, the first thing she saw, as she crept to the window and looked out, was the ruined cedar lying on the lawn. Only the gaunt and crippled trunk of it remained. The single giant bough that had been left to it lay dark upon the grass, sucked endways towards the Forest by a great wind eddy. It lay there like a mass of drift-wood from a wreck, left by the ebbing of a high spring-tide upon the sands—remnant of some friendly, splendid vessel that once had sheltered men.

And in the distance she heard the roaring of the Forest further out. Her husband's voice was in it.

Egyptian Antiquities

Once the steamer ticket is paid for, one gets anxious about the question of cabin companion. What will he be like? At such close quarters it is a serious matter, for a degree of intimacy is unavoidable, and the purses of the majority cannot manage a cabin *de luxe* for one only. You inspect his luggage shrewdly as you go below for the first time and see it strewn upon the berth. Will he snore? Will he be a good sailor or a bad? Will he come in late, and noisily, just as you are getting off to sleep after a wretched attempt to face the dining-room? Will he be—untidy? Marseilles to Alexandria is only five days at the most, but they may be a rough and uncomfortable five days, and the type of your enforced travelling companion has not a little to say in the matter. This time he was on board before me, and I anxiously scanned the rag and bag and bundle of books I saw littered on the lower berth, trying to forecast what manner of man this Mr. Jones might be. For J. J. Jones was writ large upon the labels in firm blue ink, and there was no telling what store of sin or virtue the high-crowned black billycock hanging on the peg outside the door might cover. He was already, then, in his travelling cap, a quick, methodical sort of fellow probably, and this by no means his first voyage. Also, he had not, as first comer, taken an unfair advantage of my being late by seizing all the best pegs and nooks and nets for his "extras"; again a good sign. The syren hooted, and I went above, thinking every man I went on deck must be Mr. J. J. Jones, and feeling elated or depressed according to the type I encountered. The sea was calm. I experienced that ridiculous false courage which almost persuades one all may be well; this time, after all, I shall not succumb. They say one grows out of *mal de mer* as years advance. One feels bold, and struts about, trying to appear as though this dreadful weakness was for others only. And on entering the cabin later, to get tidy for dinner, Mr. Jones I saw had just gone

354

out. In the air was that faint perfume of soap to prove it, and a different soap to my own. He was clean, at any rate, or cleanish. The billy-cock swung out so that place where it was bought became easily legible; and I read with a sense of shame that it was something semi-private, the legend of—a cheap shop in High Holborn. On the whole this was disappointing rather, not quite what I had hoped for and expected. A hat is a significant symptom; it betrays a man more mercilessly than a tie. If only I could find a necktie lying about by chance I should know Mr. J. J. Jones for what he was. But, instead of a tie, I saw the titles of his books—a Life of Clive and a standard work on Egyptian Antiquities. My spirits went up again with a rush, and, following their example, I too went up—to dinner.

But the sea became my chief interest long before the end of that ghastly ordeal—a long dinner in the saloon of a steamer when that steamer rolls and one's seat is far from any door or exit—so that I relegated Mr. Jones to the unimportant things of life, and retired early to bed. Again I had been forestalled. Jones was in bed and asleep; but, as only the top of his head, and that bald, was visible, final judgment was still impossible, even had I possessed the power or inclination to form it. In the morning, however, I woke to a steady steamer, and to the sight of my companion—almost *in naturalibus*—doing exercises. The night I shall long remember. He was a sturdy, vigorous man of over fifty, powerfully built, with a genial, merry face, and his immediate remark, "I trust I do not disturb you, sir?" was caused by my instinctive movement to protect my face from one of his tremendous sweeps of shoulders, arms, and body, which, as he apologetically informed me, he was "obliged to do every morning for the liver, sir." I agreed, somewhat feebly, perhaps, and watched the operation out of one eye, the other ready at any moment to direct a movement of my own in self-protection. His muscular development was unusual, and he looked like a prize-fighter stripped for the fray. "A difficult place to practise in," I suggested, and his reply, given breathlessly, without stopping the violent swings, "Oh, it's all right as long as we don't do it both at once," let me into a corner of his life's philosophy, I felt. He was easy-going and good-natured, yet not afraid to be himself. Wondering keenly what Mr. Jones might be in his home circle, and what his particular means of livelihood, I felt distinctly drawn to him. From that moment we got on well together. Fear of him as an unpleasant travelling companion in a small cabin existed no more. Curiosity took its place. An unlawful desire to know what he did, and how he lived, and what was taking him now to Egypt possessed me to a degree I am almost ashamed to confess. The various methods of indirect "pumping," although good breeding utterly forbids them, I put shamelessly into practice—without avail. Jones kept his own counsel. On every other subject under the sun he was voluble and readily forthcoming, but his purpose in going to Egypt remained all "wropt in mystery." There were things about him far from prepossessing, things of which the High Holborn hat was symbolical; but I overlooked them all in the hope of finding out what I wanted. And the more he concealed it, the more I wanted to know. Was he an explorer? His sunburned skin and athletic manners some-how suggested that he might be. Or a great traveller? He seemed to know Egypt from end to end. Or a professional man of sorts? His technical knowledge, geological, meteorological, and so forth, hinted at something of the sort. Or was he an archæological "crank," an Egyp-tologist, a digger in the sands? His familiarity with excavations along the Nile and elsewhere in Upper Egypt made it possible. Or was he merely travelling for his health? Denials to one and all I obtained by one means or another, directly or indirectly. He was none of these. His hints at extensive luggage in the hold, and Customs difficulties ahead, made me wonder if he were perhaps a commercial traveller of sorts; but such-like do not go first-class, or number a life of Clive and a book on Egyptian Curios among their portable baggage. Jones was no mere "drummer." I even thought of a detective, but for one reason or an-other dismissed it as equally impossible. We walked the decks together, we smoked in the odious, stuffy smoking-room, we chatted in the morning and the last thing on going to bed, but he never betrayed himself. And, unless I started a subject myself, he talked Clive, and, of all things in the world—boxing. He had been an amateur champion in his day, somewhere or other; clubs and "meetings" and boxing slang were all mixed up together, and even introduced into the life of Clive, who had done something that he considered "hitting below the belt." Yet I never fell into this obviously-laid trap of judging him a profes-sional fighting man. He was too old for one thing. His exercises were a relic of other days.

Altogether, though, I formed somehow a high opinion of the man. In the lower ranks of life, as we term them, he was somewhere noble. His calling, I felt sure, would be no ordinary, certainly no unworthy, one. Every man's mind is a seeing instrument pressed against the windows of life to see what's going on outside. From various angles they peer forth into the darkness, and one mind sees what another does not see, though all look out upon the same view. If external details of a particular seer are unpleasing, the philosopher overlooks them in his desire to ascertain what that mind may have to report from his window-gazing, and above all how he interprets what he sees. From this point of view a butler or a bootblack becomes interesting. There was much about the exterior of J. J. Jones the world agrees to call unpleasing. But, so far as I was concerned, I passed it by in my keen desire to know what he saw through the window and what he made of it. His calling in life, I hoped, would reveal the man. My interest in him was most likely due solely to proximity. Anyhow, as the voyage neared its end, my curiosity grew hourly stronger.

And then, at last, he let me in little by little towards the truth. All the time, perhaps, he had been waiting to judge me worthy or otherwise. He dropped hints, carefully at first, then, as the ship neared Alexandria, recklessly. He came out to Egypt every winter, and this was his tenth year. He was deeply interested in a certain line of trade. Last season had been "a poor one"; seasons now were not what they used to be when he was younger; people knew so much more than they used to know; and there was American competition too into the bargain. I was so on the tiptoe of expectation that I feared to say anything, lest by a wrong question I should send him into his shell again. I divined, however, that he was bursting to confide in some one. He longed for some one he could trust. And at the end my self-restraint was well rewarded.

"I'm from Birmingham," be told me suddenly. "I represent a big house there. But I do a little on my own account as well, you know." And he gave a queer, sly laugh that was clearly meant to try my value as a confidant.

"That's the only way." I agreed instantly, though knowing nothing of what he meant or what I was talking about. "Trade's gone down everywhere."

"Something terrible," he answered with a sigh. "A man can hardly make a living any more. And if he's married!—" He shrugged his great shoulders as though he meant to square them for a blow at fate.

"You've felt it in your line, too?" I ventured, sympathetically. The moment I felt sure had come. It had.

"Awful," he replied; "there's simply nothing doing. But this year ought to be better. The Durbar people coming home, you see, and all that. They all have money to spend."

"Some of it will come your way then, too," I said. It was a shot at a venture, but it went fairly straight.

"May be," he said, more hopefully. "We do a good bit in India, too. We send a lot of men out there. But my particular field is Egypt—Egyptian antiquities, made Birmingham, you know."

The Attic

The forest-girdled village upon the Jura slopes slept soundly, although it was not yet many minutes after ten o'clock. The clang of the *couvre-feu* had indeed just ceased, its notes swept far into the woods by a wind that shook the mountains. This wind now rushed down the deserted street. It howled about the old rambling building called La Citadelle, whose roof towered gaunt and humped above the smaller houses—Château unfinished long ago by Lord Wemyss, the exiled Jacobite. The families who occupied the various apartments listened to the storm and felt the building tremble. "It's the mountain wind. It will bring the snow," the mother said, without looking up from her knitting. "And how sad it sounds."

But it was not the wind that brought sadness as we sat round the open fire of peat. It was the wind of memories. The lamplight slanted along the narrow room towards the table where breakfast things lay ready for the morning. The double windows were fastened. At the far end stood a door ajar, and on the other side of it the two elder children lay asleep in the big bed. But beside the window was a smaller unused bed, that had been empty now a year. And to-night was the anniversary. . . .

And so the wind brought sadness and long thoughts. The little chap that used to lie there was already twelve months gone, far, far beyond the Hole where the Winds came from, as he called it; yet it seemed only yesterday that I went to tell him a tuck-up story, to stroke Riquette, the old motherly cat that cuddled against his back and laid a paw beside his pillow like a human being, and to hear his funny little earnest whisper say, "Oncle, tu sais, j'ai prié pour Petavel." For La Citadelle had its unhappy ghost—of Petavel, the usurer, who had hanged himself in the attic a century gone by, and was known to walk its dreary corridors in search of peace—and this wise Irish mother, calming the boy's fears with wisdom, had told him, "If you pray for Petavel, you'll save his soul and make him happy, and he'll only love you." And, thereafter, this little imaginative boy had done so every night. With a passionate seriousness he did it. He had wonderful, delicate ways like that. In all our hearts he made his fairy nests of wonder. In my own, I know, he lay closer than any joy imaginable, with his big blue eyes, his queer soft questionings, and his splendid child's unself-ishness—a sun-kissed flower of innocence that, had he lived, might have sweetened half a world.

"Let's put more peat on," the mother said, as a handful of rain like stones came flinging against the windows; "that must be hail." And she went on tiptoe to the inner room. "They're sleeping like two pud-dings," she whispered, coming presently back. But it struck me she had taken longer than to notice merely that; and her face wore an odd ex-pression that made me uncomfortable. I thought she was somehow just about to laugh or cry. By the table a second she hesitated. I caught the flash of indecision as it passed. "Pan," she said suddenly—it was a nickname, stolen from my tuck-up stories, *he* had given me—"I won-der how Riquette got in." She looked hard at me. "It wasn't you, was it?" For we never let her come at night since he had gone. It was too poignant. The beastie always went cuddling and nestling into that emp-ty bed. But this time it was not my doing, and I offered plausible ex-planations. "But—she's on the bed. Pan, *would* you be so kind—" She left the sentence unfinished, but I easily understood, for a lump had somehow risen in my own throat too, and I remembered now that she had come out from the inner room so quickly—with a kind of hurried rush almost. I put "mère Riquette" out into the corridor. A lamp stood on the chair outside the door of another occupant further down, and I urged her gently towards it. She turned and looked at me—straight up into my face; but, instead of going down as I suggested, she went slow-ly in the opposite direction. She stepped softly towards a door in the wall that led up broken stairs into the attics. There she sat down and waited. And so I left her, and came back hastily to the peat fire and companionship. The wind rushed in behind me and slammed the door.

And we talked then somewhat busily of cheerful things; of the children's future, the excellence of the cheap Swiss schools, of Christ-mas presents, ski-ing, snow, tobogganing. I led the talk away from mournfulness; and when these subjects were exhausted I told stories of my own adventures in distant parts of the world. But "mother" listened the whole time—not to me. Her thoughts were all elsewhere. And her air of intently, secretly listening, bordered, I felt, upon the uncanny. For she often stopped her knitting and sat with her eyes fixed upon the air before her; she stared blankly at the wall, her head slightly on one side, her figure tense, attention strained—elsewhere. Or, when my talk positively demanded it, her nod was oddly mechanical and her eyes looked through and past me. The wind continued very loud and roaring; but the fire glowed, the room was warm and cosy. Yet she shivered, and when I drew attention to it, her reply, "I do feel cold, but I didn't know I shivered," was given as though she spoke across the air to some one else. But what impressed me even more uncomfortably were her repeated questions about Riquette. When a pause in my tales permitted, she would look up with "I wonder where Riquette went?" or, thinking of the inclement night, "I hope mere Riquette's not out of doors. Perhaps Madame Favre has taken her in?" I offered to go and see. Indeed I was already half-way across the room when there came the heavy bang at the door that rooted me to the ground where I stood. It was not wind. It was something alive that made it rattle. There was a second blow. A thud on the corridor boards followed, and then a high, odd voice that at first was as human as the cry of a child.

It is undeniable that we both started, and for myself I can answer truthfully that a chill ran down my spine; but what frightened me more than the sudden noise and the eerie cry was the way "mother" supplied the immediate explanation. For behind the words "It's only Riquette; she sometimes springs at the door like that; perhaps we'd better let her in," was a certain touch of uncanny quiet that made me feel she had known the cat would come, and knew also *why* she came. One cannot explain such impressions further. They leave their vital touch, then go their way. Into the little room, however, in that moment there came between us this uncomfortable sense that the night held other purposes than our own—and that my companion was aware of them. There was something going on far, far removed from the routine of life as we were accustomed to it. Moreover, our usual routine was the eddy, while this was the main stream. It felt big, I mean.

And so it was that the entrance of the familiar, friendly creature brought this thing both itself and "mother" *knew,* but whereof I as yet was ignorant. I held the door wide. The draught rushed through behind her, and sent a shower of sparks about the fireplace. The lamp flickered and gave a little gulp. And Riquette marched slowly past, with all the impressive dignity of her kind, towards the other door that stood ajar. Turning the corner like a shadow, she disappeared into the room where the two children slept. We heard the soft thud with which she leaped upon the bed. Then, in a lull of the wind, she came back again and sat on the oil-cloth, staring into "mother's" face. She mewed and put a paw out, drawing the black dress softly with half-opened claws. And it was all so horribly suggestive and pathetic, it revived such poignant memories, that I got up impulsively—I think I had actually said the words, "We'd better put her out, mother, after all"—when my companion rose to her feet and forestalled me. She said another thing instead. It took my breath away to hear it. "She wants us to go with her. Pan, will you come too?" The surprise on my face must have asked the question, for I do not remember saying anything. "To the attic," she said quietly.

She stood there by the table, a tall, grave figure dressed in black, and her face above the lamp-shade caught the full glare of light. Its expression positively stiffened me. She seemed so secure in her singular purpose. And her familiar appearance had so oddly given place to something wholly strange to me. She looked like another person— almost with the unwelcome transformation of the sleep-walker about her. Cold came over me as I watched her, for I remembered suddenly her Irish second-sight, her story years ago of meeting a figure on the attic stairs, the figure of Petavel. And the idea of this motherly, sedate, and wholesome woman, absorbed day and night in prosaic domestic duties, and yet "seeing" things, touched the incongruous almost to the point of alarm. It was so distressingly convincing.

Yet she knew quite well that I would come. Indeed, following the excited animal, she was already by the door, and a moment later, still without answering or protesting, I was with them in the draughty corridor. There was something inevitable in her manner that made it impossible to refuse. She took the lamp from its nail on the wall, and following our four-footed guide, who ran with obvious pleasure just in front, she opened the door into the courtyard. The wind nearly put the lamp out, but a minute later we were safe inside the passage that led up flights of creaky wooden stairs towards the world of tenantless attics overhead.

And I shall never forget the way the excited Riquette first stood up and put her paws upon the various doors, trotted ahead, turned back to watch us coming, and then finally sat down and waited on the threshold of the empty, raftered space that occupied the entire length of the building underneath the roof. For her manner was more that of an intelligent dog than of a cat, and sometimes more like that of a human mind than either.

We had come up without a single word. The howling of the wind as we rose higher was like the roar of artillery. There were many broken stairs, and the narrow way was full of twists and turnings. It was a dreadful journey. I felt eyes watching us from all the yawning spaces of the darkness, and the noise of the storm smothered footsteps everywhere. Troops of shadows kept us company. But it was on the threshold of this big, chief attic, when "mother" stopped abruptly to put down the lamp, that real fear took hold of me. For Riquette marched steadily forward into the middle of the dusty flooring, picking her way among the fallen tiles and mortar, as though she went towards—some one. She purred loudly and uttered little cries of excited pleasure. Her tail went up into the air, and she lowered her head with the unmistakable intention of being stroked. Her lips opened and shut. Her green eyes smiled. She *was* being stroked.

It was an unforgettable performance. I would rather have witnessed an execution or a murder than watch that mysterious creature twist and turn about in the way she did. Her magnified shadow was as large as a pony on the floor and rafters. I wanted to hide the whole thing by extinguishing the lamp. For, even before the mysterious action began, I experienced the sudden rush of conviction that others besides ourselves were in this attic—and standing very close to us indeed. And, although there was ice in my blood, there was also a strange swelling of the heart that only love and tenderness could bring.

But, whatever it was, my human companion, still silent, knew and understood. She *saw*. And her soft whisper that ran with the wind among the rafters, "Il a prié pour Petavel et le hon Dieu l'a entendu," did not amaze me one quarter as much as the expression I then caught upon her radiant face. Tears ran down the cheeks, but they were tears of happiness. Her whole figure seemed lit up. She opened her arms—

picture of great Motherhood, proud, blessed, and tender beyond words. I thought she was going to fall, for she took quick steps forward; but when I moved to catch her, she drew me aside instead with a sudden gesture that brought fear back in the place of wonder.

"Let them pass," she whispered grandly. "Pan, don't you see. . . . He's leading him into peace and safety . . . by the hand!" And her joy seemed to kill the shadows and fill the entire attic with white light. Then, almost simultaneously with her words, she swayed. I was in time to catch her, but as I did so, across the very spot where we had just been standing—two figures, I swear, went past us like a flood of light.

There was a moment next of such confusion that I did not see what happened to Riquette, for the sight of my companion kneeling on the dusty boards and praying with a curious sort of passionate happiness, while tears pressed between her covering fingers—the strange wonder of this made me utterly oblivious to minor details. . . .

We were sitting round the peat fire again, and "mother" was saying to me in the gentlest, tenderest whisper I ever heard from human lips—"Pan, I think perhaps that's why God took him. . . ."

And when a little later we went in to make Riquette cosy in the empty bed, ever since kept sacred to her use, the mournfulness had lifted; and in the place of resignation was proud peace and joy that knew no longer sad or selfish questionings.

The Whisperers

To be too impressionable is as much a source of weakness as to be hyper-sensitive: so many messages come flooding in upon one another that confusion is the result; the mind chokes, imagination grows congested.

Jones, as an imaginative writing man, was well aware of this, yet could not always prevent it; for if he dulled his mind to one impression, he ran the risk of blunting it to all. To guard his main idea, and picket its safe conduct through the seethe of additions that instantly flocked to join it, was a psychological puzzle that sometimes overtaxed his powers of critical selection. He prepared for it, however. An editor would ask him for a story—"about five thousand words, you know"; and Jones would answer, "I'll send it you with pleasure—when it comes." He knew his difficulty too well to promise more. Ideas were never lacking, but their length of treatment belonged to machinery he could not coerce. They were alive; they refused to come to heel to suit mere editors. Midway in a tale that started crystal clear and definite in its original germ, would pour a flood of new impressions that either smothered the first conception, or developed it beyond recognition. Often a short story exfoliated in this bursting way beyond his power to stop it. He began one, never knowing where it would lead him. It was ever an adventure. Like Jack the Giant Killer's beanstalk it grew secretly in the night, fed by everything he read, saw, felt, or heard. Jones was too impressionable; he received too many impressions, and too easily.

For this reason, when working at a definite, short idea, he preferred an empty room, without pictures, furniture, books, or anything suggestive, and with a skylight that shut out scenery—just ink, blank paper, and the clear picture in his mind. His own interior, unstimulated by the geysers of external life, he made some pretence of regulating; though even under these favourable conditions the matter was not too easy, so prolifically does a sensitive mind engender.

His experience in the empty room of the carpenter's house was a curious case in point—in the little Jura village where his cousin lived to educate his children. "We're all in a pension above the Post Office here," the cousin wrote, "but just now the house is full, and besides is rather noisy. I've taken an attic room for you at the carpenter's near the forest. Some things of mine have been stored there all the winter, but I moved the cases out this morning. There's a bed, writing-table, wash-handstand, sofa, and a skylight window—otherwise empty, as I know you prefer it. You can have your meals with us," etc. And this just suited Jones, who had six weeks' work on hand for which he needed empty solitude. His "idea" was slight and very tender; accretions would easily smother clear presentment; its treatment must be delicate, simple, unconfused.

The room really was an attic, but large, wide, high. He heard the wind rush past the skylight when he went to bed. When the cupboard was open he heard the wind there too, washing the outer walls and tiles. From his pillow he saw a patch of stars peep down upon him. Jones knew the mountains and the woods were close, but he could not see them. Better still, he could not smell them. And he went to bed dead tired, full of his theme for work next morning. He saw it to the end. He could almost have promised five thousand words. With the dawn he would be up and "at it," for he usually woke very early, his mind surcharged, as though subconsciousness had matured the material in sleep. Cold bath, a cup of tea, and then—his writing-table; and the quicker he could reach the writing-table the richer was the content of imaginative thought. What had puzzled him the night before was invariably cleared up in the morning. Only illness could interfere with the process and routine of it.

But this time it was otherwise. He woke, and instantly realised, with a shock of surprise and disappointment, that his mind was— groping. It was groping for his little lost idea. There was nothing physically wrong with him; he felt rested, fresh, clear-headed; but his brain was searching, searching, moreover, in a crowd. Trying to seize hold of the train it had relinquished several hours ago, it caught at an evasive, empty shell. The idea had utterly changed; or rather it seemed smothered by a host of new impressions that came pouring in upon it—new modes of treatment, points of view, in fact development. In the light of these extensions and novel aspects, his original idea had altered beyond recognition. The germ had marvellously exfoliated, so that a whole volume could alone express it. An army of fresh suggestions clamoured for expression. His subconsciousness had grown thick with life; it surged—active, crowded, tumultuous.

And the darkness puzzled him. He remembered the absence of accustomed windows, but it was only when the candle-light brought close the face of his watch, with two o'clock upon it, that he heard the sound of confused whispering in the corners of the room, and realised with a little twinge of fear that those who whispered had just been standing beside his very bed. The room was full.

Though the candle-light proclaimed it empty—bare walls, bare floor, five pieces of unimaginative furniture, and fifty stars peeping through the skylight—it was undeniably thronged with living people whose minds had called him out of heavy sleep. The whispers, of course, died off into the wind that swept the roof and skylight; but the Whisperers remained. They had been trying to get at him; waking suddenly, he had caught them in the very act. . . . And all had brought new interpretations with them; his thought had fundamentally altered; the original idea was snowed under; new images brimmed his mind, and his brain was working as it worked under the high pressure of creative moments.

Jones sat up, trembling a little, and stared about him into the empty room that yet was densely packed with these invisible Whisperers. And he realised this astonishing thing—that he was the object of their deliberate assault, and that scores of other minds, deep, powerful, very active minds, were thundering and beating upon the doors of his imagination. The onset of them was terrific and bewildering, the attack of aggressive ideas obliterating his original story beneath a flood of new suggestions. Inspiration had become suddenly torrential, yet so vast as to be unwieldy, incoherent, useless. It was like the tempest of images that fever brings. His first conception seemed no longer "delicate," but petty. It had turned unreal and tiny, compared with this enormous choice of treatment extension, development, that now overwhelmed his throbbing brain.

Fear caught vividly at him, as he searched the empty attic-room in vain for explanation. There was absolutely nothing to produce this tempest of new impressions. People seemed talking to him all together, jumbled somewhat, but insistently. It was obsession, rather than inspiration; and so bitingly, dreadfully real.

"Who are you all?" his mind whispered to blank walls and vacant corners.

Back from the shouting floor and ceiling came the chorus of images that stormed and clamoured for expression. Jones lay still and listened; he let them come. There was nothing else to do. He lay fearful, negative, receptive. It was all too big for him to manage, set to some scale of high achievement that submerged his own small powers. It came, too, in a series of impressions, all separate, yet all somehow interwoven.

In vain he tried to sort them out and sift them. As well sort out waves upon an agitated sea. They were too self-assertive for direction or control. Like wild animals, hungry, thirsty, ravening, they rushed from every side and fastened on his mind.

Yet he perceived them in a certain sequence.

For, first, the unfurnished attic-chamber was full of human passion, of love and hate, revenge and wicked cunning, of jealousy, courage, cowardice, of every vital human emotion ever longed for, enjoyed, or frustrated, all clamouring for—expression.

Flaming across and through these, incongruously threaded in and out, ran next a yearning softness of incredible beauty that sighed in the empty spaces of his heart, pleading for impossible fulfilment. . . .

And, after these, carrying both one and other upon their surface, huge questions flashed and dived and thundered in a patterned, wild entanglement, calling to be unravelled and made straight. Moreover, with every set came a new suggested treatment of the little clear idea he had taken to bed with him five hours before.

Jones adopted each in turn. Imagination writhed and twisted beneath the stress of all these potential modes of expression he must choose between. His small idea exfoliated into many volumes, work enough to fill a dozen lives. It was most gorgeously exhilarating, though so hopelessly unmanageable. He felt like many minds in one. . . .

Then came another chain of impressions, violent, yet steady owing to their depth; the voices, questions, pleadings turned to pictures; and he saw, struggling through the deeps of him, enormous quantities of people, passing along like rivers, massed, herded, swayed here and there by some outstanding figure of command who directed them like flowing water. They shrieked, and fought, and battled, then sank out of sight, huddled and destroyed in—blood. . . .

And their places were taken instantly by white crowds with shining eyes, and yearning in their faces, who climbed precipitous heights towards some Radiance that kept ever out of sight, like sunrise behind mountains that clouds then swallow. . . . The pelt and thunder of images was destructive in its torrent; his little, first idea was drowned and wrecked. . . . Jones sank back exhausted, utterly dismayed. He gave up all attempt to make selection.

The driving storm swept through him, on and on, now waxing, now waning, but never growing less, and apparently endless as the sky. It rushed in circles, like the turning of a giant wheel. All the activities that human minds have ever battled with since thought began came booming, crashing, straining for expression against the imaginative stuff whereof his mind was built. The walls began to yield and settle. It was like the chaos that madness brings. He did not struggle against it; he let it come, lying open and receptive, pliant and plastic to every detail of the vast invasion. And the only time he attempted a complete obedience, reaching out for the pencil and note-book that lay beside his bed, he desisted instantly again, sinking back upon his pillows with a kind of frightened laughter. For the tempest seemed then to knock him down and bruise his very brain. Inextricable confusion caught him. He might as well have tried to make notes of the entire Alexandrian Library in half an hour. . . .

Then, most singular of all, as he felt the sleep of exhaustion fall upon his tired nerves, he heard that deep, prodigious sound. All that had preceded, it gathered marvellously in, mothering it with a sweetness that seemed to his imagination like some harmonious, geometrical skein including all the activities men's minds have ever known. Faintly he realised it only, discerned from infinitely far away. Into the streams of apparent contradiction that warred so strenuously about him, it seemed to bring some hint of unifying, harmonious explanation. . . . And, here and there, as sleep buried him, he imagined that chords lay threaded along strings of cadences, breaking sometimes even into melody—music that rose everywhere from life and wove Thought into a homogeneous Whole. . . .

"Sleep well?" his cousin enquired, when he appeared very late next day for *déjeuner*. "Think you'll be able to work in that room all right?"

"I slept, yes, thanks," said Jones. "No doubt I shall work there right enough—when I'm rested. By the bye," he asked presently, "what has the attic been used for lately? What's been in it, I mean?"

"Books, only books," was the reply. "I've stored my 'library' there for months, without a chance of using it. I move about so much, you see. Five hundred books were taken out just before you came. I often think," he added lightly, "that when books are unopened like that for long, the minds that wrote them must get restless and—"

"What sort of books were they?" Jones interrupted.

"Fiction, poetry, philosophy, history, religion, music. I've got two hundred books on music alone."

The Second Generation

Sometimes, in a moment of sharp experience, comes that vivid flash of insight that makes a platitude suddenly seem a revelation: its full content is abruptly realised. "Ten years is a long time, yes," he thought, as he walked up the drive to the great Kensington house where she still lived.

Ten years—long enough, at any rate, for her to have married and for her husband to have died. More than that he had not heard, in the outlandish places where life had cast him in the interval. He wondered whether there had been any children. All manner of thoughts and questions, confused a little, passed across his mind. He was well-to-do now, though probably his entire capital did not amount to her income for a single year. He glanced at the huge, forbidding mansion. Yet that pride was false which had made of poverty an insuperable obstacle. He saw it now. He had learned values in his long exile.

But he was still ridiculously timid. This confusion of thought, of mental images rather, was due to a kind of fear, since worship ever is akin to awe. He was as nervous as a boy going up for a *viva voce;* and with the excitement was also that unconquerable sinking—that horrid shrinking sensation that excessive shyness brings. Why in the world had he come? Why had he telegraphed the very day after his arrival in England? Why had he not sent a tentative, tactful letter, feeling his way a little?

Very slowly he walked up the drive, feeling that if a reasonable chance of escape presented itself he would almost take it. But all the windows stared so hard at him that retreat was really impossible now; and though no faces were visible behind the curtains, all had seen him. Possibly she herself—his heart beat absurdly at the extravagant suggestion. Yet it was odd; he felt so certain of being seen, and that some one watched him. He reached the wide stone steps that were clean as marble, and shrank from the mark his boots must make upon their spotlessness. In desperation, then, before he could change his mind, he touched the bell. But he did not hear it ring—mercifully; that irrevocable sound must have paralysed him altogether. If no one came to answer, he might still leave a card in the letter-box and slip away. Oh, how utterly he despised himself for such a thought! A man of thirty with such a chicken heart was not fit to protect a child, much less a woman. And he recalled with a little stab of pain that the man she married had been noted for his courage, his determined action, his inflexible firmness in various public situations, head and shoulders above lesser men. What presumption on his own part ever to dream . . . ! He remembered, too, with no apparent reason in particular, that this man had a grown-up son already, by a former marriage.

And still no one came to open that huge, contemptuous door with its so menacing, so hostile air. His back was to it, as he carelessly twirled his umbrella, but he "felt" its sneering expression behind him while it looked him up and down. It seemed to push him away. The entire mansion focused its message through that stern portal: Little timid men are not welcomed here.

How well he remembered the house! How often in years gone by had he not stood and waited just like this, trembling with delight and anticipation, yet terrified lest the bell should be answered and the great door actually swung wide! Then, as now, he would have run, had he dared. He was still afraid; his worship was so deep. But in all these years of exile in wild places, farming, mining, working for the position he had at last attained, her face and the memory of her gracious presence had been his comfort and support, his only consolation, though never his actual joy. There was so little foundation for it all, yet her smile, and the words she had spoken to him from time to time in friendly conversation, had clung, inspired, kept him going. For he knew them all by heart. And, more than once, in foolish optimistic moods, he had imagined, greatly daring, that she possibly had meant more. . . .

He touched the bell a second time—with the point of his umbrella. He meant to go in, carelessly as it were, saying as lightly as might be, "Oh, I'm back in England again—if you haven't *quite* forgotten my existence—I could not forgo the pleasure of saying how do you do, and hearing that you are well . . . ," and the rest; then presently bow himself easily out—into the old loneliness again. But he would at least have seen her; he would have heard her voice, and looked into her gentle, amber eyes; he would have touched her hand. She might even ask him to come in another day and see her! He had rehearsed it all a hundred times, as certain feeble temperaments do rehearse such scenes. And he came rather well out of that rehearsal, though always with an aching heart, the old great yearnings unfulfilled. All the way across the Atlantic he had thought about it, though with lessening confidence as the time drew near. The very night of his arrival in London, he wrote; then, tearing up the letter (after sleeping over it), he had telegraphed next morning, asking if she would be in. He signed his surname—such a very common name, alas! but surely she would know—and her reply, "Please call 4.30," struck him as oddly worded—rather . . . Yet here he was.

There was a rattle of the big door knob, that aggressive, hostile knob that thrust out at him insolently like a fist of bronze. He started, angry with himself for doing so. But the door did not open. He became suddenly conscious of the wilds he had lived in for so long; his clothes were hardly fashionable; his voice probably had a twang in it, and he used tricks of speech that must betray the rough life so recently left. What would she think of him—now? He looked much older, too. And how brusque it was to have telegraphed like that! He felt awkward, gauche, tongue-tied, hot and cold by turns. The sentences, so carefully rehearsed, fled beyond recovery.

Good heavens—the door was open! It had been open for some minutes. It moved on big hinges noiselessly. He acted automatically—just like an automaton; he heard himself asking if her ladyship was at home, though his voice was nearly inaudible. The next moment he was standing in the great, dim hall, so poignantly familiar, and the remembered perfume almost made him sway. He did not hear the door close, but he knew. He was caught. The butler betrayed an instant's surprise—or was it overwrought imagination again?—when he gave his name. It seemed to him, though only later did he grasp the significance of that curious intuition—that the man had expected another caller instead. The man took his card respectfully, and disappeared. These flunkeys, of course, were so marvellously trained. He was too long accustomed to straight question and straight answer; but here, in the Old

Country, privacy was jealously guarded with such careful ritual.

And, almost immediately, the butler returned with his expressionless face again, and showed him into the large drawing-room on the ground floor that he knew so well. Tea was on the table—tea for one. He felt puzzled. "If you will have tea first, sir, her ladyship will see you afterwards," was what he heard. And though his breath came thickly, he asked the question that forced itself up and out. Before he knew what he was saying, he asked it: "Is she ill?" Oh no, her ladyship was "quite well, thank you, sir. If you will have tea first, sir, her ladyship will see you afterwards." The horrid formula was repeated, word for word. He sank into an armchair and mechanically poured out his own tea. What he felt he did not exactly know. It seemed so unusual, so utterly unexpected, so unnecessary, too. Was it a special attention, or was it merely casual? That it could mean anything else did not occur to him. How was she busy, occupied—not here to give him tea? He could not understand it. It seemed such a farce, having tea alone like this; it was like waiting for an audience; it was like a doctor's or a dentist's room. He felt bewildered, ill at ease, cheap. . . . But after ten years in primitive lands . . . perhaps London usages had changed in some extraordinary manner. He recalled his first amazement at the motor-omnibuses, taxi-cabs, and electric tubes. All were new. London was otherwise than when he left it. Piccadilly and the Marble Arch themselves had altered. And, with his reflection, a shade more confidence stole in. She knew that he was there; and presently she would come in and speak with him, explaining everything by the mere fact of her delicious presence. He was ready for the ordeal; he would see her—and drop out again. It was worth all manner of pain, even of mortification. He was in her house, drinking her tea, sitting in a chair she even perhaps used herself. Only—he would never dare to say a word, or make a sign that might betray his changeless secret. He still felt the boyish worshipper, worshipping in dumbness from a distance, one of a group of many others like himself. Their dreams had faded, his had continued, that was the difference. Memories tore and raced and poured upon him. How sweet and gentle she had always been to him! He used to wonder sometimes . . . Once, he remembered, he had rehearsed a declaration—but, while rehearsing, the big man had come in and captured her, though he had only read the definite news long after by chance in the Arizona paper. . . .

He gulped his tea down. His heart alternately leaped and stood still. A sort of numbness held him most of that dreadful interval, and no clear thought came at all. Every ten seconds his head turned towards the door that rattled, seemed to move, yet never opened. But any moment now it *must* open, and he would be in her very presence, breathing the same air with her. He would see her, charge himself with her beauty once more to the brim, and then go out again into the wilderness—the wilderness of life—without her—and not for a mere ten years, but for always. She was so utterly beyond his reach. He felt like a backwoodsman. He was a backwoodsman.

For one thing only was he duly prepared—though he thought about it little enough: she would, of course, have changed. The photograph he owned, cut from an illustrated paper, was not true now. It might even be a little shock perhaps. He must remember that. Ten years cannot pass over a woman without—

Before he knew it, then, the door was open, and she was advancing quietly towards him across the thick carpet that deadened sound. With both hands outstretched she came, and with the sweetest welcoming smile upon her parted lips he had seen in any human face. Her eyes were soft with joy. His whole heart leaped within him; for the instant he saw her it all flashed clear as sunlight—that she knew and understood. His being melted in the utter bliss of it; shyness vanished. She had always known, had always understood. Speech came easily to him in a flood, had he needed it. But he did not need it. It was all so adorably easy, simple, natural, and true. He just took her hands—those welcoming, outstretched hands in both his own, and led her to the nearest sofa. He was not even surprised at himself. Inevitable, out of depths of truth, this meeting came about. And he uttered a little, foolish commonplace, because he feared the huge revulsion that his sudden glory brought, and loved to taste it slowly:

"So you live here still?"

"Here, and here," she answered softly, touching his heart, and then her own. "I am attached to this house, too, because *you* used to come and see me here, and because it was here I waited so long for you, and still wait. I shall never leave it—unless you change. You see, we live together here."

He said nothing. He leaned forward to take and hold her. The abrupt knowledge of it all somehow did not seem abrupt—as though he had known it always; and the complete disclosure did not seem disclosure either—rather as though she told him something he had inexplicably left unrealised, yet not forgotten. He felt absolutely master of himself, yet, in a curious sense, outside of himself at the same time. His arms were already open—when she gently held her hands up to prevent. He heard a faint sound outside the door.

"But you are free," he cried, his great passion breaking out and flooding him, yet most oddly well controlled," and I—"

She interrupted him in the softest, quietest whisper he had ever heard:

"You are not free, as I am free—not yet."

The sound outside came suddenly closer. It was a step. There was a faint click on the handle of the door. In a flash, then, came the dreadful shock that overwhelmed him—the abrupt realisation of the truth that was somehow horrible: that Time, all these years, had left no mark upon her, and that she *had not changed*. Her face was young as when he saw her last.

With it there came cold and darkness into the great room that turned it instantly otherwise. He shivered with cold, but an alien, unaccountable cold. Some great shadow dropped upon the entire earth. And though but a second could have passed before the handle actually turned, and the other person entered, it seemed to him like several minutes. He heard her saying this amazing thing that was question, answer, and forgiveness all in one. This, at least, he divined before the ghastly interruption came:

"But, George—if you had only spoken—!"

With ice in his blood, he heard the butler saying that her ladyship would be "pleased" to see him now if he had finished his tea and would he be "so good as to bring the papers and documents upstairs with him." He had just sufficient control of certain muscles to stand upright and murmur that he would come. He rose from a sofa that held no one but himself. But, all at once, he staggered. He really did not know exactly then what happened, or how he managed to stammer out the medley of excuses and semi-explanations that battered their way through his brain and issued somehow in definite words from his lips. Somehow or other he accomplished it. The sudden attack, the faintness, the collapse! . . . He vaguely remembered afterwards—with amazement, too—the suavity of the butler, as he suggested telephoning for a doctor, and that he just managed to forbid it, refusing the offered glass of brandy as well, and that he contrived to stumble into the taxi-cab and give his hotel address, with a final explanation that he would call another day and "bring the papers." It was quite clear that his telegram had been attributed to some one else—some one "with papers"—perhaps a solicitor or architect. His name was such an ordinary one. There were so many Smiths. It was also clear that she he had come to see, and *had* seen, no longer lived here—in the flesh. . . .

And, just as he left the hall, he had the vision—mere fleeting glimpse it was—of a tall, slim, girlish figure on the stairs asking if anything was wrong, and realised vaguely through his atrocious pain that she was, of course, the wife of the son who had inherited . . .

Ancient Lights

From Southwater, where he left the train, the road led due west. That he knew; for the rest he trusted to luck, being one of those born walkers who dislike asking the way. He had that instinct, and as a rule it served him well. "A mile or so due west along the sandy road till you come to a stile on the right; then across the fields. You'll see the red house straight before you." He glanced at the post-card's instructions once again, and once again he tried to decipher the scratched-out sentence—without success. It had been so elaborately inked over that no word was legible. Inked-out sentences in a letter were always enticing. He wondered what it was that had to be so very carefully obliterated.

The afternoon was boisterous, with a tearing, shouting wind that blew from the sea, across the Sussex weald. Massive clouds with rounded, piled-up edges, cannoned across gaping spaces of blue sky. Far away the line of Downs swept the horizon, like an arriving wave. Chanctonbury Ring rode their crest—a scudding ship, hull down before the wind. He took his hat off and walked rapidly, breathing great draughts of air with delight and exhilaration. The road was deserted; no horsemen, bicycles, or motors; not even a tradesman's cart; no single walker. But anyhow he would never have asked the way. Keeping a sharp eye for the stile, he pounded along, while the wind tossed the cloak against his face, and made waves across the blue puddles in the yellow road. The trees showed their under leaves of white. The bracken and the high new grass bent all one way. Great life was in the day, high spirits and dancing everywhere. And for a Croydon surveyor's clerk just out of an office this was like a holiday at the sea.

It was a day for high adventure, and his heart rose up to meet the mood of Nature. His umbrella with the silver ring ought to have been a sword, and his brown shoes should have been top-boots with spurs upon the heels. Where hid the enchanted Castle and the princess with the hair of sunny gold? His horse . . .

The stile came suddenly into view and nipped adventure in the bud. Everyday clothes took him prisoner again. He was a surveyor's clerk, middle-aged, earning three pounds a week, coming from Croydon to see about a client's proposed alterations in a wood—something to ensure a better view from the dining-room window. Across the fields, perhaps a mile away, he saw the red house gleaming in the sunshine; and resting on the stile a moment to get his breath he noticed a copse of oak and hornbeam on the right. "Aha," he told himself, "so that must be the wood he wants to cut down to improve the view? I'll 'ave a look at it." There were boards up, of course, but there was an inviting little path as well. "I'm not a trespasser," he said; "it's part of my business, this is." He scrambled awkwardly over the gate and entered the copse. A little round would bring him to the field again.

But the moment he passed among the trees the wind ceased shouting and a stillness dropped upon the world. So dense was the growth that the sunshine only came through in isolated patches. The air was close. He mopped his forehead and put his green felt hat on, but a low branch knocked it off again at once, and as he stooped an elastic twig swung back and stung his face. There were flowers along both edges of the little path; glades opened on either side; ferns curved about in damper corners, and the smell of earth and foliage was rich and sweet. It was cooler here. What an enchanting little wood, he thought, turning down a small green glade where the sunshine flickered like silver wings. How it danced and fluttered and moved about! He put a dark blue flower in his button-hole. Again his hat, caught by an oak branch as he rose, was knocked from his head, falling across his eyes. And this time he did not put it on again. Swinging his umbrella, he walked on with uncovered head, whistling rather loudly as he went. But the thickness of the trees hardly encouraged whistling, and something of his gaiety and high spirits seemed to leave him. He suddenly found himself treading circumspectly and with caution. The stillness in the wood was so peculiar.

There was a rustle among the ferns and leaves and something shot across the path ten yards ahead, stopped abruptly an instant with head cocked sideways to stare, then dived again beneath the underbrush with the speed of a shadow. He started like a frightened child, laughing the next second that a mere pheasant could have made him jump. In the distance he heard wheels upon the road, and wondered why the sound was pleasant. "Good old butcher's cart," he said to himself—then realised that he was going in the wrong direction and had somehow got turned round. For the road should be behind him, not in front.

And he hurriedly took another narrow glade that lost itself in greenness to the right. "That's my direction, of course," he said; "the trees has mixed me up a bit, it seems"—then found himself abruptly by the gate he had first climbed over. He had merely made a circle. Surprise became almost discomfiture then. And a man, dressed like a gamekeeper in browny green, leaned against the gate, hitting his legs with a switch. "I'm making for Mr. Lumley's farm," explained the walker. "This *is* his wood, I believe—" then stopped dead, because it was no man at all, but merely an effect of light and shade and foliage. He stepped back to reconstruct the singular illusion, but the wind shook the branches roughly here on the edge of the wood and the foliage refused to reconstruct the figure. The leaves all rustled strangely. And just then the sun went behind a cloud, making the whole wood look otherwise. Yet how the mind could be thus doubly deceived was indeed remarkable, for it almost seemed to him the man had answered, spoken—or was this the shuffling noise the branches made?—and had pointed with his switch to the notice-board upon the nearest tree. The words rang on in his head, but of course he had imagined them: "No, it's not his wood. It's ours." And some village wit, moreover, had changed the lettering on the weather-beaten board, for it read quite plainly, "Trespassers will be persecuted."

And while the astonished clerk read the words and chuckled, he said to himself, thinking what a tale he'd have to tell his wife and children later—"The blooming wood has tried to chuck me out. But I'll go in again. Why, it's only a matter of a square acre at most. I'm bound to reach the fields on the other side if I keep straight on." He remembered his position in the office. He had a certain dignity to maintain.

The cloud passed from below the sun, and light splashed suddenly in all manner of unlikely places. The man went straight on. He felt a touch of puzzling confusion somewhere; this way the copse had of shifting from sunshine into shadow doubtless troubled sight a little. To his relief, at last, a new glade opened through the trees and disclosed the fields with a glimpse of the red house in the distance at the far end. But a little wicket gate that stood across the path had first to be climbed, and as he scrambled heavily over—for it would not open—he got the astonishing feeling that it slid off sideways beneath his weight, and towards the wood. Like the moving staircases at Harrod's and Earl's Court, it began to glide off with him. It was quite horrible. He made a violent effort to get down before it carried him into the trees, but his feet became entangled with the bars and umbrella, so that he fell heavily upon the farther side, arms spread across the grass and nettles, boots clutched between the first and second bars. He lay there a moment like a man crucified upside down, and while he struggled to get disentangled—feet, bars, and umbrella formed a regular net—he saw the little man in browny green go past him with extreme rapidity through the wood. The man was laughing. He passed across the glade some fifty yards away, and he was not alone this time. A companion like himself went with him. The clerk, now upon his feet again, watched them disappear into the gloom of green beyond. "They're tramps, not gamekeepers," he said to himself, half mortified, half angry. But his heart was thumping dreadfully, and he dared not utter all his thought.

He examined the wicket gate, convinced it was a trick gate somehow—then went hurriedly on again, disturbed beyond belief to see that the glade no longer opened into fields, but curved away to the right. What in the world had happened to him? His sight was so utterly at fault. Again the sun flamed out abruptly and lit the floor of the wood with pools of silver, and at the same moment a violent gust of wind passed shouting overhead. Drops fell clattering everywhere upon the leaves, making a sharp pattering as of many footsteps. The whole copse shuddered and went moving.

"Rain, by George," thought the clerk, and feeling for his umbrella, discovered he had lost it. He turned back to the gate and found it lying on the farther side. To his amazement he saw the fields at the far end of the glade, the red house, too, ashine in the sunset. He laughed then, for, of course, in his struggle with the gate, he had somehow got turned round—had fallen back instead of forwards. Climbing over, this time quite easily, he retraced his steps. The silver band, he saw, had been torn from the umbrella. No doubt his foot, a nail, or something had caught in it and ripped it off. The clerk began to run; he felt extraordinarily dismayed.

But, while he ran, the entire wood ran with him, round him, to and fro, trees shifting like living things, leaves folding and unfolding, trunks darting backwards and forwards, and branches disclosing enormous empty spaces, then closing up again before he could look into them. There were footsteps everywhere, and laughing, crying voices, and crowds of figures gathering just behind his back till the glade, he knew, was thick with moving life. The wind in his ears, of course, produced the voices and the laughter, while sun and clouds, plunging the copse alternately in shadow and bright dazzling light, created the figures. But he did not like it, and he went as fast as ever his sturdy legs could take him. He was frightened now. This was no story for his wife and children. He ran like the wind. But his feet made no sound upon the soft mossy turf.

Then, to his horror, he saw that the glade grew narrow, nettles and weeds stood thick across it, it dwindled down into a tiny path, and twenty yards ahead it stopped finally and melted off among the trees. What the trick gate had failed to achieve, this twisting glade accomplished easily—carried him in bodily among the dense and crowding trees.

There was only one thing to do—turn sharply and dash back again, run headlong into the life that followed at his back, followed so closely too that now it almost touched him, pushing him in. And with reckless courage this was what he did. It seemed a fearful thing to do. He turned with a sort of violent spring, head down and shoulders forward, hands stretched before his face. He made the plunge; like a hunted creature he charged full tilt the other way, meeting the wind now in his face.

Good Lord! The glade behind him had closed up as well; there was no longer any path at all. Turning round and round, like an animal at bay, he searched for an opening, a way of escape, searched frantically, breathlessly, terrified now in his bones. But foliage surrounded him, branches blocked the way; the trees stood close and still, unshaken by a breath of wind; and the sun dipped that moment behind a great black cloud. The entire wood turned dark and silent. It watched him.

Perhaps it was this final touch of sudden blackness that made him act so foolishly, as though he had really lost his head. At any rate, without pausing to think, he dashed headlong in among the trees again. There was a sensation of being stiflingly surrounded and entangled, and that he *must* break out at all costs—out and away into the open of the blessed fields and air. He did this ill-considered thing, and apparently charged straight into an oak that deliberately moved into his path to stop him. He saw it shift across a good full yard, and being a measuring man, accustomed to theodolite and chain, he ought to know. He fell, saw stars, and felt a thousand tiny fingers tugging and pulling at his hands and neck and ankles. The stinging nettles, no doubt, were responsible for this. He thought of it later. At the moment it felt diabolically calculated.

But another remarkable illusion was not so easily explained. For all in a moment, it seemed, the entire wood went sliding past him with a thick deep rustling of leaves and laughter, myriad footsteps, and tiny little active, energetic shapes; two men in browny green gave him a mighty hoist—and he opened his eyes to find himself lying in the meadow beside the stile where first his incredible adventure had begun. The wood stood in its usual place and stared down upon him in the sunlight. There was the red house in the distance as before. Above him grinned the weather-beaten notice-board: "Trespassers will be prosecuted."

Dishevelled in mind and body, and a good deal shaken in his official soul, the clerk walked slowly across the fields. But on the way he glanced once more at the post-card of instructions, and saw with dull amazement that the inked-out sentence was quite legible after all beneath the scratches made across it: "There *is* a short cut through the wood—the wood I want cut down—if you care to take it." Only "care" was so badly written, it looked more like another word; the "c" was uncommonly like "d."

"That's the copse that spoils my view of the Downs, you see," his client explained to him later, pointing across the fields, and referring to the ordnance map beside him. "I want it cut down and a path made so and so." His finger indicated direction on the map. "The Fairy Wood—it's still called, and it's far older than this house. Come now, if you're ready, Mr. Thomas, we might go out and have a look at it . . ."

Sand

I

As Felix Henriot came through the streets that January night the fog was stifling, but when he reached his little flat upon the top floor there came a sound of wind. Wind was stirring about the world. It blew against his windows, but at first so faintly that he hardly noticed it. Then, with an abrupt rise and fall like a wailing voice that sought to claim attention, it called him. He peered through the window into the blurred darkness, listening.

There is no cry in the world like that of the homeless wind. A vague excitement, scarcely to be analysed, ran through his blood. The curtain of fog waved momentarily aside. Henriot fancied a star peeped down at him.

"It will change things a bit—at last," he sighed, settling back into his chair. "It will bring movement!"

Already something in himself had changed. A restlessness, as of that wandering wind, woke in his heart—the desire to be off and away. Other things could rouse this wildness too: falling water, the singing of a bird, an odour of wood-fire, a glimpse of winding road. But the cry of wind, always searching, questioning, travelling the world's great routes, remained ever the master-touch. High longing took his mind in hand. Mid seven millions he felt suddenly—lonely.

> "I will arise and go now, for always night and day
> I hear lake water lapping with low sounds by the shore;
> While I stand on the roadway, or on the pavements gray,
> I hear it in the deep heart's core."

He murmured the words over softly to himself. The emotion that produced Innisfree passed strongly through him. He too would be over the hills and far away. He craved movement, change, adventure—somewhere far from shops and crowds and motor-'busses. For a week the fog had stifled London. This wind brought life.

Where should he go? Desire was long; his purse was short.

He glanced at his books, letters, newspapers. They had no interest now. Instead he listened. The panorama of other journeys rolled in colour through the little room, flying on one another's heels. Henriot enjoyed this remembered essence of his travels more than the travels themselves. The crying wind brought so many voices, all of them seductive:

There was a soft crashing of waves upon the Black Sea shores, where the huge Caucasus beckoned in the sky beyond; a rustling in the umbrella pines and cactus at Marseilles, whence magic steamers start about the world like flying dreams. He heard the plash of fountains upon Mount Ida's slopes, and the whisper of the tamarisk on Marathon. It was dawn once more upon the Ionian Sea, and he smelt the perfume of the Cyclades. Blue-veiled islands melted in the sunshine, and across the dewy lawns of Tempe, moistened by the spray of many waterfalls, he saw—Great Heavens above!—the dancing of white forms ... or was it only mist the sunshine painted against Pelion? ... "Methought, among the lawns together, we wandered underneath the young grey dawn. And multitudes of dense white fleecy clouds shepherded by the slow, unwilling wind. . . ."

And then, into his stuffy room, slipped the singing perfume of a wall-flower on a ruined tower, and with it the sweetness of hot ivy. He heard the "yellow bees in the ivy bloom." Wind whipped over the open hills—this very wind that laboured drearily through the London fog.

And—he was caught. The darkness melted from the city. The fog whisked off into an azure sky. The roar of traffic turned into booming of the sea. There was a whistling among cordage, and the floor swayed to and fro. He saw a sailor touch his cap and pocket the two-franc piece. The syren hooted—ominous sound that had started him on many a journey of adventure—and the roar of London became mere insignificant clatter of a child's toy carriages.

He loved that syren's call; there was something deep and pitiless in it. It drew the wanderers forth from cities everywhere: "Leave your known world behind you, and come with me for better or for worse! The anchor is up; it is too late to change. Only—beware! You shall know curious things—and alone!"

Henriot stirred uneasily in his chair. He turned with sudden energy to the shelf of guide-books, maps, and time-tables—possessions he most valued in the whole room. He was a happy-go-lucky, adventure-loving soul, careless of common standards, athirst ever for the new and strange.

"That's the best of having a cheap flat," he laughed, "and no ties in the world. I can turn the key and disappear. No one cares or knows—no one but the thieving caretaker. And he's long ago found out that there's nothing here worth taking!"

There followed then no lengthy indecision. Preparation was even shorter still. He was always ready for a move, and his sojourn in cities was but breathing-space while he gathered pennies for further wanderings. An enormous kit-bag—sack-shaped, very worn and dirty—emerged speedily from the bottom of a cupboard in the wall. It was of limitless capacity. The key and padlock rattled in its depths. Cigarette ashes covered everything while he stuffed it full of ancient, indescribable garments. And his voice, singing of those "yellow bees in the ivy bloom," mingled with the crying of the rising wind about his windows. His restlessness had disappeared by magic.

This time, however, there could be no haunted Pelion, nor shady groves of Tempe, for he lived in sophisticated times when money markets regulated movement sternly. Travelling was only for the rich; mere wanderers must pig it. He remembered instead an opportune invitation to the Desert. "Objective" invitation, his genial hosts had called it, knowing his hatred of convention. And Helouan danced into letters of brilliance upon the inner map of his mind. For Egypt had ever held his spirit in thrall, though as yet he had tried in vain to touch the great buried soul of her. The excavators, the Egyptologists, the archaeologists most of all, plastered her grey ancient face with labels like hotel advertisements on travellers' portmanteaux. They told where she had come from last, but nothing of what she dreamed and thought and loved. The heart of Egypt lay beneath the sand, and the trifling robbery of little details that poked forth from tombs and temples brought no true revelation of her stupendous spiritual splendour. Henriot, in his youth, had searched and dived among what material he could find, believing once—or half believing—that the ceremonial of that ancient system veiled a weight of symbol that was reflected from genuine supersensual knowledge. The rituals, now taken literally, and so pityingly explained away, had once been genuine pathways of approach. But never yet, and least of all in his previous visits to Egypt itself, had he discovered one single person, worthy of speech, who caught at his idea. "Curious," they said, then turned away—to go on digging in the sand. Sand smothered her world to-day. Excavators discovered skeletons. Museums everywhere stored them—grinning, literal relics that told nothing.

But now, while he packed and sang, these hopes of enthusiastic younger days stirred again—because the emotion that gave them birth was real and true in him. Through the morning mists upon the Nile an old pyramid bowed hugely at him across London roofs: "Come," he heard its awful whisper beneath the ceiling, "I have things to show you, and to tell." He saw the flock of them sailing the Desert like weird grey solemn ships that make no earthly port. And he imagined them as one: multiple expressions of some single unearthly portent they adumbrated in mighty form—dead symbols of some spiritual conception long vanished from the world.

"I mustn't dream like this," he laughed, "or I shall get absent-minded and pack fire-tongs instead of boots. It looks like a jumble sale already!" And he stood on a heap of things to wedge them down still tighter.

But the pictures would not cease. He saw the kites circling high in the blue air. A couple of white vultures flapped lazily away over whining miles. Felucca sails, like giant wings emerging from the ground, curved towards him from the Nile. The palm-trees dropped long shadows over Memphis. He felt the delicious, drenching heat, and the Khamasin, that over-wind from Nubia, brushed his very cheeks. In the little gardens the mish-mish was in bloom. . . . He smelt the desert . . . grey sepulchre of cancelled cycles. . . . The stillness of her interminable reaches dropped down upon old London. . . .

The magic of the sand stole round him in its silent-footed tempest.

And while he struggled with that strange, capacious sack, the piles of clothing ran into shapes of gleaming Bedouin faces; London garments settled down with the mournful sound of camels' feet, half dropping wind, half water flowing underground—sound that old Time has brought over into modern life and left a moment for our wonder and perhaps our tears.

He rose at length with the excitement of some deep enchantment in his eyes. The thought of Egypt plunged ever so deeply into him, carrying him into depths where he found it difficult to breathe, so strangely far away it seemed, yet indefinably familiar. He lost his way. A touch of fear came with it.

"A sack like that is the wonder of the world," he laughed again, kicking the unwieldy, sausage-shaped monster into a corner of the room, and sitting down to write the thrilling labels: "Felix Henriot, Alexandria *via* Marseilles." But his pen blotted the letters; there was sand in it. He rewrote the words. Then he remembered a dozen things he had left out. Impatiently, yet with confusion somewhere, he stuffed them in. They ran away into shifting heaps; they disappeared; they emerged suddenly again. It was like packing hot, dry, flowing sand. From the pockets of a coat—he had worn it last summer down Dorset way—out trickled sand. There was sand in his mind and thoughts.

And his dreams that night were full of winds, the old sad winds of Egypt, and of moving, shifting sand. Arabs and Afreets danced amazingly together across dunes he could never reach. For he could not follow fast enough. Something infinitely older than these ever caught his feet and held him back. A million tiny fingers stung and pricked him. Something flung a veil before his eyes. Once it touched him—his face and hands and neck. "Stay here with us," he heard a host of muffled voices crying, but their sound was smothered, buried, rising through the ground. A myriad throats were choked. Till, at last, with a violent effort he turned and seized it. And then the thing he grasped at slipped between his fingers and ran easily away. It had a grey and yellow face, and it moved through all its parts. It flowed as water flows, and yet was solid. It was centuries old.

He cried out to it. "Who are you? What is your name? I surely know you . . . but I have forgotten . . . ?"

And it stopped, turning from far away its great uncovered countenance of nameless colouring. He caught a voice. It rolled and boomed and whispered like the wind. And then he woke, with a curious shaking in his heart, and a little touch of chilly perspiration on the skin.

But the voice seemed in the room still—close beside him:

"I am the Sand," he heard, before it died away.

And next he realised that the glitter of Paris lay behind him, and a steamer was taking him with much unnecessary motion across a sparkling sea towards Alexandria. Gladly he saw the Riviera fade below the horizon, with its hard bright sunshine, treacherous winds, and its smear of rich, conventional English. All restlessness now had left him. True vagabond still at forty, he only felt the unrest and discomfort of life when caught in the network of routine and rigid streets, no chance of breaking loose. He was off again at last, money scarce enough indeed, but the joy of wandering expressing itself in happy emotions of release. Every warning of calculation was stifled. He thought of the American woman who walked out of her Long Island house one summer's day to look at a passing sail—and was gone eight years before she walked in again. Eight years of roving travel! He had always felt respect and admiration for that woman.

For Felix Henriot, with his admixture of foreign blood, was philosopher as well as vagabond, a strong poetic and religious strain sometimes breaking out through fissures in his complex nature. He had seen much life; had read many books. The passionate desire of youth to solve the world's big riddles had given place to a resignation filled to the brim with wonder. Anything *might* be true. Nothing surprised him. The most outlandish beliefs, for all he knew, might fringe truth somewhere. He had escaped that cheap cynicism with which disappointed men soothe their vanity when they realise that an intelligible explanation of the universe lies beyond their powers. He no longer expected final answers.

For him, even the smallest journeys held the spice of some adventure; all minutes were loaded with enticing potentialities. And they shaped for themselves somehow a dramatic form. "It's like a story," his friends said when he told his travels. It always was a story.

But the adventure that lay waiting for him where the silent streets of little Helouan kiss the great Desert's lips, was of a different kind to any Henriot had yet encountered. Looking back, he has often asked himself, "How in the world can I accept it?"

And, perhaps, he never yet has accepted it. It was sand that brought it. For the Desert, the stupendous thing that mothers little Helouan, produced it.

II

He slipped through Cairo with the same relief that he left the Riviera, resenting its social vulgarity so close to the imperial aristocracy of the Desert; he settled down into the peace of soft and silent little Helouan. The hotel in which he had a room on the top floor had been formerly a Khedivial Palace. It had the air of a palace still. He felt himself in a country-house, with lofty ceilings, cool and airy corridors, spacious halls. Soft-footed Arabs attended to his wants; white walls let in light and air without a sign of heat; there was a feeling of a large, spread tent pitched on the very sand; and the wind that stirred the oleanders in the shady gardens also crept in to rustle the palm leaves of his favourite corner seat. Through the large windows where once the Khedive held high court, the sunshine blazed upon vistaed leagues of Desert.

And from his bedroom windows he watched the sun dip into gold and crimson behind the swelling Libyan sands. This side of the pyramids he saw the Nile meander among palm groves and tilled fields. Across his balcony railings the Egyptian stars trooped down beside his very bed, shaping old constellations for his dreams; while, to the south, he looked out upon the vast untamable Body of the sands that carpeted the world for thousands of miles towards Upper Egypt, Nubia, and the dread Sahara itself. He wondered again why people thought it necessary to go so far afield to know the Desert. Here, within half an hour of Cairo, it lay breathing solemnly at his very doors.

For little Helouan, caught thus between the shoulders of the Libyan and Arabian Deserts, is utterly sand-haunted. The Desert lies all round it like a sea. Henriot felt he never could escape from it, as he moved about the island whose coasts are washed with sand. Down each broad and shining street the two end houses framed a vista of its dim immensity—glimpses of shimmering blue, or flame-touched purple. There were stretches of deep sea-green as well, far off upon its bosom. The streets were open channels of approach, and the eye ran down them as along the tube of a telescope laid to catch incredible distance out of space. Through them the Desert reached in with long, thin feelers towards the village. Its Being flooded into Helouan, and over it. Past walls and houses, churches and hotels, the sea of Desert pressed in silently with its myriad soft feet of sand. It poured in everywhere, through crack and slit and crannie. These were reminders of possession and ownership. And every passing wind that lifted eddies of dust at the street corners were messages from the quiet, powerful Thing that permitted Helouan to lie and dream so peacefully in the sunshine. Mere artificial oasis, its existence was temporary, held on lease, just for ninety-nine centuries or so.

This sea idea became insistent. For, in certain lights, and especially in the brief, bewildering dusk, the Desert rose—swaying towards the small white houses. The waves of it ran for fifty miles without a break. It was too deep for foam or surface agitation, yet it knew the swell of tides. And underneath flowed resolute currents, linking distance to the centre. These many deserts were really one. A storm, just retreated, had tossed Helouan upon the shore and left it there to dry; but any morning he would wake to find it had been carried off again into the depths. Some fragment, at least, would disappear. The grim Mokattam Hills were rollers that ever threatened to topple down and submerge the sandy bar that men called Helouan.

Being soundless, and devoid of perfume, the Desert's message reached him through two senses only—sight and touch; chiefly, of course, the former. Its invasion was concentrated through the eyes. And vision, thus uncorrected, went what pace it pleased. The Desert played with him. Sand stole into his being—through the eyes.

And so obsessing was this majesty of its close presence, that Henriot sometimes wondered how people dared their little social activities within its very sight and hearing; how they played golf and tennis upon reclaimed edges of its face, picnicked so blithely hard upon its frontiers, and danced at night while this stern, unfathomable Thing lay breathing just beyond the trumpery walls that kept it out. The challenge of their shallow admiration seemed presumptuous, almost provocative. Their pursuit of pleasure suggested insolent indifference. They ran fool-hardy hazards, he felt; for there was no worship in their vulgar hearts. With a mental shudder, sometimes he watched the cheap tourist horde go laughing, chattering past within view of its ancient, half-closed eyes. It was like defying deity.

For, to his stirred imagination the sublimity of the Desert dwarfed humanity. These people had been wiser to choose another place for the flaunting of their tawdry insignificance. Any minute this Wilderness, "huddled in grey annihilation," might awake and notice them . . . !

In his own hotel were several "smart," so-called "Society" people who emphasised the protest in him to the point of definite contempt. Overdressed, the latest worldly novel under their arms, they strutted the narrow pavements of their tiny world, immensely pleased with themselves. Their vacuous minds expressed themselves in the slang of their exclusive circle—value being the element excluded. The pettiness of their outlook hardly distressed him—he was too familiar with it at home—but their essential vulgarity, their innate ugliness, seemed more than usually offensive in the grandeur of its present setting. Into the mighty sands they took the latest London scandal, gabbling it over even among the Tombs and Temples. And "it was to laugh," the pains they spent wondering whom they might condescend to know, never dreaming that they themselves were not worth knowing. Against the background of the noble Desert their titles seemed the cap and bells of clowns.

And Henriot, knowing some of them personally, could not always escape their insipid company. Yet he was the gainer. They little guessed how their commonness heightened contrast, set mercilessly thus beside the strange, eternal beauty of the sand.

Occasionally the protest in his soul betrayed itself in words, which of course they did not understand. "He is so clever, isn't he?" And then, having relieved his feelings, he would comfort himself characteristically:

"The Desert has not noticed them. The Sand is not aware of their existence. How should the sea take note of rubbish that lies above its tide-line?"

For Henriot drew near to its great shifting altars in an attitude of worship. The wilderness made him kneel in heart. Its shining reaches led to the oldest Temple in the world, and every journey that he made was like a sacrament. For him the Desert was a consecrated place. It was sacred.

And his tactful hosts, knowing his peculiarities, left their house open to him when he cared to come—they lived upon the northern edge of the oasis—and he was as free as though he were absolutely alone. He blessed them; he rejoiced that he had come. Little Helouan accepted him. The Desert knew that he was there.

From his corner of the big dining-room he could see the other guests, but his roving eye always returned to the figure of a solitary man who sat at an adjoining table, and whose personality stirred his interest. While affecting to look elsewhere, he studied him as closely as might be. There was something about the stranger that touched his curiosity—a certain air of expectation that he wore. But it was more than that: it was anticipation, apprehension in it somewhere. The man was nervous, uneasy. His restless way of suddenly looking about him proved it. Henriot tried every one else in the room as well; but, though his thought settled on others too, he always came back to the figure of this solitary being opposite, who ate his dinner as if afraid of being seen, and glanced up sometimes as if fearful of being watched. Henriot's curiosity, before he knew it, became suspicion. There was mystery here. The table, he noticed, was laid for two.

"Is he an actor, a priest of some strange religion, an enquiry agent, or just—a crank?" was the thought that first occurred to him. And the question suggested itself without amusement. The impression of subterfuge and caution he conveyed left his observer unsatisfied.

The face was clean shaven, dark, and strong; thick hair, straight yet bushy, was slightly unkempt; it was streaked with grey; and an unexpected mobility when he smiled ran over the features that he seemed to hold rigid by deliberate effort. The man was cut to no quite common measure. Henriot jumped to an intuitive conclusion: "He's not here for pleasure or merely sight-seeing. Something serious has brought him to Egypt." For the face combined too ill-assorted qualities: an obstinate tenacity that might even mean brutality, and was certainly repulsive, yet, with it, an undecipherable dreaminess betrayed by lines of the mouth, but above all in the very light blue eyes, so rarely raised. Those eyes, he felt, had looked upon unusual things; "dreaminess" was not an adequate description; "searching" conveyed it better. The true source of the queer impression remained elusive. And hence, perhaps, the incongruous marriage in the face—mobility laid upon a matter-of-fact foundation underneath. The face showed conflict.

And Henriot, watching him, felt decidedly intrigued. "I'd like to know that man, and all about him." His name, he learned later, was Richard Vance; from Birmingham; a business man. But it was not the Birmingham he wished to know; it was the—other: cause of the elusive, dreamy searching. Though facing one another at so short a distance, their eyes, however, did not meet. And this, Henriot well knew, was a sure sign that he himself was also under observation. Richard Vance, from Birmingham, was equally taking careful note of Felix Henriot, from London.

Thus, he could wait his time. They would come together later. An opportunity would certainly present itself. The first links in a curious chain had already caught; soon the chain would tighten, pull as though by chance, and bring their lives into one and the same circle. Wondering in particular for what kind of a companion the second cover was laid, Henriot felt certain that their eventual coming together was inevitable. He possessed this kind of divination from first impressions, and not uncommonly it proved correct.

Following instinct, therefore, he took no steps towards acquaintance, and for several days, owing to the fact that he dined frequently with his hosts, he saw nothing more of Richard Vance, the business man from Birmingham. Then, one night, coming home late from his friend's house, he had passed along the great corridor, and was actually a step or so into his bedroom, when a drawling voice sounded close behind him. It was an unpleasant sound. It was very near him too—

"I beg your pardon, but have you, by any chance, such a thing as a compass you could lend me?"

The voice was so close that he started. Vance stood within touching distance of his body. He had stolen up like a ghostly Arab, must have followed him, too, some little distance, for further down the passage the light of an open door—he had passed it on his way—showed where he came from.

"Eh? I beg your pardon? A—compass, did you say?" He felt disconcerted for a moment. How short the man was, now that he saw him standing. Broad and powerful too. Henriot looked down upon his thick head of hair. The personality and voice repelled him. Possibly his face, caught unawares, betrayed this.

"Forgive my startling you," said the other apologetically, while the softer expression danced in for a moment and disorganised the rigid set of his face. "The soft carpet, you know. I'm afraid you didn't hear my tread. I wondered"—he smiled again slightly at the nature of the request—"if—by any chance—you had a pocket compass you could lend me?"

"Ah, a compass, yes! Please don't apologise. I believe I have one—if you'll wait a moment. Come in, won't you? I'll have a look."

The other thanked him but waited in the passage. Henriot, it so happened, had a compass, and produced it after a moment's search.

"I am greatly indebted to you—if I may return it in the morning. You will forgive my disturbing you at such an hour. My own is broken, and I wanted—er—to find the true north."

Henriot stammered some reply, and the man was gone. It was all over in a minute. He locked his door and sat down in his chair to think. The little incident had upset him, though for the life of him he could not imagine why. It ought by rights to have been almost ludicrous, yet instead it was the exact reverse—half threatening. Why should not a man want a compass? But, again, why should he? And at midnight? The voice, the eyes, the near presence—what did they bring that set his nerves thus asking unusual questions? This strange impression that something grave was happening, something unearthly—how was it born exactly? The man's proximity came like a shock. It had made him start. He brought—thus the idea came unbidden to his mind—something with him that galvanised him quite absurdly, as fear does, or delight, or great wonder. There was a music in his voice too—a certain—well, he could only call it lilt, that reminded him of plainsong, intoning, chanting. Drawling was *not* the word at all.

He tried to dismiss it as imagination, but it would not be dismissed. The disturbance in himself was caused by something not imaginary, but real. And then, for the first time, he discovered that the man had brought a faint, elusive suggestion of perfume with him, an aromatic odour, that made him think of priests and churches. The ghost of it still lingered in the air. Ah, here then was the origin of the notion that his voice had chanted: it was surely the suggestion of incense. But incense, intoning, a compass to find the true north—at midnight in a Desert hotel!

A touch of uneasiness ran through the curiosity and excitement that he felt.

And he undressed for bed. "Confound my old imagination," he thought, "what tricks it plays me! It'll keep me awake!"

But the questions, once started in his mind, continued. He must find explanation of one kind or another before he could lie down and sleep, and he found it at length in—the stars. The man was an astronomer of sorts; possibly an astrologer into the bargain! Why not? The stars were wonderful above Helouan. Was there not an observatory on the Mokattam Hills, too, where tourists could use the telescopes on privileged days? He had it at last. He even stole out on to his balcony to see if the stranger perhaps was looking through some wonderful apparatus at the heavens. Their rooms were on the same side. But the shuttered windows revealed no stooping figure with eyes glued to a telescope. The stars blinked in their many thousands down upon the silent desert. The night held neither sound nor movement. There was a cool breeze blowing across the Nile from the Lybian Sands. It nipped; and he stepped back quickly into the room again. Drawing the mosquito curtains carefully about the bed, he put the light out and turned over to sleep.

And sleep came quickly, contrary to his expectations, though it was a light and surface sleep. That last glimpse of the darkened Desert lying beneath the Egyptian stars had touched him with some hand of awful power that ousted the first, lesser excitement. It calmed and soothed him in one sense, yet in another, a sense he could not understand, it caught him in a net of deep, deep feelings whose mesh, while infinitely delicate, was utterly stupendous. His nerves this deeper emotion left alone: it reached instead to something infinite in him that mere nerves could neither deal with nor interpret. The soul awoke and whispered in him while his body slept.

And the little, foolish dreams that ran to and fro across this veil of surface sleep brought oddly tangled pictures of things quite tiny and at the same time of others that were mighty beyond words. With these two counters Nightmare played. They interwove. There was the figure of this dark-faced man with the compass, measuring the sky to find the true north, and there were hints of giant Presences that hovered just outside some curious outline that he traced upon the ground, copied in some nightmare fashion from the heavens. The excitement caused by his visitor's singular request mingled with the profounder sensations his final look at the stars and Desert stirred. The two were somehow inter-related.

Some hours later, before this surface sleep passed into genuine slumber, Henriot woke—with an appalling feeling that the Desert had come creeping into his room and now stared down upon him where he lay in bed. The wind was crying audibly about the walls outside. A faint, sharp tapping came against the window panes.

He sprang instantly out of bed, not yet awake enough to feel actual alarm, yet with the nightmare touch still close enough to cause a sort of feverish, loose bewilderment. He switched the lights on. A moment later he knew the meaning of that curious tapping, for the rising wind was flinging tiny specks of sand against the glass. The idea that they had summoned him belonged, of course, to dream.

He opened the window, and stepped out on to the balcony. The stone was very cold under his bare feet. There was a wash of wind all over him. He saw the sheet of glimmering, pale desert near and far; and something stung his skin below the eyes.

"The sand," he whispered, "again the sand; always the sand. Waking or sleeping, the sand is everywhere—nothing but sand, sand, Sand. . . ."

He rubbed his eyes. It was like talking in his sleep, talking to Someone who had questioned him just before he woke. But was he really properly awake? It seemed next day that he had dreamed it. Something enormous, with rustling skirts of sand, had just retreated far into the Desert. Sand went with it—flowing, trailing, smothering the world. The wind died down.

And Henriot went back to sleep, caught instantly away into unconsciousness; covered, blinded, swept over by this spreading thing of reddish brown with the great, grey face, whose Being was colossal yet quite tiny, and whose fingers, wings, and eyes were countless as the stars.

But all night long it watched and waited, rising to peer above the little balcony, and sometimes entering the room and piling up beside his very pillow. He dreamed of Sand.

III

For some days Henriot saw little of the man who came from Birmingham and pushed curiosity to a climax by asking for a compass in the middle of the night. For one thing, he was a good deal with his friends upon the other side of Helouan, and for another, he slept several nights in the Desert.

He loved the gigantic peace the Desert gave him. The world was forgotten there; and not the world merely, but all memory of it. Everything faded out. The soul turned inwards upon itself.

An Arab boy and donkey took out sleeping-bag, food, and water to the Wadi Hof, a desolate gorge about an hour eastwards. It winds between cliffs whose summits rise some thousand feet above the sea. It opens suddenly, cut deep into the swaying world of level plateaux and undulating hills. It moves about too; he never found it in the same place twice—like an arm of the Desert that shifted with the changing lights. Here he watched dawns and sunsets, slept through the mid-day heat, and enjoyed the unearthly colouring that swept Day and Night across the huge horizons. In solitude the Desert soaked down into him. At night the jackals cried in the darkness round his cautiously-fed camp-fire—small, because wood had to be carried—and in the day-time kites circled overhead to inspect him, and an occasional white vulture flapped across the blue. The weird desolation of this rocky valley, he thought, was like the scenery of the moon. He took no watch with him, and the arrival of the donkey boy an hour after sunrise came almost from another planet, bringing things of time and common life out of some distant gulf where they had lain forgotten among lost ages.

The short hour of twilight brought, too, a bewitchment into the silence that was a little less than comfortable. Full light or darkness he could manage, but this time of half things made him want to shut his eyes and hide. Its effect stepped over imagination. The mind got lost. He could not understand it. For the cliffs and boulders of discoloured limestone shone then with an inward glow that signalled to the Desert with veiled lanterns. The misshapen hills, carved by wind and rain into ominous outlines, stirred and nodded. In the morning light they retired into themselves, asleep. But at dusk the tide retreated. They rose from the sea, emerging naked, threatening. They ran together and joined shoulders, the entire army of them. And the glow of their sandy bodies, self-luminous, continued even beneath the stars. Only the moonlight drowned it. For the moonrise over the Mokattam Hills brought a white, grand loveliness that drenched the entire Desert. It drew a marvellous sweetness from the sand. It shone across a world as yet unfinished, whereon no life might show itself for ages yet to come. He was alone then upon an empty star, before the creation of things that breathed and moved.

What impressed him, however, more than everything else was the enormous vitality that rose out of all this apparent death. There was no hint of the melancholy that belongs commonly to flatness; the sadness of wide, monotonous landscape was not here. The endless repetition of sweeping vale and plateau brought infinity within measurable comprehension. He grasped a definite meaning in the phrase "world without end": the Desert had no end and no beginning. It gave him a sense of eternal peace, the silent peace that star-fields know. Instead of subduing the soul with bewilderment, it inspired with courage, confidence, hope. Through this sand which was the wreck of countless geological ages, rushed life that was terrific and uplifting, too huge to include melancholy, too deep to betray itself in movement. Here was the stillness of eternity. Behind the spread grey masque of apparent death lay stores of accumulated life, ready to break forth at any point. In the Desert he felt himself absolutely royal.

And this contrast of Life, veiling itself in Death, was a contradiction that somehow intoxicated. The Desert exhilaration never left him. He was never alone. A companionship of millions went with him, and he *felt* the Desert close, as stars are close to one another, or grains of sand.

It was the Khamasin, the hot wind bringing sand, that drove him in—with the feeling that these few days and nights had been immeasurable, and that he had been away a thousand years. He came back with the magic of the Desert in his blood, hotel-life tasteless and insipid by comparison. To human impressions thus he was fresh and vividly sensitive. His being, cleaned and sensitised by pure grandeur, "felt" people—for a time at any rate—with an uncommon sharpness of receptive judgment. He returned to a life somehow mean and meagre, resuming insignificance with his dinner jacket. Out with the sand he

had been regal; now, like a slave, he strutted self-conscious and reduced.

But this imperial standard of the Desert stayed a little time beside
him, its purity focussing judgment like a lens. The specks of smaller
emotions left it clear at first, and as his eye wandered vaguely over the
people assembled in the dining-room, it was arrested with a vivid
shock upon two figures at the little table facing him.

He had forgotten Vance, the Birmingham man who sought the
North at midnight with a pocket compass. He now saw him again,
with an intuitive discernment entirely fresh. Before memory brought
up her clouding associations, some brilliance flashed a light upon him.
"That man," Henriot thought, "might have come with me. He would
have understood and loved it!" But the thought was really this—a
moment's reflection spread it, rather: "He belongs somewhere to the
Desert; the Desert brought him out here." And, again, hidden swiftly
behind it like a movement running below water—"What does he want
with it? What is the deeper motive he conceals? For there *is* a deeper
motive; and it *is* concealed."

But it was the woman seated next him who absorbed his attention
really, even while this thought flashed and went its way. The empty
chair was occupied at last. Unlike his first encounter with the man, she
looked straight at him. Their eyes met fully. For several seconds there
was steady mutual inspection, while her penetrating stare, intent without being rude, passed searchingly all over his face. It was disconcerting. Crumbling his bread, he looked equally hard at her, unable to turn
away, determined not to be the first to shift his gaze. And when at
length she lowered her eyes he felt that many things had happened, as
in a long period of intimate conversation. Her mind had judged him
through and through. Questions and answer flashed. They were no
longer strangers. For the rest of dinner, though he was careful to avoid
direct inspection, he was aware that she felt his presence and was secretly speaking with him. She asked questions beneath her breath. The
answers rose with the quickened pulses in his blood. Moreover, she
explained Richard Vance. It was this woman's power that shone reflected in the man. She was the one who knew the big, unusual things.
Vance merely echoed the rush of her vital personality.

This was the first impression that he got—from the most striking, curious face he had ever seen in a woman. It remained very near him all through the meal: she had moved to his table, it seemed she sat beside him. Their minds certainly knew contact from that moment.

It is never difficult to credit strangers with the qualities and knowledge that oneself craves for, and no doubt Henriot's active fancy went busily to work. But, none the less, this thing remained and grew: that this woman was aware of the hidden things of Egypt he had always longed to know. There was knowledge and guidance she could impart. Her soul was searching among ancient things. Her face brought the Desert back into his thoughts. And with it came—the sand.

Here was the flash. The sight of her restored the peace and splendour he had left behind him in his Desert camps. The rest, of course, was what his imagination constructed upon this slender basis. Only,—not all of it was imagination.

Now, Henriot knew little enough of women, and had no pose of "understanding" them. His experience was of the slightest; the love and veneration felt for his own mother had set the entire sex upon the heights. His affairs with women, if so they may be called, had been transient—all but those of early youth, which having never known the devastating test of fulfilment, still remained ideal and superb. There was unconscious humour in his attitude—from a distance; for he regarded women with wonder and respect, as puzzles that sweetened but complicated life, might even endanger it. He certainly was not a marrying man! But now, as he felt the presence of this woman so deliberately possess him, there came over him two clear, strong messages, each vivid with certainty. One was that banal suggestion of familiarity claimed by lovers and the like—he had often heard of it—"I have known that woman before; I have met her ages ago somewhere; she is strangely familiar to me"; and the other, growing out of it almost: "Have nothing to do with her; she will bring you trouble and confusion; avoid her, and be warned";—in fact, a distinct presentiment.

Yet, although Henriot dismissed both impressions as having no shred of evidence to justify them, the original clear judgment, as he studied her extraordinary countenance, persisted through all denials. The familiarity, and the presentiment, remained. There also remained this other—an enormous imaginative leap!—that she could teach him "Egypt."

He watched her carefully, in a sense fascinated. He could only describe the face as black, so dark it was with the darkness of great age. Elderly was the obvious, natural word; but elderly described the features only. The expression of the face wore centuries. Nor was it merely the coal-black eyes that betrayed an ancient, age-travelled soul behind them. The entire presentment mysteriously conveyed it. This woman's heart knew long-forgotten things—the thought kept beating up against him. There were cheek-bones, oddly high, that made him think involuntarily of the well-advertised Pharaoh, Ramases; a square, deep jaw; and an aquiline nose that gave the final touch of power. For the power undeniably was there, and while the general effect had grimness in it, there was neither harshness nor any forbidding touch about it. There was an implacable sternness in the set of lips and jaw, and, most curious of all, the eyelids over the steady eyes of black were level as a ruler. This level framing made the woman's stare remarkable beyond description. Henriot thought of an idol carved in stone, stone hard and black, with eyes that stared across the sand into a world of things non-human, very far away, forgotten of men. The face was finely ugly. This strange dark beauty flashed flame about it.

And, as the way ever was with him, Henriot next fell to constructing the possible lives of herself and her companion, though without much success. Imagination soon stopped dead. She was not old enough to be Vance's mother, and assuredly she was not his wife. His interest was more than merely piqued—it was puzzled uncommonly. What was the contrast that made the man seem beside her—vile? Whence came, too, the impression that she exercised some strong authority, though never directly exercised, that held him at her mercy? How did he guess that the man resented it, yet did not dare oppose, and that, apparently acquiescing good-humouredly, his will was deliberately held in abeyance, and that he waited sulkily, biding his time? There was furtiveness in every gesture and expression. A hidden motive lurked in him; unworthiness somewhere; he was determined yet ashamed. He watched her ceaselessly and with such uncanny closeness.

Henriot imagined he divined all this. He leaped to the guess that his expenses were being paid. A good deal more was being paid besides. She was a rich relation, from whom he had expectations; he was serving his seven years, ashamed of his servitude, ever calculating escape—but, perhaps, no ordinary escape. A faint shudder ran over him. He drew in the reins of imagination.

Of course, the probabilities were that he was hopelessly astray—one usually is on such occasions—but this time, it so happened, he was singularly right. Before one thing only his ready invention stopped every time. This vileness, this notion of unworthiness in Vance, could not be negative merely. A man with that face was no inactive weakling. The motive he was at such pains to conceal, betraying its existence by that very fact, moved, surely, towards aggressive action. Disguised, it never slept. Vance was sharply on the alert. He had a plan deep out of sight. And Henriot remembered how the man's soft approach along the carpeted corridor had made him start. He recalled the quasi shock it gave him. He thought again of the feeling of discomfort he had experienced.

Next, his eager fancy sought to plumb the business these two had together in Egypt—in the Desert. For the Desert, he felt convinced, had brought them out. But here, though he constructed numerous explanations, another barrier stopped him. Because he *knew*. This woman was in touch with that aspect of ancient Egypt he himself had ever sought in vain; and not merely with stones the sand had buried so deep, but with the meanings they once represented, buried so utterly by the sands of later thought.

And here, being ignorant, he found no clue that could lead to any satisfactory result, for he possessed no knowledge that might guide him. He floundered—until Fate helped him. And the instant Fate helped him, the warning and presentiment he had dismissed as fanciful, became real again. He hesitated. Caution acted. He would think twice before taking steps to form acquaintance. "Better not," thought whispered. "Better leave them alone, this queer couple. They're after things that won't do you any good." This idea of mischief, almost of danger, in their purposes was oddly insistent; for what could possibly convey it? But, while he hesitated, Fate, who sent the warning, pushed him at the same time into the circle of their lives: at first tentatively—he might still have escaped; but soon urgently—curiosity led him inexorably towards the end.

IV

It was so simple a manœuvre by which Fate began the innocent game. The woman left a couple of books behind her on the table one night, and Henriot, after a moment's hesitation, took them out after her. He knew the titles—*The House of the Master,* and *The House of the Hidden Places,* both singular interpretations of the Pyramids that once had held his own mind spellbound. Their ideas had been since disproved, if he remembered rightly, yet the titles were a clue—a clue to that imaginative part of his mind that was so busy constructing theories and had found its stride. Loose sheets of paper, covered with notes in a minute handwriting, lay between the pages; but these, of course, he did not read, noticing only that they were written round designs of various kinds—intricate designs.

He discovered Vance in a corner of the smoking-lounge. The woman had disappeared.

Vance thanked him politely. "My aunt is so forgetful sometimes," he said, and took them with a covert eagerness that did not escape the other's observation. He folded up the sheets and put them carefully in his pocket. On one there was an ink-sketched map, crammed with detail, that might well have referred to some portion of the Desert. The points of the compass stood out boldly at the bottom. There were involved geometrical designs again. Henriot saw them. They exchanged, then, the commonplaces of conversation, but these led to nothing further. Vance was nervous and betrayed impatience. He presently excused himself and left the lounge. Ten minutes later he passed through the outer hall, the woman beside him, and the pair of them, wrapped up in cloak and ulster, went out into the night. At the door, Vance turned and threw a quick, investigating glance in his direction. There seemed a hint of questioning in that glance; it might almost have been a tentative invitation. But, also, he wanted to see if their exit had been particularly noticed—and by whom.

This, briefly told, was the first manœuvre by which Fate introduced them. There was nothing in it. The details were so insignificant, so slight the conversation, so meagre the pieces thus added to Henriot's imaginative structure. Yet they somehow built it up and made it solid; the outline in his mind began to stand foursquare. That writing, those designs, the manner of the man, their going out together, the final curious look—each and all betrayed points of a hidden thing. Subconsciously he was excavating their buried purposes. The sand was shifting. The concentration of his mind incessantly upon them removed it grain by grain and speck by speck. Tips of the smothered thing emerged. Presently a subsidence would follow with a rush and light would blaze upon its skeleton. He felt it stirring underneath his feet—this flowing movement of light, dry, heaped-up sand. It was always—sand.

Then other incidents of a similar kind came about, clearing the way to a natural acquaintanceship. Henriot watched the process with amusement, yet with another feeling too that was only a little less than anxiety. A keen observer, no detail escaped him; he saw the forces of their lives draw closer. It made him think of the devices of young people who desire to know one another, yet cannot get a proper introduction. Fate condescended to such little tricks. They wanted a third person, he began to feel. A third was necessary to some plan they had on hand, and—they waited to see if he could fill the place. The woman, with whom he had yet exchanged no single word, seemed so familiar to him, well known for years. They weighed and watched him, wondering what he would do.

None of the devices were too obviously used, but at length Henriot picked up so many forgotten articles, and heard so many significant phrases, casually let fall, that he began to feel like the villain in a machine-made play, where the hero for ever drops clues his enemy is intended to discover.

Introduction followed inevitably. "My aunt can tell you; she knows Arabic perfectly." He had been discussing the meaning of some local name or other with a neighbour after dinner, and Vance had joined them. The neighbour moved away; these two were left standing alone, and he accepted a cigarette from the other's case. There was a rustle of skirts behind them. "Here she comes," said Vance; "you will let me introduce you." He did not ask for Henriot's name; he had already taken the trouble to find it out—another little betrayal, and another clue.

It was in a secluded corner of the great hall, and Henriot turned to see the woman's stately figure coming towards them across the thick carpet that deadened her footsteps. She came sailing up, her black eyes fixed upon his face. Very erect, head upright, shoulders almost squared, she moved wonderfully well; there was dignity and power in her walk. She was dressed in black, and her face was like the night. He found it impossible to say what lent her this air of impressiveness and solemnity that was almost majestic. But there *was* this touch of darkness and of power in the way she came that made him think of some sphinx-like figure of stone, some idol motionless in all its parts but moving as a whole, and gliding across—sand. Beneath those level lids her eyes stared hard at him. And a faint sensation of distress stirred in him deep, deep down. Where had he seen those eyes before?

He bowed, as she joined them, and Vance led the way to the armchairs in a corner of the lounge. The meeting, as the talk that followed, he felt, were all part of a preconceived plan. It had happened before. The woman, that is, was familiar to him—to some part of his being that had dropped stitches of old, old memory.

Lady Statham! At first the name had disappointed him. So many folk wear titles, as syllables in certain tongues wear accents—without them being mute, unnoticed, unpronounced. Nonentities, born to names, so often claim attention for their insignificance in this way. But this woman, had she been Jemima Jones, would have made the name distinguished and select. She was a big and sombre personality. Why was it, he wondered afterwards, that for a moment something in him shrank, and that his mind, metaphorically speaking, flung up an arm in self-protection? The instinct flashed and passed. But it seemed to him born of an automatic feeling that he most protect—not himself, but the woman from the man. There was confusion in it all; links were missing. He studied her intently. She was a woman who had none of the external feminine signals in either dress or manner, no graces, no little womanly hesitations and alarms, no daintiness, yet neither anything distinctly masculine. Her charm was strong, possessing; only he kept forgetting that he was talking to a—woman; and the thing she inspired in him included, with respect and wonder, somewhere also this curious hint of dread. This instinct to protect her fled as soon as it was born, for the interest of the conversation in which she so quickly plunged him obliterated all minor emotions whatsoever. Here, for the first time, he drew close to Egypt, the Egypt he had sought so long. It was not to be explained. He *felt* it.

Beginning with commonplaces, such as "You like Egypt? You find here what you expected?" she led him into better regions with "One finds here what one brings." He knew the delightful experience of talking fluently on subjects he was at home in, and to some one who understood. The feeling at first that to this woman he could not say mere anythings, slipped into its opposite—that he could say everything. Strangers ten minutes ago, they were at once in deep and intimate talk together. He found his ideas readily followed, agreed with up to a point—the point which permits discussion to start from a basis of general accord towards speculation. In the excitement of ideas he neglected the uncomfortable note that had stirred his caution, forgot the warning too. Her mind, moreover, seemed known to him; he was often aware of what she was going to say before he actually heard it; the current of her thoughts struck a familiar gait, and more than once he experienced vividly again the odd sensation that it had all happened before. The very sentences and phrases with which she pointed the turns of her unusual ideas were never wholly unexpected.

For her ideas were decidedly unusual, in the sense that she accepted without question speculations not commonly deemed worth consideration at all, indeed not ordinarily even known. Henriot knew them, because he had read in many fields. It was the strength of her belief that fascinated him. She offered no apologies. She knew. And while he talked, she listening with folded arms and her black eyes fixed upon his own, Richard Vance watched with vigilant eyes and listened too, ceaselessly alert. Vance joined in little enough, however, gave no opinions, his attitude one of general acquiescence. Twice, when pauses of slackening interest made it possible, Henriot fancied he surprised another quality in this negative attitude. Interpreting it each time differently, he yet dismissed both interpretations with a smile. His imagination leaped so absurdly to violent conclusions. They were not tenable: Vance was neither her keeper, nor was he in some fashion a detective. Yet in his manner was sometimes this suggestion of the detective order. He watched with such deep attention, and he concealed it so clumsily with an affectation of careless indifference.

There is nothing more dangerous than that impulsive intimacy strangers sometimes adopt when an atmosphere of mutual sympathy takes them by surprise, for it is akin to the false frankness friends affect when telling "candidly" one another's faults. The mood is invariably regretted later. Henriot, however, yielded to it now with something like abandon. The pleasure of talking with this woman was so unexpected, and so keen.

For Lady Statham believed apparently in some Egypt of her dreams. Her interest was neither historical, archaeological, nor political. It was religious—yet hardly of this earth at all. The conversation turned upon the knowledge of the ancient Egyptians from an unearthly point of view, and even while he talked he was vaguely aware that it was *her* mind talking through his own. She drew out his ideas and made him say them. But this he was properly aware of only afterwards—that she had cleverly, mercilessly pumped him of all he had ever known or read upon the subject. Moreover, what Vance watched so intently was himself, and the reactions in himself this remarkable woman produced. That also he realised later.

His first impression that these two belonged to what may be called the "crank" order was justified by the conversation. But, at least, it was interesting crankiness, and the belief behind it made it even fascinating. Long before the end he surprised in her a more vital form of his own attitude that anything *may* be true, since knowledge has never yet found final answers to any of the biggest questions.

He understood, from sentences dropped early in the talk, that she was among those few "superstitious" folk who think that the old Egyptians came closer to reading the eternal riddles of the world than any others, and that their knowledge was a remnant of that ancient Wisdom Religion which existed in the superb, dark civilisation of the sunken Atlantis, lost continent that once joined Africa to Mexico. Eighty thousand years ago the dim sands of Poseidonis, great island adjoining the main continent which itself had vanished a vast period before, sank down beneath the waves, and the entire known world to-day was descended from its survivors. Hence the significant fact that all religions and "mythological" systems begin with a story of a flood—some cataclysmic upheaval that destroyed the world. Egypt itself was colonised by a group of Atlantean priests who brought their curious, deep knowledge with them. They had foreseen the cataclysm.

Lady Statham talked well, bringing into her great dream this strong, insistent quality of belief and fact. She knew, from Plato to

Donnelly, that all the minds of men have ever speculated upon the gorgeous legend. The evidence for such a sunken continent—Henriot had skimmed it too in years gone by—she made bewilderingly complete. He had heard Baconians demolish Shakespeare with an array of evidence equally overwhelming. It catches the imagination though not the mind. Yet out of her facts, as she presented them, grew a strange likelihood. The force of this woman's personality, and her calm and quiet way of believing all she talked about, took her listener to some extent—further than ever before, certainly—into the great dream after her. And the dream, to say the least, was a picturesque one, laden with wonderful possibilities. For as she talked the spirit of old Egypt moved up, staring down upon him out of eyes lidded so curiously level. Hitherto all had prated to him of the Arabs, their ancient faith and customs, and the splendour of the Bedouins, those Princes of the Desert. But what he sought, barely confessed in words even to himself, was something older far than this. And this strange, dark woman brought it close. Deeps in his soul, long slumbering, awoke. He heard forgotten questions.

Only in this brief way could he attempt to sum up the storm she roused in him.

She carried him far beyond mere outline, however, though afterwards he recalled the details with difficulty. So much more was suggested than actually expressed. She contrived to make the general modern scepticism an evidence of cheap mentality. It was so easy; the depth it affects to conceal, mere emptiness. "We have tried all things, and found all wanting"—the mind, as measuring instrument, merely confessed inadequate. Various shrewd judgments of this kind increased his respect, although her acceptance went so far beyond his own. And, while the label of credulity refused to stick to her, her sense of imaginative wonder enabled her to escape that dreadful compromise, a man's mind in a woman's temperament. She fascinated him.

The spiritual worship of the ancient Egyptians, she held, was a symbolical explanation of things generally alluded to as the secrets of life and death; their knowledge was a remnant of the wisdom of Atlantis. Material relics, equally misunderstood, still stood to-day at Karnac, Stonehenge, and in the mysterious writings on buried Mexican temples and cities, so significantly akin to the hieroglyphics upon the Egyptian tombs.

"The one misinterpreted as literally as the other," she suggested, "yet both fragments of an advanced knowledge that found its grave in the sea. The Wisdom of that old spiritual system has vanished from the world, only a degraded literalism left of its undecipherable language. The jewel has been lost, and the casket is filled with sand, sand, sand."

How keenly her black eyes searched his own as she said it, and how oddly she made the little word resound. The syllable drew out almost into chanting. Echoes answered from the depths within him, carrying it on and on across some desert of forgotten belief. Veils of sand flew everywhere about his mind. Curtains lifted. Whole hills of sand went shifting into level surfaces whence gardens of dim outline emerged to meet the sunlight.

"But the sand may be removed." It was her nephew, speaking almost for the first time, and the interruption had an odd effect, introducing a sharply practical element. For the tone expressed, so far as he dared express it, disapproval. It was a baited observation, an invitation to opinion.

"We are not sand-diggers, Mr. Henriot," put in Lady Statham, before he decided to respond. "Our object is quite another one; and I believe—I have a feeling," she added almost questioningly, "that you might be interested enough to help us perhaps."

He only wondered the direct attack had not come sooner. Its bluntness hardly surprised him. He felt himself leap forward to accept it. A sudden subsidence had freed his feet.

Then the warning operated suddenly—for an instant. Henriot *was* interested; more, he was half seduced; but, as yet, he did not mean to be included in their purposes, whatever these might be. That shrinking dread came back a moment, and was gone again before he could question it. His eyes looked full at Lady Statham. "What is it that you know?" they asked her. "Tell me the things we once knew together, you and I. These words are merely trifling. And why does another man now stand in my place? For the sands heaped upon my memory are shifting, and it is *you* who are moving them away."

His soul whispered it; his voice said quite another thing, although the words he used seemed oddly chosen:

"There is much in the ideas of ancient Egypt that has attracted me ever since I can remember, though I have never caught up with anything definite enough to follow. There was majesty somewhere in their conceptions—a large, calm majesty of spiritual dominion, one might call it perhaps. I *am* interested."

Her face remained expressionless as she listened, but there was grave conviction in the eyes that held him like a spell. He saw through them into dim, faint pictures whose background was always sand. He forgot that he was speaking with a woman, a woman who half an hour ago had been a stranger to him. He followed these faded mental pictures, though he never caught them up. . . . It was like his dream in London.

Lady Statham was talking—he had not noticed the means by which she effected the abrupt transition—of familiar beliefs of old Egypt; of the Ka, or Double, by whose existence the survival of the soul was possible, even its return into manifested, physical life; of the astrology, or influence of the heavenly bodies upon all sublunar activities; of terrific forms of other life, known to the ancient worship of Atlantis, the great Potencies that might be invoked by ritual and ceremonial, and of their lesser influence as recognised in certain lower forms, hence treated with veneration as the "Sacred Animal" branch of this dim religion. And she spoke lightly of the modern learning which so glibly imagined it was the animals themselves that were looked upon as "gods"—the bull, the bird, the crocodile, the cat. "It's there they all go so absurdly wrong," she said, "taking the symbol for the power symbolised. Yet natural enough. The mind to-day wears blinkers, studies only the details seen directly before it. Had none of us experienced love, we should think the first lover mad. Few to-day know the Powers *they* knew, hence deny them. If the world were deaf it would stand with mockery before a staring group swayed by an orchestra, pitying both listeners and performers. It would deem our admiration of a great swinging bell mere foolish worship of form and movement. Similarly, with high Powers that once expressed themselves in common forms—where best they could—being themselves bodiless. The learned men classify the forms with painstaking detail. But deity has gone out of life. The Powers symbolised are no longer experienced."

"These Powers, you suggest, then—their Kas, as it were—may still—"

But she waved aside the interruption. "They are satisfied, as the common people were, with a degraded literalism," she went on. "Nut was the heavens, who spread herself across the earth in the form of a woman; Shu, the vastness of space; the ibis typified Thoth, and Hathor was the Patron of the Western Hills; Khonsu, the moon, was personified, as was the deity of the Nile. But the high priest of Ra, the sun, you notice, remained ever the Great One of Visions."

The High Priest, the Great One of Visions!—How wonderfully again she made the sentence sing. She put splendour into it. The pictures shifted suddenly closer in his mind. He saw the grandeur of Memphis and Heliopolis rise against the stars and shake the sand of ages from their stern old temples.

"You think it possible, then, to get into touch with these High Powers you speak of, Powers once manifested in common forms?"

Henriot asked the question with a degree of conviction and solemnity that surprised himself. The scenery changed about him as he listened. The spacious halls of this former khedivial Palace melted into Desert spaces. He smelt the open wilderness, the sand that haunted Helouan. The soft-footed Arab servants moved across the hall in their white sheets like eddies of dust the wind stirred from the Libyan dunes. And over these two strangers close beside him stole a queer, indefinite alteration. Moods and emotions, nameless as unknown stars, rose through his soul, trailing dark mists of memory from unfathomable distances.

Lady Statham answered him indirectly. He found himself wishing that those steady eyes would sometimes close.

"Love is known only by feeling it," she said, her voice deepening a little. "Behind the form you feel the person loved. The process is an evocation, pure and simple. An arduous ceremonial, involving worship and devotional preparation, is the means. It is a difficult ritual—the only one acknowledged by the world as still effectual. Ritual is the passage way of the soul into the Infinite."

He might have said the words himself. The thought lay in him while she uttered it. Evocation everywhere in life was as true as assimilation. Nevertheless, he stared his companion full in the eyes with a touch of almost rude amazement. But no further questions prompted themselves; or, rather, he declined to ask them. He recalled, somehow uneasily, that in ceremonial the points of the compass have significance, standing for forces and activities that sleep there until invoked, and a passing light fell upon that curious midnight request in the corridor upstairs. These two were on the track of undesirable experiments, he thought. . . . They wished to include him too.

"You go at night sometimes into the Desert?" he heard himself saying. It was impulsive and miscalculated. His feeling that it would be wise to change the conversation resulted in giving it fresh impetus instead.

"We saw you there—in the Wadi Hof," put in Vance, suddenly breaking his long silence; "you too sleep out, then? It means, you know, the Valley of Fear."

"We wondered—" It was Lady Statham's voice, and she leaned forward eagerly as she said it, then abruptly left the sentence incomplete. Henriot started; a sense of momentary acute discomfort again ran over him. The same second she continued, though obviously changing the phrase—"we wondered how you spent your day there, during the heat. But you paint, don't you? You draw, I mean?"

The commonplace question, he realised in every fibre of his being, meant something *they* deemed significant. Was it his talent for drawing that they sought to use him for? Even as he answered with a simple affirmative, he had a flash of intuition that might be fanciful, yet that might be true: that this extraordinary pair were intent upon some ceremony of evocation that should summon into actual physical expression some Power—some type of life—known long ago to ancient worship, and that they even sought to fix its bodily outline with the pencil—his pencil.

A gateway of incredible adventure opened at his feet. He balanced on the edge of knowing unutterable things. Here was a clue that might lead him towards the hidden Egypt he had ever craved to know. An awful hand was beckoning. The sands were shifting. He saw the million eyes of the Desert watching him from beneath the level lids of centuries. Speck by speck, and grain by grain, the sand that smothered memory lifted the countless wrappings that embalmed it.

And he was willing, yet afraid. Why in the world did he hesitate and shrink? Why was it that the presence of this silent, watching personality in the chair beside him kept caution still alive, with warning close behind? The pictures in his mind were gorgeously coloured. It was Richard Vance who somehow streaked them through with black. A thing of darkness, born of this man's unassertive presence, flitted ever across the scenery, marring its grandeur with something evil, petty, dreadful. He held a horrible thought alive. His mind was thinking venal purposes.

In Henriot himself imagination had grown curiously heated, fed by what had been suggested rather than actually said. Ideas of immensity crowded his brain, yet never assumed definite shape. They were familiar, even as this strange woman was familiar. Once, long ago, he had known them well; had even practised them beneath these bright Egyptian stars. Whence came this prodigious glad excitement in his heart, this sense of mighty Powers coaxed down to influence the very details of daily life? Behind them, for all their vagueness, lay an archetypal splendour, fraught with forgotten meanings. He had always been aware of it in this mysterious land, but it had ever hitherto eluded him. It hovered everywhere. He had felt it brooding behind the towering Colossi at Thebes, in the skeletons of wasted temples, in the uncouth comeliness of the Sphinx, and in the crude terror of the Pyramids even. Over the whole of Egypt hung its invisible wings. These were but isolated fragments of the Body that might express it. And the Desert remained its cleanest, truest symbol. Sand knew it closest. Sand might even give it bodily form and outline.

But, while it escaped description in his mind, as equally it eluded visualisation in his soul, he felt that it combined with its vastness something infinitely small as well. Of such wee particles is the giant Desert born. . . .

Henriot started nervously in his chair, convicted once more of unconscionable staring; and at the same moment a group of hotel people, returning from a dance, passed through the hall and nodded him goodnight. The scent of the women reached him; and with it the sound of their voices discussing personalities just left behind. A London atmosphere came with them. He caught trivial phrases, uttered in a drawling tone, and followed by the shrill laughter of a girl. They passed upstairs, discussing their little things, like marionettes upon a tiny stage.

But their passage brought him back to things of modern life, and to some standard of familiar measurement. The pictures that his soul had gazed at so deep within, he realised, were a pictorial transfer caught incompletely from this woman's vivid mind. He had seen the Desert as the grey, enormous Tomb where hovered still the Ka of ancient Egypt. Sand screened her visage with the veil of centuries. But She was there, and She was living. Egypt herself had pitched a temporary camp in him, and then moved on.

There was a momentary break, a sense of abruptness and dislocation. And then he became aware that Lady Statham had been speaking for some time before he caught her actual words, and that a certain change had come into her voice as also into her manner.

V

She was leaning closer to him, her face suddenly glowing and alive. Through the stone figure coursed the fires of a passion that deepened the coal-black eyes and communicated a hint of light—of exaltation—to her whole person. It was incredibly moving. To this deep passion was due the power he had felt. It was her entire life; she lived for it, she would die for it. Her calmness of manner enhanced the effect. Hence the strength of those first impressions that had stormed him. The woman had belief; however wild and strange, it was sacred to her. The secret of her influence was—conviction.

His attitude shifted several points then. The wonder in him passed over into awe. The things she knew were real. They were not merely imaginative speculations.

"I knew I was not wrong in thinking you in sympathy with this line of thought," she was saying in lower voice, steady with earnestness, and as though she had read his mind. "You, too, know, though perhaps you hardly realise that you know. It lies so deep in you that you only get vague feelings of it—intimations of memory. Isn't that the case?"

Henriot gave assent with his eyes; it was the truth.

"What we know instinctively," she continued, "is simply what we are trying to remember. Knowledge is memory." She paused a moment watching his face closely. "At least, you are free from that cheap scepticism which labels these old beliefs as superstition." It was not even a question.

"I—worship real belief—of any kind," he stammered, for her words and the close proximity of her atmosphere caused a strange up-heaval in his heart that he could not account for. He faltered in his speech. "It is the most vital quality in life—rarer than deity." He was using her own phrases even. "It is creative. It constructs the world anew—"

"And may reconstruct the old."

She said it, lifting her face above him a little, so that her eyes looked down into his own. It grew big and somehow masculine. It was the face of a priest, spiritual power in it. Where, oh where in the echo-ing Past had he known this woman's soul? He saw her in another set-ting, a forest of columns dim about her, towering above giant aisles. Again he felt the Desert had come close. Into this tent-like hall of the hotel came the sifting of tiny sand. It heaped softly about the very fur-niture against his feet, blocking the exits of door and window. It shrouded the little present. The wind that brought it stirred a veil that had hung for ages motionless. . . .

She had been saying many things that he had missed while his mind went searching. "There were types of life the Atlantean system knew it might revive—life unmanifested to-day in any bodily form," was the sentence he caught with his return to the actual present.

"A type of life?" he whispered, looking about him, as though to see who it was had joined them; "you mean a—soul? Some kind of soul, alien to humanity, or to—to any forms of living thing in the world to-day?" What she had been saying reached him somehow, it seemed, though he had not heard the words themselves. Still hesitat-ing, he was yet so eager to hear. Already he felt she meant to include him in her purposes, and that in the end he must go willingly. So strong was her persuasion on his mind.

And he felt as if he knew vaguely what was coming. Before she an-swered his curious question—prompting it indeed—rose in his mind that strange idea of the Group-Soul: the theory that big souls cannot express themselves in a single individual, but need an entire group for their full manifestation.

He listened intently. The reflection that this sudden intimacy was unnatural, he rejected, for many conversations were really gathered in-to one. Long watching and preparation on both sides had cleared the way for the ripening of acquaintance into confidence—how long he dimly wondered? But if this conception of the Group-Soul was not new, the suggestion Lady Statham developed out of it was both new and startling—and yet always so curiously familiar. Its value for him lay, not in far-fetched evidence that supported it, but in the deep belief which made it a vital asset in an honest inner life.

"An individual," she said quietly, "one soul expressed completely in a single person, I mean, is exceedingly rare. Not often is a physical instrument found perfect enough to provide it with adequate expression. In the lower ranges of humanity—certainly in animal and insect life—one soul is shared by many. Behind a tribe of savages stands one Savage. A flock of birds is a single Bird, scattered through the consciousness of all. They wheel in mid-air, they migrate, they obey the deep intelligence called instinct—all as one. The life of any one lion is the life of all—the lion group-soul that manifests itself in the entire genus. An ant-heap is a single Ant; through the bees spreads the consciousness of a single Bee."

Henriot knew what she was working up to. In his eagerness to hasten disclosure he interrupted—

"And there may be types of life that have no corresponding bodily expression at all, then?" he asked as though the question were forced out of him. "They exist as Powers—unmanifested on the earth to-day?"

"Powers," she answered, watching him closely with unswerving stare, "that need a group to provide their body—their physical expression—if they came back."

"Came back!" he repeated below his breath.

But she heard him. "They once had expression. Egypt, Atlantis knew them—spiritual Powers that never visit the world to-day."

"Bodies," he whispered softly, "actual bodies?"

"Their sphere of action, you see, would be their body. And it might be physical outline. So potent a descent of spiritual life would select materials for its body where it could find them. Our conventional notion of a body—what is it? A single outline moving altogether in one direction. For little human souls, or fragments, this is sufficient. But for vaster types of soul an entire host would be required."

"A church?" he ventured. "Some Body of belief, you surely mean?"

She bowed her head a moment in assent. She was determined he should seize her meaning fully.

"A wave of spiritual awakening—a descent of spiritual life upon a nation," she answered slowly, "forms itself a church, and the body of true believers are its sphere of action. They are literally its bodily expression. Each individual believer is a corpuscle in that Body. The Power has provided itself with a vehicle of manifestation. Otherwise we could not know it. And the more real the belief of each individual, the more perfect the expression of the spiritual life behind them all. A Group-Soul walks the earth. Moreover, a nation naturally devout could attract a type of soul unknown to a nation that denies all faith. Faith brings back the gods. . . . But to-day belief is dead, and Deity has left the world."

She talked on and on, developing this main idea that in days of older faiths there were deific types of life upon the earth, evoked by worship and beneficial to humanity. They had long ago withdrawn because the worship which brought them down had died the death. The world had grown pettier. These vast centres of Spiritual Power found no "Body" in which they now could express themselves or manifest. . . . Her thoughts and phrases poured over him like sand. It was always sand he felt—burying the Present and uncovering the Past. . . .

He tried to steady his mind upon familiar objects, but wherever he looked Sand stared him in the face. Outside these trivial walls the Desert lay listening. It lay waiting too. Vance himself had dropped out of recognition. He belonged to the world of things to-day. But this woman and himself stood thousands of years away, beneath the columns of a Temple in the sands. And the sands were moving. His feet went shifting with them . . . running down vistas of ageless memory that woke terror by their sheer immensity of distance. . . .

Like a muffled voice that called to him through many veils and wrappings, he heard her describe the stupendous Powers that evocation might coax down again among the world of men.

"To what useful end?" he asked at length, amazed at his own temerity, and because he knew instinctively the answer in advance. It rose through these layers of coiling memory in his soul.

"The extension of spiritual knowledge and the widening of life," she answered. "The link with the 'unearthly kingdom' wherein this ancient system went for ever searching, would be re-established. Complete rehabilitation might follow. Portions—little portions of these Powers—expressed themselves naturally once in certain animal types, instinctive life that did not deny or reject them. The worship of sacred animals was the relic of a once gigantic system of evocation—not of monsters," and she smiled sadly, "but of Powers that were willing and ready to descend when worship summoned them."

Again, beneath his breath, Henriot heard himself murmur—his own voice startled him as he whispered it: "Actual bodily shape and outline?"

"Material for bodies is everywhere," she answered, equally low; "dust to which we all return; sand, if you prefer it, fine, fine sand. Life moulds it easily enough, when that life is potent."

A certain confusion spread slowly through his mind as he heard her. He lit a cigarette and smoked some minutes in silence. Lady Statham and her nephew waited for him to speak. At length, after some inner battling and hesitation, he put the question that he knew they waited for. It was impossible to resist any longer.

"It would be interesting to know the method," he said, "and to revive, perhaps, by experiment—"

Before he could complete his thought, she took him up:

"There are some who claim to know it," she said gravely—her eyes a moment masterful. "A clue, thus followed, might lead to the entire reconstruction I spoke of."

"And the method?" he repeated faintly.

"Evoke the Power by ceremonial evocation—the ritual is obtainable—and note the form it assumes. Then establish it. This shape or outline once secured, could then be made permanent—a mould for its return at will—its natural physical expression here on earth."

"Idol!" he exclaimed.

"Image," she replied at once. "Life, before we can know it, must have a body. Our souls, in order to manifest here, need a material vehicle."

"And—to obtain this form or outline?" he began; "to fix it, rather?"

"Would be required the clever pencil of a fearless looker-on—some one not engaged in the actual evocation. This form, accurately made permanent in solid matter, say in stone, would provide a channel always open. Experiment, properly speaking, might then begin. The cisterns of Power behind would be accessible."

"An amazing proposition!" Henriot exclaimed. What surprised him was that he felt no desire to laugh, and little even to doubt.

"Yet known to every religion that ever deserved the name," put in Vance like a voice from a distance. Blackness came somehow with his interruption—a touch of darkness. He spoke eagerly.

To all the talk that followed, and there was much of it, Henriot listened with but half an ear. This one idea stormed through him with an uproar that killed attention. Judgment was held utterly in abeyance. He carried away from it some vague suggestion that this woman had hinted at previous lives she half remembered, and that every year she came to Egypt, haunting the sands and temples in the effort to recover lost clues. And he recalled afterwards that she said, "This all came to me as a child, just as though it was something half remembered." There was the further suggestion that he himself was not unknown to her; that they, too, had met before. But this, compared to the grave certainty of the rest, was merest fantasy that did not hold his attention. He answered, hardly knowing what he said. His preoccupation with other thoughts deep down was so intense, that he was probably barely polite, uttering empty phrases, with his mind elsewhere. His one desire was to escape and be alone, and it was with genuine relief that he presently excused himself and went upstairs to bed. The halls, he noticed, were empty; an Arab servant waited to put the lights out. He walked up, for the lift had long ceased running.

And the magic of old Egypt stalked beside him. The studies that had fascinated his mind in earlier youth returned with the power that had subdued his mind in boyhood. The cult of Osiris woke in his blood again; Horus and Nephthys stirred in their long-forgotten centres. There revived in him, too long buried, the awful glamour of those liturgal rites and vast body of observances, those spells and formulae of incantation of the oldest known recension that years ago had captured his imagination and belief—the Book of the Dead. Trumpet voices called to his heart again across the desert of some dim past. There were forms of life—impulses from the Creative Power which is the Universe—other than the soul of man. They could be known. A spiritual exaltation, roused by the words and presence of this singular woman, shouted to him as he went.

Then, as he closed his bedroom door, carefully locking it, there stood beside him—Vance. The forgotten figure of Vance came up close—the watching eyes, the simulated interest, the feigned belief, the detective mental attitude, these broke through the grandiose panorama, bringing darkness. Vance, strong personality that hid behind assumed nonentity for some purpose of his own, intruded with sudden violence, demanding an explanation of his presence.

And, with an equal suddenness, explanation offered itself then and there. It came unsought, its horror of certainty utterly unjustified; and it came in this unexpected fashion:

Behind the interest and acquiescence of the man ran—fear: but behind the vivid fear ran another thing that Henriot now perceived was vile. For the first time in his life, Henriot knew it at close quarters, actual, ready to operate. Though familiar enough in daily life to be of common occurrence, Henriot had never realised it as he did now, so close and terrible. In the same way he had never *realised* that he would die—vanish from the busy world of men and women, forgotten as though he had never existed, an eddy of wind-blown dust. And in the man named Richard Vance this thing was close upon blossom. Henriot could not name it to himself. Even in thought it appalled him.

He undressed hurriedly, almost with the child's idea of finding safety between the sheets. His mind undressed itself as well. The business of the day laid itself automatically aside; the will sank down; desire grew inactive. Henriot was exhausted. But, in that stage towards slumber when thinking stops, and only fugitive pictures pass across the mind in shadowy dance, his brain ceased shouting its mechanical explanations, and his soul unveiled a peering eye. Great limbs of memory, smothered by the activities of the Present, stirred their stiffened lengths through the sands of long ago—sands this woman had begun to excavate from some far-off pre-existence they had surely known together. Vagueness and certainty ran hand in hand. Details were unrecoverable, but the emotions in which they were embedded moved.

He turned restlessly in his bed, striving to seize the amazing clues and follow them. But deliberate effort hid them instantly again; they retired instantly into the subconsciousness. With the brain of this body he now occupied they had nothing to do. The brain stored memories of each life only. This ancient script was graven in his soul. Subconsciousness alone could interpret and reveal. And it was his subconscious memory that Lady Statham had been so busily excavating.

Dimly it stirred and moved about the depths within him, never clearly seen, indefinite, felt as a yearning after unrecoverable knowledge. Against the darker background of Vance's fear and sinister purpose—both of this present life, and recent—he saw the grandeur of this woman's impossible dream, and *knew,* beyond argument or reason, that it was true. Judgment and will asleep, he left the impossibility aside, and took the grandeur. The Belief of Lady Statham was not credulity and superstition; it was Memory. Still to this day, over the sands of Egypt, hovered immense spiritual potencies, so vast that they could only know physical expression in a group—in many. Their sphere of bodily manifestation must be a host, each individual unit in that host a corpuscle in the whole.

The wind, rising from the Lybian wastes across the Nile, swept up against the exposed side of the hotel, and made his windows rattle—the old, sad winds of Egypt. Henriot got out of bed to fasten the outside shutters. He stood a moment and watched the moon floating down behind the Sakkara Pyramids. The Pleiades and Orion's Belt hung brilliantly; the Great Bear was close to the horizon. In the sky above the Desert swung ten thousand stars. No sounds rose from the streets of Helouan. The tide of sand was coming slowly in.

And a flock of enormous thoughts swooped past him from fields of this unbelievable, lost memory. The Desert, pale in the moon, was coextensive with the night, too huge for comfort or understanding, yet charged to the brim with infinite peace. Behind its majesty of silence lay whispers of a vanished language that once could call with power upon mighty spiritual Agencies. Its skirts were folded now, but, slowly across the leagues of sand, they began to stir and rearrange themselves. He grew suddenly aware of this enveloping shroud of sand—as the raw material of bodily expression: Form.

The sand was in his imagination and his mind. Shaking loosely the folds of its gigantic skirts, it rose; it moved a little towards him. He saw the eternal countenance of the Desert watching him—immobile and unchanging behind these shifting veils the winds laid so carefully over it.

Egypt, the ancient Egypt, turned in her vast sarcophagus of Desert, wakening from her sleep of ages at the Belief of approaching worshippers.

Only in this insignificant manner could he express a letter of the terrific language that crowded to seek expression through his soul. . . . He closed the shutters and carefully fastened them. He turned to go back to bed, curiously trembling. Then, as he did so, the whole singular delusion caught him with a shock that held him motionless. Up rose the stupendous apparition of the entire Desert and stood behind him on that balcony. Swift as thought, in silence, the Desert stood on end against his very face. It towered across the sky, hiding Orion and the moon; it dipped below the horizons. The whole grey sheet of it rose up before his eyes and stood. Through its unfolding skirts ran ten thousand eddies of swirling sand as the creases of its grave-clothes smoothed themselves out in moonlight. And a bleak, scarred countenance, huge as a planet, gazed down into his own. . . .

Through his dreamless sleep that night two things lay active and awake . . . in the subconscious part that knows no slumber. They were incongruous. One was evil, small, and human; the other unearthly and sublime. For the memory of the fear that haunted Vance, and the sinister cause of it, pricked at him all night long. But behind, beyond this common, intelligible emotion, lay the crowding wonder that caught his soul with glory:

The Sand was stirring, the Desert was awake. Ready to mate with them in material form, brooded close the Ka of that colossal Entity that once expressed itself through the myriad life of ancient Egypt.

VI

Next day, and for several days following, Henriot kept out of the path of Lady Statham and her nephew. The acquaintanceship had grown too rapidly to be quite comfortable. It was easy to pretend that he took people at their face value, but it was a pose; one liked to know something of antecedents. It was otherwise difficult to "place" them. And Henriot, for the life of him, could not "place" these two. His Subconsciousness brought explanation when it came—but the Subconsciousness is only temporarily active. When it retired he floundered without a rudder, in confusion.

With the flood of morning sunshine the value of much she had said evaporated. Her presence alone had supplied the key to the cipher. But while the indigestible portions he rejected, there remained a good deal he had already assimilated. The discomfort remained; and with it the grave, unholy reality of it all. It was something more than theory. Results would follow—if he joined them. He would witness curious things.

The force with which it drew him brought hesitation. It operated in him like a shock that numbs at first by its abrupt arrival, and needs time to realise in the right proportions to the rest of life. These right proportions, however, did not come readily, and his emotions ranged between sceptical laughter and complete acceptance. The one detail he felt certain of was this dreadful thing he had divined in Vance. Trying hard to disbelieve it, he found he could not. It was true. Though without a shred of real evidence to support it, the horror of it remained. He knew it in his very bones.

And this, perhaps, was what drove him to seek the comforting companionship of folk he understood and felt at home with. He told his host and hostess about the strangers, though omitting the actual conversation because they would merely smile in blank miscomprehension. But the moment he described the strong black eyes beneath the level eyelids, his hostess turned with a start, her interest deeply roused: "Why, it's that awful Statham woman," she exclaimed, "that must be Lady Statham, and the man she calls her nephew."

"Sounds like it, certainly," her husband added. "Felix, you'd better clear out. They'll bewitch you too."

And Henriot bridled, yet wondering why he did so. He drew into his shell a little, giving the merest sketch of what had happened. But he listened closely while these two practical old friends supplied him with information in the gossiping way that human nature loves. No doubt there was much embroidery, and more perversion, exaggeration too, but the account evidently rested upon some basis of solid foundation for all that. Smoke and fire go together always.

"He *is* her nephew right enough," Mansfield corrected his wife, before proceeding to his own man's form of elaboration; "no question about that, I believe. He's her favourite nephew, and she's as rich as a pig. He follows her out here every year, waiting for her empty shoes. But they *are* an unsavoury couple. I've met 'em in various parts, all over Egypt, but they always come back to Helouan in the end. And the stories about them are simply legion. You remember—" he turned hesitatingly to his wife—"some people, I heard," he changed his sentence, "were made quite ill by her."

"I'm sure Felix ought to know, yes," his wife boldly took him up, "my niece, Fanny, had the most extraordinary experience." She turned to Henriot. "Her room was next to Lady Statham in some hotel or other at Assouan or Edfu, and one night she woke and heard a kind of mysterious chanting or intoning next her. Hotel doors are so dreadfully thin. There was a funny smell too, like incense of something sickly, and a man's voice kept chiming in. It went on for hours, while she lay terrified in bed—"

"Frightened, you say?" asked Henriot.

"Out of her skin, yes; she said it was so uncanny—made her feel icy. She wanted to ring the bell, but was afraid to leave her bed. The room was full of—of things, yet she could see nothing. She *felt* them, you see. And after a bit the sound of this sing-song voice so got on her nerves, it half dazed her—a kind of enchantment—she felt choked and suffocated. And then—" It was her turn to hesitate.

"Tell it all," her husband said, quite gravely too.

"Well—something came in. At least, she describes it oddly, rather; she said it made the door bulge inwards from the next room, but not the door alone; the walls bulged or swayed as if a huge thing pressed against them from the other side. And at the same moment her windows—she had two big balconies, and the venetian shutters were fastened—both her windows *darkened*—though it was two in the morning and pitch dark outside. She said it was all *one* thing—trying to get in; just as water, you see, would rush in through every hole and opening it could find, and all at once. And in spite of her terror—that's the odd part of it—she says she felt a kind of splendour in her—a sort of elation."

"She saw nothing?"

"She says she doesn't remember. Her senses left her, I believe—though she won't admit it."

"Fainted for a minute, probably," said Mansfield.

"So there it is," his wife concluded, after a silence. "And that's true. It happened to my niece, didn't it, John?"

Stories and legendary accounts of strange things that the presence of these two brought poured out then. They were obviously somewhat mixed, one account borrowing picturesque details from another, and all in disproportion, as when people tell stories in a language they are little familiar with. But, listening with avidity, yet also with uneasiness, somehow, Henriot put two and two together. Truth stood behind them somewhere. These two held traffic with the powers that ancient Egypt knew.

"Tell Felix, dear, about the time you met the nephew—horrid creature—in the Valley of the Kings," he heard his wife say presently. And Mansfield told it plainly enough, evidently glad to get it done, though.

"It was some years ago now, and I didn't know who he was then, or anything about him. I don't know much more now—except that he's a dangerous sort of charlatan-devil, *I* think. But I came across him one night up there by Thebes in the Valley of the Kings—you know, where they buried all their Johnnies with so much magnificence and processions and masses, and all the rest. It's the most astounding, the most haunted place you ever saw, gloomy, silent, full of gorgeous lights and shadows that seem alive—terribly impressive; it makes you creep and shudder. You feel old Egypt watching you."

"Get on, dear," said his wife.

"Well, I was coming home late on a blasted lazy donkey, dog-tired into the bargain, when my donkey boy suddenly ran for his life and left me alone. It was just after sunset. The sand was red and shining, and the big cliffs sort of fiery. And my donkey stuck its four feet in the ground and wouldn't budge. Then, about fifty yards away, I saw a fellow—European apparently—doing something—heaven knows what, for I can't describe it—among the boulders that lie all over the ground there. Ceremony, I suppose you'd call it. I was so interested that at first I watched. Then I saw he wasn't alone. There were a lot of moving things round him, towering big things, that came and went like shadows. That twilight is fearfully bewildering; perspective changes, and distance gets all confused. It's fearfully hard to see properly. I only remember that I got off my donkey and went up closer, and when I was within a dozen yards of him—well, it sounds such rot, you know, but I swear the things suddenly rushed off and left him there alone. They went with a roaring noise like wind; shadowy but tremendously big, they were, and they vanished up against the fiery precipices as though they slipped bang into the stone itself. The only thing I can think of to describe 'em is—well, those sand-storms the Khamasin raises—the hot winds, you know."

"They probably *were* sand," his wife suggested, burning to tell another story of her own.

"Possibly, only there wasn't a breath of wind, and it was hot as blazes—and—I had such extraordinary sensations—never felt anything like it before—wild and exhilarated—drunk, I tell you, drunk."

"You saw them?" asked Henriot. "You made out their shape at all, or outline?"

"Sphinx," he replied at once, "for all the world like sphinxes. You know the kind of face and head these limestone strata in the Desert take—great visages with square Egyptian head-dresses where the driven sand has eaten away the softer stuff beneath? You see it everywhere—enormous idols they seem, with faces and eyes and lips awfully like the sphinx—well, that's the nearest I can get to it." He puffed his pipe hard. But there was no sign of levity in him. He told the actual truth as far as in him lay, yet half ashamed of what he told. And a good deal he left out, too.

"She's got a face of the same sort, that Statham horror," his wife said with a shiver. "Reduce the size, and paint in awful black eyes, and you've got her exactly—a living idol." And all three laughed, yet a laughter without merriment in it.

"And you spoke to the man?"

"I did," the Englishman answered, "though I confess I'm a bit ashamed of the way I spoke. Fact is, I was excited, thunderingly excited, and felt a kind of anger. I wanted to kick the beggar for practising such bally rubbish, and in such a place too. Yet all the time—well, well, I believe it was sheer funk now," he laughed; "for I felt uncommonly queer out there in the dusk, alone with—with that kind of business; and I was angry with myself for feeling it. Anyhow, I went up—I'd lost my donkey boy as well, remember—and slated him like a dog. I can't remember what I said exactly—only that he stood and stared at me in silence. That made it worse—seemed twice as real then. The beggar said no single word the whole time. He signed to me with one hand to clear out. And then, suddenly out of nothing—she—that woman—appeared and stood beside him. I never saw her come. She must have been behind some boulder or other, for she simply rose out of the ground. She stood there and stared at me too—bang in the face. She was turned towards the sunset—what was left of it in the west—and her black eyes shone like—ugh! I can't describe it—it was shocking."

"She spoke?"

"She said five words—and her voice—it'll make you laugh—it was metallic like a gong: 'You are in danger here.' That's all she said. I simply turned and cleared out as fast as ever I could. But I had to go on foot. My donkey had followed its boy long before. I tell you—smile as you may—my blood was all curdled for an hour afterwards."

Then he explained that he felt some kind of explanation or apology was due, since the couple lodged in his own hotel, and how he approached the man in the smoking-room after dinner. A conversation resulted—the man was quite intelligent after all—of which only one sentence had remained in his mind.

"Perhaps you can explain it, Felix. I wrote it down, as well as I could remember. The rest confused me beyond words or memory; though I must confess it did not seem—well, not utter rot exactly. It was about astrology and rituals and the worship of the old Egyptians, and I don't know what else besides. Only, he made it intelligible and almost sensible, if only I could have got the hang of the thing enough to remember it. You know," he added, as though believing in spite of himself, "there *is* a lot of that wonderful old Egyptian religious business still hanging about in the atmosphere of this place, say what you like."

"But this sentence?" Henriot asked. And the other went off to get a note-book where he had written it down.

"He was jawing, you see," he continued when he came back, Henriot and his wife having kept silence meanwhile, "about direction being of importance in religious ceremonies, West and North symbolising certain powers, or something of the kind, why people turn to the East and all that sort of thing, and speaking of the whole Universe as if it had living forces tucked away in it that expressed themselves somehow when roused up. That's how I remember it anyhow. And then he said this thing—in answer to some fool question probably that I put." And he read out of the note-book:

"'You were in danger because you came through the Gateway of the West, and the Powers from the Gateway of the East were at that moment rising, and therefore in direct opposition to you.'"

Then came the following, apparently a simile offered by way of explanation. Mansfield read it in a shamefaced tone, evidently prepared for laughter:

"'Whether I strike you on the back or in the face determines what kind of answering force I rouse in you. Direction is significant.' And he said it was the period called the Night of Power—time when the Desert encroaches and the spirits are close."

And tossing the book aside, he lit his pipe again and waited a moment to hear what might be said. "Can you explain such gibberish?" he asked at length, as neither of his listeners spoke. But Henriot said he couldn't. And the wife then took up her own tale of stories that had grown about this singular couple.

These were less detailed, and therefore less impressive, but all contributed something towards the atmosphere of reality that framed the entire picture. They belonged to the type one hears at every dinner party in Egypt—stories of the vengeance mummies seem to take on those who robbed them, desecrating their peace of centuries; of a woman wearing a necklace of scarabs taken from a princess's tomb, who felt hands about her throat to strangle her; of little Ka figures, Pasht goddesses, amulets, and the rest, that brought curious disaster to those who kept them. They are many and various, astonishingly circumstantial often, and vouched for by persons the reverse of credulous. The modern superstition that haunts the desert gullies with Afreets has nothing in common with them. They rest upon a basis of indubitable experience; and they remain—inexplicable. And about the personalities of Lady Statham and her nephew they crowded like flies attracted by a dish of fruit. The Arabs, too, were afraid of her. She had difficulty in getting guides and dragomen.

"My dear chap," concluded Mansfield, "take my advice and have nothing to do with 'em. There *is* a lot of queer business knocking about in this old country, and people like that know ways of reviving it somehow. It's upset you already; you looked scared, I thought, the moment you came in." They laughed, but the Englishman was in earnest. "I tell you what," he added, "we'll go off for a bit of shooting together. The fields along the Delta are packed with birds now: they're home early this year on their way to the North. What d'ye say, eh?"

But Henriot did not care about the quail shooting. He felt more inclined to be alone and think things out by himself. He had come to his friends for comfort, and instead they had made him uneasy and excited. His interest had suddenly doubled. Though half afraid, he longed to know what these two were up to—to follow the adventure to the bitter end. He disregarded the warning of his host as well as the premonition in his own heart. The sand had caught his feet.

There were moments when he laughed in utter disbelief, but these were optimistic moods that did not last. He always returned to the feeling that truth lurked somewhere in the whole strange business, and that if he joined forces with them, as they seemed to wish, he would witness—well, he hardly knew what—but it enticed him as danger does the reckless man, or death the suicide. The sand had caught his mind.

He decided to offer himself to all they wanted—his pencil too. He would see—a shiver ran through him at the thought—what they saw, and know some eddy of that vanished tide of power and splendour the ancient Egyptian priesthood knew, and that perhaps was even common experience in the far-off days of dim Atlantis. The sand had caught his imagination too. He was utterly sand-haunted.

VII

And so he took pains, though without making definite suggestion, to place himself in the way of this woman and her nephew—only to find that his hints were disregarded. They left him alone, if they did not actually avoid him. Moreover, he rarely came across them now. Only at night, or in the queer dusk hours, he caught glimpses of them moving hurriedly off from the hotel, and always desertwards. And their disregard, well calculated, enflamed his desire to the point when he almost decided to propose himself. Quite suddenly, then, the idea flashed through him—how do they come, these odd revelations, when the mind lies receptive like a plate sensitised by anticipation?—that they were waiting for a certain date, and, with the notion, came Mansfield's remark about "the Night of Power," believed in by the old Egyptian Calendar as a time when the supersensuous world moves close against the minds of men with all its troop of possibilities. And the thought, once lodged in its corner of imagination, grew strong. He looked it up. Ten days from now, he found, Leyel-el-Sud would be upon him, with a moon, too, at the full. And this strange hint of guidance he accepted. In his present mood, as he admitted, smiling to himself, he could accept anything. It was part of it, it belonged to the adventure. But, even while he persuaded himself that it was play, the solemn reality of what lay ahead increased amazingly, sketched darkly in his very soul.

These intervening days he spent as best he could—impatiently, a prey to quite opposite emotions. In the blazing sunshine he thought of it and laughed; but at night he lay often sleepless, calculating chances of escape. He never did escape, however. The Desert that watched little Helouan with great, unwinking eyes watched also every turn and twist he made. Like this oasis, he basked in the sun of older time, and dreamed beneath forgotten moons. The sand at last had crept into his inmost heart. It sifted over him.

Seeking a reaction from normal, everyday things, he made tourist trips; yet, while recognising the comedy in his attitude, he never could lose sight of the grandeur that banked it up so hauntingly. These two contrary emotions grafted themselves on all he did and saw. He crossed the Nile at Bedrashein, and went again to the Tomb-World of Sakkara; but through all the chatter of veiled and helmeted tourists, the *bandar-log* of our modern Jungle, ran this dark under-stream of awe their monkey methods could not turn aside. One world lay upon another, but this modern layer was a shallow crust that, like the phenomenon of the "desert-film," a mere angle of falling light could instantly obliterate. Beneath the sand, deep down, he passed along the Street of Tombs, as he had often passed before, moved then merely by historical curiosity and admiration, but now by emotions for which he found no name. He saw the enormous sarcophagi of granite in their gloomy chambers where the sacred bulls once lay, swathed and embalmed like human beings, and, in the flickering candle-light, the mood of ancient rites surged round him, menacing his doubts and laughter. The least human whisper in these subterraneans, dug out first four thousand years ago, revived ominous Powers that stalked beside him, forbidding and premonitive. He gazed at the spots where Mariette, unearthing them forty years ago, found fresh as of yesterday the marks of fingers and naked feet—of those who set the sixty-five ton slabs in position. And when he came up again into the sunshine he met the eternal questions of the pyramids, overtopping all his mental horizons. Sand blocked all the avenues of younger emotion, leaving the channels of something in him incalculably older, open and clean swept.

He slipped homewards, uncomfortable and followed, glad to be with a crowd—because he was otherwise alone with more than he could dare to think about. Keeping just ahead of his companions, he crossed the desert edge where the ghost of Memphis walks under rustling palm trees that screen no stone left upon another of all its mile-long populous splendours. For here was a vista his imagination could realise; here he could know the comfort of solid ground his feet could touch. Gigantic Ramases, lying on his back beneath their shade and staring at the sky, similarly helped to steady his swaying thoughts. Imagination could deal with these.

And daily thus he watched the busy world go to and fro to its scale of tips and bargaining, and gladly mingled with it, trying to laugh and study guide-books, and listen to half-fledged explanations, but always seeing the comedy of his poor attempts. Not all those little donkeys, bells tinkling, beads shining, trotting beneath their comical burdens to the tune of shouting and belabouring, could stem this tide of deeper things the woman let loose in the subconscious part of him. Everywhere he saw the mysterious camels go slouching through the sand, gurgling the water in their skinny, extended throats. Centuries passed between the enormous knee-stroke of their stride. And, every night, the sunsets restored the forbidding, graver mood, with their crimson, golden splendour, their strange green shafts of light, then—sudden twilight that brought the Past upon him with an awful leap. Upon the stage then stepped the figures of this pair of human beings, chanting their ancient plain-song of incantation in the moonlit desert, and working their rites of unholy evocation as the priests had worked them centuries before in the sands that now buried Sakkara fathoms deep.

Then one morning he woke with a question in his mind, as though it had been asked of him in sleep and he had waked just before the answer came. "Why do I spend my time sight-seeing, instead of going alone into the Desert as before? What has made me change?"

This latest mood now asked for explanation. And the answer, coming up automatically, startled him. It was so clear and sure—had been lying in the background all along. One word contained it:

Vance.

The sinister intentions of this man, forgotten in the rush of other emotions, asserted themselves again convincingly. The human horror, so easily comprehensible, had been smothered for the time by the hint of unearthly revelations. But it had operated all the time. Now it took the lead. He dreaded to be alone in the Desert with this dark picture in his mind of what Vance meant to bring there to completion. This abomination of a selfish human will returned to fix its terror in him. To be alone in the Desert meant to be alone with the imaginative picture of what Vance—he knew it with such strange certainty—hoped to bring about there.

There was absolutely no evidence to justify the grim suspicion. It seemed indeed far-fetched enough, this connection between the sand and the purpose of an evil-minded, violent man. But Henriot saw it true. He could argue it away in a few minutes—easily. Yet the instant thought ceased, it returned, led up by intuition. It possessed him, filled his mind with horrible possibilities. He feared the Desert as he might have feared the scene of some atrocious crime. And, for the time, this dread of a merely human thing corrected the big seduction of the other—the suggested "super-natural."

Side by side with it, his desire to join himself to the purposes of the woman increased steadily. They kept out of his way apparently; the offer seemed withdrawn; he grew restless, unable to settle to anything for long, and once he asked the porter casually if they were leaving the hotel. Lady Statham had been invisible for days, and Vance was somehow never within speaking distance. He heard with relief that they had not gone—but with dread as well. Keen excitement worked in him underground. He slept badly. Like a schoolboy, he waited for the summons to an important examination that involved portentous issues, and contradictory emotions disturbed his peace of mind abominably.

VIII

But it was not until the end of the week, when Vance approached him with purpose in his eyes and manner, that Henriot knew his fears unfounded, and caught himself trembling with sudden anticipation—because the invitation, so desired yet so dreaded, was actually at hand. Firmly determined to keep caution uppermost, yet he went unresistingly to a secluded corner by the palms where they could talk in privacy. For prudence is of the mind, but desire is of the soul, and while his brain of to-day whispered wariness, voices in his heart of long ago shouted commands that he knew he must obey with joy.

It was evening and the stars were out. Helouan, with her fairy twinkling lights, lay silent against the Desert edge. The sand was at the flood. The period of the Encroaching of the Desert was at hand, and the deeps were all astir with movement. But in the windless air was a great peace. A calm of infinite stillness breathed everywhere. The flow of Time, before it rushed away backwards, stopped somewhere between the dust of stars and Desert. The mystery of sand touched every street with its unutterable softness.

And Vance began without the smallest circumlocution. His voice was low, in keeping with the scene, but the words dropped with a sharp distinctness into the other's heart like grains of sand that pricked the skin before they smothered him. Caution they smothered instantly; resistance too.

"I have a message for you from my aunt," he said, as though he brought an invitation to a picnic. Henriot sat in shadow, but his companion's face was in a patch of light that followed them from the windows of the central hall. There was a shining in the light blue eyes that betrayed the excitement his quiet manner concealed. "We are going— the day after to-morrow—to spend the night in the Desert; she wondered if, perhaps, you would care to join us?"

"For your experiment?" asked Henriot bluntly.

Vance smiled with his lips, holding his eyes steady, though unable to suppress the gleam that flashed in them and was gone so swiftly. There was a hint of shrugging his shoulders.

"It is the Night of Power—in the old Egyptian Calendar, you know," he answered with assumed lightness almost, "the final moment of Leyel-el-Sud, the period of Black Nights when the Desert was held to encroach with—with various possibilities of a supernatural order. She wishes to revive a certain practice of the old Egyptians. There *may* be curious results. At any rate, the occasion is a picturesque one— better than this cheap imitation of London life." And he indicated the lights, the signs of people in the hall dressed for gaieties and dances, the hotel orchestra that played after dinner.

Henriot at the moment answered nothing, so great was the rush of conflicting emotions that came he knew not whence. Vance went calmly on. He spoke with a simple frankness that was meant to be disarming. Henriot never took his eyes off him. The two men stared steadily at one another.

"She wants to know if you will come and help too—in a certain way only: not in the experiment itself precisely, but by watching merely and—" He hesitated an instant, half lowering his eyes.

"Drawing the picture," Henriot helped him deliberately.

"Drawing what you see, yes," Vance replied, the voice turned graver in spite of himself. "She wants—she hopes to catch the outline of anything that happens—"

"Comes."

"Exactly. Determine the shape of anything that comes. You may remember your conversation of the other night with her. She is very certain of success."

This was direct enough at any rate. It was as formal as an invitation to a dinner, and as guileless. The thing he thought he wanted lay within his reach. He had merely to say yes. He did say yes; but first he looked about him instinctively, as for guidance. He looked at the stars twinkling high above the distant Libyan Plateau; at the long arms of the Desert, gleaming weirdly white in the moonlight, and reaching towards him down every opening between the houses; at the heavy mass of the Mokattam Hills, guarding the Arabian Wilderness with strange, peaked barriers, their sand-carved ridges dark and still above the Wadi Hof.

These questionings attracted no response. The Desert watched him, but it did not answer. There was only the shrill whistling cry of the lizards, and the sing-song of a white-robed Arab gliding down the sandy street. And through these sounds he heard his own voice answer: "I will come— yes. But how can I help? Tell me what you propose—your plan?"

And the face of Vance, seen plainly in the electric glare, betrayed his satisfaction. The opposing things in the fellow's mind of darkness fought visibly in his eyes and skin. The sordid motive, planning a dreadful act, leaped to his face, and with it a flash of this other yearning that sought unearthly knowledge, perhaps believed it too. No wonder there was conflict written on his features.

Then all expression vanished again; he leaned forward, lowering his voice.

"You remember our conversation about there being types of life too vast to manifest in a single body, and my aunt's belief that these were known to certain of the older religious systems of the world?"

"Perfectly."

"Her experiment, then, is to bring one of these great Powers back—we possess the sympathetic ritual that can rouse some among them to activity—and win it down into the sphere of our minds, our minds heightened, you see, by ceremonial to that stage of clairvoyant vision which can perceive them."

"And then?" They might have been discussing the building of a house, so naturally followed answer upon question. But the whole body of meaning in the old Egyptian symbolism rushed over him with a force that shook his heart. Memory came so marvellously with it.

"If the Power floods down into our minds with sufficient strength for actual form, to note the outline of such form, and from your drawing model it later in permanent substance. Then we should have means of evoking it at will, for we should have its natural Body—the form it built itself, its signature, image, pattern. A starting-point, you see, for more—leading, she hopes, to a complete reconstruction."

"It might take actual shape—assume a bodily form visible to the eye?" repeated Henriot, amazed as before that doubt and laughter did not break through his mind.

"We are on the earth," was the reply, spoken unnecessarily low since no living thing was with earshot, "we are in physical conditions, are we not? Even a human soul we do not recognise unless we see it in a body—parents provide the outline, the signature, the sigil of the returning soul. This," and he tapped himself upon the breast, "is the physical signature of that type of life we call a soul. Unless there is life of a certain strength behind it, no body forms. And, without a body, we are helpless to control or manage it—deal with it in any way. We could not know it, though being possibly *aware* of it."

"To be aware, you mean, is not sufficient?" For he noticed the italics Vance made use of.

"Too vague, of no value for future use," was the reply. "But once obtain the form, and we have the natural symbol of that particular Power. And a symbol is more than image, it is a direct and concentrated expression of the life it typifies—possibly terrific."

"It may be a body, then, this symbol you speak of."

"Accurate vehicle of manifestation; but 'body' seems the simplest word."

Vance answered very slowly and deliberately, as though weighing how much he would tell. His language was admirably evasive. Few perhaps would have detected the profound significance the curious words he next used unquestionably concealed. Henriot's mind rejected them, but his heart accepted. For the ancient soul in him was listening and aware.

"Life, using matter to express itself in bodily shape, first traces a geometrical pattern. From the lowest form in crystals, upwards to more complicated patterns in the higher organisations—there is always first this geometrical pattern as skeleton. For geometry lies at the root of all possible phenomena; and is the mind's interpretation of a living movement towards shape that shall express it." He brought his eyes closer to the other, lowering his voice again. "Hence," he said softly, "the signs in all the old magical systems—skeleton forms into which the Powers evoked descended; outlines those Powers automatically built up when using matter to express themselves. Such signs are material symptoms of their bodiless existence. They attract the life they represent and interpret. Obtain the correct, true symbol, and the Power corresponding to it can approach—once roused and made aware. It has, you see, a ready-made mould into which it can come down."

"Once roused and made aware?" repeated Henriot questioningly, while this man went stammering the letters of a language that he himself had used too long ago to recapture fully.

"Because they have left the world. They sleep, unmanifested. Their forms are no longer known to men. No forms exist on earth to-day that could contain them. But they may be awakened," he added darkly.

"They are bound to answer to the summons, if such summons be accurately made."

"Evocation?" whispered Henriot, more distressed than he cared to admit.

Vance nodded. Leaning still closer to his companion's face, he thrust his lips forward, speaking eagerly, earnestly, yet somehow at the same time, horribly: "And we want—my aunt would ask—your draughtsman's skill, or at any rate your memory afterwards, to establish the outline of anything that comes."

He waited for the answer, still keeping his face uncomfortably close.

Henriot drew back a little. But his mind was fully made up now. He had known from the beginning that he would consent, for the desire in him was stronger than all the caution in the world. The Past inexorably drew him into the circle of these other lives, and the little human dread Vance woke in him seemed just then insignificant by comparison. It was merely of To-day.

"You two," he said, trying to bring judgment into it, "engaged in evocation, will be in a state of clairvoyant vision. Granted. But shall I, as an outsider, observing with unexcited mind, see anything, know anything, be aware of anything at all, let alone the drawing of it?"

"Unless," the reply came instantly with decision, "the descent of Power is strong enough to take actual material shape, the experiment is a failure. Anybody can induce subjective vision. Such fantasies have no value though. They are born of an overwrought imagination." And then he added quickly, as though to clinch the matter before caution and hesitation could take effect: "You must watch from the heights above. We shall be in the valley—the Wadi Hof is the place. You must not be too close—"

"Why not too close?" asked Henriot, springing forward like a flash before he could prevent the sudden impulse.

With a quickness equal to his own, Vance answered. There was no faintest sign that he was surprised. His self-control was perfect. Only the glare passed darkly through his eyes and went back again into the sombre soul that bore it.

"For your own safety," he answered low. "The Power, the type of life, she would waken is stupendous. And if roused enough to be attracted by the patterned symbol into which she would decoy it down, it will take actual, physical expression. But how? Where is the Body of Worshippers through whom it can manifest? There is none. It will, therefore, press inanimate matter into the service. The terrific impulse to form itself a means of expression will force all loose matter at hand towards it—sand, stones, all it can compel to yield—everything must rush into the sphere of action in which it operates. Alone, we at the centre, and you, upon the outer fringe, will be safe. Only—you must not come too close."

But Henriot was no longer listening. His soul had turned to ice. For here, in this unguarded moment, the cloven hoof had plainly shown itself. In that suggestion of a particular kind of danger Vance had lifted a corner of the curtain behind which crouched his horrible intention. Vance desired a witness of the extraordinary experiment, but he desired this witness, not merely for the purpose of sketching possible shapes that might present themselves to excited vision. He desired a witness for another reason too. Why had Vance put that idea into his mind, this idea of so peculiar danger? It might well have lost him the very assistance he seemed so anxious to obtain.

Henriot could not fathom it quite. Only one thing was clear to him. He, Henriot, was not the only one in danger.

They talked for long after that—far into the night. The lights went out, and the armed patrol, pacing to and fro outside the iron railings that kept the desert back, eyed them curiously. But the only other thing he gathered of importance was the ledge upon the cliff-top where he was to stand and watch; that he was expected to reach there before sunset and wait till the moon concealed all glimmer in the western sky, and—that the woman, who had been engaged for days in secret preparation of soul and body for the awful rite, would not be visible again until he saw her in the depths of the black valley far below, busy with this man upon audacious, ancient purposes.

IX

An hour before sunset Henriot put his rugs and food upon a donkey, and gave the boy directions where to meet him—a considerable distance from the appointed spot. He went himself on foot. He slipped in

the heat along the sandy street, where strings of camels still go slouching, shuffling with their loads from the quarries that built the pyramids,
and he felt that little friendly Helouan tried to keep him back. But desire now was far too strong for caution. The desert tide was rising. It
easily swept him down the long white street towards the enormous
deeps beyond. He felt the pull of a thousand miles before him; and
twice a thousand years drove at his back.

Everything still basked in the sunshine. He passed Al Hayat, the
stately hotel that dominates the village like a palace built against the
sky; and in its pillared colonnades and terraces he saw the throngs of
people having late afternoon tea and listening to the music of a regi-
mental band. Men in flannels were playing tennis, parties were climbing off donkeys after long excursions; there was laughter, talking, a
babel of many voices. The gaiety called to him; the everyday spirit
whispered to stay and join the crowd of lively human beings. Soon
there would be merry dinner-parties, dancing, voices of pretty women,
sweet white dresses, singing, and the rest. Soft eyes would question
and turn dark. He picked out several girls he knew among the palms.
But it was all many, oh so many leagues away; centuries lay between
him and the modern world. An indescribable loneliness was in his
heart. He went searching through the sands of forgotten ages, and
wandering among the ruins of a vanished time. He hurried. Already the
deeper water caught his breath.

He climbed the steep rise towards the plateau where the Observatory stands, and saw two of the officials whom he knew taking a siesta
after their long day's work. He felt that his mind, too, had dived and
searched among the heavenly bodies that live in silent, changeless
peace remote from the world of men. They recognised him, these two
whose eyes also knew tremendous distance close. They beckoned,
waving the straws through which they sipped their drinks from tall
glasses. Their voices floated down to him as from the star-fields. He
saw the sun gleam upon the glasses, and heard the clink of the ice
against the sides. The stillness was amazing. He waved an answer, and
passed quickly on. He could not stop this sliding current of the years.

The tide moved faster, the draw of piled-up cycles urging it. He
emerged upon the plateau, and met the cooler Desert air. His feet went
crunching on the "desert-film" that spread its curious dark shiny car-

pet as far as the eye could reach; it lay everywhere, unswept and smooth as when the feet of vanished civilisations trod its burning surface, then dipped behind the curtains Time pins against the stars. And here the body of the tide set all one way. There was a greater strength of current, draught, and suction. He felt the powerful undertow. Deeper masses drew his feet sideways, and he felt the rushing of the central body of the sand. The sands were moving, from their foundation upwards. He went unresistingly with them.

Turning a moment, he looked back at shining little Helouan in the blaze of evening light. The voices reached him very faintly, merged now in a general murmur. Beyond lay the strip of Delta vivid green, the palms, the roofs of Bedrashein, the blue laughter of the Nile with its flocks of curved felucca sails. Further still, rising above the yellow Libyan horizon, gloomed the vast triangles of a dozen Pyramids, cutting their wedge-shaped clefts out of a sky fast crimsoning through a sea of gold. Seen thus, their dignity imposed upon the entire landscape. They towered darkly, symbolic signatures of the ancient Powers that now watched him taking these little steps across their damaged territory.

He gazed a minute, then went on. He saw the big pale face of the moon in the east. Above the ever-silent Thing these giant symbols once interpreted, she rose, grand, effortless, half-terrible as themselves. And, with her, she lifted up this tide of the Desert that drew his feet across the sand to Wadi Hof. A moment later he dipped below the ridge that buried Helouan and Nile and Pyramids from sight. He entered the ancient waters. Time then, in an instant, flowed back behind his footsteps, obliterating every trace. And with it his mind went too. He stepped across the gulf of centuries, moving into the Past. The Desert lay before him—an open tomb wherein his soul should read presently of things long vanished.

The strange half-lights of sunset began to play their witchery then upon the landscape. A purple glow came down upon the Mokattam Hills. Perspective danced its tricks of false, incredible deception. The soaring kites that were a mile away seemed suddenly close, passing in a moment from the size of gnats to birds with a fabulous stretch of wing. Ridges and cliffs rushed close without a hint of warning, and level places sank into declivities and basins that made him trip and stumble. That indescribable quality of the Desert, which makes timid souls avoid the hour of dusk, emerged; it spread everywhere, undisguised. And the bewilderment it brings is no vain, imagined thing, for it distorts vision utterly, and the effect upon the mind when familiar sight goes floundering is the simplest way in the world of dragging the anchor that grips reality. At the hour of sunset this bewilderment comes upon a man with a disconcerting swiftness. It rose now with all this weird rapidity. Henriot found himself enveloped at a moment's notice.

But, knowing well its effect, he tried to judge it and pass on. The other matters, the object of his journey chief of all, he refused to dwell upon with any imagination. Wisely, his mind, while never losing sight of it, declined to admit the exaggeration that over-elaborate thinking brings. "I'm going to witness an incredible experiment in which two enthusiastic religious dreamers believe firmly," he repeated to himself. "I have agreed to draw—anything I see. There may be truth in it, or they may be merely self-suggested vision due to an artificial exaltation of their minds. I'm interested—perhaps against my better judgment. Yet I'll see the adventure out—because I *must*."

This was the attitude he told himself to take. Whether it was the real one, or merely adopted to warm a cooling courage, he could not tell. The emotions were so complex and warring. His mind, automatically, kept repeating this comforting formula. Deeper than that he could not see to judge. For a man who knew the full content of his thought at such a time would solve some of the oldest psychological problems in the world. Sand had already buried judgment, and with it all attempt to explain the adventure by the standards acceptable to his brain of to-day. He steered subconsciously through a world of dim, huge, half-remembered wonders.

The sun, with that abrupt Egyptian suddenness, was below the horizon now. The pyramid field had swallowed it. Ra, in his golden boat, sailed distant seas beyond the Libyan wilderness. Henriot walked on and on, aware of utter loneliness. He was walking fields of dream, too remote from modern life to recall companionship he once had surely known. How dim it was, how deep and distant, how lost in this sea of an incalculable Past! He walked into the places that are soundless. The soundlessness of ocean, miles below the surface, was about him. He was with One only—this unfathomable, silent thing where nothing breathes or stirs—nothing but sunshine, shadow, and the wind-borne sand. Slowly, in front, the moon climbed up the eastern sky, hanging above the silence—silence that ran unbroken across the horizons to where Suez gleamed upon the waters of a sister sea in motion. That moon was glinting now upon the Arabian Mountains by its desolate shores. Southwards stretched the wastes of Upper Egypt a thousand miles to meet the Nubian wilderness. But over all these separate Deserts stirred the soft whisper of the moving sand—deep murmuring message that Life was on the way to unwind Death. The Ka of Egypt, swathed in centuries of sand, hovered beneath the moon towards her ancient tenement.

For the transformation of the Desert now began in earnest. It grew apace. Before he had gone the first two miles of his hour's journey, the twilight caught the rocky hills and twisted them into those monstrous revelations of physiognomies they barely take the trouble to conceal even in the daytime. And, while he well understood the eroding agencies that have produced them, there yet rose in his mind a deeper interpretation lurking just behind their literal meanings. Here, through the motionless surfaces, that nameless thing the Desert ill conceals urged outwards into embryonic form and shape, akin, he almost felt, to those immense deific symbols of Other Life the Egyptians knew and worshipped. Hence, from the Desert, had first come, he felt, the unearthly life they typified in their monstrous figures of granite, evoked in their stately temples, and communed with in the ritual of their Mystery ceremonials.

This "watching" aspect of the Libyan Desert is really natural enough; but it is just the natural, Henriot knew, that brings the deepest revelations. The surface limestones, resisting the erosion, block themselves ominously against the sky, while the softer sand beneath sets them on altared pedestals that define their isolation splendidly. Blunt and unconquerable, these masses now watched him pass between them. The Desert surface formed them, gave them birth. They rose, they saw, they sank down again—waves upon a sea that carried forgotten life up from the depths below. Of forbidding, even menacing type, they somewhere mated with genuine grandeur. Unformed, according to any standard of human or of animal faces, they achieved an air of giant physiognomy which made them terrible. The unwinking stare of eyes—lidless eyes that yet ever succeed in hiding—looked out under

well-marked, level eyebrows, suggesting a vision that included the mo-
tives and purposes of his very heart. They looked up grandly, understood why he was there, and then—slowly withdrew their mysterious,
penetrating gaze.

The strata built them so marvellously up; the heavy, threatening
brows; thick lips, curved by the ages into a semblance of cold smiles;
jowls drooping into sandy heaps that climbed against the cheeks; pro-
truding jaws, and the suggestion of shoulders just about to lift the entire bodies out of the sandy beds—this host of countenances conveyed
a solemnity of expression that seemed everlasting, implacable as
Death. Of human signature they bore no trace, nor was comparison
possible between their kind and any animal life. They peopled the Desert here. And their smiles, concealed yet just discernible, went broad-
ening with the darkness into a Desert laughter. The silence bore it
underground. But Henriot was aware of it. The troop of faces slipped
into that single, enormous countenance which is the visage of the
Sand. And he saw it everywhere, yet nowhere.

Thus with the darkness grew his imaginative interpretation of the
Desert. Yet there was construction in it, a construction, moreover, that
was *not* entirely his own. Powers, he felt, were rising, stirring, wakening
from sleep. Behind the natural faces that he saw, these other things
peered gravely at him as he passed. They used, as it were, materials that
lay ready to their hand. Imagination furnished these hints of outline,
yet the Powers themselves were real. There *was* this amazing movement of the sand. By no other manner could his mind have conceived
of such a thing, nor dreamed of this simple, yet dreadful method of
approach.

Approach! that was the word that first stood out and startled him.
There was approach; something was drawing nearer. The Desert rose
and walked beside him. For not alone these ribs of gleaming limestone
contributed towards the elemental visages, but the entire hills, of which
they were an outcrop, ran to assist in the formation, and were a necessary part of them. He was watched and stared at from behind, in front,
on either side, and even from below. The sand that swept him on, kept
even pace with him. It turned luminous too, with a patchwork of
glimmering effect that was indescribably weird; lanterns glowed within
its substance, and by their light he stumbled on, glad of the Arab boy

he would presently meet at the appointed place.

The last torch of the sunset had flickered out, melting into the wilderness, when, suddenly opening at his feet, gaped the deep, wide gully known as Wadi Hof. Its curve swept past him.

This first impression came upon him with a certain violence: that the desolate valley rushed. He saw but a section of its curve and sweep, but through its entire length of several miles the Wadi fled away. The moon whitened it like snow, piling black shadows very close against the cliffs. In the flood of moonlight it went rushing past. It was emptying itself.

For a moment the stream of movement seemed to pause and look up into his face, then instantly went on again upon its swift career. It was like the procession of a river to the sea. The valley emptied itself to make way for what was coming. The approach, moreover, had already begun.

Conscious that he was trembling, he stood and gazed into the depths, seeking to steady his mind by the repetition of the little formula he had used before. He said it half aloud. But, while he did so, his heart whispered quite other things. Thoughts the woman and the man had sown rose up in a flock and fell upon him like a storm of sand. Their impetus drove off all support of ordinary ideas. They shook him where he stood, staring down into this river of strange invisible movement that was hundreds of feet in depth and a quarter of a mile across.

He sought to realise himself as he actually was to-day—mere visitor to Helouan, tempted into this wild adventure with two strangers. But in vain. That seemed a dream, unreal, a transient detail picked out from the enormous Past that now engulfed him, heart and mind and soul. *This* was the reality.

The shapes and faces that the hills of sand built round him were the play of excited fancy only. By sheer force he pinned his thought against this fact: but further he could not get. There *were* Powers at work; they were being stirred, wakened somewhere into activity. Evocation had already begun. That sense of their approach as he had walked along from Helouan was not imaginary. A descent of some type of life, vanished from the world too long for recollection, was on the way,—so vast that it would manifest itself in a group of forms, a troop, a host, an army. These two were near him somewhere at this very moment, already long at work, their minds driving beyond this little world. The valley was emptying itself—for the descent of life their ritual invited.

And the movement in the sand was likewise true. He recalled the sentences the woman had used. "My body," he reflected, "like the bodies life makes use of everywhere, is mere upright heap of earth and dust and—sand. Here in the Desert is the raw material, the greatest store of it in the world."

And on the heels of it came sharply that other thing: that this descending Life would press into its service all loose matter within its reach—to form that sphere of action which would be in a literal sense its Body.

In the first few seconds, as he stood there, he realised all this, and realised it with an overwhelming conviction it was futile to deny. The fast-emptying valley would later brim with an unaccustomed and terrific life. Yet Death hid there too—a little, ugly, insignificant death. With the name of Vance it flashed upon his mind and vanished, too tiny to be thought about in this torrent of grander messages that shook the depths within his soul. He bowed his head a moment, hardly knowing what he did. He could have waited thus a thousand years it seemed. He was conscious of a wild desire to run away, to hide, to efface himself utterly, his terror, his curiosity, his little wonder, and not be seen of anything. But it was all vain and foolish. The Desert saw him. The Gigantic knew that he was there. No escape was possible any longer. Caught by the sand, he stood amid eternal things. The river of movement swept him too.

These hills, now motionless as statues, would presently glide forward into the cavalcade, away like vessels, and go past with the procession. At present only the contents, not the frame, of the Wadi moved. An immense soft brush of moonlight swept it empty for what was on the way. . . . But presently the entire Desert would stand up and also go.

Then, making a sideways movement, his feet kicked against something soft and yielding that lay heaped upon the Desert floor, and Henriot discovered the rugs the Arab boy had carefully set down before he made full speed for the friendly lights of Helouan. The sound of his departing footsteps had long since died away. He was alone.

The detail restored to him his consciousness of the immediate present, and, stooping, he gathered up the rugs and overcoat and began to make preparations for the night. But the appointed spot, whence he was to watch, lay upon the summit of the opposite cliffs. He must cross the Wadi bed and climb. Slowly and with labour he made his way down a steep cleft into the depth of the Wadi Hof, sliding and stumbling often, till at length he stood upon the floor of shining moonlight. It was very smooth; windless utterly; still as space; each particle of sand lay in its ancient place asleep. The movement, it seemed, had ceased.

He clambered next up the eastern side, through pitch-black shadows, and within the hour reached the ledge upon the top whence he could see below him, like a silvered map, the sweep of the valley bed. The wind nipped keenly here again, coming over the leagues of cooling sand. Loose boulders of splintered rock, started by his climbing, crashed and boomed into the depths. He banked the rugs behind him, wrapped himself in his overcoat, and lay down to wait. Behind him was a two-foot crumbling wall against which he leaned; in front a drop of several hundred feet through space. He lay upon a platform, therefore, invisible from the Desert at his back. Below, the curving Wadi formed a natural amphitheatre in which each separate boulder fallen from the cliffs, and even the little *silla* shrubs the camels eat, were plainly visible. He noted all the bigger ones among them. He counted them over half aloud.

And the moving stream he had been unaware of when crossing the bed itself, now began again. The Wadi went rushing past before the broom of moonlight. Again, the enormous and the tiny combined in one single strange impression. For, through this conception of great movement, stirred also a roving, delicate touch that his imagination felt as bird-like. Behind the solid mass of the Desert's immobility flashed something swift and light and airy. Bizarre pictures interpreted it to him, like rapid snap-shots of a huge flying panorama: he thought of darting dragon-flies seen at Helouan, of children's little dancing feet, of twinkling butterflies—of birds. Chiefly, yes, of a flock of birds in flight, whose separate units formed a single entity. The idea of the Group-Soul possessed his mind once more. But it came with a sense of more than curiosity or wonder. Veneration lay behind it, a veneration touched with awe. It rose in his deepest thought that here was the

first hint of a symbolical representation. A symbol, sacred and inviola-
ble, belonging to some ancient worship that he half remembered in his
soul, stirred towards interpretation through all his being.

He lay there waiting, wondering vaguely where his two companions were, yet fear all vanished because he felt attuned to a scale of
things too big to mate with definite dread. There was high anticipation
in him, but not anxiety. Of himself, as Felix Henriot, indeed, he hardly
seemed aware. He was some one else. Or, rather, he was himself at a
stage he had known once far, far away in a remote pre-existence. He
watched himself from dim summits of a Past, of which no further details were as yet recoverable.

Pencil and sketching-block lay ready to his hand. The moon rose
higher, tucking the shadows ever more closely against the precipices.
The silver passed into a sheet of snowy whiteness, that made every
boulder clearly visible. Solemnity deepened everywhere into awe. The
Wadi fled silently down the stream of hours. It was almost empty now.
And then, abruptly, he was aware of change. The motion altered
somewhere. It moved more quietly; pace slackened; the end of the
procession that evacuated the depth and length of it went trailing past
and turned the distant bend.

"It's slowing up," he whispered, as sure of it as though he had
watched a regiment of soldiers filing by. The wind took off his voice
like a flying feather of sound.

And there *was* a change. It had begun. Night and the moon stood
still to watch and listen. The wind dropped utterly away. The sand
ceased its shifting movement. The Desert everywhere stopped still,
and turned.

Some curtain, then, that for centuries had veiled the world, drew
softly up, leaving a shaded vista down which the eyes of his soul
peered towards long-forgotten pictures. Still buried by the sands too
deep for full recovery, he yet perceived dim portions of them—things
once honoured and loved passionately. For once they had surely been
to him the whole of life, not merely a fragment for cheap wonder to
inspect. And they were curiously familiar, even as the person of this
woman who now evoked them was familiar. Henriot made no pretence to more definite remembrance; but the haunting certainty rushed
over him, deeper than doubt or denial, and with such force that he felt

no effort to destroy it. Some lost sweetness of spiritual ambitions, lived for with this passionate devotion, and passionately worshipped as men to-day worship fame and money, revived in him with a tempest of high glory. Centres of memory stirred from an age-long sleep, so that he could have wept at their so complete obliteration hitherto. That such majesty had departed from the world as though it had never existed, was a thought for desolation and for tears. And though the little fragment he was about to witness might be crude in itself and incomplete, yet it was part of a vast system that once explored the richest realms of deity. The reverence in him contained a holiness of the night and of the stars; great, gentle awe lay in it too; for he stood, aflame with anticipation and humility, at the gateway of sacred things.

And this was the mood, no thrill of cheap excitement or alarm to weaken in, in which he first became aware that two spots of darkness he had taken all along for boulders on the snowy valley bed, were actually something very different. They were living figures. They moved. It was not the shadows slowly following the moonlight, but the stir of human beings who all these hours had been motionless as stone. He must have passed them unnoticed within a dozen yards when he crossed the Wadi bed, and a hundred times from this very ledge his eyes had surely rested on them without recognition. Their minds, he knew full well, had not been inactive as their bodies. The important part of the ancient ritual lay, he remembered, in the powers of the evoking mind.

Here, indeed, was no effective nor theatrical approach of the principal figures. It had nothing in common with the cheap external ceremonial of modern days. In forgotten powers of the soul its grandeur lay, potent, splendid, true. Long before he came, perhaps all through the day, these two had laboured with their arduous preparations. They were there, part of the Desert, when hours ago he had crossed the plateau in the twilight. To them—to this woman's potent working of old ceremonial—had been due that singular rush of imagination he had felt. He had interpreted the Desert as alive. Here was the explanation. It *was* alive. Life was on the way. Long latent, her intense desire summoned it back to physical expression; and the effect upon him had steadily increased as he drew nearer to the centre where she would focus its revival and return. Those singular impressions of being watched and accompanied were explained. A priest of this old-world worship performed a genuine evocation; a Great One of Vision revived the cosmic Powers.

Henriot watched the small figures far below him with a sense of dramatic splendour that only this association of far-off Memory could account for. It was their rising now, and the lifting of their arms to form a slow revolving outline, that marked the abrupt cessation of the larger river of movement; for the sweeping of the Wadi sank into sudden stillness, and these two, with motions not unlike some dance of deliberate solemnity, passed slowly through the moonlight to and fro. His attention fixed upon them both. All other movement ceased. They fastened the flow of Time against the Desert's body.

What happened then? How could his mind interpret an experience so long denied that the power of expression, as of comprehension, has ceased to exist? How translate this symbolical representation, small detail though it was, of a transcendent worship entombed for most so utterly beyond recovery? Its splendour could never lodge in minds that conceive Deity perched upon a cloud within telephoning distance of fashionable churches. How should he phrase it even to himself, whose memory drew up pictures from so dim a past that the language fit to frame them lay unreachable and lost?

Henriot did not know. Perhaps he never yet has known. Certainly, at the time, he did not even try to think. His sensations remain his own—untranslatable; and even that instinctive description the mind gropes for automatically, floundered, halted, and stopped dead. Yet there rose within him somewhere, from depths long drowned in slumber, a reviving power by which he saw, divined, and recollected— remembered seemed too literal a word—these elements of a worship he once had personally known. He, too, had worshipped thus. His soul had moved amid similar evocations in some aeonian past, whence now the sand was being cleared away. Symbols of stupendous meaning flashed and went their way across the lifting mists. He hardly caught their meaning, so long it was since he had known them; yet they were familiar as the faces seen in dreams, and some hint of their spiritual significance left faint traces in his heart by means of which their grandeur reached towards interpretation. And all were symbols of a cosmic, deific nature; of Powers that only symbols can express—prayer-books and sacraments used in the Wisdom Religion of an older time, but to-day known only in the decrepit, literal shell which is their degradation.

Grandly the figures moved across the valley bed. The powers of the heavenly bodies once more joined them. They moved to the measure of a cosmic dance, whose rhythm was creative. The Universe partnered them.

There was this transfiguration of all common, external things. He realised that appearances were visible letters of a soundless language, a language he once had known. The powers of night and moon and desert sand married with points in the fluid stream of his inmost spiritual being that knew and welcomed them. He understood.

Old Egypt herself stooped down from her uncovered throne. The stars sent messengers. There was commotion in the secret, sandy places of the desert. For the Desert had grown Temple. Columns reared against the sky. There rose, from leagues away, the chanting of the sand.

The temples, where once this came to pass, were gone, their ruin questioned by alien hearts that knew not their spiritual meaning. But here the entire Desert swept in to form a shrine, and the Majesty that once was Egypt stepped grandly back across ages of denial and neglect. The sand was altar, and the stars were altar lights. The moon lit up the vast recesses of the ceiling, and the wind from a thousand miles brought in the perfume of her incense. For with that faith which shifts mountains from their sandy bed, two passionate, believing souls invoked the Ka of Egypt.

And the motions that they made, he saw, were definite harmonious patterns their dark figures traced upon the shining valley floor. Like the points of compasses, with stems invisible, and directed from the sky, their movements marked the outlines of great signatures of power—the sigils of the type of life they would evoke. It would come as a Procession. No individual outline could contain it. It needed for its visible expression—many. The descent of a group-soul, known to the worship of this mighty system, rose from its lair of centuries and moved hugely down upon them. The Ka, answering to the summons, would mate with sand. The Desert was its Body.

Yet it was not this that he had come to fix with block and pencil. Not yet was the moment when his skill might be of use. He waited, watched, and listened, while this river of half-remembered things went past him. The patterns grew beneath his eyes like music. Too intricate and prolonged to remember with accuracy later, he understood that they were forms of that root-geometry which lies behind all manifested life. The mould was being traced in outline. Life would presently inform it. And a singing rose from the maze of lines whose beauty was like the beauty of the constellations.

This sound was very faint at first, but grew steadily in volume. Although no echoes, properly speaking, were possible, these precipices caught stray notes that trooped in from the further sandy reaches. The figures certainly were chanting, but their chanting was not all he heard. Other sounds came to his ears from far away, running past him through the air from every side, and from incredible distances, all flocking down into the Wadi bed to join the parent note that summoned them. The Desert was giving voice. And memory, lifting her hood yet higher, showed more of her grey, mysterious face that searched his soul with questions. Had he so soon forgotten that strange union of form and sound which once was known to the evocative rituals of olden days?

Henriot tried patiently to disentangle this desert-music that their intoning voices woke, from the humming of the blood in his own veins. But he succeeded only in part. Sand was already in the air. There was reverberation, rhythm, measure; there was almost the breaking of the stream into great syllables. But was it due, this strange reverberation, to the countless particles of sand meeting in mid-air about him, or—to larger bodies, whose surfaces caught this friction of the sand and threw it back against his ears? The wind, now rising, brought particles that stung his face and hands, and filled his eyes with a minute fine dust that partially veiled the moonlight. But was not something larger, vaster these particles composed now also on the way?

Movement and sound and flying sand thus merged themselves more and more in a single, whirling torrent. But Henriot sought no commonplace explanation of what he witnessed; and here was the proof that all happened in some vestibule of inner experience where the strain of question and answer had no business. One sitting beside him need not have seen anything at all. His host, for instance, from Helouan, need not have been aware. Night screened it; Helouan, as the whole of modern experience, stood in front of the screen. This thing took place behind it. He crouched motionless, watching in some re-constructed ante-chamber of the soul's pre-existence, while the torrent grew into a veritable tempest.

Yet Night remained unshaken; the veil of moonlight did not quiv-er; the stars dropped their slender golden pillars unobstructed. Calm-ness reigned everywhere as before. The stupendous representation passed on behind it all.

But the dignity of the little human movements that he watched had become now indescribable. The gestures of the arms and bodies invested themselves with consummate grandeur, as these two strode into the caverns behind manifested life and drew forth symbols that represented vanished Powers. The sound of their chanting voices broke in cadenced fragments against the shores of language. The words Henriot never actually caught, if words they were; yet he under-stood their purport—these Names of Power to which the type of re-turning life gave answer as they approached. He remembered fumbling for his drawing materials, with such violence, however, that the pencil snapped in two between his fingers as he touched it. For now, even here, on the outer fringe of the ceremonial ground, there was a stir of forces that set the very muscles working in him before he had become aware of it. . . .

Then came the moment when his heart leaped against his ribs with a sudden violence that was almost pain, standing a second later still as death. The lines upon the valley floor ceased their maze-like dance. All movement stopped. Sound died away. In the midst of this profound and dreadful silence the sigils lay empty there below him. They waited to be in-formed. For the moment of entrance had come at last. Life was close.

And he understood why this return of life had all along suggested a Procession and could be no mere momentary flash of vision. From such appalling distance did it sweep down towards the present.

Upon this network, then, of splendid lines, at length held rigid, the entire Desert reared itself with walls of curtained sand, that dwarfed the cliffs, the shouldering hills, the very sky. The Desert stood on end. As once before he had dreamed it from his balcony windows, it rose upright, towering, and close against his face. It built sudden ramparts to the stars that chambered the thing he witnessed behind walls no centuries could ever bring down crumbling into dust.

He himself, in some curious fashion, lay just outside, viewing it apart. As from a pinnacle, he peered within—peered down with straining eyes into the vast picture-gallery Memory threw abruptly open. And the picture spaced its noble outline thus against the very stars. He gazed between columns, that supported the sky itself, like pillars of sand that swept across the field of vanished years. Sand poured and streamed aside, laying bare the Past.

For down the enormous vista into which he gazed, as into an avenue running a million miles towards a tiny point, he saw this moving Thing that came towards him, shaking loose the countless veils of sand the ages had swathed about it. The Ka of buried Egypt wakened out of sleep. She had heard the potent summons of her old, time-honoured ritual. She came. She stretched forth an arm towards the worshippers who evoked her. Out of the Desert, out of the leagues of sand, out of the immeasurable wilderness which was her mummied Form and Body, she rose and came. And this fragment of her he would actually see—this little portion that was obedient to the stammered and broken ceremonial. The partial revelation he would witness—yet so vast, even this little bit of it, that it came as a Procession and a host.

For a moment there was nothing. And then the voice of the woman rose in a resounding cry that filled the Wadi to its furthest precipices, before it died away again to silence. That a human voice could produce such volume, accent, depth, seemed half incredible. The walls of towering sand swallowed it instantly. But the Procession of life, needing a group, a host, an army for its physical expression, reached at that moment the nearer end of the huge avenue. It touched the Present; it entered the world of men.

X

The entire range of Henriot's experience, read, imagined, dreamed, then fainted into unreality before the sheer wonder of what he saw. In the brief interval it takes to snap the fingers the climax was thus so hurriedly upon him. And, through it all, he was clearly aware of the pair of little human figures, man and woman, standing erect and commanding at the centre—knew, too, that she directed and controlled, while he in some secondary fashion supported her—and ever watched. But both were dim, dropped somewhere into a lesser scale. It was the knowledge of their presence, however, that alone enabled him to keep his powers in hand at all. But for these two *human* beings there within possible reach, he must have closed his eyes and swooned.

For a tempest that seemed to toss loose stars about the sky swept round about him, pouring up the pillared avenue in front of the procession. A blast of giant energy, of liberty, came through. Forwards and backwards, circling spirally about him like a whirlwind, came this revival of Life that sought to dip itself once more in matter and in form. It came to the accurate out-line of its form they had traced for it. He held his mind steady enough to realise that it was akin to what men call a "descent" of some "spiritual movement" that wakens a body of believers into faith—a race, an entire nation; only that he experienced it in this brief, concentrated form before it has scattered down into ten thousand hearts. Here he knew its source and essence, behind the veil. Crudely, unmanageable as yet, he felt it, rushing loose behind appearances. There was this amazing impact of a twisting, swinging force that stormed down as though it would bend and coil the very ribs of the old stubborn hills. It sought to warm them with the stress of its own irresistible life-stream, to beat them into shape, and make pliable their obstinate resistance. Through all things the impulse poured and spread, like fire at white heat.

Yet nothing visible came as yet, no alteration in the actual landscape, no sign of change in things familiar to his eyes, while impetus thus fought against inertia. He perceived nothing form-al. Calm and untouched himself, he lay outside the circle of evocation, watching, waiting, scarcely daring to breathe, yet well aware that any minute the scene would transfer itself from memory that was subjective to matter that was objective.

And then, in a flash, the bridge was built, and the transfer was accomplished. How or where he did not see, he could not tell. It was there before he knew it—there before his normal, earthly sight. He saw it, as he saw the hands he was holding stupidly up to shield his face. For this terrific release of force long held back, long stored up, latent for centuries, came pouring down the empty Wadi bed prepared for its reception. Through stones and sand and boulders it came in an impetuous hurricane of power. The liberation of its life appalled him. All that was free, untied, responded instantly like chaff; loose objects fled towards it; there was a yielding in the hills and precipices; and even in the mass of Desert which provided their foundation. The hinges of the Sand went creaking in the night. It shaped for itself a bodily outline.

Yet, most strangely, nothing definitely moved. How could he express the violent contradiction? For the immobility was apparent only—a sham, a counterfeit; while behind it the essential *being* of these things did rush and shift and alter. He saw the two things side by side: the outer immobility the senses commonly agree upon, *and* this amazing flying-out of their inner, invisible substance towards the vortex of attracting life that sucked them in. For stubborn matter turned docile before the stress of this returning life, taught somewhere to be plastic. It was being moulded into an approach to bodily outline. A mobile elasticity invaded rigid substance. The two officiating human beings, safe at the stationary centre, and himself, just outside the circle of operation, alone remained untouched and unaffected. But a few feet in any direction, for any one of them, meant—instantaneous death. They would be absorbed into the vortex, mere corpuscles pressed into the service of this sphere of action of a mighty Body. . . .

How these perceptions reached him with such conviction, Henriot could never say. He knew it, because he *felt* it. Something fell about him from the sky that already paled towards the dawn. The stars themselves, it seemed, contributed some part of the terrific, flowing impulse that conquered matter and shaped itself this physical expression.

Then, before he was able to fashion any preconceived idea of what visible form this potent life might assume, he was aware of further change. It came at the briefest possible interval after the beginning—this certainty that, to and fro about him, as yet however indeterminate, passed Magnitudes that were stupendous as the desert. There was beauty in them too, though a terrible beauty hardly of this earth at all. A fragment of old Egypt had returned—a little portion of that vast Body of Belief that once was Egypt. Evoked by the worship of one human heart, passionately sincere, the Ka of Egypt stepped back to visit the material it once informed—the Sand.

Yet only a portion came. Henriot clearly realised that. It stretched forth an arm. Finding no mass of worshippers through whom it might express itself completely, it pressed inanimate matter thus into its service.

Here was the beginning the woman had spoken of—little opening clue. Entire reconstruction lay perhaps beyond.

And Henriot next realised that these Magnitudes in which this group-energy sought to clothe itself as visible form, were curiously familiar. It was not a new thing that he would see. Booming softly as they dropped downwards through the sky, with a motion the size of them rendered delusive, they trooped up the Avenue towards the central point that summoned them. He realised the giant flock of them—descent of fearful beauty—outlining a type of life denied to the world for ages, countless as this sand that blew against his skin. Careering over the waste of Desert moved the army of dark Splendours, that dwarfed any organic structure called a body men have ever known. He recognised them, cold in him of death, though the outlines reared higher than the pyramids, and towered up to hide whole groups of stars. Yes, he recognised them in their partial revelation, though he never saw the monstrous host complete. But, one of them, he realised, posing its eternal riddle to the sands, had of old been glimpsed sufficiently to seize its form in stone,—yet poorly seized, as a doll may stand for the dignity of a human being or a child's toy represent an engine that draws trains. . . .

And he knelt there on his narrow ledge, the world of men forgotten. The power that caught him was too great a thing for wonder or for fear; he even felt no awe. Sensation of any kind that can be named or realised left him utterly. He forgot himself. He merely watched. The glory numbed him. Block and pencil, as the reason of his presence there at all, no longer existed. . . .

Yet one small link remained that held him to some kind of consciousness of earthly things: he never lost sight of this—that, being just outside the circle of evocation, he was safe, and that the man and woman, being stationary in its untouched centre, were also safe. But— that a movement of six inches in any direction meant for any one of them instant death.

What was it, then, that suddenly strengthened this solitary link so that the chain tautened and he felt the pull of it? Henriot could not say. He came back with the rush of a descending drop to the realisation— dimly, vaguely, as from great distance—that he was with these two, now at this moment, in the Wadi Hof, and that the cold of dawn was in the air about him. The chill breath of the Desert made him shiver.

But at first, so deeply had his soul been dipped in this fragment of ancient worship, he could remember nothing more. Somewhere lay a little spot of streets and houses; its name escaped him. He had once been there; there were many people, but insignificant people. Who were they? And what had he to do with them? All recent memories had been drowned in the tide that flooded him from an immeasurable Past.

And who were they—these two beings, standing on the white floor of sand below him? For a long time he could not recover their names. Yet he remembered them; and, thus robbed of association that names bring, he saw them for an instant naked, and knew that one of them was evil. One of them was vile. Blackness touched the picture there. The man, his name still out of reach, was sinister, impure, and dark at the heart. And for this reason the evocation had been partial only. The admixture of an evil motive was the flaw that marred complete success.

The names then flashed upon him—Lady Statham—Richard Vance.

Vance! With a horrid drop from splendour into something mean and sordid, Henriot felt the pain of it. The motive of the man was so insignificant, his purpose so atrocious. More and more, with the name, came back—his first repugnance, fear, suspicion. And human terror caught him. He shrieked. But, as in nightmare, no sound escaped his lips. He tried to move; a wild desire to interfere, to protect, to prevent, flung him forward—close to the dizzy edge of the gulf below. But his muscles refused obedience to the will. The paralysis of common fear rooted him to the rocks.

But the sudden change of focus instantly destroyed the picture; and so vehement was the fall from glory into meanness, that it dislocated the machinery of clairvoyant vision. The inner perception clouded and grew dark. Outer and inner mingled in violent, inextricable confusion. The wrench seemed almost physical. It happened all at once, retreat and continuation for a moment somehow combined. And, if he did not definitely see the awful thing, at least he was aware that it had come to pass. He knew it as positively as though his eye were glued against a magnifying lens in the stillness of some laboratory. He witnessed it.

The supreme moment of evocation was close. Life, through that awful sandy vortex, whirled and raged. Loose particles showered and pelted, caught by the draught of vehement life that moulded the substance of the Desert into imperial outline—when, suddenly, shot the little evil thing across that marred and blasted it.

Into the whirlpool flew forward a particle of material that was a human being. And the Group-Soul caught and used it.

The actual accomplishment Henriot did not claim to see. He was a witness, but a witness who could give no evidence. Whether the woman was pushed of set intention, or whether some detail of sound and pattern was falsely used to effect the terrible result, he was helpless to determine. He pretends no itemised account. She went. In one second, with appalling swiftness, she disappeared, swallowed out of space and time within that awful maw—one little corpuscle among a million through which the Life, now stalking the Desert wastes, moulded itself a troop-like Body. Sand took her.

There followed emptiness—a hush of unutterable silence, stillness, peace. Movement and sound instantly retired whence they came. The avenues of Memory closed; the Splendours all went down into their sandy tombs. . . .

The moon had sunk into the Libyan wilderness; the eastern sky was red. The dawn drew out that wondrous sweetness of the Desert, which is as sister to the sweetness that the moonlight brings. The Desert settled back to sleep, huge, unfathomable, charged to the brim with life that watches, waits, and yet conceals itself behind the ruins of apparent desolation. And the Wadi, empty at his feet, filled slowly with the gentle little winds that bring the sunrise.

Then, across the pale glimmering of sand, Henriot saw a figure moving. It came quickly towards him, yet unsteadily, and with a hurry that was ugly. Vance was on the way to fetch him. And the horror of the man's approach struck him like a hammer in the face. He closed his eyes, sinking back to hide.

But, before he swooned, there reached him the clatter of the murderer's tread as he began to climb over the splintered rocks, and the faint echo of his voice, calling him by name—falsely and in pretence—for help.

The Temptation of the Clay

I

Some men grow away from places, others grow into them: It is a curious and delicate matter. Before now, a man has been thrown out by his own property, yet his successor made immediately at home there. Once let Imagination dwell upon this psychology of places and it will travel very far. Here lies a great mystery, entangled with the mystery of life itself, delicately baited, too. Only the utterly obtuse, one thinks, can ignore the hint offered by Nature—that there is this very definite relationship existing between places and human beings, and that the aggressive attitude is not always chiefly upon the side of the latter.

So it is that there are spots of country—mere bits of scenery, a valley, plain, or river bank, estate, or even garden—that undeniably bid a man stay, and welcome; or for no ascertainable reason reject him, and make him anxious to leave. Campers, looking for a night's resting-place, know this well; and so may owners of estates and houses,— campers on a larger scale, seeking to settle somewhere for the few years of a life-time. Neither one nor other, however, one thinks, unless he be a swift-minded poet with vivid divination, gets quite to the root of the matter.

Very suggestive are the mysterious processes by which such results are sometimes brought about, a certain pathos in them too. For the rejected owner is usually of that hard intellectual type that is utterly insensible to the fairy flails of Beauty, and seeks, therefore, in vain through all his stores of logic for a reasonable cause and effect; whereas the accepted one, exquisitely adjusted though he may be to the seduction of the place that takes him in, yet is unable to tell in words what really happens, or to express a tithe of that sweet marvellous explanation that lies concealed within his heart. The one denies it, the other makes wild, poetic guesses; but neither really knows.

Dick Eliot understood something of the two points of view per-haps, because he experienced both acceptance and rejection; and this story, of how a place first welcomed him, then violently tossed him out again, is as queer a case of such relationship as one may ever hear. But, then, Dick Eliot combined in himself a measure of both types of mind; he was intellectual, and knew that two and two make four, but he was also mystical, and knew that they make five or nothing, or a million—that everything is One, and One is everything. Neither was, perhaps, very strong in him, because life had not provided the opportunity for one or other's exclusive development; but both existed side by side in his general mental composition. And they resulted in a level so deli-cately poised that the apparent balance yet had instability at its roots.

Leaving England at twenty-two or three—there were misunderstand-ings with his University, where in classics and philosophy he had promised well; with his step-parents who regarded him as well lost; and in a sense, that yet did not affect his honour, with his country's law—he had since met life in difficult, rough places. He had lived. All manner of experiences had been his; he had known starvation in strange cities, and had more than once been close to death—queer kinds of death. But, also, he had been close to earth, and the earth had wonderfully taught him. The results of this teaching, not recognised at the time, came out later to puzzle and amaze him. For years he dwelt in the wilderness with life reduced to its essentials—the big, crude, thundering facts of it—so that he had come to regard scholarship, once so valued, as over-rated, and action as the sole reality. The poetic, mystical side of him passed into temporary abeyance. Worldly achievement and ambition led him. This, however, was a mood of youth only, a reaction due to the resentment of his exile, and to the grievance he cherished against the academic conventions—so he deemed them—that had cut him off from his inheritance.

At thirty, or thereabouts, he fell in love and married—a vigorous personality of a woman with Red Indian in her blood, picked up in some wild escapade along the frontiers of Arizona and New Mexico; and, within six months of marriage, the death of an aunt had left him unexpected master of this little gem of an estate in the south of England where the following experience took place.

This impulsive action of an aunt whom he had seen but once, due to her wish to spite the other claimants rather than to any pretended love for himself, resulted in a radical change of life. He came home, ignored by his relations, and ignoring them in turn. The former love of books revived; the imaginative point of view re-asserted itself; he saw life from another angle. Action, after all, was but a part of it, another form of play. The mental life was the reality; he studied, meditated, wrote. Once more the deep, poetic mystery of things lit all his thoughts with wonder. Corrected by the hard experiences of his early years, the philosopher and dreamer in him assumed the upper hand, though the speculative dreams he indulged were more sanely regulated than before. The imagination was now more finely tempered.

To look at, he was sometimes obviously forty-five, yet at others could easily have passed for thirty:—a tall, lean figure of a man; spare, as though the wilderness had taken that toll of him which no amount of subsequent easy living could efface. To see him was to think of men toiling in a hard, stern land where all things had to be conquered and nothing yielded of itself, where, moreover, human life was cheap and of small account. He was alert, always in training, cheeks thin, neck sinewy, knees ready instantly to turn a horse by grip alone, the reins unnecessary so that both hands were free to fight. The eyes were keen and dark, moustache clipped very short and partly grizzled; deep furrows marked the jaw and forehead; but the muscular hands were young, the fling of the shoulders young, the toss and set of the big head young as well. And he always dressed in riding breeches, with a strap about the waist instead of braces. You might see him hitch them up as he stepped back to leap the stream, or to take the pine knolls with a run downhill.

Indeed, the imaginative side of him seemed almost incongruous; and that such a figure could conceal a mystical, tenderly poetic side not one man in a thousand need have guessed. But, in spite of these severer traits, the character, you felt, was tender enough upon its under side. It was merely that the control of the body and emotions acquired in the wilds had never been unlearned, and that no amount of softer living could let it be forgotten.

About the rather grim and over-silent mouth, for instance, there were marks like the touches of a flower that sometimes made the sternness seem a clumsy mask. An intuitive woman, or a child, must have found him out at once.

II

After years spent as he had spent them among the conditions of primitive lands, Dick Eliot came back with his "uncivilised" wife, to find that with the old established values of English "County" existence they had little or nothing in common. Their ostracism by the neighbourhood has no place in this story, except to show how it threw them back intensely into the little property he had inherited. They lived there a dozen years, isolated, childless, knowing that solitude in a crowd which yet is never loneliness.

The "Place," as they always called it, took them, and welcome, to itself. The land, running to several hundred acres, was comparatively worthless, mere jumbled stretch of sand and pines and heathery hills; too remote from any building centre to be easily sold, and of no avail for agricultural purposes. For which, since he had just enough to live on quietly, both were grateful: they could keep it lovely and unspoilt. All round it, however, was an opulent, over-built-upon country that they loathed, since they felt that its quality, once admitted, would cause the Place to wither and die. The gross surfeit of prosperous houses, preserved woods, motoring hotels, and the rest would settle on its virgin face. Builders and business men would commercially appraise it, financiers undress it publicly so that it would know itself naked and ashamed. Deep down its soul would turn weakly and diseased, then disappear, and their own assuredly go with it.

For both had loved the Place at sight. She in particular loved it—with a kind of rude enthusiasm she forced, as it were, upon his gentler character. Its combination of qualities fascinated her—the old-world mellowness with the unkempt, untidy wildness. The way it kept alive that touch of the wilderness she had known from childhood, set in the midst of so much over-civilised country all about, gave her the feeling of having a little, precious secret world entirely to herself. She forced this view with all the vigour of her primitive poetry upon her husband till he accepted it as his own. It became his own; only she realised it more vitally than he did. The contrast laid a spell upon her, and she would not hear of going away. They lived there, in this miniature world, until they knew it with such close intimacy that it became identified with their very selves. She made him see it through her eyes, so that the place was haunted, saturated, invested with their moods of worship, love, and wonder. It became a little mystery-world that their feelings had turned living.

Thus when, after twelve years' happiness together, she died there, he stayed on, sole guardian as it were of all she had loved so dearly. Too vital a man to permit the slightest morbid growth which comes from brooding, he yet lived among fond memories, aware of her presence in every nook and glade, in every tree, her voice in the tinkle of the stream, new values everywhere. Each ridge and valley, made familiar by her step and perfume, strengthened recollection, and more than ever before the Place seemed interwoven with herself and him, subtle expression of vanished joys. The Past stayed on in it; it did not move away; it remained the Present. Her death had doubly consecrated the little estate, making it, so to speak, a sacrament of dear communion. The only change, it seemed, was that he identified it with her being more than with himself or with the two of them. He guarded it unspoilt and sweet because of her who held it once so dear—as another man might have kept a flower she had touched, a picture, or a dress that she had worn. Now it was doubly safe from the damage she had feared—commercial spoliation. "Keep the Place as it is, Dick," she had so often said with a vehemence that belonged to her vigorous type, "I'd hate to see it dirtied!" For her the civilised country round had always been "dirty." And he did so, almost with the feeling that he was keeping her person clean at the same time; for what a man thinks about is real, and he had come to regard the Place and herself as one.

Throwing himself into definite work to occupy his mind, he kept it as the apple of his eye, living in solitude, and cared for only by a motherly old housekeeper (years ago his mother's maid) whose services he had by fortunate chance secured. He spent his leisure time in writing—studies of obscure periods in forgotten history that, when published, merely added to the clutter of the world's huge mental lumber-room, to judge by the reviews. Once he made a journey to his haunts of youth, *their* youth, in Arizona, but only to return dissatisfied, with added pain. He settled down finally then, throwing himself with commendable energy into his studies, till the hurrying years brought him thus to forty-five. Rarely he went to London and pored over musty volumes in the British Museum Reading-room, but after a day or two would hear the murmur of the mill-wheel singing round that portentous, dreary dome, and back he would come again, post-haste. And perhaps he chose his line of study, rather than more imaginative work, because it reasonably absorbed him, while yet it stole no single emotion from his past with her, nor trespassed upon the walking of one dear faint ghost.

III

And it was upon this gentle, solitary household that suddenly Mánya Petrovski descended with her presence of wonder and of magic. Out of a clear blue sky she dropped upon him and made herself deliciously at home. Only daughter of his widowed sister, married to a Russian, she was fourteen at the time of her mother's death; and the duty seemed forced upon him with a conviction that admitted of no denial. He had never seen the child in his life, for she was born in the year that he returned to England, family relations simply non-existent; but he had heard of her, partly from Mrs. Coove, his housekeeper, and partly from tentative letters his sister wrote from time to time, aiming at reconciliation. He only knew that she was backward to the verge of being stupid, that she "loved Nature and life out of doors," and that she shared with her strange father a certain sulking moodiness that seemed to have been so strong in his own half-civilised Slav temperament. He also remembered that her mother, a curious mixture of puritanism and weakly dread of living, had brought her up strictly in the manufacturing city of the midlands where they dwelt "wealthily," surrounded by an atmosphere of artificiality that he deemed almost criminal. For his sister, fostering old-fashioned religious tendencies, believed that a visible Satan haunted the frontiers of her narrow orthodoxy, and would devour Mánya as soon as look at her once she strayed outside. She too had claimed, he remembered, to love Nature, though her love of it consisted solely in looking cleverly out of windows at passing scenery she need never bother herself to reach. Her husband's violent tempers she had likewise ascribed to his possession by a devil, if not by *the*—her own personal—devil himself. And when this letter, written on her death-bed, came begging him, as the only possible relative, to take charge of the child, he accepted it, as his character was, unflinchingly, yet with the greatest possible reluctance. Significant, too, of his character was the detail that, out of many others surely far more important, first haunted him: "She'll love Nature (by which he meant the Place) in the way her mother did—artificially. We shan't get on a bit!"—thus, instinctively, betraying what lay nearest to his heart.

None the less, he accepted the position without hesitation. There was no money; his sister's property was found to be mortgaged several times above its realisable value, and the child would come to him without a penny. He went headlong at the problem, as at so many other duties that had faced him—puzzling, awkward duties—with a kind of blundering delicacy native to his blood. "Got to be done, no good dreaming about it," he said to himself within a few hours of receiving the letter; and when a little later the telegram came announcing his sister's death, he added shortly with a grim expression, "Here goes, then!" In this plucky, yet not really impulsive decisiveness, the layer of character acquired in Arizona asserted itself. Action ousted dreaming.

And in due course the preparations for the girl's reception were concluded. She would make the journey south alone, and Mrs. Coove would meet her. Moreover, evidence to himself at least of true welcome, Mánya should have the bedroom which had been for years unoccupied——his wife's.

For all that, he dreaded her arrival unspeakably. "She'll be bored here. She'll dislike the Place—perhaps hate it. And I shall dislike her too."

IV

Eliot ruled his little household well, because he ruled himself. No one, from the tri-weekly gardener to the rough half-breed Westerner who managed the modest stable, felt the least desire to trifle with him. Even Mrs. Coove, in the brief morning visits to his study, did not care about asking him to repeat some sentence that she had not quite caught or understood. Yet, in a sense, as with all such men, it was the woman who really managed him. "Mrs." Coove, big, motherly, spinster, divined the child beneath the grim exterior, and simply played with him. She it was who really "ran" the household, relieving him of all domestic worries, and she it was, had he fallen ill—which, even for a day, he never did—who would have nursed him into health again with such tactfully concealed devotion that, while loving the nursing, he would never have guessed the devotion.

So it was largely upon Mrs. Coove that he secretly relied to welcome, manage, and look after his little orphaned niece, while, of course, pretending that he did it all himself.

"She'll want a companion, sir, of sorts—if I may make so bold—some one to play with," she told him when he had mentioned that later, of course, he would provide a "governess or something" when he had first "sized up" the child.

He looked hard at her for a moment. He realised her meaning, that the hostile neighbourhood could be relied on to supply nothing of that kind.

"Of course," he said, as though he had thought of it himself.

"She'll love the pony, sir, if she ain't one of the booky sort, which I seem to remember she ain't," added Mrs. Coove, looking as usual as though just about to burst into tears. For her motherly face wore a lachrymose expression that was utterly deceptive. Her contempt for books, too, and writing folk was never quite successfully concealed.

In silence he watched the old woman wipe her moist hands upon a black apron, and the perplexities of his new duties grew visibly before his eyes. She had little notion that secretly her master stood a little in awe of her superior domestic knowledge.

"The pony and the woods," he suggested briefly.

"A puppy or a kitten, sir, would help a bit—for indoors, if I may make so bold," the housekeeper ventured, with a passing gulp at her own audacity; "and out of doors, sir, as you say, maybe she'll be 'appy enough. Her pore mother taught—"

The long breath she had taken for this sentence she meant to use to the last gasp if possible. But her master cut her short.

"Miss Mánya arrives at six," he said, turning to his books and papers. "The dog-cart, with you in it, to meet her—please." The "please" was added because he knew her vivid dislike of being too high from the ground, while judging correctly that the pleasure would more than compensate her for this risk of elevation. It was also intended to convey that he appreciated her help, but deplored her wordiness. Laconic even to surliness himself, he disliked long phrases. It was a perpetual wonder to him why even lazy people who detested effort would always use a dozen words where two were more effective.

So Mrs. Coove, accustomed to his ways, departed, with a curtsey that more than anything else resembled a sudden collapse of the knees beneath more than they could carry comfortably.

"Thank you, sir; I'll see to it all right," she said, obedient to his glance, beginning the sentence in the room but finishing it in the passage. She looked as though she would weep hopelessly once outside, whereas really she felt beaming pleasure. The compliment of being sent to meet Miss Mánya made her forget her dread of the elevated, swaying dog-cart, as also of the silent half-breed groom who drove it. Full of importance she went off to make preparations.

And later, when Mrs. Coove was on her way to the station five miles off, dangerously perched, as it seemed to her, in mid-air, he made his way out slowly into the woods, a vague feeling in him that there was something he must say good-bye to. The Place henceforth, with Mánya in it, would be—not quite the same. What change would come he could not say, but something of the secrecy, the long-loved tender privacy and wonder would depart. Another would share it with him, a trespasser, in a sense an outsider. And, as he roamed the little pine-grown vales, the mossy coverts, and the knee-high bracken, there stole into him this queer sensation that it all was part of a living Something that constituted almost a distinct entity. His wife inspired it, but, also, the Place had a personality of its own, apart from the qualities he had read into it. He realised, for the first time, that it too might take an attitude towards the new arrival. Everywhere, it seemed, there was an air of expectant readiness. It was aware. . . . It might possibly resent it.

And, for moments here and there, as he wandered, rose other ideas in him as well, brought for the first time into existence by the thought of the new arrival. This element, like a sudden shaft of sunlight on a landscape, discovered to him a new aspect of the mental picture. It was vague; yet perplexed him not a little. And it was this: that the thing he loved in all this little property, thinking it always as his own, was in reality what *she* had loved in it, the thing that *she* had made him see through the lens of her own more wild, poetic vision. What he was now saying good-bye to, the thing that the expected intruder might change, or even oust, was after all but a phantom memory—the aspect she had built into it. This curious, painful doubt assailed him for the first time. Was his love and worship of the Place really an individual possession of his own, or had it been all these years but her interpretation of it that he enjoyed vicariously? The thought of Mánya's presence here etched this possibility in sharp relief. Unwelcome, and instantly dismissed, the thought yet obtruded itself—that his feelings had not been quite genuine, quite sincere, and that it was her memory, her so vital vision of the Place he loved rather than the Place itself at first hand.

For the idea that another was on the way to share it stirred the unconscious query: What precisely was it she would share?

And behind it came a still more subtle questioning that he put away almost before it was clearly born: Was he really *quite* content with this unambitious guardianship of the dream-estate, and was the grievance of his exile so completely dead that he would, under all possible conditions, keep its loveliness inviolate and free from spoliation?

The coming of the child, with the new duties involved, and the probable later claims upon his meagre purse, introduced a worldly element that for so long had slept in him. He wondered. The ghosts all walked. But beside them walked other ghosts as well. And this new, strange pain of uncertainty came with them—sinister though exceedingly faint suggestion that he had been worshipping a phantom fastened into his heart by a mind more vigorous than his own.

Ambition, action, practical achievement stirred a little in their sleep.

And on his way back he picked some bits of heather and bracken, a few larch twigs with little cones upon them, and several sprays of pine. These he carried into the house and up into the child's bedroom, where he stuck them about in pots and vases. The flowers Mrs. Coove had arranged he tossed away. For flowers in a room, or in a house at all, he never liked; they looked unnatural, artificial. Flowers and food together on a table seemed to him as dreadful as the sickly smelling wreaths people loved to put on coffins. But leaves were different; and earth was best of all. In his own room he had two wide, deep boxes of plain earth, watered daily, renewed from time to time, and more sweetly scented than any flowers in the world.

Opening the windows to let in all the sun and air there was, he glanced round him with critical approval. To most the room must have seemed bare enough, yet he had put extra chairs and tables in it, a sofa too, because he thought the child would like them. Personally, he preferred space about him; his own quarters looked positively unfurnished; rooms were cramped enough as it was, and useless upholstery gave him a feeling of oppression. He still clung to essentials; and an empty room, like earth and sky, was fine and dignified.

But Mánya, he well knew, might feel differently, and he sought to anticipate her wishes as best he might. For Mánya came from a big house where the idea was to conceal every inch of empty space with something valuable and useless; and her playground had been gardens smothered among formal flower-beds—triangles, crescents, circles, anything that parodied Nature—paths cut cleanly to neat patterns, and plants that acknowledged their shame by growing all exactly alike without a trace of individuality.

He moved to the open window, gazing out across the stretch of hill and heathery valley, thick with stately pines. The wind sighed softly past his ears. He heard the murmur of the droning mill-wheel, the drum and tinkle of falling water mingling with it. And the years that had passed since last he stood and looked forth from this window came up close and peered across his shoulder. The Past rose silently beside him and looked out too. . . . He saw it all through other eyes that once had so large a share in fashioning it.

Again came this singular impression—that, while he waited, the whole Place waited too. It knew that she was coming. Another pair of feet would run upon its face and surface, another voice wake all its little echoes, another mind seek to read its secret and share the mystery of its being.

"If Mánya doesn't like it—!" struck with real pain across his heart. But the thought did not complete itself. Only, into the strong face came a momentary expression of helplessness that sat strangely there. Whether the child would like himself or not seemed a consideration of quite minor importance.

A sound of wheels upon the gravel at the front of the house disturbed his deep reflections, and, shutting the door carefully behind him, he gave one last look round to see that all was right, and then went downstairs to meet her. The sigh that floated through his mind was not allowed to reach the lips; but another expression came up into his face. His lips became compressed, and resolution passed into his eyes. It was the look—and how he would have laughed, perhaps, could he have divined it!—the look of set determination that years ago he wore when in some lonely encampment among the Bad Lands something of danger was reported near.

With a sinking heart he went downstairs to meet his duty.

But in the hall, scattering his formal phrases to the winds, a boyish figure, yet with loose flying hair, ran up against him, then stepped sharply back. There was a moment's pitiless examination.

"Uncle Dick!" he heard, cried softly. "Is *that* what you're like? But how wonderful!" And he was aware that a pair of penetrating eyes, set wide apart in a grave but eager face, were mercilessly taking him in. It was he who was being "sized up." No redskin ever made a more rapid and thorough examination, nor, probably, a more accurate one.

"Oh! I *never* thought you would look so kind and splendid!"

"Me!" he gasped, forgetting every single thing he had planned to say in front of this swift-moving creature who attacked him.

She came close up to him, her voice breathless still but if possible softer, eyes shining like two little lamps.

"I expected—from what Mother said—you'd be—just Uncle Richard! And instead it's only Uncle—Uncle Dick!"

Here was unaffected sincerity indeed. He had dreaded—he hardly knew why—some simpering sentence of formality, or even tears at being lonely in a strange house. And, in place of either came this sort of cowboy verdict, straight as a blow from the shoulder. It took his breath away. In his heart something turned very soft and yearning. And yet he—winced.

"Nice drive?" he heard his gruff voice asking. For the life of him he could think of nothing else to say. And the answer came with a little peal of breathless laughter, increasing his amazement and confusion.

"I drove all the way. I made the blackie let me. And the mothery person held on behind like a bolster. It was glorious."

At the same moment two strong, quick arms, thin as a lariat, were round his neck. And he was being kissed—once only, though it felt all over his face. She stood on tiptoe to reach him, pulling his head down towards her lips.

"How are you, Uncle, please?"

"Thanks, Mánya," he said shortly, straightening up in an effort to keep his balance, "all right. Glad you are, too. Mrs. Coove, your 'mothery person who held on like a bolster,' will take you upstairs and wash you. Then food—soon as you like."

He had not indulged in such a long sentence for years. It increased his bewilderment to hear it. Something ill-regulated had broken loose.

Mrs. Coove, who had watched the scene from the background and doubtless heard the flattering description of herself, moved forward with a mountainous air of possession. Her face as usual seemed to threaten tears, but there was a gleam in her eyes which could only come from the joy of absolute approval. With a movement of her arm that seemed to gather the child in, she went laboriously upstairs. The back of her alone proved to any seeing eye that she had already passed willingly into the state of abject slavery that all instinctive mothers love.

"We shan't be barely five minutes, sir," she called respectfully when half-way up; and the way she glanced down upon her grim master, who stood still with feet wide apart watching them, spoke further her opinion—and her joy at it—that he too was caught within her toils. "She'll manage you, sir, if I may make so bold," was certainly the thought her words did not express.

They vanished round the corner—the heavy tread and the light, pattering step. And he still stood on there, waiting in the hall. A mist rose just before his eyes; he did not see quite clearly. In his heart a surge of strong, deep feeling struggled upwards, but was instantly suppressed. Mánya had said another thing that moved him far more than her childish appreciation of himself, something that stirred him to the depths most strangely.

For, when he asked her how she enjoyed the drive, the girl had replied with undeniable sincerity, looking straight into his eyes:

"The last bit was like a fairy-tale. Uncle, *how* awfully this place must love you!"

She did not say, "How you must love the place!" And—she loathed the "dirty" country all about.

Then, the first rush of excitement over, a sort of shyness, curiously becoming, had settled down all over her like a cloud. It settled down upon himself as well. But—she had said the perfect thing. And his doubts all vanished. It *was*—yes, surely—the Place she loved.

And yet, when all was over, there passed through him an unpleasant afterthought—as though Mánya had applied a test by which already something in himself was found gravely wanting.

V

With its sharp, pine-grown declivities, its tumbling streams, stretches of open heather, and its miniature forests of bracken, the dream-estate was like a liliputian Scotland compressed into a few hundred acres. All was in exquisite proportion.

The old house of rough grey stone, set in one corner, looked out upon a wild, untidy garden that melted unobserved into woods of mystery beyond, and farther off rose sharp against the sky a series of peaked knolls and ridges that in certain lights looked like big hills many miles away. There were diminutive fairy valleys you could cross in twenty minutes; and several rivulets, wandering from the moorlands higher up, formed the single stream that once had worked the Mill.

But the Mill, standing a stone's-throw from the study windows, so that he heard the water singing and gurgling almost among his bookshelves, had for a century ground nothing more substantial than sunshine, air, and shadow. For the gold-dust of the stars is too fine for grinding. But it ground as well the dreams of the lonely occupant of the grey-toned house. And he let it stand there, falling gradually into complete decay, because beneath those crumbling wooden walls—he remembered it as of yesterday—the sudden stroke had come that in a moment, dropping as it seemed out of eternity, had robbed him of his chief possession—fashioner of the greatest dream of all. The splash and murmur of the water, the drone of the creaking wheel in flood time, the white weed that gathered thickly over the pond formed by the ancient dam, and the red-brown tint of walls and rotting roof,—all were like the colour of the water's singing, the colour of her memory, and the colour of his thinking too, made sweetly visible.

Indeed, despite his best control, *she* still lurked everywhere, so that he could not recall a single experience of the past years without at the same time some vivid aspect of the scenery, as she saw it, rising up clearly to accompany it. In every corner stood the ghost of a still recoverable mood. Here he had suffered, fought, and prayed; here he had loved and hated; here he had lost and found. All the kaleidoscope aspects of growing older, of hopes and fears and disappointments, were visualised for him in terms of the Place where he had met and dealt with them for his soul's good or ill. But behind them always stood that Figure in Chief; it was she who directed the ghostly band; and she it was who coaxed the romantic scenery thus into the support of all his personal moods, and continued to do so with even greater power after she was gone.

His respect for the Place seemed, therefore, involved with his respect for himself and her. That tumbling stream had an inalienable right of way; that mill of golden-brown claimed ancient lights as truly as any mental palace of thoughts within his mind; and the little dips and rises in the woods were as sacred—so he had always felt—as were those twists and turns of character that he called his views of life and his beliefs. This blending of himself with the Place and her had been very carefully reared. The notion that its foundations were not impregnable for ever was a most disturbing one. That the mere arrival of an intruder could shake it, possibly shatter it, touched sacrilege. And for long he suppressed the outrageous notion so successfully that he almost entirely forgot about it.

This strip of vivid land whereon he dwelt acquired, moreover, a heightened charm from the character of the odious land surrounding it. For on all sides was that type of country best described as over-fed and over-lived-upon. The scenery was choked and smothered unto death; it breathed, if at all, the breath of a fading life pumped through it artificially and with labour. Heavily beneath the skies it lay—acres of inert soil.

There were, indeed, people who admired it, calling it typical of something or other in the south of England; but for him these people, like the land itself, were bourgeois, dull, insipid, and phlegmatic as the back of a sheep. Like rooms in a big club, it was over-furnished with too solid upholstery—thick, fat hedges, formal oak woods, lifeless copses stuck upon slopes from which successful crops had sucked long ago the last vestiges of spontaneous life; and spotted with self-satisfied modern cottages, "improved" beyond redemption, that made him think with laughter of some scattered group of city aldermen. "They're pompous City magnates," he used to tell his wife, "strayed from the safety of Cornhill, and a little frightened by the wind and rain."

Everywhere, amid bushy trees that looked so pampered they were almost sham, stood "country houses," whole crops of them, dozing after heavy meals among gardens of sleek tulip and geraniums. They plastered themselves, with the atmosphere of small Crystal Palaces, upon every available opening, comfortably settled down and weighted with every conceivable modern appliance, and in "Parks" all cut to measure like children's wooden toys. They stood there, heavy and respectable, living close to the ground, and in them, almost without exception, dwelt successful business men who owned a "country seat." From his uncivilised, wild-country point of view, they epitomised the soul of the entire scenery about them—something gross and sluggish that involved stagnation. They brooded with an air of vulgar luxury that was too stupid even to be active. Here "resided," in a word, the wealthy.

When he walked or drove through the five miles of opulent ugliness that lay between Mill House and the station, it seemed like crossing an inert stretch of adipose tissue, then lighting suddenly upon a pulsating nerve-centre. To step back into the fresh and hungry beauty of his pine valley, with its tumbling waters and its fragrance of wild loveliness, was an experience he never ceased to take delight in. The air at once turned keen, the trees gave out sharp perfumes, waters rustled, foliage sang. Oh! here was life, activity, and movement. Vital currents flowed through and over it. The grey house among the fir-trees, beckoning to the Mill beyond, was a place where things might happen and pass swiftly. Here was no stagnation possible. Thrills of beauty, denied by that grosser landscape, returned electrically upon the heart. With every breath he drew in wonder and enchantment.

And all this, for some years now, he had enjoyed alone. Rather than diminishing with his middle age, the spell had increased. Then came this sudden question of another's intrusion upon his dream-estate, and he had dreaded painful alteration. The presence of another, most likely stupid, and certainly unsympathetic, must cause a desolating change. Alteration there was bound to be, or at the best a readjustment of values that would steal away the wild and accustomed flavour. He had dreaded the child's arrival unspeakably. It had turned him abruptly timid, and this timidity betrayed the sweetness of the treasure that he guarded. For it came close to fear—the fear men know when they realise an attack they cannot, by any means within their power, hope to defeat.

And alteration, as he apprehended, came; yet not the alteration he had dreaded. Mánya's arrival had been a surprise that was pure joy. Its wonder almost woke suspicion. And the surprise, he found, grew into a series of surprises that at first took his breath away. The alchemy that her little shining presence brought persisted, grew from day to day, till it operated with such augmenting power that it changed himself as well. No stranger fairy-tale was ever written.

VI

Next day he put his work aside and devoted himself whole-heartedly to the lonely child. It was not only duty now. She had stirred his love and pity from the first. They would get on together. Unconsciously, by saying the very thing to win him—"Uncle, *how* the Place must love you!"—she had struck the fundamental tone that made the three of them in harmony, and set the whole place singing. The sense of an intruding trespasser had vanished. The Place accepted her.

It was only later that he realised this completely and in detail, though on looking back he saw clearly that the verdict had been given instantly. For no revision changed it. "I'm all right here with Uncle," was the child's quick intuition, meeting his own half-way:—"We three are all right here together." For she leaped upon his beloved dream-estate and made it seem twice as wild and living as before. She delighted in its loneliness and mystery. She clapped her hands and laughed, pointed and asked questions, made her eyes round with wonder, and, in a word, put her own feelings from the start into each nook and corner where he took her. There was no shyness, no confusion; she made herself at home with a little air of possession that, instead of irritating as it might have done, was utterly enchanting. It was like the chorus of approval that increases a man's admiration for the woman he has chosen.

She brought her own interpretations, too, yet without destroying his own. They even differed from his own, yet only by showing him points and aspects he had not realised. The child saw things most oddly from another point of view. From the very first she began to say astonishing things. They piqued and puzzled him to the end, these things she said. He felt they unravelled something. In his own mind the personality of the Place and the memory of his wife had become confused and jumbled, as it were. Mánya's remarks and questions disentangled something. Her child's divination cleared his perceptions with a singular directness. She had strong in her that divine curiosity of children which is as far removed from mere inquisitiveness as gold-dust from a vulgar-finished ornament. Wonder in her was vital and insatiable, and some of these questions that he could not answer stirred in him, even on that first day of acquaintance, almost the sense of respect.

Morning and afternoon they spent together in visiting every corner of the woods and valleys; no inch was left without inspection; they followed the stream from the moorlands to the Mill, plunged through the bracken, leaped the high tufts of heather, and scrambled together down the precipitous sandpits. She did not jump as well as he did, but showed equal recklessness. And the depths of shadowy pinewood made her hushed and silent like himself. In her childish way she *felt* the wild charm of it all deeply. Not once did she cry "How lovely" or "How wonderful"; but showed her happiness and pleasure by what she did.

"Better than yesterday, eh?" he suggested once, to see what she would answer, yet sure it would be right.

She darted to his side. "That was all stuffed," she said, laconically as himself, and making a wry face. And then she added with a grave expression, half anxious and half solemn, "Fancy, if *that* got in! Oh, Uncle!"

"Couldn't," he comforted himself and her, delighted secretly.

But it was on their way home to tea in the dusk, feeling as if they had known one another all their lives, so quickly had friendship been cemented, that she said her first genuinely strange thing. For a long time she had been silent by his side, apparently tired, when suddenly out popped this little criticism that showed her mind was actively working all the time.

"Uncle, you *have* been busy—keeping it so safe. I suppose you did most of it at night."

He started. His own thoughts had been travelling in several directions at once.

"I don't walk in my sleep," he laughed.

"I mean when the stars are shining," she said. She felt it as delicately as that, then! She felt the dream quality in it. "I mean, it loves you best when the sun has set and it comes out of its hole," she added, as he said nothing.

"Mánya, it loves you too—already," he said gently.

Then came the astonishing thing. The voice was curious; the words seemed to come from a long way off, taking time to reach him. They took time to reach her too, as though another had first whispered them. It almost seemed as though she listened while she said them. A sense of the uncanny touched him here in the shadowy dark wood:

"It's a woman, you see, really, and that's why you're so fond of it. That's why it likes me too, and why I can play with it."

The amazing judgment gave him pause at once, for he felt no child ought to know or say such things. It savoured of precociousness, even of morbidity, both of which his soul loathed. But reflection brought clearer judgment. The sentence revealed something he had already been very quick to divine, namely, that while the ordinary mind in her was undeveloped, backward, almost stunted, by her bringing up, another part of her was vividly aware. And this other part was taught of Nature; it was the fairy thing that children had the right to know. She stood close to the earth. Landscape and scenery brought her vivid impressions that fairy-tales, rather stupidly, translate into princes and princesses, ogres, giants, dragons. Mánya, having been denied the fairy books, personified these impressions after her own fashion. What was it after all but the primitive instinct of early races that turned the moods of Nature into beings, calling them gods, or the instinct of a later day that personified the Supreme, calling it God? He himself had "felt" in very imaginative moments that bits of scenery, as with trees and even the heavenly bodies, could actually express such differences of temperament, seem positive or negative, almost male or female.

And perhaps, in her original, child's fashion, she felt it too.

Then Mánya interrupted his reflections with a further observation that scattered his philosophising like an explosion. Something, as he heard it, came up close and brushed him. It made him start.

"In some places, you see, Uncle, I feel shy all over. But here I could run about naked. I could undress."

He burst out laughing. Instinctively he felt this was the best thing he could do. A sympathetic answer might have meant too much, yet silence would have made her feel foolish. His laughter turned the idea in her little mind all wholesome and natural.

"Play here to your heart's content, for there's no one to disturb you," he cried. "And when I'm too busy," he added, thinking it a happy inspiration, "Mrs. Coove can—"

"Oh," she interrupted like a flash, "but she's too bulgey. She could never jump like you, for one thing."

"True."

"Or play hide-and-seek. She couldn't fit in anywhere. She'd never be able to hide, you see."

And so they reached the house, like two friends who had found suddenly a new delight in life, and sat down to an enormous tea, with jam, buttered muffins, and a stodgy indigestible cake straight from the oven. His tea hitherto had consisted of one cup and two pieces of thin bread and butter. But the appetite of twenty-five had come back again.

A new joy of life had come back with it. After so many years of brooding, dreaming, solitary working, he had grown over solemn, the sense of fun and humour atrophying. He had erected barriers between himself and all his kind, hedged himself in too much. The arrival of this child brought new impetus into the enclosure. Without destroying what imagination had prized so long, she shifted the old values into slightly different keys. Already he caught his thoughts running forward to construct her future—what she might become, how he might help her to develop spiritually and materially—yes, materially as well. His thoughts had hitherto run chiefly backwards.

This need not, indeed could not, involve being unfaithful to the past. But it did mean looking ahead instead of always looking back. It was more wholesome.

Yet what dawned upon him—rather, what chiefly struck him out of his singular observations perhaps, was this: not only that the Place had whole-heartedly accepted her, but that she had instantly established some definite relation with it that was different to his own. It was even deeper, truer, more vital than his own; for it was somehow more natural. It had been discovered, though already there; and it was not, like his own, built up by imaginative emotion. Hence came his notion that she disentangled something; hence the respect he felt for her from the start; hence, too, the original, surprising things she sometimes said.

VII

For several days he watched and studied her, while she turned the Place into a private playground of her own with that air of sweet possession that had charmed him from the first. Backward and undeveloped she undeniably was, but, in view of her stupid, artificial bringing up, he understood this easily. Of books and facts, of knowledge taught in school, she was shockingly ignorant. The wrong part of her had been "forced" at the wrong time; the "play" side had been denied development, and, while gathering force underground, her little brain had learned by heart, but without real comprehension, things that belonged properly to a later stage. For if ever there was one, here was an elemental being, free of the earth, native of open places, called to the wisdom of the woods. It all had been suppressed in her. She now broke out and loose, bewildered, and a little rampant, wild rather, and over joyful. She revelled like an animal in new-found freedom.

In time she sobered. He led her wisely. Yet often she went too fast for him to follow, and slipped beyond his understanding altogether. For there were gaps in her nature, unfilled openings in her mind, loopholes through which she seemed to escape too easily, perhaps too completely, into her playground, certainly too rapidly for him to catch her up. It was then she said these things that so astonished him, making him feel she was somehow an eldritch soul that saw things, Nature especially, from a point of view he had never reached. Her sight of everything was original. A bird's-eye view he could understand; most primitive folk possessed it, and in his wife it had been vividly illuminating. But Mánya had not got this bird's-eye view, the sweeping vision that takes in everything at a single glance from above. Her angle was another one, peculiar to herself. Laughing, he thought of it rather as seeing everything from below—a fish's point of view!

Brightness described her best—eyes, skin, teeth, and lips all shone. Yet her manner was subdued, not effervescent, and in it this evidence of depth, a depth he could not always plumb. It was a nature that sparkled, but the sparkle was suppressed; and he loved the sparkle, while loving even more its suppression. It gathered till the point of flame was reached, and it was the possible out-rushing of this potential flame that won his deference, and sometimes stirred his awe. His dread had been considerable, anticipation keen; and the relief was in proportion. Here was a child he could both respect and love; and the sense of responsibility for the little being entrusted to his charge grew very strong indeed.

In due course he supplied a governess, Fräulein Bühlke. She came from the neighbouring town, with her broad, flat German face, framed in flaxen hair that was glossy but not oiled, and smoothed down close to the skull across a shining parting. Mechanically devout, rather fussy, literal in mind, exceedingly worthy and conscientious, her formula was, "You think that would be wise? Then I try it." And the "trying," which the tone suggested would be delicate, was applied with a blundering directness that defeated its own end. Her method was thumping rather than insinuating, and her notion of delicacy was to state her meaning heavily, add to it, "Try to believe that I know best, dear child," and then conscientiously enforce it. Mánya she understood as little as an okapi, but she was kind, affectionate, and patient; and though Eliot always meant to change her, he never did, for the getting of a suitable governess was more than he and Mrs. Coove could really manage. *"Der liebe Gott weisst alles,"* was the phrase with which she ended all their interviews. And if Mánya's obedience showed a slight contempt, it was a contempt he did not think it wise entirely to check.

For he himself could never scold her. It was impossible. It felt as though he stepped upon a baby. Their relations were those of equals almost, each looking up to the other with respect and wonder. Her schoolroom life became a thing apart. So did the hours in his study. Her walks with the governess and his journeys to the British Museum were mere extensions of the schoolroom and the study. It was when they went out together, roaming about the Place at will, exploring, playing, building fires, and the rest, that their true enjoyment came—

enjoyment all the keener because each stuck valiantly to duty first.

Her face, though not exactly pretty, had the charm of some wild intelligence he had never seen before. The nose, slightly tilted, wore a tiny platform at its tip. The mouth was firm, lips exquisitely cut, but it was in the dark, shining eyes that the expression of the soul ran into focus; though at times she knew long periods of silence that seemed almost sullen, when her eyes turned dead and coaly, and she seemed almost gone away from behind them. One day she was old as himself, another a mere baby; something was always escaping the leash and slipping off, then coming back with a rush of some astonishing sentence it had gone to fetch. Her physical appearance sometimes was elusive too, now tall, now short, her little body protean as her little soul.

Like running water she was all over the house, not laughing much, not exactly gay or cheerful either, but somehow charged to the brim with a mysterious spirit of play—grave, earnest play, yet airy with a consummate mischief sometimes that was the despair of Fräulein Bühlke, who wore an expression then as though, after all, there were things God did *not* know. Yes, like running water through the rooms and corridors, and tumbling down the stairs behind the kitten or round the skirts of "bulgey" Mother Coove. Swift and gentle always, yet with force enough to hurt you if you got in her way; almost to sting or slap. Soft, and very girlish to look at, she was really hard as a boy, flexible too as a willow branch, and with a rod of steel laced somewhere invisibly through her tenderness, unsuspected till occasion—rarely—betrayed its presence. It shifted its position too; one never knew where that firmness which is character would crop out and refuse to bend. For then the childishness would vanish. She became imperious as a little natural queen. The half-breed groom had a taste of this latter quality more than once, and afterwards worshipped the ground she walked on. To see them together, she in her dark-grey riding-habit, holding a little whip, and he with his sinister, wild face and half malignant manners, called up some picture of a child and a savage animal she had tamed.

But the thing Mánya chiefly brought into his garden, and so also into the garden of his thoughts, was this new element of Play. She brought with her, not only the child's make-believe, but the child's conviction, earnestness, and sense of reality.

"Tell me *one* thing," she had a way of saying, sure preface to something of significant import that she had to ask, accompanied always by a darker expression in the eyes, puzzled or searching and not on any account to be evaded or lightly answered; "Tell me one thing, Uncle: do these outside things come after us into the house as well?" "Only when we allow them, or invite them in," he replied, taking up her mood as seriously as herself, yet knowing her question to be a feint. She knew the true answer better than himself. She wished to see what he would say. Her sly laughter of approval told him that. "They're already there, though, aren't they?" she whispered, and when he nodded agreement, she added, "Of course; they're everywhere really all the time. They don't move about as we do."

But she had often this singular way of seeing things, and saying them, from the original point of view whence she regarded them—from beneath, as it were, topsy-turvy some might call it, almost a little mad, judged by the sheep-like vision of the majority, yet for herself entirely true, consistent, not imagined merely.

Her literal use of words, too, was sometimes vividly illuminating—as though she saw language *directly,* and robbed of the cloak with which familiar use has smothered it. She undressed phrases, making them shine out alone.

"Moping, child?" he asked once, when one of her silent fits had been somewhat prolonged. "Unhappy?"

"No, Uncle. And I'm *not* moping."

"What is it, then?"

"Fräulein told me I was self-ish, rather."

"That's all right," he said to comfort her. "Be yourself—self-ish—or you're nothing."

She followed her own thought, perhaps not understanding him quite.

"She said I must put my Self out more—for others. Mother used to say it too."

He turned and stared at her. The little face was very grave.

"Eh?" he asked. "Put your Self out?"

Mánya nodded, fixing her eyes, half dreamy, upon his own. She had been far away. Now she was coming back.

"So I'm learning," she said, her voice coming as from a distance.

"It's *so* funny. But it's not really difficult—a bit. I could teach you, I think, if you'd promise faithfully to practise regularly."

There was a pause before he asked the next question.

"How d'you do it, child?" came a little gruffly, for he felt queer emotion rising in him.

She shrugged her shoulders.

"Oh, I couldn't tell you *like that*. I could only show you."

There was a touch of weirdness about the child. It stole into him—a faint sense of eeriness, as though she were letting him see through peepholes into that other world she knew so well.

"Well," he asked, more gently, "what happens when you *have* put your Self—er—out? Other things come in, eh?"

"How can I tell?" she answered like a flash. "I'm out."

He stared at her, waiting for more. But nothing followed, and a minute later she was as usual, laughing, her brilliant eyes flashing with mischief, and presently went upstairs to get tidy for their evening meal that was something between an early dinner and high tea. Only at the door she paused a second to fling him another of her characteristic phrases:

"I wonder, Uncle. Don't you?" For she certainly knew some natural way, born in her, of moving her Self aside and letting the tide of "bigger things" sweep in and use her. It was her incommunicable secret.

And he did wonder a good deal. Wonder with him had never faded as with most men. It had often puzzled him why this divine curiosity about everything should disappear with the majority after twenty-five, instead, rather, of steadily increasing the more one knows. Familiarity with those few scattered details the world calls knowledge had never dulled its golden edge for him. Only Mánya, and the things she asked and said, gave it a violent new impetus that was like youth returned. And her notion of putting one's Self out in order to let other things come in filled him with about as much wonder as he could comfortably hold just then. He dozed over the fire, thinking deeply, wishing that for a single moment he could stand where this child stood, see things from her point of view, learn the geography of the world she lived in. The source of her inspiration was Nature of course. Yet he too stood close to Nature and was full of sympathetic understanding for her mystery and beauty. Did Mánya then stand nearer than himself? Did she, perhaps, dwell inside it, while he examined from the outside only, a mere onlooker, though an appreciative and loving onlooker?

It came to him that things yielded up to her their essential meaning because she saw them from another side, and he recalled an illuminating line of Alice Meynell about a daisy, and how wonderful it must be to see from "God's side," even of such a simple thing.

Mánya, moreover, saw everything in some amazing fashion as One. The facts of common knowledge men studied so laboriously in isolated groups were but the jewelled facets that hung glittering upon the enormous flanks of this One. The thought flashed through his mind. He remembered another thing she said, and then another; they began to crowd his brain. "I never dream because I know it all awake," she told him once; and only that afternoon, when he asked her why she always stopped and stood straight before him—a habit she had—when he spoke seriously with her, she answered, "Because I want to see you properly. I must be opposite for that! No one can see their own face, or what's next to them, can they?"

Truth, and a philosophical truth! Of no particular importance, maybe, yet strange for a child to have discovered.

Even her ideas of space were singularly original, direct, unhampered by the terms that smother meaning. "Up" and "down" perplexed her; "left" and "right" perpetually deceived her; even "inside" and "outside," when she tried to express them, landed her in a chaos of confusion that to most could have seemed only sheer stupidity. She stood, as it were, in some attitude of naked knowledge behind thought, perception unfettered, untaught, in which she knew that space was only a way of talking about something that no one ever really understands. She saw space, felt it rather, in some absolute sense, not yet "educated" to treat it relatively. She saw everything "round," as though her spatial perceptions were all circles. And circles are infinite, eternal.

With Time, too, it was somewhat similar. "It'll come round again," she said once, when he chided her for having left something undone earlier in the day; or, "when I get back to it, Uncle," in reply to his reminding her of a duty for the following day. To the end she was "stupid" about telling the time, and until he cured her of it her invariable answer to his question, "what o'clock it was," would be the literal truth that it was "just now, Uncle," or simply "now," as though she saw things from an absolute, and not a relative point of view. She was always saying things to prove it in this curious manner. And, while it made him sometimes feel uncomfortable in a way he could not quite define, it also increased his attitude of respect towards the secret, mysterious thing she hid so well, though without intending to hide it. She seemed in touch with eternal things—more than other children—not merely with a transient expression of them filtered down for normal human comprehension. Some giant thing she certainly knew. She lived it. Death, for instance, was a conception her mind failed to grasp. She could not realise it. People had "left" or "gone away," perhaps, but somehow for her were always *"there."*

Thus started, his thoughts often travelled far, but always came up with a shock against that big black barrier—the army of the dead. The dead, of course, were always somewhere—if there was survival. But, though he had encountered strange phases of the spiritualistic movement in America, he had known nothing to justify the theory of interference from the other side of that black barrier. The deliverances of the mediums brought no conviction. He sometimes wondered, that was all. And in particular he wondered about that member of the great army who had been for years his close and dear companion. This was natural enough. Could it be that his thought, prolonged and concentrated, formed a prison-house from which escape was difficult? And had his own passionate thinking that ever associated her memory with the Place, detained one soul from farther flight elsewhere? Was this an explanation of that hint Mánya so often brought him—that her presence helped to disentangle, liberate, unravel . . . ? Was the Place haunted in this literal sense? . . .

VIII

Yet, perhaps, after all, the chief change she introduced was this vital resurrection of his sense of play. For Play is eternal, older than the stars, older even than dreams. She taught him afresh things he had already known, but long forgotten or laid aside. And all she knew came first direct from Nature, large and undiluted.

He learned, for instance, the secret of that deep quiet she possessed even in her wildest moments; and how it came from a practice in her mother's house, where all was rush and clamour about worldly "horrid things"—her practice of lying out at night to watch the stars. But not merely to watch them for a minute. She would watch for hours, following the constellations from the moment they loomed above the horizon till they set again at dawn. She saw them move slowly across the entire sky. For "mother hurried and fussed" her so, and by doing this she instinctively drew into her curious wild heart the deep delight of feeling that "there was lots of room really, and no particular hurry about anything." Her inspiration was profound, from ancient sources, natural.

And her "play," for the same reason, was never foolish. It was creative play. It was the faculty by which the poets and dreamers re-create the world, and thus rejuvenate it. Adam knew it when he named the beasts, and Job, when he made rhymes about taking Leviathan with a hook, and sang his little heart-sweet songs about the conies and the hopping hills. In the wise it never dies, for it is most subtly allied to wisdom, and only the dreamless can divorce it quite. It is the natural, untaught poetry of the soul which laughs and weeps with Nature, knowing itself akin, seeing itself in everything and everything in itself. Mánya in some amazing fashion, not yet educated out of her, knew Nature in herself.

She did naughty things too, as he learned from Mrs. Coove, when he felt obliged to lecture her, but they were invariably typical and explanatory of her close-to-Nature little being. And he understood what she felt so well that his lectures ended in laughter, with her grave defence "Uncle, you'd have done the same yourself." Once in particular, after a fortnight of parching drought, when the gush of warm rain came with its welcome, drenching soak, and the child ran out upon the balcony in her nightgown to feel it on her body too—how could he prove her wrong, having felt the same delight himself? "I was thirsty and dry all over. I *had* to do it," she explained, puzzled, adding that of course she had changed afterwards and used the rough Turkey towel "just as you do."

But other things he did not understand so well; and one of these was her singular habit of imitating the sounds of Nature, with an accuracy, too, that often deceived even himself. The true sounds of Nature are only two—water and wind, with their many variations. And Mánya, by some trick of tone and breath, could reproduce them marvellously.

"It's the way to get close," she told him when he asked her why, "the way to get inside. If you get the sound exact, you feel the same as they do, and know their things." And the cryptic, yet deeply suggestive explanation contained a significant truth that yet just evaded his comprehension. They often played it together in the woods, though he never approached her own astonishing excellence. This, again, stirred something like awe in him; it was a little eerie, almost uncanny, to hear her "doing trees," or "playing wind and water."

But the strangest of all her odd, original tricks was one that he at length dissuaded her from practising because he felt it stimulated her imagination unwisely, and with too great conviction. It is not easy to describe, and to convey the complete success of the achievement is impossible without seeing the actual results. For she drew invisible things. Her designs, so clumsily done with a butt of pencil, or even the point of her stick in the sand, managed to suggest a meaning that somehow just escaped grasping by the mind. They made him think of puzzle-pictures that intentionally conceal a face or figure. Vague, fluid shapes that never quite achieved an actual form ran through these scattered tracings. She used points in the scenery to indicate an outline of something other than themselves, yet something they contained and clothed. His eye vainly tried to force into view the picture that he felt lay there hiding within these points.

On a large sheet of paper she would draw roughly details of the landscape—tops of trees, the Mill roof, a boulder or a stretch of the stream, for instance—and persuade these points to gather the blank space of paper between them into the semblance, the suggestion rather, of some vague figure, always vast and always very much alive. They marked, within their boundaries, an outline of some form that remained continually elusive. Yet the outline thus framed, whichever way you looked at it, even holding the paper upside down, still remained a figure; a figure, moreover, that moved. For the child had a way of turning the paper round so that the figure had an appearance of moving independently upon itself. The reality of the whole business was more than striking; and it was when she came to giving these figures names that he decided to put a stop to it.

One day another curious thing had happened. He had often thought about it since, and wondered whether its explanation lay in mere child's mischief, or in some power of discerning these invisible Presences that she drew.

They were returning together from a scramble in the gravel-pit which they pretended was a secret entrance to the centre of the world; and they were tired. Mánya walked a little in front, as her habit was, so that she could turn and see him "opposite" at a moment's notice when he said an interesting thing. Her red tam-o'-shanter, with the top-knot off, she carried in her hand, swinging it to and fro. From time to time she flicked it out sideways, as though to keep flies away. But there were no flies, for it was chilly and growing dark. The pines were thickly planted here, with sudden open spaces. Their footsteps fell soft and dead upon the needles. And sometimes she flung her arm out with an imperious, sudden gesture of defiance that made him feel suspicious and look over his shoulder. For it was like signing to some one who came close, some one he could not see, but whose presence was very real to her. The unwelcome conviction grew upon him. Some one, in the world she knew apart from him, accompanied them. A few minutes before she had been wild and romping, playing at "mush-rooms" with laughter and excitement. She loved doing this—whirling round on her toes till her skirts were horizontal, then sinking with them ballooning round her to the ground, the tam-o'-shanter pulled down over her entire face so that she looked like a giant toadstool with a crimson top. But now she had turned suddenly grave and silent.

"Uncle!" she exclaimed abruptly, turning sharply to face him, and using the hushed tone that was always prelude to some startling ques-tion, "tell me *one* thing, please. What would *you* do if—"

She broke off suddenly and sprang swiftly to one side.

"Mánya! if what?" He did not like the movement; it was so obvi-ously done to avoid something that stood in her way—between them—very close. He almost jumped too. "I can't tell you anything while you're darting about like a deer-fly. What d'you want to know?" he added with involuntary sharpness.

She stood facing him with her legs astride the path. She stared straight into his eyes. The dusk played tricks with her height, always delusive. It magnified her. She seemed to stand over him, towering up.

"If some one kept walking close beside you under an umbrella," she whispered earnestly, "so that the face was hidden and you could never see it—what would *you* do?"

"Child! But what a question!" The carelessness in his tone was not quite natural. A shiver ran down his back.

She moved closer, so that he felt her breath and saw the gleam of her big, wide-opened eyes.

"Would you knock up the umbrella with a bang," she whispered, as though afraid she might be overheard, "or just suddenly stoop and look beneath—catching it that way?"

He stepped aside to pass her, but the child stepped with him, barring his movement of escape. She meant to have her answer.

"Take it by surprise like that, I mean. *Would* you, Uncle?"

He stared blankly at her; the conviction in her voice and manner was disquieting.

"Depends what kind of thing," he said, seeing his mistake. He tried to banter, and yet at the same time seem serious. But to joke with Mánya in this mood was never very successful. She resented it. And above all he did not want to lose her confidence.

"Depends," he said slowly, "whether I felt it friendly or unfriendly; but I *think*—er—I should prefer to knock the brolly up."

For a moment she appeared to weigh the wisdom of his judgment, then instantly rejecting it.

"*I* shouldn't!" she answered like a flash. "I should suddenly run up and stoop to see. I should catch it that way!"

And, before he could add a word or make a movement to go on, she darted from beside him with a leap like a deer, flew forwards several yards among the trees, stooped suddenly down, then turned her head and face up sideways as though to peer beneath something that spread close to the ground. Her skirts ballooned about her like the mushroom, one hand supporting her on the earth, while the other, holding the tam-o'-shanter, shaded her eyes.

"Oh! oh!" she cried the next instant, standing bolt upright again, "it's a whole lot! And they've all gone like lightning—gone off there!" She pointed all about her—into the sky, towards the moors, back to the forest, even down into the earth—a curious sweeping gesture; then hid her face behind both hands and came slowly to his side again.

"It wasn't one, Uncle. It was a lot!" she whispered through her fingers. Then she dropped her hands as a new explanation flashed into her. "But p'raps, after all, it was only one! Oh, Uncle, I do believe it *was* only one. Just fancy—how awfully splendid! I wonder!"

Neither the hour nor the place seemed to him suitable for such a discussion. He put his arm round her and hurried out of the wood. He put the woods behind them, like a protective barrier; for his sake as well as hers; that much he clearly realised. He somehow made a shield of them.

In the garden, with the stars peeping through thin clouds, and the lights of the windows beckoning in front, he turned and said laughing, quickening his pace at the same time:

"Rabbits, Mánya, rabbits! All the rabbits here use brollies, and the bunnies too." It was the best thing he could think of at the moment. Rather neat he thought it. But her instant answer took the wind out of his sham sails.

"That's just the name for them!" she cried, clapping her hands softly with delight. "Now they needn't hide like that any more. We'll just pretend they're bunnies, and they'll feel disguised enough."

They went into the house, and it was comforting to see the figure of Mother Coove filling the entire hall. At least there was no disguising her. But on the steps Mánya halted a moment and gazed up in his face. She stood in front of him, deaf to Mrs. Coove's statements from the rear about wet boots. Her eyes, though shining with excitement, held a puzzled, wild expression.

"Uncle," she whispered, with sly laughter, standing on tiptoe to kiss him, "I wonder—!" then flew upstairs to change before he could find a suitable reply.

But he wondered too, wondered what it was the child had seen. For certainly she had seen something.

Yet the thought that finally stayed with him—as after all the other queer adventures they had together—was this unpleasant one, that his so willing acceptance of the little intruder involved the disapproval, even the resentment, of—another. It haunted him. He never could get quite free of it. Another watched, another listened, another—waited. And Mánya knew.

IX

Autumn passed into winter, and spring at last came round. The dream-estate was a garden of delight and loveliness, fresh green upon the larches and heather all abloom. The routine of the little household was established, and seemed as if it could never have been otherwise. The relationship between the elderly uncle and his little charge was perfect now, like that between a father and his only daughter, spoilt daughter, perhaps a little, who, knowing her power, yet never took advantage of it. He loved her as his own child; and that evasive "something" in her which had won his respect from the first still continued to elude him. He never caught it up. It had increased, too, in the long, dark months. Now, with the lengthening days, it came still more to the front, grown bolder, as though "spring's sweet trouble in the ground" summoned it forth. This sympathy between her being and the Place had strengthened underground. The disentangling had gone on apace. With the first warm softness of the April days he woke abruptly to the fact, and faced it. The older memories had been replaced. It seemed to him almost as though his hold upon the Place had weakened. He loved it still, but loved it in some new way. And his conscience pricked him, for conscience had become identified with the trust of guardianship thus self-imposed. He had let something in, and though it was not the taint of outside country *she* had said would "dirty" it, it yet was alien. It was somehow hostile to the conditions of his original Deed of Trust.

Then, into this little world, dropping like some stray bullet from a distant battle, came with a bang the person of John C. Murdoch. He came for a self-proposed visit of one day, being too "rushed" to stay an hour longer. Chance had put him "on the trail" of his old-time "pard of a hundred camps," and he couldn't miss looking him up, not "for all the money you could shake a stick at." More like a shell than mere bullet he came—explosively and with a kind of tempestuous energy. For his vitality and speed of action were terrific, and he was making money now "dead easy"—so easy, in fact, that it was "like picking it up in the street."

"Then you've done well for yourself since those old days in Arizona," said Eliot, really pleased to see him, for a truer "partner" in difficult times he had never known; "and I'm glad to hear it."

"That's so, Boss"—he had always called the "Englisher" thus because of his refined speech and manners—"God ain't forgot me, and I've got grub-stakes now all over Yurrup. Just raking it in, and if you want a bit, why, name the figger and it's yours." He glanced round at the modest old-fashioned establishment, judging it evidence of unsuccess.

"What line?" asked Eliot, dropping into the long-forgotten lingo.

"Why, patents, bless your heart," was the reply. "They come to me as easy as mother's milk to baby, and if the heart don't wither in me first, I'll patent everything in sight. I'll patent the earth itself before I'm done."

And for a whole hour, smoking one strong green cigar upon another, he gave brief and picturesque descriptions of his various enterprises, with such energy and gusto, moreover, that there woke in Eliot something of the lust of battle he had known in the wild, early days, something of his zest for making a fortune, something too of the old bitter grievance—in a word, the spirit of action, eager strife, and keen achievement, which never had quite gone to sleep. . . .

"And now," said Murdoch at length, "tell me about yerself. You look fit and lively. You've had enough of my chin-music. Made yer pile and retired too? Isn't that it? Only you still like things kind o' modest and camp-like. Is that so?"

But Eliot found it difficult to tell. This side of him that life in England had revived, to the almost complete burial of the other, was one that Murdoch would not understand. For one thing, Murdoch had never seen it in his friend; the Arizona days had kept it deeply hidden. He listened with a kind of tolerant pity, while Eliot found himself giving the desired information almost in a tone of apology.

"Every man to his liking," the Westerner cut him short when he had heard less than half of the stammering tale, "and your line ain't mine, I see. I'm no shadow-chaser—never was. You've changed a lot. Why"—looking round at the little pine-clad valley—"I should think you'd rot to death in this place. There's not room to pitch a camp or feed a horse. I'd choke for want of air." And he lit another cigar and spat neatly across ten feet of lawn.

John Casanova Murdoch—in the West he was called "John Cass," or just "John C.," but had resurrected the middle name for the benefit of Yurrup—was a man of parts and character, tried courage, and unfailing in his friendship. "Straight as you make 'em" was the verdict of the primitive country where a man's essential qualities are soon recognised, "and without no frills." And Eliot, whatever he may have thought, felt no resentment. He remembered the rough man's kindness to him when he had been a tenderfoot in more than one awkward place. John C. might "rot to death" in this place, and might think the vulgar country round it "great stuff," but for all that his host liked to see and hear him. He remembered his skill as a mining prospector and an engineer; he was not surprised that he had at last "struck oil."

They talked of many things, but the visitor always brought the conversations round to his two great healthy ambitions, now on the way to full satisfaction: money and power. Upon some chance mention of religion, he waved his hand impatiently with enough vigour to knock a man down, and said, "Religion! Hell! I only discuss facts." And his definition of a "fact" would no doubt have been a dollar bill, a mining "proposition," or a food-problem—some scheme by which John C. could make a bit. Yet though he placed religion among the fantasies, he lived it in his way. He ranked the Pope with Barnum, each of them "biggest in his own line of goods," and "Shakespeare was right enough, but might have made it shorter."

And Eliot, listening, felt the buried portion of his nature waken and revive. It caused him acute discomfort.

"Now show me round the little hole a bit," said Murdoch just before he left. "I'd like to see the damage, just for old times' sake. It won't take above ten minutes if we hustle along."

They hustled along. Eliot led the way with a curious deep uneasiness he could not quite explain. His heart sank within him. Gladly he would have escaped the painful duty, but Murdoch's vigorous energy constrained him. The whole way he felt ashamed, yet would have felt still more ashamed to have refused. He "faced the music" as John Casanova Murdoch phrased it, and while doing so, that other music of his visitor's villainous nasal twang cut across the deep-noted murmur of the wind and water like a buzz-saw with a bit of wire trailing against its teeth.

The entire journey occupied but half an hour, for Eliot made short-cuts, instinctively avoiding certain places, and the whole time Murdoch talked. His business, practical soul expanded with good nature. "The place ain't so bad, if you worked it up a bit," he said, striking a match on the wall of the mill, and spitting into the clear water, "but it's not much bigger than a chicken-run at present. If I was you, Boss, I'd have it cleaned up first." Again he offered a cheque, thinking the unkempt appearance due to want of means. His uninvited opinions were freely offered, as willingly as he would have given money if his old "pard" had needed it; given kindly too, without the least desire to wound. He picked out the prettiest "building sites," and explained where an artificial lake could be made "as easy as rolling off a log." His patent wire would fence the gardens off "and no one ever see it"; and his special concrete paving, from waste material that yielded a hundred per cent profit, would make paths "so neat and pretty you could dance to heaven on 'em." The place might be developed so as to "knock the stuffing" out of the country round about, and the estate become a "puffect picture-book."

"You've got a gold mine here, and God never meant a gold mine to lie unnoticed like a roadside ditch. Only you'll need to gladden it up a bit first. You could make it hum as a picnic or amusement resort for the town people. Take it from me, Boss. It's so."

And the effect upon Eliot as he listened was curious; it was twofold. For while at first the chatter wounded him like insults aimed directly at the dead, at the same time, to his deep disgust, it stirred all his former love of practical, energetic action. The old lust and fever to be up and doing, helping the world go round, making money and worldly position, woke more and more, as Murdoch's vigorous, crude personality stung his will, stung also desires he thought for ever dead. It made him angry to find that they were not dead, and yet he felt that he was feeble not to resent the gross invasion, even cowardly not to resist the coarse attack and kick the vulgar intruder out. It was like a breach of trust to take it all so meekly without protesting, or at least without stating forcibly his position, as though he were not sufficiently sure of himself to protect his memories and his dead. But this was the truth: he was not sure of himself. The blinding light of this simple fellow's mind showed up the hidden inequalities to himself. Another discovered his essential instability to himself. This other side of him had existed all the time; and his attachment to the Place was partly artificial, built up largely by the vigorous assertion of the departed. His love had coloured it wonderfully all these years, but—it was a love that had undergone a change. It had not faded, but grown otherwise. Another kind of love had to some extent replaced and weakened it. He felt mortified, ashamed, but more, he felt uneasy too.

The wrench was pain. "If only she were here and I could explain it to her," ran his thought over and over again, followed by the feeling that perhaps she *was* there, listening to it all—and judging him.

Behind the trees, a little distance away, he saw the flitting figure of Mánya, watching them as they passed noisily along the pathways of her secret playground. Her attitude even at this distance expressed resentment. He imagined her indignant eyes. But, closer than that, another watched and followed, listened and disapproved—that other whom she knew yet never spoke about, who was in league with her, and seemed more and more to him, like a phantom risen from the dead.

With difficulty, and with an uneasiness growing every minute now, he gave his attention to his talkative, well-meaning, though almost offensive guest, at once insufferable yet welcome. One moment he saw him in his camping-kit of twenty years ago, with big sombrero and pistols in his belt, and the next as he was to-day, reeking of luxury and money, in a London black tail-coat, white Homburg hat, diamonds shining on his fingers and in his gaudy speckled tie, his pointed patent-leather boots gleaming insolently through the bracken and heather.

And through his silence crashed a noise of battle that he thought the entire Place must hear. But clear issue to the battle there was none. The opposing sides were matched with such deadly equality. Which was his real self lay in the balance, until at the last John Casanova unwittingly turned the scales.

It came about so quickly, with such calculated precision, as it were, that Eliot almost felt it had all been prepared beforehand and Murdoch had come down on purpose. It was like a sudden flank attack that swept him from his last defences. Help that could not reach him in the form of Mánya signalled from the distance with her shining eyes, her red tam-o'-shanter the banner of reinforcements that arrived too late. For John C. stood triumphantly before him, a conqueror in his last dismantled fortress. His face alight with enthusiasm that was all excitement, he held his hands out towards him, cup-wise.

"See here," he said with excitement, but in a hard, dry tone that reminded Eliot of prospecting days in Arizona, "Boss, will you take a look at this, please?"

He had been rooting about in the heather by the edge of the sand-pits. And he thrust his joined hands beneath the other's nose. Something the size of a hen's egg, something that shone a dirty white, lay in them against the thick gold rings. "Didn't I tell you the place was a gol-darned gold mine? But what's the use o' talking? Will you look at this, now?" He repeated it with the air of a man who has suddenly discov-ered the secret of the world. The voice was quiet with intense excite-ment kept hard under.

And Eliot obeyed and looked. He saw his visitor, his Bond Street trousers turned up high enough to show the great muscles of his calves, the Homburg hat tilted across one eye, coat-sleeves pulled up and smeared with a whitish mud. There was perspiration on his fore-head. It only needed the sombrero and the pistols to complete the pic-ture of twenty years ago when Cass Murdoch, after weeks of heavy labour, found the first gold-dust in his pan. For John C. *had* found gold. It lay, a dirty lump of white earth, in his large spread hands. Those hands were the pan. The breeze that murmured through the pine-trees came, sweet and keen, from leagues of open plain and virgin mountains far away. . . . Eliot smelt the wood-fire smoke of camp . . . heard the crack of the rifle as some one killed the dinner. . . .

"Well, John C.," he gasped, as he dropped back likewise into the vanished pocket of the years, "what's your luck? Out with it, man, out with it!"

"A fortune," replied his visitor. "Put yer finger on it right now, an' don't tell mother or burst out crying unless yer forced to!" High pleas-ure was in his voice.

He stepped closer, transferring the lump of dirt into the hand his host unconsciously stretched open to receive it. It lay there a moment, looking even dirtier than before against the more delicate skin. Eliot felt it with finger and thumb. It was soft and sticky and a little moist. It stained the flesh.

Then he looked up and stared into his companion's eyes—blankly. A horrible excitement worked underground in him. But he did not even yet understand.

"You've got it," observed John C., with dry finality.

"Got what?" asked Eliot.

"Got it right there in yer westkit pocket," said the other, with an air of supreme satisfaction. His cigar had gone out. He lit it again in leisurely fashion, spat accurately at a distant frond of bracken, eyed the lump of dirt again with inimitable pride, and added, "Got it without asking; the working soft and easy too; water-power on the spot, and the sea all close and handy for shipping it away." He made a gesture to indicate the tumbling stream and the sea-coast a few miles beyond.

Then, seeing that his host still stared with blank incomprehension, holding the little lump at arm's length as though it might bite or burn him, he deigned to explain, but with a note of condescending pity in his voice, as of a man explaining to a stupid child.

"Clay," he said calmly, "and good stuff at that."

"Clay," repeated Eliot, still a little dazed, though light was breaking on him. "Bricks . . . ?" he asked, with a dull sinking of the heart.

"Bricks, nothing!" snapped the other with impatient scorn, as though his friend were still a tenderfoot in Arizona. "Good, white pottery clay, and soft as a baby's tongue. The best God ever laid down for man. Worth twice its weight in dust. And all to be had for the trouble of shovelling it out. Old pard, you've struck it good and hot this time; and here's my blessing on yer both."

Eliot dropped the lump his fingers held so long and took half-heartedly the giant hand that squeezed his own. Across his brain ran visions of slender vases, exquisite white cups and bowls and pitchers, plates and sweet-rimmed basins, all fashioned in delicate-toned shades of glaze—beautifully finished pottery—"worth twice their weight in dust."

X

And half an hour later, when John Casanova Murdoch had boomed away in his luxurious motor-car like a departing thunderstorm, Eliot, coming back by the pinewood that led from the high road, heard a step behind him, and turned to find Mánya's face looking over his very shoulder.

"Uncle, who was that?" There was a touch of indignation in her voice that was almost contempt.

"Man I knew in America—years ago," he said shortly. He still felt dazed, bewildered. But shame and uneasiness came creeping up as well.

"He won't come again, will he?"

"Not again, Mánya."

The child took his arm, apparently only half relieved.

"He was like a bit of the dirty country," she said, and when he interrupted with "Not quite so bad as that, Mánya," she asked abruptly with her usual intuition, "Did he want to buy, or build, or something horrid like that?"

"We haven't met for twenty years," he said evasively. "Used to hunt and camp together in America. He went to the goldfields with me." He was debating all the while whether he should tell her all. He hardly knew what he thought. Like a powerful undertow there drove through the storm of strange emotions the tide of a decision he had already come to. It swept him from all his moorings, though as yet he would not acknowledge it even to himself.

"Uncle," she cried suddenly, stepping across the path, and looking anxiously into his face, "tell me one thing: will anything be different?"

And the simple question, or perhaps the eager, wistful expression in her voice and eyes, showed him the truth that there was no evading. He must tell her sometime. Why not now?

He decided to make a clean sweep of it.

"Mánya," he began gently, "this Place one day—when I am gone, you know—will be your own. But there'll be no money with it. You'll have very little to live on."

She said nothing, just listening with a little air of boredom, as though she knew this already, yet felt no special interest in it. It belonged to the world of things she could not realise much. She nodded. They still stood there, face to face.

"I've been anxious, child, for a long time about your future," he went on, meeting her dark eyes with a distinct effort, for they seemed to read the shame he felt rising in his heart; "and wondering what I could do to make you safe—"

"I'm safe enough," she interrupted, tossing her hair back and raising her chin a little.

"But when I'm gone," he said gravely, "and Mrs. Coove has gone, and there's no one to look after you. Money's your only friend then."

She seemed to reflect. She moved aside, and they walked on slowly towards the house.

"That's a long way off, Uncle. I'm not afraid."

"But it's my duty to provide for you as well as possible," he said firmly.

And then he told her bluntly and in as few words as possible of the discovery of the clay.

The excitement at first in the child was so great that nothing would satisfy her but that they should at once turn back and see the place together. They did so, while he explained how "Mr. Murdoch," who was learned in strata, their depth and dip and outcrop, had declared that this deposit of fine white clay was very large. Its spread below the heather-roots might be tremendous. "My aunt," he said, "your great-aunt Julia, lived all her life upon a gold mine here without knowing it, poor as a church mouse."

This particularly thrilled her. "How funny that she never *felt* it!" was her curious verdict. "Was she *very* deaf?"

"Stone deaf, yes," he replied, laughing, "and short-sighted too."

"Ah!" said the child, as though things were thus explained. "But she might have digged!"

She ran among the heather when he showed her the place, found lumps of clay, played ball with them and was wildly delighted. She treated the great discovery as a game; then as a splendid secret "just between us two." Mr. Murdoch wouldn't tell, would he? That seemed the only danger that she saw—at first.

But her uncle knew quite well that this excitement was all false; and far from reassuring him, it merely delayed the deeper verdict that was bound to come with full comprehension. All the discovery involved had not reached her brain. As yet she realised only the novelty, the mystery, the wonder. The spot, moreover, where the great deposit showed its lip was beside the loveliest part of all the wood, and just where the child most loved to play.

At last, then, as her body grew tired and the excitement brought the natural physical reaction, he saw the change begin. She paused and looked about her half suspiciously, like an animal that suspects a trap. Her glance ran questioningly to where her uncle leaned, watching her, against a tree. She eyed him. He thought she suddenly looked different, though wherein the difference lay escaped him. He felt as if he were watching a wild animal, only half tamed, that distrusts its owner, and would next deny his mastership and wait its opportunity to spring. The simile, he knew, was exaggerated, but the picture rose within him none the less. Misgiving and uneasiness grew apace.

Abruptly Mánya stopped her wild playing and with the movement of a little panther ran towards him. She took up a position, as usual, directly opposite. With the strange air of dignity that sometimes clothed her, the figure of the child stood there among the darkening trees and asked him questions, keen, searching questions. He was grateful for the shadows, though he felt they did not screen his face from her piercing sight; but it was her imperious manner above all that made his defence seem so clumsily insincere, and the questions a veritable inquisition.

Before the flood of them, as before their pitiless scrutiny, he certainly quailed. Their keen directness convicted him almost of treachery, and he was hard put to it to persuade her and himself that it really *was* a sense of duty he obeyed in this decision to work the clay. "I'm doing it all for her," he repeated again and again to himself, and loathed, with a dash of terror, that curious sudden drive, as of a blow from outside, that sent his tongue into his cheek. But the terror, he dimly divined, was due to another feeling as well, equally vague yet equally persistent. For it seemed that while she listened to his explanations, another listened in the darkness too. Her resentment and distress he realised vividly; but he felt also the resentment and distress—of another. And more than once, during this strange dialogue in the darkening wood, he knew the horrible sensation that this "other" had come very close, so close as to slip between himself and the child. Almost—that the child was being used as the instrument to express the vehement protest . . . !

But he faced the music, to use the lingo of John C., and spared himself nothing. He told Mánya, though briefly, that workmen must swarm all through her secret playground, that machinery must grind and boom across the haunted valleys, that the water of her little stream must yield the power to turn great ugly wheels, and that perhaps even a little railway might be built to convey the loads of precious clay down to the sea where steamers would call for them. Acres of trees, too, would be swept away, and heather-land marred and scarred with pits and ditches and quarries. But the benefits in time would all be hers. He put it purposely at its worst, while emphasising as best he could the interest and excitement that must accompany the developments. The dream of many years was nevertheless shattered into bits in half an hour.

The child listened and understood. He was relieved, if puzzled at the same time, that she betrayed no emotion of disappointment or indignation. What she felt she dealt with in her own way—inside. At the stream, however, on her way home, she paused a moment, watching it slip through the darkness underneath the old mill-wheel.

"It won't run any more—for itself," she said in a low, trembling little voice, that was infinitely pathetic.

"No; but it will run for you, Mánya," he answered, though the words had not been addressed really to him; "working away busily for your future."

And then she burst into tears and hid her face against his coat. He found no further thing to say. He walked beside her, feeling like a criminal found out.

But at the end, as they neared the house side by side, she suddenly turned and asked another question that caused him a thrill of vivid surprise and discomfort—so vivid, in fact, that it was fear.

They were standing just beneath *her* bedroom window then. Memory rushed back upon him with overwhelming force, and he glanced up instinctively at the empty panes of glass. It was almost as though he expected to see a face looking reproachfully down upon him. Through him like spears of ice, as he heard the words, there shot again the atrocious sensation that it was not Mánya, the child, who asked the question, but that Other who had recently moved so close. For behind the tone, with no great effort to conceal it either, trailed a new accent that Mánya never used. Greater than resentment, it was anger, and within the anger lay the touch of a yet stronger note—the note of judgment.

"But, tell me one thing, Uncle," she asked in a whispering voice: "will the Place let you?"

XI

Motive, especially in complex natures, is often beyond reach of accurate discovery, and a mixed motive may prove quite impossible of complete disentanglement. But for the sense of shame that Eliot felt, he might never have discerned that with his genuine desire to provide for Mánya's future there was also involved a secret satisfaction that he himself would profit too. The sight of gold demolishes pretence and artifice; and deep within he felt the old lust of possession and acquisition assert itself. All these years it had been buried, not destroyed. His love of the Place, his worship of Memory, his guardianship of the little dream-estate, compared to the prize of worldly treasure, were on the surface. They were artificial.

This little thing had proved it. The child's tears, her significant question above all, had shown him to himself. If not, whence came this sense of ignominy before her own purer passion, the loss of confidence, this inner quailing before Another who gazed reprovingly, resentfully, upon him from the shadows of the past? That note of menace in Mánya's suggestive question was surely not her own. It haunted him. Day and night he heard it ringing in his brain. This new distrust of himself that he recognised read into it something almost vindictive and revengeful.

But Eliot, for all that, was not the man to give in easily. He resolutely dismissed this birth of morbid fancy. Clinging to the thought that his duty to his niece came first, he resisted the suggestion that imputed a grosser selfishness. Cass Murdoch, too, unwittingly helped; for the side of his character John C.'s visit had revived—the love of fight and energetic action—came valiantly to the rescue. To a great extent he persuaded himself that his motive was—almost entirely—a pure one. Preparations for developing the clay went forward steadily.

Mánya too appeared to help him. She said no more distressing things; she showed keen interest in the coming and going of surveyors, architects, soil experts, and the like. And Murdoch's discovery was no false alarm; the bed of clay was deep and extensive as he prophesied, its quality very fine. Men came with pick and shovel; sample pits were dug; the stuff was tested and judged excellent; and the verdict of the manufacturers, to whom "lots" were forwarded on approval, pronounced it admirable for a large and ready market. There was money in it, and the supply would last for years. The papers heralded the fortunate discoverer, and a moderate fortune undeniably was in sight.

The preparations, however, took time, and the finding of the initial capital, which Murdoch readily supplied, also took time, and spring meanwhile slipped into summer before the enterprise was fairly on its feet. Soft winds sighed lazily among the larches, and the scent of flowers pervaded every valley; the pine-trees basked in the sunshine, the pearly water laughed and sang; and at night the moon shot every glade with magic that was like the wings of moths whose flitting scattered everywhere the fine dust of a thousand silvery dreams. The beauty of the little haunted estate leaped into a rich maturity that was utterly enchanting, like wild flowers that are sweetest just before they die.

And over Mánya, too, there passed slowly a mysterious change, for it seemed as if for a time she had been standing still, and now with a sudden leap of beauty passed into the glory of young womanhood. With her short skirts and tumbled hair, her grave and wistful face, swinging idly that red tam-o'-shanter from which she was inseparable, he saw her one evening on the lawn outside his study window, and the change flashed into him across the moonlight with a positive shock. The child had suddenly grown up. A barrier stood between them.

But the barrier was not so sudden as it seemed, for, on looking back, he realised the daily, almost imperceptible manner of its growth. Its complete erection he realised now, but he had been aware of it for a long time—ever since his decision to work the clay, in fact. Here was the proof her deceptive silence had concealed. She had felt it too deeply for words, for arguing, for disappointment volubly expressed; but it had struck into the roots of her little being and had changed her from within outwards. It had aged her. Reality had broken in upon her world of play and dream. He had destroyed her childhood at a single blow. She questioned, doubted, and grew old.

But though every one grows older in identically this way, by sudden leaps, as it were, due to the forcing impulse of some strong emotion, with Mánya it brought no radical alteration. She deepened rather than definitely changed. The sense of wonder did not fade, but ripened. The crude facts of life could never satisfy a nature such as hers, and though she realised them now for the first time, they could not enter to destroy. They drove her more deeply into herself. That is, she dealt with them.

And the change, though he devoted hours of pondering reflection over it, may be summed up briefly enough in so far as it affected himself. There was a difference in their relationship. He stood away from her; while she, on her side, drew nearer to something else that was not himself. With this elusive and mysterious Thing she lived daily. She took sides with it and with the Place, against himself. It went on largely, he felt, behind his back. She grew more and more identified with some active influence that had always been at work in all the wild gardened loveliness of the property, but was now more active than before. Stirred up and roused it was; he could almost imagine it—aggressive. And Mánya, always knowing it at closer quarters than himself, was now in definite league with it. There was opposition in it, though an opposition as yet inactive.

And in the silent watches of the night sometimes, when imagination wove her pictures all unchecked, he again knew the haunting thought close beside his bed: that the mind and hand of the dead were here at work, using the delicate instrument of this rare, sensitive child to convey protest, resentment, warning. Over the little vales, from all the depth of forest, and above the spread of moorland just beyond, there breathed this atmosphere of disapproval.

Mánya, never telling him much, now told him less than before; for he had forfeited the right to know.

If it made him smile a little to notice that she had made Mother Coove lengthen her dresses, it did not make him smile to learn that she still wore her old shorter ones once the darkness fell, or that she now went out to play in her wild corners of the woods chiefly after dusk. For he saw the significance of this simple manœuvre, and divined its meaning. She felt shy now in the daylight. This new thing in the spirit of the Place had changed it all. She could not be abandoned as before, go naked and undressed as once she graphically put it. The vulgar influence from outside had come in. It stared offensively. It asked questions, leered, turned everything common and unclean.

And she changed from time to time her playground as the workmen drove her out. She moved from place to place, seeking new corners and going farther into the moors and open spots. She followed the stream, for instance, nearer to its source where its waters still ran unstained. And from the neighbourhood of the sample pits that gaped like open sores amid the beauty, she withheld herself completely. Nothing could persuade her to come near them.

Towards himself especially, her attitude was pregnant with suggestion, and though he made full allowance for the phantoms conscience raises, there always remained the certainty that the child, and another with her, watched him sharply from a distance. She was still affectionate and simple, even with a new touch of resigned docility that was very sweet, as though resolved to respect his older worldly wisdom, yet with an air of pity for his great mistake that was half contempt, half condescension. Her silence about the progress of the work made him feel small. It so mercilessly judged him. And, while the dignity he had always recognised in her increased, it seemed now partly borrowed— his imagination leaned more and more towards this unwelcome explanation—from this invisible Companion who overshadowed her. He felt as though this silence temporarily blocked channels along which something would presently break out with violence and scorn to overwhelm him; till at last he came to regard her as a prisoner regards the foreman of the jury who has formed his verdict and is merely waiting to pronounce it—Guilty. Behind her, as behind the foreman, gathered the composite decision of more than one, and the decision was hostile. It urged her on against him. Opposition accumulated towards positive attack. He dreaded some revelation through the child; and piling guess on guess he felt certain who was this active Influence that sought to use her as its instrument. The dead now, day and night, stood very close beside him.

And meanwhile, things ran far from smoothly with the work itself. Unforeseen difficulties everywhere arose to baffle him. Even Murdoch made oppressive, troublesome conditions about the money that seemed unnecessary, insisting upon details of management with a touch of domineering interference that exasperated. Obstacles rose up automatically, involving, as it were, the very processes of Nature itself. There was a strike that delayed the railway builders for a month, and when they returned the heavy summer rains had washed yards of embankment down again. Soon afterwards a falling tree killed a workman, and there ensued compensation worries that threatened a law-suit. The clay itself, too, played them sudden tricks, proving faulty the maps the surveyors had drawn; its depths and direction were not as supposed, its angle to the lie of the slope deceptive, so that an extra branch of single line for the trucks became essential. And the money was insufficient; further advances became imperative, and, though readily forthcoming, involved more delay. The spirit of lonely peace and beauty departed from the Place, hiding its injured face among the moorland reaches further up. Obstruction, with turmoil and confusion at its back, rose up on every side to baffle him.

Though the advance was steady enough on the whole, and the difficulties were only such as most similar enterprises encounter, Eliot was conscious more and more of this sense of obstacles deliberately interposed. It all seemed so nicely calculated to cause the maximum of trouble and delay. The interference was so cunningly manœuvred. He brought all his old energy and force to meet them, but there was ever this curious sense of advised and determined opposition that began to sap his confidence.

"More trouble, sir," the foreman said one morning, when Eliot went down to view the work, unaccompanied as usual by Mánya. "There seems no end to it."

"What is it this time?" He abhorred these conversations now. It always seemed that Another stood behind his shoulder, listening.

"The clay has gone," was the curious answer. He said it as though it had gone purposely to spite them like a living thing.

"Gone!" he exclaimed incredulously.

"Sunk away, gone deeper than we expected," was the answer. The man shrugged his shoulders as though something puzzled him. "A kind of subsidence come in the night," he added gloomily.

They stared at one another for a full minute with eyes that screened other meanings. Eliot felt a sort of fury rise within him. Somehow the idea of foul play crossed his mind, though instantly rejected as absurd.

"With this loose sandy bottom, and a steep slope that ain't drained properly, you're never very sure of where you are," said the man at length, feeling his position made some explanation necessary. He seemed to regard the Clay as something ever on the move.

"I see," said Eliot, grateful for a solution that he could apparently accept. They talked of ways and means to circumvent it.

"Queerest job I ever come across, sir," the foreman muttered, as at length Eliot turned away, pretending not to hear it.

And scenes like this were frequent. Another time it was the white weed—with the pretty little flower Mánya loved to twine about her tam-o'-shanter—that had gathered so thickly on the artificial ponds where the water was stored, that it clogged the machinery till the wheels refused to turn; and next, a group of men that quit working without any reasonable excuse—open symptom of a hidden dissatisfaction that had been running underground for weeks. There was something about the job they didn't like. Rumours for a long time had been current—queer, unsubstantiated rumours that those in authority chose to disregard. Superstition hereabouts was rife enough without encouraging it.

Taken altogether, as products of a single hostile influence at work, these difficulties easily assumed in his imaginative mind the importance of a consciously directed opposition. He remembered often now those words of Mánya, the last time she had opened her lips upon the subject. For she had credited the Place with the power of resisting him; only by "the Place" she now meant this mysterious personal influence that she knew behind it.

Yet he persisted in his consciousness of doing right. His duty to the child was clear; her future was in his charge; and the fact that he meant to leave her everything proved that his motive, or part of it at least, was above suspicion. From John C. he also gathered comfort and support. He had only to imagine him standing by his side, repeating that remark about religion, to feel strong again in his determination. Cass Murdoch recognised no mystery or subtlety anywhere. He discussed only facts.

The consciousness that he was partly traitor none the less remained, and with it the feeling that the very Tradition he had nursed and worshipped all these years was up in arms against him. Mánya, standing closer to Nature than himself, had divined this Tradition and, in some fashion curiously her own, had personified it. And this personification linked on with the dead. His love of the Beauty, and his love of a particular memory he had read into the Place, she had most marvellously disentangled. Both were genuine in him; yet he had suffered them in combination to produce a false and artificial Image existing only in his own imagination. There was conflict in his being. His motive was impure.

Behind them stood the giant, naked thing the child divined that was—Reality. She knew it face to face. What was it? The mere definite question which he permitted himself made him sometimes hesitate and wait, not unwilling to call a halt. He was aware that the child stood ever in the background, waiting her time with that sly laughter of superior knowledge. These obstacles and difficulties were sent as warnings; and while he disregarded them of set purpose, something deep within him paused to question—and while it questioned, trembled. For protest, he seemed to discern, had become resentment, resentment grown into resistance; resistance into hostile opposition, and opposition now, with something horribly like anger at its back, was hinting already at a blank refusal that involved almost—revenge.

Hitherto he had been hindered, impeded, thwarted merely; soon he could be deliberately overruled and stopped. Nature, ever defeating an impure motive, would rise up against him and cry finally No.

"But, Uncle, tell me one thing: will the Place let you?" rang now often through his daily thoughts. He heard it more especially at night. At night, too, when sleep refused him, he surprised himself more than once framing sentences of explanation and defence. They rose automatically. They followed him even into his dreams. "My duty to the child is plain. How can I help it? If you were here beside me now, would you not also approve?"

For the idea that *she* was beside him grew curiously persuasive, so that he almost expected to see her in the corridors or on the stairs, standing among the trees or waiting for him by the Mill itself where last she drew the breath of life.

And by way of a climax came then Mánya's request to change her room, and his own decision to move himself into the one she vacated. The reason she gave was that the "trees made such a noise at night" she could not sleep, and since it had three windows, two of which were almost brushed by pine branches, the excuse, though discovered late, seemed natural enough. At any rate he did not press her further. She occupied a room now at the back where a single window gave a view far up into the moors. And, turning out the unnecessary furniture to suit his taste, he moved into the one she had vacated—his wife's.

XII

Summer passed in the leisurely, gorgeous way that sometimes marks its passage into autumn, and the work ploughed forward through the sea of difficulties. The conspiracy of obstacles continued. There was progress on the whole, but a progress that seemed to bring success no nearer.

The beds of clay, however, were definitely determined now, and their extent and depth fulfilled the most sanguine expectations. The troubles lay with the railway, the men, water, weather, and a dozen things no one could have foreseen. These seemed far-fetched, and yet were natural enough. And they continued—until Eliot, never a man who yielded easily, began to feel he had undertaken more than he could manage. He weakened. The idea came to him that he would sell his interest and leave the development to others.

To retire from the fight and acknowledge himself defeated was a step he could not lightly take. There was a bitterness in the thought that stung his pride and vanity. There was also the fact that if he held on and first established a paying business, he could obtain far more money—for Mánya. Yet he felt somehow that it was from Mánya herself that the suggestion first had come. For the child gave hints in a hundred different ways that he could not possibly misunderstand. They were indirect, unconsciously given, and they followed invariably upon curious little personal accidents that about this time seemed almost a daily occurrence.

And these little accidents, though perfectly natural taken one by one as they occurred, when regarded all together seemed to compose a formidable whole. They pointed an attack almost. The menace he had imagined was becoming aggressive. Some one who knew his habits was playing him tricks. Some one with intimate knowledge of the way he walked and ran and moved laid traps for him. And at each little "accident" Mánya laughed her strange, sly laughter—precisely as a child who says "I told you so! You brought it on yourself!" She had expected it, perhaps had seen it coming. And now, to avoid more grave disasters, she wanted him—elsewhere. Her deep affection for him, sinner though he was in her eyes, sought to coax him out of the danger zone.

When he slipped in jumping the stream—he, who was sure-footed as a mountain goat!—and turned his ankle; and when the heavy earth, loosened by the rains, rolled down upon him as he climbed the embankment, or when the splinter that entered his hand as he vaulted the fencing near the wharf, led to festering that made him carry his arm in a sling for days—in every case it was the same: the child looked up at him and smiled her curious little smile of one who knew. She was in safety, but he stood in the line of fire. She knew who it was that laid the traps. She saw them being laid. It was always wood, earth, water thus that hurt him and never once an artificial contrivance of man.

"Uncle, it wouldn't happen if you stayed away," was what she said each time, though never phrased the same. And the obvious statement only just covered another meaning that her words contained. She knew worse things would come, and feared for him. "There's no good hiding, Uncle Dick, because it's in the house as well."

He grew to feel unwelcome in his own woods and garden, an intruder in his own moors and valleys, an element the Place rejected and wished elsewhere. The Place had begun to turn him out. And Mánya, this queer mysterious child, in league with the secret Influence at work against him, was being used to point the warnings and convey the messages. Her silent attitude, more even than her actual words, was the messenger. The hints thus brought, moreover, now troubled themselves less and less with disguise. He realised them at last for what they were: and they were beyond equivocation—threatening.

And it was at this point that Eliot made the journey up to London to see Cass Murdoch, and feel his way towards escape. Retirement was the word he used, and the sentence John C. heard in the bar of the big hotel as they discussed clay and cocktails was "sell my interest to more competent hands who will get quicker and bigger results than I can. The work and worry affect my health."

The interview may be easily imagined, for John Casanova Murdoch was more than willing to buy him out, though the conditions, with one exception, have no special interest in this queer history: Eliot was to lease the Place for a period of years. And this meant leaving it.

In the train on his way back his emotions fought one another in a regular pitched battle. He stood in front of himself suddenly revealed—a traitor. It seemed as if for a moment he saw things a little from his niece's inverted point of view, standing outside of Self and looking up. It provided him with unwelcome sensations that escaped analysis. Love and hate are one and the same force, according to the point in the current where one stands; repulsion becomes, from the opposite end, attraction; and a great love may be reversed into a great hate. There is no exact dividing line between heat and cold, no neat frontier where pleasure becomes pain, just as there is really no such absolute thing as left and right, uphill and downhill, above and below.

Mánya stood outside these relative distinctions men have invented for the common purposes of description. He understood at last that the power which had drawn his life into the Place as by a kind of absorption, was now inverted into a process of turning him out again as by a kind of determined elimination.

It was being accomplished, moreover, as he felt and phrased it to himself, from outside; by which perhaps he meant from beyond that fence which men presumptuously assume to contain all the life there is. But the dead stand also beyond that fence. And Mánya, being so obviously in league with this hostile, eliminating Influence stood hand in hand, therefore, with—the dead.

But for him The Dead meant only one.

XIII

He walked home from the station, which he reached at nine o'clock. Crossing the zone of the "dirty" country, now successful invader of the dream-estate, he entered his property at length by the upper end of the Piney Valley. A passionate wind was searching the trees for music, and handfuls of rain were flung against the trunks like stones; but, on leaving the road the tempest seemed to pass out towards the sea, leaving an unexpected, sudden hush about his footsteps. The moon peered down through high, scudding clouds. It was partly that the storm was breaking up, and partly that the valley provided shelter; but it gave him the feeling that he had entered a little world prepared for his reception. He was expected, the principal figure in it. Attention everywhere focussed on himself. He felt like a prisoner who comes out of streets indifferent to his presence and enters a Court of Law. This ominous silence preceded the arrival of the Judge.

The path at once dipped downwards into a world of shadows where the splashes of moonlight peered up at him like faces on the ground. He heard the water murmuring out of sight; and it came about his ears like whispering from the body of the Court. There reigned, indeed, the same gentle peace and stillness he had known for years, but somewhere in it a brooding unaccustomed element that was certainly neither peace nor stillness. Something unwonted stirred slowly, very grandly, through the darkness.

He paused a moment to listen; he looked about him; he pushed aside the bracken with his stick, and his eyes glanced up among the lower branches of the trees. And everywhere, it seemed, he encountered other eyes—eyes usually veiled, but now with lifted lids. Then he went on again, faster a little than before. A touch of childhood's terror chilled his blood. And it took at first a childhood's form. He thought of some big, savage animal that lurked in hiding, its presence turning the once friendly wood all otherwise and dreadful. A giant paw filled the little valley to the brim. The stir of the wind was the opening and shutting of its claws. The lips were drawn back to show the gums and teeth. Something opened; there came a rush of air. The awful spring would follow in a moment. . . .

Another hood of memory lifted then and showed him Mánya, as she played about the sand-pits—then paused when the full discovery dawned upon her mind. She had eyed him. She had given him this similar impression of an animal waiting its opportunity to spring. But now it was the Place that waited to spring. . . .

He banished the bizarre, exaggerated picture his imagination conjured up, but could not banish the emotion that produced it. The Place *was* different. Change spread all over it. Potential attack hummed through the very air. Thus might a man feel walking through a hostile crowd. But thus also might he feel in the presence of a friend to whom in a time of confidence he had betrayed himself too lavishly—a friend now turned against him with this added power of knowing all his secrets. His own imagination leaped upon him, calling him coward, traitor, unfaithful steward. Fear made him bitterly regret the familiarity that years of unguarded dreaming had established between himself and—and— His mind hesitated horribly between the choice of pronouns; and when he finally chose the neuter, it seemed that a curious running laughter passed within the sounds of wind and water. It almost was like the mockery of Mánya's laughter taken over by the dying storm.

While he evaded the direct attack, his mind, however, continued searching for the word that should describe accurately, and so limit all this vague, distressing feeling of hostility. But for long he could not find it. The new element that breathed through the sombre intricacies of the glen played with him as it pleased until he could catch it in the proper word, and so imprison it. Branches seemed no longer soft and feathery: they bristled, pointed, stood rigid for a blow. The stream no longer murmured: it laughed and cried aloud. The shadows did not cover smoothly: they concealed; and the whole atmosphere of the Place, instead of welcoming, repelled.

And then, quite suddenly, the word emerged and stood before his face: Disturbance.

Less than disorder, yet more than mere disquietude, this word described the attitude he was conscious of. In its aggressive, threatening, sinister meaning, he accepted it as true.

There was Disturbance. Somewhere in those chains of iron that bind the operations of Nature within invariable, unyielding laws, a link had weakened. Disturbance was the result—but a disturbance that somehow let in purpose. Urging everywhere through the manifestations of Nature in his dream-estate was the drive and stress of purposiveness.

The discovery of the word, moreover, announced the approach, though not yet the actual entrance, of the Judge. There were steps, and the steps were in himself. Some one walked upon his life.

He quickened his pace like a terrified child. With genuine relief at last he reached the house. But even in the friendly building he was aware of this keen discomfort at his heels. It penetrated easily. The Disturbance came in after him into the house itself. Hanging up coat and hat, he then passed into the Study, and the prosaic business of drinking milk and munching water-biscuits scattered the strange illusion for a time. It weakened, at any rate, for it never wholly disappeared. It waited.

The house was silent, every one in bed. He locked the front door carefully, stared at his face a moment in the hat-stand mirror—wondering at a certain change in the expression of the features, though he could not name it—and with his lighted candle went on tiptoe up to bed. But the instant he entered the room he was aware that the feeling of distress had already preceded him. He was forestalled. There was this dark disquiet in the very atmosphere of his bedroom. The Disturbance had established itself in these most private, intimate quarters that once had been his wife's. It was strongest here.

Dismissing a sharp desire to sleep in another room—anywhere but in the place made sacred by long-worshipped memories—he began to undress. He said to himself with a certain vehemence, "I'll ignore the thing." But it was fear that said it. A frightened child without a light might as well determine to ignore the darkness. For this thing was urgent everywhere about him, inside and outside, like the air he breathed. And the next minute, instead of ignoring it, he made an attempt to face it. He would drag the secret out. The fact was, both will and emotions were already in disorder. He knew not how or where to take the thing.

The attempt then showed him another thing. It was no secret. The terror in his heart and conscience made pretence of screening something that he really knew quite well. This aggressive, hostile Presence was a Presence that he recognised, and had recognised all along.

And instinctively he turned to this side and to that, examining the room; for space in this room, he realised, was no longer quite as usual: there was a change in its conditions. Everything contained within it—the very objects between the four walls—were affected. He felt them altered; they had become otherwise. He himself was changed as well, become otherwise. And if anything alive—another person or an animal even—came in, they also, in some undetermined, startling way, would look otherwise than usual. They would look different.

Hurriedly he sought a concrete simile to steady his shaking mind on, and his mind provided this: That, if the temperature were suddenly lowered, the invisible moisture would at once appear, otherwise—frost-crystals on the window-panes, snow, and so forth. The change would not be untrue or even distorted, no falseness in it anywhere, nor exaggeration—only otherwise. And if the presence of the dead, whom he felt so close now in this room, turned visible owing to the changed conditions of the space about him, he would see—but the thought remained unfinished in his mind . . .

He thrust the terror down into the depths. Yet the idea must have been very insistent in him, for he crossed the floor on tiptoe to lock the door securely, and stood already within easy reach of it, one hand actually stretched out, when there came a faint knocking on the panelling within a few inches of his very face. He saw the handle turn. With suggestive, dreadful stealthiness the door then opened, the merest crack at first, then gradually wider and wider. And the slowness was exasperating. The seconds dragged like hours. Had he not been spellbound he would have violently slammed it to again or torn it instead wide open.

There was just time in his bewildered mind to wonder what form this Presence from the dead would take, when he realised that the figure stood already by his side. She had crossed the threshold. With amazement he saw that it was Mánya.

She came in swiftly. She was on the carpet close against him before he could speak a word or move. And she looked, as he had expected, otherwise: she looked extraordinary. The word came to him in the way she might herself have used it, getting its first meaning out—extraordinary.

And her appearance was—might well have been, at least—ludicrous. For she was dressed to go out, but in a fashion that at any other time must have been cause for laughter. Now it stood at the very opposite pole, however. It was superb. Her red tam-o'-shanter was perched carelessly, almost gaily, on her hair, which was already fashioned into plaits for the night, and underneath the garden jacket that he knew so well, he saw white drapery that plainly was her little nightgown. She had pulled her stockings on, but had not fastened them. They hung down, partly showing her skin below the knee. The boots flapped open, with no attempt to button them. Her hurry had been evidently great, and she looked at the first glance like some one surprised by a midnight call of fire.

Yet these details, which he took in at a single glance, stirred no faintest touch of amusement in him, for about her whole presentment was this other nameless quality that showed her to him—utterly otherwise than usual. It made him wince and shudder, yet pause in a wondering amazement too—amazement that barely held back awe. He stared like a man struck suddenly dumb. The phrase the child so often used came back upon him with the force of a shock. The girl had put her Self out. This being that stood just opposite to his face was not Mánya. It was another. It was *the* other!

And both doubt and knowledge dropped down upon him in that fearful moment: knowledge, that it was the Influence she had been so long in league with, and that sought to use her as its instrument of protest; and doubt, as to exactly what—or who—this Influence really was.

For it came to him as being so enormously bigger and vaster than anything his mind could label "the dead." He felt in the presence of a multitude. He had once felt thus when seeing a single Redskin steal like a shadow round the camp, knowing that the night concealed a host of others. About her actual form and body, too, this sense of multitude also spread and trembled, only just concealed: and indescribable utterly. For the edges of the child were ill-defined and misty, so that he could not see exactly where her outline ceased. The candle-light played round and over her as though she filled the room. She might have been all through the air above him, behind as well as opposite, close in front as well. In a sense he felt that she had come to him through the open windows and from the night itself, and not merely along the passage and through the narrow door. She came from the entire Place.

He made a feverish struggling effort to concentrate his mind upon common words. He wanted to move backwards, but his feet refused to stir. The familiar sound of her name he uttered close into her face:—

"Mánya! And at this hour of the night!" he stammered.

His voice was thick and without resonance in his mouth, smothered like a sound in a closed box. And as he heard the name a kind of silent laughter reached him—inaudible really, as though inside him— sly laughter like her own. For the name had lost its known familiarity. It, too, was different and otherwise, though for the life of him he could not seize at first wherein the alteration lay.

She smiled, and her eyes, wide opened, were like stars. The breath came soft and windily between her lips, but no words with it. It was regular, deep, unhurried. There was something in her face that petrified him—something, as it were, non-human. He began to forget who and where he was. Identity slipped from him like a dream.

With another effort, this time a more violent one, he strove to fasten upon things that were close and real in life. He felt the buttons down his coat, fingering them desperately till they hurt his hands and escaped from his slippery moist skin.

"Mánya!" he repeated in a louder voice, while his mind plunged out to seek the child he had always known behind the familiar name.

And this time she answered; but to his horror, the whole room, and even space beyond the actual room, seemed to answer with her. The name was repeated by her lips, yet came from the night beyond the open window too. He had made a question of it. The answer, repeating it, was assent.

"M á n y-a . . ." he heard all round him, while the head bent gently down and forward.

The shock of it restored to him some power of movement, and he stumbled back a step or two further from her side. It might well have been whimsical and cheap, this artificial play upon a name, but instead of either it was abominably significant. This motionless figure, so close that he could feel her breath upon his face, was positively in some astonishing way more than one. She *was* many. The laughter that lay behind the trivial little thing was a laughter both grand and terrible. It was the laughter of the sea, of the woods, of sand—a host that no man counteth—the laughter of a multitude.

And he thrust out both his hands automatically lest she should touch him. He shook from head to toe. Contact with her person would break up his being into millions. The sensation of terror was both immense and acute, sweeping him beyond himself. Like her, he was becoming many—becoming hundreds and thousands—sand that none can number.

"Child!" he heard his voice repeating faintly, yet with an emphasis that spaced the words apart with slow distinctness, "what does this mean?" In vain he tried to smother the beseeching note in it that was like a cry for help.

He stepped back another pace. She did not move. Composure then began to come back slowly to him, a little and a little. He remembered who he was, and where he was. He said to himself the commonplace thing: "This is Mánya, my little niece, and she ought to be asleep in bed." It sounded ridiculous even in his mind, but he tried deliberately to think of ordinary things.

And then he said it aloud: "Do you realise where you are and what you are doing, child?" And then he added, gaining courage, a question of authority: "Do you realise what time it is?"

Her answer came again without hesitation, as from a long way off. A smile lit up the entire face, gleaming from her skin like moonlight. There were tears, he saw, upon the checks. But the face itself was radiant, wonderful.

"The time," she said, peering very softly into his eyes, "is *now*." And she took a slow-gliding step towards him, with a movement that frightened him beyond belief.

But by this time he had himself better in hand. He understood that the child was walking in her sleep. It was her little frame that was being worked and driven by—Another. She was possessed. Something was speaking through the entranced physical body. Her answer regarding time was the answer absolute, not relative, the only true answer that could be given. Other answers would be similar. He understood that here was the long expected revelation, and that he must question her if he wished to hear it. He resolved to do so, hut with a cold awe in his heart as though he were about to question—Death.

They both retained their first positions, three feet apart, standing. The candle behind him on the table shed its flickering light across her altered features. Outside he heard the trees shaking and tossing in the gusts of rainy wind.

"Who are you then?" he asked hesitatingly, in a low tone.

There was no reply. But effort, showing that she heard and tried to answer, traced a little frown above the eyebrows; and the eyes looked puzzled for a moment.

"You mean," he whispered, "you cannot tell me?"

The head bowed slowly once by way of assent.

"You cannot find the word, the language?" he helped her. "Is that it?" He still whispered, afraid of his own voice.

"Yes," was the answer, spoken below the breath. Then instantly afterwards, straightening herself up with a vigorous movement that startled him horribly, she made a curious, rushing gesture of the whole body, spreading her arms out through the air about her. "I am—*like that!*" the voice sprang out loud and clear.

She seemed by the gesture to gather space and the night into her wide embrace. She repeated it. The face smiled marvellously. Through this slim body, he realised, there rolled something ancient as the stars. It poured through space against him like a sea. It turned his little ideas of space all—otherwise.

"Tell me where you come from," he asked quickly, eager yet dreading to hear.

"From everywhere," came the answer like a wind.

He paused, breathless with astonishment. He felt himself dwindling. Here was a vaster thing than he had contemplated. It was surely no single discarnate influence that possessed the child!

"And—for whom?" It was whispered as before.

The figure stepped with a single gliding stride towards him, coming so close that he held his ground only by a tremendous effort of the will.

"For you!" The voice came like a clap of wind again, at once soft yet thundering, filling the entire room.

"For me," he faltered. "Your message is for me?"

He felt the assault of strange, violent sensations he had never known before and could not name. A boyhood's dream rushed back upon him for an instant. He recalled his misery and awe when he stood before the Judgment Throne for some unforgivable breach of trust which he could not explain because the dream concealed its nature. Only this was ten times greater, and his guilt beyond redemption.

"And I," he stammered, "who am I?"

Her eyes looked him all over like a stare of the big moon.

"You," she answered, without pause or hesitation.

"You do not know my name?" he insisted, still clinging to the clue that her he spoke with must be from the dead.

The little frown came back between the eyes. She nodded darkly.

"You," she repeated, giving the answer absolute again, the only really true one.

The girl stood like a statue, serene and solemn. She stared through and beyond him, motionless but for a scarcely perceptible swaying, and calm as a meadow in the dawn. Enormous meanings passed from her eyes across the air, and sank down into him like meanings from a forest or a sea.

From these, he realised, came her stupendous inspiration, and, so realising, he knew at last his deep mistake. For not so do the Dead return. They never, indeed, return, because from the heart that loved them they have never gone away, but only changed their magic intercourse in kind. And, had *she* known, she would have approved the wisdom of his great decision, while clearing his motive of all insincerity at the same time.

It was not *she* who brought the protest and the menace. It was something bigger by far, something awful and untamed. It was the Place itself. And behind the Place stood Nature. It was Nature that possessed the child and used her little lips and hands and body for its thundering message of disapproval.

Mánya was possessed by Nature.

And the shock of the discovery first turned him into stone. His body did not stir the fraction of an inch. In that moment of vivid realisation these two little human figures stood facing one another, motionless as columns; and, while so standing, the One who brought the Message for himself drew closer.

For several minutes he saw absolutely nothing. The approach was too big for any sensory perceptions he could recognise. And then, mercilessly, pitilessly, the power of sight returned.

He knew the touch of a giant, earthy hand was upon his arm. Beside him, in the flickering candle-light, stood Nature. He looked into a host of mighty eyes that yet his imagination translated into merely two—eyes set wide apart beneath enormous brows. He met the gaze of the Gigantic, the Patient, the Inexorable that saw him as he was, and judged him where he stood. And a melting ran through his body, as though the bones slipped from their accustomed places, leaving him utterly without support. He swayed, but did not fall. His physical frame stood upright to receive like a blow the revelation that was coming.

And then, with a curious, deep sense of shame, he realised abruptly that his position in regard to her was inappropriate. He, at any rate, had no right to stand. His proper attitude must be a very different one.

He took her by the hand and, bending his head with an air of humble worship, led her slowly across the room. The touch of her was wonderful—like touching wind—all over him. With a reverence he guided her, all unresisting, to a high-backed chair beside the open window. She lowered herself upon it, and sat upright. She stared fixedly before her into space. No clothing in the world could have stolen from her childish face and figure the nameless air of grandeur that she wore. She was august.

And he knelt before her. He raised his folded hands. A moment his eyes rested on the dispassionate little face, then looked beyond her into the night of wind and rain. His gaze returning then sought the eyes again.

And the child, sweet little human interpreter of so vast a Mystery, bent her head downwards and looked into his heart. Wind stirred the hair upon her neck. He saw the bosom gently rise and fall.

"What is it that you have to say to me?" he whispered, like a prayer for mercy. 'What is the message that you bring?'

Her lips moved very slightly. The smile broke out again like moonlight across the lowered face. The words dropped through the sky. Very slowly, very distinctly, they fell into his open heart: simple as wind or rain.

"Leave—me—as—I—am—and—as—you—found—me. Leave—us—together—as—we—are—and—as—we—-were."

XIV

There came then a sudden blast that swept with a shout across the night; and through his mind passed also a tumult like a roaring wind. Both winds, it seemed to him, were in the room at once. He had the sensation of being lifted from the earth. The candle was extinguished. And then the sound and terror dipped away again into silence and into distance whence it came. . . .

He found himself standing stiffly upright, though he had no recollection of rising from his knees. With an abruptness utterly disconcerting he was himself again. No item of memory had faded; he remembered the entire series of events. Only, he was in possession of his normal mind and powers, fear, awe, and wonder all departed. Mánya, who had been walking in her sleep, was sitting close before him in the darkness. He could just distinguish her outline against the open window. But he was master of himself again. Even the wild improbability, the extravagance of his own actions, the very lunacy of the picture that the night now smothered, left him unbewildered. And the calmness that thus followed the complete transition proved to him that all he had witnessed, all that had happened, had been—true. In no single detail was there falseness or distortion due to the excitement of a hysterical mood. It had been right and inevitable.

He lit the candle again quietly, with a hand that did not tremble. He saw Mánya sitting on the high-backed chair with her head sunk forward on her breast. Gently he raised the face. The eyes were now closed, and the regular, deep breathing showed that the girl was sound asleep—but with the normal sleep of tired childhood. The Immensity to which he had knelt and prayed in her was gone, gone from the room, gone out into the open darkness of the Place. It had visited her, it had used her, it had left her. But at the same time he understood, as by some infallible intuition, that the warning to depart she brought him was not yet complete. It had reached his mind, but not as yet his soul. In its fulness the Notice to Quit could not be delivered between close, narrow walls. Its delivery must be outside.

He looked at the sleeping child in silence for several minutes. She sat there in a semi-collapsed position and in momentary danger of falling from her chair. The lips were parted, the eyes tight shut, the red tam-o'-shanter dropping over one side of the face. Both hands were folded in her lap. By the light of two candles now he watched her, while the perspiration he had not been as yet aware of, dried upon his skin and made him shiver with the cold. And, after long hesitation, he woke her.

With difficulty the girl came to, stared up into his face with a blank expression, rubbed her eyes, and then, with returning consciousness of who and where she was, looked mightily astonished.

"Mánya, child," he began gently, "don't be frightened."

"I'm not," she said at once. "But where am I? Is that you, Uncle?"

"Been walking in your sleep. It's all right. Nothing's happened. Come, I'll see you back to bed again." And he made a gesture as though to take her hand.

But she avoided him. Still looking bewildered and perplexed, she said:

"Oh—I remember now—I wanted to go out and see things. I want to go out still." Then she added quickly as the thought struck her, "But does Fräulein know? You haven't told Fräulein, Uncle, have you? I mean, you won't?"

He shook his head. This was no time for chiding.

"I often go out like this—at night, when you're all asleep. It's the only time now, since—"

He stopped her instantly at that. "You fell asleep while dreaming! Was that it?" He tried to laugh a little, but the laughter would not come.

"I suppose so." She glanced down at her extraordinary garments.

But no smile came to the eyes or lips. Then she looked round her, and gazed for a minute through the open window. The rain had ceased, the wind had died away. Moist, fragrant air stole in with many perfumes. "I don't remember quite. I was in bed. I had been asleep already, I think. Then—something woke me." She paused. "There was something crying in the night."

"Something crying in the night?" he repeated quickly, half to himself.

She nodded. "Crying for me," she explained in a tone that sent a shudder all through him before he could prevent it. "So I thought I'd go out and see. Uncle, I *had* to go out," she added earnestly, still whispering, "because they were crying—to get at you. And unless I brought them—unless they came through me," she stopped abruptly, her eyes grew moist, she was on the verge of tears—"it would have been so terrible for you, I mean—"

He stiffened as he heard it. He made a violent effort at control, stopping her further explanation.

"And you weren't afraid—to go out like this into the dark?" he asked, more to cover retreat than because he wanted to hear the reply.

"I put myself out for you," she answered simply. "I let them come in. That way you couldn't get hurt. In me they had to come gently. They were an army. Only, nothing out of me could hurt you, Uncle." She suddenly put her arms about his neck and kissed him. "Oh, Uncle Dick, it *was* lucky I was there and ready, wasn't it?"

And Eliot, remembering that great Disturbance in the woods, pressed the child tenderly to himself, praying that she might not understand his heart too well, nor feel the cold that made his entire body tremble like a leaf. He had thought of an angry animal Presence lurking in the darkness. It had been bigger than that, and a thousand times more dangerous!

"You see," she added with a little gasp for breath when he released her, "they waked me up on purpose. I dressed at an awful rate. I got to the door—I remember that perfectly well—and then—" An expression of bewilderment came into her face again.

"Yes," he helped her, "and then—what?"

"Well, I forget exactly; but something stopped me. Something came all round me and took me in their arms. It was like arms of wind. I was lifted up and carried in the air. And after that I forget the rest, forget everything—till now."

She stopped. She took off her tam-o'-shanter and smoothed her untidy hair back from the forehead. And as he looked a moment at her—this little human organism still vibrating with the passage of a universal Power that had obsessed her, making her far more than merely child, yet still leaving in her the sweetness of her simple love— he came to a sudden, bold decision. He would face the thing complete. He would go outside.

"Mánya," he whispered, looking hard at her, "would you like to go out—now—with me? Come, child! Suppose we go together!"

She stared at him, then darted about the room with little springs of excitement. She clapped her hands softly, her eyes alight and shining.

"Uncle Dick! You really mean it? Wouldn't it be grand!"

"Of course, I mean it. See! I'm dressed and ready!" And he pointed to his boots and clothes.

"It's the very best thing we can do, really," she said, trying to speak gravely, but the mischievous element uppermost at the idea of the secret nocturnal journey. "They'll see that you're not afraid, and you'll be safe then for ever and ever and ever! Hooray!"

She twirled the tam-o'-shanter in the air above her head, skipping in her childish joy.

"And we'll go past Fräulein's door," she insisted mischievously, as he took her outstretched hand and led the way on tiptoe down the dark front stairs.

"Hush!" he whispered gruffly. "Don't talk so loud."

She fastened up her garments, and they moved like shadows through the sleeping house.

XV

That journey he made with this "child of Nature" among the dripping trees and along soaked paths was one that Eliot never forgot. For him its meaning was unmistakable. His early life again supplied a parallel. He had once seen a wretched man marched out of camp with two days' rations to shift for himself in the wilderness as best he might,—a prisoner convicted of treachery, but whose life was spared on the chance that he might redeem it, or die in the attempt. He had seen it done by redskins, he had seen it done by white. And hanging had been better. Yet the crime—stealing a horse, or sneaking another's "grub-stakes"—was one that civilisation punishes with a paltry fine, or condones daily as permissible "business acumen."

In primitive conditions it was a crime against the higher law. It was sinning against Nature. And Nature never is deceived.

Richard Eliot was now being drummed out of camp. And the child who led him, mischief in her eyes and the joy of forbidden pleasure in her heart, was all unconscious of the awful rôle she played. Yet it was she who as well had pleaded for his life and saved him.

Nature turned him out; the Place rejected him; and Mánya saw him safely to the confines of that wilderness of houses, ugliness, commercial desolation where he must wander till he re-made his soul or lost it altogether.

They cautiously opened the front door, and the damp air rushed to meet them.

"Hush!" he repeated, closing it carefully behind him. But the child was already upon the lawn. Beyond her, dark blots against the sky, rose the massed outline of the little pointed hills. There were no stars anywhere, though the clouds were breaking into thinning troops; but it was not too dark to see, for a moon watched them somewhere from her place of hiding. The air was warm and very sweet, left breathing by the storm.

"Hush, Mánya!" he whispered again, ill at ease to see her go. She ran back, her feet inaudible upon the thick, wet lawn, and took his hand. "We'll go by the Piney Valley," she said, assuming leadership. And he made no objection, though this was the direction of the sample pits. It led also, he remembered, to the Mill—the spot where she who had left him in charge had gone upon her long long journey.

They went forward side by side. The wind below them hummed gently in the tree-tops, but it did not reach their faces. The whole wet world lay breathing softly about them, exhausted by the tempest. It was very still. It watched them pass. There was no effort to detain them. And in Dick Eliot's heart was a pain that searched him like a pain of death itself.

But his companion, he now clearly realised, was merely the child again—eerie, wonderful, eldritch, but still the little Mánya that he knew so well. Mischief was in her heart, and the excitement of unlawful adventure in her blood; but nothing more. The vast obsessing Entity that had constituted her judge and executioner was now entirely gone. He was spared the added shame of knowing that she realised what she did.

Sometimes she left his side, to come back presently with a little rush of pleasurable alarm. He was uncertain whether he liked best her going from him or her sudden return. Their tread was now muffled by the needles as they went slowly down the pathways of the Piney Valley. The occasional snapping of small twigs alone betrayed their movements. Heavy branches, soaked like sponges, splashed showers on the ground when their shoulders brushed them in passing, and drops fell of their own weight with mysterious little thuds like footsteps everywhere about them in the woods.

Mánya dived away from his side. She came back sometimes in front of him and sometimes behind. He never quite knew where she was. His mind, indeed, neglected her, for his thoughts were concentrated within himself. Her movements were the movements of a block of shadow, shifting here and there like shadows of trees and clouds in faint moonlight.

"Uncle, tell me one thing," he heard with a start, as she suddenly stood in front of him across the narrow pathway, and so close that he nearly bumped against her. "Isn't there something here that's angry with you? Something you've done wrong to?"

"Hush, child! Don't say such things!" He felt the shiver run through him. He pushed her forward with his hands.

"But they're being said—all round us. Uncle, don't you hear them?" she insisted.

"I've always loved the Place. We've always been happy here together." He whispered it, as though a terror was in him lest it should be overheard and—contradicted.

Her answer flabbergasted him. Her intuitions were so uncannily direct and piercing.

"That's what I meant. You've been unkind. You've hurt it."

"Mánya," he repeated severely, "you must not say such things. And you must not think them."

"I'm so awfully sorry, Uncle Dick," she said softly in the dark, and promptly kissed him. The kiss went like a stab into his heart.

Then she was gone again, and he caught her light footstep several yards in front, as though a shower of drops had fallen on the needles.

"Uncle," came her voice again close beside him. She stood on tiptoe and pulled his ear down to the level of her lips. "Hold my hand tight. We're coming near now." She was curiously excited.

"To the Mill?" he asked, knowing quite well she meant another thing.

"No, to the pits the men dug," she answered, nestling in against him, while his own voice echoed faintly, "Yes, the sample pits." He felt like passing the hostile outposts of the Camp who would shoot him but for the presence of the appointed escort.

A sigh of lonely wind went past them with its shower of drops. And these little hands of wind with their fingers of sweet rain helped forward his expulsion. The empty wilderness beyond lay waiting for his soul. It heard him coming.

And a curious, deep revelation of the child's state of mind then rushed suddenly upon him. He knew that she expected something. And her answer to the question he put explained his own thought to himself.

"What is it you expect, Mánya?" he had asked unwisely.

"Not *expect* exactly, Uncle, for that would be the wrong way. But I *know.*"

And several kinds of fear shot through him as he heard it, for the words lifted a veil and let him see into her mind a moment. She had said another of her profoundly mystical truths. Expectation, anticipation, he divined, would provide a mould for what was coming, would give it shape, but yet not quite its natural shape. To anticipate keenly meant to attract too quickly: to force. The expectant desire would coax what was coming into an unnatural form that might be dreadful because not quite true. Let the thing approach in its own way, uninvited by imaginative dread. Let it come upon them as it would, deciding its own shape of arrival. To expect was to invite distortion. This flashed across him behind her simple words.

"You fearful child!" he whispered, forcing an unnatural little laugh.

"The soft, wet, sticky things, half yellow and half white," she began, resenting his laughter, "always moving, and never looking twice the same—"

Then, before he could stop her, she stopped of her own accord.

She clutched his arm. He understood that it was the closeness of the thing that had inspired the atrocious words. She held his arm so tightly that it hurt. They stood in the presence of others than themselves.

Yet these Others had not *come* to them. The movement of approach was not really movement at all. It was a condition in himself had altered so that he knew. Out here the veil had thinned a little, as it had thinned in the room an hour ago. And he saw space otherwise. This Power that in humanity lies normally inarticulate was breaking through. In the room its language had been a stammer; it was a stammer now. Or, in the terms of sight, it was a little fragment utterly inexplicable by itself, since the entire universe is necessary for its complete expression.

Yet Eliot did perceive the enormous thing behind—the thing to which he had been unfaithful by prostituting his first original love. And the fact that it was interwoven with his ordinary little human feelings at the same time only added to the bewilderment of its stupendous reality.

He saw for a fleeting moment just as Mánya saw—from her immediate point of view.

"It's here," she whispered, in a voice that sounded most oddly everywhere; "it's here, the angry thing you've hurt."

On either side of the path, where the heather-land came close, he saw the openings the men had dug—pale, luminous patches of whitish yellow. Between the bushy tufts they shone faintly gleaming against the night. Perspective, in that instant, became the merest trick of sight, a trivial mental jugglery. That slope of coal-black moor actually was extraordinarily near. The tree-tops were just as well beneath his feet, or he stood among their roots. Either was true. There was neither up nor down. The sky was in his hands, a little thing; or the stars and moon hid washed within the current of his blood. Size was illusion, as relative as time. No object in itself had any "size" at all. He saw her universe, all true, as ever, but from another point of view. And the entire Place ran down here to a concentrated point. The sample pits pressed close against his face.

"The pits," she whispered, with a sound of wind and water in her breath.

So, for a moment, he saw from the point of view whence Mánya always saw. He and the child and the Spirit of the Place stood side by side on that narrow shelf of darkness, sharing a joint and absolute comprehension. Her elemental aspect became his own, for his inner eye was against the peep-hole through which her Behind-the-Scenes was visible. He realised a new thing, grand as a field of stars.

For the Place here focussed almost into sentiency. Those slow moving forces that stir to growth in crystals, waken and breathe in plants, and first in the animal world know consciousness, here moved vast and inchoate, through the structure of the dream-estate he owned. Yet moved not blind and inarticulate. For the stress of some impulse, normally undivined by men, urged them towards articulate expression. Here was reaction approximate to those reactions of the nervous cells which in their ultimate result men call emotions. And this irresistible correspondence between the two appalled him.

The raw material of definite sensation here poured loose and terrible about him from the ground. In them, moreover, was anger, protest, warning, and a menacing resentment—all directed against his mean, insignificant being. From these sample pits issued the menace and the warning, just as literally as there issued from them also the soft, white clay that would degrade the immemorial beauty he had once thought he loved with a clean, pure love. The pits were wounds. They drew all the feelings of the injured Place into the tenderness of sentient organs.

But behind the threatening anger he recognised a softer passion too. There was a sadness, a deep yearning, and a searching melancholy as well, that seemed to bear witness to his rejection with a sighing as of the sea and wood and hills.

And here, doubtless, came in the interweaving of his own little human emotions. For an overpowering sorrow soaked his heart and mind. The judgment that found him wanting woke all his stores of infinite regret. It would have been better for him had he found that millstone which can save the soul, because it removes temptation.

"It is too late," breathed round him in three weeping voices that passed out between his lips as a single cry together. "It is too late."

Yet nothing happened; that is, he saw nothing—nothing translatable by any words that he could find. Time dwindled and expanded curiously. The past ran on before him, and the future grouped itself behind his back. The seconds and minutes which men tick off from the apparent movement of the sun gave place to some condition within himself where they lay gathered for ever into the circle of the Present. He remembers no actual sequence of acts or movements. Duration drew its horns back into a single point. . . . It is sure, however, that these two human beings marched presently on. They steadily became disentangled from the spot, and somehow or other moved away from the staring pits. For Eliot, looking back, recalls that it felt like walking past the mouths of loaded cannon; also that the pits watched them out of sight as portraits follow a moving figure with their expressionless stare. He thinks that he looked straight before him as he went. He is sure no single word was spoken—until they left the trees behind and emerged into the open. The Mill, the old, familiar building, was the thing that first restored him to a normal world again. He saw its outline, humped and black, shouldering its way against the sky. He heard the water running under the wheel. But even the Mill, like a hooded figure, turned its face away. It expressed the melancholy of a multitude. And the woods were everywhere full of tears.

Mánya, he realised then beside him, was making the humming sound of the water that flowed beneath that motionless wheel. Her voice became the voice of the Place—the undifferentiated sound of Nature. It was the voice of dismissal and farewell. Here was the Gateway through which his soul passed out into the Wilderness.

He involuntarily stooped down to feel her, and she lifted her face up in the darkness and kissed him. But it was across a barrier that she kissed him. He already stood outside.

And half an hour later they were indoors again and the house was still. Mánya slept as soundly as the placid Fräulein Bühlke or the motherly Mrs. Coove doubtless also slept.

But he lay battling with strange thoughts for hours. Night and the wind were oddly mingled with them; water, hills, and masses of strong landscape too. They rose before his mind's eye in a giant panorama, endlessly moving past beneath huge skies, and visible against a pale background of luminous, yellowish white. It had strange movements of its own, this yellowish background, like the swaying of a curtain on the stage; and sometimes it surged forwards with a smothering sweep that enveloped everything of beauty he had ever known. It then obliterated the world. Stars were extinguished; scenery turned to soil. The Spectre of the Clay he had invoked possessed the Place.

He lay there frightened in his sleepless bed and saw the dawn—a helpless little mortal, destroyed by his faithlessness and breach of trust. And all night long there lay outside, yet watching him, something else that equally never slept—agile, alert, unconquerable. Only it was no longer *disturbed.* For its purpose was accomplished. It had turned him out.

And it is not necessary to tell how John Casanova Murdoch soon thereafter took the work in hand and developed the Place, as he expressed it, "without a hitch." For John C. had made no promises of love; nor had he pretended to establish with Nature that intimate relationship of trust and worship which invokes the spiritual laws. Nature took no note of him, for he worked frankly with her, and his motive, if not exalted, was at least a pure one. And the Clay, as he phrased it a little later in his expressive Western lingo, soon was "paying hand over fist. The money was pouring in—more money than you could shake a stick at!"

The Goblin's Collection

Dutton accepted the invitation for the feeble reason that he was not quick enough at the moment to find a graceful excuse. He had none of that facile brilliance which is so useful at week-end parties; he was a big, shy, awkward man. Moreover, he disliked these great houses. They swallowed him. The solemn, formidable butlers oppressed him. He left on Sunday night when possible. This time, arriving with an hour to dress, he went upstairs to an enormous room, so full of precious things that he felt like an insignificant item in a museum corridor. He smiled disconsolately as the underling who brought up his bag began to fumble with the lock. But, instead of the sepulchral utterance he dreaded, a delicious human voice with an unmistakable brogue proceeded from the stooping figure. It was positively comforting. "It 'ull be locked, sorr, but maybe ye have the key?" And they bent together over the disreputable kit-bag, looking like a pair of ants knitting antennæ on the floor of some great cave. The giant four-poster watched them contemptuously; mahogany cupboards wore an air of grave surprise; the gaping, open fireplace alone could have swallowed all his easels—almost, indeed, his little studio. This human, Irish presence was distinctly consoling—some extra hand or other, thought Dutton, probably.

He talked a little with the lad; then, lighting a cigarette, he watched him put the clothes away in the capacious cupboards, noticing in particular how neat and careful he was with the little things. Nail-scissors, silver stud-box, metal shoe-horn, and safety razor, even the bright cigar-cutter and pencil-sharpener collected loose from the bottom of the bag—all these he placed in a row upon the dressing-table with the glass top, and seemed never to have done with it. He kept coming back to rearrange and put a final touch, lingering over them absurdly. Dutton watched him with amusement, then surprise, finally with exasperation. Would he never go? "Thank you," he said at last; "that will do. I'll dress now. What time is dinner?" The lad told him, but still lingered, evidently anxious to say more. "Everything's out, I think," repeated Dutton impatiently; "all the loose things, I mean?" The face at once turned eagerly. What mischievous Irish eyes he had, to be sure! "I've put thim all together in a row, sorr, so that ye'll not be missing anny-thing at all," was the quick reply, as he pointed to the ridiculous collection of little articles, and even darted back to finger them again. He counted them one by one. And then suddenly he added, with a touch of personal interest that was *not* familiarity, "It's so easy, ye see, sorr, to lose thim small bright things in this great room." And he was gone.

Smiling a little to himself, Dutton began to dress, wondering how the lad had left the impression that his words meant more than they said. He almost wished he had encouraged him to talk. "The small bright things in this great room"—what an admirable description, almost a criticism! He felt like a prisoner of state in the Tower. He stared about him into the alcoves, recesses, deep embrasured windows; the tapestries and huge curtains oppressed him; next he fell to wondering who the other guests would be, whom he would take in to dinner, how early he could make an excuse and slip off to bed; then, midway in these desultory thoughts, became suddenly aware of a curiously sharp impression—that he was being watched. Somebody, quite close, was looking at him. He dismissed the fancy as soon as it was born, putting it down to the size and mystery of the old-world chamber; but in spite of himself the idea persisted teasingly, and several times he caught himself turning nervously to look over his shoulder. It was not a ghostly feeling; his nature was not accessible to ghostly things. The strange idea, lodged securely in his brain, was traceable, he thought, to something the Irish lad had said—grew out, rather, of what he had left unsaid. He idly allowed his imagination to encourage it. Some one, friendly but curious, with inquisitive, peeping eyes, was watching him. Some one very tiny was hiding in the enormous room. He laughed about it; but he felt different. A certain big, protective feeling came over him that he must go gently lest he tread on some diminutive living thing that was soft as a kitten and elusive as a baby mouse. Once, indeed, out of the corner of his eye, he fancied he saw a little thing with wings go fluttering past the great purple curtains at the other end. It was by a window. "A bird, or something, outside," he told himself with a laugh, yet moved thenceforth more often than not on tiptoe. This cost him a certain effort: his proportions were elephantine. He felt a more friendly interest now in the stately, imposing chamber.

The dressing-gong brought him back to reality and stopped the flow of his imagining. He shaved, and laboriously went on dressing then; he was slow and leisurely in his movements, like many big men; very orderly, too. But when he was ready to put in his collar stud it was nowhere to be found. It was a worthless bit of brass, but most important; he had only one. Five minutes ago it had been standing inside the ring of his collar on the marble slab; he had carefully placed it there. Now it had disappeared and left no trail. He grew warm and untidy in the search. It was something of a business for Dutton to go on all fours. "Malicious little beast!" he grunted, rising from his knees, his hand sore where he had scraped it beneath the cupboard. His trouser-crease was ruined, his hair was tumbled. He knew too well the elusive activity of similar small objects. "It will turn up again," he tried to laugh, "if I pay it no attention. Mal—" he abruptly changed the adjective, as though he had nearly said a dangerous thing—"naughty little imp!" He went on dressing, leaving the collar to the last. He fastened the cigar-cutter to his chain, but the nail-scissors, he noticed now, had also gone. "Odd," he reflected, "very odd!" He looked at the place where they had been a few minutes ago. "Odd!" he repeated. And finally, in desperation, he rang the bell. The heavy curtains swung inwards as he said, "Come in," in answer to the knock, and the Irish boy, with the merry, dancing eyes, stood in the room. He glanced half nervously, half expectantly, about him. "It'll be something ye have lost, sorr?" he said at once, as though he knew.

"I rang," said Dutton, resenting it a little, "to ask you if you could get me a collar stud—for this evening. Anything will do." He did not say he had lost his own. Some one, he felt, who was listening, would chuckle and be pleased. It was an absurd position.

"And will it be a shtud like this, sorr, that yez wanting?" asked the boy, picking up the lost object from inside the collar on the marble slab.

"Like that, yes," stammered the other, utterly amazed. He had overlooked it, of course, yet it was in the identical place where he had left it. He felt mortified and foolish. It was so obvious that the boy grasped the situation—more, had expected it. It was as if the stud had been taken and replaced deliberately. "Thank you," he added, turning away to hide his face as the lad backed out—with a grin, he imagined, though he did not see it. Almost immediately, it seemed, then he was back again, holding out a little cardboard box containing an assortment of ugly bone studs. Dutton felt as if the whole thing had been prepared beforehand. How foolish it was! Yet behind it lay something real and true and—utterly incredible!

"*They* won't get taken, sorr," he heard the lad say from the doorway. "They're not nearly bright enough."

The other decided not to hear. "Thanks," he said curtly; "they'll do nicely."

There was a pause, but the boy did not go. Taking a deep breath, he said very quickly, as though greatly daring, "It's only the bright and little lovely things he takes, sorr, if ye plaze. He takes thim for his collection, and there's no stoppin' him at all." It came out with a rush, and Dutton, hearing it, let the human thing rise up in him. He turned and smiled.

"Oh, he takes these things for his collection, does he?" he asked more gently.

The boy looked dreadfully shame-faced, confession hanging on his lips. "The little bright and lovely things, sorr, yes. I've done me best, but there's things he can't resist at all. The bone ones is safe, though. He won't look at thim."

"I suppose he followed you across from Ireland, eh?" the other enquired.

The lad hung his head. "I told Father Madden," he said in a lower voice, "but it's not the least bit of good in the wurrld." He looked as though he had been convicted of stealing and feared to lose his place. Suddenly, lifting his blue eyes, he added, "But if ye take no notice at all he ginrelly puts everything back in its place agin. He only borrows thim, just for a little bit of toime. Pretend ye're not wantin' thim at all, sorr, and back they'll come prisintly again, brighter than before maybe."

"I see," answered Dutton slowly. "All right, then," he dismissed him, "and I won't say a word downstairs. You needn't be afraid," as the lad looked his gratitude and vanished like a flash, leaving the other with a queer and eerie feeling, staring at the ugly bone studs. He finished dressing hurriedly and went downstairs. He went on tiptoe out of the great room, moving delicately and with care, lest he might tread on something very soft and tiny, almost wounded, like a butterfly with a broken wing. And from the corners, he felt positive, something watched him go.

The ordeal of dinner passed off well enough; the rather heavy evening too. He found the opportunity to slip off early to bed. The nail-scissors were in their place again. He read till midnight; nothing happened. His hostess had told him the history of his room, enquiring kindly after his comfort. "Some people feel rather lost in it," she said; "I hope you found all you want," and, tempted by her choice of words—the "lost" and "found"—he nearly told the story of the Irish lad whose goblin had followed him across the sea and "borrowed little bright and lovely things for his collection." But he kept his word; he told nothing; she would only have stared, for one thing. For another, he was bored, and therefore uncommunicative. He smiled inwardly. All that this giant mansion could produce for his comfort and amusement were ugly bone studs, a thieving goblin, and a vast bedroom where dead royalty had slept. Next day, at intervals, when changing for tennis or back again for lunch, the "borrowing" continued; the little things he needed at the moment had disappeared. They turned up later. To ignore their disappearance was the recipe for their recovery—invariably, too, just where he had seen them last. There was the lost object shining in his face, propped impishly on its end, just ready to fall upon the carpet, and ever with a quizzical, malicious air of innocence that was truly goblin. His collar stud was the favourite; next came the scissors and the silver pencil-sharpener.

Trains and motors combined to keep him Sunday night, but he arranged to leave on Monday before the other guests were up, and so got early to bed. He meant to watch. There was a merry, jolly feeling in him that he had established quasi-friendly relations with the little Borrower. He might even see an object go—catch it in the act of disappearing! He arranged the bright objects in a row upon the glass-topped dressing-table opposite the bed, and while reading kept an eye slyly on the array of tempting bait. But nothing happened. "It's the wrong way," he realised suddenly. "What a blunderer I am!" He turned the light out then. Drowsiness crept over him. . . . Next day, of course, he told himself it was a dream. . . .

The night was very still, and through the latticed windows stole faintly the summer moonlight. Outside the foliage rustled a little in the wind. A night-jar called from the fields, and a secret, furry owl made answer from the copse beyond. The body of the chamber lay in thick darkness, but a slanting ray of moonlight caught the dressing-table and shone temptingly upon the silver objects. "It's like setting a night-line," was the last definite thought he remembered—when the laughter that followed stopped suddenly, and his nerves gave a jerk that turned him keenly alert.

From the enormous open fireplace, gaping in darkness at the end of the room, issued a thread of delicate sound that was softer than a feather. A tiny flurry of excitement, furtive, tentative, passed shivering across the air. An exquisite, dainty flutter stirred the night, and through the heavy human brain upon the great four-poster fled this picture, as from very far away, picked out in black and silver—of a wee knight-errant crossing the frontiers of fairyland, high mischief in his tiny, beating heart. Pricking along over the big, thick carpet, he came towards the bed, towards the dressing-table, intent upon bold plunder. Dutton lay motionless as a stone, and watched and listened. The blood in his ears smothered the sound a little, but he never lost it altogether. The flicking of a mouse's tail or whiskers could hardly have been more gentle than this sound, more wary, circumspect, discreet, certainly not half so artful. Yet the human being in the bed, so heavily breathing, heard it well. Closer it came, and closer, oh, so elegant and tender, this bold attack of a wee Adventurer from another world. It shot swiftly past the bed. With a little flutter, delicious, almost musical, it rose in the air before his very face and entered the pool of moonlight on the dressing-table. Something blurred it then; the human sight grew troubled and confused a moment; a mingling of moonlight with the reflections from the mirror, slab of glass, and shining objects obscured clear vision somehow. For a second Dutton lost the proper focus. There was a tiny rattle and a tiny click. He saw that the pencil-sharpener stood balanced on the table's very edge. It was in the act of vanishing.

But for his stupid blunder then, he might have witnessed more. He simply could not restrain himself, it seems. He sprang, and at the same instant the silver object fell upon the carpet. Of course his elephantine leap made the entire table shake. But, anyhow, he was not quick enough. He saw the reflection of a slim and tiny hand slide down into the mirrored depths of the reflecting sheet of glass—deep, deep down, and swift as a flash of light. This he thinks he saw, though the light, he admits, was oddly confusing in that moment of violent and clumsy movement.

One thing, at any rate, was beyond all question: the pencil-sharpener had disappeared. He turned the light up; he searched for a dozen minutes, then gave it up in despair and went back to bed. Next morning he searched again. But, having overslept himself, he did not search as thoroughly as he might have done, for half-way through the tiresome operation the Irish lad came in to take his bag for the train.

"Will ut be something ye've lost, sorr?" he asked gravely.

"Oh, it's all right," Dutton answered from the floor. "You can take the bag—and my overcoat." And in town that day he bought another pencil-sharpener and hung it on his chain.

Let Not the Sun—

I t began delightfully: "Where are *you* going for your holiday, Bill?" his sister asked casually one day at tea, some one having mentioned a trip to Italy; "climbing, I suppose, as usual?" And he had answered just as casually, "Climbing, yes, as usual."

They were both workers, she a rich woman's secretary, and he keeping a stool warm in an office. She was to have a month, he a bare three weeks, and this summer it so happened, the times overlapped. To each the holiday was of immense importance, looked forward to eagerly through eleven months of labour, and looked back upon afterwards through another long eleven months. Frances went either to Scotland or some little pension in Switzerland, painting the whole time, and taking a friend of similar tastes with her. He went invariably to the Alps. They had never gone together as yet, because—well, because she painted and he climbed. But this year a vague idea had come to each that they might combine, choosing some place where both tastes might be satisfied. Since last summer there had been deaths in the family; they realised loneliness, felt drawn together like survivors of a wreck. He often went to tea with her in her little flat, and she accompanied him sometimes to dinner in his Soho restaurants. Fundamentally, however, they were not together, for their tastes did not assimilate well, and their temperaments lacked that sympathy which fuses emotion and thought in a harmonious blend. Affection was real and deep, but strongest when they were apart.

Now, as he walked home to his lodgings on the other side of London, he felt it would be nice if they *could* combine their holidays for once. Her casual question was a feeler in the same direction. A few days later she repeated it in a postscript to a letter: "Why not go together this year," she wrote, "choosing some place where you can climb and Sybil and I can paint? I leave on the 1st; you follow on the 15th. We could have two weeks in the same hotel. It would be awfully jolly. Let me know what you feel, and mind you are *quite* frank about it."

They exchanged letters, discussed places, differed mildly, and agreed to meet for full debate. The stage of suggestion was past; it was a plan now. They must decide, or go separately. One of them, that is to say, must take the responsibility of saying No. Frances leaned to the Engadine—Maloja—whereas her brother thought it "not a bad place, but no good as a climbing centre. Still, Pontresina is within reach, and there are several peaks I've never done round Pontresina. We'll talk it over." The exchange of letters became wearisome and involved, because each wrote from a different point of view and feeling, and each gave in weakly to the other, yet left a hint of sacrifice behind. "It's a very lovely part," she wrote of his proposal for the Dolomites, "only it's a long way off and expensive to get at, and the scenery is a bit monotonous for painting. *You* understand. Still, for two weeks—"; while he criticised her alternative selections in the Rhone Valley as "rather touristy and overcrowded, don't you think?—the sort of thing that everybody paints." Both were busy, and wrote sometimes briefly, not making themselves quite plain, each praising the other's choice, then qualifying it destructively at the end of apparently unselfish sentences with a formidable and prohibitive "but." The time was getting short meanwhile. "We ought to take our rooms pretty soon," wrote Frances. "Immediately, in fact, if we want to get in anywhere," he answered on a letter-card. "Come and dine to-night at the Gourmet, and we'll settle everything."

They met. And at first they talked of everything else in the world but the one thing in their minds. They talked a trifle boisterously; but the boisterousness was due to excitement, and the excitement to an unnatural effort to feign absolute sympathy which did not exist fundamentally. The bustle of humanity about them, food, and a glass of red wine, gradually smoothed the edges of possible friction, however.

"You look tired, Bill."

"I am rather," he laughed. "We both need a holiday, don't we?"

The ice was broken.

"Now, let's talk of the Alps," she said briskly. "It's been so difficult to explain in writing, hasn't it?"

"Impossible," he laughed, and pulled out of his pocket a sheet of notepaper on which he had made some notes. Frances took a Baedeker from her velvet bag on the hook above her head. "Capital," he laughed; "we'll settle everything in ten minutes."

"It will be so awfully jolly to go together for once," she said, and they felt so happy and sympathetic, so sure of agreement, so ready each to give in to the other, that they began with a degree of boldness that seemed hardly wise. "Say exactly what *you* think--quite honestly," each said to the other. "We must be candid, you know. It's too important to pretend. It would be silly, wouldn't it?" But neither realised that this meant, "I'll persuade you that my place is best and the only place where I could really enjoy my holiday." Bill cleared a space before him on the table, lit a cigarette, and felt the joy of making plans in his heart. Francis turned the pages to her particular map, equally full of delight. What fun it was!

"All I want, Bill dear, is a place where I can paint—forests, streams, and those lovely fields of flowers. Almost anywhere would do for me. You understand, don't you?"

"Rather," he laughed, making a little more room for his own piece of paper, "and you shall have it, too, old girl. All I want is some good peaks within reach, and good guides on the spot. We'll have our evenings together, and when I'm not climbing, we'll go for picnics while you paint, and—and be awfully jolly all together. Sybil's a nice girl. We shall be a capital trio." He put her Baedeker at the far corner of the table for a moment.

"Oh, *please* don't lose my place in it," she said, pulling the marker across the page and leaving the tip out.

"I'm sorry," he replied, and they laughed—less boisterously.

"You tell me your ideas first," she decided, "and then I'll tell you mine. If we can't agree then, we're not fit to have a holiday at all!"

It worked up with deadly slowness to the rupture that was inevitable from the beginning. Both were tired after, not a day's, but a year's work; both felt selfish and secretly ashamed; both realised also that an unsuccessful holiday was too grave a risk to run—it involved eleven months' disappointment and regret. Yet, if this plan failed, any future holiday together would be impossible.

"After all," sighed Frances peevishly at length, "perhaps we *had* better go separately."

It was so tiring, this endless effort to find the right place; their reserve of vitality was not equal to the obstacles that cropped up everywhere. Full, high spirits are necessary to see things whole. They exaggerated details. "It's funny," he thought; "she *might* realise that climbing is what I need. One can paint everywhere!" But in her own mind the reflection was the same, turned the opposite way: "Bill doesn't understand that one can't paint *anything*. Yet, for climbing, one peak is just as good as another." He thought her obstinate and faddy; she felt him stubborn and rather stupid.

"Now, old girl," he said at length, pushing his papers aside with a weary gesture of resignation, having failed to convince her how admirable his choice had been, "let's look at *your* place." He laughed patiently, but the cushions provided by food and wine and excitement had worn thin. Friction increased; words pricked; the tide of sympathy ebbed—it had been forced really all along, pumped up; their tastes and temperaments did *not* amalgamate. Frances opened her Baedeker and explained mechanically. She now saw clearly the insuperable difficulties in the way, but for sentimental and affectionate reasons declined to be the first to admit the truth. She was braver, bigger than he was, but her heart prevented the outspoken honesty that would have saved the situation. He, though unselfish as men go, could not conceal his knowledge that he was so. Each vied with the other in the luxury of giving up with apparent sweetness, only the luxury was really beyond the means of either. With the Baedeker before them on the table, the ritual was again gone through—from her point of view, while in sheer weariness he agreed to conditions his strength could never fulfil when the time came. They met half-way upon Champéry in the Valais Alps above the Rhone. It satisfied neither of them. But speech was exhausted; energy flagged; the restaurant, moreover, was emptying and lights being turned out.

They put away Baedeker and paper, paid the bill, and rose to go, each keenly disappointed, each feeling conscious of having made a big sacrifice. On the steps he turned to help her put her coat on, and their eyes met. They felt miles apart. "So much for my holiday," he thought, "after waiting eleven months!" and there was a flash of resentful anger in his heart. He turned it unconsciously against his sister.

"Don't write for rooms till the end of the week," he suggested. "I *may* think of a better place after all."

It was the tone that stung her nerves, perhaps. She really hated Champéry—a crowded, touristy, "organised" place. Her sacrifice had gone for nothing. "Even now he's not satisfied!" she realised with bitterness.

"Oh, if you don't feel it'll do, Bill, dear," she answered coolly, "I really think we'd better give it up—going together, I mean." Her force was exhausted.

He felt sore, offended, injured. He looked sharply at her, almost glared. A universe lay between them now. Before there was time to reflect or choose his words, even to soften his tone, he had answered coldly:

"Just as you like, Frances. I don't want to spoil your holiday. You're right. We'd better go separately then."

Nothing more was said. He saw her to the station of the Tube, but the moment the train had gone he realised that the final wave of her little hand betrayed somehow that tears were very close. She had not shown her face again. He felt sad, ashamed, and bitter. Deeper than the resentment, however, was a great ache in his heart that was pain. Remorse surged over him. He thought of her year of toil, her tired little face, her disappointment. Her brief holiday, so feverishly yearned for, would now be tinged with sadness and regret, wherever she went. Memory flashed back to their childhood together, when life smiled upon them in that Kentish garden. They were the only two survivors. Yet they could not manage even a holiday together. . . .

Though so little had been said at the end, it was a rupture. . . . He went home to bed, planning a splendid reconstruction. Before they went to their respective work-places in the morning he would run over and see her, put everything straight and sweet again, explaining his selfishness, perhaps, on the plea that he was overtired. He wondered, as he lay ashamed and sad upon his sleepless bed, what *she* was thinking and feeling now . . . and fell asleep at last with his plan of reconstruction all completed. His last conscious thought was—"I wish I had not let her go like that . . . without a nice good-bye!"

In the morning, however, he had not time to go; he postponed it to the evening, sending her a telegram instead: "Come dinner to-night same place and time. Have worked out perfect plan." And all day long he looked forward eagerly to their meeting. Those childhood thoughts haunted him strangely—he remembered the enormous plans all had made together years ago in that old Kentish garden where the hop-fields peered above the privet hedge and frightened them. There were five of them then; now there were only two.

But plans, large or small, are not so easily made. Fate does not often give two chances in succession. And Fate that day was very busy in and out among the London traffic. Frances, hopeful and delighted, kept the appointment,—and waited a whole hour before she went anxiously to his flat to find out what was wrong. In the awful room she knew that Fate had made a different plan, and had carried it out. She was too late for him to recognise her, even. In the pocket of the coat he had been wearing she found a sheet of paper giving the names of hotels at Maloja, pension terms, and railway connections from London. She also found the letter he had written engaging the rooms. The envelope was addressed and stamped, but left open for her final approval. She keeps it still.

What she also keeps, however, more than the recollection of real, big quarrels that had come into their lives at other times, is the memory of the way they had left one another at that Tube station, and the horrid fact that she had gone home with resentment and unforgiveness in her heart. It was such a little thing at the moment. But the big, formidable quarrels had been adjusted, made up, forgotten, whereas this other regret would burn her till she died. "We were so cross and tired. But it might so easily have been different. If only . . . I had not left him . . . just like that . . . !"

La Mauvaise Riche

If seeing is believing the story, of course, is justified, and stands foursquare as a fact, for certainly both my cousin and myself saw the thing as clearly as we saw the village church and the wooded mountains beyond, which were its background. There may, however, be other explanations, and my cousin, who is something of a psychologist, availed himself volubly of the occasion to ride his pet hobby. He easily riddled the saying that seeing is believing, while I listened as patiently as possible. Although no psychologist myself, I knew that the phrase was as inadequate as most other generalisations. Indeed, there is no commoner act of magic in daily life than that of sight, by which the mind projects into the air an image, translated objectively from a sensation in the brain caused by light irritating the optic nerve. "The picture on the retina, upside down, anyhow," he kept telling me afterwards, "is not the object itself that throws off the light-rays, is it? You never see the actual object, do you? You're merely playing with an image, eh? It's pure image-ination, don't you see? It's simple magic, the magic that everybody denies."

Yet, somehow, nothing he could offer by way of explanation satisfied me. The question form of his sentences, moreover, irritated. I rather clung to "seeing is believing," and I think in his heart he did the same, for all his cloud of words.

It was evening, and the summer dusk was falling, as we tramped in silence up the hill towards the village where my cousin, with his wife and children, occupy the upper part of an old châlet. We had been climbing Jura cliffs all day; it had been arduous, exciting work, and we both were tired out. Conversation had long since ceased; our legs moved mechanically, and we both devoutly wished we were at home. "Ah, there's the cemetery at last," he sighed, as the landmark near the village came into view. "Thank goodness!" and I was too weary even to make the obvious commentary. The relief of lying down seemed in his mind. With a grunt by way of reply I glanced carelessly at the rough stone wall surrounding the ugly patch cut squarely from the vineyards, and at the formal pines and larches that stood, plume-like, among the peasant graves. "Old mère Corbillard is safe and snug in her last resting-place," he added, as we passed the painted iron gate, "and a good thing too!" There was relief in his tone, but a moment later there was vivid annoyance. "Izzie," he cried, stopping short, "what are you doing again in there? You know your mother forbade you to go any more. What a naughty, disobedient child you are!" And he called to his fourteen-year-old child to come out. She came at once, but listlessly, and not one whit afraid. He scolded her a little. "I was only putting flowers on the grave," she said. Her face wore a puzzled, scared expression, and the eyes were very bright—she had wonderful brown eyes—but it was not her father's chiding that caused the look.

She took our arms with affectionate possession, as her way was, and we all three laboured up the hill together. No more was said; her father was too tired to find further fault. "Please don't tell mother, Daddy, will you?" she whispered, as we reached the châlet and went in; "I promise faithfully not to go again." He said nothing, but I saw him give her a kiss, and I gave her one myself. The feeling was strong in me that she was frightened and needed protection. I put my arm tightly round her, giving her a good warm hug. The pleading, helpless look she gave me in return I shall not soon forget.

The memory of "old mère Corbillard" no one cared to keep alive—the wealthy peasant who had died a week ago. Known as "la mauvaise riche," because of her miserly habits, she was also credited with stealing her neighbours' cats for the purpose of devouring them—"lapin de montagne," as the natives termed the horrid dish. Her face was sinister—steel-grey eyes, hooked nose, and prominent teeth—and had the village soul been more imaginative or superstitious, she would certainly have been called a witch. As it was, she was merely passed for "méchante" and distinctly "toquée." Held in general disfavour, she was avoided and disliked, and she repaid the hatred well, thanks to her money. She lived in utter solitude, the one companion, oddly enough, to whom admittance was never denied, being—Izzie. "Oddly enough," because, while the old woman was half-imbecile, ma-

liciously imbecile, the child, on her side—to put it kindly—was unusually backward for her age, if not mentally deficient. But Izzie's defi-
ciency was of mild and gentle quality—a sweet child, if ever there was
one. And the parents, while barely tolerating the strange acquaintanceship, never knew how frequent the visits were. They always meant to
stop the friendship, yet had never done so. Izzie, true solitary, kept to
herself too much. She loved the old woman's stories. They hesitated to
say the final No. Thus, at first, they let her go to put fresh flowers,
which she picked herself, upon the grave, until, feeling that her too
constant journeys there were morbid, the ultimatum had gone forth
that they must stop. "It's queer that you should care to go so often,"
said her father. "It's not right," added her mother, the parents ex-
changing a look that meant they scented some unholy influence at
work. "But I promised to do it every day," said Izzie frankly. Then further explanations elicited the unwelcome addition: "She said she would
come and fetch me if I didn't"—and the influence of the old woman
seemed defined. "Ha, ha!" said mother's eyes to father; "so the old
wretch frightened her apparently into the promise," and they congratulated themselves that the mischief had been stopped in time.

The incident was slight enough. The imagination of the backward
child, perhaps a little morbidly inclined owing to her love of solitude,
had been unduly stimulated. It had been gently, wisely corrected, and
the matter was at an end. Yet, somehow, for me, it lingered in my
memory, as though something very vital lay at the core of it.

There followed forty-eight hours of soaking rain that kept us all
indoors, and after it a day of cloudless sunshine that made everybody
happy. We romped and played with the children, basked in the delicious heat, and were generally full of active mischief. Mother, mending
stockings and trying to write letters, had a sorry time of it. But joy and
forgiveness ruled the day, and one was ashamed to feel vexation at anything with such a sun in the heavens. Only Izzie, I noticed, kept apart;
she was listless and indifferent, joining in no games; her thin, pale face,
in contrast to the strange brilliance of her eyes, was evidence to me of
some force busily at work within. But she kept it fairly well concealed;
it seemed natural for her to moon about alone; I think no one else noticed that her behaviour was more marked than usual. With the cunning of the slow-witted she avoided me in particular, guessing that I

was ready to make advances. She divined that I understood. Hiding my purpose as well as possible, I kept her closely under observation, and after supper, when she strolled off alone down the road between the vineyards, I called to Daddy to come and have a pipe. We followed her. The moment we caught her up she turned and took her place as usual, an arm to each. How tall she seemed; she almost topped her father. She kept silence, merely walking in step with us, and holding us rather close I thought, as though glad of our presence though she had started off alone. At first Daddy made efforts to draw her into conversation—efforts that failed utterly. For my part, I let her be, content to keep her arm firmly in my own, for there was very strong in me the feeling that I must protect and watch, guarding her from something that she feared yet was unable to resist. We talked across her, I guiding the conversation towards fun, and she was so tall that we had to stoop and lean forward to see each other's faces.

Hot sun had dried the road up, and the evening was still and peaceful. We paced slowly to and fro, turning always at the village fountain, and again at the crest of the hill where the descent went steeply towards the cemetery. And here, at each turning, Izzie lingered a moment and looked down the hill. I felt perceptibly the dragging on my arm. Once, at the fountain, I made to follow the road through the village. "No," said the child, with decision I disliked intensely, "let's go back again," and we obeyed meekly. "Little tyrant," said her unobservant father.

The mountains rose in a wall of purple shadow, their ridges outlined against a fading sky of gold and crimson. Thin columns of peat smoke traced their scaffolding across it faintly, then melted out. From time to time a group of labourers from the vineyards passed us, singing the Dalcroze songs, taking their hats off, and saying. "Bon soir, bonne nuit." We knew them all. Izzie watched them go—with almost feverish interest. I got the queer impression she was waiting till the last group had gone home. She certainly was waiting for something; there was a covert expectancy in her manner that stirred my former uneasiness. And this uneasiness grew stronger every minute. I could hardly listen to my cousin's desultory talk. At last I brought things suddenly to a head, for it was more than my nerves could stand. Abruptly I stood still. The other two, linked arm-in-arm, stood with me.

"Daddy," I said sharply, "let's go in," and was going to add peremptorily, "take Izzie with you," when the words died away on my lips and the tongue in my mouth went dry. My blood seemed turned to ice. For a second I stood in rigid paralysis. For the figure between us, she whose arms were linked in ours was not Izzie, but another. A gaunt, lean face peered close into my own through the dusk as I stooped to see my cousin, and the eyes were of cold steel-grey instead of brown. The skin was lined and furrowed, and projecting teeth of an aged woman gleamed faintly below the great hooked nose. It was mère Corbillard who stood between us, hanging her withered hands upon our arms, her sinister face so close that her straggling thin grey hair even touched our shoulders.

The dreadful sight was as vividly defined as the white face of my cousin which I saw at the same instant just beyond; and by his ghastly pallor, and the water in his eyes, I knew that he had seen her too. His lips were parted, his right hand was raised and clenched. I thought he was going to strike, but instead, wrenching himself violently free, he sprang to one side with an expression of horror that was more a cry than actual words. There *was* a shriek; whose I dare not say; it may have been my own for all my scattered senses can remember. To this day what I recall was the sensation of death upon my arm, and the glare of those steely eyes that peered triumphantly into my own—then a momentary darkness.

All happened in less than a second. The figure had broken loose from between us, and was racing down the road like a flying shadow— towards the cemetery. Yet the figure we watched an instant before starting in frantic pursuit was unmistakable—Izzie.

To my cousin belongs the reward of prompt action and recapture. He simply flew. And he caught the child long before she reached the forbidden gates. Weeping, white, and frightened, we half carried her indoors, and explained to her alarmed mother that she had been taken suddenly ill, a *crise de nerfs,* as Daddy, with presence of mind, described it. It was not the first time; Izzie had been too often hysterical to cause undue anxiety. Mother will never know the truth unless she reads this story, which is unlikely, since her mending and darning leave her little leisure for newspapers. My cousin and myself have discussed the thing *ad nauseam,* and, as I have indicated, he explained it in a variety of ways.

But neither of us know what Izzie thought or felt. We, of course, dared not ask her, and the child has never volunteered a word. That she was severely frightened only is clear. She never passes the cemetery alone now, and the name of old mère Corbillard has not passed her lips a single time. My cousin's discovery of the horror, however, coincided with my own. Comparing notes proved that. He had been aware of no uneasy sensations previously, as I had been. Telepathy, therefore, was the clue he finally decided on. "It covers more ground than the word 'possession,' and has besides," as he said, "a sort of scientific sound."

Bibliography

I. Collections

The Lost Valley and Other Stories. London: Eveleigh Nash, 1910. London: G. Bell & Sons, 1910. New York: Vaughan & Gomme, 1914. New York: Knopf, 1917. London: Eveleigh Nash & Grayson, 1931. [*Contents:* The Lost Valley; The Wendigo; Old Clothes; Perspective; The Terror of the Twins; The Man from the "Gods"; The Man Who Played upon the Leaf; The Price of Wiggin's Orgy; Carlton's Drive; The Eccentricity of Simon Parnacute.]

Pan's Garden: A Volume of Nature Stories. London: Macmillan, 1912. New York: Macmillan, 1912. [*Contents:* The Man Whom the Trees Loved; The South Wind; The Sea Fit; The Attic; The Heath Fire; The Messenger; The Glamour of the Snow; The Return; Sand; The Transfer; Clairvoyance; The Golden Fly; Special Delivery; The Destruction of Smith; The Temptation of the Clay.]

Ten Minute Stories. London: John Murray, 1914. New York: Dutton, 1914. [*Contents:* Accessory Before the Fact; The Deferred Appointment; The Prayer; Strange Disappearance of a Baronet; The Secret; The Lease; Up and Down; Faith Cure on the Channel; The Goblin's Collection; Imagination; The Invitation; The Impulse; Her Birthday; Two in One; Ancient Lights; Dream Trespass; Let Not the Sun—; Entrance and Exit; You *May* Telephone from Here; The Whisperers; Violence; The House of the Past; Jimbo's Longest Day; If the Cap Fits—; News *v.* Nourishment; Wind; Pines; The Winter Alps; The Second Generation.]

The Wolves of God and Other Fey Stories (with Wilfred Wilson). London: Cassell, 1921. New York: Dutton, 1921. [*Contents:* The Wolves of God; Chinese Magic; Running Wolf; First Hate; The Tarn of Sacrifice; The

553

Valley of the Beasts; The Call; Egyptian Sorcery; The Decoy; The Man Who Found Out; The Empty Sleeve; Wireless Confusion; Confession; The Lane That Ran East and West; "Vengeance Is Mine."]

Ancient Sorceries and Other Tales. London: Collins, 1927. [*Contents:* Ancient Sorceries; The Willows; The Return; Running Wolf; The Man Whom the Trees Loved; The Man Who Played upon the Leaf.]

Strange Stories. London: Heinemann, 1929. [*Contents:* The Man Whom the Trees Loved; The Sea Fit; The Glamour of the Snow; The Tryst; Transition; The Occupant of the Room; The Wings of Horus; By Water; Malahide and Forden; Alexander Alexander; The Man Who Was Milligan; The Little Beggar; The Pikestaff Case; Accessory Before the Fact; The Deferred Appointment; Ancient Lights; You *May* Telephone from Here; the Goblin's Collection; Running Wolf; The Valley of the Beasts; The Decoy; Confession; A Descent into Egypt; The Damned; The Willows; Ancient Sorceries.]

[*Short Stories.*] (Short Stories of To-day and Yesterday.) London: George G. Harrap, 1930. [*Contents:* The Regeneration of Lord Ernie; The Sacrifice; Chinese Magic; The Land of Green Ginger; The Stranger; First Hate; The Olive; Two in One; Dream Trespass; Cain's Atonement.]

The Willows and Other Queer Tales. London: Collins, 1932. [*Contents:* The Willows; Ancient Sorceries; The Return; Running Wolf; The Man Whom the Trees Loved; The Man Who Played upon the Leaf; The Tryst; By Water; The Occupant of the Room; The Decoy; Dream Trespass.]

Tales of Algernon Blackwood. London: Martin Secker, 1938. New York: Dutton, 1939. [*Contents:* The Empty House; A Case of Eavesdropping; Strange Adventures of a Private Secretary; With Intent to Steal; Keeping His Promise; The Wood of the Dead; A Suspicious Gift; The Listener; Max Hensig; The Willows; The Insanity of Jones; The Dance of Death; May Day Eve; The Woman's Ghost Story; A Psychical Invasion; Ancient Sorceries; The Nemesis of Fire; Secret Worship; The Camp of the Dog; The Man from the "Gods"; The Wendigo.]

Tales of the Uncanny and Supernatural. London: Peter Nevill, 1949. [*Contents:* The Doll; Running Wolf; The Little Beggar; The Occupant of the Room; The Man Whom the Trees Loved; The Valley of the Beasts; The South Wind; The Man Who Was Milligan; The Trod; The Terror of the Twins; The Deferred Appointment; Accessory Before the Fact; The Glamour of the Snow; The House of the Past; The Decoy; The Tradition; The Touch of Pan; Entrance and Exit; The Pikestaffe Case; The Empty Sleeve; Violence; The Lost Valley.]

II. First Appearances of Individual Stories

"Accessory Before the Fact." *Westminster Gazette* (2 September 1911): 2–3. In *Ten Minute Stories* (1914), *Strange Stories* (1929), *Tales of the Uncanny and Supernatural* (1949).

"Ancient Lights." *Eye-Witness* 3, No. 4 (11 July 1912): 112–14. In *Ten Minute Stories* (1914), *Strange Stories* (1929).

"The Attic." *Westminster Gazette* (20 April 1911): 2. In *Pan's Garden* (1912).

"The Biter Bit." *Saturday Westminster Gazette* (17 February 1912): 3.

"Clairvoyance." *Eye-Witness* 1, No. 18 (19 October 1911): 560–62. In *Pan's Garden* (1912).

"The Deferred Appointment." *Westminster Gazette* (21 January 1911): 2. In *Ten Minute Stories* (1914), *Strange Stories* (1929), *Tales of the Uncanny and Supernatural* (1949).

"The Destruction of Smith." *Eye-Witness* 2, No. 11 (29 February 1912): 336–38. In *Pan's Garden* (1912).

"Dream Trespass." *Morning Post* (London) (24 October 1911): 6. In *Ten Minute Stories* (1914), *Short Stories* (1930), *The Willows* (1932).

"The Eccentricity of Simon Parnacute." In *The Lost Valley* (1910).

"Egyptian Antiquities." *Morning Post* (London) (9 April 1912); 2.

"The Empty Sleeve." *London Magazine* 25 (January 1911): 553–63. In

The Wolves of God (1921), *Tales of the Uncanny and Supernatural* (1949).

"The Glamour of the Snow." *Pall Mall Magazine* 48 (December 1911): 911–23. In *Pan's Garden* (1912), *Strange Stories* (1929), *Tales of the Uncanny and Supernatural* (1949).

"The Goblin's Collection." *Westminster Gazette* (5 October 1912): 3. In *Ten Minute Stories* (1914), *Strange Stories* (1929).

"The Golden Fly." *Eye-Witness* 2, No. 2 (28 December 1911): 48–50. In *Pan's Garden* (1912).

"The Heath Fire." *Country Life* 31 (20 January 1912): 85–86. In *Pan's Garden* (1912).

"Imagination." *Westminster Gazette* (17 December 1910): 15. In *Ten Minute Stories* (1914).

"The Impulse." *Westminster Gazette* (8 April 1911): 2. In *Ten Minute Stories* (1914).

"Let Not the Sun—." *Morning Post* (London) (19 November 1912): 5. In *Ten Minute Stories* (1914).

"The Man from the 'Gods.'" In *The Lost Valley* (1910), *Tales* (1938).

"The Man Whom the Trees Loved." *London Magazine* 28 (March 1912): 97–128. In *Pan's Garden* (1912), *Ancient Sorceries* (1927), *Strange Stories* (1929), *The Willows* (1932), *Tales of the Uncanny and Supernatural* (1949).

"La Mauvaise Riche." *Westminster Gazette* (30 November 1912): 3.

"The Message of the Clock." *Nash's Magazine* 2 (June 1910): 793–95.

"The Messenger." *Westminster Gazette* (9 December 1911): 3. In *Pan's Garden* (1912).

"News vs. Nourishment." *Westminster Gazette* (4 November 1911): 3. In *Ten Minute Stories* (1914).

"Old Clothes." In *The Lost Valley* (1910).

"The Prayer." *Westminster Gazette* (17 June 1911): 2. In *Ten Minute Stories* (1914).

"The Price of Wiggins's Orgy." In *The Lost Valley* (1910).

"The Return." *Eye-Witness* 1, No. 1 (22 June 1911): 18–19. In *Pan's Garden* (1912), *Ancient Sorceries* (1927), *The Willows* (1932).

"Sand." In *Pan's Garden* (1912).

"The Sea Fit." *Country Life* 27 (25 June 1910): 939–42. In *Pan's Garden* (1912), *Strange Stories* (1929).

"The Second Generation." *Westminster Gazette* (6 July 1912): 2. In *Ten Minute Stories* (1914).

"The Singular Death of Morton." *Tramp* 2, No. 10 (December 1910): 230–36.

"The Temptation of the Clay." In *Pan's Garden* (1912).

"The Transfer." *Country Life* 30 (9 December 1911): 887–89. In *Pan's Garden* (1912).

"Two in One." *Eye-Witness* 1, No. 5 (20 July 1911): 146–48. In *Ten Minute Stories* (1914), *Short Stories* (1930).

"The Wendigo." In *The Lost Valley* (1910), *Tales* (1938), *Selected Short Stories* (1945).

"The Whisperers." *Eye-Witness* 2, No. 23 (23 May 1912); 720–22. In *Ten Minute Stories* (1914).

www.ingramcontent.com/pod-product-compliance
Lightning Source LLC
Chambersburg PA
CBHW070352030726
47504CB00001B/152